D1799606

THE CLANS CONFLICT

THE CLANS CONFLICT

Chronicles of the New Earth
Book One

Sean C. Helms

Copyright © 2011 by Sean C. Helms.

Library of Congress Control Number:		2011901846
ISBN:	Hardcover	978-1-4568-6515-3
	Softcover	978-1-4568-6514-6
	Ebook	978-1-4568-6516-0

All rights reserved. No part of this book may be reproduced or transmitted
in any form or by any means, electronic or mechanical, including
photocopying, recording, or by any information storage and retrieval
system, without permission in writing from the copyright owner.

This is a work of fiction. Names, characters, places and incidents either
are the product of the author's imagination or are used fictitiously, and
any resemblance to any actual persons, living or dead, events, or locales is
entirely coincidental.

This book was printed in the United States of America.

To order additional copies of this book, contact:
Xlibris Corporation
1-888-795-4274
www.Xlibris.com
Orders@Xlibris.com
94094

DEDICATION

To my friends and family that have put up with me talking about this book and its characters for so long and which I have become so attached to over the years, and bouncing ideas around to gain their output. Special thanks goes to my brother, Kurt Helms, and to my good friend Mike Gibson, both of which read an earlier draft of this book and offered suggestions on how to make it better. This final draft arrived in part because of them. Lastly, I want to thank my wife Amy for supporting me and her encouragement toward having this book published.

PREFACE

In the year 2164 A. D. the planet Earth succumbed to a fate in which many from another generation had long feared—the devastation of global nuclear war. During the historic disarmaments of the mid-1980's few had considered the dire possibility that a surprising number of Third World countries, following the breakup of the Soviet Union, would find access to potent, sophisticated technologies. Among these, and by far the most dangerous, were the numerous nuclear warheads.

At a time when money had become the new power in the world, more so than the strength of arms, Japan literally owned over half the planet. Nations, once proud and fiercely independent, found themselves forced to band together for economic sake in order to battle the ever escalating prices from around the world for imported goods. At that time, the first of the two most needed and equally expensive commodities was the microelectronics, in which Japan excelled in producing. The second, and perhaps most important world wide, was the crude oil supplied from the lands of the middle-east. With Japan's unexpected purchase of OPEC, the small island country vaulted suddenly to the pinnacle of power and influence over earthly affairs. From their humiliating defeat in World War II, the Japanese Empire had again become a world power. This time power had not been achieved through military supremacy, but rather through their economic ruthlessness. By way of national will and frugality of monetary resources the Japanese had literally purchased a stranglehold on the entire world.

Several young nations, free and independent from the clutches of the dead and unlamented Soviet Union, with their peoples freezing, starving, and dying, turned on those whom they believed had forsaken them aid in their time of need. However, the chief direction of those nations' wrath was reserved for the contemptible Japanese who had bled their countries dry in an all-consuming drive for more and more wealth, the new currency of power and god in a corrupt society. Those poor nations lashed out with every weapon in their possession, including portable nuclear missiles and other, smaller but still lethal, nuclear devices which were compact enough to fit within the confines of a large suitcase. The dire consequences of their drastic actions was considered with due trepidation by some of those starving eastern European nations, but others, blinded by their seething hatred, gave no thought to the price of their actions.

Foremost among the countries across the globe targeted for their fury was Japan, as well as the United States. The American response to the missile launches was decisive as AmeriCan strategic defense satellites automatically answered the threat by launching Patriot III and the newly designed Patriot IV missiles to intercept the incoming ICBM's and counterattacked. Orbiting MX missiles blasted off from their platforms in space and, despite decades of neglect, locked in precisely on the trajectories of the oncoming weapons. Unerringly, the obsolete arsenal followed the flight paths directly back to the enemy launch sites to deliver their payloads of overwhelming destruction.

Among the areas most horribly struck were northwestern AmeriCan, where the orbiting defense network had not been completed; worse hit was nearly the entirety of Eastern Europe, but the most devastated of all was Japan. In an instant, the island nation ceased to exist. Following the dreadful attack all that remained of that chain of islands was a flattened wasteland of radioactive, blackened glass. Almost immediately the rest of the rocked world began to feel the affects as the huge mushroom plumes dissipated their radioactive fallout to the four winds. Ash darkened the skies and rained down upon the earth spreading contamination and wholesale slaughter.

The initial death toll, resulting from nuclear detonations, decimated the world's population; however, what followed in the days and months ahead was far worse. Slowly, over the course of the next six years, radiation sickness from the deadly fallout, which contaminated most water and food supplies, ravaged the human race and all animal species nearly to the point of extinction. The death toll continued to increase over human kind until a mere two people of every hundred survived.

Eight hundred years of deprivation and hardship followed for the remnants of the human race and their descendants as they sought to adapt to a world suddenly changed and increasingly hostile. Hardy folk survived and persevered, and as generations passed the earth began to recover and restore green living things in the wilds. Nature's recovery came more swiftly in certain areas where the natural climate was cooler, as the dissipation of radiation levels proceeded at a more rapid rate. Some such areas included: northern AmeriCan, the British Isles, Scandinavia, as well as northern Europe which included the Ukraine and Russia.

What follows is the history of a proud nation's revival and exceptional progress at the time of the age called *the Recovery*. That country's name in its storied history has been Alban and Alba, as well as Caledonia, although you reading this would most likely know that nation by the name of Scotland.

Perhaps, due in part to certain factors, such as the Scottish people's resilient nature and way of life, their sense of family, God, and honour of their proud clans, they rebuilt anew their government and nation upon old principles and proven traditions that they had never forgotten. Through oral tradition of bards many important things were remembered and passed down throughout the centuries, including: the ancient rivalries and animosities between the clans; general history; old allies as well as their enemies. Each respective clan retained a sense of itself and knew the territories and borders of their ancestral lands—lands which they still held, or those lost in battle or by guile to covetous neighbors. In short, Scots have long memories.

I now take all of you to Scotland, in the Twentieth-third year of the Recovery, near the village of Dunmoore . . . .

SCOTLAND

CHAPTER ONE

E arly afternoon sunlight splashed elaborate designs through the green branches of the hardy Scotch pines surrounding the perimeter of the glade. Grazing placidly within that sleepy dell was a large, healthy flock of black Scottish sheep still wearing their thick curls of wool that had kept them warm through the northern country's harsh winter. Spring would soon arrive, however the cold season stubbornly refused to loosened her grip upon the land as frosty drafts of mountain air ruffled through pine needles.

Two young men dressed in heavy tartan kilt, quilted leather boots, and thick wool cloak quietly attended to the content flock. Each clansman attentively kept watch for predators, four legged and two, that might assail their charges. Both men had long, light colored hair that they kept pulled back in a border braid, and a downy growth of whiskers that did not quite make the equivalent of true beard. Though not yet twenty years of age, the weapons they bore were a man's weapons. Each leaned upon the thick shaft of a six foot long spear, it's steel head honed to a sharp point; a quiver of a score cloth yard arrows rested at each man's hip, while a longbow slung across the back waited for the opportunity to fire the arrows with deadly force.

*   *   *

"Ye heard the lads—see to yer weapons! The bloody Camerons wi' be a coming, but they wi' hae none of our sheep!" bellowed Lyam, the grizzled old chieftain of the MacNeish family.

The House of MacNeish, being a sept of the MacGregor clan, had the important responsibility of protecting a portion of the clan's northern border, as well as their own flocks, against the Camerons and any other raiders that might seek to infringe upon their territory. It had happened before and it surely would happen again, just as it appeared would be occurring once more this day.

"James, prepare a score of the lads with bow and the gulls. We wi' set an ambush for the thieving bastards in the far forest surrounding the stony glen," the old chieftain instructed his son, a hard glare creasing his forehead and blue eyes so cold that the man's stare was known to chill his enemies blood in their veins. The fierce glower was not directed at his son, but the younger man nevertheless swallowed audibly in the face of his father's cold fury. "Make sure ye return in one piece, I'll nae hae ye haunting me in the night, nor yer mother flaying me in the day with the rough side of her tongue!"

Suddenly the weathered old chieftain smiled. "Whip some Cameron arse for yer old man and send them home with a tail between their legs. When ye return I wi' be sure to reward the scouting lads for their watchfulness."

Less than an hour following the report from the border sentries, the MacNeish clansmen, bristling with their weapons, were in their positions. Hidden within the thick, dark green embrace of fragrant Scotch pines they waited in silence for the approach of the reaving Camerons. They did not have long to wait as soon a silent alarm, delivered by hand signal, went out from man to man. The enemy moved slowly into sight and as they came closer the size of their band proved to be thirty men strong; a sizable force to be sure, but not so much as to cause the MacNeish clansmen any worry.

Young James watched attentively as the intruders, some mounted though most walking, came closer and closer and finally milling around furtively while their leaders dismounted from sturdy highland bred horses. Before the reavers could disperse among the grazing sheep to round up the wary animals the chieftain's son raised his gloved hand and yanked it down in the command to draw and let fly their gull fletched arrows.

In unison, twenty longbows snapped forward letting fly a hissing tide of long gray fletched shafts. Immediately following the deadly rain of steel tipped quarrels that washed down among the Camerons, screams of pain and agony followed by shouts of surprise and fear could be heard all too well. From within the hail of arrows, however, no further sound came from the throats of nineteen Cameron men as death had been dealt instantly by arrows slamming through chest, neck, or other vital places. Out of the remaining reavers only nine had escaped from any wound.

James' clansmen required no further orders as they surged forward, with chilling warcries, from their hiding places within the pines and down the shallow hillock to fall upon the remaining enemy. Swords raised before them, James' extended family rushed ahead with anticipation to deal more death on the raiding clansmen. Soon the opponents merged together into a sometimes graceful dance of battle as they clashed. The chill air was filled with the sharp clanging and shrieking of steel on steel; the heavy thud of weapons chopping into thick wood and leather shields and the rivaling battle cries of the fierce Cameron clansmen and the MacGregors.

The bloody skirmish was fought viciously and without mercy, as limbs along with heads were severed from bodies. Fighting, that seemed to last an eternity but in reality persisted for only moments, came to an abrupt halt as James finished off the Cameron leader with his claymore's keen blade slamming several inches deep through the middle of his young adversary's chest. The spirit from the remaining reavers vanished and, with sorrowing eyes for their fallen lord, began a hasty retreat. Of the Cameron raiding party a mere five survived to escape, and three of those nursed wounds.

With the brutal fighting at a sudden hasty end, cheers spontaneously broke out among the victorious though exhausted MacGregor clansmen. The hale slapped each of their fellows on the back in congratulations at running off the thieving enemy and also for living to survive through the melee. Cheers of victory and relief soon changed to roars of approval for their young master as he planted his foot on his dead opponent's chest and pulled free his heavy sword from the man's breast. His sword dripping with bright blood, James gripped the basket hilt with both hands and leveled a strike at the dead man's neck. The severed, tawny-bearded head of the Cameron lord bounced away from the shoulders after one economical blow.

Late that afternoon, following their triumphant return, a celebration banquet was held in honour of the chieftain's son and his brave war party. The feast lasted well into the night and the entire village turned out to stuff themselves, drink toasts to the warriors, sing songs, and listen as the bard told and retold the *Victory of Forest Down*. That night all of Dunmoore had a merry old time with plenty to eat, and often too much various spirits to drink.

The next morning came much too soon for many as they complained of aching heads from their over indulgence of beer, wine, and Scotch whisky. It was the weekly day of the hunt in which all able bodied men of Dunmoore set out to bring in meat to feed the entire village for the next week. Longbows strung and at the ready, they left shortly after dawn. It was the month's big hunt and a hawk feather was the prize for whoever brought down the largest deer. Nearly one hundred and fifty clansmen struck out with their aged chieftain and his only son and heir James Alexander, who would in time, inherit lairdship of Dunmoore and the surrounding lands.

"Today seems a bonny fine day for a hunt, do ye nae think so lad?" Old Lyam casually asked his son. His manner today had been much more relaxed; he was relieved in the knowledge that his son was returned safe from battle, but his cheerfulness seemed somewhat forced, in James' opinion. They had been riding through their forested lands eastward for the past hour, and indeed the weather had been agreeable enough: a crisp, sunny day with only wispy clouds high in the azure sky.

James glanced over at his proud father as the unease that he had been feeling all morning climbed his spine and made the hair on his hairs raise. *Perhaps Da is feeling the same thing; as if something is just nae right*, he considered to himself.

"Oh, aye. It does indeed seem like a bonny fine day, Da, but—"

Lyam turned a piercing blue stare on his only son. "Aye? Speak yer mind, laddie; ye hae been far tae quiet for yer wont this morning."

James shrugged his slender shoulders. "I'm nae sure what it is, Da. Just a feeling, I suppose, but *something* has been making me feel uneasy since we left the village," he admitted with a grimace. "It's like feeling the cold, dead fingers of the Fiddler sliding up and down my spine."

*   *   *

"Ready yer clansmen, Alfred Cameron! We soon ride out to exact the blood price of vengeance for ye, for the murder of yer rash son!" stormed Lord Robert Campbell, his voice full of contempt and blood lust. "Hasten! My clansmen are waiting and eager to fight alongside the Camerons to spill the blood of the MacGregor dogs."

"Of course, my Lord," The Cameron replied through tight lips. Turning, the man marched from the hall to seek out his warleader. "This Campbell pup barks just like his buggered father the old Duke Domeric," he muttered to himself. "And may the god that my people worship be with us all."

The Cameron chief was still muttering indignantly to himself when he, quite unexpectedly crossed paths with the man. "There ye are. I hae been looking for ye; the Campbell puppy is insisting on starting a war and is shamelessly twisting the blade of honour and vengeance to force my cooperation in it," growled Alfred, bristling eyebrows drawn down over glaring green eyes.

"Alfred, ye must calm yerself, ye'll hae a stroke," chided Edward Cameron, the able warleader of the Camerons, as he came alongside his chief and moved into step with him. "Ye must nae let that whelp of a Campbell ruffled ye sae much old friend." Pointing toward where their clansmen were moving into a mass formation on horseback, Edward went on, "We hae precisely two hundred and three fighting men combined to lead into battle. Over half of those are Campbell clansmen; let the buggers fight as they wi', I wi' nae let our lads be wasted. I promise ye that, old friend."

Not long after the Cameron leaders had joined the head of the formation, the command was shouted to move out. The joint force moved out from their staging area at a quick trot that within the hour found them within the MacGregor's territory. Hastening their pace, once reaching the lands of their enemy, the force would reach the village of Dunmoore in just over the space of a couple hours. The two bristling columns of mounted warriors continued to ride steadily on unmolested, and without pause to rest as anticipation of the coming battle grew. Soon they reached their destination and quietly the troops were put into position.

Nervously eager warriors were well hidden within the trees at the edge of the forest where the large raiding party waited for the command to charge. The young lord of the Campbells crept among his men encouraging them and repeating his generous offer of two gold coins in exchange for the head of Lyam MacNeish or his son.

"Lord, we await yer command to commence the attack," reported Campbell's lieutenant, a glint shining in his dark eyes. "The lads are eager to be spilling a fair share of MacGregor blood for ye today, sair."

"Good," Robert said, baring his even white teeth in a feral grin. "Good. They hae my permission to spill as much as they want. Begin the attack."

"Aye!" Saluting, the lieutenant darted off to relay the command.

*　　*　　*

"It was a bonny good hunt we've had today," observed Lyam, relaxing in the saddle. "Perhaps ye should ride on ahead, James, with some of the lads ye led yesterday, to just check on the village folk and ease yer mind about things."

"Aye, that I would for sure, Da!" James readily agreed, flashing a thankful smile up at his father. He was at the moment down on his knees as he finished gutting the large buck he had feathered and which he and father had tracked to this spot. "Thank ye, Da. I wi' head out just as soon as I finish here."

"Och," grunted Lyam, hitching his leg up and sliding to the ground from his seat. "Off with ye, laddie. I'm nae sae old that I can nae gut a deer by myself."

James climbed to his feet and brushed leaves and dirt from his knees. "I'll see ye at the village," he said, moving eagerly toward his horse where grazed contentedly on a patch of sweet clover.

A few minutes later, James had rounded up several of his father's retainers and with a party of thirty in tow he headed off at a canter. Soon he and his swiftly moving band had quickly left behind the main hunting party.

The uneasy feeling James had been experiencing all morning had not gone away as the day progressed, but rather had become even more intense. *At this pace we should reach home in about half an hour,* James calculated in his mind even as he urged more speed from his mount as his group came upon a well used game trail he recognized. *I wonder if this feeling of dread is what Da calls the* Second Sight?

The young MacNeish was still pondering those thoughts as he and his men neared Dunmoore, but suddenly all such thoughts were driven from his mind as the screams of terror first reached his ears through the green of the forest. His gray eyes flashing, James and his band, of one accord, kicked anxious heels into their horse's flanks demanding more speed. They could hear the mounting horrified screams, sounding as if they were being ripped from the throats of the village women.

In the village of Dunmoore all was chaos. Mothers and wives ran, scrambling about in every direction with babes in arms, striving to find their older children and seek any safe place in which for them to hide. Murdering raiders, clad in the distinct tartans of the Campbell and Cameron clans, appeared to be everywhere. Their assault on the village had been had come at the worst possible time for the poor villagers, who were left alone to defend for themselves. Already several structures were ablaze from torches flung by the attackers, while many folk had been indiscriminately cut down as rampant violence swept through the streets and homes.

Some young clanswomen, to proud and outraged at the senseless carnage to seek safety in hiding, fought back with anything and anyway that they could. At the same time, eldermen of the village, too old to be out hunting and such things, hastily emerged from their homes after uncovering the worn weapons of their youth. Hands gripped hafts of axes and hilts of swords with old familiarity after years of storage. The elders strode forward and banded together with the fellows of their youth for one final battle, to defend their homes and families with a stoic and proud resolve. Few were their numbers, no more than twenty or thirty in all, but courageously they fought with strength of the young lions they had once been. Calling upon the wiles gained of experience, the elders battled with the younger enemy. So effectively did they fight, that for a time, the old clansmen were able to hold the raiders at bay and allow some of their fellow villagers to escape into the safer confines of the surrounding forest. Such were the numbers of the enemy; however, it soon became obvious that despite their valorous stand that they would soon be overwhelmed and brought down like a proud stag by a ravenous pack of wild dogs.

Determined to fight even until their deaths, the old warriors continued to battle on, struggling more fiercely as they ever had in their younger years. Then swiftly the attackers rushed them in a concerted wave, surging forth like waters through a burst dam and swept through the brave old warriors. Although those that remained fought on, many of the enemy swarmed past them to sack and ravage the rest of the highland village, slaughtering as they went anyone still in the streets and any found hidden away. Homes and shops were looted indiscriminately for anything of value. At one point, a few raiders began taking captive unlucky young women that they fancied and forced them onto the back of horses they were riding. Death is an expensive price for lust as several of the enemy warriors discovered as the MacNeish women fought back with a passion borne from fear and outrage. Drawing forth short but very sharp skean dhu daggers from within pouches at their waist or beneath skirts, they buried the keen blades into their abductor's backs or reached around to viciously slit their throats from behind.

Despite these instances of bravery and desperation many clans' folk of the village were slain that fateful day at the hands of some men whose thirst for blood could not be slaked, no matter the quantity spilled.

Soon, James and his companions were near enough to the village that they could first smell and then see the smoke rising above the tops of the trees. One huge bear of a man that everyone called Redwood noticed the smoke first and pointed it out with a surprised shout, "James! Look ahead man! There's a lot of smoke billowing from the forest before us—oh, dear Lugh! That could nae be our village, could it?"

Just at that moment a loud shriek rent the air, coming from the likes of a young girl scared beyond her wits, until it was abruptly cut off.

Following their master's unvoiced command, the group of companions charged homeward. Digging heels into their horse's flanks they demanded an unsparing speed in their distress and urgent need.

A few minutes later, James saw with a stricken expression what he had been fearing most of all. He halted his men with a raised and clenched fist. He found he could not pull his astounded eyes away from the burning village that was his home. His dry mouth worked for a second before he could speak, but when he did his voice was harsh with violent emotion.

"The Camerons hae come upon us, and they hae brought the bloody Campbells with them!" he growled fiercely. "The bloody bastards wi' tasty out steel for this, I swear it by the Morrigan! Dismount, we wi' sneak up on them from the rear and attack them with the vengeance of the Battle Raven! Our surprise over them must be complete, my friends, fore they greatly outnumber us and we must hold them until our laird and the rest of our clansmen can return."

James and his companions dismounted and after tethering each horse to trees well back into the forest each man armed himself with javelin, longbow and quiver taken from saddle holsters. The companions were all similarly armed with personal sidearms of dirk and the distinctively highland claymore broadsword.

"Come, lads, we hae nay time to waste," urged James, fighting to hide the surge of battle fear from his friends. "Remember that we are nae doing this for personal glory, but for the lives of our kith and kin."

Moving together, like on one of their hunts, the MacNeish warriors crept forward as quietly as if stalking a deer and fanned out toward the enemy. On through the pines they went with the stealth of the expert woodsmen and hunters they were until they had snuck to within throwing range of their javelins.

Campbells formed a sort of rearguard that was intended to ward against any enemy that might approach while their main force sacked the village. There appeared to be twelve men, but they were careless in their duty as they walked about, passing along skins of ale and complaining about being left out of the fun the other clansmen were having. None had an inkling of the danger they were in until it was too late. They died to a man without so much as seeing an enemy or the slender lengths of shaved saplings with their heads of sharpened steel as they arced gracefully through the cool air.

Rushing forward, James and his companions dislodged their javelins from the limp bodies they had pierced. Some of the dead showed expressions of surprise on their face, but most were just contorted in the brief agony that snuffed out all life.

"That was easy," observed Redwood. Reclaiming his lengthy javelin he wiped the steel leaf shaped tip clean on his victim's kilt.

James glanced at him sharply. "Do nae get over confident; these men were just meat for our slaughter," he chided. Jabbing his own javelin through the loop of a wine skin, he raised it for the big man to see. "Look. They were drinking on duty, but ye can be sure that the rest are sober and full of fight."

Redwood bobbed his great curly-haired head in chagrin. "Ye're right, James. These drunken bastards never had a chance," he confessed, his tone regretful.

"Do nae worry, Redwood," James chuckled grimly, slapping his tall friend on one broad shoulder. "I'm sure there's plenty more just waiting for us beyond these trees; ye'll hae yer share of them."

Redwood's expression brightened considerably.

"Alright, lads. Listen up," ordered James, turning to address to others. "Nine of ye with yer bows wi' accompany me. The rest of ye wi', under the cover of our arrows," he explained his plan of action, "strike off toward the right flank, where I believe they wi' be keeping our flocks. Redwood wi' lead ye lot, and yer first duty is to recover them at whatever the cost if our folk are to survive starvation. May the honour of the House of MacNeish and of Clan Gregor guide ye and protect ye all. Ye wi' ken our diversion when it comes; that is when ye'll ken to make yer move."

Waiting in their concealed position along the outer ring of the forest's trees, James and his squad of archers prepared for the right moment to attack. Each of the ten men had a first arrow nocked with another dozen stuck lightly, point first into the ground before them. They did not have long to wait before a group of mounted Campbells trotted several yards away of their hidden position. When the horsemen passed directly before them, James raised his longbow with as men following his lead, and without much apparent effort at taking aim, let fly his arrow. Nine more arrows followed immediately, the twang of bowstrings singing in unison. The effect of their attack was lethal as each targeted rider near the rear of the column suddenly found, to their astonishment, a gull fletched, cloth-yard arrow sprouting from his neck. Each rider toppled bonelessly from his horse, dead before hitting the ground.

To James' pleasant surprise, the tactic of attacking those to the rear of the column had gone completely unobserved as the others continued on without pause. Nodding to his men the young leader nocked another arrow and together they systematically chose targets to the rear of the mounted column. The next wave of arrows dropped ten more warriors from their saddles, but this time the attack did not go unobserved as Campbell and Cameron alike gawked about in shock at their fallen companions. Another wave of hissing arrows dropped ten more warriors from the now disorderly column and finally, this brought the desired reaction that James had been waiting for.

The column of reserve horsemen fell into complete disarray as the enemy began ducking behind their horses, each other, and anything else that might offer them cover some cover from the deadly hail of arrows raining down upon them.

The second group of MacNeishs, in a position far off on the right flank, watched the effect of their fellow clansmen's arrows on the enemy with earnest attention. Seeing their enemies cowering away from the deadly barrage of missiles, and having all of their attention drawn in that direction, the MacNeish men saw the opportunity that they had been waiting for and prepared to seize it.

"Alright lads, come on, it's time now to earn our keep," ordered redwood, a thick red beard of whiskers bristling as he spoke. "None of those sorry bastards wi' be poking his head out to look around for awhile. Let's to it."

Moving in silence, as only natural hunters can do, the score of companions broke cover from their position just within the treeline. Sprinting across the dangerously open area of pasture fields, rich in nothing but clover, they hastened for the welcoming shadows of woods waiting directly across from their previous hiding place. At last they had each plunged in to the safety of the wood's underbrush, the enemy taking no notice of their headlong run as they remained wary of the lethally accurate arrows..

Catching his breath, Redwood watched briefly as a younger Campbell tartan clad man rode up to the horsemen's pinned down position. Even from as far away as he was, the huge, muscular MacNeish man could clearly see the look of seething rage contorting the young gentleman's sparsely bearded face. Still grinning to himself, Redwood led his fellows off toward where they believed the raiding clansmen had moved and would be guarding the village flocks.

Spread out and moving with patient hunting stealth, Redwood and his comrades flipped off into the woods, stalking their human prey. Well before they might catch sight of their quarry, the mournful bleeding of frightened sheep reached the clansmen's ears and helped guide them on. Soon, as they crept silently closer, the MacNeish retainers caught glimpses of the black coated sheep they sought, through narrow openings in the thick woodland growth, as the anxious animals grazed half-heartedly on patches of tough yellowed grasses that had survived through the winter. Standing idly among the massive combined MacNeish flocks, a dozen Camerons kept watch over the rich prize of their surprise raid, to see that none of the unpredictable animals wandered off.

*   *   *

"Cowards! The whole lot of ye are nothing but cowards!" shrieked the incensed Lord Robert Campbell, his whole body shaking in reaction. Endeavoring to dampen the rage that he felt the young lordling closed his dark eyes as took a deep breath.

Reopening his eyes, he glanced over the bodies of his clansmen and those of his ally and sighed in disgust. "I want a count of our dead," he ordered tersely. "Is there any man *jack* among ye that could *possibly* tell me just how many times the bloody arrows fell upon ye? Or are ye all tae lily-livered to even recall that detail?"

Nervously, a black bearded veteran Cameron warrior cleared his throat. Strong fingers gripped the hilt of his sword as he met the young lord's fierce glare with a calm one of his own.

"Speak," Robert ordered curtly.

"My lord," began the Cameron, with forced respect, "three times it was that the enemy fired volleys of arrows upon us that I witnessed, and nae counting individual arrows that feathered targets of opportunity. However, since the initial attack, I hae discovered another squad of our warriors lying dead close to those woods just there," the Cameron reported, pointing a thick calloused finger toward the treeline where James and his band of archers had been hiding.

"My lord," interrupted an aide of the Campbell lord, sketching a hasty salute as he received the annoyed attention of his master. "My lord, the total body count from this column is twenty-eight dead and two wounded."

Robert Campbell nodded his head with grim solemnity. "I see. Does yer count also include that group of our clansmen that lay over there toward the treeline?" he asked stiffly, pointing where the Cameron officer had just directed his attention.

The young aide swallowed audibly in dismay as he followed the line of his lord's finger to where several tartaned heaps lay unmoving. "Nay, nay, my lord, they hae nae been counted yet," he answered in a quavering voice. "Please excuse my mistake, Lord Robert, I wi' return shortly with a proper count."

Turning his back on the camp aide with a look of disgust, the frustrated Campbell lordling dismissed him with a haughty wave of his hand.

His attention quickly returned to the burly Cameron officer still waiting near at hand, and Robert raised his hand in an unneeded gesture to gain the notice of all those nearby. "Brave warriors! Take heart in the news that ye hae been attacked and pinned down by a lusty group of about ten clever archers hidden within the edge of that wood. They hae slain, I would guess, upward of forty warriors just among ye," he paused dramatically for those numbers to sink in. "It is wise to believe that, if they hae assaulted ye from that position, their small band of archers hae also eliminated those stalwart souls we left behind as our rearguard.

"Ye can be sure that these MacNeish archers ken all these lands like the back of their hand," admitted Robert, grudging respect for his foe hidden in his cold clinical tone. A hard glint in his eyes, he added, "I do nae care how many of ye it takes, nor how long, but I want them all dead. I want each of their heads taken as trophies for my officer's javelin. Ye," he pointed imperiously at the black bearded Cameron officer, "are in charge of seeing my orders carried out. Choose as many men as ye desire, Randall, but before I leave ye to it, ken this: return successful and I wi' promote ye myself, but if ye do nae come back with those heads, do nae bother to return at all.

Tossing his head arrogantly, Robert turned and mounted his chestnut charger, the horse having been brought up by another aide. Pointing his mount toward the smoking village of Dunmoore, the Campbell lord missed the look of contempt that was directed at him by Randall Cameron and several others among their number.

Immediately, upon the young Campbell lord's leaving earshot, quarreling broke out among the Camerons and Campbells, involving who would be those chosen to go out on this mission with Randall.

The squabbling was so vociferous that from their position James and his band of archers could not help but share amused grins among themselves while gathering up their remaining arrows. Soon the group of MacNeish men was quietly scampering off through the woods, following the sweep of forest as it angled around the village. As they moved beyond the left flank of the enemy they slowed but continued on until they were near a point where they hoped to enter the village unobserved.

When James and his retainers were finally able to sneak within the confines of their village they were appalled and outraged at what they witnessed, while at the same time felt their hearts fill with pride. Before them lay the scattered bodies of the dead and wounded: men, women, and children. The carnage was horrific as friend and foe alike lay where they had fallen among the blood and gore. The stench of that gore along with the foulness of released bowels was nearly enough to turn their stomachs.

Several of the village's wooden buildings were ablaze, billowing thick, black smoke high into the air. The MacNeish men watched with growing indignation as folk they had known all his life were robbed and bodies of the slain were looted of anything that might be of value. Beyond the looting and pillaging, however, was a different scene altogether as in the village common a small group of eldermen still fought valiantly to protect their home. Despite the fact that they were completely ringed about and greatly outnumbered by their enemies, while being taunted and jeered by Campbell and Cameron clansmen alike, they resolutely refused to yield even in the face of death.

"Ha, when are ye auld men going to give up?" Robert Campbell mocked them from where he sat comfortably astride his horse. "Ye can nae possibly believe that ye can hold out against us. Yer village is in flames; yer flocks are ours. Ye hae already lost, but if ye wi' lay down yer arms I may still choose to be merciful."

"To hell wi' ye, ye arrogant lordling!" growled one elder. "I would rather be cut down where I stand than surrender to the haughty pup of an ignoble bastard!"

"Come and try yer *skill* against *me* if ye dare!" barked another of the old warriors, his face worn like old leather with a thick dark beard peppered through with gray. He spat on the ground in contempt as he menacingly hefted his imposing battleaxe.

A sudden flush of seething rage colored the Campbell lord's sallow face crimson. Sputtering with indignation, he pointed a shaking finger at the bearded old warrior and cried, "Kill him! I want his ugly head on a stick—ugh! Oh, my God!" Robert's eyes went wide, bulging in frightened surprise as his face abruptly drained of color. Glancing down in shock he stared at the long shaft of a barbed arrow protruding from the center of his chest. His last breath groaned from his lips with a spatter of bright blood just before he tumbled bonelessly from his tall stallion; the duke's heir was dead before landing in a heap at the feet of his shocked retainers.

All of a sudden the chill smoky air was alive with the hiss of flying arrow shafts. Many of the missiles flew true, finding their mark in the bodies of Campbell clansmen and their allies wearing the Cameron tartan. Without delay the armed eldermen surged forward, showing a vigor that belayed their age, and savagely attacked their tormentors. In short order, they dispatched the remaining immediate enemy that had survived being cut down by the shower of arrows fired by James' band. The vicious melee ended with no enemy left alive to report their defeat or the death of their young master.

Even as James and his exuberant archers ran forward from their hidden positions to greet the valiant eldermen, the grizzled old warrior, wielding his massive battleaxe, relieved the Campbell lord of his sparsely bearded head with a single deft swing of his great axe. Holding aloft the severed head of his enemy, he cried out triumphantly to the ancient Celtic god named Nuada, "Thanks to ye, High King of the Sidhe, for this bonny trophy of my over-proud enemy."

Another of the eldermen welcomed James with a hearty slap on the shoulder. "Well met, lad. We are glad at yer timely appearance," he said with feeling. "I did nae ken how much longer we could hae lasted without yer sudden aid, Jamey-lad. How did ye happen to return hame sae early?"

"Never mind that now," the axe wielder broke in abruptly. "The bastards first came upon us, upward of an hour ago, like a swarm of reaving locusts. We auld bastards fought them like the warriors of our youth, valiantly, I might add, and though we did lose sixteen of our twenty-eight still able to fight," the burly axe wielder related with a grim smile, "we left twice that many of them dead at our feet."

The grizzled elder's smile widened before continuing, "And then ye showed up, my bonny Nephew, with these fine archers, and helped my lot by killing fourteen more of these thieving bastards!"

Crimwal, the aged axe wielder and James' own uncle, grinned again and slapped James exuberantly on the back. Starting to chuckle, the MacNeish chieftain's brother, reveled in the fatigue he felt in long unused muscles. Feeling young again, his laughter became infectious as his friends chuckles joined in with his.

Answering the eldermen's laughter with a determinedly grim smile, James spoke up resolutely, "We must drive the rest of them from our lands, Uncle. From what the lads and I hae seen, they still clearly outnumber us. I do hae a plan that may work; if we put the Campbell lordling's head on the end of a spear and show them that their leader is dead, it may prompt the rest of them to give up and flee."

"Yer dear father is right about ye, James," Crimwal replied with approval. "Ye hae a good head on yer shoulders, even at yer tender age. I believe that ye wi' make a formidable chieftain when yer time comes. It is a clever idea ye propose, lad, and I think it just may succeed. Come, lads, let's do as James has said."

As it turned out, the plan worked even better than James had hoped. While the combined party marched through the ravaged village, toward where the allied enemies were marshalling the bulk of their warriors, they were sighted straight away. Swiftly a band of the raiders were alerted to their approach and hurried forward to intercept them, brandishing drawn weapons and howling with anticipation.

Watching the enemy clansmen rapidly approach, Crimwal calmly hoisted up his borrowed spear with the Campbell lord's head unceremoniously impaled upon the tip. With growing curiosity the group of Campbell tartaned warriors continued to close with the MacNeishs, wondering what they were up to. Suddenly, one in the approaching band, cried out in dismay as he recognized at last whose head rode upon the spear. Anguished cries quickly spread from man to man as each could see that their duke's son and heir was slain by their enemies.

As the Campbell clansmen milled together in consternation, James punctuated his point and ordered Crimwal to heave the top heavy spear in their direction, returning the dead lord's head to them in disgrace.

Taking two loping bounds, the old warrior flung the burdened spear toward the bewildered Campbells. The laden spear swept high into the air and had almost borne down upon them before someone shouted a startled warning, but by then it was too late. The spear arced downward in its flight and struck one of their officers square in the chest. The keen spearhead pierced through the attached skull and only halted it's momentum after punching clear through the unfortunate man with several inches of bloodied steel slicing clean through the back of his chain armor and protruding from his back. As the officer slumped to his knees, the split skull rolled to a stop before him and its blank gaze seemed to glare up at the stricken soldier. The horrified warriors stared at the accusing skull with superstitious fear; several of the Campbell clansmen instinctively crossed themselves with consternation.

Casting nervous glances amongst themselves, the Campbell retainers muttered fearfully while they waited as one of their number carefully retrieved the mutilated head of their Lord Robert and placed it gingerly into a canvas bag. Once the trembling warrior had secured the battered trophy, he cast a wary glance back at his lord's killers, the man shouted at the others and together they ran back to the safely of their lines.

James waited with his party, and shivered as he listened to the undulating wails of mourning for the young lord rising from the Campbell encampment. He was grateful for the distraction when Redwood and his part of his band appeared, cautiously approaching from behind one of the few mostly undamaged structures left in the village.

Questions were in the huge clansman's eyes when he gripped James' hand, but he withheld his queries until he reported of the success of his raid.

"They outnumbered me and the lads, of course, but we took them unawares," he said, grinning broadly. "We killed ten of the bastards and left the other two wounded and trussed up and gagged, hanging well up in a tree, just in case ye wanted to question them later. We herded the flocks into one of our alternate, secluded pastures with half of the lads left behind to guard them."

"Did ye lose anyone?" asked James.

Redwood grinned again. "None. We took some cuts and gashes, but nothing tae serious. Sae, tell me, what is all that wailing about?" he demanded, unable to contain his curiosity any longer.

"Ach, the bloody Campbells are crying because they just got a taste of their own medicine and do nae care tae much for the flavor," growled Crimwal.

"They're mourning for their duke's son, Robert, that we slew," elaborated James. With a shrug, he added, "They're nae taking it very well."

Crimwal snorted. "I do nae see why any man could feel the need to mourn the passing of such an ill-mannered, disgraceful bastard as Robert Campbell. He is much tae much like his bloody father," interjected James' stalwart uncle, obviously still smarting from the Campbell lord's tongue.

"Someone's coming, James," noted one of the archers.

Coming from the Campbell lines, two men mounted on impressive tall steeds, plodded slowly toward where the MacNeish warriors waited on the main village street. The riders came on with an escort of six marching warriors, as protocol allowed under the truce flag one horseman bore, in plain view, on the head of a spear. Reaching the mid point between the two groups of combatants, they halted and waited, eyeing James and his men with a calm but wary demeanor.

"Let's hear what they hae to say," ordered James. Trudging ahead, the chieftain's son was joined by Crimwal and Redwood, along with four other retainers. About a dozen paces away from the parleying adversary they halted and looked over the men before them, noting the wealthy appearance of the apparent leader.

"Greetings, I am Alfred, Chief of Clan Cameron," spoke the richly armored, elder gentleman. Handing off his reins to one his men, Alfred dismounted smoothly, stepping forward to address James on even footing. "I desired to speak wi' ye before we leave yer borders, and to warn ye of something—"

"Ye warn us? Ye certainly hae some gall Cameron!" Crimwal stormed furiously, hefting his battleaxe with intended menace.

"Uncle!" barked James. "Put away yer weapon, we are met under a flag of truce. Do nae stain yer honour or the honour of our family with such behavior," he commanded in a tight steely voice.

Gradually, Crimwal regained his composure and with a heavy thump, grounded the broad head of his axe between his feet. Only when he had done so did the Cameron retainers, sent to guard their chief, release white-knuckled grips on their weapons, though they continued to trade angry glares with the grizzled axeman.

"Ye were saying, Lord Alfred?" James prompted calmly.

"Aye. I'm nae here to threaten ye," assured The Cameron, "but ye should ken that although ye hae fought nobly today against the impetuous and dishonourable ways of the young lord of the Campbells, the duke wi' nae see it that way. He whose head ye hae so unceremoniously returned on the head of a pike was the eldest son of Duke Domeric of Clan Campbell. And ye would be wise to be prepared for his wrath.

"In exchange for my warning, I would ask a boon of ye," he added. "The granting of what I request costs ye nothing, but would mean the world to me."

"What would ye hae of me?" James wondered in puzzlement.

"I would ask for the body of my own son," explained Alfred. "He was the leader of the raiding party yesterday, and he did nae return hame."

James nodded in sudden understanding and immediately ordered two of his men to go and retrieve the body and its severed head.

When the men returned, they bore the young man's body wrapped in thick cloths and the head washed, bound in gauze and placed in a lidded basket. In silence, the two packages were turned over to the Cameron men and in turn secured to the back of the second rider's horse with utmost care.

When the visibly aged Cameron chief spoke again, it was in a voice softened with grief and a certain amount of meekness. "I thank ye for yer kindness, Laird Dunmore; do ye ken who ended my son?"

Again James nodded. "Aye. I did the deed, sair," he admitted, "but I am nae laird of this place yet; my father is chieftain of the House of MacNeish. I am James MacNeish, son of Lyam MacNeish, Laird of Dunmore.

"Yer son fought bravely and died the same way, as befitting the son of a chief," he said, looking the man square in the eye. "It was a quick ending, without undue pain and suffering, I swear to ye on the honour of House MacNeish."

Hearing those kind words, Alfred almost smiled, in gratitude but also with pride in the manner of his son's honorable comportment and the knowledge that he had died bravely in combat at the hands of a worthy opponent.

Alfred nodded his appreciation. "We wi' be leaving yer lands peacefully, in short order," he promised. "Truly, I held nay grudge against ye or yer kin. This horrid attack launched against yer village was commanded by Duke Domeric, of whom it is my misfortune to obey as liege lord. It is clear that he wished to use the death of my son as his excuse to make war upon ye and yer clan," he explained, some heat coming into his voice at the indignity of it all. "He cared nae at all whether *my son* died, nay more than he would care if *I* had come to grief today. Ye see, wi' the death of myself and my heirs, the Cameron lands and title would be his.

"Fare well, James," he said, offering his hand in friendship. "We must be going now, before the Campbell officers grow suspicious about the length of this parley with ye. May we meet again under more peaceful circumstances."

"I pray that it may be so," agreed James, accepting the chief's hand.

The lord of Clan Cameron remounted his proud horse. Accepting the reins from his waiting retainer, and with a departing nod, Alfred wheeled his steed about with the deft touch of a born rider, and set forth. Without a backward glance, the chief rode off toward his lines while his retainers followed in his wake past the dead bodies of their unlamented Campbell allies.

Once The Cameron and his men had returned to their encampment, Alfred could be seen personally helping the wounded and with gathering the dead from his clan for transportation back to their own territory for funeral rites.

*   *   *

Later on that rainy evening, the fires throughout the village had been quenched, and once the wounded of Dunmore had been attended to, the time for grieving over the loss of loved ones began. The dismaying sounds of girls and women keening for their dead husbands and sons slain during the savage attack, and for daughters that had been brutally raped, filled the gloomy evening with profound sadness. Funeral pyres were built for the dead and set ablaze to cleanse the Earth and to release those Christian souls to fly free of a useless husk and ascend to heaven, to join God there for an eternity of peace that they had not known during their mortal life.

The funeral fires lighted the grim night as old Lyam honoured the beloved slain by leading the passing rites of the dead. Once those sad rites had been completed the bravery of the eldermen was also given a proper tribute, along with that of James and his gallant band of archers, for their courageous stand against the overwhelming numbers of the ruthless enemy.

It was into the chill night before most of the mourners had exhausted themselves with their grief and had at last bedded down where they could. James did not find an opportunity until then to speak privately with his father, finding the aged leader at last alone, in his longhouse, warming himself before a crackling fire.

"Da, I must speak wi' ye about something."

Startled, the weathered chieftain glanced up sharply from the pewter tankard cupped between his sinewy fingers and eyed the one which disturbed his reverie. The rebuke that leapt to his lips vanished as he realized the intruder was his son. His angular face shifted from anger to a somewhat wary expression as James moved toward his father's side before the stone hearth.

"I thought to myself that ye would be coming to see yer ole Da soon, Jamie. Sit yerself down, laddie, so I do nae hae to get a crick in my neck looking up at ye," ordered Lyam in his usual brisk manner, pointing to a comfortable wooden, padded chair next to the one he occupied.

"Who led the Campbells and Camerons against us, lad?"

The abrupt question caught James by surprise and he lowered himself into the offered chair before answering. "Well, I ken that Lord Alfred came with his Camerons, and Robert Campbell, the duke's eldest son led his clan," he related slowly. "The overall command of the war party seemed to fall to Robert, despite the Cameron chief being in attendance. I ken that Lord Alfred was in command for their retreat once I had properly feathered the cocky Campbell brat."

Considering the young man's earnest expression the tired old chieftain could not help but grin in response. He affectionately remembered how he had been, all those years ago, when he had still been a virile young man.

"Aye. Aye, James," he agreed, slowly nodding his head. "Ye surely did that. A fine archer ye hae grown to be; one of the finest I hae ever seen. But, unfortunately for all of us, that pompous old fool, Duke Domeric Campbell wi' nae be so pleased with yer choice of targets. Mark my words, James: the duke wi' be out to exact blood vengeance for the death of his eldest son and heir. As things were, he was already waiting for just such an ideal excuse to start a full-blown border war with our clan, and now I believe he has just discovered one, all wrapped and tied up with a bright bow, that the king can nae merely wave away," Lyam confided.

With a sigh, the old chieftain raised the tankard to his mouth and quaffed down the remainder of his ale. "Ach. The king wi' be totally impotent to intercede, even more so because our Lord Gregor is wedded to His Majesty's daughter."

"Ye must let me ride straightaway for Glenorchy!" exclaimed James, earnest in his desire to try and make amends for the deed that had brought about the coming storm of war. "Lord Gregor has to be warned about the Campbells that he may prepare a ready defense of the clan borders!"

Paternal pride and a certain grim satisfaction shone in Lyam's weathered face as he intently regarded his son's eagerness to accept responsibility for his actions, and take the initiative to warn the clan of danger, while also placing himself in a position to face their chief's possible wrath.

"Ye are my son and we are of a like mind about this," agreed Lyam, his leathery face stretching into a fond smile. "The sooner ye are on yer way the better, lad. Choose yer escort, Jamie, and make it a full warband. It wi' show of our commitment to totally rally with our clan, if it should come down to a full blown border war with the bleeding Campbells and their allies.

"How soon can ye be ready to ride out, lad?"

Already on his feet, James was eager to be out and selecting the men that he would be riding out with. His mind already racing, James distractedly glanced down at his father and said, "We wi' be equipped and ready to ride out by nay later than early tomorrow morning—with Redwood's help, of course."

Flashing his beloved father a cheerful, although, excited smile, James rushed from the longhouse and into the night. Stalking forth at a purposeful gait he was impatient to seek out the fellows that he would have at his back. Equipment had to be collected and provisions packed ahead for the busy morning coming that was a mere few hours away. The first among his friends that he sought out was the stalwart Redwood, who would be his trusted lieutenant of the MacNeish warband as they made their hasty journey to their lord's stronghold nestled in the beautiful hills of Glenorchy.

Beneath the clear starlit night, the MacNeish chieftain's son James laboured tirelessly. His mind was still fast at work choosing an additional ten warriors that would make the expedition, along with himself and the original thirty brave hearts, to give warning to Lord Gregor MacGregor and their clan of the eminent threat from their enemy in the person of Duke Domeric Campbell.

CHAPTER TWO

The new morning dawned with a crispness in the air that did not dissipate until it was close to mid-morning, fleeing upon the arrival of the welcomed bright sunlight that was at last revealed from high and fast moving clouds.

James and his band of hand chosen clansmen had moments before finished the job of loading supplies and personal gear onto their tough mountain ponies. Now they bid their goodbyes to the family, friends, and sweethearts that they might not see for perhaps a long time. No one spoke of the possibility that, if there truly ended up being a border war with their enemy, the Campbells, some of them may never return.

It was a grand send off and it appeared as though the entire village had turned out to offer their best wishes to the brave band soon to set off. Fathers offered last minute advice while friends shouted encouragement; mothers made sure sons had plenty of food and extra clothes, while sweethearts and wives offered heartfelt tears and kisses and tokens of love to take along with them.

"Fare ye well, lad," said Lyam, embracing his son with a wiry strength. "Take heed of stout Redwood's advice in the days to come, James. He's proven himself a fine hunter and warrior, with a good head on his shoulders, just as ye do. The lad has a good heart as well, he wi' nae let ye down.

"It's time now that ye were on yer way, lad. May God guide yer path," the old man offered a parting blessing, "and Lugh's long arm protect ye."

Giving his sire a final grim smile, the young lord climbed onto his rugged pony and motioned for his warband to follow suit. Proudly riding at the head of his weapon bristling band, James led his forty men forth out of Dunmoore to the sweet skirling sound of *Scotland the Brave* played by a lone bagpiper.

The immense Redwood rode a hard pressed pony, which occasionally cast an accusing glance back at the large man, at his friend and leader's side. Sighing, he looked away from his grimacing mount and quietly said, "Ye ken, James, there's nothing that sounds so bonny fine as the pipes, and nay place I hae more wanted to return and visit than our chief's Glenorchy. Tae bad it was nae under other circumstances."

James chuckled softly as he regarded the mournful animal plodding at his side before addressing his friend. "I went there as a wee lad with my Da, but I was tae young to really remember much about it."

"Och, it was the finest most wonderful place I had ever seen," Redwood assured him. "The castle seemed to be as big as nearly half of our entire village. It had walls, that Da said were forty feet tall, that surrounded the whole bastion and there was also another shorter wall that ringed the town sprawling below the castle, on it's hill," the bearish warrior told his companion, a rapt look in his slate gray eyes, as he again beheld the place in his mind's eye. The memory of his earlier visit stood out clear in his mind as he thought about the old glory of their clan's seat of power.

"Just wait, Jamie, ye wi' see for yerself," promised Redwood, a gleam in his eyes. "Ye ken, even if the walls of Caer Glenorchy were somehow breeched, the great keep itself would never be taken. Storming the keep would be sheer suicide for any attacker; a handful of resolute men could hold off an army by themselves," he assured with the devout faith of a missionary. "Ye wi' be impressed and proud tae, Jamie."

"Aye, I'm sure I wi' be, if Glenorchy so impressed ye, Redwood," agreed James, nodding his head. "Before we speak on, I hae a matter that must be resolved. I had nay time to speak with ye about it before we departed this morning."

"Aye? Go ahead and speak yer piece."

"Well, father and I talked a bit before our departure and we agreed that, if ye are willing, ye should be my lieutenant of this mission and from now on. What say ye? Wi' ye do this for me?" James asked, studying the big warrior's face.

The man's broad face abruptly split into a huge grin, even white teeth gleaming through a forest of wild bushy red whiskers. "Of course I wi' do it, Jamie! Ye are my best friend and ye honour me with yer trust, and I swear that it is a trust that wi' never be betrayed as long as I hae breath!"

"Ach, I ken that, ye great ox," replied James in reassurance. "Nay man ever had such a loyal friend as like I hae in ye, Redwood. And truly, if events lead us to indeed hae a border war to fight, I would rather hae none but ye guarding my side and watching my back. I value yer advice as well as yer strength, so remember to always feel free to share yer council with me," he said, the sincerity within his voice choking the joy Redwood had felt and replacing it with the true gravity of his new responsibility.

All day did the MacNeish warband ride, stopping only briefly every couple of hours to water the ponies and have a bite to eat themselves. It was past dusk before they finally stopped to set up camp for the night.

Early the next morning the band rose before dawn and broke their fast on rations packed carefully within saddlebags. Shortly thereafter, the forty broke camp in whispered silence and continued on their journey.

Over the following days they traveled on with the same discipline, each man sore from hours in the saddle. Short breaks they made during each day to rest the ponies and let them graze on lush green grass and clover, while the men enjoyed the respite to hungrily eat food they carried with them. Each night the party of warriors stopped only when it was too dark and footing too dangerous to continue farther.

It was now their third day of travel and James' warband had stopped toward mid day to rest their ponies. The ponies contentedly grazed, while the MacNeish men eagerly munched on ripe red apples that hanged from laden trees that grew close along the banks of a gurgling little creek.

On towards evening that day, James and his warband first heard and then saw a mounted patrol of MacGregor tartaned soldiers charging toward them at a dead gallop, having presumed to have discovered a band of raiders or bandits. James halted his party, hastily throwing up a gauntleted fist. Throwing a quick glance at his master, Redwood unobtrusively guided his mount between where James waited and began to reach for the enormous axe strapped across his broad back.

"Nay weapons!" snapped James, pitching his voice loud enough for everyone to hear him. "They're friends; they just do nae ken it yet."

Swiftly the newcomers, following their leader, closed the shadowy distance with the anxiously waiting MacNeish men. Their hooves drummed the earth like thunder and fading sunlight cast the occasional gleam from drawn swords.

Slowly drawing his sword, James waited until he knew the patrol's captain was near enough to see him clearly. Carefully then, he raised the shiny blade by the hilt and sharp tip with both hands above his head to let the stylized thistle tassel, which represented his family within the clan, flutter in the mild breeze. He hoped that the clan officer would recognize the symbol.

He did.

It was a mere few hours ride, it turned out, to reach Glenorchy but in the company of the hard faced soldiers it seemed a lot longer than that. The clan patrol escorted James and his men the rest of the way to their destination, though it seemed less a friendly escort and more like a detail of armed guards sent to conduct villains to gaol. The captain leading the patrol rode beside James, and though he honoured the symbol that had been shone, he had not lost his grim disposition towards his new charges.

The dour captain removed his helmet and lifted an end of his plaid to wipe a bead of perspiration from his brow. His hair was thinning and iron gray, which surprised James as the man appeared hale and fit with no sign of graying in his thick mustaches.

"I'm a soldier, nae a bloody diplomat," he stated blandly, as if he spoke to the air with no one else about to hear. Reseating the unadorned helm upon his head, he turned cold eyes to regard the young man riding beside him. "I am nae persuaded by the mere appearance of a MacNeish symbol that some stranger may wave in my face," declared the captain. "Ye lot could very well hae murdered the true holder of that token."

James glared at the man but bit his tongue at the last minute, realizing that what the hard bitten officer had said was something that had possibly happened before. "I can see yer point, Captain," he admitted.

"Ye and yer men wear the MacNeish markings," acknowledged the captain, "but ye wi' only persuade me that is who ye truly are by answering a question for me. Tell me truthfully or I wi' ken it," he challenged, fingering his own tasseled sword hilt.

His face red with anger, James tersely nodded his head. "Ask yer question, Captain, I grow tired of this distrust and insult to my honour."

"Very well, laddie," the officer agreed. "Tell me then: there is a man of our clan called Crimwal. What can ye tell me of him?"

The stony expression melted from James' face so swiftly to be replaced by a grin that the captain raised his eyebrows in wonder.

James snorted and shook his head. "Aye, I ken somewhat of this old Crimwal, considering that he is my own uncle!"

"Truly? What did ye say yer name was laddie?"

"I am James Alexander MacNeish, eldest son and heir to the MacNeish chieftain and laird of Dunmoore, Lyam MacNeish," he said proudly. "Crimwal is my father's own brother. Now, Captain, are ye quite satisfied or would ye prefer to continue on with yer interrogation?" he asked, annoyance thick in his tone.

The officer chuckled to himself. "Young master, ye would nae enjoy it so much if ye were *interrogated* by me; of that ye can be sure. This was but a pleasant conversation. Ye do seem to hae inherited ole Crimwal's temper, something I had nay problem with, but which had a way of landing ole Crimwal into his share of hot water," he admitted, trying to hide a smirk behind his whiskers. "I am Captain Gaston Grant. Crimwal and I, of old, are great friends and hae long been sae from when we served in Lord Gregor's Household Guard together some years ago.

"I remained in the Guard, it's what I ken best," he admitted without regret, "but Crimwal returned home to Dunmoore, where some lovely wench beguiled him. I hae nae seen the ole rascal for some time; how is h doing?"

"He is well," replied James. "He is still more than capable with the axe, as he sure proved less than a week past."

"I hear the makings a story in that last statement, young master," Gaston pointed out with curiosity. "Perhaps the story I hae nae heard yet is the reason behind why ye and yer warband are traveling to Glenorchy?"

James nodded solemnly. "Aye. I am the bearer of grim news; that, unfortunately, is the purpose that brings me and this warband to Lord Gregor's hall." He continued on with his report before the captain could interrupt, "The Campbells are seeking to start a border war with our clan. They hae already led an attack, with their ally the Camerons, on Dunmoore and hae killed villagers while also firing a number of buildings in the process before our weekly hunting party returned to discover them and run them off. In the fighting, the Campbell duke's son, Robert was slain by an arrow. My arrow," James related, shrugging his shoulders ruefully. "The bastard *did* hae it coming, but it appears that through my actions, I may hae given the duke all the excuse he needs to wage the war he has been longing for."

As James had explained what had led him to Glenorchy, Gaston's face had grown ashen and troubled by the time the chieftain's had finished speaking.

"I'm sure Robert did deserve his fate," agreed the veteran officer. Pausing to compose his thoughts as much as anything else, he removed his heavy helmet and wiped at the sudden sweat beading his brow. Slowly he returned the helm to his head, hiding once more the only sign of his sixty odd years.

Gaston nodded decisively, more to himself than to the young man near his side. "I wi' hae ye before Lord Sean immediately.

He is the clan's warlord," he explained for James' benefit. "He wi' ken what to do about this muddle more than anyone else, besides he is the personal friend of Lord Gregor."

It was not long before the first view of Glenorchy came into sight. The size of the town dwarfed that of Dunmoore, but the streets were laid out with care and a surprising order. The structures were neat and well cared for, while the streets themselves were tidy and free of rubbish. Surrounding the entire town was a thick stone wall about twenty feet tall where guards could be seen on patrol along its length. The heavy iron bound gates were currently open for folk to come and go as they pleased, under the watchful gaze of the constabulary. Looming above all this was Caer Glenorchy. Situated upon a natural hill of considerable size in the center of the town, which had grown up around it, the castle was an impressive fortress of pale granite with its own tall and mighty bulwarks. Flying proudly from the towers were the banners of Scotland and below it Clan Gregor. The upper most flag was a field of blue with the white saltire cross of Saint Andrew. The flag beneath was more intricate, bearing the arms of the clan on gold with the stylized roaring lion wearing a crown.

James felt a shiver of pride as a beheld the seat of Clan Gregor's power, and as he glanced around he saw that his companions were feeling the same emotion. It was then that Redwood trotted his weary mount up to James' left side, a wide grin fairly splitting his face in two, and saluted his leader.

"I told ye that she was beautiful," he said joyfully. "She's the most impressive sight I hae ever beheld; she makes me proud just to gaze upon her."

"Aye," James wholeheartedly agreed, his smile a match for the one on his friend's face. "Just seeing Glenorchy makes me feel safe."

The large band of armed warriors, with their escort of Household Guard, entering Glenorchy and riding up the main thoroughfare garnered the interest of the townsfolk and soon everyone along route was turned out to witness the arrivals firsthand. Several shouted to Captain Grant asking what was going on. The officer waved but offered no response to the curious inquiries.

The large group was soon admitted within the thick gates of the stronghold where they were met in the courtyard by a number of soldiers and stablemen.

Once their mounts had been attended to, the MacNeish men were parted from James. Redwood went with them and took charge as they were shown to the barracks, where they were promised some welcome hot food, and would be bedded down for their stay at Glenorchy. Seeing that Redwood had things well in hand, and along with the MacNeish men was being welcomed, shown around and introduced to the soldiers who were currently off duty, James followed Gaston into the keep. Somewhere inside, James knew that Lord Sean MacSean awaited his arrival, and also knew that the clan's warlord would be expecting an explanation for a war with the Campbells.

Marching down a long hallway, James followed Captain Grant as the officer guided him through the bowels of the extensive keep. Soldiers flanking a broad wooden door snapped smartly to attention as the captain neared.

Standing aside, one soldier opened the door and said, "Please go in, Lord Sean is inside and expecting ye, sair."

Gaston and the young laird strode through the portal, entering the room with its high ceilings and walls well appointed with martial paraphernalia. As they entered a tall athletic man rose from a lavishly carved wooden chair, which sat behind a heavy oak desk, to politely greet his visitors.

"Welcome to Glenorchy, Master James," he said in a rich baritone voice. "I am Sean MacSean, please come in and be seated. Captain," he said, turning to the waiting officer, "thank ye for escorting my guest. Yer diligence is appreciated but I wi' nae keep ye any longer from yer men."

"Thank ye, my lord," he acknowledged the dismissal with a crisp salute. Turning, the officer withdrew, his steps echoing slightly as he marched off down the hallway until one of the soldiers outside quietly closed the door.

Lord Sean stepped around his desk and reclaimed his former seat. "I hae heard much about Laird Lyam and this Crimwal.

Crimwal served in the Household Guard when I was a captain. He was quite a rascal, yer uncle. I trust they are both well?" he asked, genuine warmth in his tone.

Ever since entering Lord Sean's wardroom, James had been unable to help but perceive the impressive stature of the warlord and the commanding bearing that the man exuded, which was more than slightly imposing. His face was not what one might call handsome, but rather hawkish with its long aquiline nose and slender features and bright eyes that were blue and green at the same time, depending on the lighting, and had a quality that made them seem to be boring into one's soul. Red-blonde hair topped his lean hollowed out face and was pulled back into a tight border braid. He appeared to be about thirty-five years of age, though those piercing eyes seemed to hold greater years, James thought to himself, as he mentally sized up the clan's warlord.

"Aye, they are quite well, my lord," James replied. "Thank ye for asking."

The warlord graciously inclined his head. "From the information I hae received, I am given to understand that ye hae urgent news for Lord Gregor."

"Aye," he agreed, nodding his head emphatically.

"Ye may impart this news to me. I am our chief's representative when he is engaged with other matters," explained the Warlord.

"Very well, my lord; I bring ye grim tidings," he began, and went on to relate to the attentive warlord all that he had previously told to Captain Grant. Now he gave a full account of what had taken place in Dunmoore days before and which had prompted his speedy trip to inform the clan leadership.

" . . . so ye see, Lord Sean, why it is I hae come," James finished.

"Aye," Sean quietly concurred, deep in thought as he unconsciously smoothed the red whiskers at his chin. "Aye, I do indeed. The Campbell duke wi' surely pursue his vengeance, while at the same time having a persuasive argument to take before his allies and furthermore, for keeping the king from interfering.

"He may very well take the field against out clan and our allies; in truth, he has waiting for such an opportunity to do so for quite some time," MacSean explained. "If ye wi' excuse me, I must pull Lord Gregor from the matters he is attending and inform him of the situation, along with my field officers regarding this urgent matter. In the name of the clan, I thank ye for yer promptness in coming forth with this information," he said, rising from his seat and moving around the desk. "I'm sure that Gregor wi' wish to thank ye himself, when he gets the opportunity. Meanwhile, please be welcome to dine in the castle with me this evening; I shall hae returned by that time.

"Now, Master James, if ye wi' excuse me?" he said, already moving toward the door, where he donned a heavy crimson and dark green cloak.

"Of course, my lord," murmured James, hastily coming to his feet, and moving toward the door as well with a dip of his head.

"**James!** James, wake up man!"

From deep within the dark depths of James' dreamless sleep, a familiar booming voice penetrated into the young laird's skull, until he suddenly sat up, his mind still in a foggy daze of sleep. I was only then, that he at last recognized the voice as being Redwood's echoing in the strange room's dark confines.

"Redwood? What in Lugh's name do ye want?" James muttered irritably, his tone bewildered, as he strived to fully awaken.

"Get up, James!" ordered his hulking friend, while tossing the man's clothes onto his lap. "The Warlord has returned—and with terrible news. Come quickly, Jamie; I was sent to bring ye to the hall," Redwood added anxiously.

Stumbling into kilt and riding leathers, James followed his burly lieutenant back toward the hall where a large number of people could gather without restriction.

Already gathered inside were the Warlord and four others that the young laird had not yet met. Three of that number of gentlemen seemed to James' eye as being of an age comparable to that of Lord Sean. The fourth gentleman was older, though he appeared to still be in excellent fighting form. Gray at his temples added a distinguished look to his long auburn hair, which was pulled back in a thick border braid and fell to the middle of his broad back, adding to his already regal bearing.

"Ah, there ye are. Good evening Master James," the Warlord greeted, raising a beckoning hand for him to approach.

"I would like to introduce ye to some important people. First," he indicated the three younger men standing to his right, "let me present to ye, Lord Kirkland, our close ally of Clan MacPherson; and Duncan MacSean, my brother; and Lord Dgunal Fraser, son of Earl Mhoram Fraser."

James nodded politely to each of the men and clasped each by the hand. "I am pleased to make yer acquaintance gentlemen."

As each man was introduced to the young MacNeish, he could feel himself being sized up and measured, but not so much so as when he was at last introduced to the distinguished gentleman to the Warlord' left. "And finally," he indicated, bowing slightly toward the older man, "this is Lord Gregor of MacGregor, my uncle."

Clear emerald green eyes held his own, until with a suppressed gulp, James dropped to one knee in homage to the clan chief.

"My Lord."

"Please rise, James. I do nae stand much on ceremony except when I absolutely can nae avoid it, young warrior," said Lord Gregor, not unkindly. "I hear that it was ye who are responsible for slaying a son of The Cameron *and* of our old friend Domeric Campbell. I see that ye hae been quite busy, lad."

"Aye, My Lord," admitted a sheepish James.

"Yer bravery has certainly been proved beyond a doubt, and other circumstances I would be proud to reward yer actions on behalf of our clan," divulged the clan chief, as he regarded the young before him.

"That is nae necessary, My Lord," said James, ducking his head contritely. "In the course of doing my duty, I hae brought our clan ill consequences."

A pleased smile flashed across the chief's usually stern but handsome face before he glanced aside at his warlord. The two leaders seemed to converse one with the other without speaking a word aloud, but merely with the passing of familiar well-read facial expressions and body language.

Turning back once more to the waiting young border laird, hands clasped behind his back, Gregor smiled and said, "Ach, ye do deserve some fitting reward for ridding us of that arrogant whelp of Domeric Campbell and ye wi' be granted it accordingly.

"I would hae such a leader, with proven loyalty and a brave heart, as a captain to other warriors," he said on, "so that they may learn and follow his example. What say ye, James? Wi' ye accept a commission by my hand to serve in my army?"

In a fruitless attempt to control the surprise struck expression seizing his youthful features without much success, James broke into a wide delighted grin that threatened to split his flushed face. "Of course, My Lord! I am honoured to accept such, but if I may, I would request something more of ye for the sake of the folk of Dunmoore," he added quickly, less his nerve fail him.

"I'm listening lad; go ahead."

"If it please ye, I would first lead the company ye hae offered as my command to Dunmoore," he requested soberly. "The Campbells wi' surely be out to seek their first vengeance against the MacNeish folk before any others, and Dunmoore can nae withstand another such an assault again sae soon. If they are supported by an additional company of strong hearted, well-armed men to reinforce those warriors already there, who are willing to die before a Campbell can ever again steal MacGregor land, then ye can deny the duke of his retribution," James fervently explained, a passion in his voice that surprised even himself.

"Well said, lad," said Gregor, nodding his head in approval. "Very well, Captain MacNeish, I place in yer command a company of two hundred soldiers that are in service to our Clan Gregor. Yer company wi' be assembled for ye within a day; I leave it for ye to select yer officers, but do so with care. Ye hae three days from tomorrow to hae yer company in order and ready to move out. My first order for ye is this: march yer command straightaway to Dunmoore and prepare that place for battle.

"I expect much from ye, James and I trust ye to nae disappoint me," Lord Gregor mildly admonished the eager young man. His normally stern visage softened somewhat as his eyes twinkled with kind amusement at the new captain's enthusiasm. "May ye hae good fortune and God go with ye."

"Thank ye, My Lord," said James, ducking his head. "I wi' nae let ye down; ye hae my word as a MacNeish," he pledged, a determined glint of pride showing fiercely in his wide iron gray eyes.

Acknowledging the oath of his eager young retainer with a brief nod, Lord Gregor dismissed the newly commissioned captain from the chamber before beginning his war council in earnest.

Early the next morning, before the sun had yet to penetrate through a thick blanket of mist, James along with Captain Grant and the stalwart Redwood stood before a mustered formation of two hundred and eighteen clan soldiers. Each fighter was girded with leather baldric holding a scabbarded claymore broadsword, along with a strong recurve bow slung purposely across their back. These men were an elite company of warrior/archers and were each a sworn MacGregor retainer.

"Good morning to ye," James addressed those gathered before him. "I am Captain MacNeish and I hae been placed in command of this newly organized company. We hae been given a simple directive by our Lord Gregor, and that is to defend the lands and people of our clan. More specifically, our orders are to reinforce the village of Dunmoore and eradicate any Campbells and their allies as may present themselves.

"It is my understanding that each one of ye hae volunteered to join this unit," he continued cheerfully. "For that, I thank ye one and all. These gentlemen that stand with me before ye are my lieutenants. Some of ye may already be acquainted with Gaston Grant," he indicated toward the older man. Directing his attention toward his childhood friend, James went on, "This other fellow is called, Redwood. Ye wi' be delighted to ken that my brawny colleague here is in charge this morning and wi' direct today's unarmed combat training. Ye are dismissed to break fast. Be back here in formation in one quarter of an hour.

"All sergeants wi' report immediately for a briefing. That is all," the new captain ordered briskly, ending his first act as commander.

Following the usual banter and discussion of a fairly typical staff meeting, James directed the conversation toward the matter of choosing a banner for the new unit and a name by which it would be known. Pressed for time, the young captain released his cadre to return to the unit, but urged each to think on the matter and to discuss it with the men they were in charge of. In the evening they would all dine with him and present any ideas that they might have garnered.

What followed was a full day as James participated in the training exercises that Redwood used prepare the soldiers of their unit. The young captain was not without his share of bruises before the exhausted soldiers were finally released for the day. Redwood informed them that the training would continue the next day and there were a number of groans from the assembled men. James could sympathize as he gingerly rubbed his ribs where his friend had landed a hearty punch not so long before.

Over dinner, James broached the subject he had left the cadre to mull over since breakfast. "So, gentlemen, are there any suggestions on the matter of a company standard or an appealing name for us?"

The cadre of sergeants was for the most part a hard-bitten lot of tough career soldiers, whose dour demeanor usually frightened their subordinates into obedience more so than having to rely on normal punishment. The topic of a unit banner and name however, had peaked their interest and they showed true enthusiam now that conversation had begun concerning it.

Several imaginative ideas were put forward in a short period of time and each contributed with good natured banter before the issue was decided. It was agreed, after no small amount of debate, that the unit's name would be, *Border Dragons*, and that the standard would be a black border with Saint Andrew's cross overlaying a background of gold, and finally have an ebony dragon crouched in the center.

In the end, all seemed to be rather pleased, although some were more so than others. The design was forwarded to a reputed tailor in Glenorchy for its crafting and informed that speed was of the essence as the unit was slated to move out in less than two days time. Extra coin was offered in an effort to ensure the tailor's alacrity.

Morning came too soon for many in the newly organized unit, but Redwood was eagerly ready for the rigors of the day. By the end of another long day of hard training, with the burly warrior supervising the troops, he at last declared them fit and ready for the threatened combat to come. The forty that James had led to Glenorchy had joined in with the training and numbered among the clan soldiers to depart in the morning. Orders were issued for each member of the unit to find their bunks early as they would be depart early the following morning once all supplies had been collected and loaded.

Their withdrawal from Glenorchy Castle began as the sun had peaked the horizon and the journey to Dunmoore got underway in good order. In the mind of each clansman was the knowledge that war was inevitable, as the Campbell duke's army would be coming to seek vengeance against the slayers of that clan's ducal heir.

*   *   *

"**My son?!**" Domeric Campbell stormed, his wrath evident in his enraged scowl as much as his lashing words, as he learned of his eldest son's death. "Where is Robert's body, vermin? Ye did nae leave it in the hands of those MacGregor dogs, did ye?"

The two officers kneeling before their duke cowered fearfully before that lord's furious diatribe, wishing the floor could swallow them up. At last, one of the men dared to speak up, rather than risk further wrath by not doing so.

"Yer Grace, Lord Robert's body was retrieved from his killers and has been laid in his rooms to await funerary services," he reported, hoping that news would mitigate the fury that raged from his lord.

The officer kneeling beside his fellow now found his voice. "Yer Grace, our enemy did nae fight with honour, nor show any to yer son. Lord Robert was, well, he was feathered, Yer Grace," said the man, paling before the baleful stare of the duke, but did manage to continue, his voice pleading. "There was nothing that we could hae done, it happened so fast. Please forgive us, Yer Grace."

"Get out of my sight," Duke Domeric hissed in a deceptively quiet voice. "Get out before I run ye through and remove both of yer worthless heads!"

The shaken officers fled the chamber in one direction while the duke stalked out, his boot heels beating a staccato of thundering steps as he made his way toward his fallen son's apartments. The lord's visage was so twisted by grief and fury that none, no matter their rank, dared to cross his path.

"Oh, Robert . . . my son, my son," Domeric openly wept as he entered the dimly lit apartment. Dropping to his knees, beside the bed upon which his dead son lay with such dreadful wounds that spoke of his sad end, the grieving father sobbed disconsolately. One hot tear rolled down his lined cheek onto Robert's lifeless hand, a hand that Domeric held tenderly in both of his own.

"The MacNeishs did this to ye, my beloved son. I wi' avenge ye, Robert, I swear it," he promised in a fierce whisper. "Nay matter what it takes."

Regaining his feet, Domeric stepped out onto the balcony that adjoined his son's bedroom and leaned against the railing. He stared up into the star filled night sky, dark eyes smoldering with a rage and hatred that found voice as he shouted into the night, "Ye MacGregors wi' pay dearly for this, every last one of ye! I wi' collect this debt of blood from yer entire accursed clan; I wi' claim all yer bleeding lands as my own, whilst bringing slaughter to each and every one of yer thrice damned kin with sword and fire, as all the gods are my witness!"

"My Lords, I hae called ye all here over a matter of grim importance to each of us," Duke Domeric Campbell began, wasting no time but coming straight to the point of his hasty summons. "As ye all ken by now, I hae long waited, desiring an acceptable way to legally engage in a war with the bloody MacGregors and those misguided clans that are confederated with them. Truly, I hae for years now, yearned to eliminate Gregor and his grasping ambitions for power," he admitted in a smoldering voice. "Now he and his ill begotten race hae crossed the line into madness!

"Most of ye hae already learned of the savage MacNeishs of Clan Gregor, and how they hae slaughtered Lord Cameron's son and a number of his fine men," he said, pausing before going on. "Now they hae forced war upon me by brutally murdering my eldest son and heir, Robert. If that were nae foul enough, they even denied the lad an honourable opportunity to fight, but rather preferred to cut him down with an arrow," he told his peers with an outraged growl. "Nae proper steel, oh nay, but rather a cursed gull fletched arrow! I tell ye now, I want their blood for this! I demand it!

"Now, gentlemen, if ye are with me, let us throw down the gauntlet and declare war on the thrice-damned MacGregors and all those who may be foolish enough to stand with them. What say ye?" Campbell demanded of them.

A brief discussion took place as the gathered lords spoke amongst themselves, although the decision was already a forgone conclusion, but as they did so Lord Alfred Cameron spoke up to address their host.

"Yer Grace," he said, standing in his place at the long table, "my clan as long been an ally with Clan Campbell, and we wi' stand with ye now if ye want Camerons to fight by yer side. But I do hae a concern," he confessed in a solemn tone.

Domeric gave a long sigh and scrubbed a hand at his lined forehead. "Very well, Alfred, please regale us with yer words of wisdom. What is it that concerns ye? I ken that ye hae nay dread of combat," he prodded, adding the last in an effort to take some of the sting out of his initial response.

The chief of Clan Cameron stared darkly at his troubling ally a brief instant before speaking. "As ye hae said, I hae nay fear of combat. I hae seen tae much of it to let it hae any hold over me. What I hae concern about is this: the king taking the field. What if His Majesty should rally to Lord Gregor's defense?"

That question drew everyone's attention back to Duke Domeric. The chamber grew instantly quiet as each lord waited for their leader's response.

Domeric was not taken by surprise, however, for he had considered that very prospect as he had awaited for his ally's arrival. He had expected that Lord Alfred would be the one to broach the subject and was not disappointed. The chief of Cameron had always been methodical in all his dealings; a shrewd man, he was never one to commit to action in haste, but thoughtfully considered every option and angle before carrying out any plan of action.

Domeric appeared to consider his answer before speaking, though he had already formulated his response the evening before.

"That is a serious concern, one that can nae be ignored," he assured Cameron and his other peers. "King William is a shrewd politician and wi' seek the advice of his Royal Council when this border war breaks out. His councilors understand how William wi' be sympathetic toward the husband of his own daughter," Domeric explained. "Wise voices wi' argue that the situation is delicate because blood has already been shed, particularly the blood of a senior noblemen's heir. Furthermore, if the king were to come in force to Gregor's aid under such circumstances, it would show preference on his behalf which could lead to an uprising against him.

"William's logical plan of action wi' be to investigate and seek to stop this war by calling for a truce and try to mediate peace between myself and Gregor," he told his rapt listeners. "It would be foolish for the king to enter the conflict, but if he were to do so," he paused before going on to elaborate. Careful to keep his voice calm he went on, "I am prepared to carry on and, if needs be, fight against a king who would play at being a tyrant rather than being the wise ruler that Scotland deserves."

Alfred Cameron slowly nodded his head, carefully considering the duke's words before responding, as several sets of inquiring eyes settled on him. "I wi' lead my clan at yer side to fight against the MacGregors and their allies. However," the old chief paused, glancing from one man to the next before returning his steady gaze back to that of the Campbell duke, "if the king should take the field, either to keep the peace or to lend aid to Lord Gregor, I should find myself compelled to withdrawal my clan from action. My vow of fealty to King William demands nay less."

Domeric nodded his head in acceptance but could not hide the scowl that pulled down his brows in foul humor. "Very well;

ye gentlemen hae all heard Lord Alfred's answer. Now I would hear what the rest of ye hae to say."

Their response was not as wholehearted as Domeric would have hoped, but it was good enough as each confirmed their support without reservation. Although the Cameron had put a damper on the proceedings, still some of the Campbell allies showed a level of enthusiam that improved Domeric's temper somewhat.

Allowing himself a tight smile of triumph, Domeric thanked each of his peers in turn, including Lord Alfred, who watched him warily. Losing no time, the duke set forth to immediately begin a war council in earnest.

"Lord Campbell," began the Duke of Hamilton, "we hae at our collective disposal a force of some thirteen thousand men. They are, of course, within each of our own territories and waiting for the order to march forth," conveyed Hamilton, his deep voice confident as he addressed his equal. "With yer approval, each allied clan may begin to immediately marshal their troops within yer borders."

"Of course, Lord Hamilton," Campbell readily agreed, his head nodding in approval. "Gentlemen, ye may begin immediately."

"We wi' see to it right away," Hamilton promised, glancing quickly around the table at his fellows. "Where shall the marshalling point be, Lord Campbell?"

Domeric grew thoughtful for a moment before bestowing the man with a grim smile. "Doomfield. We shall gather our armies together outside Inveraray at Doomfield in one fortnight. Let the name of our rallying point be an omen of MacGregor's own fate, shall we? This meeting is concluded," he stated, slapping his hands down sharply on the arms of his tall chair. "Each of ye are invited to sup with me this evening."

Turning on his heel, Duke Domeric Campbell strode purposefully, with a steady thumping of boots on tile floor, from the council chamber to find his armorer. He had to be fitted for his new enameled helm and breastplate; after all, one had to look their best when riding out on campaign did one nae?

*   *   *

Not long ago, James MacNeish had left Dunmoore in charge of a warband of forty men, but now he returned at the head of better than two hundred soldiers, along with the rank of captain. It was all due to the thanks and generosity of Lord Gregor, the powerful chief of the MacGregors.

The company of soldiers covered the distance from Glenorchy to Dunmoore in a matter of two and a half days, not bad time at all considering the size of the war party compared to the much smaller one on James' first trip through the rocky foothills. The trek back home was an easy one, blessed with uncommonly mild weather, instead of the typical rain squalls and thunder storms of the season. All this made for cheerful moods as each troop was thankful for not having to slog through mud to their destination.

Lazy clouds turned to soft shades of pink and lavender as the bright sun began its slow descent behind the heather clad hills. Captain MacNeish and his company were steadily making their own decent into the glen where Dunmoore straddled a modest brook of cold fresh water that flowed from the mountains.

Soon the company of MacGregor retainers was greeted warmly by the friendly villagers of Dunmoore and by their laird, the MacNeish chieftain. In short order, James' men were garrisoned on the village green in tents that they quickly erected with practiced skill. Meanwhile, James and his officers were given lodging in the chieftain's own home. The MacNeish men that had accompanied the chieftain's son returned to their own homes and families and sweethearts for the night once Lyam, the laird of Dunmoore, had supervised the bivouac of the reinforcements.

Mid way through the following morning, Captain MacNeish mustered his Border Dragons into an open rank formation before the hosting laird, who also happened to be the proud father of the new company commander. James, along with his two lieutenants, Redwood and Gaston Grant followed behind as Lyam began his inspection.

Laird Lyam MacNeish was getting up in years and had better than forty years when his lamented wife had given birth to his son James. He carried the years well however, his back still straight as he strolled down the long ranks and critically gave the troops a once over. He was a tall man by European standards, standing at just under six feet tall. Still muscular, but in a wiry sort of way, he weighed no more than thirteen stone; if his shirt were off, one would have been surprised to see corded muscles ripple on Lyam's chest and his ropey arms. Part of his continued strength came from his daily use of the same stout longbow of his youth and it's one hundred pound pull. His eyesight was more keen than many a younger man and could still drop a running stag at seventy five paces, a feat few could duplicate on their best day.

The inspection concluded, the proud chieftain strode purposefully back to the front of the formation with the three officers following in tow. Once there, Lyam turned and gave his son an approving nod.

"Captain," Lyam began, speaking loud enough for anyone remotely near could over hear what he said. "These lads of yers are a fine company and I am right honoured to hae ye and yer soldiers with us in our modest village. Fighting skills is something that I'm sure we'll need very soon," he stated soberly, before going on in a lowered voice for James ears alone, "please bring yer officers and meet me once ye hae dismissed these handsome soldiers of yers."

"Of course, Da," agreed James, offering a smart salute.

The old laird had just started away toward the village meeting hall when he was stopped short and brought around by a shout of the assembled war fighters.

"Hail MacNeish!" They thundered enthusiastically in unison, saluting Laird Lyam with right fist covering each man's heart. The honour they did him flushed the chieftain with pride, especially when he saw his brother, Crimwal, witness the acclaim.

A pleased smile brightening his gaunt-like face, Lyam acknowledged the honour they bestowed on him with a gracious bow and a return salute before continuing on from the green common area toward the hall where Crimwal was now waiting for him.

They are a bonny group of lads. I truly wish that I did nae hae the need for them to fight off those bloody Campbells, but unfortunately, it appears that I wi' hae nay choice in the matter, the old chieftain gravely thought to himself. *If Domeric sends his clan against us none of us wi' hae any choice at all.*

On the village green, James dismissed his company of clan soldiers while having his small cadre corps remain behind. With those hard-bitten sergeants in tow he and his lieutenants made their way to the hall where Lyam awaited them.

Moments later, Captain MacNeish and his staff found themselves seated around a long table that dominated the interior of the village meeting hall. The old table was still impressive despite its age or perhaps because of it. Crafted of heavy English oak, the boards were two inches thick and fifteen feet long, while the width was a notable ten feet. Along its length the stout table was scarred from age and extensive use.

Mulled wine was already sitting on the table with several glasses around a large pitcher which still steamed from being heated. Lyam, the residing laird, was already sitting in a tall hand carved chair at the far end as he beckoned the newcomers to take their seats. Around the table to the chieftain's left hand, old Crimwal sat impatiently drumming his blunt fingers against the hard wood surface.

"Gentlemen, a good day to ye all," Lyam greeted them cordially. "Before we get down to the business at hand, I wanted to thank ye for allowing me that wee inspection. Please ken that I am most satisfied to hae yer company here in Dunmoore," he declared, allowing a small smile to lighten his grave demeanor. "I thought it wise to hae a council of war, so to speak, that we might discuss a strategy for the defense of Dunmoore and the borders it is our duty to attend, in order to prevent our lands from being overrun.

"It is my understanding, James, that yer bonny company has a total strength of some two hundred lads. Is that correct?" he inquired.

"Aye, sair," James confirmed, nodding his head.

"We wi' need every one of them when the Campbells return," stated Lyam. "Our village may be relatively small, but the border we watch is another matter entirely. It may be most prudent to pull our border patrols back to within a mile of Dunmoore or we risk our forces being tae strung out to be of any avail when the bastards do come."

Glancing down the long table, Lyam found James' burly red haired lieutenant and caught his eye. "Redwood, ye should ken this better than anyone else present, how many lads hae we in Dunmoore and the outlying farms that can be depended on to give a good fight, if and when we find ourselves invaded and under attack?"

"Well, uh, sair," the big man faltered, somewhat at a loss at suddenly being thrust into the midst of such an important discussion. "Well, sair, if ye mean to exclude all the lasses from the battle, we wi' hae lost almost eighty bonny fighters," Redwood remarked, warming to his favorite subject with a wide grin seeming to split his bushy face. He had been the one to offer training for any woman desiring it, and a surprising number had come forward to accept his proposal. The grin visibly wilted as he noted the withering gaze aimed at him from his chieftain. "Uh, aye, sair; just the lads. We hae about another two hundred good lads that we can depend on."

"Thank ye, Redwood," Lyam muttered dryly, noting the usual mock contriteness in the man's sheepish expression. Shaking his head slightly he returned his attention back to the others sitting about him before losing control of the grin he was suppressing. Lyam picked up the discussion where he left off.

"What I am proposing is that my retainers be called in to supplement the brave soldiers ye hae brought to garrison here," he explained. "My lads combined with yers wi' give us a fighting force of about four hundred warriors—nae counting, of course, those bonny fighting maidens . . ." he trailed off, the expression on the old laird's leathery face one of rare open amusement aimed in Redwood's direction.

The remainder of Lyam's war council continued on smoothly enough, although it dragged on throughout the afternoon. Arrangements were agreed on that would have a series of hasty breastworks and pickets erected as a parameter around the village, as well as a rotating schedule of sentries to stand watch every hour, day and night. A regular patrol was also established, with the best riders assigned to range up to a mile outside of Dunmoore in a ring to scout against the enemy. They were to serve as an early warning against any enemies seeking to come and strike Dunmoore by surprise.

Everyone involved in the planning knew that although everything was quiet, for the time being, it would not remain so for long. No one knew when the Campbells and their confederates might attack, but each was certain the enemy would not keep them waiting much longer.

Throughout the day life in the modest village continued as usual, as folk went about their daily chores. A sprinkling of cool rain began to fall late that afternoon and on into the evening, while a breeze rustled through the trees. It was a calm scene of tranquil serenity that most folk realized was a blessing that could be shattered at any moment when the chaos and thunder of war arrived to destroy it. Most folk still hoped for peace to endure, but steadfastly prepared for war. Those who had been acquainted with the nature of war knew that it left a swathe of blood and death in its wake, along with the unforgettable stench of gore and oily smoke from burned and gutted villages just like Dunmoore. Those things had ever been the legacy of every armed conflict that had taken place down through the ages.

A week had passed since Captain MacNeish had departed, from the Clan Gregor capital of Glenorchy, along with his company of Border Dragons; and the fortress town was a place bustling with activity as the populace girded themselves for war.

Losing no time, Lord Gregor had quickly summoned his councilors and military commanders to make preparations for war. Along with his own confidants the powerful chief invited representatives from each of the several clans, whom were allied with the MacGregors, to participate in the war planning.

Under the unified authority of the allied war council, each of the aligned clans was instructed to hasten the mobilization of their armed retainers to muster within their respective territory. Once each allied clan had their troops marshaled, they were to stand fast and ready to march, on short notice, for Glenorchy.

The gathered leaders found themselves all in agreement that the Campbells and their own alliance of confederated clans would, without a doubt, move swiftly against Clan Gregor. The most likely point of attack was believed to be Dunmoore, where the MacNeishs had already stood up to the enemy seeking to avenge the duke's slain son. Beyond those points, there was much debate without resolution and no amount of discussion was going to discern when or how the enemy would strike. Prior experience with the wily nature of Domeric Campbell had them all uncertain and restless as they were forced to wait and see what the duke had up his sleeve.

Late, in the deep of the night when even the most restless were fast asleep, Lord Sean lay in peaceful slumber and dreamed of days in his youth. Abruptly those pleasant dreams were shattered as he was set upon by his excited younger brother, insistently shaking his shoulder and urging him to awaken.

"Sean! Sean, ye must wake up man!" Duncan insisted, his voice anxious. He was about three years younger than his brother, but no one could have missed the family resemblance between the two men. Although his hair was lighter, without red shining in it, and he was clean-shaven, they shared the same features and nose, and most could not discern between their voices, having the same tones and inflections. "One of my men has just now returned . . . get up for God's sake!"

The warlord forced his eyes open and tried to sit up. "Wha-?"

"The lad killed his horse to get here as swiftly as possible," he said, quieter now that his brother was roused. "It's the Campbells!"

"Campbells? What's all this about the bloody Campbells, Duncan?" Sean hissed, glaring up at his agitated brother through slitted eyes. He was just now coming fully awake and was none too pleased in the manner of the rousing. Before Duncan could give response, Sean threw back the bed covers and sat up, swinging his legs over the edge of the comfortable bed. *This had better be bloody important*, he grumbled silently.

As Warlord of Clan Gregor, Sean was always the first to be informed about any activities having to do with the other territories and particularly all troop movements that happened near MacGregor borders. *Unfortunately*, he grumbled to himself, *everything always seems to happen in the dead of the bloody night*. The minor title, with the power and influence that came with it, were not always worth the bother. He no longer kept track of the many nights that he had been denied sleep.

"All right, brother of mine, I'm awake now," he assured. "Calm down and quiet yerself before ye wake the entire castle. I wi' get dressed and then ye can take me to yer scout so I can question him," he muttered, glancing about for his tunic.

Once he was dressed an impatient Duncan led his ill humored brother to where the scout was waiting. Both men tramped along sconce lighted, stone corridors down into the castle near the kitchens. Striding through opened, wide wooden doors, the duo entered the refectory and stopped short to watch in awe as the young spy stuffed food into his mouth as fast as he could swallow it. He continued to eat, oblivious to the men staring at him, and showed no signs of slowing down.

Sean raised an eyebrow at his brother. "Impressive."

Smirking, Duncan strode on into the hall and slid onto a bench across from the hungry lad. The scout almost choked when he saw the two gentlemen, and hastily rose from his seat, a hunk of cheese in one hand and a chicken leg in the other.

"Sit, lad," Duncan ordered, eyes twinkling in amusement.

"Sean, this hungry lad is Robert Petrie. He is in my employ and a laddie of many talents, as ye can see," Duncan introduced, fighting the urge to grin and failing.

"So I can see," observed Sean. "I trust yer other *talents* are as keen as yer appetite young Master Petrie. I hae roused from a comfortable bed to hear yer report."

"Aye, sair," he said, bobbing his head respectfully.

"Petrie, this is Warlord MacSean, my brother," said Duncan, indicating toward the man at his side. "Please relay yer report to him. The warlord needs to hae every detail about what ye hae seen and heard. Leave nothing out," he ordered.

"Aye, my lord," replied the spy, wiping his greasy hands off on his faded tunic, before directing his undivided attention to the warlord.

Clan Gregor's military leader sat down alongside Duncan and made himself as comfortable as he could no the hard wooden bench and wished for something strong to drink. This was going to be a long night.

"Lord, it's the Campbells," reported the spy, his tone one of mixed anger and fear. "They march on us as we speak, sair. They're coming right up the vales and across our border, pretty as ye please, heading for Glenorchy!"

"What?!" exclaimed Sean, glancing at his younger brother.

"They're marching here," Petrie confirmed. "After spying on their army I wasted nay time but sped here as swiftly as my horse could carry me, to deliver this news. Their army, at the pace they maintained, wi' be here in less than two days time. Ach, and sair, it's nae just the Campbells. Warriors wearing the tartan of the Hamiltons are with them, along with Kennedys and Carlyles as well.

"The entire force numbers at least four thousand; most of them are infantry, but there are several hundred mounted soldiers tae," he imparted, the young spy's voice cracking in dismay. "I'm sorry, my lord. I would hae gotten this ill news to ye quicker if I could hae, but I rode my poor horse to death getting here as soon as I did."

"That's alright, lad. Ye did all that could be asked of ye," replied a troubled Lord Sean, giving the young spy a reassuring nod before turning to Duncan. "Find yer young master Petrie a bed and fill his sporran with coin for his vigilance.

"Ye did well, lad," said the Warlord. Standing he came around the dining table and offered the scout his hand. "We need more good men like ye, Petrie. The time ye hae given to us, to prepare, may prove the difference between victory and defeat in the days to come. Ye hae my thanks and the gratitude of our entire clan," Sean declared, slapping Petrie on the back with approval.

The young man beamed with pride and shot a grin at his patron before following Duncan from the dining hall and to a waiting bunk. *Wait until I tell my Da and Ma that I had my hand shaken by Warlord MacSean! They'll nae believe it!*

It was just past dawn once the warlord left Duncan, to see his man taken care of, and he had a lot to get done before briefing the chief. Letters were dictated to blurry eyed secretaries and within the hour relay couriers sped from the castle with dispatches to all of the clans of their alliance. All that was left to do was share the gathered information with Lord Gregor and prepare the defenses, while waiting for a positive response from each of their allies.

Just after dawn the following morning, with three answering dispatches tucked in his belt, Warlord MacSean again briefed his liege lord of the overall situation, including the replies of their closest allies.

"My Lord, our troops stand at high alert and are ready for whatever the Campbells throw at us," Sean reported to the chief. "The MacAlpines, MacLeans, and Clanranald hae answered the summons. Each of those clans should reach us here before the enemy does, and Clanranald should arrive by tomorrow morning with a thousand troops.

"Our own forces, mustered at Glenorchy, total fifteen hundred, plus an additional four hundred ready militia as a reserve," the warlord informed his attentive chief.

The two MacGregor leaders started in surprise as a travel worn courier burst, unceremoniously, into the chamber. "My lords! I bear grave news for the clan!" he cried breathlessly, adrenaline the only thing keeping the exhausted man on his feet. "Lord Gregor, Glengyle and Dunmoore are both being marched upon. The prongs of the attack wi' hit each at virtually the same time."

"That's impossible, man! *We're* being marched on," the harried Chief of Clan Gregor hissed, his voice low and dangerous.

The news bearer visibly blanched. "But, My Lord, it is true! I am a spy in service to Duncan MacSean," he cried in a near pleading voice, risking a glance at the man he knew to be his employer's brother. Sinking on wobbly legs, to his knees before his fierce eyed chief, the man added bleakly, "Those armies wi' be converging on Glengyle and Dunmoore in a day and a half at best; I swear it!"

The brief look exchanged between the Gregor and his nephew was every bit as bleak as the one borne by the messenger and bore with it a meaning that words could not give true weight to. The fresh burden pressed down on the chief's shoulders as if it were an actual mass of stone.

"My dear Lugh," sighed The MacGregor.

"Has Duncan already heard this news ye bear, lad?" asked the Warlord, seeking to divert the spy's attention from the shocked chief, as much as to have an answer.

"Aye, My Lord," he affirmed with a brisk nod. "Lord Duncan has dispatched fast riders to speed news of this to the Frasers and MacAlpine, requesting immediate support for Dunmoore, but especially Glengyle.

"How can it be that the Campbells hae such numbers to send against us, Lord?" the spy asked in a frightened tone. "Are there truly sae many clans that hate us?"

"Nay. There are nae sae many that hate us," Sean assured the man, "but, the duke of the bloody Campbells surely does. And his influence drives others to follow his will, while others wi' do his bidding out of fear from threat of retaliation."

"Do nae worry yerself over it, lad," Gregor told the courier, snapping out of his momentary reverie. "Our clan can handle the bloody Campbells any day of the week, and anything in which they choose to throw at us."

"Duncan did well to take the initiative about this," Sean noted approvingly. "The time he has saved, even if it be but moments, could make a difference. I was nae aware that my brother had such a network of spies in his service, nor ones that were such loyal men. Did ye ken, Gregor?"

"Nay," said Gregor, shaking his head. "But, Duncan is a good man, and he has proven himself a fine leader. Perhaps it is time that ye should try him in a field command position, Sean. We already ken his men trust him, and he has shone, in the past, a head for strategy. Yer brother has some interesting ideas regarding tactics and although they can be a bit unconventional, they hae nevertheless been effective," Lord Gregor said, an approving energy in his words. "Considering what is coming, I believe we wi' need every talent and resource at our disposal. Do ye nae agree?"

"Aye," concurred the Warlord. "I wi' see to it immediately."

In the same hour that Glenorchy and the Clan Gregor leadership received the news about armies marching on Glengyle and Dunmoore, Laird Lyam MacNeish at his home in Dunmoore, received word about the situation unfolding at the clan capital. That old man's response was a very similar disbelief like that of his chief.

"By Nuada!" exclaimed Lyam. "Nae only are we marched on, but Glengyle and Glenorchy are as well—and all at the same time! I can nae believe it. That auld bloody Domeric Campbell must hae some grand army to be able to split it into three parts, and still hae such numbers for each attack," his bellow holding an appalled note.

James was shocked as well. The father and son had been having a private dinner when the messenger had arrived in the care of a looming Redwood. Plates of food now sat on the old table, forgotten as they thought about the prospect of a war that offered scant hope of any further reinforcements from the soon to be hard-pressed clan.

"We must start arming the fighting maidens to aid in the defense. Redwood, ye wi' see to it immediately," James commanded.

"Aye, sair," he replied, nodding his great head.

"This is going to be a very bloody business, James. Mark my words," muttered Lyam, the look he directed toward his son full of worry. "Domeric wi' nae be satisfied until our whole clan is finished and trod until his heel."

"Aye, Da, that as may be," James quietly agreed, "but we wi' just hae to put such an anguish in the hearts of his clan that he wi' be forced to withdrawal."

CHAPTER THREE

It proved to be a long, anxious day in Dunmoore. Redwood and his small scouting party had returned early from their patrol of the new pulled-in boundaries that surrounded the tense village, to the southeast. That had been the previous point in which Campbell raiders had led their foray to pillage Dunmoore, and now it was watched diligently as a likely place for their next approach into MacNeish lands.

Before making his way to the laird's longhouse, Redwood dismissed his scouts to eat and relax, wishing he could join them, as his stomach rumbled in protest. Reaching his chieftain's house, the huge warrior was forced to wait, if somewhat impatiently, as Lyam was finishing an interview with a man wearing the Fraser tartan.

"And when should I be expecting yer vanguard to arrive, lad?" Old Lyam asked, at once noticing the impatient, looming form of his most trusted retainer. Redwood had remained respectfully back close to the entrance, but just the sheer size of him made it next to impossible to be overlooked.

"Sair, ye should anticipate our lead elements sometime before dawn," replied the Fraser forward scout. "The main column follows nay more than an hour behind those in the vanguard. My lord commanded that I relay his personal promise to ye: depend on the troops of Clan Fraser to be ready to stand by yer side. Together we wi' bloody our swords and bring slaughter upon 'the thieving dogs' of Duke Domeric," said the scout, relaying the spirited words of his chief.

A sudden grin stretched the leathery skin tight across Lyam's worn face. His chuckle was dry but good humored as he clapped the Fraser on the shoulder. Turning in his seat, Lyam beckoned his waiting retainer into the room with a wave of his hand.

Not one for wasting any time on pleasantries, the powerful warrior stepped into his laird's presence, still covered in sweat and smelling of horse and leather, from his hurried return to Dunmoore with his report.

"Sair, it is bonny news to hear of our Fraser allies coming to join cause with us," stated Redwood, claiming a seat next to his laird. The wood protested under his weight and creaked as if it might shatter at any time. "Unfortunately, all is nae good news this day. As ye already ken, the bleeding Campbells are camped at the border; well, sair, in addition to them," he reported somberly, "my lads and I hae spotted warriors belonging to other clans. We saw large groups of Gordons and MacNeils in the camp as they sat pretty as ye please sharpening their weapons.

"The encampment was warded by a heavy watch," Redwood continued evenly. "Alert as the sentries were, the lads and I could nae draw very close to observe much, or hear anything worthwhile, without the risk of alarming them to our presence. From the size of their camp, I estimate a few thousand men and an equally substantial number of horse. I also spotted several wagons laden with supplies."

The weary old laird shook his gray head gravely at Redwood's news before fixing his steely gaze on the Fraser scout. "They wi' be marching against us at dawn," he said with certainty. "I trust ye are correct with yer information, laddie.

"Redwood," said the laird, his voice betraying no signs of weariness. "Find James and his man Grant, and bring them to me straightaway."

"Aye, sair," said the huge man, offering a respectful nod.

The scout had left the village and gone to rejoin with his lord, whom led forth a contingent of Frasers to assist the MacNeishs. Not long after he had gone, the four men who currently led the defense of Dunmoore met and sat together in the laird's longhouse. Under the glow of smelly, oil burning lamps—the sun had suddenly disappeared behind a thick blanket of dark clouds—they discussed what should or could be done about the new developments that had taken shape.

James took the time to fill his tankard, along with each of the other men's, with nice warm, mulled wine while fresh rain pattered outside and drummed on the roof. Once he was seated, all eyes turned to the chieftain that had summoned them.

"All right, lads," Lyam began, after taking a pull at his tankard, "we hae a wee bit of planning to do. Although we hae the benefit of the Frasers coming to lend a hand, the coming of the Gordons and the MacNeils changes things somewhat as they sit on our border along with the bloody Campbells.

"Our enemies wi' surely move against us at sunrise, I hae nay doubt about that; and our ally, the Frasers are supposed to arrive at nearly the same time," he said for the benefit of those that had not already been informed. "We, therefore, must take some measures to somehow delay our enemy's approach.

"The Frasers wi' nay doubt be done in with fatigue, due to their long hurried rush to our aid," said the chieftain, raising the steaming tankard to his mouth. Taking a long drink, he went on, "Personally, I never much liked depending on others to help me in the performance of my duties, if ye lads follow my meaning. But we must nae act rashly, a solid plan of action is vital for success."

The old laird raised his tankard again and drank it to the dregs in one long pull. Sitting the heavy mug back down before him, Lyam glanced from one man to the next, suppressing an amused grin at his own aggressive nature.

"To my mind, I think some sort of late night foray aimed against the enemy sitting pretty on our border as merit," he suggested, before adding, "but I would hear whatever advice ye might hae as to what form the raid should take. Do any of ye lads hae any ideas that we can consider?"

The plan of action they finally decided on was the most simple, at least in theory: stealthy soldiers would infiltrate the enemy camp, quietly eliminating the sentries on duty before the bulk of the warband advanced into the oblivious encampment.

Once there, each man would go about the grisly business of killing whatever enemy he could. On the event that they were discovered, the marauding clansmen were to cause, in whatever fashion as they saw fit, as much chaos as possible among the enemy to aid in the retreat of himself and his fellows.

The warriors chosen to go on the raid were quickly selected, largely on their merits as hunters and the stalking of prey. The three score men picked out followed their officers out of the village on horseback and quickly disappeared from sight into the dark embrace of the forest's shadowy arms. Standing under the eaves of his home, Lyam watched them go as he puffed intently on his pipe. He wished each departing man a silent farewell and good fortune on a mission that he yearned to have been still young enough to lead, rather than delegating the post to his swiftly maturing son.

Each of the men comprising the raiding party quietly urged their mounts forward on the slow silent ride to the southern clan border. The night trip to meet the enemy took what seemed like an eternity, but after about two hours in the saddle, James passed the order to dismount. He had chosen a well-sheltered, partial clearing at the base of a tall slope. It was a safe distance from the enemy camp and a secure place in which to leave a single person to have the horses hidden and ready.

"Listen up now," commanded Captain MacNeish, standing tall in his stirrups to gain each man's attention and to be seen by each of his men. In the dark of the forest, he noted with approval, he and his men looked like moving shadows as they all wore black leathers and cloaks to better blend into the night.

"All right, lads, the time has come," he addressed the closely gathered warband, his tone calm but fiercely confident. "The enemy is near and hae come to make war upon us, but we shall nae wait like sheep to be slaughtered. We now meet them head on and it is we who wi' do the slaughtering! Each of ye ken yer instructions; follow those orders to the letter. Ye hunters ken best how to blend into the shadows, pair up with those who are nae so skilled. All of ye remember to stay within sight of those on either side of ye," he reminded them all.

"Now, I require thirty volunteers," James added. "Sergeants, bring the thirty to me as soon as ye hae them. We move out as soon as ye hae them."

The group of volunteers was swiftly collected and brought to the captain. Waiting with his commander, Redwood stood and listened attentively as the young officer issued him his instructions.

"Lads," the captain addressed the thirty waiting men. "Lieutenant Redwood wi' be in command of yer part of this raid. I leave it to him to explain what yer part of the plan wi' be. But ken this, yer coming actions wi' be vital to our success tonight. If ye should fail, many of us wi' surely perish.

Turning to his towering companion, James extended his hand, "Good fortune to ye, Redwood. May Lugh's long arm protect ye. I wi' see ye after," he said quietly, so that only his boyhood friend could hear. Silently, James wondered if he would ever see his burly friend again or if he was sending the man to his death.

Redwood grinned. "Morrigan always favors the brave and she wi' favor us this night, Jamie. I wi' see ye after."

The men of Redwood's command soon vanished into the night, separating from the remainder of the warband, trailing behind their confident leader. As time seemed to pass in slow motion in the dark of the forest, Captain MacNeish and his group of hunters waited with a growing restlessness.

At last, word was relayed to the MacGregor commander that Redwood and his band were in position. Having become restive himself, Captain MacNeish immediately rallied the remaining black clad warriors to his position. Under the direct command of Lieutenant Grant, they were eager to be put into action.

"All of ye ken yer duty and hae received yer instructions," MacNeish told them. "What ye are called on to do this night is as distasteful to me as it wi' be to ye, but it must be done. Tonight we wi' nae only intimidate our enemies, but we shall show them that we are nae afraid. One last thing: at the first shouts of alarm are raised, begin yer retreat and knock over any tent that ye pass, but do nae take unnecessary risks. May Lugh grant us all good hunting," he concluded.

Gaston offered the captain his hand in a firm handshake. "They're all good lads, sair; we wi' nae let ye down. I wi' see ye after."

Watching the men trot off, James drew his blackened blade and followed them as they moved to confront the unsuspecting enemy.

The sentries posted around the parameter of the invader's encampment, though alert, had no chance at all as a quiet but deadly flight of well-aimed arrows hissed in to strike through the night's damp mist. No shaft was wasted as each shot flew true and buried its deadly steel head deep in the flesh of the enemy pickets.

Hidden within the comforting embrace of familiar thick woodlands, MacNeish archers waited for any signs of alarm or uproar. At last satisfied that the enemy remained oblivious to the attack, they stealthily moved forward to make sure none of the sentries was yet alive and then set about pulling the slain out into the forest where they would not be discovered. As that part of the mission was accomplished, Captain MacNeish, who remained in direct command of the archers, gave the go ahead signal to the waiting Lieutenant Grant and his men. Silently, the aging officer and his band slipped from their concealed positions deeper within the forest, toward the sleeping camp, like so many ghostly wraiths mantled in cloaks of mist.

Seconds stretched into minutes and those minutes slowed for the tensely waiting archers into what seemed like an eternity. They knew that their comrades, who had infiltrated the adversary's camp, were busy, going about the grisly duty of moving amidst the canvas tents and cutting the throats of the sleeping enemy. Although each warrior who held an arrow nocked to his bowstring held no love for Campbells or their lackeys, they were relieved to not have their fellow warriors' gruesome task.

Abruptly, the stillness of the night was shattered as a loud hysterical cry of fright split the air. As suddenly as the scream began, it was hastily silenced, but not before it had roused the astonished enemy warriors.

"That's done it, lads. Be ready, but hold yer fire until Grant and his lads hae safely retreated past our position," ordered the captain. Swiftly, the command was passed down the line of hidden archers as they prepared to cover their friend's withdrawal.

The entire camp was soon in a chaotic uproar as more and more shouts and cries of outrage sounded along with spreading flames among the close packed tents. A number of the enemy tents could be seen to collapse by Captain MacNeish, entangling many of the occupants with fallen canvas and tie ropes. For some of the more unfortunate soldiers just awakening, they roused to find themselves trapped and covered by their smoking and smoldering shelters; those men's cries were the most horrific of all, as they were slowly burned alive.

For James, it seemed a lifetime before Grant and his men were streaming from the excited camp toward the relative safety of the woods. Their retreat was hurried but otherwise in orderly fashion. He watched as the infiltrators skirted around his crouched archers, many was their face blanched of color, some with tears on their cheeks, an after reaction to the vile task they had performed. More than one tough Scotsman was violently ill, vomiting on the needle covered ground.

Back in the camp, half-dressed soldiers were emerging from unmolested tents and helping those ensnared in burning shelters, while others were running about and waving swords at an invisible enemy with impotent rage and fear.

James swallowed a lump in his throat as the last of Grant's men had safely exited the last ring of tents and bolted for the trees. Even from where he waited, James could see the wide eyed horror on the young man's face—a face not so different from his own—as he grimaced in revulsion at the bloody dirk in his hand before casting it away.

Several soldiers within the camp spotted the fleeing MacNeish warrior at nearly the same instant and gave pursuit, issuing bloodcurdling warcries. Their screams seemed to act as a focus for their fellow clansmen, and many of the bewildered warriors began rallying toward the small knot of men they saw charging towards the forest.

Raising his longbow, James drew back on the string until the feathers brushed softly against his cheek and shouted, "Ready the gulls to fly . . . Loose!" Releasing his own shaft he heard his archers follow suit, the thrumming of snapping strings sounding all the way down the line. The mist chilled air was suddenly filled with the hiss of flying, deadly arrows, but that sound was quickly replaced as the miserable sounds of the wounded and dying choked out everything else.

The enemy charge from their camp instantly faltered as their comrades began to drop all around them. Their charge had been too frenzied to have actual ranks, but now total chaos reigned as frightened and confused clansmen wavered and looked to anyone, someone for leadership.

It was then that Redwood and his band thundered into the enemy camp from the opposite direction, the timing given as much to luck as anything else.

Already shaken and barely beginning to recover, the bulk of the Campbell army was just rallying to officers that sought to regain control of the situation, as they found themselves beset by a second attacking force. Platoons of the recently rallied troops broke and ran in all directions, ignoring the commands of the outraged officers. In stark terror, all organized resistance and attempts at order futilely vanished as men sought to do nothing but save themselves.

Leading his men from the front, the mighty Redwood charged through the midst of the panicking camp, wielding his two-handed claymore sword to excellent effect among the fear stricken enemy soldiers. And, all the while, the fearsome MacNeish retainer howled, his bloodcurdling battle cry issuing forth in a booming shout that rent the cool, misty highland air. *"The Woody Heights!"*

The ancient battle cry of the MacGregors thrilled the hearts of all the warriors of that proud clan and spurred them on with greater determination. Taking the warcry to heart, Captain MacNeish and then each of his clansmen repeated those words until it became a full throated chant. Soon the warcry echoed gloriously all over the area, from the camp and the forest, and the sound of it struck fear into the hearts of even the most battle-hardened of the enemy's veteran soldiers.

"Captain!" shouted Grant, trying to be heard over the chanting, as he attempted to make the after action report regarding his raid. "Captain, the raid went about as well as anyone could hae expected. By my tally, we sent at least fifty of the Campbell bastards to the gates of hell. We did lose one of our own, and another two were wounded, but all are accounted for. That includes the slain lad; we carried him back with us," he pointed out, proud in the fact that none of his men was left behind. "The two lads wounded were able to return under their own strength."

"Well done, Lieutenant Grant. Return to yer men and fall back to the horses, and await the rest of us there," instructed James, nodding with approval.

"Aye, Captain," responded the veteran officer with a sharp salute. Pivoting on his heel the old soldier proudly strode away to carry out the new orders, bellowing out to his own orders as he went.

Remaining in his original position, James watched as the enemy camp began to show signs of a renewed rally. Troops there began to gather and form into cohesive ranks under the commanding authority of several hard-bitten non-coms who were ranting and screaming obscenities at any soldier who did not comply swiftly enough with their orders. Seeing enough, James re-formed his detail of archers into two staggered ranks and soon a fresh rain of arrows began to fall among the rallying soldiers.

Three devastatingly accurate volleys were sufficient to disintegrate the formation before it could do any harm. Although the enemy troopers were once again reduced into a chaotic mob, the sergeants there were not cowed. Even as the MacNeish archers began choosing individual targets and continued a suppressive fire that kept the heads of enemy archers down, the non-coms kept their wits about them. One gray bearded sergeant had somehow found a group of armored knights eager to retaliate, and from the relative cover of some untouched tents they began to mount up for a counter attack.

Realizing the sudden danger, James briskly ordered his archers to retreat, as they stood no chance against mounted knights. "Fall back! Fall back to the horses, we hae worn out our welcome!" He could wait no longer for Redwood. He and his men would have to make it out on their own. *Morrigan help us!*

Following their captain's orders, the archers fell back slowly, in good order and continued to loose deadly shafts at intervals. Meanwhile, as previously ordered, each man kept a rough count of how many of their foes they added feathers to. Moving away, deeper into the dark forest, the trees soon prevented any clear shots on target and at that point they turned and quickly trotted toward the rally position.

Captain MacNeish and his men had just joined with the waiting warriors under Grant's command and were climbing into saddles when they heard the crashing of horses coming from direction they had just emerged from. Several archers cast worried glances at each other and their captain as they hurriedly scrambled to mount up.

James caught Gaston's eye and nodded with grim determination as he drew his basket hilted claymore. "Pull steel and rally to me!" he shouted.

In scant seconds, James found himself ringed about by a solid wall of horseflesh and forbidding defenders, each of which wielded before them three feet of sharpened Scottish steel. The crashing became louder as the horsemen swiftly closed the distance, and suddenly bursting into the open rode Redwood and his late coming band.

"Ho! James! 'Tis a great angry batch of hornets ye hae stirred up!" exclaimed Redwood with a laugh, his smiling face flushed with excitement. Only after the large warrior had spoken did he realize the consternation his mad dash had caused. With a growl, Gaston slammed home his sword into leather scabbard.

"Nae exactly the welcome I had expected," Redwood muttered, seeing the stern faces between he and his friend. "Sorry I'm late, but the lads and I found ourselves somewhat delayed by a cheeky group of knights. That lot was in a foul humor, especially when they discovered we had stolen these fine horses from their picket lines."

James shook his head in sudden bemusement. "At ease, men. Redwood is one of us, even if he is a great oversized rogue!" he quipped, unable to stop himself as a relieved smile lightened his taut expression.

The raiding party once again united, they quietly evacuated the area and quickly left behind the disorganized forces sent to harry them. As the distance they put between themselves and the enemy camp grew the mood of the men improved. Most of those involved marveled at the incredible success they had enjoyed, though there were others that would never be able to forget the terrible deeds they had performed.

Some two hours later, and still well before the coming of dawn, the tired and exuberant company rode through the welcoming gates of Dunmoore.

James was pleased to note that the sentries were alert and the village well guarded as he and his warband had approached. The advance warders were Gaston's idea and designed to give some advance notice to sentries, to allow them time to summon forth a quick reaction force. Dozens of defenders manned the wall and the night bristled with the sharp metal heads of their readied arrows.

Once within the safe confines of home, James led his company on to the village green where their camp had been set up. To his surprise and the delight of the men, they were greeted by what seemed like the entire village populace, and along with them they brought enough food and drink for all the returning warriors. Eagerly the town folk had gathered and set up makeshift tables, to hold the impromptu feast with benches at every side for the brave men to rest.

Following a necessary formation, in order to count heads and gather a rough tally of enemy losses, James quickly dismissed all of his men, except for his two lieutenants, so that they might enjoy the villager's hospitality. They all deserved a well-earned rest and the folk's merriment would help take minds from less pleasant things.

Redwood gazed longingly at the food laden tables and pretty girls passing out mugs of frothy beer and sighed heavily. Together he and Gaston followed their captain to a large tent set up in the center of the small sea of crisp canvas tents.

The inside of the commander's tent was spartanly furnished. A small camp desk was set up in the center that sported a number of leather cups sown to the sides and currently held a number of rolled up maps. Ranged about the table, in no particular order, sat three foldable stools made of wood and canvas. A heavy, fur lined sleep coverlet lay neatly spread over a folding, wooden cot.

"I would invite ye gentlemen to sit," said James, moving to the opposite side of the portable desk, "but wi' nae keep ye from the gathering any longer than I must. Details may wait until later, but ye both are aware of what I need to ken."

Once the information had been garnered from Redwood and Gaston, the young captain released his two capable and very different officers, to join the others before all the food vanished along with the pitchers of dark local beer and ale.

James wished he could join them, but knew he needed to catch up with his father and give him a report about the mission. Soon he caught sight of the old chieftain as the laird walked through the rows of tents, visiting the temporary army encampment. Calling out, James waved to draw his father's attention and headed toward the man.

"Ah, James," he greeted with a nod of his head. "I was just making my rounds to check on the lads about camp.

"I'm pleased to see ye safely returned without injury," he said, looking his son over with critical eye. "Walk with yer old Da and tell me how everything went. I'm eager to hear about the success of yer raid on the accursed Campbells."

As the two strolled through the camp the older man led them slowly toward where the rest of the war party relaxed, eating and drinking with their hosts.

"Tell me, did we hae many losses?"

"Nay, Da," James shook his head. "One lad was killed in the attack and two more were wounded, but wi' nae miss the fighting to come. I had hoped that none would fall, but, truly the raid could nae hae gone much cleaner. The Campbells wi' be licking their wounds after the way we hurt them."

"Men wi' always fall in battle, it is The Morrigan's way," Lyam told his son matter-of-factly. "The death of friends and allies is something ye must learn to harden yerself to if ye wish to become a true leader. Sacrifice is often necessary in battle if one is to triumph over the enemy. I do nae mean to sound uncaring," he said, glancing over at his heir. "Ye must value the lives of all those that follow yer commands, but ye wi' hae to distance yerself from sorrowful guilt and nae allow the loss of each dead warrior to hang like a weight around yer neck or it wi' brake yer heart. If ye let that happen ye wi' soon find that ye hae lost the spirit to fight on and others wi see it. Should that ever happen ye would be a wise man to hang up yer sword and let someone else lead."

"Aye," said James, his head nodding in understanding. "I recognize the wisdom of yer words, but it's still tough to cope with the sudden loss of someone that ye hae known all of yer life. Ach, anyway, I hae a loose count of the enemy dead; the total is nae bound to be perfect, but it should be fairly reliable," he qualified ahead of time. "The lads feathered upwards of four hundred enemy soldiers, while Gaston and his band of infiltrators accounted for over fifty more of the foe slain in their sleep. That exploit by itself should effect the Campbell's and their ally's morale most of all.

"By that tally, we hae seriously crippled the invading force with little loss to our own fighting strength. With any luck we hae stunned them enough that they may hae to withhold their advance a day or two to lick the wounds we gave them."

"Mayhap, James," said Lyam, shrugging his shoulders, "but do nae underestimate yer opponent. They may do as ye hope, however they may also press ahead with a new resolve to exterminate us all. Speculation means nothing. We must be diligent and ready for what ever may happen.

"Ye make me proud at how well ye hae shown yerself as a leader of men, and I am sure that in the coming days ye wi' further prove yer mettle," said James' approving father, gripping the young man's shoulder with fierce affection.

"Come now, let's avail ourselves of some of this bonny feast before Redwood eats it all . . ." Lyam's voice trailed off as the thundering noise of many horses drew everyone's attention. Abruptly, the village green erupted into action as wide-eyed soldiers darted for their tents to arm themselves and sergeants bellowed orders.

"See to yer men!" barked the old chieftain, not looking at his son as he trotted toward where the village folk milled about the food laden tables in apparent confusion. Quickly he had them all rounded up and headed for the cover of their homes, the party forgotten in an instant.

James drew his sword and held it aloft to attract attention. "MacGregor! MacGregor, rally to me!" he shouted fiercely.

A grizzled soldier rushed on foot toward where James waited as the rally point. "Sair! There be Frasers here!" he exclaimed and the captain directed his attention to the man in surprise.

"Sair, the Frasers hae arrived and wait outside the gates," he reported, offering a quick salute. "Their leader says that he has come to reinforce us against the Campbells, and he has brought with him fifteen hundred soldiers."

A sudden grin flashed across James' relieved face.

"Sair, Lord Mhoram wishes to meet with ye and Laird Lyam," the last he added as both men saw the chieftain hastening toward them, a bared sword in his hand.

"I heard," he said curtly, veering spryly toward the gate. "Follow me, we should nae keep our guests waiting out in the night."

Together, the three men hurried to meet their allies. Climbing up onto the wall, Lyam and James gazed down upon the host of Frasers and the small contingent that sat astride their mounts before the closed portal.

Instantly recognizing the Earl of Inverness, Lyam barked a hasty order and soon the main gate was opening in welcome to the waiting lord.

Lyam beamed down at familiar figure of the Fraser chief. "My lord, it is good to see ye and yer lads. Please be welcome in Dunmoore."

Waving, the nobleman kneed his horse forward and led his party within the walls of the MacNeish village. He was dressed for war, a fine hauberk of mail and strategically placed plates of steel armor protecting him and a finely wrought, plumed helm resting on his head. The martial dignity of the earl was unmarred by the mud and road dust that covered him from head to foot. His garments were raven's wing black, with the Fraser ensign on the fine surcoat embroidered in crimson.

The MacNeish chieftain and his son descended from the wall and strode to meet the dismounting lord. Lord Mhoram was quite tall, James realized, something that had not been evident while seated on his impressive horse.

The Fraser turned to face the two men approaching. His long hair, bound back in a border braid, was a glossy black with wings of silver showing at each temple. A thick beard and mustaches held the distinguishing flecks of silver in them as well. Resting under his black gloved fingers rested a remarkable sword that was of a size to equal the stature of it's master. The black leather scabbard, fully four feet in length, rested at his hip. The much used hilt was wrapped in worn dark leather and capped in blackened steel with a large crimson gem set in it and fashioned for a one handed swing, and a generous cross-guard swept out to stylized, hollow crosses.

"Lyam! It's good to see ye again," he greeted in a deep voice, a smile coming to his lips as the whiskers parted to reveal even white teeth. The towering warrior-lord let his dark eyes travel curiously to regard the young captain at the chieftain's side. "And ye must be James. Ye hae the look of yer father about ye. I understand that congratulations are in order for yer first command.

"I am Mhoram Fraser. I and my troops are pleased to hae arrived in time to aid ye in the coming battle," he informed both men and tugged off one heavy gauntlet to free his right hand. He offered his hand first to Lyam and then to James, the massive paw all but engulfing each of theirs in turn.

"We are most pleased to hae ye and yer lads with us," Lyam welcomed, accepting the offered hand in a firm handshake with a gracious smile. "I am also pleased to be able to offer ye some pleasant news that ye likely hae nae heard about yet, my lord. Earlier, this very night, a warband led by Captain MacNeish, my son here, attacked the enemy sitting on our borders. Using the cover of darkness and the skill of stealth he caught the Campbells and their allies by surprise, and with but three score lads dealt a fearsome blow against that camped host. Our lads, under the gallant command of my son, struck them so mightily that more than four hundred of the enemy warriors fell before them and they are most likely still licking their wounds from such a defeat," he pronounced with an unmistakable note of pride. "One of our lads did fall in battle—poor shame that—for any of our blood to be spilled by the thrice damned Campbells."

The chief of Clan Fraser raised thick eyebrows in astonishment. "By God! Ye hae drawn first blood and struck down the dogs before I could even get here! I shall be sorely disappointed if ye hae nae saved any for me!" Mhoram exclaimed.

"It was ye who commanded the attack?"

"Aye, my lord," replied James.

"The plan was formed by our chieftain," he modestly diverted credit, "while the lads fought with skill and bravery."

"Yer modesty is admirable, Captain MacNeish," Mhoram approved, "but soldiers typically only perform with such bravery when well led. And, it seems, that ye are the man that has sought to deprive my lads and I of our fun, uh?" he demanded gruffly, glaring down at the much shorter man briefly before his broad face broke into a sudden, amused grin. "Well done then, lad. Ye hae shown plenty of brass to take the attack to the Campbells like that. I believe that I wi' enjoy fighting by yer side, Captain."

Following the initial pleasantries, Lyam offered the hospitality of his long house to his noble guest and to those officers accompanying their lord. At the host's invitation, Lord Mhoram strode confidently into the rustic dwelling of Dunmoore's laird, ducking his head under the doorway to accommodate his impressively tall frame. Once inside, they discovered James' officers already within and waiting patiently.

Soon James and his lieutenants had been introduced and acquainted with their counterparts from Clan Fraser. Lyam invited all those present to join him and be seated at the large table dominating the main chamber. And it was there that they presented ideas and together coordinated the tactics for the upcoming battle. Taking into account their hasty confluence, the planning went much more smoothly than most of those gentlemen would have expected.

In the meantime, Lord Fraser's retainers were quietly marched, with orderly haste, inside the walls and swiftly erected bulwarks of Dunmoore and out of sight from any scouts the enemy may have dispatched to reconnoiter the area. The village green was suddenly a very crowded place as the Fraser troops set up camp and pitched their tents alongside those of their Clan Gregor allies. Sergeants among the new arrivals kept tight rein on their subordinates and ordered them to obtain as much sleep as they could. They received little argument as the men were fatigued from the hard, ambitious march they had embarked on from the north. And as they bedded down to restore themselves from the arduous journey, troops of the Border Dragons kept a vigilant watch. The Frasers were not the only ones grateful for the chance to rest, however, as those men of Captain MacNeish's raiding party were just as eager to find their cots following the long, bloody duty they had endured in taking the fight to the enemy.

Morning came and went and slowly the mild afternoon hours passed as well, until the sun began it's steady descent toward the horizon that evening. The much expected attack failed to materialize and all remained pleasantly quiet. The mood of the waiting MacGregor troops became somber as they became more on edge as the hours passed and wondered what the enemy had in store for them.

Sentries atop the walls were doubled as the sun faded beyond the surrounding forest and cast fingers of darkness that crept forward to engulf Dunmoore, along with the surrounding lands and approaches. Those men on duty became ever more cautious as the possibility of a night attack grew in their minds, for surely, old Domeric Campbell would retaliate of the one they had launched against him. However, the night remained quiet and the enemy made no showing of themselves.

The allied leaders made advantageous use of the time given them and together, formed an alternate plan that could be used, if no attack had materialized, by an hour past midnight. The initial strategy was proposed by the freshly arrived earl and was expanded and improved by James and Redwood. It was a daring stratagem that included an option in the event of their force being accidentally intercepted by an advance picket, or the more likely probability of an enemy force moving toward Dunmoore, to launch a late night attack of their own. If such a scenario were to unfold, their warband would split up into a number of small, mobile teams and commence with quick hit and run attacks on any targets of opportunity that might presented itself; in this way, they could strike again and again from several places at once. This tactic would work to disorganize and demoralize their enemy, while giving themselves the opening to break away from the adversary and return safely to Dunmoore.

The bold main plan formulated by the gathered officers and leaders was directed in an attempt to use the Campbell's own preparedness against them. Another sneak attack in the night versus them would never succeed again, as they would be doubly watchful and wary of such a repeated tactic.

No enemy attack materialized out of the darkness and as the midnight hour came and went, Lord Mhoram and Captain MacNeish assembled their combined force, minus five hundred troops who would remain behind to defend the walled village. In total, a force of one thousand, four hundred warriors marched forth from the gates of Dunmoore in hushed silence. Soon the army, all on foot, pushed forward in orderly columns and disappeared within the brooding, mist shrouded forest.

During the long three hour march, the joint force of MacGregors and Frasers wended their way cautiously through the primeval Scottish forest, ever vigilant for the appearance of a waiting enemy. When, at last, their army had reached the designated site, James favored the lord marching at his side a tight grin.

"This is the place where we wi' engage our enemies," he declared. "The clearing here is just large enough to suffice for our needs. One thousand men in two ranks across this natural clearing will prevent any coordinated attempt at flanking us," he told the attentive lord, pointing out the location with a gloved hand. "A generous reserve force can easily remain hidden in those thick trees off to our left flank."

Lord Mhoram followed the line of dark trees indicated by the captain's finger and nodded his approval. "I agree, Captain. Yer extensive knowledge of these wooded lands is impressive," he complimented.

"It would be my honour to see to the arraying of the main battle lines," he offered politely, "if ye be willing to see to the placement of the reserves. I and my lads would enjoy the opportunity to garner a measure of glory on the bodies of our mutual enemy," the Fraser chief added.

James inclined his head. "I'd hae it nay other way." Saluting his co-commander, he strode off and called Redwood and Gaston to his side for a hasty conference. With his orders given, James and his burly lieutenant set about moving the MacGregor forces into their position within the deep shadows of the towering evergreens. Meanwhile, Gaston gathered his much smaller band, a token force numbering a mere thirty warriors, and waited until the command to proceed was given.

The battle lines were soon in position and the troops settled down to rest while they had the opportunity to do so. The hefty reserve force was swiftly situated out of sight from the clearing, and hunkered down about a dozen yards from the edge of the tree line until they would be called on to assist their comrades. Everything arranged to his liking, James left Redwood in charge of the reserves while he proceeded through the darkness and mist to locate his other lieutenant and the band that would be bait for the trap. Near the forward edge of the clearing he found them huddled around Gaston.

"Everyone is in position and ready to give our enemy a greeting he'll nae soon forget," James told the waiting men. "Their camp is about a quarter mile away; we are all depending on ye lads to stir things up enough that they chase ye, but be sure that they nae lose ye in the dark. That lot must come directly to us or it may be *us* that are on the receiving end of a nasty surprise."

"We'll get the job done," Gaston assured his commander. "Every lad that is part of this mission is familiar with these lands. Except me, of course," he added, earning a chuckle from the men gathered around.

James offered the veteran lieutenant his hand. "Nay unnecessary risks, gentlemen. God speed ye all on yer way and I'll see ye soon."

Moments later, Gaston and his thirty men set out and quickly were swallowed by the darkness. A MacNeish tracker led the way through thick woodland terrain as if he could see in the dark. Gaston followed with the other men, putting his trust in the hunter's ability, hoping that he did not become separated from the others.

The area of the enemy camp they were bound for was made up mostly of Gordon and MacNeil clansmen and Gaston hoped that they were spoiling for a fight. He knew if they did not take the bait the whole night march would have been in vain.

The veteran woodsman interrupted the lieutenant's thoughts as he was suddenly standing before him. "Sair, we are near the enemy camp. We must be very quiet as we move closer to the treeline," he reported.

"Thank ye, Sergeant," Gaston replied. "Things are going to start happening fast once we are in position, so stick with me or I'll get lost for sure."

The tracker nodded and winked at the officer. "Do nae worry, sair, I'll make sure that I get ye back safe and sound; I ken ye wi' want to be around when the fun starts."

A full compliment of sentries was on duty about the enemy camp; many could be seen moving along the parameter in watchful attentiveness, but there were others as well that warded the area from hidden positions. It was one of these that cried out the first alarm before one of Grant's men could silence him with a dagger through the ribs.

A prepared and waiting reactionary force burst forward almost immediately from tents in groups in answer to the call to arms. Hundreds streamed out into the night, much like angry bees from a hornet's nest, shouting enthusiastic warcries as they came. Several fell with arrows suddenly sprouting from their body, but otherwise the volley had little effect as enemy soldiers charged through the mist towards the wood line.

Realizing the threat of quickly becoming overwhelmed, Gaston ordered his men to loose one more volley and retreat. Following his own directive the lieutenant promptly fled with his band back into the murky forest. His standing order had been to feign fear, as if fleeing for their lives, but there was little pretending needing done as with real fright the small band scampered away from the howling foe. The group's sudden flight drew the enemy reaction force after them in a heckling, headlong rush that could not be reigned in by the accompanying officers. An unrestrained mob of warriors swarmed in to the forest with no thought beyond meting out a measure of revenge on those that dared to shed the blood of so many friends and allies. Rapidly, the ranks of the pursuers became disorganized and continued on in small groups as they chased after the sounds of those fleeing before them.

The ruse, now in earnest, of Grant's platoon worked almost better than he would have desired as the pursuing troops came after them deep into the ancient forest. Ragged breaths wheezed from the veteran officer and he would have sighed with relief, as he at last burst from the thick undergrowth and into the clear, if he had had the breath for it. As it was, Gaston labored on toward where he knew safety awaited. As he drew nearer, the welcome sight of friendly battle lines came into view through the gloom. He had never realized just how beautiful the sight of bristling battle lines was.

The waiting ranks of Fraser clansmen opened narrow corridors at intervals along their neat lines at a shouted command from their commander. Grateful for the sign of welcome, Gaston and his weary band bounded to safety and only halted once they had reached the area where the two senior officers waited. Behind them, the ranks of Fraser warriors closed smartly to reform a solid front.

Before the panting lieutenant could report, shouts of command rang out up and down the lines as officers caught their first sight of the enemy emerging of the trees. They came on, heedless of the danger awaiting them, racing after their quarry.

A staccato command rang out and suddenly the thrumming of bowstrings snapped as the rank of archers, protected by kneeling spearmen, let loose a concentrated volley of deadly cloth yard shafts at the oncoming soldiers. Surprised, but undaunted, and caught up in their bloodlust, the running and the occasional mounted adversary broke into a sprint as they brandished weapons and shouted jeers of derision.

Scores began to fall lifeless to the ground as they charged ever forward, including several mounted knights whose chain armor could not withstand the hard hitting, steel arrow heads. Many fell in that first chaotic rush for vengeance before they realized the true danger they were in; belatedly they witnessing clearly an army waiting for them with fully arrayed battle formation and not the ragged skirmish line as expected.

A distant horn rang out a silvery set of notes that hanged in the misty air. The enemy charge immediately faltered in confusion and most of the warriors halted their rushing advance and began to retreat back to rally around their commander. However, several ignored the signaled command and continued to press on. Quickly dispatched by well aimed arrows, they never had the chance to realize their error in judgment.

Across the clearing from where the retreating skirmishers had sought refuge, the young, ranking officer, dressed in the tartan of Clan Gordon sat calmly astride his well trained mount. He held a telescoping glass to his eye and perused the orderly ranks of his adversary while awaiting the regrouping of his forces. He would not berate his officers before the men for allowing such a disgraceful display of pandemonium to occur, as the MacNeil clansmen had shown they were a discouraging influence with their lack of proper military leadership, but he promised himself that each of his subordinate officers and non-coms would have the proper motivation to prevent anything like it from ever happening in the future.

The Gordon commander was tall and golden with a chiseled jaw and the bearing of a prince who wore well the mantle of command. He proved himself once again, before his subordinate officers, an able leader as he prodded the returning troops into a cohesive fighting formation that joined with the force he had brought through the forest. The mob that had rushed headlong into the waiting foe had lost, he estimated, over a hundred of their number. It was a loss he regretted, but what was done was done. Soon, a disciplined fighting formation had rallied before him and awaited his orders. Returning the field lens to a worn leather pouch at his trim waist he coolly issued clear and concise commands to the officers gathered about him before sending them to relay those directives to their men. Those orders were soon passed on down the chain of command.

Bringing the ornate horn of his fathers again to his lips, the laird of the Gordons signaled the advance. Orderly ranks of his clansmen trotted forward across the clearing toward the waiting opponent under his watchful eye as he kneed his horse to keep pace with them. He blew another note from the horn and his modest army broke into a loping run, charging on a full front, but massed much more heavily toward the distant left flank of the Fraser lines as they had been ordered. The gallop of the proud, charging cavalry quickly outstripped the men storming ahead on foot and hurled themselves valiantly against the ranks of veteran Fraser soldiers. Those soldiers presented a deadly hedge of spears, grounded to receive a charge, and bravely stood their ground as the horses and riders bore down upon them. The lines of spearmen rippled violently as the cavalry smashed forcefully into them. The sound of the concussion echoed throughout the clearing as the Gordon knights tried to press their advantage with a strength gained from pent up frustration. The bristling wall of spears seemed to waver for a heartbeat before the furious onslaught until the stoic infantrymen grimly reasserted the embattled position and reset their ranks. As they had been repeatedly drilled, the Gordon cavalry disengaged and smartly regrouped to again charge the beleaguered flank. This time the press of charging horsemen was too much as the hard hit flank began to buckle under the onslaught of the ferociously fighting attackers and superior numbers as the foot soldiers arrived to drive home an attack the cavalry had begun.

The clash of battling warriors was brutal, and on both sides combatants were falling at the feet of their struggling fellows. The Gordon and MacNeil foot soldiers pressed forward relentlessly and the embattled Frasers anchoring that flank began to give ground as the attack turned more and more in the favor of the aggressors while the MacGregor allies were being cut down at an alarming rate. Already the spilled blood and carnage reeked in the still air along with a stench that came from released bowels of the dead. Footing became ever more hazardous as those fighting on were forced to awkwardly step around the bloody, hacked remains of fallen comrades and foe alike.

Witnessing the precarious plight of his ally's left flank, James personally took command of the waiting reserve force and, with Redwood's comforting presence at his side, drew his sword. "The

Woody Heights!" he roared. Springing forward he brandished his claymore and charged from the hidden position with alacrity to lend much needed support to the struggling Frasers.

"Stand fast there! Stand yer ground and fight my bonny lads! Help is on the way," Lord Mhoram chivvied his men, shouting to be heard above the din of battle. "Captain MacNeish is coming to lend a hand. Let's show these devils what Fraser men are made of!" Grimly the lord waded back into the thick of the fighting, without regard to his own safety, wielding his mighty black bladed sword as it dripped enemy blood. The heavy weapon hummed through the air with effortless, deadly strokes as Mhoram cut a swath through enemy troops. He sliced off the offending arm of first one opponent's sword arm and then parted another's head from his neck, life blood pumping in great spurts as the body dropped bonelessly to the sodden ground. The severed head hung in the air briefly, the eyes bulging in fascinated disbelief as the dying man witnessed the fall of his own twitching body.

Soon however, and to the earl's chagrin, the press of enemy soldiers faded from around him as they began to avoid facing his ferocious onslaught. Drawing a deep breath, Mhoram paused to wipe sweat from his face. His hand came away with as much blood as it did perspiration and he chuckled without humor. Glancing down he shook his head as he saw blood from his encounters coating every inch of his tall frame.

Raising his fearsome sword before him, Mhoram moved menacingly toward the closest knot of fighting men. Eyebrows drawn down in a fierce scowl he shouted out an indignant challenge, "I can nae believe my eyes! Is there none among ye willing to fight me or are ye all tae cowardly to face me?"

Distracted by the bellowed challenge of the towering, blood-drenched warrior bearing his great black and bloody sword, the opposing infantrymen failed to take notice of the new threat. Storming eagerly into their own left flank swept the fresh MacNeish reinforcements brought on by Captain MacNeish and his red haired lieutenant.

"The Woody Heights!" Screamed the attacking MacGregor clansmen, falling with vigor upon the surprised Gordon and MacNeil clan troops. The entire reserve continued to stream from the shadows of the evergreens even as the leading elements were converging on the left and rear side of those soldiers attacking the Frasers.

Astounded soldiers fell like scythed wheat before the momentum of the fierce charge, the enemy clansmen turning to face the new threat with the beginnings of fright showing in their wide eyes. Caught now between the lethal pinch of two fronts at once they panicked, despite their gallant commander's valiant attempts to stabilize his forces. His efforts soon failed as he saw the previously hidden reserve drive a fatal wedge into his exposed flank, turning the tide of battle dramatically, into a bloody slaughter. Raising the horn at his side, to his lips, Gordon sounded the retreat and hoped to lead the battered remnants of his army across the clearing where he hoped to rally them.

It was not so much a retreat, but rather a full-blown flight as the panicked MacNeil heard the horn blast as a sign of permission to save themselves and caused the entire formation to dissolve. Confusion reigned as desperate men sought to escape the jaws of their enemy's trap and fled without regard to anything except saving one's own skin. In the turmoil that took place the Gordon warriors fled as well, unwittingly abandoning their proud, young laird.

The Gordon commander remained behind to help cover the disorganized retreat of his army and fought bravely to buy them time to escape, although many were still cut down from behind as they fled the field. In the process he quickly found himself cut off and surrounded by a number of enemy troops. His stallion was war trained and for a time the fighting pair held their own, but even the strongest of warriors will become weary of constantly defending against overwhelming numbers. A spear jabbed in from his off side and pierced his mail to drive deeply into his shoulder. The soldier wielding the spear used the leverage gained by the puncture to topple him from the saddle.

Showing surprising toughness and dexterity, Gordon vaulted to his feet with sword still in hand and faced his attackers using his riled mount to protect his left side. Left behind and alone by his men, the abandoned commander stood his ground amid a field of stinking carnage and a multitude of slain bodies. He knew he was going to die; it was just a matter of time as he weakened from blood loss and faced off single handedly versus the triumphant MacGregor/Fraser army. His bloody broadsword he clutched with both hands, held in a loose high-guard position across his mailed chest so that the long blade could rest lightly next to his bloodied shoulder.

Despite the near blinding pain radiating from his torn shoulder the Gordon leader fearlessly refused to back down, a studied look of flat defiance plain on his handsome features as he faced the ring of hostile warriors around him. Secretly, he prayed that they would get on with it and let him die an honourable death.

"I am a commander of Gordons, and I demand the rite of single combat with one of ye whom also is a captain of soldiers," he declared in an even tone, although he gritted his teeth against the anguish of his wound. He held his golden head high with pride in spite of the shameful fact that he had been left behind by his own clansmen. As he waited for a response the weakening man noted the steady approach of the formidable black clad warrior that had cut down so many of his troops, along with another man wearing the MacGregor tartan who he supposed must be the local leader.

"Ye surely be more than just a captain, I'd wager, laddie. Is that nae so? Or is it that ye would be denying yer own birthright?" Lord Mhoram chided, stepping forward through the press of fellow soldiers that respectfully parted for him. Halting a few paces from the injured man, he took care to remain out of the reach of steel shod hooves that lashed out from the spirited horse.

Coolly appraising the young commander with a critical eye the towering clan chief crouched to casually wipe a quantity of drying blood from his glistening, long black blade onto the dusty kilt of a fallen foe. His blade now dry and free of blood, Mhoram slowly straightened to his impressive full height which allowed him to tower over every man there, including the seemingly fearless Gordon.

"Ye are Conall Gordon, Laird of Clan Gordon, the right given ye by dictate of yer crippled and albeit honourable father, Conan, the Duke of Huntly," declared the Fraser lord, an engaging smile on his lips. "I hae the acquaintance of yer father and I believe he would be rightfully proud of the determination and courage that ye hae shown upon this bloody field of battle."

The defeated laird did not return the smile, however courtesy and respect were as much a part of his character as bravery and pride. "I thank ye for those kind words, sair, but ye hae me at the disadvantage. Ye ken who I am, so would ye be so kind as to grant me the same privilege?" he asked wearily. His shoulder wound continued to profusely bleed, dripping a steady flow of red blood from his bent elbow, as he still managed through strong of will, to hold up his increasingly heavy sword. Dried blood was caked copiously over the wounded man, although the majority of it was not his own, but rather the lifeblood of numerous opponents.

"Captain MacNeish, would ye be sae kind as to introduce me to this noble young man?" Fraser asked politely.

"Of course," assented James, "it would be my pleasure." Moving forward, he stepped slightly between the two warriors while being careful to give the war trained mount a wide berth before continuing. "Laird Gordon," he said, inclining his head, first to the bloodied enemy commander, with due respect to his rank before raising a hand to indicate his notable ally. "I hae the honour of introducing Lord Mhoram Fraser, chief of that name and Earl of Inverness. His lordship or myself should be sufficient to meet the qualifications of single combat ye hae demanded."

"Hold, James. Before matters progress to such a drastic climax I hae something in mind that may prevent more unneeded bloodshed," said Mhoram reasonably, keeping his gaze fixed to that of the Gordon. "Laird Conall, could ye first explain to me what it is that fuels the feud that ye harbor against The MacGregor and his clan sae much that ye hae brought yer clan to invade their borders?"

The golden warrior frowned slightly, the unexpected query catching him a little off guard. "Lord Mhoram, what right hae ye as my enemy to question my motives?"

Mhoram shrugged his massive shoulders. "Perhaps just the curiosity of one leader to another as to why we must shed one another's blood. It would seem a poor waste of good men to fight for nay particular reason."

The Gordon took a deep breath and grimaced in pain as the movement aggravated his wound. "The quarrel is nae our own, Lord Mhoram," he admitted mildly. "We were goaded into this by our Campbell overlord. My ailing father was compelled to comply with Lord Domeric's demands or we were to be treated the same as the MacGregors. And as we are surrounded on nay less than four borders by stout allies of the Campbells, there was nought else that we could do but submit.

"For my part, I hae nay love for the Campbells or their duke," he confessed, his face tight with indignity, "especially when they use my clansmen, like sae much cheap fodder, to be butchered in the front lines of their own war! Would that I were home with my clansmen, but duty brought us to this place; I can nae think of just the wellbeing of my soldiers when the safety of my entire clan is at issue," the laird finished heavily, his stricken body shaking as he sought to contain his rage and grief for his dead clansmen, along with his own pain. Hot tears of sorrow, for his fallen clansmen, rolled unheeded down his proud dust and blood caked cheeks as he suddenly cast down his sword in a bitter show of defeat.

"I grieve with ye, lad," sympathized Mhoram. "Yer clan has been ill used by the Campbells, but tell me, what would ye do if ye found yerself free of the indignant hold that Duke Domeric has imposed?"

"Lord, if that were possible, may all the gods protect them!" he cried vehemently, raising his haggard eyes to stare at the Fraser chief. "The Gordons would fall upon that thrice-accursed duke and his mongrel clan with sword and fire to avenge every one of our clansmen that he has led to their deaths, and for the wicked stranglehold he has kept upon us these past years since gaining his foul and misbegotten overlordship over my clan. Ach, a pox on Domeric Campbell!" he spat with unconcealed hate.

During Conall's tirade, Mhoram and James surreptitiously exchanged a knowing nod. As the Gordon cursed their mutual enemy, the Earl of Inverness solemnly returned his attention back to him and said, "I am one lord among others in a confederacy of allied clans who all aligned against the Campbell Alliance, and I hae the authority to grant yer clan the protection promised to all members if ye wi' join cause with us, Conall. All that is required for my satisfaction is yer solemn word of honour," he offered with gracious dignity, sliding his terrible black sword back into its long scabbard and straightening his heavy, black, oiled cloak so that it covered both broad shoulders. "Freely give to me yer word of honour, Laird Conall, and we wi' fight side by side until the Campbells are nay longer a blight in our beloved highlands."

A measure of weariness melted from Conall's noble features as a grin curved his lips. Hiding his obvious pain behind a grim mask he reached down to retrieve his sword and slowly knelt behind it as he grounded the blade. Resting his forehead forward against the cross guard hilt, he spoke with quiet dignity, "I, Laird Conall Gordon, acting under the authority given me my father, Duke Conan of Huntly, do solemnly swear by this cross on my honour and that of my clan, that Clan Gordon wi' nay longer wage war nor offer any hindrance to Clan Gregor or any of the clans confederated them. I also pledge to ye that nay aid and comfort should be given to Clan Campbell nor to any of those clans that make common cause with them. Furthermore, Gordons wi', as we are able, bring to the Campbells war in their territories with sword and fire. May all the gods, but especially the one God, bless our endeavor in the name of the Holy Christ," he added in a fervent and reverent whisper as he leaned forward to kiss his soldier's cross.

"So mote it be," James and Mhoram intoned together.

The morning came early for the defending army, as following their withdrawal to Dunmoore along with the Gordon laird and the surviving portion of his men that had been part of the large reaction force, as they prepared to receive the enemy's attack. The leaders gathered there conferred without rest; planning out the next step of resistance.

"So, ye are acting in yer father's stead as Laird of Clan Gordon," Lyam stated bluntly, appraising the bandaged young laird with a critical eye. "Can ye be sure that yer clansmen wi' harken to orders after ye hae abandoned yer original mission. Some might consider yer decision to join with us an act of cowardice or even betrayal."

Genuine doubt clouded Conall's haggard features as he shook his blonde head, clearly wrestling with how to answer, but at last he muttered forlornly, "I can nae offer ye any guarantee as to how they wi' respond."

Lyam nodded his head thoughtfully while admiring the man's honesty. "Very well, lad. Our plans must be drawn in such a way as to be prepared for the possibility that the Gordons may nae choose to follow the young laird. Gentlemen, let's go over every option that we hae available to us," Lyam suggested, "perhaps something wi' present it self to us that we may hae overlooked before." Within the hour, much to the relief of all those involved, the war council was interrupted for breakfast.

It was still early morning, but as the first rays of the sun stretched long shadows across the ground and obscured the ominous face of a blood-red moon, the damp mists began to burn off. Vigilant soldiers, of each allied clan, were fully armed and already at their designated posts in preparation for an eminent attack. The defenders were not to be kept waiting long as scouts soon began to stream in on lathered mounts to report on the advancement and disposition of the marching enemy.

Hardly more than an hour passed before the enemy army had advanced to within view of the defenders of Dunmoore. Marching closer, they made a great display of their orderly ranks and of the proud banners borne of each clan present. And all the while a score of bagpipers played, the martial skirl of their instruments wailed in the brisk morn and urged on the columns of colorfully clad clansmen.

Standing atop the bulwarks, Lord Mhoram and Captain MacNeish attentively watched as the enemy forces were deployed in full view of the village. They formed into the precise ranks and files of an infantry core and in this formation were the archer corps blended in, while companies of pikemen held the outer edges as a ward to any attacking cavalry. Stationed outside of the ranks of foot soldiers were squadrons of their own cavalry, both light and heavy.

"Their commander puts on a pretty parade," disdainfully snorted the earl once the army had ground to halt no more than a thousand yards away, and carefully beyond the range of

Dunmoore's bowmen. "This is it, James. Order yer lieutenant's attachment to escort our young Laird Gordon outside the wall, and make sure they do nae place Conall in danger by moving tae close to their archers," Fraser instructed.

"Do ye expect a betrayal of a truce flag?"

The powerful leader shrugged his massive shoulders. "Who knows? But, when ye hae any dealings with a Campbell always keep one hand on yer sword."

Captain MacNeish nodded in grim agreement. Turning he descended from the new wall and quickly found the men he had been looking for. "Redwood, are ye and yer lads ready to begin our little ceilidh? Good," James said briskly, replying to his burly lieutenant's nod. "Remember to keep the truce flag raised high so that our friends out there won't be tempted to attack ye; and be ready for anything. Ye do nae ken how they wi' react once Laird Gordon makes his appeal."

"Aye, sair," replied Redwood, saluting his friend and captain.

Momentarily, the main gates of Dunmoore opened and Laird Gordon along with his twenty man escort rode forth at a slow trot. They continued their measured pace until reaching a point near midway between the invading army and the fortified village. The white parley flag snapped briskly as Redwood rode, bearing it high for all to see.

The group stopped and waited for a reaction from the aggressors. The red haired lieutenant glanced over at the nobleman waiting by his side. "Now would seem as good a time as any to get this party started, sair."

"Aye. This is it then," murmured Conall, before raising himself up to be seen by standing in his stirrups. In place of his usual steel helmet, he wore a highland bonnet upon his golden head which sported the distinctive Gordon crest with it's impressive stag's head along with a single proud eagle feather, the ancient denotation of a clan chieftain. Gazing boldly out upon the army, which he had so recently been a part of, the Gordon laird easily spotted the proud battle standard of his clan.

Lifting the end of his long Gordon tartaned cloak above his head he addressed himself to the soldiers positioned about his clan's banner in a practiced parade ground voice. "Hear me men of Clan Gordon! I am Conall, son of our lord and chief, Conan Gordon," he proclaimed loudly. "If ye would follow yer rightful laird, ye wi' follow me! All who are Gordons and loyal to yer chief rally to me! To me, Gordons! Rally to me, I command it!" he urged them.

Within the orderly ranks of the opposing army there was an immediate stirring of reaction as confusion and disarray broke out as Gordon clansmen broke ranks to better see who it was that had summoned a rallying of their clan. Soon there were cries of joy ringing out as many of the Gordon warriors suddenly recognized the anxious figure of their missing leader. Most had believed their chief's eldest son was dead, fallen in the battle that had occurred during the past night.

"Tis Conall . . . that is our bonny laird . . . we must rally to his call . . ." Those were the most common and loudest voices that reached the ears of Conall and his escort as he waited with false calm for the clan's answer.

"To me Gordons! It *is* I, Conall, and I *surely* live yet!" Again the laird shouted while waving his bonnet, his golden blonde hair shining in the morning sunlight, like a halo about his head.

The laird's waving and shouting caused more unrest within the enemy ranks and by now Conall had been recognized by all those present that were acquainted with him, especially when they caught a glimpse of his uncovered head. More than just breaking ranks now to see what was happening, the Gordon clansmen opened large gaps in the army's formation as they rushed from their positions and rushed across the barren meadow to their leader's side. The remainder of the bewildered army, following the mass defection, was barely two-thirds of it's original complement, and found itself suddenly not so sure of itself.

Outraged officers among the remaining Campbell and MacNeil army hastened to bring order to their stricken army and shouted terse commands. Bows snapped as archers released their quarrels after the deserting Gordons. Several fell with arrows plunging into their exposed backs, but the rest continued on with greater urgency to be reunited with their laird and the hope of sanctuary behind the village walls.

Waving his bonnet, Conall kneed his mount around and cantered with his escort toward Dunmoore as the gates swung open in offered hospitality. The Gordons ran on in the wake of their leader and soon streamed into the village and refuge from the vindictive officers and men they had left behind.

The gates were safely closed and secured once the mass of over three hundred Gordon clansmen had entered. None of those clansmen looked back, but instead gathered in a circle around their golden leader—the man whom nearly all had believed slain in the nighttime battle. Eagerly they gazed at him and waited to hear what he had to say, being more than a little curious about why he had ordered their unexpected switching of sides on the virtual brink of battle.

Before anyone else could speak up, one tall and wire thin warrior, his stout bow flung across his back, stepped forward wearing a broad, happy grin. "Conall! It is ye, thank the gods! I had come to believe that ye were dead after that battle yester eve," he exclaimed, pleased to have been wrong. The second Conall had dismounted and had his feet on the ground, the archer was there to throw his arms enthusiastically around the man and clap him on the back. "I'm so glad ye are alive, Conall; I still had nae decided on how I was to break the news of it to Father."

Conall chuckled and returned the backslapping. "It *is* me, brother, and I am fine. Actually, I am more fine than I hae been in a long time," confirmed the laird, his tone carrying more significance than just his health. "I need to speak to ye, to all of ye," he said loud enough for all gathered nearby to hear, "on a matter of great importance.

"Our reaction force was defeated last night by a canny opponent that was fighting to protect their lands. My beaten lads, along with those of the MacNeils, fled the field deep in the MacGregor's forest; and in the process of attempting to cover their retreat I was left behind in the hands of the opposing army. Wounded and without hope of rescue, I demanded the right of single combat in order to die an honourable death," he proudly explained. "Instead of death, I was greeted by Lord Mhoram, Earl of Inverness, the chief of Clan Fraser, and offered an alternative. That alternative was nae just for myself, but for our entire clan. That lord offered, in exchange for my word of honour to discontinue battling against the MacGregors, to admit our clan into their confederacy and with it the protection of those united clans. In essence, a mutual pact that is opposed to our mad overlord, the ever arrogant and high-handed Domeric Campbell.

"All of us must be aware that my father has never harbored any love for the thieving Campbells," he intimated, his direct gaze moving from man to man gathered there and coming to rest on his younger brother's serious face. "I believe our chief would agree with my decision if he were here. Nay longer wi' we be required to spill our blood and die at the whim of that fool duke. Ye are all kin to me, and since I carry with me the power invested by my father I hae chosen to oppose our oppressor.

"Are ye with me?" he demanded, again sweeping his intense gaze across the group of his assembled clansmen. "I renounce Duke Domeric's heavy yoke; wi' ye still follow me and fight for the pride and honour of Clan Gordon?"

No one spoke up at first and Conall began to feel disappointment as his greatest fear seemed to be coming true—that his clansmen would reject his leadership. At last, however, his brother came to his rescue and filled the silence. "I am Donald, youngest son of Conan our chief," he declared, although every man there knew very well who he was and not just for who his father was, but for the reputation he had won for himself by his superlative skill with the bow. "For my part, I say we *should* break from the duke and his bloody Campbells! We hae before us the opportunity to repay him and his clansmen for all the hardships they brought upon us. Would ye all prefer to remain cowed by their threats or stand with Conall and I to win back our pride?"

Donald's fiery argument stirred the Gordon warriors and like wildfire agreement spread through the gathering. Before long, every one of those Gordons was shouting enthusiastic support for their brave laird. The sound of sword hilts pounding against targs was carried far beyond the walls of Dunmoore to the ears of those soldiers arrayed to do battle versus the defenders within the small village.

All was chaos within the devastated ranks of the remaining army of MacNeils and Campbells. In their eyes, they had been horribly betrayed by the sudden and unexpected defection of a trusted ally who had turned their coats to join with the enemy on the eve of battle. A heated conference took place between the MacNeil chief and the commander of the Campbell troops; in the end, the two outraged leaders found themselves forced into a distasteful decision. Convinced that they now held no chance of any sort of victory, against the overwhelming force now at their enemy's disposal, they reformed their disheartened troops into long columns and gave the order to march. And as they marched away, the happy sounds of celebration rang in their ears with shame.

Standing atop the village's bulwarks, Lord Mhoram turned a grim smile on James as he climbed up to join him on the wall near the front gate. "I still say that we could hae whipped the lot of them, even with the Gordons on their side of the wall," he declared stoutly. Turning his head he watched the invading army march from sight much like a dog with its tail between its legs.

"We'll never know," admitted James, shrugging his shoulders. "It does nae matter anyway. What does matter is that we hae won a nearly bloodless victory while punishing those that would come and threaten us in our homes.

"Aye, perhaps we could hae done it, but I'm pleased to nae hae to," he added, sighing deeply. "But now we hae one more ally to rely on in this war that the flaming Campbells hae brought against us." Turning away from the view of the departing enemy, James faced the lord at his side and thrust out his hand. "We hae all come through this remarkably well and we MacNeishs hae ye and yer clan to thank for it, my lord," he said as Mhoram firmly gripped his hand in friendship. "What wi' ye do, now that Dunmoore is free from Duke Domeric's foul attention? Wi' ye go now to throw yer support behind Lord Gregor in Glenorchy?"

"Aye, we wi' be taking our leave of ye later today," he affirmed, nodding his head slightly. "I believe Lord Gregor wi' be in need of my lads to help turn back Domeric's main army, if my guess is correct. The old duke's army wi' nae be sae easy to deal with as this one proved to be. I would dearly love to be present to see his pocked face when he receives the news of today's outcome," the earl said, a guffaw erupting from his lips.

CHAPTER FOUR

For hours, following the time that Lord Mhoram led his clan troops away from Dunmoore, the fighting continued without pause at the walls of Glenorchy. Just as it had begun at dawn, with zeal and ferocity, the fight for that city's thick walls persisted with neither side gaining and keeping any clear advantage. MacGregor soldiers still held the wall and Campbell troops remained determined to take it from them.

The angry-looking red sun descended as Scotsmen battled fellow Scotsmen until its glare fell beyond the mountainous horizon. Only then, with the growing darkness, did the fierce fighting gradually subside as the stubborn Campbell duke at last ordered a withdrawal from the formidable walls. In their wake remained the piteous cries of wounded soldiers and dying comrades. The loud keening of newly made widows filled the night with their sorrow for loved ones lost to the great sleep.

Exhausted soldiers gratefully found what rest there was to have, knowing that come the morning the fighting would resume anew. Meanwhile, smoke from many fires wafted into the night sky about Glenorchy like a gray haze that matched the mood of many soldiers and citizens of that place. This was but the first day of war for them, however, most realized that it was likely to just the beginning of what could turn out to be a long and drawn out siege. Men were already dying of wounds given them by enemies wielding weapons, but a long siege could bring just as cruel a death to the young and old alike when supplies of food began to run out.

All during the chill overnight hours, field surgeons labored feverishly as they went about the grim task of mending the wounded or in many cases sought to bring some comfort to the mortally wounded men's final hours. Surgeons from both sides did the best they could, while mourning afresh the loss of vast amounts of medical knowledge that abounded before the Time of Destruction along with the warriors that knowledge could have saved. In their heart, each healer laid the blame of the deaths of hundreds of warriors at the feet of those men and women long dead during a past age. It was they whom were ultimately responsible for the nearly complete annihilation of the human race then, as well as the deaths that bled the ground red now.

To the surprise and delight of Lord Gregor and the Warlord Sean MacSean, the army of Clan Fraser arrived following their chief, Mhoram Fraser, little more than an hour after full dark had fallen. The besieging army was just as stunned as the arrivals drove a wedge through their lines and fought determinedly to enter the city. MacGregor forces quickly assembled a mounted legion and sallied forth to aid in clearing the way for those friendly troops to reach safely within Glenorchy's fortifications.

A pleased smile warmed Mhoram Fraser's broad face as he sat his horse on the main city thoroughfare with his army stretched out behind him. Surrounding him were the friendly faces of throngs of citizenry and soldiers alike, cheering him and his men for the unexpected arrival to reinforce their home. Ahead of him, the beaming earl watched as Lord Gregor and his warleader slowly made their way towards him, through the crowd, on well-bred destriers as he delighted in the warm reception. Dismounting, Mhoram patted his horse once he was on his own feet, and stretched his back with a quiet groan before turning to see his ally approach leading his horse by the reins.

"Welcome, Mhoram!" The Master of Glenorchy heartily greeted his longtime ally and boon friend, grasping the burly earl in an enthusiastic embrace. "I am surprised to hae ye here with us; ye were nae expected for at least another fortnight, if then. What news of Dunmoore? The last word that we hae received was of an army numbering some fifteen hundred warriors of the

Gordons, MacNeils, and Campbells, which were invading the border near there," said the MacGregor chief.

Lord Mhoram nodded his head sagely. "Aye, Gregor. Yer information was indeed correct, however, yer Captain MacNeish had matters well in hand by the time my lads and I arrived. Apparently, young Master James had led a very successful raid on the enemy camp one night and handily disposed of a few hundred of the invaders men before we ever got there to lend a hand. Ye should count yerself fortunate to hae leaders such as him fighting for ye. He's a very resourceful lad, James is.

"Anyway, once my lads were camped in Dunmoore, the young captain and I led a very satisfying outing one night," he said, a pleased grin threatening to split open his face as he spoke. "Our ambush thoroughly routed a detachment of Gordons, and in the process we captured the Gordon's laird."

"Oh, what a stroke of luck!" interjected Sir Sean.

"Indeed. And it gets better yet," Fraser added, a foxy smile creasing his bluff face as he glanced from one man to the other. "I had a wee conversation with that laird, right on the spot, and persuaded young Conall Gordon to ally himself and his clan with our bonny confederation against the bleeding Campbells! Hah, very soon, I am sure that the lad wi' hae his Gordons wreaking havoc within Domeric's own borders!"

The powerful earl laughed heartily at the shock registering on the faces before him. "Ach, I would delight in seeing the old duke's face when he discovers that some of his *own* towns are under attack!"

Lord Mhoram's laughter was infectious and soon Gregor and the Warlord joined him in mirth at their adversary's expense. Surrounding faces regarded the leaders as they enjoyed a good laugh, and wondered at their merriment.

Not long afterward, Gregor welcomed his friend to join him at the castle and led him directly to his great hall where they could talk in private and dine together. Sir Sean went with them as he was the joint force's field commander and wished to glean further details about the enemy that he might require.

Ensconced in Glenorchy's great hall, Sir Sean looked up from his steaming plate of roasted lamb and potatoes and regarded the earl. The three gentlemen sat together at one of the hall's long oak trestle tables, and the big man shoveled hot food into his mouth like he had not eaten in days. Sean regretted having to interrupt the hungry earl's repast, but addressed himself to the man anyway. "My lord, it is a genuine delight to hear what ye hae told us of the Campbell's misfortune, but please tell me, how many of yer bonny warriors hae ye brought to reinforce Glenorchy?"

"My whole army, minus, of course, the score and nine lads fallen at Dunmoore," replied Mhoram, pausing in the act of stuffing a warm roll into his mouth. "I marched from Inverness with every lad answering the flaming cross."

"Well, we can certainly make full use of ye, come morning," said Gregor. "The duke threw everything he had at us today. I believe he wi' nae resort to cutting us off to besiege Glenorchy, but rather prefer to take us by force. I had expected a more cautious approach, but Domeric has proven me wrong and seems undeterred by the bloodshed we hae dealt his army. Thankfully, Sean was well prepared for the onslaught."

Sean rolled his shoulders and modestly said, "The duke sought to surprise us and drive home a furious attack while he believed us nae at full strength. He knows that we are nae undermanned now, especially with the timely arrival of Lord Mhoram and his dowdy clansmen. A wily commander wi' adjust his tactics accordingly. He wi' now be wondering what *our* next moves wi' be."

"Aye," Mhoram agreed, nodding his head.

"Those are my thoughts as well," Gregor concurred, and turned his eyes to his nephew. "We must hae the clan council gathered to consider all these things. I would hear what the others hae to say; perhaps between us a clear path can be found in dealing with our old enemy. Please see to it, Sean," the chief of the MacGregor clan ordered as he pushed away his empty plate and raised his tankard for a drink.

Not long after the three were joined in their host's study, which served these days as his war room, by the other allied lords and their respective field commanders that were already at Glenorchy. The other clans in attendance were the MacAlpine,

Clanranald, and MacLean. As yet, the mighty MacDonalds had not arrived.

A satisfactory plan of action was quickly resolved among them and Lord Gregor, as the residing host, adjourned the meeting soon afterward in order for his allies to find their beds and catch what sleep they could before battle resumed in the morning. Wasting no time, Gregor retired to his own bed and no sooner did his weary head came to rest upon the soft pillow but he fell into a deep sleep.

Dawn came too early for many of the fatigued warriors, of each opponent, as they were chivvied from their slumber by cursing sergeants that were long awake and dressed before their men. The sun was just rising above the horizon and already it was blazing like a giant fireball as it glared at the besiegers and besieged alike. Not a single cloud was aloft in the azure sky, as below, the arrayed army of Duke Domeric Campbell scrambled across the already trampled pasture fields lying outside the protective ring of Glenorky's walls. Waiting for them was an army of defenders already drawn up in battle formation in the shadow of those lofty battlements.

Resilient clansmen of the Campbells and their allies charged enthusiastically through the mud to meet the defenders, waving keen edged swords with bared teeth, as behind those men, bagpipers encouraged them on. Bagpipes screamed defiance before them as well, as MacGregor pipers played valiantly to counter the martial music of the other side. The initial charge faltered briefly as the attackers were assaulted by a deadly swarm of arrows loosed from men atop the stout wall. Scores of soldiers fell under the steady buzz of arrows, but many more flooded around and over the dead and wounded to close with those arrayed before them.

The morning wore slowly on as the opposing armies squared off against one another and the blood of their soldiers mingling on a battlefield that was quickly ground to a quagmire of reddish mud. It was not until about mid-morning that either side began to show any sign of an advantage. Capitalizing on a momentary gain in momentum along his right flank, Duke

Domeric rushed a company of his crack household troops into that area to concentrate on the weakening Clanranald men. The influx of fresh veteran troops began to have the affect the duke desired almost immediately. The Campbell Household Guards surged forward in a relentless tide, taking a heavy toll against the beleaguered Clanranald infantry. Slowly, but with a steady push, the veterans commenced to rolling up the overwhelmed flank with lethal efficiency.

Warned of the sudden danger to the beleaguered Clanranald troops and the very imminent collapse of that flank, Earl Alister, chief of Clan MacAlpine, acted with his usual brand of alacrity. Taking command of the situation, along with the initiative, he led forth his squadron of heavy cavalry to come to the relief of his embattled ally. Without any regard to the danger he placed himself in, Lord Alister personally led his knights on the counterattack as they swept in to confront the enemy. The heavy horse charged the Campbell pikemen with the MacAlpine chief at the head of the wedge; shouting their warcry the horsemen hurled a volley of barbed javelins into the packed mass of pikemen before slamming into the enemy ranks with devastating effect. The surprised foe found themselves all but helpless as the regalvanized infantry fought back with renewed vigor and determination, in the face of the sudden attack.

Falling like wheat before a well swung scythe, their own long pikes rendered ineffective at such close quarters, the veteran Household Guard was routed and those that were able to, hastily withdrew before the onslaught. For many, however, there was no retreat as they were efficiently cut down by the mass of MacAlpine cavalry. Those that were able to escape the pressing melee were harried by clusters of pursuing cavalry until a tardy troop of Kennedy horsemen charged from the rear and came to rescue the fleeing Campbells. Hot as his blood was with battle fever, Lord Alister was still able to keep his head, and wisely called off his trooper's pursuit. In good order, the Earl of Atholl led his force triumphantly back to the security of their previous position.

Hidden within the dense confines of the ancient forest that stretched thickly along the southwest of the lush glen, Sir Duncan

MacSean watched with keen interest as the battle progressed. He nodded his blonde head with approval and a slight smile curved his lips as he observed the professional manner in which Lord Alister had dealt with rallying the weakened flank. Quietly he turned from his observations and trotted deeper into the fragrant forest that he regarded as home.

Every woodland had its secrets but even the thickest and most foreboding forest contained trails that may be followed if one knows what to look for. Duncan was far from being a stranger to these woods, having spent many hours and days under the great forest's canopy, and prided himself in the intimate knowledge he possessed. It was the untamed wildness that attracted him the most as several species of fauna made this place their home. He never hunted or trapped here, unwilling to sully the tranquility that he had always found in its depths. His lightly armed cavalry that had followed him here was not so deep into the forest as he usually frequented, but they were secreted far enough within the ancient coniferous tract for his current purpose.

Following an old deer trail, Duncan moved out silently on buckskin boots until he suddenly stepped into a small clearing that was presently occupied by one hundred and three score of his well-trained, mounted archers. They were alert and awaiting his return, but still they were startled by his sudden appearance. A grim smile curved his lips, but did not quite reach his ice blue eyes as he accepted hasty salutes from his officers.

"It's our turn now, gentlemen. Order yer lads to mount up and follow me," he quietly commanded. As the Warlord's younger brother as had already held a position of some authority, but now he had been honoured by Lord Gregor with the rank of general, and this was his first independent command.

He waited patiently as his troopers mounted up and as they formed up loosely, Duncan accepted the reins of his sleek, blood-bay stallion from a waiting warrior and swung himself up into the saddle. "Follow me, lads. Do nae talk or stray from the path that I blaze. Stealth is our most valuable ally," he conveyed, guiding his mount to the forefront of his warband. "Without surprise we'll nae hae much chance of living through the day.

Remember also that nay quarter is to be given, and expect none from a Campbell as they are come here to destroy us all."

Trotting his horse to the edge of the clearing, General Sir Duncan MacSean edged forward into the surrounding pines and followed the track back the way he had recently come. In his wake quietly trailed the men of his command. Each of those clansmen was armed with a short recurve bow, a generous supply of arrows that was held at the ready in a quiver slung across each back, and secured within each saddle-holster waited one of the great Scottish, two-handed claymore swords.

The path wound through the tall trees and as Duncan led the way he loosened his shoulders trying to dispel the tension that grew within him. At last, he saw before him the thinning boundary of the forest and ushered the following troopers into position without leaving the protective screen of young trees and brush.

"Stay in tight formation and follow me," he whispered fiercely. Brandishing his bow with an arrow already nocked to the string, Duncan broke cover and with his mounted archers in a wedge behind him, charged across the field. Before them stretched the massed Campbell army with its rearmost right flank anchored nearest them by a troop of dismounted heavy cavalry. Unerringly, they closed on the unaware enemy until they were within a hundred yards, and the range of their short bows. Slowing, but not halting, the MacGregor horsemen veered sharply to the left in a flanking maneuver that permitted the force to loose a concentrated volley. The flight of arrows flew accurately towards the enemy reserve cavalry and yielded excellent results as they found their marks in the bodies of both horses and riders.

Duncan's satisfaction was short lived as he stretched his horse back to a gallop to continue the maneuver in a large circle. In his wake, the general heard the blowing of horns as the enemy signaled a desperate alarm and knew immediately that the element of surprise was gone. His time was limited before other troops of enemy cavalry arrived to relieve their fellows; if he was to deliver more of a telling blow, his initial tactic would have to be modified to the situation.

Silently cursing his ill luck, Duncan bellowed his new orders and hoped that he was not endangering his men with unnecessary bravado. Completing the wide circle for another concentrated volley the mounted archers loosed a second fusillade at the enemy's mobilizing heavy cavalry. For a second the young general watched the withering rain of arrows descend into the ranks of knights and their horses. The effect was much as the first had been, and although that once fearsome force was badly mauled they somehow maintained a remarkable cohesion as they set themselves in pursuit of their fleet footed opponents. Leading his horsemen away from the pursuit of the Campbell's heavy cavalry, Duncan set an easy pace and drew his men behind him, riding at a smooth canter parallel to the long enemy ranks of infantry. Nocking and loosing arrow after arrow into the tight packed foot soldiers the MacGregor troopers began to take a heavy toll.

He had delivered what damage that had been within his ability, but Duncan was not yet satisfied. He wanted to make a difference in the battle, not merely be a nuisance to his clan's enemies. The newly commissioned general quickly came to a decision. "Lads! Prepare to charge!" he shouted the command.

Just as General MacSean was ordering his men to put away their bows in favor of the massive two-handed claymores, the ranking officer commanding the enemy rear was valiantly shouting his own commands to the rear ranks to have them reverse the face of their formation. Barking his orders furiously, the officer demanded obedience of those soldiers as he knew the tall shields could deflect many of the deadly missiles. So loud were those commands, that Duncan's mounted troops could hear most of what he was bellowing to the foot soldiers.

Standing tall in his stirrups, Duncan roared, "Keep yer formation tight, lads! At the gallop . . . charge!"

Charge they did. With the ancient MacGregor warcry issuing from each of their mouths they bore down on the infantry. "Ard Choille!" *The Woody Heights!*

Lacking any throwing javelins or the longer, heavier pikes, the troopers under Duncan's command had drawn and now brandished before them the heavy two-handed claymore, the favored weapon of many highlanders. The long fleet strides of their sleek mounts carried the one hundred, sixty men crashing into the shield wall that had been hastily thrown up by the inexperienced foot soldiers. The thick, door-like shields were the only thing that saved the Stevenson clan from being crushed and routed, but even still, the charge cut a deep swathe into their ranks. One of the first men cut down was the singular officer that had tried to prepare his inexperienced clansmen.

The first four ranks of the overmatched Stevensons were, quickly and with great efficiency, slaughtered by the mounted warriors. Sir Duncan and his men wielded their monstrous five foot long swords like deadly, giant sickles and skillfully laid waste to any within range of those long blades. Each of those swords held a keen edge, and was as sharp as a well-honed razor that, when swung by a determined warrior, could easily slice through flesh and bone, and even armor, with equal effortlessness. Henceforth, as those warriors, in Sir Duncan's command, pressed their attack from the advantage of horseback with such vicious weapons, the hapless enemy on the muddy ground, were methodically butchered or broken beneath the kicking and stamping destrier's steel-shod hooves.

Aware of his brother's planned attack, Warlord MacSean seized the moment and pressed for what ever advantage he could from the opportunity. Committing nearly half of his ready reserves, Sir Sean aggressively assailed the Campbell army and pressed his assault to pinch the enemy forces between himself and Duncan's cavalry. Personally leading the reserve brigade, Sir Sean exploited the weakness of the enemy's flank where his brother's attack had bloodied and drawn away the Campbell cavalry. Lacking the protective screen of heavy horse, the general's warriors swung around the exposed flank and for a brief time opened a second front against the Campbell infantry.

It appeared that the flank would be overcome and except for the prompt action of a mounted officer, the gambit would have succeeded. That Campbell officer kept a cool head about him and wisely ordered up a sufficient number of his own reserves to come to the relief of their fellows. They had bent but not broken.

The Warlord ordered the withdrawal sounded and skillfully disengaged his forces from the embattled enemy flank and returned to his previous position. The enemy reserve force, in the mean time, arrived too late to do more than postulate before their officer ordered them to turn back.

Unaware of what was taking place elsewhere on the battlefield, Sir Duncan and his cavalry littered the ground with the bodies of Clan Stevenson. His mounted warriors were superior to the previously untried men he fought, but the press of numbers had at last blunted his attack and the momentum was beginning to shift. Sensing this shift, the general finished off one last opponent and turned the nose of his brave mount.

Standing tall in the stirrups, Duncan yelled at the top of his lungs, "Retreat! MacGregors! Retreat and follow me!" Spurring his horse away from the bloody swathe of ground, liberally covered by dead and dying men, the general drew back and brought his horsemen with him. It was not so much a retreat but a strategic withdrawal and he led his exhausted troopers away from the enemy ranks. What followed was a surprisingly easy fighting withdrawal as the Stevensons, for the most part, allowed their adversary to depart with hardly an effort made to stop them.

To Duncan's relief, the threat of heavy cavalry had never materialized, having already been otherwise engaged. Speedily he surveyed the field and decided to lead his force back in the way they had come and seek to join with friendly forces where the reserves were being marshaled, near the city wall.

Kicking spurred boots to his horse's flanks, the cavalry general led his remaining troopers along the enemy rear and toward their bloodied right flank. His men, requiring no order, loosed into the enemy ranks whatever arrows that remained in their quivers as they streamed swiftly behind their gallant leader. Their flight to the relative safety of the rear was mostly uncontested as they easily bolted around the slower and depleted enemy heavy cavalry, leaving them behind to shake their fists with impotent fury.

For the weary soldiers of both armies, the second day of fighting seemed to last for an eternity. It was a terrible day of blood, sweat and tears, and most of all, death. The preceding day had been merely a taste of what was to follow; and whereas it had been one that had ended a virtual draw, this one did not. The bloodied armies fought stoutly on into the afternoon and into the evening, but the tide of battle had now swung in the favor of Clan Gregor and her allies. A dominating reason for that swing was due, in large part, to the daring raid of those courageous mounted archers following the intrepid leadership of General Sir Duncan MacSean.

The red, glaring sun was just beginning its slow but inexorable drop toward the mountainous western horizon when Duncan at last gave the order to dismount. A ragged cheer went up from them and the weary clansmen gratefully complied, sliding from the sweat-stained and blood encrusted saddles of their equally fatigued battle steeds. Waiting groomsmen stepped forward to take care of those lathered horses and led them away to be watered and fed. Offering a grateful smile, Duncan handed over the reins of his proud mount to an eager page, and after inquiring to the location of his brother, headed off in that direction to offer his after action report.

Soon afterward, the rocky highlands surrounding Ben Novis that bordered the long glen swallowed up the last of the sun's amber rays, casting long, gloomy shadows across the much trampled and bloody battlefield. Once again the army of each opponent was forced to retire until the coming again of dawn's early light.

The coming of evening and the cession of battle found Lord Gregor and the other members of the confederated war council gathered together in his well appointed study. Over a light meal of cold, roasted quail and rabbit, along with crusty bread and cheese, they discussed events that had taken place throughout the long day. Lord Mhoram was just in the act of praising the actions of Duncan MacSean and his cavalry when the earl was unceremoniously interrupted as an excited page burst into the chamber.

"My Lord! I hae glad tidings!" the towheaded young messenger exclaimed in a high voice and sketched a hasty bow to

Lord Gregor. Forgetting to wait for permission, before speaking further, he blurted, "Lord MacDonald has just now arrived in Glenorchy with an escort of his clansmen. The rest of his army is coming tae. They hae landed with his fleet and even now are marching to join us."

Coming to his feet as the boy spoke, Lord Gregor motioned to the door with an indulgent smile tugging at his lips. "Perhaps ye should go and bring the gentleman here to join us, laddie. I would nae hae my friend miss supper."

"At once, My Lord," saluted the page before slipping beyond the heavy door.

A wide welcoming smile brightened Gregor's normally sober mien as the island lord ambled into the room, ducking under the doorway for his head to clear the opening. He beamed amiably as Gregor came to greet him and quipped, "I see I've arrived just in time." His gaze scanned over the food laid out on a large desk before centering on the face of his friend.

"Donald! Well come, old friend. I am glad to see ye," warmly greeted the Master of Glenorchy, embracing the man heartily. "Come and sup with us; ye *hae* arrived just in time to share our repast."

The huge, looming form of the Chief of the MacDonalds, slapped Lord Gregor cheerfully on the back. "Gladly," he said, accepting the invitation. "I wi' nae deny that I'm famished. It truly is good to see ye again after sae long, but it's a pity that I should hae to come under such ill circumstances." He grasped Gregor by the shoulders and held him out at arms length. "Ye look good, Gregor, and ye do nae seem to hae changed at all since last I laid eyes on ye. When we hae a moment to ourselves, ye must tell me how that bonny godson of mine is doing."

"I wi'," agreed his host. "Later tonight I wi' bring ye to see him, but for now come and join us. We were just discussing the events of the day."

"Ach, I'll wager old Campbell wi' surely be surprised when he first lays eyes on my banner. What do ye think? I'd love to see his ugly face," MacDonald said, laughing jovially and slapping his friend stoutly on one broad shoulder. Ach, Gregor, I must tell ye a thing before I forget: ye *really* should do something about all the short doorways around here. Some day I'm gonna forget to duck my poor head and knock it a good one!"

Gregor chuckled. "My poor doorway, ye mean! Come on, ye tall bear and eat with us; ye *must* be famished after yer long journey."

Donald MacDonald, the powerful Lord of the Isles, was a towering mountain of a man in height and mass. Standing close to seven feet tall, his huge frame all but dwarfed Gregor, who was no small man in his own right, being a few inches over six feet and being a healthy and robust figure at about eighteen stone. The MacDonald chief boasted a powerful bulk and outweighed his friend by an impressive one hundred pounds, a fact that forced him to ride as a mount only the largest and strongest of the mighty Clydesdale breed of Scottish horse.

Approaching the outsized desk, Donald nodded to each of the other men as one by one they rose to offer their own greetings. "I find myself in good company," he said to the room in general, settling onto an empty, cushioned chair which chose that moment to creak threateningly under the burden.

Once they were all seated and eating the tasty dinner, conversation resumed along with the sounds of their hardy consumption of the food.

"I hae an idea for the deployment of yer troops, Donald, and I would hear yer thoughts about it," said Gregor, around a mouthful of tender rabbit. Twirling a wine glass filled with a ruby colored vintage between long, calloused fingers, he raised his blue eyes to glance over at MacDonald. "In today's battle, following our Warlord's plan, we used a light force of hidden cavalry to surprise the Campbell rear. I propose that we do it again, but just a little differently. Earlier, Sir Sean's brother, Duncan MacSean commanded an attack aimed at the enemy's rear with some success in bloodying the Stevenson clan. What if we could divide yer clansmen into two separate forces, before the old duke realizes ye are here, and position them within the surrounding forest along *both flanks* of his army. In concert, the ambush could be sprung with both forces attacking simultaneously. The duke wi' likely be expecting some kind of trickery from us after today, but I doubt he and his officers could be prepared for such trickery on so large a magnitude," Gregor paused briefly, after outlining his idea and fix his eyes on Donald. "What think ye?"

Lord Donald shrugged his massive shoulders. "It's a bold plan and potentially a very risky one as well. What does our Warlord hae to say? Does this strategy hae merit in regards to the wily old duke?"

From where Sir Sean lounged, at ease in a comfortable chair, the canny battlefield commander permitted a slow, foxy grin to spread across his ruddy face. His cool, azure eyes twinkled in merriment as he looked across the remains of their dinner table at the two inquiring leaders.

"Oh, nay. I well ken that look, Donald," Gregor said, groaning audibly. "My dear nephew has something nasty in mind. Well, Sean, what is it?"

"Ach, nothing tae nasty I think, Uncle."

The MacDonald chief chuckled deep in his throat. "Ach, I *like* nasty," he grinned, baring sharp, white, predatory teeth like a great shaggy bear. "This should be good. Tell me what ye are thinking, Warlord."

Lord Donald's grin only widened as he liked what he heard. No sooner had the new plan of action been voiced but everyone present agreed to it. The new proposal was a rather practical compromise with a calculated difference.

*   *   *

"My Lord, with the Frasers of the Earl of Inverness standing with the MacGregors we nay longer hold any advantage of numbers, and without those numbers we hae little chance of defeating them. Even were we to win the field, they would hae only to retire within those stout walls and let us die trying to batter our way inside. I believe, sair, it would be only prudent to withdraw for the time being and summon more support before launching another fruitless assault," General Wilfred Campbell advised his duke.

Duke Domeric snorted angrily. "That's what ye would tell me? Nay! We wi' nae crawl away with our tail tucked between our legs, Cousin. I would look like a weakling and a fool in the eyes of our misbegotten enemy, nae to mention our own allies. Nay, that is nae going to happen," cried the outraged duke.

"But, Domeric, this is *their* land and they ken it like we never can," argued the general. "Thus far, they hae only begun to use that intimate knowledge to their benefit, but they wi'. I ken that I certainly would! I like nae this thick forest stretched all about us; it has already brought the Stevensons grief-"

"Nay! Yer insufferable whining wi' nae change my mind, kinsman," retorted the angry duke. "We did well enough these two days in spite of the little surprise raid aimed against our rear. Within days, the MacClellans and Carlyles wi' arrive to join forces with us. What we *do* need to do is give our clansmen a rest.

"At dawn tomorrow, I wi' ride forward with an escort and parley with our bloody enemy for a temporary truce," the duke informed him. "If that's nae to their liking, then perhaps a symbolic single combat between a champion from each side, with the victor winning the day for his army would be. It might even prove amusing," he went on with a cunning grin creeping onto his face. "I wi' leave it to ye to select a proper champion for us, General. Tae bad MacGregor could nae be talked into fighting it personally. Seeing him fall with Campbell steel in his guts would go far toward making up for our loss at Dunmoore and the stealing away of my Gordons. Ah, well. Even Gregor is nae so foolish as to do that," he mused, shrugging forlornly. "Very well, Wilfred, be off with ye. Ye hae yer orders; see that ye take care to chose well."

"As ye wish, Yer Grace."

The duke missed the grimace of disdain that flashed across the officer's face as he walked away. *He's an old fool,* thought the general as he returned to his pavilion, *he should worry more for the well-being of his soldiers and clansmen, and less about his blasted pride! Ach, may the claws of the Raven take him and good riddance. He wi' wish he had taken my advice before this is all over.*

On his way to his striped tent soldiers avoided the general when they noticed the angry scowl darkening his brow. Reaching the field headquarters housed within his tent, Wilfred called for an orderly to come inside.

"General?" the young orderly asked meekly.

"Aye, Adam. I want ye to find Sir Roger Scott, lad, and hae him report personally to me, here, within the hour," he instructed curtly. "If he asks, and he wi', tell him that the duke has a task well suited to his talents."

"I wi' see to it at once, sair."

"Very good; see that ye do. Ye are dismissed," said the gaunt general, throwing up his right hand in a weary, mechanical salute.

Reclining onto his portable cot, Wilfred tried to relax and groaned with relief as he took the weight from his booted feet. Reaching out to a strategically placed camp stool located nearby, the general retrieved a squat, gallon-sized, earthenware jug. With an ease coming from much practice, he sat up and unstoppered the jug, then slinging the sloshing and already half-empty decanter into the crook of his cord-muscled arm, brought it up to his chapped lips. The smoky, amber colored liquid trickled into his waiting mouth and he swallowed it. Quickly lowering the jug and its potent contents, his brown eyes bulging as he gave an involuntary gasp. The single malt whisky, being what it was, burned a slow path of fire down his throat into his empty stomach, where it sat hotly.

"Phew," the man exclaimed, shaking his graying head. "There's nothing like good scotch to warm up yer insides," he remarked for his own benefit. "I'm glad those lads of the MacNeish's held out. Nay one distills better single malt than they-"

A sudden raw scream from somewhere outside in the camp broke the Campbell general's train of thought, and nearly dropping his jug of spirits as he bolted upright. Sitting down the jug, he moved to the tent entrance and pulled the flap back to peer outside just in time to watch as Sir Roger Scott fell in a heap, joining his young orderly, lying unmoving on the ground. Both men lay face down in a growing pool of their mingled blood. Grimly, the general noted with alarm, the telltale arrow shafts that protruded prominently from the neck of each fallen comrade.

Recovering from his momentary shock, General Campbell cupped his shaking hands together before his mouth and shouted loudly, "Campbells rally to me! The enemy is upon us! To arms, to arms!

"Lieutenant, call out the crossbowmen, at once!" Wilfred shouted his earnest command, when he saw a mounted officer trotting into view. The general drew his sword and waved it wildly over his head to catch the man's attention. At last his shouting and waving caught the mounted man's notice and with a harried salute, cantered off to do his superior's bidding.

General Campbell's attempt to rally the camp's reactionary force proved to be in vain, as the persistent raiders struck time after time, and like phantoms, would disappear before any resistance could be brought to bear against them. Standing by, helplessly, all the Campbell general could do was watch furiously as several fleet-footed wraiths faded rapidly into the night, scampering toward the mist shrouded forest.

Once the last of the enemy warriors had vanished from sight, the only sign that the raiders had ever been within the confines of the army's camp was the many corpses of recently slain soldiers. Dead bodies sprawled on the trampled ground wherever the chagrined general looked, each of his soldiers with one or more arrows sprouting from their lifeless body.

It was a long time before morning dawned on the bloody battlefield.

Even though Wilfred knew that another attack in the night was unlikely, the old general nevertheless doubled the parameter sentries for the remainder of the hours of darkness. Only after he had taken care of that duty personally did Wilfred return to his tent to find what sleep he could salvage. *I'm tae old for this shite*, he grumbled under his breath, pulling woolen covers up to his chin. Although he was weary and knew his body required rest before another grueling day, sleep eluded him for a long time.

When the new day dawned, it brought with it a deep and unsettling sense of foreboding for the Campbell general. Wilfred sat easily astride his familiar mount and watched attentively as his junior officers moved their individual platoons and companies into battle formation. At last, when all was at readiness, he nudged his horse into a trot up to his lord's side.

"Yer Grace, the army stands ready for yer command," the tight-lipped general reported gruffly, dark rings showing starkly under his eyes, as he sketched a salute.

"Good. Hae the commanders advance smartly with their men," ordered the duke. "Ye wi' personally lead a squadron of my heavy cavalry. With yer squadron, Cousin, ye wi' patrol our rear to prevent a similar folly from happening like befell us yesterday," he commanded with disdain, a clear note of contempt creeping into his voice as he eyed his stiff-backed field commander.

Checking his anger, Wilfred nodded, "Aye, Yer Grace."

Disappointment battled with anger as the general put spurs to his horse and rode away from his liege lord and kinsmen to carry out the man's orders. A familiar sign of irritation warned his subordinate officers of his ill humor as he approached, the twitching of muscles prominent in his jaw, along with his black scowl, proved enough to quiet even the most outspoken of those officers. Wilfred relayed the duke's orders in a clipped tone that brooked no discussion. Once he moved off to join with and take command of the Campbell's knightly force, the gathered officers glanced around at one another with raised eyebrows before moving to join up with their respective units.

Duke Domeric Campbell watched the general's brief interaction with the lower ranking commanders, a frown beetling his brow with concern. *Other than the short lived raid the bloody MacGregors conducted against me last night, nothing unusual has come about that I can perceive,* he mused, continuing to follow the general with his eyes, *but something feels amiss. Keeping those heavy cavalry in a patrolling reserve makes me feel somewhat better, but I hope I made the correct decision in continuing the fighting, rather than the parley I was going to attempt. But, how could I parley for a truce after the raid they conducted last night, without losing face? In everyone's eyes, I would appear as a wee lass afraid of specters in the night. Still, perhaps I was tae harsh with Wilfred; I'll hae make it up to his pride somehow.*

The morning wore slowly on, and to Duke Domeric's surprise, the ever fickle tide of battle seemed it be in his army's favor. Under the direct leadership of Duke Fergis, the Chief of Clan Hamilton, of whom the Campbell lord had replaced his cousin, the army appeared to be succeeding in buckling the left side of the enemy line. The MacLeans that battled against Hamilton's surge seemed to remain in dire straights, in spite of the reinforcements that had come on two occasions to assist them.

By the middle of the grinding afternoon, Duke Fergis had still failed to roll the flank anchored by the bloodied MacLeans. Changing his tactics, the lowland lord had, with substantial losses to both sides, pressed what advantage his stubborn troops had won and slowly was driving a wedge into his opponent's formation. The MacLeans fought on with vigor, but the tactic was succeeding in starting to divide the defender's lines; if his warriors were able to do so, Domeric hoped fervently, the whole enemy left would be splintered away from the rest of their army.

Duke Fergis was growing more confident as the day wore on, knowing that if he could just force his wedge just a little further into the confederacy's skirmish lines, that the day would be his. The splinter, he would have caused, would be cut off and without support from the main force and easily routed or could even possibly be completely and utterly slaughtered if fortune smiled favorably. *With such a fine show of my command abilities,* Fergis contemplated arrogantly, *that flinty ole Campbell wi' be forced to recognize my talents as a superior general to his over-cautious cousin and grant* me *the field command for the duration of this stupid war.*

The Duke of Hamilton did not realize that his luck was about to run out.

General Wilfred Campbell could hardly believe his eyes as he beheld a force of cavalry emerge from the forest, in just the same location as on the previous occasion, to charge towards his duke's army. From where he sat his horse, the general watched them charge forward with readied weapons. *They're actually going to attempt the same tactic as they did yesterday,* he mused in surprised disbelief. *Well, the MacGregors are in for a nasty shock if they think we'll be duped like that again!*

Lifting a signal horn to his lips, General Campbell blew a long note that carried across the battlefield. The strident sound alerted the officers of the army's rear echelon, of the impending danger, just as the enemy lowered their lances for the charge.

Drawing his sword, Wilfred stood in his stirrups to address himself to the nearest of the infantry officers. "Ready yer lads to accept a charge by lance!" he bellowed, his voice a whipcord of authority. "Let's show these vermin what we're made of, and avenge our fallen brethren that fell before them in yesterday's battle!"Turning to his cavalry officers he waved his sword above his head and kicked spurred heels into his mount's flanks. Leading his squadron of knights forward the general set a course to intercept the oncoming enemy horsemen. "Charge!" he screamed.

The infantry officers shouted their urgent commands as the Campbell heavy horse thundered off; with alacrity the ground troops pivoted to face the threat. They watched hopefully as the old general led his knights to meet the charging horsemen.

Riding at the head of his men, Wilfred gasped in dismay as he heard the enemy's warcry ring out from many throats: '*A Donald! For Lord Donald!*' Simultaneously, he could distinguish the billowing plaids of the MacDonald clan. Foreboding, like an icy hand clenching his heart, seized the general seconds before the two opposing sides clashed thunderously together. Steel tipped lances struck in unison against raised shields, armor and yielding flesh alike. Many a lance splintered in brutal impact a mere heartbeat before men and horses alike collided with bone crushing force. Scores of men fell under the terrible onslaught, along with their brave mounts, but the enemy was well met.

Seeing an opportunity to assist their comrades, infantry officers shouted out fresh commands to their men and charged to the aid of the battling cavalrymen. Reinforcing their knightly comrades, the disciplined foot soldiers swiftly stabilized their new lines to the harsh voiced commands of veteran non-coms. The stunned cavalry soon rallied and began to reassert themselves with new vigor.

The unexpected MacDonald horsemen had immediately discarded lances that had been rendered useless. As each warrior drew their long, heavy claymore to continue the attack and to hack down the opposing knights at close quarters, the infantry swarmed in to steal away their momentum. Seeing an opportunity, General Campbell withdrew his mounted troopers from the melee and regrouped for another charge, this time into the exposed side of the MacDonalds, while they were still bogged down by the infantry. With lances couched and ready, Wilfred raised his sword above his head and swept it around it prelude to commanding the charge, but suddenly disaster struck.

Wilfred heard what was happening before he saw it. Whirling about in the saddle to peer across the writhing body of the battling armies, the stunned general gasped in disbelief as a second mounted force attacked from the other end of the battlefield. The new threat stormed toward the other flank with hundreds of warriors shrieking as if with one voice. Half of those attackers plunged into the left side of the Campbell army, while the remainder swarmed around the army's rear and bore down on the cavalry commander and his knights like avenging angels ready to deal death and slaughter.

Screaming frantic commands in a voice near panic, Wilfred turned the face of his cavalry ranks to confront the latest threat, seeing in it his own looming death. His only chance to save the army from imminent doom sent a chill down his back as he realized he must sacrifice himself and his remaining cavalry.

He aimed his heavy mount at the converging foe and thundered toward them with a wordless scream. Wilfred did not remember commanding the charge, but his men were stretched out to either side of him urging their warhorses to a gallop. The explosion of noise was incredible as the two sides came together in a bloody tangle of men and horses. Almost immediately, upwards of half the Campbell force was struck down under the swarming charge of enemy horsemen. As those cavalrymen filtered through the bloody swathe they had cut through the midst of his command, General Campbell shouted for the remnants of his squadron to rally about him. Grimly, he prepared to stand and to fight the foe, face to face and to the death, with honour and pride.

We gave them a good fight, at least, thought the beaten general, *and they'll ken that they fought a noble opponent.*

He had no more time for though as the opposing horsemen bore down on him once again, melee erupting all around him. By ones and twos the general's cavalrymen fell before the superior number thrown against them, until Wilfred realized, to his horror that he alone remained of his entire force. Wondering why he had not been cut down as well, he watched with a strange calmness as what appeared to be his counterpart walked his handsome mount toward, stopping just a few paces away.

"Yer knights were worthy adversaries, Campbell," the man confided. "For the sake of honour, I offer ye yer life in return for the gift of yer name."

Wilfred grimaced and pulled the helmet from his head; lowering the unadorned headpiece to his waist he wiped the sweat from his brow. Returning his attention to the man that had addressed him, he said, "For my honour's sake, I must refuse yer kindly offer. However, I wi' nevertheless give ye my name, that ye may remember at least this one old Campbell lord with a certain amount of respect, instead of the contempt that my cousin, the Duke of Argyll, has earned," the general replied, a sad dignity shading his tone with solemnity. "I am Baron Wilfred Campbell.

"Might I hae the pleasure of yer name in return, MacGregor?" he asked curiously. "Who is the general that has the honour of commanding a host of MacDonald men, but is nae of their clan?"

"I am Duncan MacSean, lord baron."

Wilfred arched an eyebrow, his sole show of surprise. "MacSean. Ye do nae look much like Sidhe to me," he said, slowly drawing the name out. "Is Sir Sean kin of yers?"

"Aye, he's my brother," Duncan confirmed, wondering at the muttering.

"So. Nobility and skillful leadership runs strongly in yer family," Wilfred said, the compliment sounding strange coming from his lips. "When next ye see Sir Sean, please convey to him my compliments."

Duncan nodded his head. "Of course."

Slowly dismounting, Wilfred stepped away from his horse and deliberately raised his helmet to seat it once again on his head. "Well met, Sir Duncan. I hae but one final request of ye: wi' ye grant my plea of single combat?"

"Aye," he agreed. "The usual forms wi', of course, be observed. And if ye desire it, I shall personally meet ye in the circle."

Wilfred smiled gravely. "Thank ye for yer understanding, Sir Duncan, and I do accept yer noble offer. This is the only course my honour wi' allow, I fear, otherwise I believe that ye and I could hae been friends."

Duncan dismounted smoothly and passed his reins off to a sergeant waiting along side him. Drawing his sword, he saluted his vanquished counterpart by raising the basket hilt to his face with the double-edged blade shining upward in the sun. Patiently, the MacGregor officer waited for his opponent to draw his own sword.

The duel proved to be a short fight, but a fierce one as the two warriors circled one another. Each swing and thrust, parry and riposte wove a deadly net of singing steel between the combatants. In their graceful dance of death, each sword was wielded like an extension of its master's arm, both fluid and lethal.

When it was all over, Wilfred lay in a growing pool of blood at the victor's feet. As the fallen general struggled for breath, he spoke but the words came out as a whisper that Duncan could not hear.

Kneeling down on the green pasture beside the man he had just killed, who under different circumstances could have been his friend, Duncan bent his head close to the man's mouth to better perceive what the Campbell was trying to tell him.

"Ye fight well, my friend," Wilfred managed his say, coughing up bright blood that bubbled from his lips. "Honour me in yer memories."

"The bards wi' ken of yer noble end, friend," Duncan promised, squeezing the man's hand. Carefully, the victor returned the man's forgotten sword to him and helped wrap his fingers around the hilt. "Farewell in the life following this one, and may God in heaven gather up yer soul on swift wings."

"Aye, swift wings," Wilfred agreed weakly. Drawing in another ragged breath the general's stricken body shuddered feebly, then with a final sigh the breath left his lungs rattling faintly as he died.

A hand came down and gripped Duncan's shoulder lightly. "Come away, sair, we should rejoin the fighting. If the Morrigan smiles upon us, so that we can corner the wily old duke, then ye can inform him of his cousin's honour before we cut him down for his lack of it," Duncan's lieutenant whispered harshly.

"Aye. A bonny suggestion," Duncan murmured, allowing Redwood to pull him to his feet. "See to it that the baron's body is wrapped and hae it brought with us. I would see our noble opponent given an honourable burial; do ye understand, lieutenant?"

"Aye, sair. I feel the same way."

The resounding defeat of the Campbell army's rear had spread fear like wildfire throughout the invading army, even as Duke Fergis Hamilton was preparing to fully commit his main force to capitalize on the vulnerable breach that he and his men had fought to wedge open since early in the afternoon.

Bloody hell! Fergis raged in impotent fury. *I was sae close! And now, it has been all for nothing. What more can I do if bloody Domeric Campbell wi' nae follow my advice? One more push and I'm sure we could hae split their army in two, but nay, he leeches away my men to protect his own arse!*

As their momentum grounded to a halt on the front lines, the Campbell's allied forces were slowly pushed backward. Soon they had been forced to yield all the ground they had fought hard to win, and the hard-pressed MacLeans were quickly relieved by fresh reserves, much to those clansmen's weary and bitter joy. At the same time, the hardy center of the MacGregor led army surged forward with renewed vigor under the Warlord's personal command banner of crimson and dark green. Fluttering in the air, it advanced side by side with that of Lord Gregor, which sported a crimson field bordered in black, with the ancient coat-of-arms of Clan Gregor in the center.

That Warlord MacSean had chosen to fight in the center, where the battle was most ferocious, was no mistake. He knew all was well under control elsewhere about the battlefield, and as a living symbol among the soldiery he gave heart to them as they saw him fighting alongside them. Sir Sean also knew that if he could break the Campbells in the center, his army would carry the day.

Guiding his snorting battle trained mount expertly with his knees, Sir Sean swung an imposing two-handed claymore with effortless skill. Aiming killing slashes down to lay low any enemy soldier who foolishly attempted to cut him out of the saddle, MacSean plodded forward, forcing the troops of Clan Kennedy to give ground.

An interminable amount of time passed as the battle waged hotly all about the Warlord, when suddenly the enemy was running away. The Campbell front appeared to just disintegrate as their forces broke ranks and sought to flee. Their flight was hampered only by the press of bodies from behind, as the rear elements of their army remained locked in mortal combat with the MacDonald cavalry led by Sir Duncan and the daunting Lord Donald MacDonald. For the time being, Sir Sean found himself virtually alone in an empty pocket of trampled battlefield; alone save for the fallen warriors of both sides. He had become separated from his own troops, having advanced beyond any of them, as he had locked in close and vicious combat. Now, several yards behind the Warlord, the tired infantrymen caught their breath and waited anxiously for his order: whether to pursue the enemy immediately or to close ranks first, before giving chase.

Some time later, once he had managed to extricate his army from the opposing forces and had retreated from the fields about Glenorchy, until he sat now, astride his well-groomed mount. Duke Domeric Campbell continued to nervously glance back in the direction from where his army had fled, scanning for any sign of pursuing forces. Seeing none again, however, did not ease his agitation, and the duke's emotional disposition was communicated directly, through the saddle, to his horse. Sensing its master's unease, the well-bred animal became nervous, and skittishly pranced sideways and bobbed its sleek head in agitation.

"Stop yer dancing, blast ye!" growled the foul tempered duke. Sawing savagely on the reins to control the beast's skittish sidestepping, he succeeded only in making it worse as the bit tore into his mount's tender mouth. Uttering an unholy oath, Domeric vaulted with deceptive agility from the saddle and threw the reins at his aide. "Here. Take this bloody, temperamental beast and calm him down, wi' ye?"

Not waiting for a response, the irritated duke stalked away and headed toward where his latest field commander, Duke Fergis, was riding along his retreating army's ragged and disheartened column. The proud advancing columns had vanished and been replaced with soldiers that hung their heads and nursed fresh wounds, both to the body and to the spirit. *Thanks to that blasted* Sidhe *Warlord of Gregor's.*

"My lord, why are ye afoot?" asked the Duke of Hamilton, once he turned to face the front and took notice that the warrior approaching was his leader.

Domeric ground his teeth and glared up at the general. "I love walking," he growled sarcastically. "Never mind why I'm walking, Fergis. This pathetic rabble needs to rest and lick their wounds. The MacGregors and their allies hae shown nay sign of giving pursuit, therefore I want ye to order a halt for the-"

"Is that wise?" interjected Duke Fergis. "Surely Lord Gregor and his Warlord wi' be hot in pursuit soon enough. They wi' nae allow their enemies to quarter and find rest within their borders, my lord."

"In the future, Hamilton, do nae speak until I hae finished and never question my orders. Is that clear?" the angry Campbell duke demanded crossly, glowering up at the chagrined general. The man could do nothing but give a stiff nod. "Good. Now, as I was about to say, I want pickets cut and erected around our camp parameter. Furthermore, I want a triple complement of sentries assigned before we begin setting up the camp. Do ye think that ye can carry out my instructions, Hamilton?"

The general's handsome face froze in a pale mask of i.dignation. "Now see here, Campbell!" Duke Fergis snarled, vault)ng down from his tall horse. "Ye push me tae far, and I hae had`quite enough of yer high-handed manner! Ye only command my clan`for as long as I agree to follow ye. It is nay wonder to me now, that the MacGregors hate ye sae and were able to beguile the Gordon clan to switch to their side! Just ye remember one thing, Campbell: if ye wish to retain the privilege of having my clansmen follow yer banner in this misbegotten war, ye had better put aside yer petty arrogance or ye wi' hae much less of an army to lead. Furthermore, in the future, I demand that ye give me the rank that I am due; a rank, which I must remind ye is equal to yer own."

For a long moment the two leaders continued to glare blackly at each other in mutual distaste before Domeric at last broke the stalemate. "Very well, *Lord* Hamilton. I shall attempt to curb my tongue," Campbell muttered acidly. "However, do nae ever think to question my judgment or my orders in front of the common soldiers of this army, discipline must nae be compromised by such insubordination. Is that understood?"

"Of course, *Lord* Campbell," Fergis smirked, savoring his victory.

"Good. Ye hae my permission to carry out yer instructions," ordered the older duke, barely containing his contempt. With a curt nod he began walking back the way he had come, along the marching column. Belatedly recalling something, Campbell stopped and called over his shoulder, "One more thing, Fergis: I need a head count taken in order to ken how many warriors were lost this wretched day. When ye hae the tally, see that it is sent to my pavilion straight away. I wi' be expecting it by midnight."

*   *   *

In the mean time at Glenorchy, the wounded were being cared for, while a number of blazing pyres were erected by the able-bodied warriors, for the burning of the scores of fallen foes and their comrades alike. As this grisly task was being carried out, the various clan lords gathered together, at the Warlord's request, to take stock of their situation and make a hurried decision on what would best serve their cause.

"The army is battered and wore with fatigue, but they are stout lads and would nae balk at pursuing the Campbells to rid us of Duke Domeric once and for all," Sir Sean pointed out. "The most direct way of killing a snake is to remove its head."

Lord Gregor shook his head. "I appreciate the direct method, Sean. However, even though the king has distanced himself from this conflict, I ken that he would prefer to avoid having his son-in-law from slaying one of his most powerful lords. If there is a way to end these hostilities without resorting to killing the Duke of Argyll, I'm sure His Majesty would favor that more warmly."

"My ships lay at anchor within a few days march of here," Lord Donald reminded his peers. "They are at our army's disposal, Gregor. Filled to their capacity, my fleet could transport better than two thousand of our warriors wherever ye would hae them. For instance, we could sail south along the coast; the Irish Sea is placid enough this time of year. With those troops we could strike back at the Campbells on their own territory. If I may, I would suggest the Campbell held island of Arran, or perhaps the neighboring peninsula to attack the fortress city of Campbeltown as well.

"The luck of Lugh favoring the endeavor, we could take and hold either position until more of our forces could be ferried down to reinforce those troops already there," the burly Lord of the Isles recommended thoughtfully.

The Chief of Clan MacLean looked at the sea lord evenly. "Arran. Is that to be the price of yer aid, Donald? Another island to add to yer holdings?"

Donald smiled coldly at his rival. "Price? Nay, but if at the end of this war that island were offered to me I would nae refuse the proposition."

"Short of chasing down the old duke and slaying him," the Warlord spoke, partly in order to divert the direction the debate had taken, "I agree that this idea has merit. Were we to take Campbeltown, Domeric's army would be in nay position to try and drive off out. From where their fortress lies, we would be in an excellent strategic posture to drive inland from the peninsula across Campbell lands and through the Carlyle as well. From there, the duke's capital of Inveraray would be fruit ripe for the picking," he looked up at the others, his finger tapping on the map under his hands. "When the wily duke realizes what has happened he'll die of vexation.

"I agree with yer recommendation, my lord," Sir Sean approved, grinning with delight across the table at Lord Donald before turning to his chief. "The final decision is yers, Uncle, and ye gentlemen," he added, glancing around the table where the other clan chiefs stood in thought, "but I endorse the idea."

All heads around the room nodded in agreement, although The MacLean's was a trifle lower than the rest. Lord Gregor pondered the idea for a moment longer before he nodded as well. "Very well, gentlemen. Let's discuss how we wi' put this plan into action and work out all the details. We must decide what lads wi' comprise the expedition and who wi' be in command. Please be sure to exclude yerselves from that roll, as each of ye wi' be needed with the main force." With that understanding foremost in the mind of each man, they got down to business.

Lord Donald was accurate in his summation of the Irish Sea. Good weather held out for their enterprise and the short sea voyage south aboard the MacDonald ships was a smooth one. Even with a number of last minute changes instituted by Lord Gregor, the departure came off without a hitch.

Reaching their destination, in the wee hours of the night, the expertly sailed ships dropped anchor in the inky darkness and prepared to off load their cargo of soldiers. In addition to the darkness, the first force was further aided by a thick, swirling fog that made the ships invisible to anyone on shore that might being watching the coast. The efficiency of the ship crews hastened the unloading of troops and quietly rowed the one thousand, five hundred combined clansmen of the MacGregor, MacDonald, and Fraser to the gravely shore near the rich, coastal fortress city of Campbeltown. While this was taking place, additional ships continued their journey and skirted around the horn of the Campbell held peninsula, onward to their destination to the west and the island of Arran. Landing there the second force, consisting of six hundred more soldiers of clans: Gregor, MacPherson and MacLean, planned to take and secure the castle at Brodick. It had been decided that, despite Gregor's earlier requirement, Lord Kirkland MacPherson would command this force along with General Duncan MacSean, as a large portion of the force was comprised of MacPherson clansmen.

Arran island proved to be a forebodingly quiet place except for the pounding surf; billowing fog, even more thick than the more familiar highland mists, seemed so dense that it could have been cut by the soldier's swords. Shivering clansmen cursed quietly as they made their way further ashore, fine gravel crunching under their boots. Hastening forward the small army quickly disappeared from the beach and into the surrounding underbrush, eager to strike a blow against their enemy in his own territory.

Once the army was safely ashore and hidden within the woodlands beyond the thick brush bordering the beach, Duncan informed his fellow commander of it was he planned to do, and soon slipped away. Making use of his talents as a tracker and scout the general moved away from the waiting army and moved inland to survey the lay of the land and any obstacles, human or otherwise, which may await them.

More than an hour later, Kirkland paced around his veiled position with more than a little impatience. "Duncan should hae returned by now," he fretted. "Mount up, lads," the chief ordered suddenly, "let's go find him."

Following the lead of the young chief, the clansmen mounted up and rode off in his wake, following the initial direction in which MacSean had taken. All remained quiet in the night, for a while, as they silently and with drilled caution made their way through a dense copse of somber, smooth-barked, gray, beech trees. In the midst of their masking foliage a hasty alarm was passed back the ranks by hand signal.

"Ach, we hae company," Kirkland murmured under his breath. Drawing rein, the lord halted his advance and stood in his stirrups to peer ahead for a better look.

Kneeing his mount expertly, a grizzled veteran soldier, moved alongside his chief for a better look as well. A veteran of several border wars, General Robert MacEwan was the MacPherson clan's warleader and Kirkland's trusted friend. Following the aim of his chief's finger, as it pointed toward a foggy ridge rising before them, he peered into the darkness ahead with a pronounced squint. Silhouetted against the starry sky, a solitary rider could be distinguished through the murk. *The rider appears to be alone, but he also seems to be waiting for something or someone,* the general surmised. *If he has seen us, he sure is nae in a hurry to run and tell anyone.*

"I see 'em," MacEwan rumbled quiet as a bumblebee. Raising his hand in a curt signal to halt those following columns of mounted soldiers weaving laboriously ahead through the populous woods, the stocky, rather flat-faced general returned his attention to where the unidentified stranger had been.

"He's still there, but just a little further ahead. There, in the lee of that clump of squat trees," Kirkland whispered helpfully. "The shadows there are obscuring his outline somewhat. I still can nae tell if there's anyone else out there or nae. What do ye think we should do?" he asked.

MacEwan stared out at the unwelcome guest and grunted. "Ye ken, Kirk, that if we can see him, he has most likely spotted us as well," he muttered, speaking as much for his own benefit as in response to his chief. Idly, he toyed with the worn leather wraps of his much-used sword hilt.

"Aye. Sae much for appoaching Brodick Castle unobserved," Kirkland replied, his tone sardonic. "Perhaps . . . Rob! Look at that fool; what on earth is he trying to do?" he exclaimed, eyes going wide in disbelief.

The lord's astonishment was intended for the unknown rider on the foggy ridge, as the stranger had suddenly, and for no apparent reason, exploded from his position and veered directly for toward them. Seemingly heedless of the danger of his headlong flight, the rider plunged down a mist shrouded slope and through the impeding thicket. At each ponderous lurch forward, the snorting horse threatened to send both its rider and itself crashing to the ground, even as tree branches whipped and clawed at the bolting pair.

"Is he *trying* to break his fool neck?" Kirkland gasped.

Even as the MacPherson chief spoke, the horse stumbled and nearly went down, and it was then that he and his warleader could discern the reason for at least a part of the lathered animal's belabored advance. "I can nae believe it," Kirkland muttered, his words little more than a stunned whisper. "He's riding *double* at that speed, through this thick undergrowth; he ought to be flogged for treating his horse like that!"

"Mayhap aye, mayhap nay. To be riding double at that pace in this terrain, on a horse that is sae obviously spent, the devil himself must be chasing them," commented the watching general. "Sair, would ye care to perhaps give the pursuing devil a bit of sport before the man kills himself?"

Lord Kirkland raised one eyebrow in askance at the blunt general's borderline blasphemy, for just an instant, before an amused grin crept onto his boyish face. "That fellow does appear to be a trifle spooked by something," he finally admitted. "Why nae? We *are* here to aid in the halt of spreading evil."

The Chief of Clan MacPherson was well aware that his clansmen were spoiling for another fight, and he was certainly not going to deprive them of one. *I just wonder what has befallen Duncan. I pray he has nae been captured.* Dismissing those grim thoughts from his mind, he turned his focus to leading his men. Drawing his keen sword, Kirkland raised it over his head with a flourish. Casting a hasty glance back toward where the standard bearers were busy shaking out the cloth folds of the MacGregor and MacPherson battle flags, he smiled grimly around at the readied troops. Kirkland gave the general a slight nod and MacEwan bawled out his orders.

"Forward at the trot, and fan out!" commanded the general, standing tall in his stirrups and pointing out directions to his subordinates with his battle-worn broadsword. A long, ugly scar stood out lividly across his face where it stretched from before his right ear and cut toward his wide mouth, before ending in the graying goatee covering his chin. The long healed scar pulled the general's fierce grin into a snarling smirk.

"I think that whoever's chasing that stranger toward us is going to hae one nasty bit of a surprise, especially when they see the hornet's nest they hae stirred up!" he called over the noise, winking at his chief.

Spurring their mounts forward, Grigor, Lord Gregor's young son and heir, along with another young squire named Setanta, rode up to Lord Kirkland's left and right. The folds of the MacGregor's scarlet and green, and the MacPherson's green and white, billowing in the misty air as they flew unfurled with inspiring martial beauty.

The angry hiss of steel slithering from oiled scabbards joined the jingling of bits and spurs, and the creak of saddle leather as General MacEwan personally led the men of the right flank. His cavalrymen swiftly broadened out their ranks with practiced ease and outriders spurred ahead to circle widely around the advance to reconnoiter. The distance that had lain between the fleeing rider and the invading army's position had proven to be deceptively further than at first expected, due to the rolling and hilly terrain. Because of the treacherous footing, the advancing troops did not increase their speed to more than a trot. As they reached the base of one hill and began moving up the slope, the fleeing rider was suddenly careening down. He was nearly upon them and close enough to see that the front passenger on the lathered horse was a woman, her flame-red hair streaming behind her in the face of the man seated behind her. The man reached up and pushed the long hair from his eyes and it was then that Kirkland recognized him.

"It's Duncan!" Kirkland exclaimed in astonishment, even as the man raised one arm to wave enthusiastically in happy recognition.

Then Duncan was in the midst of his relieved comrades, laughing out loud with obvious relief, despite his fatigue. Reining in his mount, Kirkland maneuvered his horse to stand against Duncan's faltering mount to aid in supporting it. Meanwhile, the rest of the warband swept on up the hill to fend off any pursuers. Soon enough, General MacEwan returned after quickly establishing a defensive line at the top of the hill.

"Steady," said the general, his voice adopting a soothing tone. He halted his beast close beside Duncan and coaxed the floundering animal's great head close to his armored thigh with a gentle touch and then caught the reins deftly as the big bay stumbled. The general's mount anxiously tried to sidestep as the other animal scrambled for footing to right itself. "That's it," he crooned, stroking its long nose, "you're fine. We'll take care of ye, brave laddie."

"Here; take this wildcat!" Duncan demanded, laughing weakly. "And watch out for her claws. She's already got me with them, and they're wicked sharp," he warned, trying to lift the struggling woman to a more secure perch in front of MacEwan's saddle. "Her name is Heather; she's Duke Domeric's niece. Her father's men were behind me. I had thought they lost my trail for awhile, but they found me again."

"How many of them are there?" Kirkland demanded, as he pulled Duncan up to sit in the saddle behind him. Hooking his fingers into the back of Kirkland's broad belt to steady himself, Duncan shook his unkempt hair out of his eyes. "Maybe a hundred; nae enough to give our lads much trouble, Kirk."

Duncan suddenly chuckled to himself. "Ach, I went out to do a bit of scouting and I happened upon the lass, apparently sneaking away from a party to meet her sweetheart. I recognized her from a gathering in Edinburgh, so I snatched her up. It was almost more trouble than it was worth until ye came along. That was a wee tad tae close for comfort!"

"I'm glad we were here to bail ye out of trouble," Kirkland replied, his response distracted as he allowed a fleeting grin to cross his lips. His main attention was drawn to the top of the hill where their soldiers were waiting.

Lord Kirkland expertly wheeled his own bay stallion to face the slope and turned his eyes toward the crest of the long hill where he could see their troops spread out. Speaking over his armored shoulder, he said, "I'm sure ye are correct, Duncan, about the number of men sent to hunt ye down, but it would still be prudent to make certain that yer count is accurate.

"General, I expect ye to stay out of the fighting unless the fighting comes to ye. Follow behind but do nae allow yerself to be separated," Kirkland instructed, sparing a quick glance away from the hill crest for his warleader. "Ach, forgive my poor manners, Lady," he continued, bowing slightly at the waist. "I am Lord Kirkland MacPherson, and I bid ye welcome to what little hospitality I may offer in the names of the clans: MacPherson and MacGregor. I'm sure Lord Gregor wi' be eager to welcome ye himself, but alas he is currently busy elsewhere at this time."

MacEwan could feel the girl stiffen suddenly in his arms when she heard the name of his comrade's clan. The flame haired maiden howled through her gag and began to thrash about, kicking her legs, and managed one well-landed heel that caught the man in the ribs. The general grunted but tightened his grip and adjusted her struggling form more firmly into the curve of his shield arm. He shook his head sourly and urged his mount up the hill, in the wake of the force's duel leaders. Tapping spurs to the horse's flanks, he trotted up the slope and drew the sword from his hip. Naked steel held up in the general's gauntleted hand drew the girl's wide eyed attention and worked to quickly quiet her struggles. Sighing with relief, as well as in offense, MacEwan allowed the reins to continue hanging free and guided his battle-trained warhorse with his knees.

Deployed ahead of their approaching commanders, the large warband awaited the men with shouts of delight when they saw for themselves the returned Duncan. MacSean beamed at the shouting soldiers and waved, sliding from his friend's mount to go and join them by walking through their ranks.

General MacEwan had not quite reached the top of the ridge when he became aware of raised voices converging on their position. The cries he heard, of a sudden, were filled with surprised dismay and fear, as Duncan's pursuers found more than what they had been bargaining for: a whole army of clansmen that, to their alarm, bore the banner of their fiercest enemy, the dreaded MacGregors.

The brief melee was over almost before it began, as the combined clan force held the high ground and charged with howled abandon down upon the hapless foe. Surprise was the undoing of the Campbell force and swiftly the survivors were put to flight in the face of their swarming enemy. Scores of clansmen, wearing the Campbell tartan, littered the surrounding woodlands at the feet of their victorious attackers.

Such was the gory scene as the general, with his subdued charge, came to a halt at the crest of the ridge and surveyed the skirmish site. Locating his chief, face flushed with triumph, the general kneed his mount to join the young man. From his new vantage point, MacEwan could see down into the next fog filled vale and their army's exultant cavalry, as they remained in hot pursuit of a couple dozen or so stragglers still hoping to escape. The remainder of the routed opposition, what little that yet lived, was in full retreat far ahead. Close to three score bodies, all clothed in the Campbell plaid, littered the damp ground.

Another eighteen sat or lay in a group nursing their wounds, under the watchful eyes of several dismounted MacPhersons.

Having claimed a new mount from the vanquished foe, Duncan rode down into the occupied valley and silently thanked God that none of the slain warriors were wearing the MacGregor, nor the MacPherson tartan. He took the time while he was busy checking the fallen, to roundup and collect a number of riderless horses. His thorough search for any wounded allies turned up none, so with the horses trailing along behind him on a tether, he returned to join Kirkland and the man's scowling general. On his way back to the summit, Duncan at last acknowledged the cheers coming from the exultant warband, which proudly acclaimed him for the valor he had demonstrated in the fight.

At last reaching his friend's side, Duncan exchanged a knowing grin with the man as he drew and waved his sword aloft in answer to the heartfelt cheering. Turning to look up the color bearers, Duncan signaled for Grigor to sound the battle horn and call for the pursuing cavalry to halt their advance and return. Still grinning with the pleasure of being at the center of a decisive, winning battle, albeit a small one, and without loosing a single warrior, Duncan tried to contain his enthusiasm.

"A rare and happy circumstance, Sir Duncan," acknowledged General MacEwan, reflecting on the fact of no friendly casualties, as he kneed his mount abreast of the two young leaders. "Do nae allow yerself to grow accustomed to it. Each battle can hae a mind of its own and the most ye can do is adapt to it. I do nae mean to piss on yer victory or take anything away from it, but remember what I hae told ye. Overconfidence breeds failure; the next time it could be us who are surprised and outmaneuvered."

Duncan and Kirkland each nodded their understanding, but even the general's wise, and however grim, words could not erase the joy they shared in their victory. "We hae met the enemy and the first victory is ours," Duncan spoke up first. "However, we hae lost the element of surprise and we should expect the garrison at Brodick Castle to ken that we are here and be prepared to repel us."

The MacPherson chief mutely nodded his agreement.

Soon the forward elements of the cavalry had returned and the combined clan army prepared to continue their advance through the foggy woodlands. The prisoners had been looked after by field medics in the intervening time; afterward, MacPherson men tied and bound each of them to separate trees until it was time to move out. At that time, they would be strapped to spare horses, which had been rounded up from the slain enemy, and led along behind the main force by designated guards.

The MacPherson general sat his mount between those of his chief and General MacSean, as they waited for the last of the prisoners to be secured to a tree. MacEwan glanced down in amusement at the fair-skinned and freckled girl who had chosen that moment to begin wriggling in his arms, one he finished checking the edge on his sword and had to reach around her narrow waist to slide it back into the scabbard.

"Ye hae brought us a rich prize, Sir Duncan," commented the scarred general, grinning down at the green eyed maiden. "Now that ye hae her, what are ye going to do with her? Keep her as a hostage?" The girl paused in her thrashing about all of a sudden, interested in hearing the answer as well.

Making note that the girl could not see him from the direction she was forced to remain in as the scarred general held her, Duncan caught MacEwan's eye and winked at him. "Actually, I hae been thinking about that. Heather is a very pretty lass, and with her family connections, would make quite a desirable bride."

MacEwan peered down at Heather as if examining a horse for sale. "If ye say so, Duncan, but she's tae skinny for my taste and I prefer my women a little less feral. Marry this one and ye better keep one eye on yer cutlery," he advised.

Kirkland could not contain his mirth and burst out loud with laughter, and then all three men were laughing together. The outraged maiden shrieked through her gag at them for using her as the butt of their joke. Her kicking and screaming only made them laugh all the harder until the soldiers all around them were looking to see what was happening.

"Ach, I needed that," Duncan declared, trying to stifle his chuckling. "To answer her question, Robert, I believe the duke might be willing to ransom such a wild flower merely to keep her out of the hands of such barbaric MacGregors."

MacEwan nodded sagely before having to grip her more tightly as she redoubled her efforts to squirm out of his grasp. "Now, now, lassie. There's nay point in struggling," chided the amused general. "Ye'd best save yer strength for the long trip still lying ahead of us. A wilted flower is such a sorry thing to behold."

At last she managed to work the gag from her pretty mouth. "Unhand me ye ugly brute! My father wi' rescue me and hae yer guts for garters before he's through with ye!" Heather cried venomously. "Ye were lucky to take him by surprise. Yer lot is nay better than highwaymen; what kind of men are ye to abduct innocent women?"

"Och, that's a cruel barb coming from a lass sneaking away from her home to go for a secret rendezvous with her lover," Duncan scolded her sternly. "Yer father should thank me for saving yer *innocence* by taking me into my care, lass.

"And as to yer father being taken by surprise," Duncan went on, the grin returning to his handsome face, "that's the whole point when it comes to war, is it nae, my lady? One *should* take his enemies by surprise whenever possible. I would be a poor example of a commander if I were to send my lads into battle, in enemy territory, without using every advantage at my disposal," he said, his tone mildly reproachful. "I am sure, if yer father were able, he would hae done the same." While he spoke, Duncan brought his mount slowly around to MacEwan's opposite side so that he might better see her face.

"Well, I ken that he wi' nae just sit by and allow ye to get away with this," the comely firebrand spluttered in anger, "this outrage! He wi' rescue me, and let me tell ye something else, sirrah; nay respectable Campbell wi' ever peacefully live in harmony, side by side with one of yer ilk. My people wi' furthermore nae suffer a misbegotten clan such as yer filthy MacGregors to remain and soil the land of our fathers. My uncle, the duke, wi' suffer *nay* MacGregor to live!" she spat hatefully.

The taunt was an annoyance to the MacPherson men, who from childhood had become accustomed to ignoring such affronts by the arrogant Campbells, but Duncan reacted as if he had been slapped. He had not been expecting such a foul insult from such an innocent seeming, young maiden. Kirkland, sitting his horse near his friend's side, watched the deliberate affront strike home, and Duncan's reaction as his blue eyes instantly grew cold and narrowed dangerously in flashing warning. The MacPherson chief could sense the obvious tension and sat straighter in the saddle, ready to act in case his friend decided to do something rash. He watched as Duncan visibly forced his anger back under control before allowing himself to relax.

Once the words had leaped from her mouth, the Campbell maiden gasped and went suddenly pale, as she realized *what* she had done and to *whom* she had done it. Her green eyes were wide and frightened as she stared up at Duncan. Great pools of moisture gathered in those eyes and suddenly spilled down her freckled cheeks. While this was happening, General MacEwan waited as calmly as a coiled spring, his eyes riveted on Duncan's, as he retained a firm hold on his charge. In silence, he waited to see how MacSean would handle the situation and his own temper.

General MacSean drew a deep breath and let it out. "In the future, my *lady*," began Duncan, in a deceptively quiet voice, his cold blue eyes impaling the frightened maiden, "I should take better care of my choice of words, were I ye, sae as nae to overly provoke those who hae mastery of ye." The outraged MacGregor general was still furious and continued to stare daggers at the girl until she began to squirm uneasily beneath that unwavering cold glare before he went on. "If ye believe all the foul tales told of my clan and find our entire race abhorrent, then ye should also be aware that at least some of those tales told about various members of Clan Gregor might be true. Every man has a point in which he may break, and I, myself, am nae made of stone. If ye are wise, my lady, ye wi' nae press the virtue of my patience any farther."

Duncan pulled his drilling stare away from the shaken maiden and made himself watch the army forming into orderly ranks before them. Temporarily released from the intensity of his chilling gaze, Heather drew a deep shuddering breath, but the respite did little to reassure the frightened girl. She withdrew into MacEwan's arms, trembling like a rabbit hiding from the eyes of a stalking cat.

Kirkland's stiff posture spoke volumes; surprised as anyone by the tight and iron willed control his friend exerted over his deep and abiding fury. The Duncan that he had grown to admire and respect was suddenly someone, he was forced to grudgingly admit, that held a supreme power of will over himself and everyone around him.

When he looked back at the maiden, Duncan's expression was far more mild, but Heather still recoiled into the suddenly, strangely reassuring grip of the stocky general that restrained her. "Ye wi' nae come to harm in our tender care, my lady," Duncan said, in formal reassurance. "By my honour, I swear it. If my earlier words seemed harsh, I apologize. I am a soldier more than I am a gentleman, and we hae traveled long and are weary. Furthermore, I had truly nae thought to hae so gentle a captive in our company. Although yer ill spoken words did provoke me to wrath, my quarrel lies nae with ye, but with those whom hae filled yer heart with such blind hatred," he admitted, speaking his mind, not just for her benefit, but for the two men present as well. "Even so, ye wi' still abide in our care. Now, if ye wi' grant me yer pardon, my lady, I must see to my men. We hae an island to conquer."

The new mount that Duncan had chosen for himself was strong and long-legged, its sleek coat a glossy white that all but vanished into the swirling mists as Sir Duncan led the way deeper into Campbell territory. Confidently, the army followed his lead and not long afterward had left behind the site of their first success as aggressors.

General MacSean set an almost leisurely pace, and MacEwan rode near his lord's side, both men a few horse lengths behind as the other man guided them. Heather had remained subdued since Duncan's outburst, to which, her keeper was grateful as he stole a glance down at her. *Ye had me worried there for awhile, Duncan ole boy, but ye kept a handle on yerself just fine,* MacEwan idly thought to himself. A little smile played on his lips. *Better, I'm sure, than I could hae done.*

The Campbell retainers that had been in pursuit of Heather's captor, despite being surprised and routed by the combined clan's warband, proved to be more tenacious than Lord Kirkland had given them credit for. They had wholly abandoned their mission to rescue the maiden. The MacPherson chief was one of the first to see them. Kneeing his horse forward for a better view, he examined the lightening glen with interest. Dawn had come unexpectedly and became more noticeable as he neared the treeline. Milling in a tight group a few hundred yards out, a haphazard contingent of bedraggled Campbell clansmen appeared to argue among themselves, obviously trying to decide what it was they should do next. What was most surprising about the men arrayed before them was that they all seemed to be clothed in rich court attire. None of them appeared to wear any armor, and the weapons belted about each waist looked out of place; some were not even girded about with a sword belt, but merely carried a sword.

As Kirkland looked on, Duncan commanded a troop of regular cavalrymen to the front to interpose themselves between the marching soldiers and the Campbells. Soon the cavalry troopers were in position, posted in two long ranks, as they rested at ease, ready to repel any renewed attack while they waited for further orders.

Kirkland shot a questioning glance over at his friend. "Did ye interrupt some kind of festive occasion, Duncan? Those men out there are nae dressed for a fight, but look as if they hae just come from a ceilidh," he said, riding up to his fellow commander.

"Aye. A party is what *they* called it," Duncan replied sourly, along with a loud disparaging snort. "Heather's father, Lord Oliver Campbell, was throwing a fine feast to commemorate the duke having declared war on my clan." All of a sudden, Duncan's face lit up with a thought. "Kirkland, would ye do a thing for me?"

The lord gave his a puzzled look. "Of course. What would ye hae of me?"

"Bring forward the prisoners of the skirmish. An idea just came to me," Duncan admitted, swallowing a hopeful grin.

Moments later the tethered prisoners were sitting before the MacGregor general as he scrutinized each face. Suddenly his gaze halted upon the familiar sullen features of one youthful captive. "Ha! Lady Morrigan is indeed smiling upon us!" Duncan exclaimed with delight, moving closer to the young man to get a better look. The captive had his hands bound behind his back and a rope halter lay around his neck and was tied securely to the saddle horn.

"Someone ye ken?" MacEwan curiously asked, as he felt his charge tremble as silent sobs of horror shook her body. Tears rolled down Heather's fair cheeks as she saw who one of the prisoners was.

General MacSean laughed with evident delight, and turning, clapped the man on the shoulder with a smile, his past ill humor suddenly forgotten. "Ken him? Aye. Aye, I surely do," he confirmed. "This is rare luck we hae on our side today."

Shifting his focus to his wondering friend, Duncan said, "Kirk, it is my pleasure to bring to yer acquaintance Lord Tolliver, the eldest son of Lord Oliver and the duke's nephew, as well as this young lady's brother." He paused to sweep a broad gesture in Heather's direction. "We hae two prizes now to bargain with, should the need arise."

Lord Gregor's son beamed with pride, sitting his mount beside the prisoner.

"Well done, Grigor," Kirkland praised the young warrior. "Yer Da wi' be pleased with yer performance. Did ye capture him yerself?"

Grigor drew himself up importantly, pleased at the status of his seething prize, "Of course I did. Tolliver Campbell, ye say?" he inquired, surveying with disdain the young Campbell lordling, from head to toe. "At the start of the fighting, I presented the colors and grounded the pole in the ground. After they were secure, I charged off into the melee and joined the fighting while there still some of them left. That's how I got this one. He tried to run away, but I chased him down and had to club him over the head with the hilt of my sword to get him to stop."

"Ye never would hae taken me if my saddle girth had nae snapped earlier during the battle," Tolliver retorted hotly, glaring over at his captor, his cheeks growing red. "My father wi' return for me, doubt it nae! And for the insult ye hae done to our family and clan, he wi' make ye pay dearly."

"Aye, but he'll only come under a parley flag," snorted Duncan, directing with a gesture, everyone's attention to a party heading toward his line of cavalry. One member of the approaching group waved a white handkerchief over his head. "Hardly a dashing rescue mission, laddie, but we'll go ahead and hear what they hae to say anyway. Sick at heart, the young nobleman could only turn in his bonds and watch the cautious advance of his father's small party.

"My sister and I hae done nothing against ye," he pleaded desperately, his eyes shifting from his father to his sister and then to Duncan. "Ye hae nay right to hold us as if we were mere commoners."

"Hae I nae? Did ye nae raise arms and join in an attack against my men?" Duncan asked convivially, leaning forward and resting his forearms on the high pommel of his saddle with feigned interest. "And just what should I do, as Lord Gregor's representative, with those who are our sworn enemies? Or those who defy our legal borders, steal our flocks, and resort to using fire and sword against innocent farmers and villagers? How would yer duke respond, I wonder?"

"But that land ye hold is legally ours; ours is the more legitimate claim," Tolliver protested fruitlessly. "The Campbell claim is valid-"

"I hae heard all about the claim ye supposedly possess," Duncan interrupted the lordling. "The matter was fairly settled following the 'Terrible Times', as ye well ken; ach, it was sae settled before either of us was ever born."

Turning away from Tolliver with a look of distaste, General MacSean watched as one of the MacPherson squires rode toward him from the cavalry's defensive lines. As he shifted his gaze toward the knot of Campbell riders slowly approaching under their white flag, something caught his attention further away, but he could not make out what it was. Standing up and leaning forward in his stirrups, he strained his eyes to peer further out into the still foggy glen and caught a glimpse of what appeared to be advancing torches.

"Kirk-"

"I see them," Kirkland volunteered, noting the number of torches the distant force was bearing, as he gazed through the retractable field glass he always carried. Calculating in his head, he estimated the time it would take to close with their halted expeditionary army. "They'll be Oliver's reinforcements, of course. He must hae sent back for his city militia before we found this glen. We had best make this parley a brief affair, Duncan, or we're going to hae another fight on our hands before we even hae the chance to reach the castle at Brodick," he advised thoughtfully.

Duncan nodded his agreement. "My thoughts precisely." He waved off the squire with a salute and kneed his beautiful mount in the direction in which the Campbell lord was now waiting. Arriving a moment later, General MacSean offered the lord a stiff, shallow bow from the saddle.

"Greetings, Lord Oliver," he addressed his adversary. I am General Sir Duncan MacSean. Ye must be here to arrange the release of yer son and lovely daughter. I regret that I hae only a short time in which to listen to yer proposal, but I think ye can determine what forces me to hurry along this parley of yers. Do ye wish to see yer bairns?"

At his enemy's curt nod, Duncan motioned for General MacEwan's attention, where the man waited just behind the line of cavalry along with his chief. "Robert, hae the lads prepared to ride as soon as we hae finished with this parley," he ordered. Finding his lord's son, he said, "Grigor, come forward about halfway with yer prisoner. Robert, ride out with the lass and accompany Grigor, if ye please. Perhaps our *host* may be more inclined to reason if it is known that they're safe and unharmed."

Hastily lighted torches sputtered in the weak pre-dawn morning as Tolliver and his sister were brought forward to where their father could distinguish them. Heather sat stiffly, and fought to hide her fear, as she remained bound by the arms of the resolute MacEwan. Meanwhile, Grigor and Setanta closely flanked the mounted Tolliver and tightly held the guide rope, while four cavalrymen assisted the escort with two riders before and another two following behind him.

Numbered among the Campbell party, Duncan knew Lord Oliver, of course, as well as his other son, Richard. All but the three leaders drew rein several yards away from the meeting place; Lord Kirkland riding out alone to join Duncan and the Campbell lord of Arran Island.

Duncan broke the strained silence that had taken hold as they waited for his order to be carried out. His spoke in a deceptively quiet voice, "Clan Gregor has done little to cause ye harm *yet*, Oliver Campbell, but before I hear yer proposal, I find myself forced by curiosity to ken one thing."

"And what, pray tell, might that be?" demanded Lord Oliver, taking a haughty tone as he regarded Duncan with distaste.

Arching an eyebrow at the man, Duncan shook his head in amazement. "Why is it that yer despicable brother, the Duke of Argyll, attacked Clan Gregor? He must ken that he has nay lawful reason to found his actions upon," declared the general, forcing his emotions to remain constrained from his voice. "His son, whom ye can be sure was nay innocent, was slain by one of my fellow clansmen. Aye, he surely was, but it happened as he was leading a pillaging raid within MacGregor borders to attack one of our villages, Dunmoore being its name!"

Lord Oliver cast a cold, disdainful glance at the MacPherson chief before he returned his attention back to Duncan. "Clan Campbell has never agreed with the claims yer clan put forth to territorial borders, in spite of the Crown making its unwise ruling in yer favor. Furthermore, although ye hae persuaded some of the lesser clans to be yer lackeys and to go along with yer claims, be certain in knowing that my clan wi' never back down. Those lands are ours, and wi' always be so."

"Ye are a hard-headed lot, I'll give ye that, Campbell," Duncan replied, chuckling a humorless laugh. "Sae be it. I trust that I am correct in assuming that ye wish to verify yer bairn's safety and good health?" he asked amiably. "Take a good look. They are both here and as ye can see, they hae nae been harmed," he added with false cheerfulness, carefully watching his enemy's reaction.

Lord Oliver's tight-lipped glance flickered to his embarrassed son and the man's cheek muscles twitched in anger as he beheld Tolliver, the young man anxious but also hopeful in his bonds between his captors. The Campbell's eyes slowly shifted to regard his daughter with a pained look that pinched his eyes.

"I want them back, MacGregor," he growled, fairly grinding his teeth in seething impotent wrath, forcing himself to not look at either of his children again.

Duncan inclined his head slightly. "Well, of course, ye do. What good father could nae want otherwise, my lord? And, their release can easily be arranged, although the price wi' be somewhat painful to yer pride. But I wi' assure ye, for honour's sake, that I do nae quarrel with mere children, even if they happen to hae the ill fortune to be Campbells. Sae, if ye do decline my offer, be comforted that they wi' be well cared for."

"What hostage price do ye require?" Lord Oliver demanded.

"I hae only one demand," Duncan replied mildly. "I ask only that ye hae every living person evacuate yer fortress at Brodick. I give ye until one hour before the setting of the sun today. Do that and ye shall hae yer bairns."

Sheer astonishment widened the lord's eyes, his hard face flushing suddenly as he realized that his adversary was serious. Oliver shook his gray head emphatically as he exclaimed, "I can nae do that!"

Duncan's expression did not change as he regarded the man and slowly shrugged his broad shoulders. "But ye hae to, my lord. I believe I understand yer misgivings, sae I wi' offer ye one thing more. If ye agree to do this thing, I promise ye a general amnesty that shall include ye and all of yer *immediate* family. In addition to this, I wi' agree to give ye my personal guarantee of safe conduct from this island. All of these things, ye hae my solemn word on."

"And if I refuse?"

"In that case, should ye unwisely refuse my generous offer, I fear that ye wi' very likely never see yer bairns again," Duncan bleakly replied, holding the man's eyes with his own. "Soon my esteemed brother, the Warlord of the clans aligned against yer clan, wi' be leading an army through Campbell lands. They wi' scour the duke's territories until every member of yer family and that of the duke's house are found, and in all probability put to the sword.

"My question is this: how much do ye love yer family?"

Lord Oliver's eyes flickered involuntarily to his daughter and back to his calmly waiting mortal enemy. He trembled as he fought to contain his powerless fury. "Sir Sean would never do that!" the Campbell lord gasped. "The King would never permit such an atrocity, even if *ye* could!"

"Are ye referring to the wearer of the same crown that ye, just moments ago, so railed against? Ach, do ye really wish to put such belief to the test, my lord?" Duncan countered blithely. "I fear that we digress; however much I might enjoy debating with ye, I must return to the immediate issue. Ye wi' evacuate Brodick Castle and relinquish her to me and my army, and I wi' fulfill everything that I hae offered in exchange. There is nothing further we hae to discuss, my lord."

"But these are nay terms at all!" Lord Oliver bellowed furiously, leaning forward over the neck of his horse and spitting contemptuously in the grass before the hooves of Duncan's mount. "Ye must truly take me for an idiot, MacGregor! Nay sane man would agree to this; my brother would hae my guts for garters!"

The army commander arched an eyebrow. "Then I wisely suggest that ye had better go a little bit insane, Campbell!" Duncan retorted, losing his patience. He cast a glance toward where the torches were slowly advancing. They appeared closer by half since the last time he had watched them. "I would be mad myself, if I allowed this army to tarry here any longer to debate the issue with ye. My offer stands but one minute longer, and I expect ye to give me yer answer without any further reflection or argument."

"But what of my bairns?" bleated the desperate Campbell.

"The same conditions still apply," Duncan assured the lord. "My army shall storm and take yer fortress, one way or the other; but I wi' hae it. If I am forced to take Brodick in a clash of arms, yer bairns wi' be unharmed but I wi' see that they are imprisoned as guest in yer own dungeons. My Lord, Gregor, may hae them released when this war is concluded, or he may nae," Duncan promised darkly.

"I told ye, I can nae do such a thing-"

"Then ye had better go to yer men; and be prepared to fight and die!" thundered the angry general, cutting the lord off in mid sentence, his patience finally gone. Quick to follow his friend's lead, Lord Kirkland wheeled his horse around smartly and cantered briskly back to their lines. If the Campbell had thought to entertain any ideas of following to perform some kind of lethal mischief, his opportunity was swiftly lost as both leaders safely withdrew to the security of their waiting soldiers.

Left alone between his paltry band and the drawn up lines of his enemy, Oliver cast a hopeless glance back toward where his approaching reinforcements were. They were still a quarter hour too far away to make any difference. Returning his attention toward the hostile army that invaded his island, the Campbell lord cast about for a last and forlorn stare after his captured children. Deeply shamed and disconsolate, Oliver lowered his head and bit back a sob before turning his mount to return to his men.

Heather saw her father slowly ride away and burst into a fit of distraught weeping, despite all of General MacEwan's attempts to console the hysterical maiden. Hot tears streamed down her cheeks as her fair skin grew splotchy from her distress.

"Nay! Ye can nae abandon us," she screamed between gasping sobs, struggling to wiggle and fight free of the general's relentless hold on her. "Father! Father, do nae leave me! Come back for me—please come back!" The desperate attempt was futile, of course, but having to deal with a hysterical woman was the last thing MacEwan wanted on his hands if a battle was to be fought, or even if they made a run for it. He sympathized with the girl, for the situation she found herself in, but at the moment he wanted nothing more than to be rid of the maiden and have someone else tend to her.

From behind where General MacEwan restrained the wailing girl, Duncan could hear the angry shouts coming from Lord Oliver, and turned his mount to better hear what the man was bellowing about.

"MacGregor! I *will* remember ye! And ye wi' pay for this, I promise ye," the lord cried, waving his fist angrily. "May the bloody Raven hear my call and rake yer soul! May she take yer soul in her talons, along with every other MacGregor's soul and deliver them to Hades for an eternity of suffering!"

"Ye hae pushed my patience tae far, Campbell!" Duncan bellowed back at his nemesis. "I am done with ye, but hae a care for yer bairns. If ye believe that I am damned already, I do nae hae anything further to lose or gain by personal restraint! Even though ye choose nae to believe what I say, I tell ye that it is my intention to deal with ye and yer children in an honourable manner."

Lord Oliver maintained his glare of tearful defiance for several seconds more, measuring it against Duncan's calm but icy gaze and then the contact was broken. The Campbell at last bowed his head, his broad and proud shoulders slumped in abject defeat as he turned his horse and rode slowly away.

"I wi' watch with great pleasure as yer corpse feeds the crows, foul MacGregor!" Tolliver piped up, pitching his words so that his father might hear them. If the man did hear his son's shout, he gave no sign of it as he continued his unhappy withdrawal to the waiting circle of restless retainers.

Duncan turned a measured gaze upon the captive youth and shook his head with obvious scorn. "Grigor. Please see to the whelps bonds and make them secure. Oh, and if he speaks one more word, stuff a rag into his and gag him," he politely ordered the son of his chief and sighed deeply.

Turning his handsome mount sideways, General MacSean stole another long look at the encroaching enemy reinforcements, before raising one gauntleted fist into the air as a signal to the officers waiting for orders.

Aware of Lord Kirkland's willingness to defer this type of tactic decision to his judgment, Duncan pitched his voice so that it carried to all of the eagerly awaiting troops gathered in a loose formation. Every eye was directed on the dashing general as he spoke to them, saying, "It is time that we made a tactical withdrawal; we could easily defeat the forces coming to confront us, but the time is nae right, just yet, to water the ground red with more Campbell blood. We wi' fade away for the moment and attack them at a time and place of our own choosing, my brave warriors!" Duncan's last shouted words were answered by the combined voices of the MacGregor and MacPherson troops shouting with approval and pride.

CHAPTER FIVE

The bright orange disk of the sun sank lazily toward the western horizon and drew with it lengthening shadows as evening marched ever closer. Nocturnal wildlife began to stir and make their presence known as they awoke and crept forth to hunt. Owls hooted and watched with keen, wide eyes for the appearance of mice and other rodents to slake their hunger. Other raptors also called the tall dominate trees of the woodlands home, as game for their hunting was in bounteous supply.

The large hunting birds of prey were not the only predators out in the night. Kilted warriors also crept quietly among the trees and growing darkness, stalking their human prey on the island of Arran.

Reaching their positions, just within the heavily shadowed outskirts of the woodland treeline, General Sir Duncan MacSean and his co-commander, Lord Kirkland MacPherson watched the looming walls of Lochranza Castle. The Campbell held castle, on the northern tip of Arran Island, was flanked by a prosperous coastal village that did trade with the mainland by way of a ferry. The village was quiet this late in the evening, the folk tucked away in their homes for a late meal after a long day of toil and trade. The castle was equally tranquil, except for a small number of sentries, which went about their duty of patrolling the stout stone walls. The only sound was the forlorn cries of seagulls as they wheeled through the air overhead and drifted gracefully in the cool misty air as they scanned the waters for their next meal.

Occasionally, one would swoop rapidly to the briny surface and flap away with a wiggling fish in its talons.

"The lads are in position and ready if ye are," whispered Kirkland, as he rested in a crouch posture beside Duncan.

Duncan nodded without taking his eyes from the castle walls. "Aye, let's nae wait any longer. It's time to begin making the duke pay for his little war. Good fortune to ye, Kirk, and I hope to celebrate in the castle's hall with ye after," he said quietly, pulling his plaid more snugly about his shoulders, vainly trying to ward off the chill sea air.

Silently, Kirkland crept away to join with his sizable detachment of troops. His part of the plan was crucial to the overall success of Duncan's strategy. The lord was a little nervous, as he always seemed to be before a fight, but he looked forward to showing his worth as a leader in the field.

Lord Kirkland's officers had their soldiers ready when he joined them, and looked toward the young MacPherson chief for his next command. Every officer there was at the least, a few years older than the chief and some were many years older, but none dared question his authority as Kirkland was their respected chief.

"It's time, Major," he whispered, addressing himself to a distinguished, rugged looking officer that wore his rank insignia on his bonnet.

Offering his leader a wordless nod, the major winked and trotted away to join a squad of handpicked clansmen, chosen to light up the night. Soon, Kirkland watched as a score of shadowed forms detached from the forest and loped away, bearing down on the peaceful village. Moments passed before several torches flared to life and spread through the quiet streets and allies. The torch bearers ran from building to building using their brands to light aflame the structures. Flames quickly grew from all around the village, as they hungrily consumed wooden shops and storehouses, and spread in every direction. The night became filled with smoke, and growing fires lit up the darkness.

Frightened voices wailed in the night and suddenly an alarm began to sound from the castle wall as sentries witnessed the spreading disaster. The ringing bell was soon answered by others, and garrisoned soldiers were roused from their bunks. Officers ran to the castle walls, belting weapons to their waist, to see what the commotion was about. From the walls, they had a commanding view of the growing fires and were stricken to see that half the village below was already ablaze. Villagers were scrambling from their homes and forming a bucket brigade from the nearby waterfront.

A command was shouted and the stout castle gates began to open as an officer gathered together what warriors he could find. A hastily assembled company charged from the fortress behind a young officer, intent on helping their clan folk to extinguish the fires raging from one end of the town to the other.

Watching from his hidden position, Lord Kirkland grinned and climbed atop his horse. He drew his sword and silently urged his warriors forward, leading them across the fields toward the burning village. Reaching the outskirts of Lochranza, the clan chief paused and shouted for his piper to announce their arrival. Almost immediately, the droning of the bagpipes sounded their martial notes into the smoky air, skirling the notes of *Scotland the Brave* for all to hear. The familiar song heartened the MacPherson men as they marched down the main street to confront the Campbell soldiers.

Surprise and dread shone clearly on the Campbell's faces as Lord Kirkland led his warriors forward in a wild highland charge. They fell upon the bewildered enemy troops with shrill battle cries and exultant hearts, caring not whether the foe had thought to bring a weapon or not.

The battle outside of Lochranza Castle was over quickly and the victory belonged to Lord Kirkland and his clansmen. Having taken fully advantage of the Campbell's surprise and lack of discipline, the MacPhersons offered no quarter to any of the vanquished enemy that was found armed. A handful was able to escape into the countryside, but not enough to merit sending troops to round them up.

Seeing that his task was accomplished, Lord Kirkland ordered his subordinate officers to have the warband regroup. It took several minutes to force the triumphant warriors into orderly ranks, as they were eager to storm the castle. Once they were in formation, the chief could see that they had lost some of their original compliment, but the losses were not excessive and were indeed, quite light. The scowling faces of the soldiers brightened as they discovered that they were to be given that wish. With the promise of more Campbells to fight and kill, they eagerly settled down and reformed their ranks to advance.

The skirl of bagpipes accompanied them as they quick marched toward the gates of the castle to assist their comrades.

Turning to his aide, Duncan murmured a string of rapid instructions and sent the officer off into the night, before turning and whispering to the waiting Colonel Alasdair Gregory, his second-in-command. "It's our turn, colonel. Come, let's nae keep our host waiting for his guests."

Once he was mounted, General MacSean gave the signal to advance. Appearing as a forest of writhing shadows, the main force of three hundred warriors afoot trotted ahead with as much stealth as they could manage. Moving out and screening both flanks of the foot soldiers, rode fifty cavalrymen, as they closed in on the unwitting garrison. The gates had been left yawning open and as Duncan's forces came within reach of the unbarred portal, Colonel Gregory signaled for the MacGregor bagpiper to sound his instrument of war and let the enemy know they were coming. A raw chorus of warcries joined with the scream of the skirling bagpipes as Duncan led the charge through the castle gates and into the open courtyard lying beyond.

Desperate shouts rang out from within the courtyard and other places as Campbell soldiers witnessed the unthinkable happening. The tried to force the heavy oaken gates closed before the invaders could all surge inside, but to no avail. Others, seeing that their fellows had failed, attempted to release the portcullis; however they were stopped as well by well placed arrows that suddenly sprouted from their bodies. At last, the attacking clansmen finished surging into the courtyard and swarmed like angry hornets to swiftly overcome the first hastily formed ranks of assembled defenders.

Archers from atop the wall's battlements fired earnestly down into the melee to help their clansmen and scored a number of well placed shots. Anyone moving within the confines of the open courtyard could be fired upon by at least one archer, from positions along the wall. The castle defenses had been designed for just such an emergency, but it proved to be too little too late. The enemy was too numerous and the defenders too few, as many had gone to help fight the fires raging in the village.

Making note of the archers shooting down into his cramped ranks, Duncan cast about for his lieutenant and found Colonel Gregory near the castle stables. The officer was wiping off his dripping blade on the plaid of a dead Campbell that lay at his feet.

"Alasdair!" shouted Duncan, until he gained the man's attention. Once he had the colonel's notice, he pointed emphatically up at the walls. "Take as many men as ye need and clear those walls of archers! We're sitting targets for that lot!"

Colonel Gregory was in the process of carrying out his commander's orders when the MacPherson warriors began streaming through the gates at the back of their gallant chief. The sight of more enemy soldiers was too much for the already embattled troops trying to hold the castle, and much to the chagrin of the newcomers, the Campbells threw down their weapons and pleaded for mercy.

"Well met, my lord," Duncan warmly greeted his friend, clasping his hand. "I can safely assume that all went well for yer lads, down in the village?"

"Aye. It played out much as ye had hoped it would," Kirkland affirmed. "Ye ken, my clansmen are more than a little disappointed with me. They were determined to come on in to help ye take the castle, but I forced them to reform first before charging in here to help yer lads. They think I cheated them of some of the glory."

"Ach, I'm sure they do nae feel that way," declared Duncan, frowning slightly. "Yer lads love ye, and ye ken it well."

Lord Kirkland grinned. "Well, of course they do. I'm their chief."

The pair walked a little apart and surveyed the carnage. Scores of dead littered the courtyard; most of them were Campbell defenders, but several wearing the MacGregor tartan also laid stretched out in death and covered by their bloody plaids. Fellow clansmen were busy collecting the remains of their comrades and carefully placing them together in one area where they would be honourably burned on a funeral pyre.

"Duncan, we still hae to find the lord of this place before he can make good his escape along with his family," the Chief of Clan MacPherson told his fellow commander. "There were nay noblemen among the Campbells we fought outside, so he must still be cowering in the keep somewhere."

"Aye," agreed Duncan. "Let's go flush him out."

The keep was the innermost and heaviest fortified part of any castle, and it took quite a while for a rotating crew of brawny highlanders to batter down the thick oaken doors and the braces that had been put in place from within. Leaving behind the bulk of their forces to finish securing the rest of the castle, Duncan and Kirkland led a heavy platoon of dowdy MacGregor warriors into the tall, granite keep.

The inner stronghold was a massive, ancient tower constructed of huge blocks of pale green granite, and was a place created for defense. A score of defenders could have held out against a much larger force for days if they were determined. The castle keep of Lochranza appeared to have been abandoned as Duncan's warriors started at the ground floor and worked their way up, scouring through each room, chamber, and storage cell. The fortified structure remained empty throughout the first three levels.

"There must be another stairway hidden somewhere," Kirkland complained in disappointment, striking an armored fist into a wall in irritation. "If this ancient place was built with concealed rooms and passages, the lord of this place has most likely fled already and sailed to safety. I could take days to find the hidden places."

"My lords, I think I hae found something," called one of the warriors, a note of excitement in his voice. "Over here. See behind this old cabinet? Look there; ye can see where the dust has been disturbed. Most likely it was sae unsettled by the cabinet's edge sliding out from the wall and back again."

"Good lad!" exclaimed Kirkland, slapping the grinning warrior's mail-encased shoulder enthusiastically. "Ye hae the eyes of a hawk. Once we hae finished capturing this island from the bloody Campbells, I wi' buy ye a bottle of scotch."

The warrior's grin broadened. "Thank ye, my lord; I'll hold ye to it."

Putting their broad shoulders to the heavy oak cabinet, Duncan and Lord Kirkland strained to move massive piece of furniture, manhandling the big piece away from the wall. As it grudgingly moved, the antique screeched with protest across the unpolished masonry floor setting both men's teeth of edge. Glancing behind the cabinet, Duncan saw a flicker of faint torchlight through the revealed opening, just before his warriors, headed by Grigor rushed through it and up a curving stairway.

"Why did nae we just hae the lads do this?" groaned Kirkland, swiping at the sweat beaded up on his forehead. "That's part of why we hae them, ye ken."

"Aye," agreed Duncan, good-naturedly, "but I little bit of hard work keeps a man honest. It's good for our men to see their leaders put forth some effort once in a while instead of depending on them to always do it. Besides, it'll give them something to talk and laugh about—seeing us sweat a little."

The young lord frowned at his friend. "Aye, perhaps, but I for one do nae take being laughed at very well."

"Humility is good for the soul," replied Duncan, offering him a wry smile. "Come on, before we miss all the fun."

Entering the previously hidden entranceway with swords drawn and held before them at the ready, the generals started up the dusty steps. Kirkland cast a quick glance over at his companion. "Humility may well be fine with ye, but it's humiliation that I can nae tolerate. A chief must hae the respect of his clansmen."

"Of course," Duncan agreed. "But I think that the men that follow our commands wi' hae that much more respect for a leader who wi' get his hands dirty, toiling right alongside them."

"Perhaps, ye are right," the lord admitted, if somewhat grudgingly.

They had gone about halfway up the curving stairway when both men heard a scuffle that sounded not too far ahead. The two general's shot a quick glance at the other and hastened forward and upward, taking the stone steps two and three at a time. They reached the top of the stairs at a dead run and pelted ahead stride for stride, the tardy leaders rushed without hesitation toward the nearest chamber. Stepping over the body of a dead Campbell retainer to enter the room, Duncan arrived in time to watch as an older Campbell was overpowered by young Grigor. Kirkland, half a step behind, skidded to a sudden halt to avoid running into his friend's back.

Maneuvered into a corner, her back pressed against the wall, the lord's wife was clutching a wicked, hook-bladed dagger in her fist. Waving the sharp weapon before her, the lady gaped around the room with eyes wide in terror. Trying to coax the dagger away from her, Setanta nearly lost several fingers as the terrified lady lashed out suddenly with her blade. Swearing imaginatively, Saer made a sudden lunge at the trembling woman and slapped the weapon from her hand; in the next instant, Grigor's fellow squire in training, in one swift move dragged the protesting lady to the floor and skillfully bound her wrists to the sturdy leg of a heavy oak bed that occupied part of the room.

As all of this was happening, Duncan found his eyes drawn back to the man that Grigor had subdued and bound. The man's face was hidden by the long graying hair that had escaped the thong holding it back. Leaning forward the general used his fingers to push aside the masking hair, and recoiled in astonishment at the face that grimaced up at him from the floor. Duncan crouched and rocked back on his heels, appearing to be deep in contemplation as he regarded Grigor's prisoner.

General MacSean chuckled quietly to himself and cocked an eye up at his cousin. "Grigor, lad, ye hae a genuine knack for taking important captives. Do ye ken who it is, this time, that ye hae taken prisoner?"

Grigor shook his head, frowning at the bound Campbell. "He does seem familiar to me, but nay. I do nae ken the man."

"It is bonny fine to see ye again, Lord Oliver," remarked a gloating Duncan to the prisoner, wearing his most infuriating grin. "I had never, in my most hopeful fantasies, expected to find ye *here!* But this is perfect. Bonny well done, Grigor; yer father wi' be justifiably proud of ye. When this little war is concluded, I believe Lord Gregor wi' agree ye are ready for the accolade of knighthood. Perhaps ye as well, Setanta. Well done."

"Thank ye, sair," replied a beaming Setanta.

Duncan continued smirking at the Campbell lord. "I must say, my lord, that it appeared as if yer lady put up a better struggle than ye did," he chided, allowing his grin to bloom into a wide, amused smile.

A moment later, Kirkland returned to the chamber, having gone down the secret hallway to check the remainder of the rooms located beyond the one of most interest. Hard on his heels entered Colonel Gregory, along with the two siblings they had captured late the previous evening. Heather and Tolliver were tightly bound and gagged as they were led into the room behind their temporary keeper.

"General MacSean," said Gregory, making his presence known. "What would ye hae me do with these prisoners? I do nae mean to complain, but I am nae cut out for baby sitting children. Shall I escort them both to a cell, or should I hae the lass locked away in more comfortable accommodations?"

Duncan nodded his head. "Aye, go ahead and hae Heather put up in one of the more comfortable quarters. And once ye hae her all tucked in, please return here so that ye can escort our dear friend Lord Oliver, here, along with his charming son down for a stay in the dungeons," he instructed. "I've heard the accommodations are excellent this time of year."

"I wi' make sure they are as exceptional as ye would expect, sair," replied the colonel, his expression so bland that Duncan almost laughed out loud.

As the lord's daughter was led away, Duncan returned his attention back to the father. "I wonder what has become of yer other bairn, my lord? Or the true lord of this castle," he speculated out loud. "I hae nae seen either of them. Is the boy still hidden here somewhere or did he manage to escape? Perhaps in yer wisdom, ye left him in command of Brodick Castle?" A slight frown creased the general's forehead.

"Does nae knowing worry ye, MacGregor?" Oliver taunted with a smirk.

Suddenly the smirking lord cringed forward as Grigor cuffed him sharply to the back of the head, sending Oliver reeling at Duncan's feet. "Ye would do well to keep a civil tongue in yer head! General MacSean asked ye a question, dog of a Campbell. I strongly suggest that ye answer it."

"Ye wi' pay for this, MacGregor!" Oliver spat defiantly, dividing his stony glare between Duncan and Grigor. "My brother is the Duke of Argyll, and when he learns of this fiasco, I assure ye that he wi' hae ye all-"

Grigor stepped into the swing this time and the cuff across the back of the lord's head pitched the man face first onto the floor, prone nearly senseless. The son of the MacGregor chief squatted down close to the groaning lord and pulled his head back with a handful of hair. "Ye had better start listening better, scum! The general did nae ask for any of yer lame threats," growled the incensed young warrior, handling the prisoner a bit more enthusiastically that what Duncan would have preferred. "General, I can *pry* the answer out of this wretch if ye like."

"Nay, Grigor," declined Duncan, shaking his head. "Nae yet anyway, but ye can do me the pleasure of removing this fool from my sight before I throw up. Perhaps he wi' hae a change of heart as ye and Colonel Gregory conduct him and his whelp to their new accommodations in the bowels of this place."

"Aye, of course, Sir Duncan," Grigor replied, not bothering to conceal his grin as he forcibly hauled the shaken prisoner to his feet. "Right this way, my lord, yer quarters await. I wonder if ye wi' hae very many rats for roommates?"

After Lord Oliver had been dragged from the chamber, the MacPherson chief cast a speculative look at his fellow commander. "Ye should really consider some of yer own theories, Duncan. What if Oliver's son or the lord of this place *has* escaped and is even now fleeing to the duke to plead for reinforcements to reclaim the castle? We do nae hae the forces needed to make a stand here by ourselves."

Duncan shrugged dismissively. "We hae time enough to let Oliver sweat in the dungeons a spell. Even if he did nae send his son to the duke, he would hae sent someone else. That's what I would hae done," replied the general. "It was bound to happen, what ever we may hae preferred.

"As it is," continued Duncan, "we currently hold Lochranza and the ferry that leads to the mainland. Plus, we hae pulled the fangs from the Campbell tiger that could hae shipped from Arran to plague the main advance through their territory. The island must only be held for a week or sae before we are to join back with my brother's army.

"In the mean time, this castle must be prepared sae that it may be razed to the ground at out departure," advised a thoughtful Duncan. "And, while we are here, we may as well search this place for whatever treasure it holds. What booty is found wi' be put to good use in supplying provisions for the army and in rewarding our clansmen for their time and effort away from their homes and fields."

Lord Kirkland nodded his head in avid agreement. "A splendid idea. To the victor goes the spoils," he quoted the ancient maxim.

Before the commanders left the chamber, Duncan removed the Lady Eleanor's bonds and laid her on the bed and covered her up with the thick quilts. Once he had taken care of the lady's comfort, he exited the chamber and pulled the door shut behind him. Outside, in the hall, Duncan ordered a sentry posted to guard against the lady from trying to escape. Having done with that precautious, Duncan and Kirkland each claimed one of the neighboring rooms for their personal use and together, they headed off in search for the kitchens. They were both hungry and hoped to scrounge up something to eat along with a tankard of something wet to wash it down.

By morning, the majority of those Campbell warriors that had survived the night before, and had evaded capture, had been hunted down and taken prisoner or wiped out. Those that escaped initially had been scattered into small pockets of ineffectual and disheartened resistance. At the same time, other Campbells that served in the castle as servants and other such capacities found themselves evicted from the fortress that now rested in the hands of their hated enemies, namely the MacGregors.

Waking early that morning, after successfully snatching a couple precious hours of sleep, General MacSean indulged in a bath to rid himself from the dirt, blood and stink that had clung to him like a disgusting second skin. Feeling refreshed and in good humor, he had just finished donning his armor when he heard a knock at his door.

"Come in," he called, as he continued adjusting his bracers.

"Morning," greeted Kirkland, striding inside. The lord was already clad in his armor, as well, and grinned over at his friend as he claimed a comfortable cushioned chair with a matching footrest near one of the room's windows.

"We did bonny well last night, Duncan," he commented, leaning forward in the chair to reach a side table and pouring himself a goblet of steaming mulled wine. "Better than I would hae expected, actually. Our lads fight and work well together; and yer plan was simple but highly effective."

"Aye, our clansmen work well together," Duncan agreed, nodding his head. "I've been wondering how matters are proceeding with the main invasion force. We are in the dark over here and that bothers me, I admit. Although I'm confident that my brother is meeting with success, I still wish there was a way to coordinate with him."

Kirkland took a sip and his hot wine and nodded sagely. "The same thoughts hae bothered me as well, but I see nay way of allaying the situation. It seems that all we can do for now is finish subduing this island," he said reasonably. "The Campbells still hold Brodick Castle, and though General MacEwan has them hemmed in, that condition wi nae hold unless he is reinforced soon. Eventually, they wi' realize that our entire force is nae arrayed against them. We must act soon."

"I agree," replied Duncan, moving to stand and gaze out the window. "Hae ye an estimate of our casualties?"

Lord Kirkland nodded behind his goblet. "Our combined losses were relatively light with twelve lads killed and another twenty wounded. The Campbells on the other hand found things a bit more severe," he reported, a smirk growing into a pleased smile of his handsome face. "We accounted for the better part of three hundred of their lads. Last night, before I turned in,

I walked about and counted the bodies littering the walls and courtyard, as well as outside in the village where my dependable lads absolutely crushed the poor bastards."

"Good, bonny good," replied Duncan, his smile a mirror of the infectious one on Kirkland's lips. "I trust our clansmen wi' nae be to disappointed to discover they wi' hae to march another ten miles today."

The MacPherson chief arched a quizzical eyebrow.

"I intend to march south before the enemy realizes that MacEwan is undermanned and alone," Duncan intimated, returning his attention to the seaside view that stretched beyond the window. "A light garrison of about one hundred soldiers should suffice to hold Lochranza, don't ye think, Kirk?"

"Aye. A hundred lads should be plenty to hold and to accomplish the tasks of the razing the castle, as well as securing the ferry and scuttling the other boats," agreed the lord, relaxing in the comfort of the chair. He suddenly raised his refilled goblet up toward his fellow commander and added, "How about a toast to our victory?"

*   *   *

The simultaneous invasion that took place at Campbeltown, along with the nearby stronghold of Saddell Castle, had also ended up a success for the clans confederated with the MacGregors against their mutual adversary. The price of those victories proved to be much more costly than those triumphs won on Arran Island.

Although the Campbell garrison of Saddell Castle had been surprised by the sudden appearance of armed invaders, and caught off-guard, the stout defenses of that fortress were well maintained. The troops themselves were of better quality being well trained and more disciplined than their counterparts of the neighboring island. All of this was in large part to the conscientious officers and a solid cadre of non-coms that proudly formed the professional backbone of their standing forces.

Under the overall command of Warlord Sean MacSean, the main invading army had succeeded in capturing, by storm, the enemy castle. It had been proved from the outset, however that the victory would not be an easy nor a quick one.

The initial attacks had been beaten back, a determined resistance from the well led defenders stymieing every attempt at the walls. Each side took terrible losses that first day, especially the MacGregors and their allies, who had not the benefit of stout and high walls on their side. The siege continued nevertheless, and the opposing forces strove on, battling against one another for a further twenty-four hours before the MacGregor led army at last breached the castle's defenses. Into the stronghold, they stormed through the splintered and torn down gates, and spilled into the enemy's courtyard. That was when the battle should have ended, but the Campbell defenders refused to concede in the face of their officer's brave but foolhardy stand.

The castle defenders stood to a man against the invading soldiers, and during the bitter fighting were crushed mercilessly under the heels of their exhausted enemies. No quarter had been asked for and none was given, but those Campbells that fell that day, unwittingly extended the opportunity for many others of their clan to escape certain death. Numerous folk fled through hidden and long-unused passages that took them into the countryside where they scattered inland with their families. Meanwhile, men of the militia formed into bands that vowed to return and harass the aggressors with the tried and true highland tactics of hit and run.

On the second morning, after the hard won capture of Castle Saddell, returning ships of the MacDonalds began arriving at the peninsula's harbor along with the added assistance of a number of ships belonging to the MacLean and Clanranald clans. Their cargo was more soldiers, numbering nearly four thousand, which were ferried ashore in a multitude of smaller craft. Once the host was assembled, the leadership quickly came to the realization that the reinforcements could not possibly fit within the confines of the castle. The city of Campbeltown offered little comfort either, as a portion of it had been burned, and the entire city occupied before the storming of the dominating fortress. The freshly arrived reinforcements were forced to camp outside the castle, before the broken gates, and wait until they received the awaited marching orders.

Several hours following the additional clan warriors safe arrival ashore, to their surprise and gratitude, they found themselves enjoying a bounty of food and drink that was provided to them by the uncertain citizens of Campbeltown. Slowly at first, but then with more regularity, city folk came to the army encampment with foodstuff in hopes that their hospitality would prevent looting and any burning of homes and businesses. The army, under strict orders that the city and her citizens would under no circumstances be molested or despoiled in any way, nevertheless took full advantage of the people's peace offerings, along with a more than a few bribes offered by fearful city officials.

A full blown feast was underway among the tents of the reinforcements, which stretched broadly outside the repaired castle gates, several days later when several ships sailed without warning into the bustling harbor. Those ships were soon disgorging row boats that stroked toward shore full of armed clansmen.

Troops were hastily pulled away from their feast and raced to form battle lines along the beach and docks to confront the approaching boats, but to their surprise the men coming toward the shore waved and hollered greetings. The first boat to reach the docks contained the recognizable figures of General Duncan MacSean and Lord Kirkland MacPherson leading a large number of their returning contingent.

The unexpected appearance of the respected leaders, at the head of their some four hundred warriors, added to the merriment of the feast. They were first welcomed by the troops sent to intercept them at the shore and by the harbor sentries as boat after boat offloaded men and horses, along with a substantial amount of locked strongboxes and chests. Once all were ashore, the regiment formed neatly into columns and proceeded to press forward through the well guarded parameter of the sprawling army encampment. They rode into the camp amid a chorus of shouts welcoming them and happy cheers from the hosting troops that knew that they had met the enemy and lived to tell of it.

Leaving behind their men in the capable hands of the officers and non-coms, who had orders to allow the weary troops to join in the feast, Sir Duncan and Lord Kirkland rode on with a score of clansmen that each led a heavy laden horse into the cobblestone courtyard. Dismounting and allowing their horses to be taken for stabling by attentive retainers, the two commanders bade the attending clansmen to wait with the horses that bore the locked chests, and strode into the ancient castle keep to find Lord Gregor and the Warlord and make their report.

Negotiating the network of corridors, the walls covered by a notable amount of banners and tapestries, they at last found the center of the impressive keep. Entering the greathall, Sir Duncan spotted his brother immediately and went towards him with a grateful smile at seeing him unharmed. Striding across the large hall, Kirkland pointed out what had instantly drawn his attention.

"Duncan, look there," he said, a catch in his voice.

Where he had indicated, toward one wall where light streamed in through a lovely stained glass window, colored light illuminated a handsome suit of armor. The gold plate of the armor stood on a stand, intricately overlaid with silver enamel; although it had obviously been crafted for ceremonial purposes only, the burnished suit was clearly worthy of a king's ransom.

Several warriors and officers, along with the other lords and chiefs lingered, apart from their expedition leader, talking quietly amongst themselves while eating a light repast. An occasional glance from one or more men was cast furtively toward where the MacGregor chief and his warlord stood, before returning their attention back to the others sitting at table about them.

Before a tall but narrow window stood Lord Gregor, staring thoughtfully outside at the green countryside and seemingly uncomfortable in the dark purple robe that he wore over his usual black leathers and tunic. Standing quietly near his uncle's side, and appearing more somber than he typically was, Sir Sean turned at the sound of approaching boot steps.

"There's Lord Gregor and yer brother," Kirkland said needlessly, pitching his voice barely above a whisper. "They do nae appear much like men that hae met the enemy and won a smashing victory, do they?"

"Nay, they do nae."

"Duncan!"

The knight's face suddenly lit up with a broad smile as Sean swept forward to embrace his brother and pounded him on the back heartily. "Duncan, I'm happy to see ye safely back with us!" he greeted warmly. "Did all go well?"

Duncan forgot his momentary worry and caught up his brother's hand in a firm warrior's grip, still smiling at his elder sibling. "Aye, and it could nae hae been better done. Our lads put the fear of Morrigan into the bastards," Duncan remarked, his smile grown a trifle grim at the remembrance. "I can see from the army outside and ye within this castle that ye were successful, as well, but I began to wonder if something were afoot as I saw the solemn mood between ye and Uncle Gregor. Is all well?"

"Aye," chimed in the observant Kirkland, wearing a slightly worried frown. "I saw the troubled looks on yers and Lord Gregor's face. He appears to hae the weight of the world bearing down on his shoulders, even though yer brave warriors feast in victory, outside the castle walls, as we speak."

The Warlord's face suddenly grew grim. "We received a report, nae many hours following our taking of this castle, bringing dreadful news from Edinburgh. The army has nae been told yet and nay one else has been informed of it, except for the other lords with us that allied with Uncle Gregor," confided Lord Sean, drawing the two men away so that they did not disturb their leader's grim contemplations. "A messenger arrived from Edinburgh, as the king was fully aware of our plans, bringing grave tidings.

"King William, the Stewart, was found after a fall from his horse and is reported dead from his injuries," he paused to let the dour news sink in, as Duncan and Kirkland exchanged a shocked look. "There is more, I fear. On that same dreadful day, the heir apparent, Prince David, also perished. The Prince was killed as he sailed off the coast of Saint Andrews. His ship was witnessed to hae floundered in high seas and crashed into the rocks before sinking with all hands. All were drowned; Prince David's body along with a several others was recovered some hours later by local fishermen."

"My God!" gasped a horrified Duncan, crossing himself. "May The Lord give rest to their souls. I can nae believe such a tragedy could strike sae brutally!"

Another thought gripped the stunned MacPherson chief. "Is it to be civil war then, Sean?" he breathed, his hands suddenly shaking as his normally ruddily handsome face blanched of all color.

"Aye, that is very likely, but for different reasons than ye are probably thinking of, Lord Kirkland," gravely replied the stalwart Warlord. "The late king's Royal Council has already named their legal choice for Scotland's next king, and they hae the authority to do sae, as our laws dictate under such circumstances. As ye ken, any who oppose their carefully considered decision stand guilty of treason against Scotland," he explained in a tone completely devoid of emotion.

"Who hae they chosen?" demanded Kirkland with a sudden rush of impatience. "Surely nae Domeric Campbell, of all people?"

"Nay, my friend," Sir Sean reassured, "nae him, thank The Morrigan! Nay, but by the authority of the Royal Council, and the Grace of God, Gregor MacGregor, Chief of Clan Gregor and by right of his marriage to Elizabeth, eldest daughter of the late King of Scotland, has been called upon to take up the mantle of ruler and reign as our new king. As ye can see, he is still trying to come to grips with this unexpected and unsought for duty, which has been thrust upon him."

Turning from the window and away from his own reflections, the new king caught the eye of his warlord and signed for that man to attend him. Inclining his head in a respectful nod, Sir Sean excused himself from the two recently returned commanders to join his waiting liege.

All throughout the greathall, hushed conversations abruptly ceased as Gregor, who had moved to the head table, rapped on the wooden surface with the bronze hilt of his dagger. The lord's face remained grave as he looked out at the expectant faces turned to regard him. Resting the heels of his hands on the edge of the long oak table, Gregor studied the old scars marring the wood briefly before taking a deep breath and raising his troubled eyes back to his silent audience.

"My fellow lords and commanders," began Gregor, his voice strained by sorrow and weariness. "As ye ken, I hae received a message; that message is from Edinburgh. In a moment, Lord Sean wi' read the communiqué from the balcony," he pointed to indicate where two doors, although momentarily closed, led outside to overlook the courtyard, "for ye and all of our army to hear. The news contained in the message is of grave import and rightfully belongs to every one of us, nae just we privileged few."

Striding out onto the high terrace with his bearded nephew at his side, amid not a few murmurs of curiosity and concern from the, as of yet, uninformed leaders that hurried to closely follow behind, Gregor moved to the weathered stone railing and waited where anyone outside and looking up could see him clearly.

"Attention! Attention!" bellowed the Warlord, his voice crackling with authority and all of the parade-ground force he could muster. "Lord Gregor has recently received a message from the capitol in Edinburgh which he demands I read for all to hear."

Below, in the courtyard and outside the castle walls, soldiers whether feasting or on duty, paused to look up from whatever they were doing to locate the source of the command and instantly grew quiet. The army of highlanders turned their attention toward where they found their leaders gathered above them on the keep's balcony.

"Important news from Edinburgh has reached us that all must take notice to!" the Warlord continued, a few heartbeats later, in a booming voice. "Less than a fortnight prior to this day, our king, William the Stewart died from a tragic fall from his horse. On that 6ery same fateful day, the Crown Prince David was also been laid low, drowned as his ship floundered off the coast of Saint Andrews," Sean was forced to pause as a great wail of lamentation arose from his shocked countrymen. "The king and his direct heir are dead, but by the legal authority granted them by Scottish law, the Royal Council hae chosen for us a new king! The king is dead! All hail our new king; all hail King Gregor, King of Scotland! Long live the king! Long live King Gregor!"

Astonishment and stunned silence greeted Lord Sean's announcement for several long seconds as the highland troops sought to comprehend this unexpected news. At last, one grizzled soldier doffed his border bonnet and raised a clinched fist to his heart and shouted, "Long live King Gregor! Long live the king!"

Suddenly many other voices joined with that of the grizzled older soldier's, until the chant spread and boomed into the sky with immense enthusiasm from the entire army gathered below. Almost as one, the soldiers drew their swords and sank to their knees behind the grounded blades, in homage to their king.

His blue eyes shining with unshed tears for the king he had loved as if he were his own father, Gregor, now that man's successor, raised his hands above his head beckoning the host to silence. Only after the gathered highlanders had quieted sufficiently did Gregor lower his shaking hands and address those below.

"I would begin by saying this: it was never my intention to ever be king. In truth, the idea seemed ridiculous with such a robust ruler and his own proud heir just coming into the prime of his young life," he confided, voice grim with suppressed emotion. "I well-loved William as both, my king and father-in-law, and it grieves me that I shall never again enjoy his company. However, I wi' undertake the burden handed to me, to the utmost of my ability, and strive to be a good and just king for Scotland and for all her peoples, as he did, for as long as I live," pledged the new king.

Many an eye shed tears even as the army again took up the chant of: 'God save the king; long live King Gregor!'. Sorrow mixed with jubilation among the soldiers as they witnessed firsthand the end of one king's reign and the beginning of another.

At the renewed clamor, curious citizens of the captured coastal town peeked out from windows in wonder, while others, more bold, stepped out into the streets to witness better what was happening. Children, fearless as only children can be, glanced up distractedly at the clamor from their games of marble shooting and rowdy matches of hurley, but for the most part all but ignored the hubbub raised by the occupying army that gloomy, cloud filled afternoon.

Raising his right hand in recognition of the respect and homage that was paid himl Gregor touched his clenched fist to his heart in salute to his loyal followers. Nodding slight,y to his warlord, the as of yet, uncrowned king spun smartly on his heel atop the terrace and strode with regal bearing back into the castle's greathall.

Following closely in the steps of his king and uncle, the Warlord paused briefly as Gregor sat heavily upon the finely carved throne-like chair set before the long council meeting table. The impressive chair, crafted of cherry wood, gleamed with a fine polish to its deep red grain as it rested on a stately two step high dais. It was before this and the man that sat upon it, that Sir Sean carefully knelt on both knees. In his off hand, Sean drew his heavy claymore broadsword from its old and battered, worn leather scabbard. The steel gleaming dully in the muted lighting of the large chamber, the Warlord cradled the sword on his upturned palms. Extending long muscular arms toward the seated man, he presented his offering of steel to the king.

"My lord King," the distinguished warrior began, bowing his head in respect. "As ye hae ever been my kinsman, lord and chief, I humbly kneel before ye and freely offer ye homage due to the rightful King of Scotland. My loyal heart and strong sword-arm are yers to command for good or ill. Allow this length of good Scottish steel, wielded in my hand, ever serve to bring justice in yer name to all of our sundry peoples, and furthermore to be the feared scourge of the lawless, wherever they may hide."

The king's face was stern as he regarded his nephew with a steady gaze. "Ye offer to bear a responsibility few would welcome, Nephew, but I ken of nay better man to carry such a burden," Gregor allowed. "Ye hae shown yer metal many times in the past on my behalf, and it has ever proven strong and true. Yer worth to me is indispensable, as I hae particularly become aware in these dark times of late. So be it," King Gregor agreed softly, nodding his distinguished head.

Arising from his ornate chair, the unexpected king stepped forward and accepted the expended sword. Raising the glinting claymore to eye level on his own palms, Gregor looked down the length of sharp, much used steel before returning his keen gaze to the man kneeling at his feet.

"This well-used sword, which I now hold in my hands, has ever been wielded faithfully in my service. I now declare that it signifies the right hand of the King's justice, both high and low. Into the capable hands of Sir Sean of Inversneed, do I offer this sword, for as long as loyalty and fidelity and honour remain within he and his heir's hearts," Gregor stated solemnly, raising his voice for the benefit of all those gathering in the hall that they be witness to his declaration.

Grasping the leather wrapped basket hilt in his calloused right hand, Gregor fluidly swung the balanced sword into the guard position. Expertly the king brought the heavy blade sharply down, first upon Sean's left shoulder and then his right, the flat shiny edge of the broad blade smacking solidly against the kneeling warrior's blackened chain armor. Concealing a wince, Sir Sean raised his eyes to steadily gaze up at his king as the man went on to address him.

"Sir Sean, Baron of Inversneed, *we* charge ye with enforcing the laws of Scotland and upholding *our* justice for the good of all the sundry people of Scotland, whether they be highlander, lowlander, or of the isles, noble born and the common," commanded the king in a stern tone, his sharp eyes unwavering from those of his nephew. "The justice of the king must needs be swift and furious, but always tempered with fairness, and when merited, a reasonable amount of mercy."

"All that ye command of yer servant he wi' do, to the maximum of his ability, so help me God," murmured Sir Sean.

"*We* judge that yer shoulders are broad, Sir Sean," Gregor continued, his words taking a lighter tone and giving a slight wink that only Sean could see. "Yer duty wi' be two fold, as a king must also hae a respected general to marshal and lead his armies upon the field of battle. In that capacity, arise Sean, *our* lord Marishal and provisional Marquess of North Northumbria!"

Following Gregor's command, a stunned Sean rose slowly to his feet. "Uncle—my king—I am most honoured by the trust ye hae placed in me. I wi' nae fail ye, sire," said the bewildered new marquess, color flushing his face a ruddy hue.

After the Warlord, become Marishal, had moved away to stand a respectful pace behind and to the right shoulder of the throne, King Gregor resumed his previous seat and proceeded to accept the vows of homage offered from each of the waiting lords, chiefs, and the ranking officers of the army. Once the oath taking was complete the king bade everyone present to have a seat around the long table, where he descended from the dais to join them at the head of that table. Soon a platoon of scurrying servants was busy as they laded the length of the table with platters of steaming food and pitchers of wine and ale for filling each plate and tankard.

Midmorning of the following day found the king standing at the top the broad stone steps of the keep facing the filled cobblestone courtyard packed with soldiers. It was raining again, as it did most every day during the Scottish spring. Sir Duncan and his fellow commander, Lord Kirkland, strode purposely through the growing puddles toward the steps from their position at the head of their gathered highlanders.

Returning from where he had been making his rounds atop the castle wall, Lord Sean spotted his king and bounded down from the interior steps of the wall by twos and joined Gregor. Together, the king and his marishal presented a bright splash of MacGregor tartan against the grim gray stone rising at their back.

The Marishal of Scotland stood at his king's right shoulder as the commanders approached from their front rank. A drummer suddenly began to beat a brisk drum roll and at that signal, the squire Setanta, from his place of honour stepped forward to join the advancing officers bearing with him the new battle standard. Bright as a cardinal in his color-bearer's surcoat over mail and leather, Setanta carried the banner unfurled for the first time, the sleek silk of it spilling down the saltire-cross tipped staff and billowed over his gauntleted hands.

Smiling up at the sight of the new banner, Duncan reached up and caught a handful of the silk as he, Lord Kirkland and Setanta continued to the foot of the broad keep steps, halting only when they reached the base, below the waiting king. Kneeling on the bottom-most step, Sir Duncan carefully held the standard clear of the damp ground as Setanta dipped the staff in respectful salute to King Gregor.

Approaching, all but unnoticed, a black cloak thrown over the purple finery of his office came Alistair Fletcher, the Archbishop of Edinburgh and a ranking member of the Royal Council. He had previously stood quietly behind the king, but now came down the stone steps to offer a blessing on the new specially made banner that would be borne into battle in King Gregor's name. The archbishop, whom had accompanied the royal messenger from the capital, paused for Lord Kirkland and Sir Duncan to kiss the amethyst worn on his left hand. Quietly the two commanders waited, with Duncan fixing his gaze upon the fluttering symbol of a crossed sword touching the trunk of a huge uprooted oak at the upper left hand corner of the banner. Situated to the upper right was another symbol that held Kirkland's attention: red stars scattered brightly over a field of blue and white which stretched down to form the tail of the pennon. Those stars represented the MacPherson's commitment to the coming venture, while the sword and oak denoted the equal commitment of the MacGregor clan. A regal, rampant lion in gold on scarlet at the center signified the support and sponsorship of Gregor as King of Scotland and their overlord.

Following in the wake of the high ranking priest, the king laid his hands briefly on the standard, and as he did so a hundred lances dipped in salute. The mass of handsome pennons of blue and silver nearly brushed the wet cobblestones as the knights showed their high regard.

"Bear ye with honour and fidelity this standard, knowing that it is blessed with the blessing of the Holy King of Heaven," intoned the archbishop, his eyes cast skyward as he invoked a title of the Most High God.

"Accept this banner with the heart felt blessing of yer earthly king as well; honour it always and bring honour to us all," Gregor commanded solemnly, helping Setanta to raise his burden aloft as the latter stood. "May the sight of these colors and symbols always strike terror into the hearts of all our enemies. And, may the Lord above grant all whom follow this proud banner the grace and power to shatter the ranks of those enemies with all bravery and valor."

"In the name of Christ, amen," sounded the prince of the church, signing the cross before the writhing banner.

The golden rampant lion danced in the damp breeze as Duncan released his hold on the fine silk. The deep azure and silver of the bold banner's tails cloaked his shoulder in a mantle of proud MacPherson stars. Gravely, Sir Duncan bowed and inclined his head to receive an unexpected gift from his king. The gilt chain of office was finely crafted of wide, hammered links of red-gold and seemed weightless as King Gregor placed it over his head and let it lay loosely about his neck. Flushing with pride, Duncan offered the king, who was his uncle, his joined hands in token of his homage.

"Accept from *our* hands this token and seal of the Earldom of Breadalbane, my faithful nephew," said Gregor, clasping Duncan's hands between his own after slipping the heavy signet onto his finger. "With this hereditary title and lands comes a burden of responsibility, and thus I command that ye be our Lord-General of our Northern Army. Rise, Lord Duncan," he said, favoring his younger nephew with a fleeting grin, and still clasping his hands the king thereby assisted in raising the man to his feet.

"Gladly wi' I do sae, my Liege, and solemnly swear to serve ye faithfully with honour. This I pledge to ye before all these witnesses and God above, upon mine honour and mine life," Duncan vowed, his voice suddenly gone quavery.

"MacSean!" suddenly shouted Duncan's men, rattling lances and broadswords against shields as he exchanged a formal kiss of loyalty with the king.

Moments later, once Lord Kirkland had also received the blessing of the king, both leaders, with Setanta bearing their war-banner between them, returned back to the waiting ranks of their highland army. Pausing briefly, the ennobled Duncan braced the standard against his hip while a proud young Setanta swung nimbly up into the saddle on his mean-spirited, blood bay. Concealing a good natured smirk, the lord-general watched as the spirited stallion screwed its head around to bite at the rider's hand and with a curse, Setanta slapped the horse sharply on its tender nose. Dancing abruptly sideways, the rebuked horse had to be smartly curbed before it could be maneuvered close enough for the squire to reclaim the offered battle standard.

Beyond the immediate spectacle of Setanta's misbehaving mount, the recently arrived Devlin, whom had traveled in the company of the archbishop, waited patiently on a more temperate rust colored mare that nearly matched his hair. Clad in brigandine and armed for battle the young men held the reins of Duncan's gray charger loosely in one hand, a suppressed grin twinkling in his clear blue eyes.

A smile bloomed on his freckled face as Duncan, his noble father, accepted the reins from his hand and mounted. Once astride his horse the lord-general raised a hand toward Gregor and Sean as those two men headed down the steps of the keep and made toward where their mounts were led out and steadied for them.

A modest escort, to be personally led by the king, was already assembled and waiting which would accompany Lord Duncan and his lieutenant-general, along with the newly commissioned Northern Army for the first few miles for their journey.

While one army prepared to depart, another was already assembling from a number of clan ships bobbing at anchor in the busy harbor. Some of the gathering troops would be disappointed as they received orders to remain behind to garrison Saddell Castle and neighboring Campbeltown. Other highlanders, already occupying the castle and commanded to hold the stronghold for the king, watched attentively as their king and his marishal fell in smoothly alongside Duncan, his son, and Kirkland. Together those leaders wheeled about their mounts and followed the MacGregor and MacPherson heavy cavalry squadrons, led by their officers, already beginning their exodus from the crowded courtyard and through the unbarred passage through the repaired gatehouse.

News of this departure was spread like wildfire throughout Campbeltown and did not take long to advance into the countryside and deep into the Campbell province. Even before King Gregor, and the army commanded by Lord-General Duncan MacSean, had ridden more than a few miles north a flurry of organized Campbell spies sped on fleet mountain ponies to carry report of it across the territory and to mountainous passes near Sloy and where their chief was purported to be with his forces.

*   *   *

The Alliance Army under the overall command of Duke Domeric Campbell were already converging on the lands about Kinlochlaich, preparing to meet the invading army that was moving northward. Campbell warriors and their rallying allies had recovered from the earlier defeat at the hands of the enemy, and now their picket lines were established and bright pavilions with many squad campfires sprang up like strange exotic flowers against the vibrant green of spring among the surrounding meadows. Flush with a burning hope to finish off his enemy, namely the hated MacGregors, and roust them forcibly from his lands, Duke Domeric campaigned among his troops and fanned their zeal. That zeal grew quickly as the duke's words found fertile ground in the ears of his men. Promises of support from allies and the additional military forces they were bringing came first, but then the exaggerated news of the capture and 'killings' of his noble kin, namely Heather and her brother Tolliver at Brodick on Arran Island. Clansmen swarmed in from the more northern strongholds-always on uneasy terms with their neighbors-and from lands as far east as the friendly provinces held by the Kennedys and the Hamiltons. By the time word reached them that Gregor was on the move, more than two thousand troops had arrived to reinforce the rebel duke and were camped before the walls of Kinlochlaich, northernmost stronghold in the Campbell territories.

Numbering among those reinforcements was a battalion of three hundred elite Steveno mercenaries of Clan Stevenson. Those war fighters were the princely gift from the duke's old friend, Lord Tearlach Stevenson, and a gesture meant to restore honour to his clan and redeem the poor showing his folk had exhibited at Glenorchy. In addition to his own elite warriors, Lord Stevenson had also been diligent in recruiting others to stand with the Campbells in opposition, to what he considered an upstart and illegal sovereign, in Gregor of Glenorchy. Numbering amount those he led to the rebel army and Domeric Campbell were such notorious border chiefs, particularly: Reginald MacNab, Sir Thomas Carleton, and Johnnie Armstrong of Gilnockie, each man the leader of bands of disparate men comprised of hardened brigands, bandits and reivers. These bandits did not offer their aid to the rebel duke out of the goodness of their hearts, but rather for the promise of booty and a signed contract from the Duke of Argyll, which agreed to pay them and their men on a weekly basis for the continued services they offered.

So fighting men had come to Kinlochlaich, for all the myriad reasons that have always drawn men to war, to stand against those who were fellow countrymen. Over a course of several days they gathered, and prepared to embark on an attempt that they hoped would overcome the, as of yet, uncrowned king, but if it failed would undoubtedly see the vast lands and estates of their benefactor forfeited along with that man's life.

On a day when the rays of the sun had fought constantly to shine through slim gaps between threatening gray clouds, the fiery glow of that burning orb had just reached its zenith. Beneath that silent war happening in the heavens, soldiers under the banner of the Duke of Argyll formed into straight, uniform ranks before the gates of Kinlochlaich and anxiously awaited the coming of the rebel duke, in which they had allied themselves with. Banners drifted bravely in the gentle breeze that swept from east through the passes from the mountains surrounding Ben Novis. Proud officers stood or waited calmly on snorting horses, exuding confidence before their men, knowing that all was at readiness for when the enemy would come and offer battle.

Just outside the yawning gates, beneath the shade of an open-sided blue and white pavilion situated between twin, ancient elms, a portable altar had been erected for the ceremony of the rite of blessing. Such as it was, the forthcoming ritual was not dissimilar in intent from those rites conducted at Saddell Castle outside of Campbeltown only days before with the Royal Army-for surely the Campbell's cause was the just one, and God was on their side. All of the gathered priests, assembled under the generous pavilion for mass, had told the rebel soldiers so the night before. The previous evening those priests had patiently made their way through the sizeable encampment and explained the rights of the Duke of Argyll for the crown, while they had stopped to hear the confession of any warrior that desired absolution on the eve of battle.

Scouts, posted miles to the south of Kinlochlaich, began bringing word on fast horses to the rebel leaders of their enemy's advance as that army marched north. Riding lathered mounts, the outriders returned and were pleased to see their fellow warriors all at the ready-standing tall and resolute in the face of invasion.

Sitting astride his powerful bay charger, at the head of the Grand Army of the Alliance, waited the Duke of Argyll. Close at his right hand sat Duke Domeric's chief aide and advisor, Lord Tearlach Stevenson. Of unusual swarthy complexion, particularly for one of such northern climes, Stevenson swiveled his head to gaze up and down the orderly ranks formed behind him. He inspected those troops with a perpetual scowl that made his darkly handsome face fierce with its intensity.

Lord Stevenson and his band of warriors were mercenaries in the truest form as they used the unbridled ambition of The Campbell, though the rebel duke did not realize the extent of that lord's purpose. Having nothing to lose, Stevenson had strategically put himself in a position to ride the duke's coattails toward the power he craved, but would never have been able to attain, if successful in this uprising against King Gregor. Likewise, if Duke Domeric were to fail in his bid for the crown, as a true soldier for hire he knew when it was time to retire from a hopeless fight and recoup his losses. The chief of Clan Stevenson was determined to not allow his kin to be pulled down in defeat with any ally or employer, no matter how powerful.

Turning back to face forward, Stevenson became aware of the duke studying him with a direct stare. "Yer Grace?" he asked, forcing his tone to be deferential, as he met the man's intent stare.

"Are ye my friend, Lawrence?" the duke asked directly. "Or are ye merely another man that hopes to profit from a situation I hae brought to pass?"

The chief flashed a charming smile at the older duke. "Can nae a friend seek to profit for his kin while assisting his kith?"

Domeric snorted and favored his ally a wan grin. "Well said. I leave the army in yer capable hands; it is time for me to attend the churchmen and graciously receive their blessing before Gregor makes his appearance," he explained briefly, turning the head of his horse toward the bright pavilion. "I wi' return shortly."

Situated just within the gates of Kinlochlaich the rebel lords, whom had answered the call to support the Campbell's claim to the Scottish crown, waited to escort the self-proclaimed Scottish royal family from the fortress to the pavilion that had been erected and prepared for the occasion. Once the army had gone to meet their enemies, only the Bishop of Glasgow, Angus Sutherland would remain behind with a modest garrison to attend their pretender's queen and await with hope the news of the MacGregor defeat.

Sequestered within the stone heart of Kinlochlaich Castle, Catherine Campbell, the would-be Queen of Scotland met with the closest of her family while awaiting her husband. Key advisors also attended the small gathering, for one final conference before facing their supporters and sending off an army that carried all their hopes. The chamber they met within was dark save for the burning torches hanging in holders all along the smooth stone walls. On this particular morning, the stark surroundings were a suitable setting for the heated conversation that was taking place.

"I still maintain that Gregor's rampage through the south, even if it include the taking of Inveraray, is nae nearly as great a threat as that of his lackey Duncan MacSean, who even now is marching with the intent of cutting the head off the snake, as it were, as he comes north," complained Reginald, Chief of Clan MacNab, glowering darkly as no one even deemed to respond to his outburst. Growling under his breath with disgust he began to restlessly pace the length of the stone chamber, his boots echoing hollowly on the tiled floor lying under the faded, woven rugs used to adorn the austere room. He would be the one truly leading the gathered forces under the nominal command of the Duke of Hamilton, and did not want anything to undermine his chances of victory.

"I can harry Gregor and I believe that I should be able to slow his rampage a great deal without offering a full scale battle and sustaining any major losses," Reginald went on, clasping his hands behind his back as he faced those sitting around the long, knotted pine table. "If I must, I wi' even lay waste to yer own lands in the south, if that's what it takes to slow him down and buy ye what time ye need.

"However, everything still boils down to one incontrovertible fact," he paused to bring emphasis to his next words. "In the end, if yer lot does nae or can nae stop Duncan MacSean's northern army before he can snare us between himself and Gregor's main army in the south under Sir Sean, we hae nae got a prayer to the master of heaven or that of hell to help us!"

A second prince of the church, but by no means less important than his colleague, sat near the right hand of the Duchess of Argyll at the council table and cast a glare over at the irreverent lowlander chief. His icy blue eyes smoldered with the indignant and dangerous ferocity of a fanatic, a look that was known to make the most stout man quaver with fear, as he twisted the amethyst studded bishop's ring on his left hand. His fierce look was a sure precursor of an impending tirade.

"Yer words tread tae dangerously close to blasphemy for the well being of yer soul, MacNab," hissed Henry Colquhoun, the Archbishop of Saint Andrews. "Ye would do well to yer wagging tongue before yer foolish words damn ye beyond redemption. As for yer constant whining and arguments, they hae long passed the point of tedium and I believe we hae better things to consider.

"Furthermore," continued Colquhoun, taking the bit between his teeth, "can ye nae speak of nothing but those thrice-damned spawn of the Sidhe, the jumped up generals MacSean? I'm sickened by the continual hearing of that bloody name!"

Caught in the effort of pulling on well used armor, MacNab gave one leather and steel buckle under his shoulder a final angry tug and shot the archbishop a sharp look. "Ach, for the love of God, can ye nae put aside yer blazing hatred for just a short time, Colquhoun? What if they are Sidhe? It matters nae a whit to me; the only thing about those men that concerns me is how well they command their warriors on the battlefield!" barked the fuming chief.

"Reginald is nae the only one who is becoming tedious, Yer Grace," finally spoke Catherine, her tone holding a note of rebuke. "Those 'jumped up generals' are nae less competent for yer constant berating on their parentage or the state of their souls. Hatred, I hae learned in the kirk, is also a sin, Henry."

Colquhoun turned to face the duchess with a look of startlement. "Ye speak as if the state of their souls was of nay consequence, Yer Highness. Their hellish race *is* the primary reason that I hae come here and offered yer husband my support, along with the aid of the ecclesiastical warriors I command," he countered frostily.

Arriving unseen and unannounced, Duke Domeric stepped into the chamber from where he had been attentively listening in the doorway. "The souls of Sean and Duncan MacSean," the duke spoke up as he entered, "is nae a factor I would use in determining how hard a fight they wi' give us when battle is again joined. Their cleverness, already proven at a dear price to us, along with intelligence, is what matter to me. Sir Sean has already proven his value in battle, and if his fair-haired brother is anything at all like Gregor's warlord, he wi' be a most formidable opponent," he elaborated for the benefit of everyone present. "Canniness in battle, combined with the soundness of their strategy and tactics are what matters the most about our enemies until this war is at an end and has been decided, whether in our favor, or in favor of our adversary.

"In my opinion, I believe we wi' triumph over Gregor and his followers, nay matter that some of them may be Sidhe; that is, if ye with yer kirk soldiers and those fine Steveno mercenaries of Lord Lawrence, do what they are here to do," said the duke, his stern gaze of admonishment stabbing out at the archbishop.

"They wi' do as I and Stevenson command," Colquhoun replied icily, "and that means ye can depend on them to wrest the crown out of Gregor's hands, sae long as the rest of the army under my Lord of Argyll does what *it* is required to do. Once Duncan MacSean has been lured into our trap, there wi' be nay escape, as God is my witness. I am nae the fool Lord Oliver proved to be," added Archbishop Colquhoun with a smirk.

"Watch yer flickering tongue, ye viper in churchman's clothes," Domeric snapped as his tone took a sudden sharp edge, "or *ye* wi' find nay escape as my dirk cuts it from yer vile, over-sized mouth!"

Ignoring the scowling duke's threat, Colquhoun retorted, "Do ye mean, like the way the younger MacSean invaded and breached all security on Arran Island and stole away yer dear niece, Heather, from right under the nose of yer dear brother?"

Uttering an inarticulate cry of rage and indignation, Domeric drew his long, ebony handled dirk and launched himself at the offending archbishop. The triumphant smirk that had risen to his thin lips was suddenly stillborn as Henry, too late, realized he had at last gone too far. Grabbed none too gently by the front of his pale blue and white surcoat, Henry found himself easily lifted off his feet and thrown with brutal force onto his back on the unyielding tile covered stone floor. The enraged duke followed through with the attack and bore down on the shocked man, driving a knee into his groin.

Shining, well-honed steel flashed as Domeric swept the sharp dirk toward his victim's throat with a guttural growl. Fear replaced shock in the archbishop's eyes as they widened at the menacing sight of the serrated edged blade moving steadily closer to his vulnerable neck. Although he fought desperately to hold back the weapon, Henry could not match his attacker's strength. Grasping the duke's thick wrist above the gleaming dirk with both hands until they turned white with effort, the frantic archbishop began to panic as his death stared him in the face, manifest in the form of the infuriated duke.

"Please, someone! I'm a priest! For God's sake, please help me-do nae let this madman kill me!" cried a frantic Henry, thrashing about wildly, seeking some way to escape from beneath the attacker whose weight bore down relentlessly on his chest. "My lady Catherine, I beg ye! Reginald! Please help me!"

The chief of MacNab snorted with contempt and turned away to warm his hands before the crackling flames dancing in the hearth.

Catherine, the duke's wife and hopeful queen, regarded the archbishop with a measure of disdain and sighed as if the whole episode bored her. "Oh, very well. Domeric! Really, ye must nae go about throttling anyone who happens to anger ye, however much they may deserve it. And Henry *is* a priest after all, albeit an arrogant and haughty one," she chided her husband, though her tone held a note of amusement. "Do let the poor man up, Domeric, before he dies of fright."

"Nay, Aunt, he *does* deserve a throttling!" interjected Richard, the youngest son of the Lord of Arran Island and the only one of that noble family to have escaped before the northern fortress had fallen. "I demand that this dog first give apology for the cold-hearted insults that he sae freely offered concerning the capture and probable slayings of my family!" cried the red-faced young man, the sharp tip of his unwavering broadsword pressed grim intent against the archbishop's neck. Murder was in his eyes as the sword drew a drop of scarlet blood from the man's dimpled flesh.

Catherine regarded her bereaved nephew for a moment, her wide hazel eyes filled with sympathy. "Sae be it, dear Richard, ye hae the right," she allowed. Turning to the prone archbishop, the duchess snapped, her words coming like a whipcord, "Do as my nephew demands, Henry Colquhoun; honour must be satisfied. Furthermore, if ye desire to save yer life and remain in service to the next king of this land, I strongly suggest ye beg *most humbly* the lad's forgiveness if ye would hae his mercy."

"As ye wish, my lady," croaked a sweating Henry, forcing his eyes to leave the sword above him and glance at the duchess. Too frightened to swallow, with the blade pushing harshly into his throat, he found his mouth gone dry as if it were full of cotton.

Blinking tears from his eyes, the gray haired archbishop returned his attention to the young man standing over him whom wielded the heavy claymore at his neck, before sliding a quick glance over to find the duke still glaring down at him.

"I meant nay offense to ye with my hasty words, my lords. Truly I spoke without first giving proper thought, for I deeply regret the untoward fall of yer noble kinsmen of Arran Island, to the bowels of my heart. And if they hae been foully murdered, I shall offer my fervent prayers for their souls may be at rest and find peace in the arms of our loving God," rasped Henry, his words seeming to carry genuine remorse.

"Yer apology is acceptable to me," grunted the duke with an approving nod, before turning to look at his nephew. "Do ye accept it as well, Richard?"

"Aye, Uncle," the lad affirmed grudgingly, removing the tip of his sword from Colquhoun's bloodied throat and slamming the blade back into the scabbard hanging at his side. "Just remember this, archbishop: yer vaunting ecclesiastical rank means nothing whatsoever to me. If ye ever speak disparagingly of our family again, neither yer rank nor yer God wi' be able to stop me from the vengeance I wi' deliver upon ye. God has already turned His back to me and now I do the same to Him," Richard grated bitterly, raking everyone in the room with his burning gaze. "Stand up; ye are forgiven this *one* time, Archbishop Colquhoun. I give ye yer life."

Ashen faced at the young man's deliberate blasphemy, even more so than from his close, personal brush with death, Henry climbed unsteadily to his feet and sketched a hasty bow to Duke Domeric. Offering a nod to Lady Catherine, the horrified priest fled the chamber without looking back, afraid of seeing the young lord stricken down for the blatant affront that had been so abhorrently made to the Almighty.

"Uncle," Richard began once the bishop had gone, "I wish to be with the forces that wi' be going into battle with Duncan MacSean. I want the coward's blood, regardless of what yer pet bishop may hae in store for him. The rightful claim of blood debt is mine and I respectfully demand it."

Duke Domeric appeared to consider the appeal for a moment, but shook his head in denial. "Nay, I'm sorry, Richard, but I can nae allow it. Ye wi' ride with The MacNab, to harry the main MacGregor force, as one of his officers," he said, holding up a hand to forestall the young man's argument. "If I brought ye along with my army, ye might end up losing yer head and what good judgment ye hae, in the pursuit of personal vengeance and jeopardize the overall success of our mission.

"I promise ye that he shall be dealt with, Richard," added the duke. "And, if it is within my power, I wi' hae that man captured sae that ye may draw his blood yerself and hae yer share of justice."

Later in the day, once he was sure that the fiery young Campbell lord was absent, Colquhoun ventured forth from his quarters to return to the conference chamber. He had arrived within only minutes before he heard a liveried page announce the arrival of his collegial associates: Archbishops Angus Sutherland and Randolph Campbell. Both of those churchmen entered in dignified solemnity, wearing a long purple cope over their priestly vestments. Elderly Sutherland looked venerable as ever and frail, as he leaned on the supporting arm of his one-time student and protégée, though still stately in the full panoply of his archbishop's regalia. Leading the elderly prince of the church forward, Randolph looked no less regal for his young age, in his own stately raiment of purple.

Leaving Sutherland in Colquhoun's respectful care, Randolph stepped forward and bowed over Duke Domeric's gnarled hand before moving to bestow a familiar kiss on his aunt's cheek. The young bishop's red-gold hair blazed like fire as he passed into the pool of sunlight shining upon the duchess from a high, narrow window. He appeared to take no notice as he was received with resentful glances cast his way by Colquhoun or the rebel chief of MacNab, once he moved back to offer an arm to his mentor. Accepting the arm of the younger man, whom he regarded like a son, Sutherland shuffled forward to stand before his host and would be king.

"Yer Highness," wheezed Sutherland, consumption making a bubbling noise from his lungs as he sketched a slow, solemn bow. Straightening, the senior archbishop offered his amethyst graced hand to be kissed and waited patiently until the duke had done so. "The procession is assembled and prepared to escort ye and yer queen to the leave taking ceremony. Yer loyal subjects await ye."

Flashing a withering glance in Colquhoun's direction, Domeric noted with grim pleasure that bishop's discomfort, as he rose from his throne-like chair and offered his arm to his wife and soon to be queen. "Thank ye, Archbishop Sutherland. We are quite ready, if ye would be sae kind as to lead-"

"Excuse me, dearest husband," interrupted Catherine, a little smile playing at the curve of her lips, "I believe that ye are forgetting something of some importance.

Domeric glanced quizzically down at his lovely wife's twinkling hazel eyes. She winked at him. "A surprise, my love." Turning from the wondering duke, Catherine cast her gaze about the chamber until her eyes alighted upon a particular knight. Nodding significantly, she commanded, "It is time; bring them forward."

A moment later as Catherine unconsciously re-adjusted the fine silk veil of white that wrapped her coiffured hair, the designated knight approached with a large, intricately carved, mahogany casket. Dropping gracefully to both knees, the knight whom was also the lady's personal protector opened the rectangular box and lifted it up for the couple to behold the contents.

Domeric's eyes widened in astonishment before raising eyebrows at his pleased wife. A soft peal of laughter escaped her lips as she reached into the box and lifted out a crown that had lain nestled upon a pillow of plush scarlet velvet. Suppressing a sigh of appreciation at the crowning jewel's workmanship, Catherine passed it to the patiently waiting, elderly archbishop. The golden circlet gleamed in the rays of the sun and bright colors flashed from the myriad of emeralds, rubies, and sapphires that liberally studded it as the crown rested in the churchman's hands. Shining brightest of all was the incredible diamond supported at the pinnacle of the dazzling crown; it had been costly, to be sure, but never had the duchess seen anything so magnificent. Reaching into the casket once more she pulled forth another crown, somewhat smaller and more modest than the first, but still breathtaking as delicate chains of platinum held an array of emeralds, each the size of a generous pearl, which would drape across her smooth forehead. This crown was given into the keeping of a stunned Randolph.

The ceremony that followed was simple but dignified as Angus Sutherland, the Archbishop of Cromarty, crowned Domeric and Catherine as king and queen of Scotland, in defiance of the dictates issued from the Royal Council.

For his part, Domeric felt odd with the unfamiliar weight resting on his head as he settled the heavy crown into place. Such did not seem the case with his wife as the delicate circlet rested gently on her head, centered above her finely sculpted eyebrows, the golden chains held more than a score of dark green emeralds. The crown seemed to transform Catherine from her normal self, endowing her lovely, though hollowed out features with a regal beauty and an irrefutable stateliness.

In an instant, that seemed to stretch for an unaccountable amount of time, Catherine appeared every inch a queen and much more dignified than Domeric felt for his part. She caught her husband gazing raptly at her and smiled warmly up into his dark adoring eyes. Sitting side by side before a modest group of intimates the couple reached for the other's hand, and beamed with a love for each other that made the rest of room seem to fade from awareness. Everyone assembled in the chamber before them, without exception, sank to their knees. Even Colquhoun gave homage, although he was loath to do so-not from any misgivings, but rather from stubborn pride.

At last Domeric cleared his throat and turned his stare to those gathered before his throne. "Even as I hae ruled over my beloved Clan Campbell, sae shall I rule sovereign over the whole of Scotland with my royal wife and queen. Sae do I swear it and sae shall it be, as long as I live! By God do I swear this oath!" exclaimed Domeric, standing and raising up his queen. Holding her slim fingers gently in his calloused ones, the rebel king kissed her hand before turning it over to intimately kiss the smooth palm.

"All hail the king and queen," wheezed Sutherland with approval, words that were quickly echoed by Randolph and then, more slowly by a thoughtful and much more restrained Henry Colquhoun.

Once the rebel rulers had received the sworn homage of their subjects gathered immediately within the chamber, Domeric escorted his lady wife from behind closed doors, the three high ranking clerics preceding them. Following behind came

Richard along with several clan chiefs that were allied with the Campbells, as well as other leaders that had pledged their support in exchange for payment. Among those men following behind and bringing up the rear, muttering buzzed as they complained about having to follow a 'king' that trailed behind the overly proud and arrogant Archbishop Colquhoun.

Chapter Six

The long days of summer stretched into weeks which quickly brought home the rigors and hardships of a protracted war. No one was spared from the privation and fatigue which came from little sleep and even less comforts, while being destitute of the company of wife and children. On those counts, the royal and highland troops following King Gregor were no different from those rebels that followed Domeric Campbell and were pledged to his service.

Being fully aware that a convergence of King Gregor's northern and southern Royal Armies, at a time of their own accord, could very likely spell the beginning of the end to their lord's claim to the Scottish throne, the commanders of the Campbell Alliance proceeded with alacrity their agreed upon campaign of harassment and ambush.

The force under the command of Reginald MacNab, with the Duke of Argyll's nephew Richard in tow, had marched into the southern Campbell territories weeks ago and now moved at random throughout the lands surrounding Stirling. Their apparently haphazard tactics continued to foil any attempts of Gregor and his army to engage them in a true battle, while they harried the royal army and offered nothing but scorched earth to occupy along with fruitless foraging. In this way, and according to the plans that had been laid out in advance, MacNab effectively slowed the king's army to a crawl.

Meanwhile, further north in the Lochaber region, the self-styled King Domeric, leading the remainder of his Alliance forces which included: a regiment of heavily armed warrior-monks, along with temple knights, as well as the elite Steveno mercenaries that Lord Stevenson had brought to the rebel banner. All of these veteran troops at his beck and call, the pretender to the throne played a cat and mouse game among the highlands of his northern territory. Relying on expertly conducted maneuvers and rapid movements, Campbell and his officers, particularly Colquhoun, Stevenson, and Hamilton, eventually hoped to lure the army of Duncan MacSean, and especially that general himself, into their carefully planned trap.

*   *   *

From the very first encounter with the forces flying the Campbell colors, events had taken place that Marishal MacSean had not expected, considering his past experience with the duke's generals. The initial encounters puzzled Gregor more than anything else and left him shaking his head with a deeply furrowed brow. Try as he might, the king could not fathom Domeric's motivation in all but abandoning much of his lands while burning valuable crops in the field.

"I had fully expected Domeric to confront me long before now. Nae only that, but I had thought we would hae met a more traditional resistance from gathering clansmen, especially here in the heart of long held Campbell territory," he confided one dismal day to his Marishal. A troubled frown creased the king's sweaty brow, having just a short time ago personally aided in repelling yet another nighttime raid by Campbells that relied on quick hit and run attacks on the periphery of the camp. "These small raids are nothing but a nuisance and easily countered. Even were Domeric afraid to commit his army to another battle, I expected more from independent highland bands, but we hae never seen more than a hundred warriors or sae at any given time," Gregor shook his head, a sure sign of growing frustration. "I find myself beginning to wonder whether we are dealing with an army at all. A growing fear for Duncan has begun to gnaw within me as well, Sean; what if yer brother is facing the full brunt of Domeric's might?"

Marishal Sean MacSean, the fearless and sometimes frightening warlord to the highland troops of his command and to those of the rebel duke, clamped his teeth fiercely together as he watched a light cavalry sergeant forced to put down a brutally wounded chestnut mare. The horse was only one of nearly a dozen mounts deliberately hamstrung by the enemy raiding party during the most recent skirmish. He stifled a grimace as a spray of blood fountained black in the torchlight while Barak, his son and personal page, buried his young tear-streaked face unabashedly into his side.

Sean nodded to his uncle, his own thoughts darkly mirroring those of Gregor, but with the added insight to realize just what the enemy was doing. "I agree with ye for the most part, Uncle. The real army is *nae* here, but there are ample forces abroad and nearby tae I should think, that are devoted to harry our advance without engaging in a real battle. They can nae give battle because they ken we would annihilate them," Sir Sean muttered darkly, comforting the lad with a hand stroking his silken gold hair. "Each new skirmish has shown me signs of different leadership and none of them with the generalship of the duke's usual staff of able commanders. At the very least, Domeric has divided his army into at least two parts and maybe more; the ones we seem to be encountering are a fast and highly mobile raiding warband. Hoping to slow and wear us down with numerous guerrilla raids. It's a typical borderer tactic that typically is used against the English, but always highly effective unless it is used on an opponent that is familiar with countering it," added the blonde haired Marishal.

"Sire! My Lord!" shouted Shane, one of King Gregor's personal squires, as he approached the conferring leaders at a hasty trot. "Lord Donald commanded me inform ye that he has taken a prisoner, but that ye should hurry if ye want to wring any particular information from him. It is highly unlikely that the captive wi' live much longer, as he is grievously wounded and the surgeons can do nothing!"

They followed behind young Shane at a quick trot as he led them beside an old weathered tent where one harried looking battle surgeon was working inside, spattered blood staining his arms up the elbows, a look of resignation in his shading his eyes. The enemy raider lay gasping for breath, on the back of a short, flat-bedded supply wagon, pale and shaking from loss of blood. Clothed in worn leathers along with his clan plaid, his tunic was sliced open and a bandage was dark with severe bleeding. His body was rigid with agony as his hands clawed desperately at the wad of blood soaked bandage which the surgeon was trying to keep pressed to the gaping wound in his belly. The clansman moaned piteously through clenched teeth and he seemed to be crying out distraughtly for his mother.

Gregor and Sean did not push forward but watched silently from a vantage point out of the other's way as Archbishop Fletcher knelt at the man's head and gravely made the sign of the cross upon the dying raider's forehead with blessed oil from a bottle kept stowed within his wide sleeved bishop's frock. Tight-lipped, Fletcher slowly drew back and shook his head with a forlorn sigh before quietly chanting a litany in Latin.

Walking quietly up to the wagon and climbing onto the back, Gregor cautiously sank to his knees beside the mortally wounded man and laid his hands on the stricken warrior's pallid forehead. Gently he lifted the closed eyelids with his calloused thumbs to peer at a pair of unevenly dilated pupils. Clucking softly the king shook his head with a sigh of resignation and allowed the eyelids to close.

"He's nae going to make it, Sire," belatedly offered the gore spattered surgeon, Father Drummond, as he moved to adroitly catch the wounded man's suddenly flailing arms by the wrists and restraining them as Lord Sean crouched opposite his king.

Sean caught his uncle's eye and raised his eyebrows in mute question. The king's answer was a grimace followed swiftly by a sharp nod of his head.

Bracing himself, the king's Marishal slid one hand underneath the blood saturated bandage while his other slipped smoothly inside the front of the unlaced leather jerkin to check for the rhythm of the weakly beating heart. The heart raced like that of a frightened rabbit, but the pulse was so shallow as to do the man no good.

The warrior's futile struggles were beginning to diminish even as his condition deteriorated with every thready heartbeat. The pulse of life blood was hot between Sean's fingers, and bright crimson, as the patient labored even harder to draw air into his lungs; he had lost so much blood already that the Marishal wondered how the man had lasted as long as he had. In one last desperate attempt to at least slow the inevitable, Sean forced his hand deep into the wound, clear to the knuckles, to halt the flow of blood. Even as he did so, he knew the act was pointless.

"It's nae good, Sean. He's going," Gregor whispered in resignation and closed his eyes sadly. Seconds later the stricken warrior sighed softly, twitched, and then lay still. At the end the man had withdrawn from the pain racking him, and now his face was relaxed and appeared to be at peace.

"Sae," Gregor muttered darkly, his low pitched voice was taut and just a little indignant as he jumped from the wagon and peered up at his nephew. "As ye can see, this lad's plaid is nae the Campbell, nor is it any that I can readily identify; perhaps ye may ken it, ye hae more experience among the other clans than I do. Aye?"

"Aye, Sire," admitted the scowling Marishal MacSean. "It is the MacLaren. They're a border clan that is allied loosely with the Hamiltons."

Gregor hawked noisily and spat a thick wad of phlegm onto the ground in a sign of disgust. "MacLaren this time. Ach, how many more clans wi' betray their king to stand and fight for the bloody Campbells before this is done with?"

Sighing resignedly, Lord Sean pulled his blood drenched hands slowly from the dead man's wounds. The coppery stench of gore and loosened bowels made the general particularly grateful for the basin of clean water and towel offered him by the surgeon, as he hopped from the rear of the wagon.

"Ye are nae really all that surprised about it are ye, my King? The Duke of Argyll is a wealthy man, and he was the coin and influence at his disposal to surely promise many special favors to anyone that wi' throw in with him and support his preposterous claims toward yer throne," snorted the Marishal. Wrinkling his nose at the smell clinging to him, he mechanically washed his gory hands clean, and with a force of will relaxed his clenched jaw and recomposed his thoughts. "All of this goes towards explaining my idea about the raiding tactics and altering leadership I wondered about."

Abruptly the MacDonald chief came to Gregor's side and crouched down beside the king with a loud creak of protesting leather. "Cursed new leathers, wi' they never get broken in?" Lord Donald growled, mostly to himself. Without ceremony he suddenly held out a ragged piece of torn and bloodstained tartan. "Here's another token left behind by the raiders that ye may hae, Gregor. Do ye recognize the pattern? Nay? How about ye, Sean?" he asked gruffly.

At the Marishal's affirming nod, Lord Donald grimaced and retrieved the bloody plaid to toss contemptuously over the dead enemy soldier's face. "MacNab. Reginald is their chief, and he is a bloody bastard, of that ye can be sure. Better yet, one of my scouts saw someone that he swears was Johnnie Armstrong of Gilnockie! All these things tie together my belief that Domeric Campbell has been recruiting a great bunch of bloody outlaws into his camp!"

"More likely, Archbishop Colquhoun has been recruiting them for him; he has ever held a grudge against our clan, nae to mention his unhealthy hatred toward Sean and his brother Duncan," Gregor retorted, climbing wearily to his feet. "He harbors a belief that they are evil and damned for their diluted Sidhe bloodlines, or some such shite. Besides all that, Colquhoun and that Lord Stevenson fellow hae always been like two feathers plucked from the same bird in their dealing with those of an unsavory sort. Henry has never liked to get his priestly hands dirty, sae he *would* hire this bunch of rogues and bandits, and all those others like Armstrong, who love to."

Sir Sean said nothing, keeping his own council, as he finished drying his hands, and laid the damp towel over the arm of an awaiting attendant. Nodding his thanks to the man, the Marishal silently withdrew and returned to his tent.

Later, once most of the camp had calmed down and again retired for the night, Lord Sean summoned a trusted retainer to attend him. Issuing orders to the man to act as his special courier he sent the clansman to relay a sealed letter which contained his and Gregor's growing suspicions to Duncan in the north, where his brother was commanding the king's Northern Royal Army.

It turned out to be several days later when Duncan took receipt of the letter from his older brother, and was able to read Sean's penned warning. It read: *'Greetings to ye Duncan; Our Uncle and I begin to hae misgivings about Duke Domeric's true intentions and suspect that the main Campbell army is nae in the south at all. To this point, all the action we hae encountered sae far has been skirmishes by warbands of nae more than a hundred warriors at any one time. I surmise it is by design, knowing of their weakness, they dare nae strike us in the open, but seek to hinder our movement and wound us in whatever manner they may. The duke may very well hae his main strength waiting in the north to seek ye out and annihilate yer command while beyond the reach of our support, sae beware. Duke Domeric is a wily and cunning adversary and wi' hae a plan thought out and prepared in advance; he surely knows that he would be hard pressed to win any type of victory on the battlefield should our armies converge on whatever position that he might hold, and pinch his forces between the two of ours. Until I see ye: be cautious and be well, and may Christ and the Morrigan keep ye.*

Yer Loving Brother,
Sean

The same day that Duncan received that letter urging for caution, the growing uncertainty of the strategic situation in the southern Campbell territories was beginning to fray tempers as frustration gnawed at soldiers and leaders alike. An army, no matter how well trained and motivated, could not defeat its enemy if that enemy refused to fight. The Marishal soon realized that new tactics would be called for in order to remedy the unsatisfactory strategic state of affairs that currently persisted.

"How can my army hope to defeat an enemy that we can nae bloody see, let alone fight?" the irritated king complained bitterly. This came as he and his commanders led the royal forces in a route that skirted the mountains west of Sloy and marched north, even as they continued to be beleaguered by the enemy's guerrilla attacks. "Having four thousand and more troops does nae do us any bloody good when we are unable to use more than a few hundred at a time!"

The scorched-earth policy that the bleeding Campbells hae been using is nae reassuring either; despite the fact that we hae penetrated deep within Duke Domeric's province, the burning of all foodstuffs and fields has nae diminished, but instead the destruction has become more complete, with each additional step we take into his lands, Gregor considered darkly. *He willingly beggars his own folk to hinder me.*

"We hae nay real provisioning problems just yet," offered General MacReady, seeming to read the king's mind. "However, if this continues for much longer, there wi' be," the supply officer added, giving his report at the staff meeting one evening that was attended by King Gregor's key commanders whom were gathered around a fire blazing outside the royal pavilion. "As long as decent forage can be found to supplement what provender we hae remaining for the horses, we can feed them and our lads until about midsummer, but nay longer. With an army of this size we move slow enough, but with the constant harassment we tread that much more sluggishly. Sire, if ye wi' pardon my opinion, would it nae be better if we steal a lesson from our enterprising enemies and break into smaller and more manageable warbands? In this part of the highlands could we nae do sae with little danger and increase our effectiveness?" speculated the rather portly quartermaster, his tone inquisitive.

Marishal MacSean nodded his head approvingly as he regarded the usually quiet officer. With little further debate, the general staff agreed to the suggestion and Gregor was swift to concur with the decision.

Before dawn arrived the following morning the royal army was divided up among four semi-autonomous field commanders: lords: Donald, Fraser, and MacLean, and the Marishal MacSean-with the king riding in the latter's warband. The day passed without event and by late in the afternoon the warbands had dispersed. Stretching out across the line of advance, the warbands placed a distance of a couple hours between each other; close enough to be supportive, but spaced apart so as to cover a much larger front while having an independent area in which to forage. A regular relay of couriers kept each unit in contact with the others while keeping all apprised of any new developments. The new tactics earned dividends right away as skirmishes with the formerly phantom-like enemy began to yield more definite and positive results, while at the same time producing more desperate counter measures from the raiding enemy.

"I dare say, we wi' be seeing a lot more of this and worse, Sire," said the Marishal to his fiercely scowling monarch, as they rode together through the devastation. Morning had dawned hot and sultry, particularly by highland standards where on the very hottest of summer days scarcely exceeded seventy degrees Fahrenheit. Not yet noon, the swelter seemed determined to easily overtop that figure, and it was that, at least in fair measure, that was behind the ill humor of many, including their king.

Gregor and his Marishal were currently riding a less burned track through yet another smoldering field of scorched grain, obviously razed to keep it from supplying the Scottish King's advancing army. Cautiously approaching the outskirts of what once had been a seemingly prosperous village of respectable size, the blackened stubble of those fields still smoked to either side of them and the army. Black smoke as well curled into the mountain air from beyond soot smudged walls and likewise from the modest and thatch roofed cottages within the village.

"By Lugh! This is the worst we hae seen sae far," growled Gregor, as he agitatedly slapped his leather gauntlets against one armored thigh. His effort to try and vent some of his prodigiously dark temper did little good as the proper target for it was not yet within his grasp. Turning suddenly he looked directly into the face of his Marishal and pitching his voice low, he spat, "With the Raven as my witness, Domeric Campbell wi' receive little mercy from me; nay, nae a lord who would do thus to his own people. The only mercy he wi' get from me is a quick death. His head is forfeit."

"Aye, it shall be as ye command it," replied Lord Sean, "but the traditional way of dealing with a treasonous rebel is to hae him hung by the neck like a common criminal. If that rebel should also be a lord of the realm, the sentence is more harsh because of the elevated station abused during the treason; in such cases the offender is to hae his entrails drawn from his belly and quartered while he hangs and remains alive. I hae found written in some of our histories where especially evil prisoners even had their intestines roasted by hot coals on a brazier before their very eyes."

"Merciful Christ, Sean! That's ghastly!" exclaimed Gregor, his face going a shade or two more pale and crossing himself, while forgetting a measure of his pent up wrath. "Domeric is a cold hearted bastard, but he need nae fear that last penalty as least. Ye are telling me that a Scottish king actually used such a method on someone?"

"Nay. Nay Scot, though the penalty is legally allowed," Sean admitted. A grim smile tugging at his lips, he added, "However, one of our kings used worse, some even I could nae condone, they were sae bloodthirsty. Curdle my stomach they do."

"Well, if they can curdle *yer* stomach, I would rather nae ken what *they* were!"

"A wise decision, Sire. Food stores are in tae short supply to waste them by throwing them up on the ground," agreed Sean, smoothing his red-gold mustaches with his fingers in order to conceal an amused smile.

They had been slowly advancing through enemy territory for the past week and a half, and although every field the royal army had come across had been put to the torch, the terrible devastation had worsened. No longer was the destruction confined to those fields and the occasional ransacked storehouse as in the beginning. Now that desolation was being extended to the very citizenry of the Duke of Argyll's own clan. Each new day found Gregor's allied warbands passing through more gutted villages and small towns. Populated by ever more pitiful refugees-innocent commoners, the ultimate losers in any war, as they tried to carry on with their lives once both sides in the clan's conflict had gone on their way. Those destitute folk cared little for what king might sit on the throne, so long as they and their children could rebuild their lives unmolested by anyone and without the dread of their families starving in an unforgiving land.

King Gregor hid his anguish behind a stony mask, but could not help feeling the accusing eyes of the common folk following him as he and his Marishal rode with a small lead escort into the burned village. To the front, Setanta led the way, bearing the bright banner of his king, which drew many glares as they rode through while staying on the cleared dirt thoroughfare. One old highland man, braver than most, stepped aside as the banner—bearer passed and spat in the dirt just ahead of the squire's horse. The mounted young warrior stiffened in outrage, but mastered his anger and rode on, refusing to turn and give vent to the disrespect shown the king's standard.

For security sake, a light cavalry unit had already swept through, in advance of Gregor and his party, assuring that the area was safe for the king. No enemy stragglers had been found within the village, just those hardy folk that refused to leave and would remain to stubbornly rebuild their burned homes.

Even now, the townspeople were beginning to appear more abundantly, standing in doorways and behind shattered windows. Another bold old man, leaning heavily on a cane, hobbled to the edge of his porch. His eyes were hard and filled with hate as he saw the royal banner; squinting up at the riders following that flag he hawked contemptuously and dared any to rebuke him with a fierce glare. One spiteful-eyed woman with a dirty infant sucking at her bare bosom glared out at Gregor from the sheltering doorway of a cottage, which had lost most of its roof to one of the torches thrown by the heartless raiders. Regarding her with an expression of pity on his proud face, the king continued on even as she hissed venomously at him while offering his party a rude gesture.

Sick at heart, Gregor shook his head and lowered his eyes in helpless shame as he pondered about how noblemen could behave so foully toward those that depended on them for help and safety. He only wished that there were some way besides war that could keep the peace in his recently inherited kingdom.

"I think that perhaps this is the worst part of war," Gregor murmured, glancing aside at his nephew, as they allowed their battle chargers to pick the best path through the narrow, rutted thoroughfare. "Why is it that the simple folk, the salt of the earth, always hae to suffer most for the folly of their masters?"

The Marishal snorted with contempt. "These folk are nae suffering for the folly of their master; they're suffering *because* of it!" he exclaimed.

"However, such has ever been the grim and constant trapping of war since time immemorial, Sire," the king's nephew quietly added. "If we were sae desperate, as the bloody Campbells apparently are becoming, we might also be forced to such measures, though I hope that I might be more compassionate-" Suddenly he stiffened, his words faltering in his throat as he stood tall in his stirrups to peer keenly ahead.

"What's wrong, Sean?" asked Gregor with a worried frown, following the line of his nephew's gaze.

Near the end of the street, in which the king's party currently rode upon, a score of the king's light cavalry mounts waited in a group near the foot of a set of steps which led up to the charred and blackened entrance of the village's modest kirk. The place of worship had obviously been recently vandalized; the main structure had been erected of rough cut stone that had been painstakingly white-washed, but now were blackened by soot. The surrounding wall, though tall enough, had been constructed more for privacy more than anything else and never designed for true defense. That ineffectual wall had been breached in several places; its wrought iron gate, decorated with intricate Celtic knot work and other designs, hung cockeyed from it's battered and twisted hinges. Beyond the ruined gate and broken down walls, black smoke curled lazily upward to mar the lovely blue and virtually cloudless sky from the smoldering kirk as well as from parts of the adjoining nunnery.

"I do nae like the looks of that," Lord Sean muttered darkly, indicating ahead with a finger towards the kirk and the several agitated-looking cavalrymen which had emerged from a shattered, private side door of the nunnery. Even from their considerable distance away, the king and his Marishal could hear the enraged, red-faced troopers shouting with indignation, but could not make out the actual words.

Simultaneously, King Gregor and Lord Sean kicked spurs to their mount's flanks and moved out at a brisk trot. Passing to either side of a startled Setanta and the banner he proudly bore, the two leaders clattered on ahead with the royal escort trailing closely behind and loosening swords within their scabbards in case they might be needed.

Gathering within the compound, not far from where they had exited the nunnery, the cavalry troopers had regained some semblance of composure by the time Gregor's party pulled up within the kirk's ruined walls. Although the cavalrymen were no longer shouting, the faces of those warriors, which turned to acknowledge and salute the king and their marishal's arrival, were tight jawed with bleak, hooded eyes. One of the younger lads staggered and dropped to his knees, bowing his bared head close to the singed grass and preparing to be sick at what he had witnessed. At the same time, the troop officer in command raised his scowling and outraged face toward his general, as Lord Sean reined to a halt beside the king. Grabbing at the halter of the general's horse, to keep from getting trampled as he approached, the lieutenant adroitly hopped back from the steel shod hooves. The close call served to snap the officer out of the rage that had literally shook through his body at what he had beheld inside the building.

Stumbling up behind the cavalry officer, his face tinged a sickly green, the king's squire Shane came forward to greet his royal master. The king's personal squire looked as if he could cheerfully have killed the first person who dared cross him, now that he had thrown up the contents of his stomach.

"Well do nae just stand there, Lieutenant! What's happened here that has ye all sae agitated?" Sean Lord Northumbria demanded, swinging down from his tall mount and pulling off his plumed helmet.

The grizzled cavalry officer nodded his head, handing off the reins of the Marishal's horse to one of his men, while steadying the king's mount as Gregor slid out of the saddle as well, before turning his undivided attention to the glowering general.

"Sair," he said, offering a sharp salute with a fist smacking his chest plate. "It was a dastardly raid led by the traitor Reginald

MacNab. I'm sure he is very proud of himself right now-he and his bloody men did a right thorough job against a group of helpless priests, monks, and nuns," reported the lieutenant, a grimace twisting his broad face. "This was nae just a kirk. There is a nunnery here also, and housed several residential sisters, along with several more novices here in training or retreat, that hae nae yet taken vows. Some of those poor lasses wi' never hae the opportunity to do sae now; what else is there to say? The cold-hearted bastards did nae just pillage the kirk of its gold and relics, which is bad enough, but they also-" he swallowed suddenly. "Well, sair, ye wi' hae to come and see for yerself; I hae nae the words to describe the barbarity of what has taken place here," he explained indignantly.

"How is it that ye ken it was MacNab, Lieutenant?" Gregor demanded, removing his helmet and pushing back the mail coif from his sweaty forehead.

By the king's calm tone and casual way in which he cradled the helm under his arm, Sean surmised that the foul implications had not yet become obvious to his uncle. That Gregor had little experience with the evil that men were capable of committing under the excuse of war was becoming obvious, as the Marishal decided it wise to keep his own council for the time being. Redirecting his attention to the agitated officer, MacSean waited with interest for the man to answer the king's query.

"Ach, it was MacNab all right, Sire," Lieutenant MacHenry assured him archly, unveiled contempt for the very name so thick in his voice that Lord Sean could almost taste it on his tongue. "The poor sisters here do nae ken a bloody lick about coats of arms or devices and such, but one of the surviving monks from the kirk was able to offer me a good description of a man who seemed to him to be in command. The likeness proved to me that it was nay other than the thrice damned MacNab!" He gave his head a sudden shake and took a deep breath. "I'm sorry, Sire; I ken that these things happen in war, but I hae a family tae and can nae ever seem to get used to it. By God, it is awful, and the dogs that hae done this must be hunted down and punished!"

"What things?" Gregor demanded, agitation edging into his voice. "Murder and pillage, aye, they shall be held to account for those things; but ye are right, those are a dirty business which happens in war. Ye, however, seem to be referring to something else, sae do nae mince words with me and spit it out!" The king's tone was growing angry, not wanting to believe what he was starting to realize on his own, though he still needed to hear the truth. "Well? What is it ye are nae telling me?"

The chastised cavalry officer looked at his king with a wounded expression. "Sire, forgive me, but the raiders, they raped the sisters *and* the novices," MacHenry whispered hoarsely, his mind's eye returning the brutal vision and sounds he had witnessed to full bloom, and the haunted expression in his brown eyes was sobering. "They even killed some of the women after taking their vile pleasures of them.

"MacNab and his men did nae stop with defiling the sisters, but they went on to desecrate the kirk! The bloody bastards forced some of the women into the kirk and there rutted with them in the very aisles," MacHenry went on in a blunt and measured tone, an undying outrage smoldering in his deep-set eyes. "Some damned soul among them even had the audacity to rip the holy crucifix from above the altar and, well, it was plunged between the legs of one poor aged nun!"

The lieutenant paused for a second, as the king went suddenly pale, and shrugged with unabashed Highland frankness, although the haunted look in his green eyes spoke eloquently of the effect the sight had inflicted on him. "Ye demanded to be told, Sire, and there are nay pretty words nor any easier way of telling ye. This is an ugly business with nothing appealing or noble about it, Sire, nor about any man who would perform such atrocities. If ye hae never seen something like this before," he paused again, grimly shaking his head, "well, then I guess it is probably time ye did! Meaning nay disrespect, Sire, but ye should ken at first hand the kind of animals ye're dealing with.

"Although I surely hae nay reason to hae any love for Duke Domeric, I'd bet a season's wages that he would hae a cow if he knew what has happened here!" offered the officer. "This sort of behavior does nothing but alienate his own clans folk."

"Aye, ye are probably correct in yer opinion, Lieutenant," Gregor replied coolly. "However, Duke Domeric is the one who hired these villains, and therefore he is fully responsible for them and whatever actions they take! He shares their sins in my eyes and wi' share in whatever form *our* high justice demands!"

MacHenry's outraged explanation left little doubt in the Warlord's mind about what they could expect to find within the gutted kirk and the nunnery. Tightly leashing his own kindled temper, he passed off to one of the royal escort his sturdy helmet with its telltale coronet of rank, and bade the grim-faced Gregor to do the same. Composing his own face into a mask of indifference, MacSean held that façade in place as if his face were chiseled from a piece of unyielding granite.

Reconciled to what they were about to observe firsthand, the king and his faithful warlord shouldered their way past the shaken cavalry officer and the still green-tinged Shane to climb up the littered stone steps, which were covered with soot and the debris of shattered stained glass windows and chunks of fallen stone.

As they neared the ruined entrance, the distraught cries of the injured, bereft and those brutally traumatized could be heard from within the violated sanctuary; the piteous sounds emerging from within traveled clearly on the still and breezeless heat of mid-day and could easily be heard out in the small courtyard. Along with that distressing sound, mingled the stench of smoke, excrement, and the sharp coppery odor of spilled blood. None of these things, however, could prepare properly the dour king and his nephew for what lay inside.

All types and methods of rape was a heinous crime at any time, neither condoned or practiced by any knight nor any other man of honour. No less atrocious was defiling a consecrated kirk with unholy desecration along with the rape of women until holy vows. Although the former occurred all too often in times of war for it, in and of itself, to be regarded as more than an uncommon offense, the rapine of Saint Michael's, as Lord Sean soon discovered the place was called, was all the more despicable because chief among the victims had been nuns whose consecrated status generally preserved them from a fate most often reserved for common women. Despite the fact that only about half of the population of Scotland considered themselves of the catholic faith, on the main everyone considered a nun to be a servant of God, and therefore unmolested for fear of offering offense to God. The attack upon Saint Michael's was unheard of and showed that those responsible had no respect for holy ground or fear of the Almighty.

While the two leaders paused just inside one of the lesser damaged side chapels, which was currently commandeered as a hospice for the injured, one of the woolen robed sisters stopped Sean with a trembling hand upon his arm. "My lord, if only ye could hae come sooner this would nae hae happened. We begged them to spare us, but they only laughed at us before forcing both the young and elderly-" an involuntary sob caused the old woman to pause before continuing. "We gave them all they demanded: our supply of food stuffs, grain, water and even the consecrated wine! We emptied our storerooms out to them, but it was nae enough. We did nae dream they would damn themselves by such a violation of the sanctity of the kirk or its sanctuary to . . . to force us and take their filthy, perverted pleasures on our bodies!"

"They were nothing but brutal, savage barbarians," interjected another nun that had overheard the first. Her anger was at stark odds with the physical attitude of prayer as she knelt and watched over a bruised and tottering old monk give the Rite of Extreme Unction to another sister, bloodied and sprawled unmoving in the doorway leading from the kirk proper to the vestry chamber. The kneeling nun cast a furious look over her soot covered shoulder and exclaimed, "They were worse than animals! And may God forgive them for what they hae done this blighted day, for I never shall, even should it cost me the bliss of paradise!"

Once past the initial shock of such carnage within a house of God, King Gregor weathered the difficult inspection reasonably well considering the circumstances. Passing mostly unrecognized among the survivors, although somewhat suspiciously received, he understood that to be due simply for being a man more than anything else. Perhaps the most difficult part of it all was meeting the haunted eyes of those women violated but who had survived the brutal encounter. At a loss for what he could possibly say that could console any of them, Gregor remained silent and allowed the sorrow in his eyes convey the sadness and regret that he felt for each of them.

To the mind of most that saw the distinguished lord taking stock of the situation, they beheld Gregor's scarlet brigandine with its golden rampant lion and automatically linked him vaguely with being some sort of royal official-perhaps a marshal or one of the king's generals by his age and stiff military bearing. Certainly a king would not appear to personally assess even a tragedy, especially one such as this.

Much more unrecognizable than the king's crest was Lord MacSean's own martial garb and insignia he wore as he followed at Gregor's right hand. None of the victims and citizens there, in such a small community of cloistered nuns, tucked away in the foothills of southern Argyll could have been expected to be familiar with it. He appeared to be just another nobleman assessing the damage with a crown official.

"Ach, they were highborn lords, such as yerselves, as well as common soldiers," came the unanimous accusation from each person questioned with hardly any variation. "Most of their officers wore shiny armor and such, just as ye are wearing." Others, more observant than their fellow survivors, recalled seeing men with their long hair tied back in border braids and wearing clan tartan and crest; these eyed Gregor's own border braid and the MacGregor crest and tartan that he proudly wore, with more than a little suspicion, but said nothing against it.

Time after time, Marishal MacSean ventured to question the survivors about what they had seen, and for any details that they could remember about designs on the enemy's shields and surcoats, colors of the tartans, and symbols on their crests. Any little bit of added information could have been of help in identifying the attackers.

Most, however, proved to still be too dazed, too cowed, or both to recall any truly useful details about the enemy. Not until MacSean took his questions into a secluded corner of a ruined garden did the pattern of responses shift. There the investigation began to show some significant progress.

In that isolated corner the king and his marishal found what at first appeared to be yet another repeat of the same grim story:

a hysterically sobbing and trembling young girl with her head bent over her chest and masses of long, curly auburn hair falling forward and covering her face. The girl cowered in the arms of another woman as she heard the approach of the two warriors. Both young women wore the white of and gray habit of novices of their order, although only the latter was decently wearing the proper head covering. Neither appeared to be older than about sixteen.

Gently, MacSean repeated the same questions that he had asked on several earlier occasions, with more optimism than he truly felt.

"Oh, please!" retorted the one girl. "What does it matter who he was? The beast took all that he wanted, and *that* is all that really matters, sair!" came the unexpected and defiant reply of the girl consoling her friend, as she raised a tear-streaked face to glare up at the two armored men. "The foul miscreant told her that he was sick and tired of having to knuckle under to arrogant bishops and priests, and that he was going to show them that he was a man. A man-ha!" Outraged fire flashed in her dark eyes.

"Ach, aye! A big, important man indeed was he to rape a young innocent girl who could nae protect herself!" she went on in righteous anger. "She had nothing to do with any of those bishops and priests who had supposedly offended him. Now, speak ye truly, who wi' marry her? She is violated and her betrothed wi' surely never accept her now with her purity stolen!"

"Her betrothed? Gregor asked, forcing calm into his voice as he crouched d/wn before them. "This *is* important, sister; who was this hater of bishops and priests? And the lass, she is nae a sister of yer order?"

"The Duchess Lauralee?" The young woman shot the king an amazed look with eyebrows raised and blinked at his obvious surprise. "Oh, now I see. I thought everyone knew by now. Please forgive my poor manners, sair."

Grimacing to herself, for the duchess had redoubled her hysterical weeping at the sound of her name and title, the more composed and spirited girl pulled off the smudged coif covering her hair, turned it inside-out and thoughtfully pressed it into Lauralee's hands to use as a handkerchief.

Released from its covering, a thick, blue-black braid tumbled free across the chest her rumpled and soot-stained habit. Absently, she pushed a sweat dampened tendril of loose hair from before her eyes with the back of one grimy hand before glancing back up at Gregor with a touch less belligerence than before. Her other arm remained protectively around the sobbing duchess. MacSean needed no intuition to realize that she had no idea to whom she was speaking so bluntly to.

"Well then, my lords. Where shall I begin the sordid tale?" she wondered aloud, making a brave attempt at nonchalance. The lilting accent in the novice's voice spoke of her origins being northern Ireland, possibly Ulster or Connaught.

"The Duchess Lauralee is the only daughter of the Duke of Ulster," she said, pausing for affect before continuing. "The duchess was on her way to be wedded to the Scottish prince, David of Stewart, and had stopped here briefly for a prenuptial retreat. It is customary for foreign bride-candidates to wear the habit of a novice during their stay here. And that would be why her beastly attacker thought that she was a member of the order of Saint Michael," she added tartly.

Catching the swift exchanged glance between the two kinsmen, the fiery dark haired novice demanded, "What is it? What do ye ken, my lords, that ye should look at each other so?"

Sinking to his knees, with a creak of protesting leather, beside Gregor before the novice, the MacGregor Warlord looked closely at the quavering duchess. "Is she actually injured or simply badly frightened, Sister?" he asked gently. "The news we bear is ill, and it may be tae much for the poor lass to hear at this time. I would nae desire to cause her any more unnecessary pain."

The intense novice shook her head with close to contempt and drew the weeping Lauralee still closer into the circle of her bracing arm in a vain attempt to comfort the shaken noblewoman. "Well, of course, she is *hurt*, brutalized as she was," she snapped, aiming a glare at MacSean. "But I do believe that she is mostly still frightened and *very* understandably distraught from suck a heinous violation," the novice admitted, then in a whisper, she added, "she-she wi' nae speak much of it."

"And ye, lass, hae ye been injured as well?" MacSean persisted.

The girl suddenly sniffled and bowed her dark head over Lauralee's and rubbed her face into the auburn curls. "I was untouched," she murmured through her friend's wave of hair. "I was well hidden with two other sisters when the band of brutes came. We hid like cowards. They did nae discover us, but they did find sister Constance as she hid near us, and raped her. Poor Constance! Four of them forced themselves on her! She was quite old, and so kind; why would they do that to an old woman? She died; I do nae believe her heart could take such violence."

Lifting her accusing eyes to regard MacSean, she sneered defiantly, "Ye hae nae yet told me what difference any of this makes to the likes of ye. Do ye ask out of genuine concern and Christian charity, or merely to excite yer own animal lust?" she challenged, her rage overcoming good reason.

Lord Sean stared to her in briefly in shock; no one, man nor woman had ever so blatantly called his honour into question until now.

"I ask because I hae three sisters and a goodly number of close female kin that I would die to protect from such a horrid fate," MacSean answered her in a soft even voice, refusing to be provoked. "And because I pray that other men in such a situation, such as I am now, might show similar compassion to them if they were to ever suffer what ye and the duchess hae had to endure." He went on, "I also thought that I might be able to help in some small way, since I hae some ability as a healer and surgeon to offer."

"Oh, do ye, sair?" the novice's eyes flashed as she retorted. "Well, I and all of the sisters here hae some ability as healers ourselves. Has nae one told ye? We are, what are left of us, a hospitaller order. We were founded to tend the sick and injured and victims of war sae common to this country." Her dark brown eyes went softly unfocused and began to brim with hot tears as she gazed out at the ruined garden beyond MacSean. "We exist to give comfort and succor to the ill and injured, doing nae harm to any man or woman. What more fitting reward could we ask, than to hae the same . . ."

Her voice braking with a sob, tears streamed from her eyes and she buried her face once again in her friend's hair. Easing a little closer, MacSean tentatively reached out to lay a gentle hand on her arm. At the same time, Gregor saw to the duchess, but as he tried to do so she cringed away suddenly and gasped at his approach.

"Nay! Please-" Lauralee wailed with fear.

Hastily, Gregor reached out and seized on of her wrists to keep the frightened duchess from pulling away and passed a hand insistently before her bloodshot eyes. Using an ability of the Sidhe he expertly touched her mind and whispered, "Sleep now." Suddenly she was slipping to the ground as Gregor scrambled close enough to catch her before she could collapse into a thorny bush, the girl a dead weight in his arms.

"I wi' send some of my battle surgeons that they may assist ye and yer sisters," Gregor promised the wide-eyed novice as he quietly shifted his red haired burden to his nephew, "and provisions as well for ye and the town outside. Details wi' be worked out to help with the clean up here, as well to assist with whatever necessary burials that needs to be conducted for yer fellow sisters and the monks here."

The raven haired novice stared at Gregor in near shock. "What did ye do to her?" she gasped.

"She sleeps peacefully; it is all that I can do her."

The novice nodded numbly. "Thank ye and may God bless ye, sair."

Once the king had departed the secluded garden to issue the appropriate orders, MacSean climbed to his feet and gingerly carried the sleeping Duchess Lauralee into the kirk with the dark haired novice at his side giving him directions. Those directions led him to an elderly nun that turned out to be the presiding abbess.

Bowing respectfully, the marishal addressed the slight woman. "Mother, if there be anything further that the king's men may do in Christian charity for ye or those under yer charge, ye hae but to ask for Lord Sean MacSean and name it," he promised, and added, "any soldier with us wi' ken the name."

Two bright green eyes, sharp as a bird's, fixed on the king's Warlord before the diminutive mother superior gave him a sudden curt nod of acceptance, and apparently as well of dismissal as MacSean abruptly found himself being ushered away to the nearest egress by the little abbess.

Turning in the doorway to take his leave of the compound, MacSean glanced back as the dour abbess addressed him.

"Yer gracious offer is appreciated, my lord, and I do nae want to seen rude in the face of yer kindness, but I would thank ye more to be on yer way from here with yer army. What we need more than anything else is time to put this atrocious event behind us, and offer fervent prayers to the Almighty. Only He can ease the pain and heartache that ye hae seen in this place," she admonished sadly. Abruptly she nodded her head as if coming to some inner decision and added, "There is one thing ye may do once yer army has taken leave of this sad place, and hae God's blessing in seeing it done."

Lord Sean nodded. "On my honour, ask and it shall be done, Mother."

"Very well," she said, fixing him with those piercing eyes, "Be the blade of God. Find those responsible for the crimes perpetrated here and avenge the innocent with the blood of the wicked."

Later that evening, once an encampment had been erected a bare mile north of the Saint Michael's Kirk, Marishal MacSean joined Gregor in his tent. There they dined on cold field rations that were supplemented by a generous portion of roasted venison of some red deer stags that the foragers had brought in earlier. Following the fortifying meal they listened to reports from their commanders followed shortly by the scout captain's recommendations on the probable route taken by the rebel band that had pillaged the kirk and nunnery, and burned a portion of the town around them. Once those briefings were complete, MacSean and a brooding, grim-faced Gregor rode back to the kirk in order to check on the progress of the cleanup as well as the duchess' health.

"The lads are doing a masterful job of clearing away the bodies for interment and cleaning up the smashed relics of the kirk," Bishop Fletcher reported as he came to greet them through a side entry. The access in which he led them had had its door kicked off the hinges and the bishop shook his head sadly. "There wi' still be much work to be done before all is right, however."

Inside, the three were met by a haggard looking Father Lail, the wiry little priest who served as the bishop's own battle surgeon and personal chaplain. Nodding wearily to the king and his marishal he addressed himself to his religious superior, "Yer Grace, the cleanup within the kirk proper is nearly complete. With the grace of God, I should be able to reconsecrate the kirk and its altar before we move on in the morning."

"And the sisters? How do they fare this evening?" MacSean queried.

Fletcher shrugged his shoulders, fielding the question, and sighed, "That is nae sae easy a question to answer, compared to the physical surroundings, Sean. I suppose they are doing as well as can be expected sae soon after what happened. It was nae until a short time ago that I was given an actual list of casualties from the abbess. She is a most strict mother superior, I must say," he observed with a wan smile.

"How many were killed?" demanded Gregor.

"Fortunately, nae as many as we first thought," the tired bishop replied, his little smile vanishing. "Casualties were highest among the men, of course. Half a dozen lay brothers and a monk were killed outright when they tried to defend the women; a few more were roughed up pretty badly-the usual sort of thing. Regrettably, one of the sisters also perished during the assault; and two others still suffer as a result of the shock and internal injuries inflicted when they were sexually violated," he reported miserably, and then added, "to my surprise, more seem to hae escaped harm than nae. It was only by the grace of God that sae many were overlooked."

"Thank God for that," Gregor murmured, before shifting his dour attention to the younger priest. "We ken there was nay considerable amount of slayings throughout the town. But, tell me Father Lail, how fares the duchess?"

The typically happy faced Father Lail, his ever-present surgeon's satchel slung at a cockeyed angle over his shoulder, glanced furtively back in the direction from which he and Bishop Fletcher had emerged and heaved a great sigh. "She slept well until about an hour ago, but awoke hysterical and near to shock. I hae given her a sedative to calm her sae that she rests quietly again for now. Physically, I'm sure she'll mend quickly enough, but other than that I cannae say with any certainty," he admitted, raising his hands in a helpless gesture. "That auld biddy of an abbess here could hardly be persuaded to allow me near her, of course, but she's young and strong of body at least. Plus, there is that little novice friend of hers, who is constantly by her side, and she claims there are nay serious injuries that need my tending," he added with another heavy sigh.

"Her other hurts, the psychological ones, wi' be those that I fear wi' take the most time and care to heal. Her mind is in a fragile state; it is tae bad there was nae something anyone could do to just cause her to forget the whole event. Or is there?" he wondered aloud, glancing expectantly first at his king and then at MacSean. The priest had, on other occasions, seen both men work with a skill that they had referred to as *hypnosis*, along with other things involving the mind. "Ye could make her forget, could ye nae? Or show me how, that I might do sae?"

As King Gregor suddenly found great interest in the dust gathered on his tall boots and was unexpectedly remote, MacSean cleared his throat quietly and drew everyone's attention away from the reluctant king and back to himself. He would ask his uncle about it later when they had some privacy.

"What ye ask is a very delicate thing," Sean admitted reluctantly. "Tampering with someone's mind, especially without their consent, is a very serious undertaking under any circumstances, Father. However, within the bounds of propriety and everyone's consent, we wi' certainly do what we can," he reassured the priest, while at the same time trying to puzzle out the reason behind Gregor's sudden strange behavior. "Ye do realize, of course, that if the abbess would nae allow a bishop's own chaplain and selfsame battle surgeon touch her charge, Father Lail, what her response wi' be to us?" he said, gesturing with a hand between the king and himself. "Can ye nae imagine how she wi' feel about a couple of warriors tending to the duchess?"

"We wi' speak with the mother superior," interjected Fletcher, flashing his purple stoned ring like a weapon. Turning, he stalked away and a surprised Father Lail had to rush to catch up with his superior.

"And what if she wi' nae let us see the Duchess Lauralee?" demanded Gregor, his question echoing his nephew's own once the clergymen had gone.

Lifting his broad shoulders in a noncommittal shrug, MacSean followed in the wake of his tight-lipped king toward the small chapel in which the duchess had been taken for privacy and quiet. "By Lugh," Gregor whispered fiercely, "I should hae done it when we first found her and I had the best opportunity! But nay! My own scruples would nae let me do sae."

"Done what?"

Gregor glanced at his nephew. "Read her memories, what else?" he snapped. "Do ye remember what that fierce Irish novice said; Maeve I believe was her name. She said that the duchess' attacker ranted about some arrogant bishops and priests. Who most likely fits such a description than that bastard Colquhoun?"

"Hmmm, the description does fit him," MacSean agreed.

"Ach, of course, it does! What other bishop do ye ken that has allied himself with the Campbells and could inspire such hatred from one of that ally's own family?" asked Gregor with a derisive snort. "Besides that, even if he were nae speaking of bloody Henry Colquhoun, he may hae said something else that could give us some clue as to who *is* leading the rebel warbands in this area. As the Lord is my witness, and by Lugh's long and bloody sword, I want those bastards found and exterminated!"

"Nay, nay, a thousand times nay!" Maeve whispered fiercely.

The young sister and a stony faced Gregor stood glaring at one another across the sleeping form of the duchess, the small cot their own personal battle ground. MacSean remained silently in the chapel doorway watching the combatants verbally spar. The abbess had left Maeve in charge of Lauralee's care before setting out on her rounds with the bishop and his chaplain in tow, and the novice was proving to be quite a sufficient defender for the slumbering duchess.

"Sister, please, I promise it would be done quickly; she need nae even be awake to do what I must-" pleaded Gregor, his impatience growing.

"Nay, my lord! Can ye nae understand?" Maeve retorted. "What ye ask is nae seemly. Nay. It is nae even seemly that ye should be here at all. Has her ladyship nae been sufficiently violated already at the hands of unscrupulous men? To what good purpose would it serve to subject her to this *probing* of her mind?"

This was one argument Gregor was prepared for. "It would serve the rule of law and my honour as the defender of Scotland and her people, citizen or nae. I am the lawful King of Scotland, and my sworn and sacred duty is to see that all men, guilty of such evil deeds, are brought to justice for their crimes! Ye are guilty of obstructing that justice if ye wi' nae give way, sister. Now, stand aside!"

The fierce novice was not cowed. "Ah, then do ye mean to use physical force and overpower me then o' high and mighty lord?" hissed Maeve, taking a step back in feigned fear when Gregor started to raise a hand in entreaty. "I suppose that wi' also serve yer vaunted sense of honour and justice?"

"What?" demanded an exasperated Gregor.

"That is the choice I offer ye O King. If ye intend to force me away from my charge, there is nothing I can do to prevent it, of course," she continued coldly, "for ye are two well armed warriors and I, but a helpless lass and as defenseless as she is to stop ye," Maeve taunted. "Well, go ahead and overpower me! Unless ye do sae, I swear that is the only way ye shall lay hand on the duchess and use yer strange abilities on her!" she stated, raising her chin in defiance.

Gregor snorted. "Ye are far from being helpless, what with yer tongue! I dare say, it is as sharp as the sword at my side."

The novice's eyes widened in indignation. "How dare-"

"It is an ability, nae some arcane and foul art as ye seem to believe, my dear," MacSean interjected from the doorway.

"Sister, please just try to be reasonable," pleaded Gregor, trying to keep a firm grip on his worn patience. The king had no experience in dealing with such an outrageous and disrespectful woman, but he doggedly continued to seek a logical assault against her unreasonable justification for preventing him from his duty. "If I can but ken specifically who is responsible for what happened here, that information would tell me a great deal about my enemy and allow me to see justice is done. And I shall find him however long it takes, and then I shall mete out to him the just fate he deserves," he promised coldly.

"Shall ye then, Lord King?" inquired the waspish girl, her voice deceptively quiet, although her dark eyes still burned with passion. "And shall ye then take yer vengeance upon the villain? Wi' that restore what the Duchess Lauralee or anyone of the others hae lost this day? *Vengeance is mine, I shall repay,* saith the Lord of Heaven," she went on, piously quoting scripture to the exasperated king. "He wi' repay. The Lord of all Heaven and Earth wi' do this, Yer Majesty; nae the Lord of Scotland!"

Rendered nearly speechless with pent up anger, the novice's glaring impertinence was almost maddening enough for Gregor to reconsider using force to bodily remove her from his path. Icy blue eyes narrowed with anger and frustration, the king forced his fists to unclench and shoved each thumb inside the wide leather sword belt about his waist. Shooting a quick glance in his nephew's direction for any hint of guidance that might be offered, he saw Sean silently mouth the needed advice in a way so the novice could not see the furtive exchange.

Thankful for the inspiration, Gregor returned his attention to the defiant girl and allowed a sour look to come over his already grimly set face as he silently regarded her for a moment. While he did so, his mind sifted through his memories with a concentration that was keenly sharpened by a type of self-hypnosis that he and his nephew had been practicing. Although he was in a kind of trance, Gregor could still function and remained fully aware of all that was happening around him.

For Gregor, the world seemed to slow all around him as he focused his intelligent mind to dredge up the information held within that he required. The insolent novice seemed to impatiently glare at him for long minutes, but in actuality only a few short seconds had passed before the king roused himself from the self-imposed trance. Keeping a tight rein on his expression lest he give the girl any warning of his satisfaction he prepared for his attack.

"It is nae vengeance I seek, but justice," he replied, keeping his strong voice low and without expression. "*Give the king yer judgments, O God, and thy righteousness unto the king's son.* Do ye believe that ye are the only student of the Bible who can quote scripture to support yer arguments, young lady?"

Her mouth opened and closed once in astonishment. Clearly, the shocked novice had not expected such a response and suddenly the fight seemed to go out of her. Without uttering another word, Maeve started to turn away, but Gregor would not be thwarted and bounded forward a single long step after her and seized her upper arm in a firm grip. Whirling her around to face him again, the king stared into her frightened eyes.

Effortlessly the king held the venom-tongued novice before him, and with his noble expression set like immoveable granite, he spoke once again in a voice devoid of all warmth, "Ye may turn yer back on me as ye dare, young lady, but ye can nae turn yer back on the sacred writings of the Holy Bible to pick and choose whatever ye wish of it! Every word; every I dotted and each T crossed within that text is inspired by the Lord God Almighty. And if ye hae any respect for what the habit ye wear means then ye must agree with, heed and revere every word that it contains!" Gregor challenged, his icy tone brooking no further argument.

"*And now, I beseech thee, let the power of the Lord be great*", he quoted once again. "*And if any man shall take away from the words of the book of this prophesy God shall take away his part out of the book of life.* I want, as is my God given duty, to bring those that are responsible for these crimes to justice. Under law, Maeve. Do nae forget the words uttered from our Lord Jesus' own mouth: *Render to Caesar the things that are Caesar's, and to God the things that are God's.* I must nae countenance this sort of barbarous behavior in my kingdom, especially nae from the same lords who hae been sworn to uphold those same ancient laws of Scotland! Nay person may consider themselves above the law, nay matter high or low their station."

"Then kindly take yer hand off of me, my lord," she said frostily, more than a little piqued, "if ye, that is, hae any respect for the habit I wear."

Gregor expelled a longsuffering sigh and released her, sensing that he had at last bested her in their verbal exchange. "Respect for yer habit I do hae, but I question the wisdom of those that hae allowed ye to wear it," he growled.

Ignoring the dangerous look Maeve shot at him, Gregor turned to glance first at the slumbering Lauralee and then MacSean still standing at ease, leaning against the door of the chapel. He had won the battle, but he knew that he could not quite let matters rest as they were; the war was not over. Not yet.

"I ask ye one more time, if nae for my sake then for hers," he indicated the young duchess lying asleep, keeping his voice low to mask the impatience he felt.

The novice shook her dark-tressed head. "Nay, my lord. She remains under my protection. The Duchess Lauralee has none other to defend her honour; her chaperone is dead. There is just me, and I for one wi' nae betray her."

"If that be the case, and ye wi' nae permit our *king* to read her memories directly, lass, then ye do it," demanded MacSean, standing in the doorway. "I for one am heartily tired of all this arguing. Nay, do nae start with me, lassie! I hae nae the patience for any more of yer barbed tongue; now, please do me the great favor of saving yer breath about respecting the habit ye wear," he said sternly. "Aye, ye wear the habit, but only that of an uncommitted novice which has taken nay sacred vows. Ye, in fact, are nay more a nun than is my little sister," stated the marishal, his tone full of the calm, cool assurance in which he was known for. "There is something else that I am confident about, now that I hae been in yer presence this little while. Ye hae the Sidhe blood in ye, just as much as I and my uncle, the king hae. Wi' ye deny it?"

The novice's confident demeanor began to crumble in the face of MacSean's cool rebuke, and she clasped her hands together to hide their shaking before returning her attention back to the waiting king.

"I can read her memories from ye, lass, if ye wi' but allow it," Gregor reassured the obdurate girl. "All I require is for ye to open yer mind to me and show me the attack; any pertinent information wi' be from that time. I ken that I am asking a great deal from ye, but it's the only other way to obtain what I need. It's important nae only to see that justice is done, but also to find the guilty and put a stop to their crimes before anything like this can happen again!"

Following the sweep of his hand, which indicated all of the violated abbey and the blackened, desecrated kirk, with her red rimmed eyes, Maeve nodded sadly.

"If ye would permit me a moment of prayer to calm myself?" she asked demurely.

"Of course," Gregor graciously obliged.

Turning away and sinking to her knees, Maeve bowed her dark head and clasped her fingers together, pressing them to her lips as she offered a silent prayer to God for guidance and courage. When she was ready the novice stood and faced the king.

"Are ye willing to offer me yer word of honour that ye wi' take from my mind only that in which ye need? I hae never allow anyone into my mind and nay nae how to block ye from doing sae, and I freely admit my fear of it."

Gregor nodded his understanding. "Of course. I give ye my word of honour, as a knight and as a king."

MacSean watched as some of the stiffness eased from her shoulders and saw a hint of a smile, timid as it was, touch her lips. Inwardly relaxing, he allowed a brief smile of his own ease his stern visage as he waited in silent vigil.

"It seems I had lost sight of the larger picture for awhile in my stubbornness, my lord," she admitted, forcing herself to meet Gregor's straightforward gaze. "I had refused to think of how many others had been wronged, or about those that still may suffer at the hands of those craven beasts who hae wrought their evil here," she declared, bowing her head in shame. And then, with her voice barely a whisper, Maeve added, "I wi' do as ye request, but I . . . I must ask that this thing be done in absolute privacy. Lord MacSean, I mean ye nay disrespect, but this wi' be a very difficult undertaking for me; if ye would leave us for a few moments until it is done?"

"I understand," MacSean replied simply, glancing aside at his uncle and sketching a little bow. "Shall I wait outside to ensure yer privacy, my King, or shall a return to our camp and await ye there?"

"Go ahead and be off to the army's camp. Please wait for me in my pavilion and I wi' share what I learn on my return," Gregor instructed, never taking his penetrating eyes from Maeve. "I wi' be along directly."

Once the marishal had taken his leave, pulling closed the door behind him, Maeve let out a pent up sigh and bent down to smooth a curly lock auburn hair from her charge's brow. Glancing up at Gregor suddenly, much like a frightened child who was both fragile and vulnerable, Maeve sank to her knees on the polished though dusty stone floor beside the low cot with a weary groan. Feeling that she needed a strong shoulder to lean on, the king would have gone to her, but the zealous novice sensed his intent and shook her dark tressed head while further halting him with an upraised hand.

"Please, my lord, I merely need a moment to compose myself before we proceed," Maeve whispered, her pretty face looking strained in the dim light of a single candelabra standing beside the bare white stoned altar. Moments passed as she closed her eyes and calmed herself with a brief prayer.

"I am ready, my lord," Maeve said at last, shifting to kneel over the far side of the small cot. "Do only what ye must to enable me to gain access to Lauralee's memories. She wi' nay doubt be angry and frightened, as well as more than a little embarrassed. If she even guessed that *I* was about to ken what all she suffered and endured, she would feel all those things. Sae, I am sure ye can imagine what she would feel if she knew that a man was privy to those same horrid facts."

Gregor nodded understanding. "Aye. The joining of two minds is always a very intimate thing; my gentle mother, God rest her soul, was who taught me how to join and I assure ye her touch was most tender," the king reassured her. "When ye are settled, I must first put the duchess into a sort of hypnotic trance and only then may I guide ye in as well. She wi' remain asleep just as surely as ye wi' remain in a wakeful state and aware of all that happens around ye. In such a fashion ye may then ask her questions that shall allow ye to gain the information that I need. However, beware," paused Gregor, staring into her eyes to impart the seriousness of his warning, "ye may see and feel things through the link just as she did firsthand, and it wi' be terrible to bear. If that should happen and it becomes tae much to endure ye may cut yerself off from it. Prepare yer mind to open and close like a door; when ye hae seen enough simply slam shut the door of yer mind. Do ye think ye can do that, lass?" he asked kindly.

"Aye," she said, giving a firm nod of her head. "I am ready, my lord. Let's get this over with before fear makes me change my mind."

Gregor chuckled warmly. "Very well. Ye wi' do just fine," he said, moving close to the cot and dropping down onto his knees across from the novice. "Be at ease, lass, and place one hand on Lauralee's brow and place yer other on my shoulder. Aye, just like that," he commended, once she had done so. For his part, Gregor placed his free hand on the duchess' head with his fingers gently touching her near temple. "Now I wi' first place Lauralee in a receptive trance, since she wi' be the easiest. Remain calm and silent."

Adjusting his hand slowly from the young duchess' forehead, Gregor reached out with thumb and forefinger to pull open one eyelid. In his other had the king produced a small pendant of iridescent blue-green crystal that seemed to shimmer with every shade of the rainbow as it caught the flickering light of the candelabra.

Speaking so softly that Maeve could not make out the words in which he said, just the soothing rhythm and cadence of his voice, Gregor swept the gleaming crystal slowly before the sleeping girl's eye. He let it spin slowly back and forth while Lauralee watched it with rapt attention. Abruptly, with a quick motion of his hand, the duchess closed her eye with contented sigh and a serene expression touching her lovely face.

"Lauralee is ready," murmured Gregor. "Now it is yer turn."

"She looks sae peaceful. Yer magic is strong, my lord," whispered Maeve, more than a touch of awe entering her voice.

"It must be white magic to hae such a tranquil affect on my lady. Ye are truly blessed by God."

The king snorted. "A blessing? Aye, some may call it sae, but many others name it a curse and witchcraft. If magic it was, it would be the white. However it is nae magic at all, but a science long forgotten mixed with my Sidhe blood," he corrected. "The ancients from about the Great Apocalypse used this science of the mind to work wonderful cures, in which I and only a handful of others are now just beginning to use again with a certain amount of confidence," he explained, with more passion than Maeve had yet witnessed from the sober spirited leader. "It may even be possible, if I hae the sufficient skill, that I might erase the entire memory of Lauralee's assault from her mind sae that it wi' nay longer trouble her in the future."

Maeve caught her breath in astonishment. "But, if that is sae, why hae ye nae taught this wondrous science to others sae that the practice may again be used to cure the mind sick? There are many who could benefit from its use," she stated.

"Ach, there my dear, ye hae hit it squarely on the head," he pointed out. Gregor shook his head sadly, an expression of distaste narrowing his piercing blue eyes. "Why indeed. Ye must understand how some think about such things; for instance, the Bishop of Dundee, Henry Colquhoun, is in his own perverted way a religious fanatic. He knows about this formerly lost science that my clan and some others hae rediscovered, aye, and he has decreed that it is blackest witchcraft given to me and mine by Satan himself! Sae, now tell me true, do ye still wish to go through with this or wi' ye take auld Colquhoun's word for it as the Holy Bishop of Dundee?"

A mischievous smile curved Maeve's lips. "It seems I am nae the only one here with a bit of a defiant streak in them. It also appears we share the same opinion of that detestable man! I may only be a non-committed novice, but I form my own opinions, as ye well ken. The bishop has visited Saint Michael's before; unfortunately, I hae met this *holy man* and for all his pious and self-righteous words I can attest that he is nothing but a lecherous, old man. He actually had the gall to try and seduce *me* to his bed when he was staying here for the night, and I dressed chastely wearing this habit!"

Gregor could not help but laugh openly at the thought of it. "I'm sure that his ears were burning by the time ye finished with him! By God, I needed a good laugh, Maeve. Why that old fool must be nearly four times yer age," the king exclaimed, chuckling once again, and this time Maeve's laughter joined his.

"Sae, should I presume that ye are still willing to help me?" Gregor asked, once he had regained his composure.

"Aye," agreed Maeve, grinning still. "I trust ye."

"I'm gratified to hear ye say sae," he replied sardonically. "And all it took was an auld fool like Colquhoun to make it happen."

Maeve shook her head. "Nay, that was nae what did it. Ye started winning my trust when ye spoke to me as an equal and nae just some simple lassie that should bow and scrap to ye, my lord. This country is lucky to hae such a king."

"Yer Majesty, ye are blushing."

"Of course I'm nae," he winked at her. "Perhaps we should begin."

She grinned without saying a word.

"Sae, ye remember this crystal bauble that I first showed to Lauralee? It is a focus for use in hypnotism," he explained, dangling from his hand by its cord the iridescent crystal which spun slowly before the novice's dark eyes. "The colors are beautiful, are they nae?" Gregor whispered, already drawing her into the first stage of a trance. "Every lovely hew of the rainbow dancing as if each are alive with swirling skirts. Hear their happy music as if a babe's lullaby. It is making ye sleepy, sae contentedly sleepy. Yer eyes are growing heavy, sae very heavy that it is difficult to keep them open. As ye drift to sleep ye wi' continue to hear my voice, knowing all is well and ye are at peace. Ye wi' follow all my reasonable commands. Sleep now.

"Remaining in yer sweet, peaceful reverie open yer eyes and look closely down upon yer sleeping mistress. Does she nae look calm and at peace?"

"Aye," she intoned. Peaceful as a babe."

Silently, Gregor slipped the crystal back into the pouch at his waist. "Very good, Maeve. Now, once ye hae heard me leave and the door is shut behind me, ye may ask Lauralee the questions that I hae already requested that ye ask of her. Once ye are finished learning what must be known, come to the chapel door and knock upon it softly, that I may ken that I may return to ye. Do ye understand what I hae told ye?"

"Aye," came her dreamy reply.

Some moments later, upon hearing the soft rapping on the inside of the chapel door, Gregor let himself into the room. Once again producing the crystal pendant from his belt pouch, he released Maeve from her trance with a simple command and a loud snap of his fingers.

"It worked, did it nae?" asked an awed Maeve. "I can just faintly remember ye speaking to me through the crystal."

"Aye. I believe it worked just fine," Gregor agreed, nodding assurance. "Can ye tell me everything that Lauralee imparted to ye through her trance?"

"She did nae ken her attacker's name," she replied slowly, a disturbed expression clouding her face. "I'm sorry, my lord. I hope ye are nae tae disappointed. I could see his face clearly, however, and I can describe to ye what he looks like as well as the design of his surcoat. Do ye think that wi' be enough to identify the vile man?"

Gravely, King Gregor nodded, not trusting himself to speak just yet, and held out his hand for the girl to take.

Equally serious, Maeve placed her slightly shaking hand tentatively into his. It was only then that Gregor made his decision to trust her.

Maeve's hand was cool and submissive in the king's light grip, her skin soft with youth in contrast to the worn calluses of his own due to the long use of his sword on the practice field and in battle. "There is another ability that I hae, along with my close kin and a few others from ancient times," he confided, distracting himself with the softness of her hand as he spoke his secret. "They called it *telepathy*, which is the ability to speak mind to mind with another, without the need for speech."

He pulled his eyes away from her slender hand and forced himself to look her in the face. "Trust in me; trust that I am yer friend and would never do anything to harm ye. Look deeply into my eyes, Maeve," instructed Gregor, his voice taking on a quiet and soothing quality. "Let us see if ye tae can communicate this way; yer Sidhe blood is nae sae strong as mine, but it is still Sidhe. Fear nae, ye wi' nae come to any harm while in my care. Ye hae my word on it."

As their eyes met, brown gazing into blue, the king cleared his mind and in one infinite second, Maeve suddenly had the queasy feeling of falling for an eternity without end as she became lost in the depths of Gregor's azure eyes.

She gasped in growing panic. Seconds stretched into time without end as Maeve's world was swallowed by unending blue; nothing else existed except the blue of Gregor's eyes. She felt her existence slipping away; losing herself and merging into a world as blue as the sky. Becoming frightened and then terrified, Maeve screamed in her mind. She screamed like she had never screamed before.

"Stop that! Stop that, NOW!" roared Gregor's pained voice inside her head, sharp enough to cut through her shrieks. Suddenly she was not falling any more, the voice was an anchor in which she could grab a hold and steady herself. Cold sweat beaded on her forehead and she panted with an exertion born from fear.

"By Lugh, do nae *ever* do that again," the shaken king rebuked her. "By some miracle we are still partially linked, but yer blasted shrieking nearly split my bloody head in half and part of our link was instantly severed, Maeve. Now, if ye hae calmed down enough I suggest that we continue."

"Oh, aye, I'm calm now and everything is right as rain, Yer Royal Majesty, but ye could hae given me a hint of warning about what was going to happen!" Maeve countered waspishly. "Tell me, just how well did ye cope on yer first attempt?"

"Touché. Ye are right and I apologize. If ye wi' follow my voice I shall talk ye through it," Gregor's voice in her mind suggested firmly. "Open yer mind to me and let yerself drift; aye, just like that. Ye are doing just fine, lass. There wi' be a feeling come over ye that is like ye are floating, a sort of lightness of the body-do nae fear it for this is normal. Ties of the body do nae exist in this mental state."

Drifting along in a world of endless blue with only the sound of Gregor's mind voice to accompany her the young novice could sense the outside, corporeal world start to recede. Her vision began to tunnel and the tunnel started to narrow more and more until all that she could see was the widened pupils of the king's eyes. The blue was gone and replaced with utter blackness. Her fear returned suddenly, a fear of being all alone in a world of darkness. Soon, however, even the knowledge that the blackness was Gregor's pupils disappeared as Maeve allowed her eyelids to close to despair. Suddenly she was floating alone in a void. She was beyond hope and fear, but then, although her eyes were closed, Maeve unexpectedly became aware in another point of perspective. In her mind's eye a form began to take shape before her; the vision was one that Gregor shared with her as their minds became firmly linked together. The rapt king watched the vision take form and a shape approached closer into view, and when it did so he could hear Maeve's gasp of fear as it resolved into the form of a snarling young lord.

The man coming closer, so as to loom over them, would have been handsome had his face not been contorted with unbridled rage and a foul, burning lust. He appeared to be young as well, not much older than the duchess herself, but abruptly the terrified girl's memories would only allow general impressions to filter through her terror: light brown hair that was clipped close in the common style of lowland warriors, matted down with sweat. His coif of fine polished mail was pushed back to hang between his somewhat slender shoulders as he grabbed her wrists. A wet, leering mouth moved maliciously with hate as he spouted out at his helpless victim a string of crude obscenities about bishops and priests, and about being forced to obey those same clerics.

The rapist's hate-filled brown eyes burned with the insensate heat of near madness as he stared at his powerless victim. Gregor could feel himself shudder helplessly, an echo of Lauralee's terror filled trembling, as he relived through the duchess' memories her sadistic violation as they were passed on by Maeve. A scream threatened to burst from his mind as a gauntlet encased hand savagely grasped at soft, white, cringing flesh, bruising it purposely and then that hateful face suddenly loomed closer to force a savage kiss from the poor girl.

A sense of vertigo threatened to overwhelm Gregor as he saw through Lauralee's eyes the young warrior wrench at a waist buckle to release the sword belt hw wore. Only with a surge of tightly controlled will did the king finally manage to wrench his mind away from the actual attack and fix his gaze upon the coat-of-arms embroidered on the man's dusty surcoat.

The blazon that Gregor observed on the attacker's chest was that worn only by the lords and senior household of Clan Campbell.

CHAPTER SEVEN

The part of Gregor that was King of Scotland, the dispenser of her laws and the bringer of justice, noted and recognized Duchess Lauralee's attacker immediately, with an attitude of disgust and loathing held under tight control by a supreme exertion of his iron strong will. Forcing his mind to calm once again, as much to shield the novice from his thoughts and prevent her from being frightened by them, Gregor marked Lord Richard Campbell in his mind's eye for the appropriate punishment that he so richly deserved once he was taken into the royal custody.

Adding even more to the bottled up rage that King Gregor felt as he witnessed the brutal rape of the duchess from his secured point of view, was the fact that he was only receiving a small portion of what Lauralee herself had suffered through a filter in which he had woven to protect himself. However, even through his filter, the king could feel her outrage and he shared that fully.

By the time the memories had come to an end, Gregor's heart was pounding with Lauralee's remembered horror despite his safeguards. And although he was unaware of it through his link with Maeve, the king was drenched with icy perspiration. Later, once the link between himself and Maeve had been severed, Gregor sat back on his heels panting, his hand clutching Maeve's so fiercely that a part of him was amazed that the young woman had not cried out in pain.

Moaning despite himself, Gregor forced his fingers to open and release her hands, clapping his own hands against his temples in agony as he sagged back against the altar step. Sitting heavily with his legs splayed before him, his heart still pounding, the king shuddered in after reaction before he at last regained a hard fought for self control. He had never known such fear and helplessness; those things were emotions that he fervently prayed to in no way experience ever again.

Gradually, even as the agony in his head cleared and his heart rate slowed to a more normal level, King Gregor realized that Maeve had passed on to him far more than just the information that he had requested of her. The novice had also allowed at least a fair measure of the terror and violation that the frail, young duchess had experienced and still lived with to surge through the bond.

"I'm sorry for allowing sae much of Lauralee's emotions to rush forward through the link, my lord. Ye did nae deserve that," she whispered sincerely, flinching away from his eyes as his gaze fell upon her. "I sought only to try and to make ye understand what she felt and still feels. Ye are a man after all, sire. Ye could nae comprehend what it can mean to be a woman and the fear of being used in such a barbaric way. The duchess had lived her entire young life sheltered and cared for in a loving household; protected and watched over against any such abuse. Now she is alone, her virtue stolen. Sae blemished wi' she return to her family and live in despair, knowing nay man of proper station wi' wed her. And if she be with child, what then?"

Gregor glanced quickly away from Maeve as her voice trailed off, forcing himself to draw another deep, ragged breath into his lungs as he rubbed the heel of both hands over his stinging eyes.

"Ye may be right, but nae if I hae anything to say about it," he said at last, casting a furtive glance at the sleeping duchess, gratified that she did remain asleep. "She must be checked to see if she is with child; I ken the way of it, thanks to my mother. If Lauralee is spared such a fate, I promise to do my best to blur all the memories that she has of the attack, if ye believe that I should. But I wonder, my dear, who wi' be sae kind as to blur yers and mine?"

Maeve shook her head and heaved a forlorn sigh. "One who gives all of one's self to a life of healing must expect to bear such burdens, my lord. Most likely just as another who bears the heavy weight of a jeweled crown must even feel that burden. Is that nae sae, sire?" she added gravely.

It was indeed. However, accepting that fact for the truth that it was did not make Gregor's obligation any lighter nor help alleviate any of those other emotions he still felt churning just at the surface of his awareness. He would help the girl find a suitable mate before sending her back home in dishonour, as in his eyes, Gregor knew that she was not dishonored at all, but remained an innocent. It did help in one sense that the man Lauralee had come to wed was already dead, although she did not yet know it.

"Maeve, there is a bond between us now that very few hae ever shared," said Gregor, smiling faintly. "I consider ye a ward even more sae than the duchess. If ye are called to become a nun, I can hae ye appointed wherever ye choose; and if nae, when ye decide to marry I can help with that also and provide for a generous dowry."

Maeve blinked in surprise. "Ye are tae generous, my lord. I am nothing but a girl who speaks tae much and thinks nae enough."

"That may be true," Gregor agreed, chuckling to show he meant no offense, "but I stand by my friends; and I consider ye to be one of them. Ye my call upon me any time, whether ye are in need or if ye wish merely to spar words with me. I shall look forward to seeing ye on either count."

Later, once King Gregor had taken his leave of his young friend, he rode back to the army's encampment and spent the better part of an hour just wandering aimlessly about the quiet camp alone. Every now and then Gregor was challenged by alert sentries posted around the parameter and throughout the bivouac site and passed on with the respectful salutes of each guard he came into contact with. Walking along the picket lines and murmuring greetings to the tethered warhorses, Gregor occasionally stopped briefly to rub the soft muzzle of those same horses which wickered their own welcome to him and nuzzled at his arm for a treat.

Despite all this, everything still blurred in the face of what had occurred earlier in the fire blackened kirk. Finally realizing that his wandering was doing him no good, Gregor at last decided to head back to his tent and the council of his nephew who was his closest confidant, knowing that he would be anxious for his return.

"Sire?" MacSean called, sword already in hand, as he and young Barak rose at once as the king drew aside the entry flap and stepped inside.

"Aye. It's me, Sean."

The two had been passing the time cleaning and oiling Sean's leather harness while they waited for the king's return. As was usual, Barak was correct and proper in his page's livery, while currently working a polish onto a well used spur. In contrast, Sir Sean had stripped off his dusty tunic and had drawn on about his broad shoulders a sleeveless mantle of emerald green linen. Soft, comfortable deer moccasins that rose to his knees helped ward off the chill night air. The high cavalry boots that the marishal had been wearing earlier, along with the steel studded brigandine glistened in the light of several lanterns that more than adequately illuminated the spacious tent. Lying neatly on the marishal's camp bed, and as always, near at hand was his discarded sword with the heavy leather, black baldric wound loosely around the oiled scabbard. And, although Gregor could not see it he knew the long blade had already been re-sharpened and polished as well with the typical loving care it received after any use.

"Barak, lad, ye can go to bed now," MacSean said fondly, sending his son on his way as soon as he had glimpsed the dull, haggard expression on his uncle's face. "We can finish this in the morning. Go get some sleep."

"As ye wish, Da," the boy said, obediently laying aside the spur and polishing cloth. Stepping up beside the blonde warrior, Barak kissed his father's bearded cheek. "Good night, Da. I wi' bring yer breakfast with me when I return in the morning, once ye are awake. Good night, Uncle Gregor," said the lad, favoring the king for a grin, before darting out through the tent flap to seek his own tent.

"Good night, lad. Sleep well," called Sean, as the flap fell back into place. Sean smiled over at Gregor and said, "I do nae ken what I would do without him. I see his poor mother in his eyes and in every expression each time I look upon him."

"Aye. Barak is a good lad, and I also can his mother in him, God rest her soul, but I see ye in him as well," Gregor added in agreement.

Pouring a cup of hot spiced wine that had not been asked for, but one that Sean knew the man needed, he offered it to his weary uncle.

"Thank ye, Sean," Gregor murmured, and gratefully gulped down nearly half of the wine before sinking down onto a camp chair with an exhausted sigh. Set up before him stood a small, foldable table with maps of the area spread across it, and as the king glanced over it, Sean silently moved his own stool over to sit beside him.

It was not until after having taken another deep draught from the pewter tankard, and emptying it to the dregs, that Gregor felt ready to speak of what had happened earlier in the kirk. He knew that he needed to speak of it with Sean; it was just that he did not know exactly how to explain it all.

"I returned to our camp some time ago and hae been walking for a while to clear my head," the king said softly. Setting his empty tankard on the portable table, Gregor unbuckled his sword belt and allowed sword and belt slip to the straw matting at his feet. "I just needed some time alone to think before coming back here."

MacSean did not say anything as he regarded his troubled uncle, waiting patiently for Gregor to continue as the brooding monarch stared into the flames licking upward from the lantern set on the table between them.

When the king finally spoke he did not look up from the flickering flame. "It was Richard Campbell, the ill-gotten son of Oliver Campbell, and Domeric's nearest heir with the death of his own son at Dunmoore," he murmured tonelessly. "There is nay doubt that he was the one who raped the poor duchess. I saw his face as if I was there, and I swear on my own life that he be brought to justice and pay for his crimes."

MacSean remained silent, only leaning an elbow on the rough wooden table and propping his chin thoughtfully on that hand. The fingers of his other hand were wrapped firmly around the handle of his own tankard where it sat, unfortunately as empty as the king's own, but he did not even consider refilling it. Instinctively, Sean knew that there was more to the story that just the discovery of the attacker's identity, just as he realized that Gregor was not quite ready to discuss what it was yet. His uncle would speak of it when he was ready and Sean knew not to force the issue.

After what seemed a very long time of shared silence, Gregor roused himself from his stillness and glanced up uncomfortably, half turning on his stool to stare at the tent wall off to the side. His disturbed face in profile, Gregor spoke in a voice bearing more than a whisper and asked, "Sean, hae ye ever raped a woman?"

MacSean's eyes widened in shock, barely forcing down the angry response that leaped to his lips. A fierce scowl of indignation twisted his handsome face as he flushed crimson at the offending question before he was finally able to lower a stony mask over his outraged features. "Nay, Sire. I hae nae, nor ever would. And, giving *ye* the benefit of *yer* honour, I do nae believe ye ever hae either," he answered coldly.

A grimace soured Gregor's expression at his nephew's tone and he met Sean's narrowed eyes. "I'm sorry, Sean. Ye are unworthy of such a question; it was nae wisely asked, as ye deserved the benefit of yer honour as well." Shaking his head at his own thoughtlessness, Gregor stood and went to retrieve the forgotten pitcher of heated, spiced wine. Returning to his seat the king poured some for the both of them. "I hae never done such a thing," he murmured, sitting the pitcher aside. "I confess that I hae never even been tempted either. Those sorts of appetites are nae normal in my eyes."

"I agree and nor should they be for any moral man, but unfortunately it is a harsh fact of war, Sire," MacSean said quietly, his anger extinguished. "Nay honourable man, lord or commoner should condone such, but rather deal with it due severity. I ken what penalty *I* would enact were I the judge of such vile conduct."

"Aye," concurred Gregor, knowing well how his nephew's mind worked. Lifting his tankard the king took a deep swallow and issued forth a heavy sigh. "Sean, hae ye ever wondered what it must be like-for the woman assaulted?" he asked haltingly. "I admit I never had given it any thought. But, I ken now."

Sean whistled softly between his teeth. "That obstinate novice finally showed ye the duchess' memory, did she? I was nae sae sure that she would. By yer manner, since returning, it must hae been particularly unsettling."

Gregor turned a bleak profile to his nephew's scrutiny. "Aye, that she certainly did, and more. I nae only saw the attack through Lauralee's eyes, but felt it as well. If it was nae for the filters I hastily threw up to shield myself, I would be far more than merely unsettled right now. It was horrific. Truly horrific," he confided softly, lifting the tankard to his lips and draining it to the dregs in one long pull. "Ye can read my moods tae well, Sean. I wi' hae to work on better schooling my emotions."

Sean snorted. "What would be the fun in that? Anyway, this is nae the first time I hae come upon the scene of rape, Sire. I deemed that she would give in to ye eventually," he added, shrugging his shoulders. "Ye hae that effect on people."

"From the troubled expression ye hae bore ever since returning from the chapel, I surmised that the knowledge ye gained was the reason for it. It is truly a dreadful thing to read from someone's memories that has gone through such an ordeal as the duchess has," allowed the MacGregor Warlord, his tone one of commiseration. "That was the reason for my suggesting that ye nae read any of the other victims this afternoon. If ye had been any less skilled, ye could hae been pulled in to her traumatized mind and found yerself with nay way of escape. As it is, ye may find that her memories wi' haunt yer dreams as if they are yer own remembrances," he added.

"Ach," Gregor groaned, shaking his weary head. Closing his saddened eyes for a few seconds the king reflected on the disturbing events before looking down at his intertwined fingers, still agitated by it all. "I've never beheld such a thing before, Sean. It was absolutely horrid! And Richard wi' pay for it with his life!"

Marishal MacSean woke the next morning to a day that had already dawned and was bright and chilly-typical highland weather-with a slight breeze from the west that had already blown away the last stubborn vestiges of the early morning fog. Outside the tent he could hear the sounds of the army camp already at work with sergeants yelling their orders and troops rushing to carry them out.

Rubbing sleep from his bleary eyes, MacSean noted without any real surprise that Gregor had already dressed and gone. Normally, the king would be about the camp to see that all was in order, but he knew better. *Of course. He's gone back to that plucky novice to try and blur away as much of the duchess' memories of that whole nasty business as he can,* he surmised, even as he grabbed his freshly shined boots sitting beside his cot and began pulling them on.

"Shall I bring ye some breakfast now, Da?" asked Barak, coming to his father's side to kneel and fasten the man's spurs to his boot heels. "I believe there are griddle cakes and bacon to be had, if ye like."

Sean shook his head thoughtfully. "That sounds good, but nay. Instead, I need ye to go and relay to each of the senior officers my compliments and that I require them here as soon as possible; be sure to hae the lads ready to tear down the tent this morning, I wish to be ready to depart when the king has returned from his other business," ordered the preoccupied Warlord, as he buckled on his polished leather baldric and settled the long length of his sharpened sword into its housing of supple, oiled leather. "Oh, and do nae forget to snatch yerself some breakfast, laddie," he said, looking up the a fond smile, "a growing lad like ye must keep a full stomach if ye wish to grow tall and strong like yer uncle and become the mighty knight that I expect ye to be."

The boy readily returned his father's smile with one of his own. "My belly would nae allow me to forget, and besides that, I want to grow up to be just like ye."

"Good," he said, winking. "Now, ye had best be going, laddie."

Several minutes later, while the king's Marishal sat on his cot finishing a cup of tea, the officers that he had summoned began arriving outside the large tent that he and Gregor shared. He heard them comradely greetings among themselves as he arose and sat his empty cup on the small table beside the rolled maps.

Swinging open the entrance flap, MacSean bade them a bonny morning and asked them to come inside. "Please, help yerselves to some tea. It's strong and hot," he offered, with usual highland hospitality, indicating the kettle hanging above a small brazier in the center of the tent.

"Major Peters, what is the status of our supplies? How are they holding out since our redeployment; has foraging improved?" he inquired, addressing himself to the stout officer whose spectacles had slide down his prominent nose.

The officer so singled out swallowed and immediately sat aside his steaming cup of tea. "My lord, we seem to hae solved the problem for the time being," the major answered, a line creasing his worried brow, "however, if the Campbells continue this strategy of their's and we can nae pin them down soon-well, I'm nae sure how long the king's army can carry on. Water is nay problem, of course, but grain for the horses wi' begin to run perilously low very soon; perhaps as soon as a fortnight."

"We could plunder one of the Campbell's towns for the supplies we need; could we nae, my lord?" suggested the eager, young cavalry officer standing beside Peters, his tone full of brash enthusiam.

"We may be forced to such a course, Captain MacDonoll, but we hae nae reached that point yet," interjected King Gregor, brushing aside the entry flap as he briskly strode inside. "Ye must remember, captain, that I am nae just another clan chief now, but the king of every clan. That includes Clan Campbell as well, despite what their chief may say. Once this rebellion has been put down we must nae forget that the Campbell people wi' be my people as much as any other citizen of Scotland. To a great extent, the common folk of Clan Campbell are innocent of what their duke is doing. They continue to run their crofts and mills and farms with nay part of Domeric's schemes. And I hae nay desire to start a general revolt, for to do sae would only give additional aid to the rebel duke at a time when I most need the good will of our people," Gregor reminded the captain and his other officers. "I trust ye wi' all remember that, if and when the time comes in which we must resort to seizing any needed provender."

The duly chastised captain bobbed his head in respectful acceptance.

"Bonny good. Let's step outside gentlemen, it is tae stuffy to remain inside a tent with sae many of us," ordered Gregor.

Once the group was outside the remainder of the staff meeting proceeded swiftly as usual military affairs were addressed and orders were issued straightaway.

"Well, gentlemen, the morning has nae waited around for us and we're beginning to lag tae much behind our usual schedule. Hae yer lads finish packing away the tents and loading the wagons. I expect to be in the saddle within the hour," commanded the king, then after a brief pause, added, "We can nae let the Campbells hae any respite; we hae an urgent appointment to keep with Duke Domeric and his misbegotten nephew, Richard, and I do nae intend to keep them waiting!'"

Shortly afterward, the officers having dispersed to carry out the king's orders to their respective units, King Gregor and his marishal returned to the confines of their tent to swiftly pack away an assortment of important maps and documents. In the rush to break camp all failed to take note of a solitary border scout as he slipped away from his fellows. Neatly the borderer made his escape, disappearing covertly beyond the neat line of pickets and using the bustle of busy soldiers breaking camp to obscure his getaway.

In the wearying fortnight that followed, Gregor and his retinue failed to personally catch sight of the quarry they so intently hunted, however the king's scouts did report sightings of Reginald MacNab and of other rebel leaders as they moved north. The Royal Army penetrated steadily deeper into the rugged hill country which lay between them and Lochay, but by end of those two weeks march even the smaller warbands that Gregor had divided his force into were finding it difficult to properly re-supply themselves. So it was that the king was disposed to send his quartermaster general and his squadrons of heavy cavalry, along with elements of foot, in a more easterly direction. In that way did they press on toward the Campbell's supposed base of operations, over a somewhat longer but flatter and better negotiated plains approach. Meanwhile, the impatient king and Marishal MacSean found it necessary to break down the remainder of the army into even smaller warbands to press on through the craggy hill country, as they continued their hunt for the elusive rebel forces led by Richard Campbell and his ally MacNab.

Onward the royal forces progressed doggedly northward, although that advance was punctuated by the onset of more aggressive and increasing skirmishes from warbands of a similar size and disposition as each of the previous they had encountered. The king's troops could still not force any decisive battles, and further frustrating Gregor, they could find no definitive trace of the crafty Campbell lord. Remains of looted villages and burned out fields abounded however, and the increasing scarcity of forage for both man and beast confirmed that the king had chosen wisely in sending the bulk of his forces on a different route of march.

The lengthening absence of any reports or correspondence from General Duncan MacSean's army already in the north was beginning to sow further seeds of worry in the minds of his brother and the king. Not knowing the northern army's current position nor whether it may have already met with defeat or rout in the field ate away at both leaders to the point where they secretly feared for the success of the war. Both knew as well, that should the northern army have met with defeat, the fate of Duncan was equally in doubt as he had ever been one to lead from the front.

Sagging wearily onto their cots at the end of another long day on the march, King Gregor and his marishal continued to worry over the persisting silence from the north. Fear that their strategic edge might already be fatally blunted by the increasingly possible loss of Duncan's army was the king's greatest nightmare as he promptly fell asleep but was plagued by his unease, tossing and turning on his narrow cot.

The MacGregor Warlord lay awake staring at the slanted roof of the tent, his restless thoughts denying him the rest his body craved. *Eventually the Campbells must be forced to stand and fight.*

We wi' soon be hammering at the very gates of Lochay; they hae nae much more ground to give. We should be there within the week, if we continue at the pace we hae set. Ach, Duncan, and wi' ye be there to greet me, brother?

Suddenly, Sean's head was ringing as if someone were hammering upon it with a shovel! All thoughts were driven away as he pressed his hands to his head in agony; never had he felt such torment. *"Sean! Do ye hear me, brother?"* boomed an unexpected voice in the marishal's mind, relentlessly demanding a response.

"Duncan? Is it ye?" Sean thought back in aghastment.

"Aye, it is, brother!" the voice in his head returned. *"I did nae ken if this would work from such a distance, but I had to try. I hae sent couriers with dispatches for the king and hae been awaiting further orders, but nay riders hae returned and began to fear for ye. Is all well with ye?"*

"Aye. All is as well as can be expected," returned Sean, a well of relief opening within his mind. *"The Campbells refuse to fight us openly, relying on mobile warbands to harass us with small skirmishes and attacking from the shadows. I hae been concerned about ye as well. Is all well with ye, brother?"*

"Well enough," his brother assured him. *"The Campbells hae an army lurking somewhere before us; we've found traces of their abandoned camps, but can nae discover their army as of yet! If it is auld Domeric directing their northern strategy he's good,"* Duncan warned. *"My lads are beginning to jump at every shadow and chirping cricket; at this point, the suspense is worse than if we were to pin them down and face a full-scale battle. Increasingly, I feel as if they are playing some game of cat and mouse with us, Sean! I'm sorry, brother, but I must break off contact with ye for now. The strain of using telepathy at this distance is tae much to maintain for very long."*

"Very well, brother," thought Sean, regretfully. *"Contact me again when ye are able. Keep thee well and pray success is ours."*

"Aye. Keep thee well also, Sean, and please pass on my regards to the king, our uncle. Farewell, dear brother," sent Duncan, his mind-voice strong and clear until it vanished completely from the marishal's buzzing head.

*   *   *

"Thrice damned be the bloody MacGregor!" ranted an angry Richard Campbell to no one in particular. For the time being the lordling was safely harbored behind the stout walls of Lochay, but also well aware of the fact that MacGregor's army was no more than a day's march south. With only the city's namesake-a wide but somewhat shallow river—that flowed between Ben Challum eastward until it met the River Dochart before pouring into the western part of Loch Tay, the River Lochay would pose only a minimal hindrance to the army that Gregor brought against them.

The young Campbell lord drew off his steel helm and impudently let it drop with a resounding clash to the stone floor."Aunt, we hae harried the cursed man, burned out our own people along with their fields; we hae ambushed him on several occasions, nipped at his flanks every step of the way and still he comes!" Richard cried, exasperation filling his voice along with an undertone of dread as he moped sweat from his forehead with a shaky hand. "We hae done everything that *could* be done and all has failed to halt Gregor and his army. I say that it is time to be realistic; we should begin evacuating the city, and withdraw to the safety of Inveraray Castle."

Shocked, the pretender Queen Catherine, who stood just within the doorway, felt suddenly faint and leaned against the polished wood doorframe for support as she stared at her nephew in disbelief. Lady Catherine said nothing at first while she paused to regain her composer. On her head rested the pretender crown of a queen, having just come from the formal welcome of her nephew back to Lochay, along with the rebel bishops that had pledged her husband their support. Each of those churchmen appeared as frightened as their queen looked appalled.

Standing behind Richard, the cunning chief of the MacNabs attempted to remain unnoticed as he fidgeted nervously, staring out a small window of the palace toward the southwest and the direction in which the king's army would be advancing from.

"Nay, Richard. We wi' make a stand," Catherine insisted, stepping forward to close the distance between herself and her agitated nephew, touching his shoulder with a tentative hand. "Domeric wi' stop General MacSean in the north and then come to our aid here. We can withstand The MacGregor for that long; we must and we shall! Hae faith in our cause, Richard, for we are destined to triumph."

"'Tis a chancy undertaking that ye propose, Yer Highness," MacNab remarked, unable to remain silent any longer. Hastily the hard-bitten chief offered a placating bow to the duchess as she turned to glare coldly at him. "I'm sorry to be the one to offer ye such a bitter pill to swallow, but we would be in a better position in Inveraray. The move would nae be difficult," he continued, unfazed by her glower, "we could march to Loch Awe and cross near Annat where there is a proper ferry that wi' deliver us to the other side. And then from Portsonachan we would hae but a couple days march south to stout defenses of Inveraray and the thick city walls around her.

"Once we hae reached that bastion it should be of little effort to bring in more mercenaries to fight for yer cause," MacNab continued, ignoring the flush that was rising from the duchess' neck to her cheeks. "The water supply is more dependable there tae on Loch Fyne; where it sit's the enemy could in nay way cut off our supply, and there wi' also be plenty of fish to be eaten if they should besiege us. If it should come down to The MacGregor laying siege to us there, we could hold out almost indefinitely."

"Reginald is right, Aunt," Richard eagerly agreed, thoughtfully nodding his head as he yanked at the upper buckles of his stiff leather brigandine to ease the chafing at his neck. "If we remain here, we may be able to hold out until our duke returns to relieve us, but perhaps nae. Our soldiers hae nay lack of fighting spirit, but starvation and lack of water wi' swiftly bring us low. Inveraray wi' buy us and our beloved duke some valuable time to coordinate a plan to recoup our losses," he prodded gently. "MacNab and I can mount a rearguard action to slow down the MacGregor advance while Lochay's garrison is evacuated, and ye with the bishops head east to the ferry at Annat."

"And I should just leave ye behind?" she asked, her eyes large.

Richard sighed and turned away from his aunt's pleading gaze. Resting his calloused hands on the raised sides of the narrow window slit the lordling glanced out across the plain beyond the sparkling waters of the Lochay river. He was a man now and growing old before his time, he knew, and not the same immature boy who had ridden out to do battle so confidently several weeks before. "Am I Prince and heir in truth to ye and King Domeric, or merely a convenience of birth?"

"Well, of course ye are, Richard," she stated, somewhat nonplussed by the sudden question. "What sort of thing is that to ask?"

"Then by all that ye hold holy, let me do my duty; it is my responsibility!" Richard snapped, turning back to face her squarely and lifting a hand in supplication. "If there's any chance at all for us to force a reversal of fortune and take back and hold our lands from The MacGregor, then I must stand and fight! Ye must escape, ye and those bishops that support ye, to Inveraray and rally our forces to the Campbell banner! MacNab and I wi' follow when we can. If I hae to, I wi' burn all of Lochay to the ground to frustrate yer pursuers, but ye must nae stay here," Richard promised, his face set and his voice fervent. "Ye must remain alive and free if Domeric is to be king indeed and nae just name; his hopes must be kept alive for him to come and defend us once he has achieved his victory over MacSean in the north!"

"And just suppose that Domeric has already met with defeat in the north, outfoxed by the Sidhe general, and can nae relieve us? What then, Richard?" demanded Catherine, not one to be badgered into any decision, not even by her kin. "Am I to stand by and lose both of ye? I hae lost a son already to stubborn arrogance and wi' nae do sae again! I wi' nae see ye cut down like my poor Robbie. We must persevere and stand against those who would see us brought low, but we must nae do sae rashly by sacrificing one of our most important chess pieces to the opponent. We wi' nae win this war by such forfeitures, but by outfoxing the enemy like my Domeric seeks to do."

"Ye shall, Yer Highness; a king could nae ask for a more suited queen to act in his absence and marshal is forces," Archbishop Sutherland reassured soothingly, daring to intrude on the family argument by speaking for the first time. "Lord Domeric wi' come to our rescue is he is but given sufficient time to do sae. I've received dispatches just this morning, stating that even now Archbishop Colquhoun and Lord Stevenson are drawing young General MacSean and his army nearer to their doom," he belatedly reported. "Once those MacGregor forces in the north are crushed, Henry and His Majesty wi' join us as soon as they are able. However," the elderly churchman paused, wheezing to catch his breath, "their aid wi' be of little avail to us if we hae decided to remain in Lochay's most perilous position and perhaps fallen to The MacGregor's forces. It is nae my place to be sae bold as to volunteer tactical advise, but there it is, Yer Highness."

Lady Catherine listened quietly to the ailing bishop's speech, one dainty, slippered foot tapping impatiently against the stone floor, before casting a grim glance at her cousin Randolph, the other bishop in attendance. "Well. Ye hae heard what Angus thinks about my plan to stay in Lochay. His Grace disagrees with my wishes; what say ye Randy? If we were to retreat, Richard would remain to fight a delaying action. If he is lost, ye would be our nearest heir to the throne of Scotland," Catherine stated, her tone bland. "That is provided, of course, that our other nephew Oliver is truly dead at the hands of Gregor. Is that what ye want?" she demanded.

Blanching, the young bishop averted his troubled eyes. "I wish only to serve God, as I hae always done and always hae wanted to do, Catherine. I believe, however, that the archbishop has given ye wise and honest advise," declared Randolph, saddened though he was by not being able to support her. "For the sake of the Campbell cause, I agree that ye should fall back to the stronger bastion of Castle Inveraray. Ye, more than any of us, must nae be taken my dear cousin or all is lost beyond redemption."

"I see," Catherine allowed, her proud shoulders slumping forward and her head bowing in defeat. "It appears that none of ye wi' be swayed. I understand yer concerns, but it seems that all of ye fail to see mine," she murmured, taking a deep breath before letting it out with a great sigh before meeting their waiting eyes again.

"Very well," she began without inflection. "Richard, I place all military matters in yer hands. Ye and yer lieutenant wi' hae command of whatever force ye deem necessary to conduct a proper rearguard action," the duchess finally agreed. "Tell me what ye need me to do and I shall see that it is done."

Richard glanced suddenly at MacNab for advise, uneasy in his abrupt command, particularly when it came to telling his domineering aunt what to do. The baron caught the questioning look and nodded his understanding.

Squaring his shoulders, Reginald MacNab hooked his thumbs through his wide sword belt, but remained silent a moment longer as he pondered over the situation which lay before them all.

"Yer Highness, ye and the bishops should leave under escort at once, carrying with ye only that which ye deem absolutely necessary, before MacGregor and his forces are close enough to observe yer withdrawal," MacNab abruptly began. "We wi' see that ye hae a strong detachment of the household guard to escort ye safely to Inveraray. The remainder of the household guard, along with the castle garrison wi' join forces with the warbands we already command. They're fresh and wi' serve Lord Richard well as he goes to lead a vigorous moving defense that wi', with any luck, stymie any pursuit ole Gregor wi' mount against us."

"We shall go and seek refuge at Inveraray then," Catherine affirmed dully.

"Aye, Yer Highness, it is for the best. Ye wi' be well protected by yer family's strongest castle and its formidable garrison; in addition, those of the household guard riding with ye as escort wi' compliment Inveraray's impressive defenses," said Reginald, his tone confident and optimistic. "If fortune turn against us and prevent our forces from rejoining ye at Inveraray, the reinforced garrison wi' hold firm, more than able to protect ye until relieved by friendly forces. His Majesty and Bishop Colquhoun wi' nay doubt hae won the victory from their base at Kinlochlaich and come swiftly to yer aid with the bulk of their troops. Never fear, Yer Highness, all wi' be well."

"I hae nay fear of anything for myself, *Master* Reginald," the pretender queen replied coolly, regarding the chief with an even stare. "Now, if each of ye would please excuse me, I would like a few moments alone with my nephew. Once we are finished, I shall take my leave of this place."

The others immediately took their leave, offering the lady hasty bows of respect, and soon only Catherine and Richard remained standing within the chamber. With an air of stately grace the duchess paused to enjoy the sudden silence, looking upon the young face of her nephew and memorizing it, should she not see it again.

Sighing at last, Catherine pulled off her lustrous golden crown and turned it idly in her hands to forlornly admire its workmanship. "I do nae regret what Domeric and I hae done, nor the decisions we hae made," she confided in so soft a voice that it was barely above a whisper. "The dream of a Campbell kingship might hae been, and still might be accomplished should the Almighty smile upon us, Richard. Nay one can ken the future and what may take place. All any of us can do is exert power over our actions and take responsibility for them, come what may."

Forcing a brave smile onto his face for the duchess' benefit, Richard placed his hands gently where the crown had rested on her brow and traced his fingers along the line where the metal had rested on her pale skin. Bending forward, a tender expression softening his features he lightly kissed his aunt's forehead. "The dream shall still come to pass, Aunt, I ken it," he said reassuringly. "It is only right that Domeric and Catherine Campbell should be sovereigns of this realm, and all of us wi' see this to its end as ye both take yer rightful place in Edinburgh."

As Richard drew away to look into his aunt's still comely face she lifted the gold crown between them then reaching up with it, Catherine lowered it onto his head. "I pray that it shall be sae, dear Richard-nay! Do nae pull away!"

"Please," he cried in sudden dismay, "do nae put it upon my brow, Aunt. A crown is nae for me to wear, but only for ye and my noble uncle."

She made a clucking sound. "Now, now; wear it just for a wee moment, for the benefit of an old woman, that I may see that ye shall hae worn it if something should-" her voice drifted off suddenly. Catherine knew what she had almost said and gauging by the look frozen on Richard's face, she knew he had heard her unspoken words also.

Heeding the lady's plea, Richard reluctantly allowed himself to sink to his knees before his aunt so that she could place the polished, golden crown upon his sweat covered brow. The young warrior flinched as he accepted the weight of it on his head and as the lady removed her hands he caught both in his own and kissed the lady's palms in a fervent show of homage. As he did so a low sob escaped Catherine's lips and she pulled her nephew up into an affectionate embrace, holding him for what might be the last time and altogether indifferent to the fact that her fair but careworn cheek was pressed tightly against the cold and unyielding metal of the crown.

Lady Catherine once again wore the elegant crown when she and Richard retired from the tower chamber a few minutes later. By the time they emerged, both had taken care to wipe away their tears and walked with proud heads held high.

Some time later when the sun had risen past its zenith into a sky that threatened rain to come the Lady Catherine, Duchess of Argyll, along with a well armed force of just over seventy loyal household guards, rode out of the gates of Lochay. They immediately headed eastward toward their first objective at the ferry near Annat on Loch Awe, the first leg of their flight leading to the destination at Inveraray. Seeing Lady Catherine and the bishops off and remaining behind were the pretender prince Richard and his lieutenant, Reginald MacNab to command the Campbell rearguard forces and ward them from any pursuit that their enemies might mount against them.

By nightfall, the remaining defenders of Lochay had melted away to hide in the surrounding hills to await the approaching adversary's army. All sign of the fleeing *royal* passage had been carefully erased by skilled scouts once they were gone, and the castle and town of Lochay were burning, black smoke of their flames issuing into the sky even as the expected rains began to fall.

*   *   *

The billowing smoke rising high into the sky spoke of the fiery death of Lochay as it was seen well to the south as the cloud draped sun dipped beyond the vast Campbell plain. It was then that King Gregor decided to call a halt and ordered his weary army to set up camp with night soon upon them. Climbing to stand atop the vantage point of a small hillock, the king gazed out across the rolling plain and in the distance could see the crystalline waters of River Lochay for the first time, which separated him from one of the Duke of Argyll's most key towns. Gregor followed the directing finger of one his clan's scouts with keen interest. The scout's hand pointed unerringly toward their destination, and the king's eyes widened in shock as oily, black smoke rolled upward into the pale light of dusk and blotting out the emerging moon. The ember glow of the raging fires which consumed Lochay was still faint, but they grew brighter even as Marishal MacSean joined his uncle on the rise and peered to the north. Pulling a unique, slender tube from a long pouch hanging at his waist, MacSean extended the tube until it had doubled in length and raised the narrowest end to one eye. Contained in the tube pressed to his eye was a small, transparent lens, while at the other end resided a larger lens of the same quality, this the Warlord aimed toward the growing ocher glow.

"I suppose it must be Lochay," MacSean growled, lowering his spyglass suddenly and handing it off to Gregor with an exasperated hiss. "Jamie," he addressed the waiting scout, "are there any other sizable towns in that direction, which ye ken of? I can nae think of any, but my geography of this area is a bit lacking."

The experienced MacGregor scout shook his head. "Nay, my lord. There is nae a blessed village located within a few miles of Lochay. The lads and I hae been outriding well ahead of the vanguard, and there's nay mistaking it," he affirmed. "The Campbells hae torched one of their main strongholds along with the town surrounding it, plain and simple as honest fear. We made a cursory check of the roads leading from Lochay, as we were in somewhat of a precarious position sae far ahead of ye, but I believe a substantial party must hae rode away to the east before the fires started. Of course, it could hae just been a caravan of refugees or a merchant train, but it seemed to my eyes as if someone had tried to hide the track of their passing," the scout reported. "Whatever it may hae been, they were already far out of sight before we arrived."

"More likely than nae, it was Catherine Campbell high-tailing it to the sanctuary of Inveraray, with nay regard for the broken fortunes of her own folk left behind," Gregor muttered darkly, watching the brightening glow through his nephew's handy field glass, an angry frown wrinkling his forehead.

"The auld duchess could nae hae taken her entire force with her though," added MacSean, wearing a ferocious grin. "Our scout here would hae surely taken note of such a movement of troops. Correct, Jamie?"

"Aye, that is true, my lord," readily agreed the senior scout. "Our presumption is that the duchess' army remained behind to slow our advance; perhaps they hae dispersed into smaller companies to avoid us, or maybe they just do nae hae enough soldiers left to stand and fight. For all we ken, some may very well hae deserted the duke after we beat them before. We hae still nae found any evidence of a large gathered force; nay sign of tracks or campsites. The lads and I hae been starting to wonder if they even hae much of an army with their Lord Richard."

Gregor scowled as he lowered the field glass from his eye and smacked it into his other hand thoughtfully. "Perhaps, but I very much doubt Domeric would leave Catherine sae exposed or with sae few troops. Alright, if the army is nae here, then where in all of bloody hell is it? The Campbells play the fox to my hound. Sir Duncan, commanding in the north, has nae discovered the duke's army there either," the king growled in growing annoyance. "We must bring them to ground before they can be crushed."

The MacGregor Warlord shrugged. "Perhaps the grand Campbell army nay longer exists as a true army any longer," he muttered mostly to himself, accepting the spyglass back from Gregor and slipping it into the case. "Maybe auld Catherine Campbell just gets her jollies by haeing us chase after her skirts and laddies all blessed summer! All joking and hopeful speculation aside, this *is* the sort of war I would fight if I were outnumbered and on the defensive, and if I had the same stubborn ambition as what they do. They ken that their future in totally wrapped up in this bid for supremacy; the stakes in this game of theirs is all or nothing. The Duke and Duchess of Argyll ken there can be nay surrender as a headsman's sword awaits them if they fail."

Allowing himself an irritated snort, Gregor wrapped his calloused fingers around the wide sword belt around his waist to steady his hands and continued to gaze out at the orange stain growing in the coming night. He knew better than to believe that such tactics would persist; there was a trap somewhere and soon it would be sprung.

"I might and ye most probably would do sae as well, Sean," admitted the king with a sigh. "Bloody hell, even Domeric might play such a fox if left to his own devices, but that bastard Colquhoun would never do sae for tae long, and I ken that he is nae doing sae now, nae without much wailing and gnashing of teeth," Gregor charged with valid conviction. "I believe he's been screening Domeric and the all tae real Campbell army and their allies the whole time we hae been chasing at bloody shadows! Duncan may nae hae discovered the enemy's true army, but I'd be willing to wager that he's seen signs of one's passage by now. I ken it's got to be out there somewhere and waiting for the right opportunity to pounce," growled the king, pointing an accusing finger toward the north, "and we *must* find it before it finds us. It is out there, sitting and waiting, between Duncan and us, Sean. Ye can be certain of that and if we let ourselves be drawn after Catherine's fleeing rabbit going to ground at Inveraray, I fear for what wi' become of Duncan and his army. If we were to chase after the bait, Domeric and his allies could manage to deal a severe blow to Duncan while we were out of position to offer any reinforcement. Should we underestimate our enemies all could be lost, and that is something that I wi' nae allow to happen," stated the determined king.

"Ye are right, of course, Sire. We must play our own game and nae react the way they wish us to. We wi' flush out and eliminate whatever force Catherine has left behind to ward her escape, here in Lochay and then head north to join forces with or rescue my brother, whichever it may turn out to be," agreed MacSean, dismissing the waiting scout with a wave of his hand. "Thank ye, Jamie. Ye may go to yer supper, but be ready come morning. Ye and yer scouts wi' be our eyes as we march into Lochay."

The Warlord caught Gregor's eye and with a quiet assurance added, so only he could hear, "There is a Campbell army hiding from our sight and we shall find it. And with any luck we may be able to catch it between our hammer and Duncan's anvil."

A thoughtful Gregor nodded in weary agreement even as the scout leader slipped away into the growing darkness. "Sae, ye agree then, that Domeric's army roaming about in northern Argyll and seemingly avoiding Duncan is the more dangerous threat?"

"Aye."

"Good. I had hoped that we would be of an accord; I value yer advice more than I can say, Sean," confided Gregor, favoring his nephew with a brief smile. "Very well. With that decided, I intend to take the opportunity to flush out Richard Campbell and his band of miscreant thugs and make them pay in blood for their loathsome actions at the kirk of Saint Michael's. Ye are my best tactician, sae I wi' leave the details to ye, but I do nae believe it wi' be tae difficult to draw out the Campbell puppy now that Catherine has abandoned Lochay."

"Aye," agreed MacSean. "I ken just how to bring him to us."

"Once we hae finished our business here, we head north to pin down Domeric and his army there. If luck should smile upon us, that bloody bastard Henry Colquhoun and his ecclesiastical troops wi' be united with The Campbell when we strike sae that we may deal with them all at once," said the king, striking a fist into his open hand. "Once we hae done all those things, and only then, wi' we march on Inveraray to lay siege and wait until Domeric's blasted wife starves or surrenders."

"It wi' be as ye command, Sire, and in the end every wrong which hae been perpetrated wi' be set right," promised MacSean. Breaking into a sudden, forced smile, he added, "Let us put these matters aside for a time, Uncle. I hae invited Bishop Fletcher to dine with us this evening. I'm sure he wi' cheer ye up."

"Ach, I doubt even he can do that," retorted the gloomy king. "I would hardly dare to call it dining, considering the dismal state of our food supplies. If I should never again set eyes upon another bloody-hard trail biscuit it wi' be tae soon!"

An ironic smirk twisted his lips as Gregor glanced over at his kinsman as they started down from the hill. "At least the company should be civilized for a change," he said, slapping MacSean affably on the shoulder with the first real smile he had had all day. "Nay talk of drawings or quartering or other bloodletting, eh, Sean? Come on; are ye ready to wash the stink from ye? Or would ye prefer to continue smelling like some great sweaty horse?"

Sean's hearty laughter accompanied the two, as they descended from their vantage point. The jovial sound floated on the whisper of a breeze that rose up to join them, which acted to relieve some of the day's unusual heat, and mingled with the comforting sounds of the army settling into camp for the night.

Making their way toward where the royal pavilion had earlier been diligently erected, the two leaders returned in comradely silence, wading across a sadly shallow stream which rose to no more than their ankles. The cool waters were already becoming muddied by the booted feet of busy soldiers leading thirsty horses to drink their fill as the two crossed the narrow rivulet and entered the sprawling camp. Individually, each man stopped to speak briefly with troops that hailed them and young squires which rubbed down and brushed still more heavy mounts before they made their way down one final small incline to reach the large tent that was already erected and ready for them. At the entrance, the two guards posted there snapped to attention as the king approached, and smartly saluted the man that was their respected ruler.

Waiting and ready inside was young Barak who had clean towels and basins of heated water for them, steaming by each man's cot. Tankards of strong ale stood on the campaign table toward the center of the tent, already somewhat cooled by the nearby stream. All conversation ceased between Gregor and his nephew and was quickly replaced with grunts of delight and unabashed sighs of relief for the men as Barak and Gregor's squire, Shane, helped relieve the tired leaders of their heavy armor and placed cool moist towels about their respective necks. Immediately after bathing away the dust and grime from the days travels, fresh clothing was donned and soon after that several swallows of the cold refreshing ale were quaffed as they awaited their guest to arrive for the evening meal. By the time Bishop Fletcher appeared to join them, both men were beginning to feel considerably better and hungry enough to consume whatever food was offered, even the much loathed trail biscuits.

*   *   *

Miles to the north of King Gregor's encamped army, in another military campsite loyal to the rightful king of Scotland, General Sir Duncan MacSean along with the ever faithful Lord Kirkland MacPherson, his Marshal-General MacEwen and Captain James MacNeish, commander of the Border Dragons, had just concluded a gathering within the command tent to discuss their worsening state of affairs. Uncertainty pervaded as Duncan and his commanders sought some way in which to deal with virtually unceasing guerilla attacks they were suffering at the hands of Domeric's quick striking allies.

For the previous two days, the royal forces led by Sir Duncan MacSean had been beleaguered by an unrelenting barrage of fast striking raids of mounted Stevenson archers led by their tireless chief, Lord Tearlach Stevenson. Meanwhile, other more brutally engaging attacks, would oftentimes strike at the same time but always elsewhere along the army's flank. These more aggressive assaults were conducted by the battle hardened and well-disciplined warrior-monks under the command of the dour Archbishop of Saint Andrews, Henry Colquhoun.

Thus far the royal forces had only suffered light casualties, but the unremitting skirmishing along with the unusually hot weather was already taking a toll, especially among the short tempered highlanders.

As night fell, Duncan's immense encampment stood prepared and ready for the assaults they knew would not abate because of darkness. Diligent officers had assigned a double contingent of sentries to ward the parameter with watch fires blazing at regular intervals to aid in rallying the defenders. Four strong companies of ready reaction troops were posted at key sites within the camp, to rush at a moment's notice, to deal with any attack that may come until the sleeping army could rally to arms. In order for those men to get their rest as well, the night was divided into two hour shifts and thus was the duty spread fairly among the troops. Feeling more secure because of the added precautions, the remainder of the army slept more soundly.

Sound sleep evaded General MacSean; although his body craved such rest, his troubled mind would not allow such luxury. Conceding defeat, Duncan irritably threw off his covers and sat up in his bunk with a muttered oath. So as not to wake anyone he snatched up a full winesack and a cup, grabbed one of the camp stools, and quietly strode from the tent. Taking a seat just outside the entrance the general leisurely sipped his wine and pondered the events that had been taking place while enjoying the gentle breeze. He did not permit himself to worry; worry was a useless waste of time that helped no one, just as his brother always said. Planning and action were a leader's responsibility, and a sharp mind was his best tool.

The tent flap rustled open behind Duncan and his son stepped outside to join him, stretching his back with a crack. "Do ye think they wi' come tonight, Da?" Devlin asked softly, his voice muffled as he pulled a clean tunic over his head.

Duncan shrugged his shoulders and took another sip from his cup before speaking. "It seems likely, but I do nae ken. Hae some wine?"

The young warrior accepted the proffered wineskin and with practiced ease raised it above his upturned face and squeezed, squirting a stream of the red liquid into opened mouth. After swallowing several healthy gulps of the watered wine, Devlin lowered the substantially lighter skin and sighed with appreciation. "Thank ye, I needed that. I never thought watered wine could taste sae good!" he exclaimed.

Chuckling, Duncan shook his head at his son's antics. "Aye, I suppose sae. How I long for some chilled MacNeish to drink, sitting within my own home, and nae stinking like a bloody horse!" he carped grumpily.

Devlin grinned and dropped down to take a seat on a patch of trampled grass as he said, "What kind of highlander are ye? We *all* smell like horses by now; I barely even notice the fragrance anymore."

"Yer sweetheart would," snorted Duncan. "I daresay she would nae delight in a kiss and snuggle with ye right now, laddie. Besides, I am nay longer just any highlander, but a knight in the service of the king, as well as one of his faithful lords. The accommodations should be better," he claimed with false arrogance.

The general's son rolled his eyes heavenward. "Ach, I take it all back; ye are a highlander after all. Only a true highland man could take such relish in complaining about being elevated to the nobility; it being such a dratted terrible job!" he laughed.

"I hae always heard that complaining is the sworn duty of all soldiers, as it does provide a pleasant diversion after laboring through a bloody rotten day. Ask any lad here and see if it is nae sae," retorted Duncan, waggling a finger at his son.

"Ye are right, of course," agreed Devlin wearing a roguish grin, "and since it is my duty, I must state that the grumbling of my stomach is terrible and demands that I do something about it. Perhaps, in the name of Lord Duncan, I might manage to scrounge up a late night snack to stave off our starvation?"

"Ye hae my blessing to try, but hunger is nae what plagues me," stated the earl. "What does vex me is that we hae an enemy who is all tae eager to harass us but has nay wi' to stand and fight us like men! I ken wishes are cheap and of nay value, but I *do* wish Campbell would hae the stomach to offer us a real battle to fight."

"I ken how ye feel, Da. I feel the same way, as does every man marching under yer banner," Devlin replied gravely. Standing he washed his hands over his face and pushed loose hair from his eyes. "This whole situation *is* beginning to wear on the men, and I'm sure that is just what Domeric wants. Frazzled nerves do us nay good, especially when our enemy does decide to offer us battle.

"Perhaps we should send out another courier south to try and contact Uncle Sean's army," he suggested. "Maybe he and the king hae learned new intelligence that would help us gain a fresh perspective on this campaign."

Duncan shrugged tiredly. "It could do nae harm, although I doubt another rider wi' get through when all the others seem to hae failed. For now, go and see what snack ye can round up; I think I wi' see if my cot is any more welcoming."

The haggard general did not realize it at the time, but sometimes one should be more discrete in what they wish for, because it could come true, although not necessarily in the way in which they might have desired.

CHAPTER EIGHT

In Glenorchy, the capital of the Clan Gregor territories, all was not as well as it could have been. The devastating news about the death of not just her father, the king, but of her elder brother David as well, brought a grief to Lady Elizabeth MacGregor that she could never have been prepared for. Not only did she find herself suddenly bereft of such close kin, but she also found herself abruptly thrust into a position as queen that she had never desired, much less aspired to. Elizabeth, now Queen of Scotland, unexpectedly found she had a kingdom to administer in the absence of her beloved husband and a grieving heart that she could not publicly show, nor alone give vent to her sorrow without benefit of the strong arms of Gregor to give her comfort.

The new queen was not the only individual who found the startling events a shock even as Scotland fractured into open civil war. Young Lord Grigor, the only son of Lord Gregor, Baron of Inversnaid, immediately found his life changed. No longer was he just the heir to his father's barony and next in line to be chief of Clan Gregor, but found himself thrust into the much greater role of the Prince Royal, heir apparent to the throne of Scotland. It was a role that he found himself completely unprepared for, as he had not even completed his training for the knighthood, much less been properly tutored in the turbulent political affairs of his country.

The new-found royal family was not the only ones that were having a difficult time dealing with the MacGregor's unforeseen elevation. Others, refusing to support the start of a dynasty belonging to their enemies, sought to bring a quick and brutal end to the fledgling power before it could truly be established by means of assassination. This latest intelligence had not yet reached the ears of the prince, but the household spies dutifully reported the news to their mistress, Elizabeth, mother of the youth.

Elizabeth hastily wrenched off the end of the leather scroll tube that her chief spy had delivered into her hand. Extracting the cylinder's contents she urgently unrolled the parchment to read the message written upon it. As the petite, copper-haired queen swiftly skimmed through the lines scrawled within, the words brought a gasp to her lips as her heart leaped sickeningly and stuck in her throat.

'-plans proceed on schedule . . . men to pose as merchant traders . . . with access to . . . prince . . . assassination is certain . . . be diligent-'

Having read enough, Elizabeth raised dove gray eyes full of stunned shock to meet those of her old friend, Captain MacAdam, Commander of the Royal Household Guard. "Someone wants to kill my Grigor? Who?" she asked in a whisper. "When?"

"That, I do nae ken yet, Yer Majesty, except to point a finger at the most obvious culprit, the Campbells," offered the stocky officer, shrugging his shoulders helplessly. "As to when? It wi' nae be attempted this morning with the guard on high alert, I hae seen to that already, but nae given a particular reason for it. I gather ye had nay suspicion that anything of this sort was stirring?" queried the captain.

"Nay," she responded weakly, "though it seems foolish that I should nae hae been expecting such from our enemies. The Campbells and their loyal allies remain in the field to dispute the succession, after all. I should hae realized it could come to this."

"Ye hae my word that I wi' personally take special care with all the security precautious at my disposal, my Queen. Do nae worry any further about it, the prince wi' be kept as safe as if he were my own son," Captain MacAdam reassured her, gently laying a calloused but comforting hand on the shaken queen's shoulder. "It might be wise to hae a quiet word with Prince Grigor and explain to him yer concerns and reason for them. My duty in protecting the prince wi' be much simpler if the lad is willing to cooperate with the precautions I must impose."

Elizabeth nodded her head solemnly. "Very well, Fingal. I shall do as ye request, though I ken nae how he wi' respond to this added burden."

"He's a bright lad; the necessity wi' be clear to him."

Meanwhile, King Gregor with his staunch allies continued their campaign deep in their enemy's ancestral territories. Dawn's early light burned away what meager fog that had descended during the night and found the army's divided warbands beginning to make a convergence as they marched from the foothills southwest of Lochay. The need of a united army now outweighed the necessity of a spread out force.

Standing several paces away from anyone else so none other could overhear them, Gregor and his marishal had drawn aside the young enthusiastic scout, named Arthur Whyte, to hear what he had to convey. It was clear he was eager to share his news.

"We were nae spotted, Sire. We remained hidden until it was safe for me to creep away and make my way back to ye," he promised confidently. "At first they appeared to be just another warband like those that hae been harassing us, but more and more came into our viewing. There could be more, but nae many, hidden within the valley beyond our sight. It must be the Campbell rearguard left behind to ward their escape from Lochay. There are about four hundred of them; all well-armed and all mounted. If ye act promptly, we can move against them and the surprise wi' be ours this time. It would be bloody marvelous to give them a dose of their own medicine!"

"Aye," agreed MacSean thoughtfully. "And none of ye could draw close enough to take a good look at this valley ye mentioned?"

"Nay, my lord," said the scout, shaking his head ruefully. "Jamie deemed it tae risky to do sae without drawing their attention."

MacSean nodded. "He was right to be cautious and nae gamble losing the element of surprise. How far ahead of us is this warband ye saw, lad?"

"Nay more than an hour's hard marching, my lord," the scout replied confidently. "Two men seemed to be in command; the older man in a tartan we did nae recognize, and the other appeared as young as myself wearing the Campbell colors."

MacSean raised his eyebrows and glanced at the king significantly before returning his attention back to the scout. "Ye hae done well, Arthur. We wi' rely on ye to guide us to the enemy without being spotted before we are ready, but in the mean time, please give the king and I a moment to speak alone."

Accepting the marishal's compliment, Arthur grinned and with a respectful bow that took in both leaders, turned and slipped away toward the halted column. Once a good distance away to ensure their privacy he stopped and waited in place, prepared to come when they called for him.

"What are yer orders, Sire?" inquired MacSean.

Gregor's face appeared made of stone. "Is it a trap, ye think?"

"Perhaps. It's what I would do," the marishal stated baldly. "However, Jamie Gregory is one of the finest scouts and trackers that I hae ever known, Sire, and I do nae believe he could miss the signs of an ambush nor lead us into one."

"I shall require all ye can muster of Lord Donald's heavy horse along with our own, and the Gordon light cavalry," the king decided. He shook his pensively and added, "It's tae bad we do nae hae the use of Duncan's light cavalry and horse archers; this type of situation would be perfect for their talents."

"Aye."

The king's expression hardened, though that seemed impossible from where his nephew stood quietly. "The scout's description of the enemy leaders sounds very much like Reginald MacNab and Richard Campbell; if that is sae, the time of retribution is at hand and we can nae fail in our duty. Our hounds hae cornered the hare and now it is up to us to strike the decisive blow."

"Do nae let hate overcome caution," MacSean warned. "Hate can blind even the most reasonable of men. If it is Richard, young though he may be, it is possible that he could possess a measure of his uncle's cunning.

Gregor speared the marishal with his piercing eyes. "It is nae a trap. If Domeric's army were sae close as to use his nephew as bait in a trap our scouts would hae seen sign of it," he declared coldly. "Nay. Richard has finally made the error we hae been awaiting, and I for one plan to see that it is a fatal one for him and his misbegotten band of bandits and cutthroats. It is time to pound a spike through his black heart!"

"Aye, Sire," the MacGregor Warlord murmured, troubled by the king's growing obsession with catching the young Campbell lord, but wisely knowing better than to speak further of his concern with his king in such a frame of mind. "Do ye wish to hae our commanders summoned or would ye hae me issue yer orders, Sire?"

Gregor caught his nephew's troubled expression and a fond smile twitched at the corners of his lips, mitigating some of his earlier severity. "I am the King of Scots and lead this army, but ye are my Earl Marishal. Nay man has more talent or skill for war than ye, Sean. Ye command Scotland's armies upon any field of battle far better than I ever could hope to do. I trust in ye to issue whatever orders ye see fit, to once again lead us to victory, General MacSean," he stated with total sincerity, before allowing his keen gaze to wonder toward the gently rolling plains that led to blackened Lochay; in his mind, the king envisioned the high justice he sought to mete out.

*   *   *

Richard Campbell squared his shoulders resolutely under the weight of his armor, arrogant chin held high to disdainfully look down his nose at the stubborn inhabitants of Lochay, which refused to abandon the city as they had been ordered to. Lochay was all but silent as he and MacNab rode down a blackened street, many of the homes and buildings charred, some still burning even three days after the razing had taken place. His bodyguard were quiet as well, except for the jingle of harness and clop of steel-shod hooves, as they flanked their lord and his lieutenant.

The lieutenant rode sullenly at his lord's side, his blunt, broken-nosed face a mask as he tried to contain the contempt he felt for the younger man's inaptitude towards even basic tactics or strategy. Of all places to choose to ambush The MacGregor, he had to choose the one place where they had the least advantage of success!

Glancing off to his right, MacNab watched in disbelief as a squad of Campbell troopers emerged from one building, that had mostly escaped destruction, carrying more plunder than they would be able to fit into their saddlebags. *Bloody hell! The bairn should hae gone with his mother; he shows more concern for seeking to teach his own folk a lesson in obedience than he does in preparing to fight for his bleeding life! This place is more suitable to trapping us than doing sae to Gregor,* he thought darkly, gritting his teeth as he shot a look at his commander. *He's gonna get us all killed, as sure as night follows day. I hae to find a way out of this,* he cast another fleeting glare at Richard. *I did nae join the bloody Campbells just to throw my life away for nay good reason, and I'll nae die for this pup!*

Oblivious to his lieutenant's glowering looks, preoccupied instead with the stiff necked folk of Lochay, and the lesson he was teaching them, the Campbell lord gave no consideration to the possibility that he might be the mouse to another's cat and that someone more clever might be coming to teach *him* a lesson. Overconfident to the point of stupidity, Richard continued to believe he could lead his enemy by the nose into any trap that he chose. He had been a thorn in Gregor's side for weeks now. Even the Sidhe, Sean MacSean, had not been able to counter his tactics, after all.

Someone speaking to him broke the young leader from his reverie. "Yer Highness, I must insist that ye reconsider what ye are doing!" MacNab growled, his deep voice sounding as if his throat were full of gravel. "We must leave this place unless ye wish to be cornered here like a rat; I ken we are the ones drawing our enemy into an ambush, but we wi' be the ones snared. Any ambush sprung knowingly can quickly turn against us and be our demise. Gregor could be canny enough to do sae, and MacSean certainly is crafty enough a tactician to turn the tables on us," the MacNab chief stated adamantly.

The words were barely out of MacNab's mouth before a Campbell outrider burst through the lingering smoke and into the city square, urging his lathered mount toward the two leaders. Several paces away the scout's horse suddenly fell, its front legs giving way under it, and sending the rider up and over the roan's head. Picking himself up on unsteady legs, the disheveled scout staggered up to his lord's side and grabbing the stirrup to maintain his feet.

"My lord, companies of cavalry, heavy and light, hae come upon us nae long ago and are headed this way," he reported bleakly. "They hae already found and annihilated the hunting band outside of town searching for game."

"How many?" demanded Richard.

"There are scores of them," said the breathless scout. "At least four hundred, but maybe more and they are moving fast and directly toward Lochay. Somehow they must hae found us out and ken where we are. My lord, I'm sure I saw The MacGregor!"

"Well, of course ye saw The MacGregor, he's their bloody chief! Who the bloody else would be leading his misbegotten clansmen, dimwit?" snapped Richard, his face gone white with dread as he vented his frustration on the hapless scout.

"Blast it all, ye young fool!" roared MacNab, glaring at Richard. Urging his agitated mount among the booty laden soldiers now milling uncertainly about in the street in shock. "If ye bloody idiots value yer pathetic lives drop that loot, mount up, draw yer weapons and follow me before its tae late!"

Seeing his shouted orders virtually ignored, the seething MacNab chief drew his sword and flourished it above his head for emphasis as he screamed at the confused mob of troops. In his tirade the chief's attention was drawn to multiple flashes of sunlight reflected off metal coming from the north. What MacNab saw made his mouth go dry with dismay as his worst fears were coming to pass.

"Richard!" he cried, pointing with his sword as he caught the young Campbell's attention. "Gregor is encircling us! If we do nae act swiftly all wi' die here today. He is tightening the noose about our necks while we sit here. What are yer orders?"

Trying to swallow but unable to for the lump in his throat, Richard could hardly pull his gaze away from the second force of cavalry that was rapidly closing in on them. "What can we do but surrender?" he asked, climbing from the saddle. "I do nae ken why I believed we could ever fight and defeat an enemy versed in sorcery."

The fierce glower that MacNab leveled at Richard should have struck the young man dead where he stood. "Do ye believe Lord Gregor wi' allow any of us to surrender without taking vengeance for what ye did at Saint Michael's kirk? Ye can cower before him and die, begging for mercy, but I for one plan to sell my life as dearly as I can, just as any warrior worthy my wielding a sword should, ye pathetic coward!" rasped the outraged chief, raking his furious gaze across the man with disgust.

*   *   *

It was not sorcery or any other type of magic that had been used to discover the Campbell forces, but a much more mundane method employed by skilled trackers.

For a time, the forces commanded by Richard Campbell had successfully evaded those of the king as they abandoned the heavy forests within the Lochay glen and moved back to a position within the ruined city. It was the one place in which none believed they would go, as no capable commander would have done such a thing. Scouts, a breed of independent souls which in times of peace led a life as hunters and trappers, could follow the spoor of any wild animal and now had led their king and his army on the track of their human prey after only a brief delay as they searched for sign. The spoor they found had led them directly, though surprisingly, to the scorched city of Lochay.

Now, with his quarry cornered within a trap of their own making, King Gregor and his marishal began to skillfully draw tight the noose they had set about the Campbell town, like a party of hunters would stalking a fox.

Settling his battered helm securely on his head, the king meaningfully drew the long glinting blade which had belonged to his grandfather's grandfather and raised it high above his head. Gazing determinedly at the razed town with clear blue eyes that glittered like windowpanes iced over with winter frost, he raised his visor for all to better hear him as he addressed his eager troops.

"Honourable defenders of Scotland," he began, his shout ringing clear and true as he brandished his claymore, "inside those fire blackened walls are the vermin we hae been searching for. They are nae soldiers, but merely bandits of the worst sort. They are the same vermin that sacked a holy place and slaughtered priests and raped defenseless sisters of the cloth!" charged Gregor, his voice dark with rage. All about the king, soldiers crossed themselves and called for the blood of those responsible. Raising his other hand for silence, Gregor continued, "A Campbell lord led these scum and leads them still; his name is Richard Campbell! I want this Richard, alive if possible, sae that he can be made to pay in full for his crimes. Justice must be served for the high as well as the low, as true justice must be nay respecter of station," he cried with conviction. "Justice wi' be served this day, and for Lord Richard that justice wi' be a most swift and dreadful punishment! There is another who is likely with the Campbell lord; he is a rebel chief and a bandit in his own right, named Reginald MacNab. Take them both alive if ye may.

"Now," the king paused a beat, "ride bravely for the honour of Scotland!"

"For Scotland and King Gregor!" the enthusiastic host cried in one voice, the metallic rasp of steel leaving scabbards loud as the united clansmen of several noble clans drew their sharpened blades and saluted by pounding sword against round targe.

*   *   *

Lord Richard's force, under the more capable command of Reginald MacNab, had been rallied into order through much shouting and threats by the red-faced chief. That the Campbells were set in order before the royal army could actually enter the streets of the burned town was a testament to their fear of the belligerent warrior. In moments, MacNab had the collected troops of the warband gathered on the deserted and blackened village green in formation to make a desperate stand.

Sitting his skittish mount beside the fierce chief, Richard entertained no illusions about his command's chances of surviving the afternoon. They scarcely numbered three hundred, even counting the surprising added support of some city folk, which trickled in to supplement their ranks. All those joined them came on foot but all were armed with one sort of weapon or another.

Shouting his orders in a bull roar, MacNab commanded all but the officers to dismount, and ragged ranks were formed on the green that gradually took the appearance of orderly troops. The fighting square resembled a Roman phalanx, except with the center open where the officers could see all about them and issue commands as needed. This fighting formation was the only one simple enough for the mostly untrained and freshly arrived volunteers to understand and be a help rather than a hindrance.

Watching his lieutenant take charge seemed to have no affect on Richard as he could not pull his attention away from the advancing royal troops for long. The young Campbell lord knew he was beaten; forced to fight in the open gave all the advantage to The MacGregor's heavy mounted forces, as he would use them to devastating effect on his cornered and bewildered warband.

Both hands clutched his reins in a white knuckled grip as Richard sat his restless horse beside the cursing MacNab within the fighting square. Wide brown eyes riveted to his approaching hated nemesis the young lord saw his death draw near with no means of avoiding it. Professionally calm and silent, grim of mien and unrelenting, the royal heavy cavalry came forward in supple mail and shiny plate armor. Draped in MacGregor tartan they pressed on, slowly closing off any hopes of flight, as in the meantime, from the flanks came more heavy horse draped in a different tartan. From the rear of the square came still more cavalry, lighter armed but more fleet. These wore a tartan that Richard recognized as that of Clan Gordon, formerly an ally, albeit a reluctant one.

Immediately following the tightly packed, impressive ranks of armored knights came one that caused a shiver of fear, despite the heat of the day, to run up his armored back. Heralded by the crimson, white and gold arms of Scotland, clad in burnished but somewhat dented armor, with his clan's distinctive tartan of red and green crossed with a line of white draped proudly over his broad shoulders and falling as a long cape down his back, came King Gregor.

Spotting the king at the same time as Lord Richard did so, MacNab bellowed a sudden command to the awaiting warband and spurred his mount forward as the entire phalanx surged ahead with him. Taking up a loaded crossbow hanging from his saddle and bawling insults at the royal enemy, the MacNab chief sighted down the bolt and with a gentle squeeze loosed the quarrel at Gregor's kingly silhouette. The bolt raced out with a smooth grace, but before the bolt could find its target the king was briskly shouldered aside by the mount of the plumed helmeted officer at his right hand. His heavy shield was speedily raised and interposed to effectively ward off the deadly quarrel.

Cursing luck's cruel fickleness, MacNab failed to recognize who it was that had saved the king, but Richard had not. The would-be prince felt his stomach suddenly grow queasy as he laid eyes on the infamous man. In a long cape of black and vermillion, and wearing a bright swath of MacGregor plaid draped across his chest and attached by an intricate silvery brooch of Celtic craftsmanship, he sat his horse proudly. A silver coronet denoting his title of marquess, this soldierly figure could be none other than the feared and infamous Sidhe lord, Sir Sean MacSean: the king's eldest nephew, warlord, and most staunch supporter.

Richard hardly dared to breathe as his band of warriors clashed uselessly with the immovable knights arrayed before them. Many fell in that initial rush, lying wounded and dying from grievous injuries inflicted by glittering steel lance tips. The fruitless assault, brashly led by Reginald MacNab, was repulsed with an ease that sickened the young lord as the foremost rank of knights lowered their lances and met the rebel charge. Within a matter of seconds a score of the earnest rebels had fallen at the feet of their enemy; those few wounded, but crying out in agony, quickly had their agony cut short as the royal elite signaled men-at-arms to come forward and administer the coup de grace.

Unaccustomed to the realities of actual combat the rest suddenly began to falter and then retreat, much to the ire of the lowland chief. Finding himself unexpectedly exposed in the foremost rank of battle as the rest ran away, MacNab cursed belligerently and before he could taken prisoner swung his mount around and spurred away. Through the ragged ranks of his men he rode without regard to whom his warhorse shouldered violently out of the way. By the time he had reached Richard's side, red in the face with uncontained fury and foul oaths, the survivors of the ill fated charge had been regrouped by their sergeants into a somewhat more compact fighting square.

For what seemed to be an eternity to Richard and his men but in reality was but a few seconds, the only sounds to be heard on the green were the jingle of bit and bridle, the dull stomping of steel shod hooves on the already trampled and singed grass as riders settled their mounts, and the snap of battle pennons in a brief breeze that kicked up for a moment and carried with it the acrid odor of smoldering wood. To the Campbell lordling none of those things compared to the thundering in his ears of his own racing heart, a sound which threatened to drive him mad.

Across from the green royal lance heads gleamed in the sun with grim and deadly promise, several glistening with bright red blood; it struck would-be prince that what he saw was a presaging of the coming afterlife awaiting his and his men's souls. Richard shuddered with renewed fear at the omen. Another breeze blew through the ruined town and briefly whirled the colorful lance pennons as he watched in a spellbound reverie. The Royal Standard of Scotland snapped in defiance as if the rampant lion itself was gnashing his sharp teeth together; black dust kicked up and eddied toward the east, but not a whiff of it reached Richard as he shifted uncomfortably under the weight of his armor and felt sweat trickle down his forehead and neck from under a helmet that felt as it was going to cook his brains before any sword or lance could claim that privilege.

When that frightening moment at last passed it was brought to an end by a means that Richard had not been expecting. Surrounded by an impressive knot of personal guards, a huge warrior that he did not recognize, with his tartan draping across his barrel thick and immensely broad chest, rode forth from the ranks of heavy horse positioned to the right of the rebel square.

Kneeing his huge mount, no less than the mighty Clydesdale breed required to accommodate his own great stature, the impressive lord carefully wound his way between the still combatants with a massive sword held in one fist and raised to rest casually on a broad shoulder. The coronet circling his helm proclaimed him an earl, and when he raised his visor to speak a wild tangle of bright copper whiskers covered the majority of his grim face, liberally peppered with gray and bristled with sweat.

"Ach, it *would* hae to be *him*," Reginald muttered grimly, more to himself than for the young lord mounted at his side. "The giant ye see before ye is yet another hammer in which Gregor is using to smash any hopes yer family has of living through this ill fated rebellion yer uncle has persuaded me to throw in with."

"I do nae ken the pattern of tartan he wears," commented Richard, as he curiously cast an inquiring glance toward his ally.

"That," Reginald breathed stoically through clenched jaw, "is Lord Donald, The MacDonald and Lord of the Isles; he is a right deadly bastard to any seeking to oppose him in whatever he puts his mind to. And, he dearly *hates* Clan Campbell."

"Why? I hae never laid eyes on the man."

Reginald snorted and shook his head wryly. "At this point it does nae really matter does it? However, sae ye ken, it seems that long before The Recovery, even back in the ancient times, yer Campbell ancestors did a great wicked deed against the MacDonalds of Glencoe," he replied bleakly. "While a military band of Campbells enjoyed the offered hospitality of the MacDonalds, they crept from where they had been given to sleep for the night and massacred their hosts-every man, woman, and bairn living within the keep. Plus before making their escape from MacDonald lands they torched the keep and stole their flocks. Now, despite all the years which hae passed, Lord Donald still claims the right of blood vengeance against yer family and kin until the honour of that slaughtered family of his wronged clan has been avenged."

"Ye must be joking; surely his clan would hae done sae already, eh?" asked the surprised lord with raised eyebrows. "The crime was committed sae long ago, it surprises me that he should even remember it, much less seek revenge for it."

"Perhaps his clan at that time was tae weak or possibly yers was tae politically powerful to allow their retribution. Who can ken it for sure?" shrugged Reginald with an air of indifference, while gazing across the way at the nobleman they spoke of. "All I can say for sure is how his being here affects us, Richard. Donald makes a very fine friend, but an implacable enemy, and he's known for hating yer uncle with a passion. I ken nae what the cause is for the personal animosity, but it is nae a recent thing."

"Is he a mightier enemy than MacSean?"

The MacNab chief's grin bore no trace of humor. "I'm nae sae sure that I would quite say that, Richard, but ye would be wise to nae fear Sean MacSean sae much that ye forget about yer other foes. Especially ones the like of Donald."

Offering his compatriot a curt nod, Lord Richard returned his avid attention to the drama unfolding before him. Gathering every bit of courage that remained within him to face the inevitable with at least a show of calm, he returned The MacDonald's flat stare with one of his own.

Guiding his huge mount closer to the Campbell lines with an ease of superior skill honed over decades of riding, Lord Donald never allowed his hard and relentless stare to waiver from the young Campbell lord's face. Drawing to a halt the giant warrior sat tall and utterly quiet for several seconds, allowing his baleful gaze to bore mercilessly into Richard's eyes before clearing his throat to speak.

"Sae. *This* is what the terrible Clan Campbell is reduced to," he began, his deep voice harsh and full of disdain as he shook his head in mock sadness, "a frightened rabble led by a wee bairn nae long from his mother's tit. I came to help my friend fight an enemy that I myself thoroughly despise and instead of bloody Domeric, I find a puppy playing at war as if he knew what he was doing."

Richard bristled at the deliberate insult but bit back the caustic words that leaped into his throat and settled for baring his teeth in a feral grin.

The powerful earl laughed openly at the weak display and again shook his head with unconcealed contempt. "As much as

I would be perfectly happy to annihilate the whole lot of ye, my friend, Gregor has bade me offer the misguided followers of the Duke of Argyll terms of surrender. This offer is tendered only to officers and men, but nae to those that lead ye, namely yer lordling and the rebel chief at his side," he clarified with a self-satisfied smile.

"For the benefit of those that do nae ken me, I am Donald MacDonald, Lord of the Isles," he introduced himself. "Ye lot hae seen with yer own eyes how yer kinsmen hae fallen at the taste of the keen steel lances leveled against ye. Do ye also wish to feel their cool caress or do ye hae better judgment?" asked Donald with blunt curiosity. "Ye do nae hae to die today even if yer master does nae hold any honour. Any man among ye who wi' throw down his weapon and step forth wi' nae be harmed, ye hae my word on it. If yer master does still possess some scrap of honour, I wi' personally meet him or the rebel named MacNab in single combat. To the death. If either wi' fight me and should prove victorious, King Gregor has agreed to allow every one of ye safe passage from this place with a three hour head start," he explained, a fearsome smile appearing on his whiskered face. "However, if I should prove the victor, if must agree to surrender unconditionally with the promise that if there be any further hostile action on yer part, yer numbers wi' be decimated and the rest of ye cast outside the law."

All those present knew that to be cast outside the law was a brigand's life without comfort as it would be legal for anyone to hunt them down with fire and sword. No law would protect such men from the wrath of anyone who desired to slay them. They would be a castout from society, with no rights or protection, and whom no honest merchant or crofter would buy, sell or trade with.

These thoughts ran through the minds of the rebel Campbells as some cast furtive or open glances of wonder at their young master, and awaited his response to the open challenge offered by the mighty island lord.

Before Richard could stop him, the red-faced MacNab chief raised his sword in furious defiance and spurred his mount away from his tremulous leader, forward through the Campbell ranks to the forefront. Halting opposite the MacDonald lord, he glowered at their antagonist with open hostility.

"I am Reginald MacNab, and I accept yer challenge in the name of Lord Richard Campbell. In truth, I would accept it if only to stand in opposition to The MacGregor who seeks to usurp the Scottish throne!" cried MacNab. "I for one am nay sheep that wi' go willingly to the slaughter without giving an accounting of myself like any self respecting Scottish warrior should, nor wi' I cower before ye or yer master like some whipped dog. I am surely nae a Campbell, but I am nae given to believe the destiny and future of my beloved Scotland, neither her highlands nor her lowlands belongs in the fist of a bloody MacGregor. I can speak for my clan when I say," he went on stubbornly, "we wi' never swear homage to the likes of this so called King Gregor nor any other MacGregor sae long as I draw air into my lungs!"

"The MacNab! At least ye hae more bark than the Campbell puppy," Donald said amicably, greeting his opponent. "I am nae surprised ye hae joined cause with Campbells, yer clan has ever found delight in hating their betters. I see thee and wi' meet thee gladly in single combat, Reginald MacNab, sae that I may silence yer wagging tongue and put an end to yer lungs wasting bonny Scottish air!"

"And I yers, ye great ox!" countered Reginald.

"Better for me to be an ox rather than a conniving weasel simpering before a rebel bairn for scraps from his table!"

Uttering a growl of outrage the MacNab chief kicked spurs into his mount's side causing it to surge forward the length of its body before common sense made him brutally curb his attack with a vicious yank on the reins. Casting a scornful scowl at his hulking adversary, MacNab waited for him to formally state the standard customs and rules in regards to the single combat.

For his part, Lord Donald remained unmoving through the other man's display of temper, and a predatory smile bared strong, white teeth as his lips parted, skinning back in a wolfishly hungry expression.

"Shall we dismount first, MacNab? I would nae wish to assert such a vastly unfair advantage that I would hae with my battle steed over yer poor pony."

"Aye. I *graciously* accept yer offer," Reginald said sardonically. "And, let us hae a circle drawn in the ashes, that we may learn who is the superior warrior in this dance of death," suggested the lowland chief.

"As ye wish."

Waiting silently from where he sat his horse, King Gregor watched with interest as both combatants dismounted while the impromptu fighting circle was drawn on the ash dusted ground around the two warriors. Gregor was already well aware of his friend's martial prowess in both melee and single combat, but knew as well that Donald was aging just as he himself was. The hard bitten Reginald MacNab was an unknown commodity, in that Gregor had never personally fought the man, seen him fight, nor so much as heard of his fighting ability with a sword. Nevertheless, Gregor did not harbor much fear over the well being of his old friend, as he and Donald had been involved in duels for a very long time, and Donald, that great giant of a man had never been so much as bloodied, much less seriously wounded at ant time.

Although Gregor's powerful ally had now weathered over forty winters already, The MacDonald remained as surprisingly quick as a striking snake with his infamous two handed claymore, which he still wielded with only a single hand. Its long, massive blade measured over four feet of honed steel sharp enough and sufficiently heavy that-tales of it are told, at any rate-it could and *had* cleaved a warhorse clean in half, through the saddle and all! Although Gregor had been present to witness the feat for himself, Donald had admitted with a sly wink, that he did have to swing the enormous sword with both hands on that particular occasion.

Thinking back on that fond remembrance, the king could still clearly recall Donald's laughably false modesty and it brought a smile to his lips. The two had been fast friends since childhood when Gregor had been fostered, in the highland way, to the then chief of Clan Donald for a year before he had gained his formal standing as a laird. The young men had not just become friends, but blood brothers as well, as the old scar on his palm reminded him.

Across the green on the opposite side of the completed fighting circle, Richard sat astride his mount as well, lost in brooding thoughts, but with no such faith in his own champion. Even as he fidgeted in his saddle for a more comfortable position the young Campbell lord caught sight of the king's distracted smile. An air of foreboding, as cold as a breeze sweeping in from the North Sea, filled him with such a sudden sense of dread that he had to curb an urge to swing his mount away and flee in desperation.

Standing within the completed fighting circle Donald waited nonchalantly, his long claymore grounded before him as he rested his broad hands on the plain, well-used hilt of wrapped leather. Waiting across the circle from The MacDonald stood his cunning opponent with bared steel at the ready, albeit not so calmly, as he glared with a mixture of anger and fear at the impassive island lord.

Both warriors were clad in their armor; Lord MacDonald in heavy back and breast plate while Laird MacNab wore a simple breastplate and chain, a concession he made to not be overly constrained by too much weight. Instead of wielding such a cumbersome weapon, Reginald held in one hand his well used basket hilted claymore and highland dirk in the other to counter the mightier but more taxing blade of his foe.

Holding aloft a leather gauntlet for all present to clearly see, the appointed judge bowed gravely to each of the waiting combatants and threw down the glove he held, signaling the formal onset of the dire contest before hastily backing out of the circle.

Swift to bring his attack, Reginald leaped toward Donald even before the judge could completely exit the circle. As his blade whistled fiercely in a savage cut towards the huge man's head, Donald's own sword swept up and smoothly parried the stroke, but as he did so, Reginald's dirk darted inside his guard and scored a raking blow across his foe's mail clad arm that skittered harmlessly off the sturdy, oiled links as it was turned aside. Cursing, Reginald swayed back just in time to avoid the large claymore's fearsome back swing as it flashed out at his chest and narrowly missed.

The MacDonald's smile was wolfish as he laughed with delight. "Well done, ye hae struck the first blow, MacNab! There's nay man who lives that could boast of that. Now ward yerself, it's my turn!"

In an amazing feat of strength and skill, Donald hefted his massive sword and still using only one hand, swung it into action cutting figure eights through the air between himself and MacNab laughing all the while. The sharp steel flashed in the sunshine as Donald marched at his retreating adversary. Fearsome in sound as well as in sight the island lord's mighty blade howled lustily as it scythed through the air before striking with it's very tip against his foe's breastplate and leaving a deep furrow carved in it as steel screeched on steel. The sinister sound of his armor being ravaged brought the flustered Reginald back to his senses just in time to block Donald's follow through cut, crossing sword and dirk to intercept and stop the blow. Needles of pain rushed up both his arms as he dropped down on one knee under the force of the strike and was forced to drop and roll away to avoid another ferocious assault that came so frighteningly fast. Bounding to his feet behind The MacDonald, Reginald took advantage of his agility to leap forward and aim a swift lunging attack which drove into the mail protecting the big warrior's shoulder, and drawing bright blood, as even those strong links could not withstand his sword's keen point. Following his sword strike by no more than the wink of an eye, the MacNab chief stabbed up at Donald's lightly protected neck with his dirk, but at the last instant the giant warrior twisted away and the single edged blade raked harmlessly away across the side of his helmet. In pain that was mingled with more than a little surprise, Donald bellowed incoherently and lumbered hastily out of range of his foe's weapons.

The Lord of the Isles' right arm burned with sharp burning lances of agony that shot down from his wounded shoulder even as he was forced to switch to the more traditional two handed stance as he braced to meet his opponent's fresh assault. Eyes that winced to mere slits with the fresh pain he bore as he was compelled to use his wounded shoulder, Donald parried each stroke leveled at him, but in doing so he also was forced to give ground before the smaller man's new and more confident advance. Although still wary the lowland chief no longer showed any sign of fear as he pressed his attack.

Slowly and grudgingly surrendering ground a step at a time under the onslaught of raining blows, Donald failed to note the forgotten gauntlet which had been thrown down by the judge at the start of the contest. Taking another grudging step backwards, Donald's foot caught on the glove causing him to stumble; losing his footing the huge warrior fell heavily to the ground on his back in a loud clash of armor. Crying out in surprise as his breath escaped him, Donald could feel the Morrigan coming for him and reaching out to take him into her cold embrace.

The stunned cries of shock which sounded from the royal troops and the sudden cheers of hope issuing from the Campbells were all beyond the hearing of the fallen island lord as all he beheld was the ferocious, triumphant sneer transforming Reginald's cruel lipped mouth leering down at him. Then, in a smooth motion of his enemy's wrists, the sword was quickly reversed and set to plunge savagely down through his breastplate and thunderously pounding heart!

The Lord of the Isles momentary fear suddenly burned away and in its stead a feverishly cold rage took root as Donald watched the blade descent in what seemed like slow motion toward his heaving chest. Once again able to draw breath, and regaining control of his limbs, the huge warrior reached swiftly up with one gauntleted hand and knocked aside the intended death blow of MacNab's sword. With the other, his good one, Donald sat up abruptly and cuffed his enemy a powerful blow to the side of his helmet which so stunned Reginald that he stumbled sideways under the force of it and set the smaller man's ears to ringing.

The pain from his wound momentarily forgotten, Donald scrambled to retrieve his fallen claymore and grunted with relief as his fingers wrapped around the familiar hilt. Climbing to his feet before his opponent could recover, the great island lord hefted his sword and with his legs set he began to weave a net of steel before him. Effortlessly, like an extension of his own arm, Donald whirled the keen weapon through the air as if he had never been wounded. That shiny, four foot long blade seemed to sing as its path split the air, humming a song of promised death; suddenly the music changed notes as the sharp steel cleaved through MacNab's armor as if it were not even there. Striking deep into the lowlander's flesh with a sickeningly moist thud, the heavy blade cleaved its bewildered victim from shoulder to navel. In horrified disbelief, the MacNab chief stared down at his severed sword arm as it lay twitching at his feet.

Reginald's agonized scream barely registered through The MacDonald's fearsome berserker rage. Eyeing his stricken enemy through a red haze of fury as he wrenched free his blood drenched sword, Donald howled wildly and in one graceful motion whirled around to execute a deadly roundhouse. The powerful backhanded blow easily severed MacNab's head from his already dying body, arterial blood spurting violently into the air as the head flew madly away with wide eyes, and landing after a sickening bounce outside the fight circle only a few paces from the hooves of his former master's horse.

Lord Richard gawked in horror as his comrade's head came to a rest, the eyes already glazed over, seemed to glare up at him in accusation as he swallowed the sore bile threatening to erupt from his lips. He could feel the eyes of everyone gathered on that village green riveted to his deathly pale face, clearly waiting with expectation to observe what he would do now that his champion was obviously dead.

Swallowing a great lump that had risen in his throat, Richard kneed his mount and slowly edged his way toward the front of his uneasy troops and closer to those of his sworn enemies, forcing himself to meet Gregor's impassive stare.

"I am Richard Campbell and I speak for my clansmen here along with those others here who hae pledged their support to my noble uncle," stated the nervous young leader. "My chosen champion has fallen in honourable combat before the might of yer's, Gregor. As spoken by yer champion, ye hae given oath that my men wi' nae be slaughtered if they should lay down their weapons."

Gregor nodded slightly. "That is sae."

"Very well," Richard sighed despondently. "I shall hold ye to that oath then, and formally surrender these forces under my command to yer care."

"My oath is my honour, Campbell, and I accept yer surrender," replied the king solemnly. "Any of yer troops who peacefully lay down their arms wi' be treated properly and without malice. Ye, however, do nae warrant such leniency as ye are thoroughly culpable for yer rebellious actions taken against the crown and responsible for other crimes, most notable among them being those shameful liberties carried out upon the kirk of Saint Michael and the innocents there. The laws of Scotland must be upheld and due punishment meted out for the breaking of them, Richard Campbell," said Gregor, his tone cold and dire with no hint of mercy. "Ye hae much to answer for."

"Laws of Scotland? Surely ye must instead mean 'laws of Gregor'?" demanded Richard venomously. "Shall I nae be judged by my peers? I do nae hae to answer to yer laws, MacGregor! Nay, nae from the man who usurps the crown of Scotland; who has nae been seated upon the Throne of Scone; and who is nae the true, rightful and legitimate successor to the sovereign station, of which my uncle is the proper claimant!"

"Enough! The Royal Council convened in Edinburgh some weeks past. Their decree dictated that the legal and lawful succession of Scotland's throne should pass to myself and my wife, whom ye seem to hae forgotten is the eldest daughter of our late King William the Stewart. Elizabeth stood second in line to the throne, only behind the poor deceased Prince David, who perished the same day as his father," Gregor retorted angrily. "Perhaps yer uncle, the Duke of Argyll and his lady wife hae some lesser claim, but it should be clear even to a simpleton that our claim is the greatest!"

Richard hawked and spat on the ground contemptuously. "Only should yer lady wife agree to divorce ye would Clan Campbell consider backing down from its claim. A MacGregor as our king would never, nae even in a thousand years, be acceptable to the folk of our proud clan!" cried a furious Richard.

"Then yer clan wi' be exterminated."

The mild tone of Gregor's voice as he uttered those stinging words sent a shudder of dismay through the Campbell ranks, and Richard's sullen countenance blanched as if someone had spat directly in his face.

"Ye would nae dare!" gasped the stunned lord.

"Indeed I would, should yer clan's rebellion persist," the king reassured him. "Yer lawless deeds and outright criminal actions are like a disease in this land, and I wi' nae tolerate such treatment of innocents. Nor can I allow those who wi' nae bend the knee and give proper homage to their king live to undermine my authority."

"What innocents? There are nay such in war, MacGregor," countered Richard, his tone mocking as he shook his head in denial. "These lands that ye and yer army tread upon are Campbell lands, as they ever hae been, and subject to the rule and writ of my uncle, the Duke of Argyll. All the cities and towns, every village and villager, and others which reside herein are answerable to his whim and prerogative."

"Ach," spat Gregor with growing impatience. "And does that *prerogative* now extend to God's own kirks and abbeys? I think nae. Is Clan Campbell now sae godless that the sanctuary of the kirk means nothing to ye?"

If it were possible, Richard's already ashen face would have gone even more pale at the king's pointed accusation. "What do ye mean, MacGregor? We hae nae violated the sanctuary of any kirk," he denied with widened eyes.

The king's own eyes grew hard as flint. "Ye are a liar of the most foul sort and a loathsome rapist of women, Richard Campbell! Ye are without honour, nor do ye seem to even ken what it is. It is my decree that ye are worse than a brigand, and are from henceforth considered outside the law," Gregor stated tonelessly, his hard gaze boring mercilessly into the frightened face of the felon.

The suddenly outlawed man felt himself flush with shame as his clansmen and allies began murmuring angrily among themselves, looking anywhere but in the direction of their convicted master.

"I wi' nae hae it said that becoming a king has turned me into a tyrant," Gregor went on after a moment. Pitching his voice so he could be heard by those beyond their young master, he said, "Ye highlanders who are kinsmen to The Campbell and ye others, allied with the same, hear me. If ye wi' throw down yer weapons and swear an oath of obedience to me now, I give ye my word of honour that only those found guilty in taking part in the vile debacle at Saint Michael's kirk wi' receive due punishment for their crimes. Yer master, Richard, stands already convicted of the most heinous of offenses: the rape of a young innocent woman wearing the habit of a novice. That she was also Lauralee, the Duchess of Ulster only compounds an already grievous offense in my eyes; her family, as yet, does nae ken. When they discover what has taken place I intend to tell them that swift justice was done no her behalf."

Deliberately the king returned his hard gaze to the disgraced lord. "Do ye persist in denying yer crime or would ye prefer to face yer accuser?"

Richard shivered before whispering, "I admit my guilt; God help me."

"God may be merciful on yer wicked soul, wretch, but I shall hae nay such mercy for yer corporal body," stated Gregor, his tone unyielding. "As king it is my duty to see that high justice is dispensed for my people. Therefore, I declare before God and these witnesses that the life of Richard Campbell is forfeit for his crimes perpetrated against God and against Scotland. Sentence shall be carried out one hour before the setting of the sun this very day.

"Now," said the king, turning his attention back to the rebel soldiers standing beyond the condemned lord. "Wi' ye all submit yerselves to the authority of the Crown or shall I be forced to order an attack upon ye which wi' result in yer annihilation? Well, which is it to be?" Gregor demanded sternly.

The metallic sound of swords, axes, and other weapons clattering to the ground was a better answer than any words the rebels could have expressed. Soon the only one of enemy retaining his sword was Richard. Sitting astride his horse the outlawed Campbell lord watched mutely as the king's marishal, without uttering one word, ordered a platoon of royal troops forward. These soldiers began moving amongst the enemy ranks collecting the discarded weapons, while others of the king's men began accepting oaths of surrender and dividing the rebels into small groups where they could more easily be watched over.

Once taken into custody, those rebel troops wearing armor or any type of personal ensign were segregated apart from the others to be interrogated about their conduct and orders while in the service of Lord Richard.

Alone and powerless, with no soldiers awaiting his command, Richard looked on with dread as the hard-faced king, flanked by his two closest advisors, rode slowly toward him and halted a mere length of his horse away. Donald, on the king's left, looked ill-used but otherwise still imposing as he leveled a scowl of distaste to him. On Gregor's right came the infamous Lord Sean MacSean, the Royal Warlord and much feared Sidhe. Richard shuddered as he forced his eyes to meet the cobalt gaze of the Sidhe lord, unconsciously squeezing his fingers more tightly around the reassuringly familiar hilt of his sword resting within its scabbard.

"I wi' take yer sword now, Campbell," quietly demanded MacSean, deceptively mild mannered as he held out his hand in expectation.

"Sae, I finally meet The MacGregor's pet sorcerer," commented Richard, forcing a measure of lightness into his tone as he grudgingly returned the warlord's frank gaze. "I hae long speculated what the mighty Sidhe general would be like. I wonder, what would ye do if I decided to deliver up my sword blade first into yer guts? I think yer blood would run as red as my own. But would ye perhaps strike me down with yer hellish magic before succumbing to yer wounds?" asked the captured rebel lord, smirking as he raised one elegant eyebrow. "I hae heard many rumors about the fearsome magic ye possess from the detestable Archbishop Colquhoun. Are ye and yer brother as omnipotent as that raving old man fears and believes ye to be?"

The king's marishal barked a laugh that held no humor before answering. "Auld Colquhoun is a fool and a lunatic. Duncan nor I am a sorcerer of any sort and we wield nay magic. I *hae* rediscovered what the ancients referred to as a type of science. It is just that, a science of the mind, in which I hae mastered only in part."

Nodding slightly and with what seemed a disappointed sigh, Richard slowly drew his sword with his off hand and extended it hilt first across his saddle. "I believe ye, for what it's worth, MacSean. Nay man would hae another think him as less powerful that what he is. Henry *is* a fool and mad. If only my uncle did nae depend sae fully upon that old bird's support in this war of ours," he added, shrugging forlornly. "Is there naught that I can do in which to hae my life spared? What if I were to willingly offer to renounce my support to my lord duke in his bid for the crown?"

Sean shrugged noncommittally. "I am nae the king, nor would I presume to ken his mind. If ye wish to plead and barter for yer life, ye must do sae to His Majesty," he replied, inclining his head in Gregor's direction.

"Yer Majesty?" queried the marishal.

Richard's blood ran cold with despair as the king's crowned helm moved slowly from side to side in negation. "That is nae near enough. Ye know longer hae any standing in which to bargain with, Campbell. Yer contrition comes tae late, neither is it sufficient to make up for the innocent lives ye hae taken, nor for the innocent victim that ye did personally force to bare yer vile pleasures," Gregor said grimly. "I do pity ye, Richard. And indulging that pity, because ye are sae young to hae yer life taken from ye, I find myself moved to be merciful with ye. The punishment for treason, as ye should already ken, is to be hanged and as ye swing from the rope yer entrails would be drawn from yer belly as ye watch and fried upon a brazier. Following that, although ye would most likely already be dead, yer arms and legs would each be tied to a horse; those horses would receive a lash to set them running and in doing sae would tear yer body asunder into quarters. Following all that, the head would be severed from yer body."

His already ashen face had slowly blanched of all color as Gregor explained, without inflection, the method of execution to the fallen lord until his complexion was the shade of snow. Sobbing, Richard slipped off his horse and fell to both knees before King Gregor, clasping his hands together in supplication. "Please, O high and mighty king, hae mercy upon me! I beg yer forgiveness before God; it was a mistake I made in fermenting rebellion against ye and a terrible sin I inflicted upon that poor duchess. I hae long lived with regret of my actions regarding my shameful use of that girl; I beg nae for my life, as I deserve it nae, but only for a better death," pleaded the young lord.

Gregor's stormy blue eyes intensely regarded the seemingly contrite Campbell kneeling before him. "As I said before, I wi' be merciful. Ye wi' be given whatever time ye require with a priest to make yer peace with god and seek to hae Him expunge the taint of yer sins from yer immortal soul," murmured the king. "As for the punishment ye wi' be dealt, my mercy shall be extended in that regard as well. Ye wi' nae be hanged, drawn and quartered, as by law I could hae administered on ye; rather, ye wi' receive the mercy of a quick death by the headman's axe. Nay further penalty shall be done to ravage yer body. Furthermore, I wi' see that all of yer remains are restored to yer family, that they may give ye a proper burial."

Richard wept with relief. "Thank ye, Yer Majesty."

King Gregor inclined his head slightly. "Guards, please escort Lord Richard to Father Lail; keep a close watch over him, but ye do hae to bind him, unless he should seek to escape his fate," commanded the king.

Once Richard had been led away, MacSean turned to his uncle. "I did nae expect ye to be sae merciful with that young fool, considering the manner in which ye hae had us hunting for him and his band of cutthroats," he said quietly.

"I did nae expect to be either," muttered Gregor in agreement. "It was nae for him sae much as for what he is: a bloody fool out for whatever revenge he could obtain. He is sae young tae; sae bloody young."

"Aye."

*   *   *

Meanwhile, in Glenorchy, Prince Grigor presided over some minor business of the kingdom from his father's throne-like chair, on the slightly raised dais in the greathall of Caer Glenorchy. The prince had departed for home the same day in which the king's army had marched north from Campbeltown. He had arrived home some weeks earlier, at the behest of his father, to gain some experience in such matters at his mother's side; and in doing so had been spared witnessing the tragic events which had taken place at the Kirk of Saint Michael and the adjoining nunnery.

The prior evening, before his first time sitting in his father's stead to officiate over matters of state, the prince's worried mother along with Captain MacAdam, commander of the Royal Guard had come to his chambers to relate to him the news which they had intercepted. Reasonably troubled about the fact that he was the target for assassination, young Grigor hid his uneasiness well as he now sat and listened to the petitioners coming before him for various judgments. Shifting slightly on the hard seat he silently prayed that the added defenders were vigilant about their duty.

The identity of the assassins was unclear, so it had been necessary for Grigor to use himself as bait to lure the would-be killers into a trap. Well hidden, but prepared for what could come at any time, a full score of archers was positioned along the balconies at the front and rear of the greathall. At the same time, a dozen additional guardsmen armed but without uniform or MacGregor tartan roamed casually about the hall, mingling quietly with each group of petitioners or posing as servants or clerks seeking to organize the suppliants as they arrived. These guardsmen wore only the dirk, as highland custom dictated, so as to not raise any suspicion.

All had remained quiet throughout the morning and into the afternoon since the day's business had begun and Grigor was thoroughly bored. He raised a goblet of wine that had gone warm to his mouth for a casual sip to wet his tongue before pronouncing judgment on the current petition awaiting his decision. He schooled his expression to one of interest as he regarded the men standing patiently before him.

"It seems that yer petition is reasonable enough, but I must read over this pact at length before making an equitable judgment," commented the prince, once the elderly chamberlain had finished highlighting the main theme of their request. "If ye gentlemen wi' return on the morrow, I wi' hae my decision for ye then."

The group of supplicants as a whole looked slightly pained at having been put off until the following day, but quickly hid their frustration behind feigned smiles and bowed respectfully to Prince Grigor before quietly filing out of the hall.

Feigning a smile of his own as the next trade delegation approached, the bored prince stifled a yawn and sought to keep a long suffering expression from showing on his beardless face, squaring his shoulders resolutely. As the crown prince dutifully settled in to hear the next petition he cast a sidelong glance at his mother as she sat watching from her padded seat off to his right side. Noticing her son's poorly disguised expression of glumness, Elizabeth smiled with understanding and winked covertly over at him before returning her attention to those approaching the dais.

Oh well, thought Grigor with forced cheerfulness, *when the assassins do finally decide to launch their attack, it wi' at least relieve me of this dreadful boredom!*

About five days hard ride due west of Glenorchy, the royal army led by Grigor's cousin Sir Duncan MacSean was anything but bored. For the past several days Duncan had taken personal command of his army's cavalry, while leaving to General Kirkland MacPherson the command of the slower moving infantry as he continued his tenacious pursuit of hastily withdrawing elements of the Duke of Argyll's army. Numerous running skirmishes had been fought with the duke's rearguard, which appeared to be comprised predominately of lowlanders and Lord Stevenson's tough clansmen.

Determined to force the rebels to stand and fight, General MacSean brashly left behind Kirkland's infantry in favor of speed. Leading a few hundred heavy cavalry and bringing along Captain James MacNeish's company of fleet Border Dragons, the brash general's tactic was working as they gained ground on the enemy, while gradually drawing away from his main army.

Although the duke's army continued to give ground in their retreat, the royal army unrelentingly closed the gap, but not nearly so quickly as the smaller force of horsemen led by Duncan. Before long they had closed to within just several hundred yards of the enemy's rear-most trailing elements.

Peering ahead, Duncan could see the rebel forces begin to descend into the end of a wide canyon stretching before them. Hoping to use the ravine to box in the retreating rebels, the blonde haired MacSean relayed a command to his officers to prepare for the coming assault, but instantly waved off the courier has he caught sight of the perplexed expression on Captain MacNeish's face.

Spurring his mount to within shouting distance of the captain, Duncan called out to him, "What is it, Jamie?"

The young MacNeish shook his head with a frown and closed the distance with his commander. "Sair, all of this is tae easy. Why should they flee sae readily from sae few of us, and into such a place as this?" he paused thoughtfully. "Would this canyon nae make a fine place to lure our advanced vanguard into an ambush while we are out of range of ready support from our main army?"

The captain's words made Duncan hesitate as he considered them. "Aye, ye make a fine point, Captain," agreed Duncan, attempting to conceal his chagrin with a lopsided smile. "We would do well to proceed with more caution from here on out. Thank ye for yer council, Jaime; yer instincts as a hunter serve me well."

Only when his cautiously advancing cavalry had crested the rim of the canyon did the general realize just how correct the MacNeish captain had been. Awaiting them and arrayed within the sloping gully, dismounted rebels had taken cover behind bushes and rocks. Halted on the ridge the king's men made excellent targets as waiting archers loosed their deadly shafts at the startled horsemen. Milling about in confusion as several long seconds a number of saddles were emptied by enemy marksmen.

"Bloody hell and damnation!" exclaimed Duncan, hauling his round shield around to protect himself from a sustained hail of arrows. Peering over the iron banded rim of his targe, Duncan stood in the stirrups, stretching to gain a better vantage point in which to gauge the rebel's strength and disposition. As he did so with a growing dread, the general was able to pick out the flying cross banner of the Holy See of Saint Andrew at the head of a squadron of heavily armored warrior-monks, followed by two troops of light cavalry wearing the colors of Clan Colquhoun. "Jamie-"

The general was cut off as three arrows thwacked into his stout shield nearly at the same time. Cursing under his breath, Duncan wrenched the missiles one at a time from the boiled leather facing and threw them aside. "Pull yer clansmen back to where those bastards shooting at them can nae see their targets." Following his own order the general hauled his mount around and fell back several yards away from the defile.

Safe for the time being, beyond the rim of the canyon, Duncan signaled for his officers to form their troops into battle formation to meet the enemy. While they followed his orders he twisted in the saddle and gestured for one of his couriers to attend him.

"Find my son and bring him to me without delay. I hae a mission for him."

"Aye, sair," the message rider acknowledged with a nod, before kicking spurs to his fleet mount and cantering away.

Turning to Captain MacNeish, Duncan said quietly, "I think this is it, Jamie. The duke must be out there and near, or Colquhoun would nae hae suddenly turned to give us the fight we hae been looking for. He set his trap well and I would hae fallen completely into it if it were nae for ye. As it is, we are at the disadvantage here and tae far removed from our main force. If the battle turns against us I wi' give ye the signal to disengage and flee from here with whatever men remaining under yer command. Do nae interrupt," he growled, making a chopping motion with his hand. "If I give the command ye must track after my son and see that he gets word safely to the king. King Gregor must ken what has happened and come with all speed to our assistance."

"As ye wish, sair," muttered James unhappily. "But I do nae like running away in the face of the enemy we hae been sae long seeking; nor wi' my lads."

Duncan forced a grin. "I did nae think ye would."

"My lord!" cried one of Duncan's cavalry captains. "Ye had better see this, sair. Look to the east."

Following the line of the officer's pointing finger, Duncan turned his head and saw something that made his heart leap into his throat. The disadvantage he was aware of suddenly took an alarming turn for the worse.

"Dear mother of God!"

"What is it-" Captain MacNeish's voice abruptly cut off as he witnessed a massive column of additional mixed cavalry units emerging from a cunningly hidden secondary egress of the twisting canyon. "They're going to completely cut us off from the main force if we can nae stop them," he murmured, his voice full of dread. "There may be nay escape from this place for any of us."

Standing mutely before King Gregor were a dozen rebel officers of Lord Richard Campbell's warband, anxiously waiting to hear the king's verdict in regards to each of their culpability in the rebellion and for war crimes. Each man had been interviewed by Gregor and his feared warlord, MacSean, but none had been informed beforehand of their fate until this moment.

Ranging behind and flanking the seated king stood Marishal MacSean and the daunting Lord Donald of the Isles. Both men were grim-faced and silent as wary troops guarding the prisoners herded the officers forward and forced them, none too gently, to kneel on the blackened ground before Gregor.

The tried officers awaiting sentence had previously been stripped of all their rank and insignia, with all their armor and weapons confiscated; now they waited fearfully to learn their doom with ankles bound with rope and wrists lashed behind them.

"Here I sit, King of Scots, forced to dispense justice when I would much rather be with my wife and family celebrating my son's birthday," began Gregor, his frank gaze sliding disdainfully over their number, as he sat stiffly on a small camp chair as if it were a throne. "I hae pondered over what I should do with ye. All of ye are subordinates in one degree or another, and subject to the commands of yer lord and superiors. All those things I hae taken into due consideration, however some actions are simply unconscionable even if one is ordered to perform such things.

For those crimes, ye wi' be held accountable," said the king, his countenance hard and grim.

"For the most part, these were yer own clansmen and simple folk trying to go about their lives that ye dealt with sae harshly, by Lugh!" the king went on severely. "To murder and rape are crimes that at any time are inexcusable, and ye which hae been found guilty of those felonies wi' be hanged for those sins."

"I beg ye, Sire, hae mercy," suddenly cried one younger man. "Please, in the name of God, hae mercy mighty king; I am nae guilty of such-"

"Silence!" commanded Gregor roughly. "I wi' nae be interrupted by yer sad pleas. I ken which of ye are guilty and which are nae. Yer subordinates hae been interrogated and they hae told us enough to determine which of ye most deserves *our* ire. Nae one of ye are completely without blame, however royal justice must be tempered with a degree of compassion or become less than just.

"Ye," pointed the king at one bearded man of their number. "And ye, and ye also," indicated Gregor to two other officers kneeling before him, "hae been found guilty of murder and rapine in defiance of *our* law and the laws of God. Ye are to be hanged by the neck until ye are dead. If ye wish to pray with a priest to confess yer sins before God, it wi' be allowed. May God Almighty hae mercy on yer souls."

The three officers condemned to death had gone instantly pale as Gregor indicated each one with an accusing finger and so sealing their fate. Two of the damned men hauled roughly to their feet remained stoically silent with downcast despairing eyes, but the other, a leathery and grizzled middle aged man, broke into unabashed tears as pitiable sobs of fear overwhelmed him.

Disgusted by the sobbing man's show of such weakness two soldiers caught him by the arms and hoisted him brusquely to his feet. Turning, they dragged the unmanned officer away to where the condemned would await the arrival of priests that had been summoned to attend to their final confessions.

Several moments later all three condemned officers were hanging from the end of ropes, their bodies twitching with indignity, until each life came to an end. While King Gregor watched those men being strung up and sentence carried out, the fellow officers of those doomed men turned away to avoid watching their comrades slowly die.

"Ye wi' watch," commanded the king. His face was like carved planes of granite as he beheld the more fortunate rebels. "Any one of ye could be hanging up there beside them, sae watch and remember. I wi' brook nay treason nor any foul crime perpetrated under the pretext of war or any other reason." At a look from the king, soldiers moved to enforce his command if any sought to refuse. None did.

When the executions were completed, Gregor turned his austere attention back to the remaining group of officers. "Nae a one of ye were found totally innocent of some offense or another, nor, I believe, be foolish enough to dare claim to be sae. Following orders offers only sae much excuse for yer conduct. Therefore, I decree this judgment for the lot of ye: each of ye are sentenced to receive twelve lashes of the whip, and then to be handed over to the tender mercies of the townsfolk still residing in this desolate place," he pronounced coldly. "However, in lieu of the latter portion of yer sentence, should any of ye choose to renounce yer support of those leaders remaining in defiance of my royal crown and give homage to me, I wi' be merciful. If ye should sae decide to do that, ye wi' be conscripted into this army and demonstrate yer new loyalty by bearing arms against yer former lord and master."

Gregor waited expectantly, flanked by Marishal MacSean and the towering Lord of the Isles, peering into the prisoner's faces. Some of those faces revealed a sudden hope while in others uncertainty and fear. The majority, however, simply watched their judge with varying degrees of suspicion as they contemplated his offer.

"As I stated before, with the exception of the lashes ye hae justly earned, amnesty shall be granted in return for a sincere oath of allegiance and yer steadfast service. *We* hae been lenient with ye far, but deal falsely with *us* in this regard and ye shall feel just how harsh *we* can be. Ye would be foolish to sae test *our* resolve."

Consternation and anxiety rippled amongst the bound prisoners as the king's words touched upon the inner thoughts of each man. Not one of them failed to cast a wary glance at the Sidhe lord standing silently at Gregor's right shoulder. The rebels did fear the physical ramifications of falsely swearing to the king, but even more so did they dread what Sidhe might do to them. Each had been present for at least a few of the Bishop of Dundee's raving sermons about the unholy powers of Lucifer wielded by certain men of Clan Gregor, particularly the brothers MacSean. The frightening words they had heard from the old bishop's lips were difficult to believe, but was Henry Colquhoun as a bishop not to be believed in all things spiritual? In addition to the bishop's sermons, each man had heard rumors abound about The MacGregor and his closest advisors and kinsmen being able to ascertain a man's inner thoughts. Now that same man sat before them and brought those misgivings starkly to mind.

From where he stood beside his regal uncle, Sean was forced to restrain a smirk of ironic satisfaction from reaching his lips. Gregor's judgment was indeed a lenient one, considerably more lenient than he would have been if he sat in judgment. However, it was a shrewd method he had used to hint at some mysterious Sidhe power. The judgment he offered showed a mercy contingent on each man's own honesty as the rebel prisoners each feared what might be read from their thoughts.

One by one, the rebel officers were brought forward to kneel before the king as they agreed to renounce their former lord and give Gregor their oath of allegiance. All came willingly, but most knelt with an obvious fear in their eyes. The solemn oath taking was quickly and smoothly done, much to the king's satisfaction, and although many had to visibly force themselves to meet Gregor's unwavering gaze, the warlord could not detect any sigh of subterfuge from any of them.

Once the former rebel officers had been separated and hustled away to join their new companies, Gregor turned to his nephew with a shake of his head. "Do ye think I was tae harsh with them, Sean?"

The Warlord shook his blonde head. "Hardly, sire. Those men swinging more than deserved their fate. As to the rest, if anything, ye were more lenient than I had expected and certainly more merciful than I would hae been," MacSean admitted quietly. "I did like how ye hinted at some mysterious ability to ken if they swore falsely to ye, however ye may later wish that ye had allowed the *evil sorcerer* stigma to fade away. Nay matter how talented Colquhoun is at stirring up his personal brand of hate, if we would just be a little more circumspect most people would forget all about it."

"Aye, ye hae a point, I suppose."

"As it is," MacSean added, allowing a forbearing smile to play at the corner of his lips, "the bloody auld fool has done all he could to besmirch my name and reputation, and although many already think I must be Satan's own son, most folk with a modicum of intelligence do nae believe his odious prattle."

"It must be tiresome for ye to constantly bear, living sae branded by a leader of the kirk," sympathized Gregor, squeezing his nephew's shoulder. "Perhaps when all of this unpleasantness is finished yer life wi' return to normal."

Sean shrugged noncommittally as he met his kinsman's frank blue gaze. "Perhaps, but I'm getting used to it by now, I suppose, although it does get old. Still, I ken my heart is free from any taint of dark magic and that is all that really matters," he sighed ruefully, before his usual cheerfulness reasserted itself to cast away his brooding thoughts. "Do nae worry yerself for me, Uncle, I wi' be just fine. I hae honour in our clan; a family to love and be loved by; and many bonny friends to sport with and to fight beside. It is all any man needs in this world. Nay, do nae allow my troubled path cast a shadow over all ye hae left to accomplish, Uncle. I am content."

Towards the end of that same day as the sun began its descent and while King Gregor, his officers, and the morbidly curious looked on, a crack squad of Lord Donald's infantry escorted a very subdued Richard Campbell across the village green to the shade of a large oak tree. A moment passed as a heavy log was placed into position where a hooded headsman stood by with a great double-bitted axe.

Pale but otherwise composed, the young Campbell lord knelt with resignation before the log with hands tied behind his back and leaned forward to give the executioner an easy target to aim for. A basket had been located and placed on the ground, filled with wood dust, in which to catch his severed head. A drum began to beat a slow cadence as the headsman hefted his axe and stepped into position beside the condemned lord. The drum quickened its beat until it began a grim drum roll.

Abruptly the drum halted and the heavy bladed axe flashed downward from its high arc to cleanly sever Richard's head from his body. As the head bounded into the waiting basket a lone piper began to blow a forlorn tune, its moving melody sounding harsh in the otherwise quiet village green as it heralded the man's demise.

CHAPTER NINE

Several hours of tedium passed uneventfully within the greathall of Glenorchy as Prince Grigor held court in his absent father's stead. Making decisions for the good of the people was a needed and understandable responsibility, but the prince had passed the point of being thoroughly bored some time ago and it showed on his haggard face. He had already begun to believe that, those sources which spoke of a plot to murder him, were wrong or perhaps playing a morbid joke at his expense. So many trade delegations and various other suppliants had come and gone earlier in the day, Grigor could no longer recall all of the various requests that had been made of him.

The unusual heat did not spare those with business inside the greathall, which had been getting increasingly warm and stuffy since before the noon hour. By mid-afternoon, it was simply hot and bordering on stifling as the additional bodies within the stone walls just served to increase the temperature. Waiting for the next party of petitioners to come forward, Grigor used the pillow he had been sitting on to fan himself.

Giving the sweating and ill-tempered chamberlain a bored nod to proceed while a harried clerk finished passing over the last of the relevant documents, the prince absently ran a finger around the collar of his tunic to loosen it a bit and let in some air. Noting that even his mother, who was trained for such things in the late king's court, squirmed a little uncomfortably in her padded chair also brought a faint smile to Grigor's lips. Returning his attention to the business at hand, the king's heir ignored the chamberlain's black glare at having to start over and reread the last couple of paragraphs of the current petition, and absently wiped a fresh trickle of sweat from his brow.

After that party had departed, apparently satisfied with his judgment in their case, Grigor watched the latest suppliant approach. The older man appeared to be a clergyman of some sort, what with the white clerical collar he wore, covered by a black collarino, mimicking that of the catholic cassock. Aside from that he wore no kirk garb, dressed in black breeches and black shirt which had buttons down the entire front.

The scowling chamberlain cleared his as the clergyman bowed before the prince and mopped his damp forehead with a thread-worn handkerchief. "Yer Highness, before ye comes Reverend Hugh MacAlastair of Ballikinrain Kirk. The man is despondent over the matter of his cow being taken."

"Highness, that is correct," the minister began, with another bow. "If ye'll forgive an old man; I do nae wish to waste yer time but for a minute."

Grigor smiled encouragingly. "Go ahead, Minister and speak yer piece. Please let us discuss yer matter and see what might be done to relieve yer despondency."

"Thank ye, Highness," he said, his voice quavery as a hint of a smile stretched his tanned and leathery face. "Ye see, I made bargain with yer Da when he was simply a chief and laird of these lands, and I tremble to bring such a slight problem before ye with sae many more important people seeking yer judgment."

"Minister, ye hedge around the issue like some auld, forgetful woman!" exclaimed Grigor, his former smile gone. "As far as my Da goes, he is King of Scotland now, and ye should do well to address him with suitable respect and give him his proper rank. Am I clear about that, Mister MacAlastair?"

The prince's rebuke had the desired affect on the minister, and a murmur of quiet approval came from around the hall as others heard him speak.

The chastised man all but choked on his tongue as he bowed his head. "Ach, nae offense was meant, Highness, I assure ye;

t'was but a slip of the tongue, as I hae only the highest regards for, ur, King Gregor."

"Very well, ye may continue, Minister."

"Aye, Highness. Thank ye, Highness," he said, bobbing his gray head. "As I was saying before, I had entered into an understanding with His Majesty when he was but our laird. The matter was in regards to the few small cattle I hae about my poor kirk. About a week ago my best little milking cow came missing one morning."

"Do ye ken who has taken the cow, sir?"

MacAlastair swallowed audibly. "Aye, Highness; The MacGregor's men did sae."

Grigor raised his eyebrows. "Was that nae the agreement ye made? Are ye like others who has had our protection and been spared theft, but now cry foul? I would think a man of God would hold to his word without complaint," he stated sadly, shaking his head in lament. "If I should restore yer cow to ye then everyone else would cry foul to gain the same thing. However, I wi' nae hae it said that The MacGregor does nae hae respect for God's kirk and His servants, therefore ye may go from here and choose *two* beasts from our herd as a free gift and an offering to yer kirk from my father, the king."

The old minister goggled up at the prince in astonishment and gratitude. "Thank ye, Highness! Yer generosity is most becoming in a royal son. May the Lord bless ye and keep ye and may His light shine down upon ye!" As the old minister departed, a spring was in his step that was not there before, and if he had been able to, Grigor thought he might have skipped for joy as he left the hall.

When the expected attack finally came, it arrived at an inopportune time for the would be killers, as Prince Grigor was no longer so bored following his exchange with the whining minister. Garbed in the tartan of the friendly Clan Donald, the disguised party of assassins suddenly rushed towards the dais on which the prince sat. As they came the killers drew curious, little, one-handed crossbows from beneath their kilts and sought to level them at their intended target. Genuine petitioners cried out in alarm and scattered all directions to get out of harms way, bowling over others in their haste to escape.

Face contorted in immediate rage, Grigor barely dodged away from his seat in time to avoid the steel-tipped dart one assassin fired at him as it thunked solidly into the throne just beside his head. Diving behind the carved oak throne with a venomous curse the prince heard several more of the deadly quarrels smack into the stout oak, and drew his sword while shouting for his guards.

Glancing around the throne, Grigor nearly lost his head as an assassin's sword whistled down at him in a vicious chop. Bringing his claymore hastily up to deflect the blow, the prince cursed and in one fluid motion drew and stabbed the man through the ribs with a skean dhu he kept in his boot. Leaving the short blade where it protruded from his attacker's chest, Grigor turned and lunged to skewer a second assassin with the long blade of his broad sword.

Off to his right, as the prince paused to catch his breath, he was reassured to hear the strident voice of the veteran Captain MacAdam of the Royal Guard ordering troops into the fray. At that same instant the hidden archers moved to action from their lofty positions along the front and rear balconies. In a matter of seconds, the great hall of Caer Glenorchy was alive with the lethal hiss of clothyard arrows being loosed down upon the enemy. As Grigor looked on from relative safety behind a ring of four royal guardsmen who had moved in to bracket him, the fight raged on and several hapless assassins fell with arrow feathers sprouting from their chest before they could find time to react to the new threat coming from the galleries above. The survivors continued to stoically fight on, grappling with other MacGregor retainers, too intermingled with them for the archers to risk shooting into their midst for fear of cutting down a comrade.

Within moments, however, the melee was over as the remaining would be killers were disarmed or slain, the few survivors closely guarded by loyal Royal Guard troops and snarling Gregorach. Fresh troops arriving too late to participate in the fighting were hastily assigned to cordon off the hall by one of Captain MacAdam's lieutenants, while the captain marched up to his prince's side to report. Patiently he waited, a couple paces away, while Grigor sat close to his mother with an arm around her trembling shoulder to comfort the shaken woman.

"Aye, Captain?" inquired Grigor, once he had moved from his mother's side, leaving her in the care of her ladies-in-waiting.

"My Prince, all of the assassins nae dispatched in this wee fight hae been taken into custody," MacAdam reported briskly. "Ten were slain outright and another four were wounded, of which two might live long enough to be interrogated. The lads captured another two members of the *delegation* who seem to hae nae taken a hand in the fighting, and nay weapon was found on them, although it would hae been simple enough to cast aside a dirk or such. What shall ye hae me do with them?"

"Detain them for the time being sae they may be questioned," instructed Grigor thoughtfully. "I would like to interrogate the lot of them as soon as I may. If they refuse to give me the answers I seek, ye may use whatever persuasions deemed necessary to extract any information they wi' nae give willingly."

Sketching an incipient bow to the prince, MacAdam departed to rejoin his men as they finished thoroughly binding the prisoners. Leading their captives in tow, the Royal Guardsmen under the watchful eyes of their captain, escorted their battered charges from the greathall. Before long, each of the surviving assassins had been hustled away toward the castle dungeon and safely locked away to await the prince's pleasure.

The wounded, meanwhile, were attended by a priest and men of the clan skilled in treating battlefield injuries. Those men who did not have life threatening wounds were treated and their wounds bound. The badly wounded, who were judged beyond the surgeon's ministrations were carried from the hall with an attending priest and given the coup de grace to mercifully end their misery.

Those who had intended the murder of Prince Grigor were not the only ones who numbered among the slain and wounded. One of the Royal Guard had been killed with a dart to his exposed neck, while another had lost two fingers of his left hand as he fought one of the attackers. Another man, one of the Gregorach, had been stabbed in the side by an enemy dirk but stood proudly with his fellows while he was bandaged, bragging about how he had used his body to shield his chief's son.

*   *   *

A much larger and more savage battle was being waged a few days ride to the west between the forces of Domeric, Duke of Argyll, with his chief ally Archbishop Henry Colquhoun and the hard pressed army of General Duncan MacSean.

Duncan cursed to himself as he took a brief glance at the scene developing before him. *How could I hae been sae foolish? I snapped up the bait laid out for me with nay more thought than some untried lieutenant! Even Sean wi' berate me for such an error in judgment, when he hears what I've done-provided, of course, that I'm able to affect an escape from this terrible debacle still wearing my bloody head.*

The fighting had been fierce as the sworn enemies tangled in brutal combat, but with such superior numbers nothing had been able to withstand the growing momentum of the bristling wedge of heavy cavalry that Colquhoun had driven between the main body of the royal army and its vanguard. Duncan had soon discovered, to his disgust, that his overextended force was now effectively cut off from any hope of support, and that he had no one to blame but himself. *I pray Devlin is able to reach the king in time.*

Cut off from the main army as they were Duncan's field commanders had tried valiantly to affect a breakout through the renegade bishop's widening wedge and afford an escape for their general, but to no avail. At last they were constrained to grudgingly admit failure. Having been tactically required to retreat east of the canyon and forgo any further attempts of fighting their way through the enemy force, Duncan led his troops into a defile that unexpectedly slanted up again after a few hundred yards. With his men, the harried general reached a broad rocky crest that could be better defended than the position he had previously occupied. From his vantage point, Duncan directed his gaze to where he could see the advance of Colquhoun's and Lord Stevenson's cavalry, barely a quarter mile away on the plain below.

The narrow defile in which Duncan's men had already negotiated proved, after being scouted, the only way up to the crest they held for over a mile in any direction. The general smiled with satisfaction as he realized the advantage he currently held. As he did so, a desperate plan began to form in his mind. Decisively, Duncan issued orders for his officers to marshal their men at strategic points along the hilltop to best take advantage of the natural terrain of their position.

"We may be outnumbered and cut off with only a few hundred lads, but they are a stalwart band that we lead. We should be able to hold our position, against all who come against us, for some time," declared General MacSean, baring his teeth in a fierce grin at his commanders. "Even if they should attempt an all-out frontal assault, their numbers wi' nae mean much as they are funneled up the narrow trail and it wi' cost Colquhoun dear to use up his precious warrior-monks in the effort to take this hill!" Turning to find the face he sought, Duncan asked, "Captain MacNeish, hae yer lads got those bonny big boulders in position yet?"

"Aye, sair," a subdued James replied.

"Here they come again," stated James. The captain was not quite as relaxed as he was pretending to be, as Duncan noticed sweat making muddy trails through the dust coating his rugged face, despite the coolness of the heights as the sun made its descent. *He's a good leader despite his youth, and his men love him; I'm lucky to hae him with me, nay matter what the circumstances.*

The renewed attack came forward with mounted warrior-monks supporting twice as many infantry. The oncoming foot soldiers were armed with equal amounts of pike and sword, and were advancing somewhat raggedly after already failing in three previous attempts to take the MacGregor held hill. Doggedly they came on anyway, perhaps more fearful of their commander than they were of the waiting enemy.

"If they keep coming at us like this there wi' nae be enough of them left to spit at after our archers chew them up again," commented Duncan with a wry grin as he shook his head. Close to the bottom of the narrow track that led up to the hill's mostly level summit, Lieutenant Petrie, commanded a detachment of the dismounted horse archers. Even as Duncan looked on, the archers fired with deadly precision into the loose ranks of infantrymen. Three such volleys was all the advancing enemy could stomach before they turned and ran, leaving behind nearly a hundred of their comrades lying dead or wounded on the rocky hill. The dust in that area was no longer brown or gray, but stained with the blood of so many, now appeared black.

Duncan shook his blonde head again. "Colquhoun wi' nae tolerate much more of this kind of abuse. He's already lost nearly five hundred clansmen and warrior-monks that he prizes sae much, for absolutely nothing," the general muttered mostly to himself. "About now the old bastard must be practically foaming at the mouth."

Captain MacNeish's unexpected shout jolted the general out of his reverie just in time for him to watch Lieutenant Petrie and his archer's loose one volley toward the base of the trail before beating a hasty retreat toward their second line of defense where their light war mounts had been left behind.

The second line of defense was situated about halfway up the hill where the slope began to rise sharply. Posted at that point were another of Duncan's personal light cavalry who were likewise dismounted, but instead of wielding bows those troopers were armed with ten foot long lances tipped with several inches of keen steel. In moments the archers had achieve a safe position behind the ranks of lancers who used their weapons, in this situation, like pikes. It was then that Duncan could make out the reason for the hasty but orderly withdrawal from their first defensive line. Marching slowly up from the base of the rocky slope came a company of heavy infantry behind a shield wall the width of the track and several ranks deep. These were Colquhoun's crack troops, while behind them came another couple hundred of his clansmen.

"March prettier than the last lot," James quipped.

With an impatient nod the general wave the captain to silence, his gaze fixed with hawk-like intensity on the latest threat as they advanced toward his men. *Well, ye knew Colquhoun would nae endure much more slaughter, nor stomach failure in eliminating an evil Sidhe such as myself,* he thought grimly.

"I hae need of one of yer swiftest riders to carry a message to Lieutenant Petrie for me, Jamie," stated Duncan.

"Aye, sair."

After scanning the terse dispatch, Petrie acknowledged his new orders by facing up the hill and crisply saluting his superior with his gleaming sword. Turning back to face the advancing enemy huddled behind their imposing shield wall, he sighed and wondered if he would make it home to see his beautiful wife again. As he watched, Petrie had to admire the professionalism of the warrior-monks. Marching out in precision lock step and without hesitation, each with his rectangular white shield designed with a blood red cross, they came steadily forward, rank after precise rank to do battle. Only the ecclesiastical troop's crimson enameled helms were visible as a viable target as those hardened warriors peered above the rim of their shield with steely eyes intent upon their enemy waiting for them not much farther up the trail.

"Loose!" cried Petrie, once the approaching enemy came into range.

Resolutely, the veteran warrior-monks marched on through the vicious rain of arrows descending upon them and beyond their shield wall as well. Petrie could make out the startled and painful cried of the following highland clansmen as they felt the lethal bite of his archer's barbed arrows. The tall, heavy shields made the first several ranks of soldiers virtually impervious to ranged attack except for the lucky or very skilled shot, but those following did not have the same luxury.

Answering the Gregalach cheer coming from up the slope, the undaunted warrior-monks took up singing a martial hymn in a strong voice that would have chilled the blood of less enthusiastic opponents.

From his vantage point sitting astride his charger atop the rocky hill, Sir Duncan watched intently as Petrie's archers loosed volley after volley of deadly clothyard arrows over the shield wall and into the unprotected ranks behind. The lethal rain was certainly taking a heavy toll among the lightly armed highlanders, but onward they pressed despite the severe cost in life *They seem almost eager to meet their Maker,* reflected Duncan with reluctant admiration. *It's time, Petrie; let's see if their shield wall can stand up to several thousand pounds of galloping horseflesh!*

Even as Duncan silently urged him, Petrie whirled his sword in the air in signal to his archers and pikemen. Responding as if drilled to it, the pikemen shifted to right and left to leave an avenue open down their center. Into that generous gap the archers, using lances as levers, pushed and pried at more than a dozen heavy boulders which had previously been moved into place. Slowly the massive rocks began to move until gravity took over the work and sent them rolling thunderously down the trail.

The advancing enemy troops could clearly see what the Gregalach had in store for them once the pikemen opened ranks, but with such a narrow path to negotiate there was no where to go and nothing they could do to avoid what was coming. Bracing themselves for the impending impact, the warrior-monks halted and grounded their heavy shields, hunkering down behind them and waited.

The sound was terrible as the boulders rumbled down the hill picking up speed as they went until they collided with the soldiers barring the way. The clamor of the impact was immense as unyielding stones smashed through shields and men, and relentlessly continued through the scattering ranks of the more nimble highlanders. The first two ranks of warrior-monks had been immediately pulverized by the onslaught and a score more fell and did not rise as death rolled over them. Many more men were grievously wounded as limbs were smashed and mangled beyond hope of mending. Still others were knocked senseless but otherwise unharmed by God's mercy or merely the fickle hand of fate. Even the professionalism of the kirk knights could not assist them much as their ranks had been completely ravaged and order dissolved into chaos.

Lieutenant Petrie furiously stalked among his cheering men, his gleaming sword still clinched in his hand. "This battle is nae yet done, ye bloody idiots! Archers! Loose yer bleeding arrows among them while they are yet unorganized," he thundered. "Pikes! Let's chase them off our hill-follow me!"

Ard Choille! Sounded the ancient Gregalach battle cry as the company of pikemen rushed down the trail toward their devastated enemies. Over the heads of the charging clansmen, a hail of arrows flew in hissing flight to fall with deadly effect among the foe that never saw them coming. Two more such volleys followed with equally destructive result before the pikes hammered into the disorganized enemy. Military discipline dissolved in the face of the unrelenting assault and Colquhoun's remaining force on the hillside fled, but not many survived to reach the base of the hill.

Exultant in their victory the MacGregors were slow to be reined in from further pursuit, but at last Lieutenant Petrie and his officers were able reassemble their force and return to their position. Only then did the lieutenant allow a satisfied smile to bloom on his ruddy face and accept the congratulations from his cheering subordinates.

"Well done, lads," he declared, brandishing his sword. "Let that teach the dogs a lesson about fighting the Gregalach! *Ard Choille!*"

"Ard Choille!" they all shouted heartily as one.

An hour passed in which Duncan was able to see that fresh troops were rotated in to take the places of Petrie's tired men. Amazingly, none had received a wound of any sort so those pulled off the defensive line were able to rest and eat and refill their nearly spend quivers of arrows. A second hour had nearly gone by before a signal was sent from Lieutenant Petrie's position, where he remained in command, of a renewed stirring of Colquhoun's troops at the base of the narrow trail.

Moments passed before the crimson armored warrior-monks marched into view, once again silent and imposing behind their shield wall except for the tramp of their boots as they advanced up the rocky hill's trail. Duncan sighed as he watched them come and knew that he had no more surprises in store for them. A few more large rocks had been manhandled into position, but there had not been enough time to secure further before the enemy had begun pressing forward once again.

"Be ready, Jamie," warned Duncan. "Without the benefit of all those fine boulders yer lads equipped us with before, things are going to get very bloody and the outcome my well depend on the speed in which we react to what happens in the next minutes."

The studied lack of expression showed the captain's concern as he saluted his general. "Aye, sair. My lads are ready."

All too soon the fighting became hand-to-hand as the kirk soldiers stoically closed ranks around their comrades, shattered by the thundering path of what boulders had been unleashed, and eagerly closed to engage with the prepared ranks of makeshift pikemen. The Gregorach archers with their bows already slung across their backs drew claymore to assist their comrades in a desperate defense of the hill.

Now that the battle was joined in earnest, those troops held in reserve by their general were enthusiastically waiting for the order to rush down to assist their kinsmen in the frenzied melee. Soon they would have their wish.

For long moments Lieutenant Petrie's company fought the implacable foe to a stand still, but all too soon the experience and skill of the warrior-monks began to show as they continued to hammer at the Gregorach lines. Slowly at first, the crimson clad soldiers started to gain the upper hand, and then began to push back the hard fighting highlanders one step at a time.

Perceiving the tide beginning to turn against Petrie's beleaguered troops, General MacSean called for his mount and signaled for his officers to order all their troops to mount as well. Once astride his warhorse he called out in a loud voice, clear enough for all those waiting on the hill crest could hear. "Fire the signal! Come then, Gregalach! At the trot, forward for King Gregor and Scotland! Couch lances! *Charge!*"

In an instant a single flaming arrow flew high into the air and sped over the heads of those fighting a few hundred yards below. Glimpsing the arranged signal, Petrie seized his horn and sounded the retreat, its bass rumble echoing clearly. As they had been alerted beforehand to do, the agile highlanders hastily, but in good order, backpedaled away from the shield wall and peeled back toward either side of the steep trail. In performing the maneuver they opened a clear avenue for the charging friendly cavalry as they thundered, like an avalanche, down from their lofty position.

Sweeping down from the summit, Duncan's cavalry charged down on the enemy formation in a roar of hooves and battle cries with steel lance heads flashing in the late day sun. Then they were suddenly clashing against the enemy shield wall, their sheer weight and momentum punching through the ranks of warrior-monks and beyond into the loosely bunched Colquhoun clansmen following close behind. The shrill clash of steel on steel was deafening as lances smashed through shields and armor to pierce the yielding flesh beyond. Although the cavalry charge dealt a serious blow to the warrior-monks and enemy clansmen, the assault also took its toll among the racing horses and their riders, as the cries of the stricken soon overwhelmed even the martial sounds of the fiercely fought battle on the narrow rocky pass.

Meanwhile, Lieutenant Petrie's force, which had withdrawn to allow Duncan's heavy cavalry assess to the enemy, had retrieved their mounts and eagerly followed in the general's stead in an attempt to cut their way to freedom. Following his superior's lead, Petrie ordered his own charge, albeit much less devastating than the knights which led the way, through the confused enemy ranks. This second charge forced its way through the hole torn through the buckled shield wall and swept into Archbishop Colquhoun's own clansmen, cutting a bloody swathe.

Through in ensuing confusion, Captain MacNeish led his fleet company of Border Dragons and succeeded in emerging virtually unbloodied through the melee until he was able to link up with General MacSean's knights and then the surviving troops arriving with Lieutenant Petrie. Before them, pouring into the defile from the plain to reinforce the badly mauled bishop's men, were Lord Tearlach Stevenson's clansmen and more of his hired mercenaries. These new troops arriving were all fresh and mounted, and ready for a fight. Riding at their head was the hated Archbishop of Saint Andrews himself, and The Stevenson rode at his right hand. Colquhoun's stormy countenance clearly showed his outrage at the carnage in which the despised Sidhe lord had inflicted on his elite troops and clansmen. Murder showed in his eyes as he sought out the target of his ire.

"Alas, we are still penned in," Duncan declared bitterly. "It seems we still hae more fighting lying before us, Jamie, and my doom becomes clear to me. I do nae see a way of escape, but perhaps some of us may still fight our way free, even through sae many fresh soldiers arrayed against us," he added, sweeping his arm to take in the tide of enemy reinforcements still arriving from the plain. "We must try to cut our way through to Kirkland. Before God, we must give a fair accounting of ourselves and pray for the best. I wi' nae go down without one hell of a bloody fight, and Colquhoun wi' ken that his mortal enemy fought like a lion and spilt sae much of his clan's blood this day, even more sae than our ancestor did sae long ago at Glen Fruin!

"Jamie," Said Duncan, turning in the saddle to solemnly regard the brave captain of the MacNeish Border Dragons, "now is the time I spoke of to ye earlier. Ye, and as many of yer stouts lads as ye can lead in yer tail, must flee when the opportunity presents itself and track my son. I charge ye with finding Devlin and escorting him with all haste to the king's army before it is tae late. Yer company may be able to escape this trap, as it is me that Colquhoun most desires to hae as his trophy. When I order the charge, take ye away in the confusion of battle to fulfill the responsibility I lay upon ye."

"Sair, I must nae leave ye to-"

"Ye must!" commanded the general intensely. "Gregor *must* ken of the straights we are in and our location. Those are yer orders, Captain MacNeish! Do nae fail in this duty, or ye wi' hae failed the king and every man who fights in his name!"

There was no more time to argue further as the enemy marshaled their fresh forces to renew the battle. Duncan stood tall in his stirrups and brandished his sword so that all could see him. Shouting, he chanted some of the auld words of the MacGregor Gathering, "Come then, Gregalach! MacGregor has still both his heart and his sword! Then courage, courage, courage, Gregalach! *Ard Choille!* For the woody heights!"

The opposing forces were soon joined again in desperate battle, and whether by design or by chance, Captain MacNeish and his stalwart company were steadily separated in the heat of the fighting from their general. The focus of the enemy attack was clearly on the position in which Duncan fought under his personal banner. Fighting was most fierce there as the general laid about him, on his rearing horse, with his crimson stained sword and war hammer.

The knot of bodyguards defending General MacSean fought valiantly to defend their leader and though continuing to hold their own, they were slowly being worn down one soldier at a time. Beleaguered as he was, Duncan had no opportunity to observe as more troops arrived near the mouth of the pass and converged on Colquhoun's position and gave salute to their zealous leader.

When he did realize what was happening, Duncan swore to himself. *Ach, that is all we need now; yet another nail in our coffin,* he thought grimly, noting that the newest arrivals were lightly mounted troops and armed with a weapon similar to those used by some of his own light cavalry: the short, evil looking horseman's bow.

While the battle continued to rage all about him, Duncan bleakly noted as more and more of the bodyguard knotted around him fell under warrior-monk's and Stevenson swords. The enemy soldiers began to press ever closer about him as the protective knot of defenders about him shrank under the onslaught. *This is much like a hangman's noose closing around the neck of the condemned,* he observed dolefully.

The general was suddenly startled from his reverie as from his right side a short lance wielded by a Stevenson clansmen on foot stabbed up at him, but missed its intended target and instead, pierced deeply into the heaving flank of his horse with a sickening thud. Before Duncan was able to jump clear of his dying mount another lance thrust in at his head with deadly intent. Desperately he parried the weapon safely aside with his heavy shield and sliced clean through the thick wood haft with his claymore, the shock of the blow making his wrist go partly numb. From his left came a sword stroke that the general parried weakly as his wrist still tingled madly from the previous jolt. Hastily, Duncan shouted for a horse as his mount died beneath him and crashed to the rocky ground, red blood vomiting from its mouth.

Answering the embattled general's call for a horse, one of his remaining defenders maneuvered his mount to his commander's side and helped Duncan mount up behind him. Even as Duncan escaped the poor fate of being trampled under steel shod hooves, the situation all around him was deteriorating by the second. Risking a quick scan of the battle ground, Duncan was relieved to find no trace of Captain MacNeish or any of his company remaining within eyesight. Slowly a fierce smile crept onto his grime and blood streaked face as he dared to hope.

The relieved smile did not live long on his haggard face as the encouraged enemy, sensing victory near at hand, closed around Duncan and his two surviving bodyguards until they were completely boxed in by bodies and bloodied weapons. Determined to take down as many of the enemy with him as he could, General MacSean struggled on with a renewed vitality. Laying about him with thoughtless resolve he whirled his claymore with deadly skill at any foe within reach of his three feet of sharp steel and meted out as much carnage as he could, without any thought for his own safety as a battle rage took him. Both of the general's final bodyguards feel unbeknownst to him as amid the slaughter of his own frenetic blood letting while under the spell of a berserker's fury. A ring of slain adversaries lay at Duncan's feet and all around him, but as more enemies reluctantly moved in to oppose him he had eyes only for them.

His rage empowered strength began to slowly wane and as it did so the blood rage began to recede from his mind. Clear thought started to return to Duncan, even as a stark weariness he had never experienced before threatened to overwhelm him. As he fought doggedly on, the weakening general suddenly realized that whenever an attacker had an opportunity to cut him down they were holding back their attack. Duncan had no such compunction as he continued to chop, slice and disembowel any one standing against him without so much as a thought. He became quickly aware that his entire bodyguard had been killed already, even as he obviously was not.

Apparently these poor bastards hae orders to nae kill me, but to take me alive instead, and to hell with the cost. Colquhoun's doing, of course, Duncan surmised dryly. *Aye. I can see it in their eyes. They want very badly to kill me, but are afraid to earn the wrath of the bloody bishop. Sae, he wants me alive.* he grimaced as a high thrust from his sword pierced the throat of another soldier, and bright arterial blood spurted out in a red arc that caught the general a direct hit on his battered breastplate. *Ach! Auld Colquhoun must want to play with me a bit before having me executed. Swell.*

All of a sudden an arrow struck the cross guard of the surrounded general's sword even as he raised it to deliver another killing blow. Instantly his already aching wrist went completely numb with the unexpected force of impact, and Duncan's sword dropped from his nerveless fingers to the trampled ground at his feet. Another arrow struck a glancing blow off the crest of his helmet, causing his ears to ring resoundingly. Immediately after, a third arrow, this one flying true, struck squarely against the side of his dented helmet and caused the sturdy leather strap under Duncan's chin to snap. The force of the blow temporarily dazed the general as the helm was swept from his head.

Seeing spots and with gray starting to shade the edges of his vision, Duncan felt rough hands seize his shoulders and force him to his knees. Shaking his head to clear the cobwebs the general had no means to resist his captors. Despite his mental attempts to fight free he could not seem to make his body follow the commands his foggy mind was sending it, though he did retain power of his voice and used it.

"Fight me ye bloody curs! Are ye all cowards just like yer master, or do they truly geld all ye monks?" Duncan heard himself say drunkenly, taunting the kirk knights that surrounded him as he swayed on his knees and tried to stand.

"Shut yer filthy mouth, demon! The good Bishop Colquhoun has special plans in store for ye—singular plans developed just for foul sorcerers like ye," growled someone who grabbed him by a handful of hair, but who Duncan could not focus on. Without any warning, the general was punched cruelly in the face with a gauntleted fist. Blinding pain exploded through his skull and Duncan's blurred vision was washed red with agony, but all those things were immediately replaced with a growing darkness that closed in over him. And then Duncan MacSean felt nothing at all.

No more than a couple of miles away and heading rapidly south, James MacNeish was furious that he and his company had been ordered by General MacSean to abandon the field of battle. Having put that impotent fury to good effect, James had succeeded in leading his men through the chaotic enemy lines, some of which not realizing that his band was part of the opposing force. In their scramble to escape the trap set by the troops led by Colquhoun, Captain MacNeish nor his company witnessed the fall of the general's personal bodyguard or the capture of their desperately battling commander.

Urging his mount to speed once the din of battle had been left behind, James led the largely intact company of Border Dragons to the south away from the Mamores Hills and slightly eastward to skirt around Loch Leven. The captain diligently tried to keep his mind from dwelling on thoughts of the general's plight, but it was no avail. There had been no time to inform his men, not even Redwood, of General MacSean's orders, and from the looks shared among his men as well as those directed his way, and James knew he was in for a difficult time once they halted to rest. He hoped they would not doubt his word about the orders given, particularly his trusted lieutenant Redwood, but he knew without hesitation that were all seething over fleeing the battle for any reason.

Every one of them must think I'm a bleeding coward, James fumed angrily, hiding his emotions beneath a stony mask. *Ach, the way Redwood is glaring at me, ye would think I had a hand in personally killing the general myself. Hell and damnation! In a way, he would be right to think such. I should hae ignored Duncan's orders to stayed to fight, nay matter the dressing down he might hae given me; it would be better than having the lads think me a coward. If only I had stayed . . .*

Several hours of hard riding later found young Captain MacNeish and his men pitching a cold camp near the southern edge of Loch Leven, and within an old grove of ancient oaks. Any pursuit of the company had been shaken long ago, but deciding on the side of caution, rather than discovering reason to regret it later, James posted a watch with double sentries on duty throughout the pleasantly cool night.

Pangs of doubt and loneliness afflicted James despite the company of his fellow soldiers and kinsmen, for their presence was a cold and silent one as they muttered among themselves while setting up the camp. No one had spoken to their young captain for most of their long dash of escape nor even once he ordered a halt for the night. Cold rations were shared around and still they regarded him with cold, accusing eyes; all of which further added to his feelings of self-doubt and recrimination.

"Wi' ye all believe me a coward or worse without even hearing me out?" growled James, marching to the center of the camp to stand before them.

"What is there to ken, Jamie?" demanded Redwood severely. "All of us were there when ye abandoned the general in his time of greatest need. A man of honour would nae leave his commander in the midst of battle to save his own neck; nae only that, but ye hae made all of us do the same. We hae all lost our honour because of ye.

Redwood shook his great shaggy red head. "For shame, Jamie, ye of all people I would nae hae thought to hae yellow staining yer soul! Yer Da would be sae ashamed of ye right now, if he knew of what ye hae done. Why did ye do it? Tell us what excuse ye hae of doing it; by Lugh's long arm, *I* want to ken!" demanded the big man in a hoarse growl, his eyes betraying the distress he felt.

His childhood friend's words struck James like a blow, and his misery showed clearly in his hurt expression, so much so, that his accuser was forced to look away.

Meanwhile, General Duncan MacSean, fallen and captured during the boisterous battle of the defile was drifting in and out of consciousness as he lay bound and gagged, and held under close guard. Even though he was taken captive and not dead as most of his officers and troops believed, Duncan, in those moments when he was lucid enough for thought, wished fervently that he were dead. His existence was one of unremitting pain; pure, white-hot pain that was unrelenting and merciless. Henry Colquhoun remained on hand to make sure that, and to benefit from his foe's misery.

The torture had begun once the battle had concluded. He did not know how long he had been under the skilful hands of his toad-like tormenter, but it seemed as if it were an eternity. His toenails had been very slowly pulled out one at a time, first from the left foot and then the right. The agony had been so intense that he had passed out. When next he awoke, the nails from each of his fingers had been extracted with the same slow care as had been shone to his raw and throbbing toes. Somehow, and regrettably so, Duncan retained consciousness throughout the long and drawn out process. As a reward for his endurance the general was made to stand on his ravaged feet, tied to a post, and there received a ruthless lashing from the hands of Bishop Colquhoun himself with a wickedly contrived cat of nine tails. The brutal instrument had been made just use on him by his captor and consisted of shards of glass tied to the end of each separate, leather tail. With no shred of Christian mercy showing in his gleeful face, the bishop lashed his helpless prisoner until, his body a bloody ruin, Duncan fainted into a fevered unconsciousness with a throat raw from screaming.

Some time later, cool wetness splashed into Duncan's bruised face and brought him unwillingly from the darkness in which he had escaped. Swimming back through a red haze of torment to consciousness, the ill-used general realized someone must have thrown a bucket of water onto him. Opening his dark rimmed eyes, Duncan glanced about the tent in which he was confined. He was strapped down to a rough cot and found that he could not move his arms or his legs, but could raise his head and discovered Stevenson's master torturer peering down at him with a gap-toothed smile. *This is a taste of what hell must be like*, he thought disconsolately, even as he forced his battered mouth into a crooked smirk of defiance. "Aye, I'm awake again, bastard. What bonny things do ye hae in store for me this time? Something more original this go around I trust; ye see, I always thought ye torturers were supposed to take pride in yer unholy craft and show a bit of artistry," he croaked through parched throat and mangled lips.

The fat torturer merely smiled all the broader.

"Och, he is only beginning, I assure ye," said a familiar gloating voice. Stepping to Duncan's side with hands clasped behind his back was Henry Colquhoun, and to his right stand his cohort Lord Stevenson, with former having spoken as he regarded his prisoner with unconcealed contempt.

"Ye wi' beg me to release yer black, sorcerous soul to hell before we hae finished purifying yer body, Duncan MacSean," Colquhoun assured calmly, in an oily tone, as he spitefully tapped his riding crop against the inflamed flesh of the general's mangled toes. "Ye wi' feel such an exquisite anguish as nay one alive has ever experienced before I permit ye to die. And I promise to enjoy every lingering moment of it," Henry laughed, savoring his enemy's scream of agony.

"Satan take ye, Colquhoun," Duncan gasped, in spite of the hot needles of pain lancing up his legs from his nail-less toes.

"Seeking to summon yer foul master are ye, MacSean?" goaded the bishop. "He can nae help ye now; God has given ye into my hands and ye shall nae escape me. Soon enough yer master wi' receive ye into his dark embrace and feed on yer evil soul. Soon. I wi' see to that, ye can depend on it!"

Turning to the mute torturer, Colquhoun motioned impatiently to draw the ugly brute's attention. "Break his toes, Toby. Break them one at a time. Snap every joint. I want to hear how loud this wicked fool can scream," the archbishop expressly instructed with a cold smile coming his thin lips. "Do ye understand?"

The gap-toothed grin widened as Toby nodded.

"Good. Ye may proceed."

It was not long before Duncan MacSean's screams of agony could be heard once again throughout the entire rebel encampment. Even the most hardened of veterans could not help but shudder at the sound of it and feel sympathy; some men began thoughtfully pondering the idea that it was their bishop, rather than the captured general, which was truly the evil one that they should fear.

Not much more than an hour later, though what seemed like an eternity in the mind of Duncan, the tortured screams abruptly ceased as he once again succumbed to the dark fevered embrace of unconsciousness.

Relishing his task, fat Toby had set out to prove that he was indeed a master of his art as he plied his craft. The prisoner was completely at his mercy, and he had none, but found delight in degrees of pain he could inflict. Every scream his *patient* issued was one to be savored and judged by its individual pitch and duration. Toby privately considered himself a connoisseur of screams, much like others were connoisseurs of wine, as they brought joy to his twisted heart and a gleeful smile to his pudgy face.

Several more times over the following days would the master torturer be given the opportunity to subject his victim to his indelicate ministrations. Toby had never had such an entertaining recipient to play with, and he was spurred on to his best work to show his gratitude to his vengeful sponsor who was, of course, Bishop Colquhoun. Although he had never had much use for priests or any other clerics, Toby found that he liked this bishop which professed to do all in the name of God. He had never tried praying before, but he was tempted to pray to this bishop's god if it allowed him to find delight in the torment of others. That was a god he could worship.

Above, from His majestic throne in heaven and unbeknownst to the mad priest or his deranged torturer, the Lord of Heaven raged and His angels wept over the unhinged bishop's false and hypocritical worship. If only that wicked priest and bishop of the kirk had been aware of God's wrath and indignation or the form in which the most high King of Heaven's righteous retribution would take at his unholy behavior, he would have cringed and wept with fright. Colquhoun would have hidden his face from God in shame, cowering in fear before the Almighty.

Lost in his vendetta and the joy of his victory over a hated enemy, Colquhoun was in fine humor and took to his padded cot with a smile gracing his lips. Sleep came easily to him that night and the next few nights as well, and what dreams he had were peaceful ones though he could not recall them.

CHAPTER TEN

Lord Sean MacSean, Marishal of Scotland, Marquess of Northumbria and elder brother of the captured Duncan, stood idly in the entrance of the large tent King Gregor shared with him. Not long before, within that tent which served as their headquarters in the field, he had finished questioning two Campbell spies that had been captured while lurking about the royal army's camp.

"I did nae care overly much for the manner in which ye dealt with those men, even though they were spies," said Gregor, picking with little interest at his share of the dry meal ration with his skean dhu.

The marishal shrugged. "Spying is a tough business and I'm sure both of those fine gentlemen knew the risks involved. What would ye hae had me do? Ye ken the dire predicament we are in with rationing this army, Uncle; we can nae afford to further deprive our own lads by taking prisoners that we would hae to feed, nor could I just let them go free to report to their master," Sean replied with a stony glance over his shoulder to his leader and kinsman sitting within.

Allowing his attention to wander back to the nearby ancient oak tree standing only a few yards outside the tent. Those men which had drawn the short stick and were now busy with burial detail, were cutting the down the bodies of the two men hanged as spies, and which the king and he had just been discussing. The marishal, more commonly called Warlord by his MacGregor clansmen, felt no remorse. *And why should I?* he thought coolly. *Our spies would receive the same reward from the Campbells if they are caught, and most likely hae. They all ken the price of failure should they be captured. People die in war and that's a fact that wi' never change.*

Both bodies had been cut down and the burial party was in the process of digging their graves as MacSean looked on. *Uncle Gregor's main conundrum is that he is tae kind-hearted at times to be a true warleader,* the Warlord observed thoughtfully, toying idly with the hilt of his plain, serviceable, old dirk. *He has nae yet learned to be ruthless enough in dealing with his enemies; nae like I hae,* Sean thought somberly, a wan smile tugging at his lips. *Perhaps that also makes him a better man than I.*

"Ye are right, I suppose," grudgingly admitted the king, pushing the still half full plate away with a grimace. "I am just nae as ruthless as ye are when it comes to these types of things, Sean. In the future I wi' nae question yer judgment involving such matters, as they do fall under yer purview. My word on it."

Leaving his place at the entryway, the burial party had completed their detail with typical highland élan, MacSean moved back inside the tent and slipped around Gregor to claim a stool opposite of him. Issuing a sigh the tall blonde haired warrior sat down and stretched out his legs, absently stroking his trimmed red beard in thought. The king rose and graciously poured a tankard of cool tangy wine for each of them before resuming his own wooden stool.

"*Slainte!*" exclaimed both men, touching their tankards together, before each of them took a healthy swig of the tart red drink. For some time the two leaders just sat and enjoyed the peace and quiet, occasionally sipping their wine.

Sitting his heavy cup aside, MacSean cast a glance over at his uncle and pulled out an old oiled leather pouch. Quietly he drew out his pipe and thumbed tobacco into it before offering Gregor the pouch. "I hae received some correspondence today that ye wi' take pleasure in hearing."

"Oh? Please speak on, I'm all ears."

Lord Sean grinned wolfishly. "Do ye recall when our bonny friend Lord Mhoram spoke to ye of the attack on the Gordons, toward the start of all this? Well," the grin broadened on the Warlord's face as the king nodded, "it seems that the young Gordon laird has been keeping up the end of his agreement since joining our cause, to the great detriment of our enemies. The word I hae received is that the Gordons hae been giving the Campbells, east of here, all kinds of devilment; thieving cattle and sheep like border reivers, and causing all sorts of havoc. Come this winter, if the Duke of Argyll is still breathing the sweet air, he's going to be hearing it from his holders; ye can be sure of a mighty stink," Sean said, laughing with delight and which Gregor joined in. "I would love to be there when the duke hears of how his coerced ally has turned on him, and then has become sae cheeky as to dare raid The Campbell's lands!"

"Aye! I can see Domeric's face turning red even now," replied Gregor, a raucous guffaw bursting from his lips. "Mayhap he wi' hae a stroke right then and there, and save me the trouble of having to put him down myself!"

"Mayhap, but I do nae think our luck is quite that strong."

The king's jovial grin faded. "Aye. Tae bad though, it would make everything a lot easier for all of us. I'm sure I do nae hae to ask, but has there been any further word from yer brother? I worry about what might be happening with Duncan," stated Gregor, suddenly changing the subject.

"Nay; nothing at all and I tae am concerned."

Well, at least they are speaking to me again, ruefully thought James with an inward sigh, *and they seem to believe me.*

In fact, his lifelong friend Redwood and the other MacNeish troops of the Border Dragons did believe the explanation their young laird had given, but despite the reason and orders to do so, they still held James responsible for fleeing in the face of the enemy. The fact that General MacSean had ordered the captain to escape with his company to locate and escort his son to the king was largely disregarded as the stubborn MacNeish retainers deemed such an order as one to be ignored under the type of conditions they had been under. The harried general was only human after all, and sought to guarantee his son's safe passage; it was an act of love from a father for his son. That, however, was no excuse for the captain, let alone a highland born one, to actually follow the order and abandon the field in favor of seeking to play nursemaid!

The young Laird of Dunmoore and his gloomy band reclined miserably on saddles arranged about the small, smokeless fire, the first fire they had risked since shaking the latest pursuit of enemy trackers, and ate hardtack rations in the hushed stillness of late evening. Each man ate his dry ration with a cup of water, in which to dip the hard biscuit and soften it enough to chew without breaking a tooth, and wished for better fare. The only sound came from the occasional snort of a horse and the gentle crackle with issued from the glow of the burning elm logs.

While James glumly ate his share of the cold, unappetizing supper he could feel the palpable opinions of scorn and doubt from his soldiers about his leadership, and it lay like a curtain between the young laird and the other men. Swallowing the final bite of his tasteless meal, the captain stared into the fire, lost in his thoughts.

I can nae blame them, nae even Redwood. If I were in their place I would likely feel the same way, he agonized. *They did nae hear the general's order or the manner in which it was given me, after all. If only they knew what obedience of that order had cost me to perform it! I did nae want to abandon the field or all those that remained to stand and fight-they should ken me better than that!*

Pulling his weary legs under him, James stood and tramped away from the brooding silence of the sheltered camp and made his way to the nearby gurgling creek the ran lazily in the direction that they traveled. At the edge of the shallow rivulet he crouched and cupped his hands to bring some of the icy clear water to his parched lips. Having slaked his thirst, the laird splashed more water over his head and the back of his neck before bending down to dunk his sweaty head fully into the frigid stream with an involuntary gasp at the coldness of it. *By Lugh's long arm, this should help revive my wits sae that I can try to persuade that grim lot to believe that I had nay choice but to follow the general's bloody orders*, thought James, coming back to his feet.

Before rejoining the others around their little fire the captain went quietly to his horse and produced a stiff bristled brush from a pouch at his waist. Currying his grateful and equally loyal mount soon calmed James' restless mind as all thought was turned to the task at hand, and the horse whose trust was unconditional. The stocky sable gelding's handsome head nudged his shoulder affectionately, which elicited a fond grin from the troubled lad and he paused in his brushing to search his pouches for a treat.

"Ah, here ye go, boy," he said, offering his palm to the soft muzzle of his horse with one of the cubes of sugar he still had. "I do nae hae many of those left, Shadow, sae I hope ye savor it. Maybe tomorrow I'll find an apple for ye."

As the grateful horse crunched the sweet between its strong teeth, James stroked the silky nose for a moment. "At least ye are still my friend; it's tae bad those that I travel with were nae sae trusting as ye are."

Finished with caring for his mount, James gave Shadow a pat of farewell. Shaking a shower of cool water from his head he slowly made his way back to the fire and his band of grim companions. His thoughts were more calm than before as he reached his spot and opened a saddlebag to pull out a towel to run over his damp hair.

No one glanced up as their captain returned nor when he dried his hair before once again reclining on his familiar saddle. James could feel the discontented group purposely not paying him the least attention, and the meager warmth of the fire did nothing to help warm the coolness emanating from those around him.

Picking up his mostly empty cup and then sitting it down again, James thought sourly, *I've had about enough of this bloody shite!* He glanced down at the toes of his boots and up again to scowl at the others ringing the fire. "I ken all of ye believe ill of me and think I'm wrong for having left the general in such dire straights, but as God is my witness, he sent me away for a reason. And whether or nae ye are tae keen on that reason it is nae excuse to judge me out of hand. I hae my orders. I am yer commander and those are my orders to ye grumpy lot tae, sae get over it!"

Looking up with a scornful glance Redwood regarded the young laird. "Go ahead, Jamie, then please tell us this excellent excuse ye hae for deserting our bonny general in the midst of such a desperate battle," the big man growled in undisguised disgust. With a sneer, he added, "We're all listening, sae ye'd better make it good."

"Blast ye for yer infernal distrust, Redwood MacGregory!" shouted James, his outrage pulling him suddenly to his feet. "Ye bloody sheep-shagging dolt! If I sought to merely flee from our enemies would I nae fly for home? But nay, instead we rush quick as ye please straight for King Gregor and his army under command of Duncan's fearsome brother! General MacSean was beaten and he knew it. He had already dispatched his son in hopes of finding the king with news of our position and situation before the battle had properly begun. My orders, and yers, are to find, protect, and deliver Devlin safely to the king, with the hopes that Gregor might arrive in time to reinforce the northern army under the command of Lord Kirkland before they also are chewed up like sae much dogmeat. God kens what the duke and Colquhoun's overwhelming forces did to us! If we can reach the king soon enough, with or without the general's son, maybe they can still arrive in time to divert a complete disaster.

"The whole bloody lot of ye could hae guessed my reasons for yerselves if ye had nae been sae busy believing me to be a faithless cur," James continued in a rush so no one could interrupt. "Now, if ye still refuse to believe me-sae be it. I do nae expect yer belief, but I do yer cooperation and obedience, just as the general expected mine!"

From the hangdog expressions gracing most of the men's faces, James began to hope that they might come around after all, and prayed it was so as he glanced from face to face and waited for their response.

"Now, Jamie, I would like to believe what ye-"

"Do *nae*, 'now Jamie' me, Redwood!" the Laird of Dunmoore growled furiously. "Ach, of all people, ye sound as if ye would rather believe me a coward! Bloody hell, ye great idiot; ye are one stubborn goat, do ye ken that? Look at me," he commanded, his face red with anger. "Wi' ye persuaded to believe me if I should swear a blood oath to the total honesty of every word that has passed my lips?"

Redwood's eyes narrowed, unaccustomed to be spoken to in such a manner by anyone, and scowled at his friend while the others gasped with surprise at the words and the offer their laird had made. All Highlanders and even men from the Isle of Mist (once known as Ireland), knew that no one ever dared break a blood oath offered before the Morrigan and lived beyond the length of a fortnight.

"Nay, James. I would nae hae ye give blood oath on my account," whispered the big red-haired retainer, lowering his eyes in shame. "Please forgive an old friend of his stubborn foolishness. I had nay right to sae question yer honour, and I swear that it shall never happen again."

"Redwood may be sae easily bluffed, but nae me," spoke up one of the older retainers, his face hard and tough as old boot leather. "We all ken the two of ye hae been fast friends since the time ye were pups, but I am nae convinced. To my eyes it sure appeared that our Laird MacNeish turned tail and ran. For the good of this company, I wi' accept yer blood oath," the graying man declared. There was no malice in his tone, but neither was there any compassion. "May God and ye forgive me if ye hae been honest with us, but I wi' accept the oath of blood before the Morrigan."

James swallowed the hard lump that suddenly formed in his throat, but he gave a sharp nod as he drew the dirk from his side. "Very well, ye shall hae it."

"Conner, nay! Ye can nae ask the young master to do this," cried another family retainer. "Mayhap he did run from the fight, I do nae ken what to think for sure, but I ken that he is our laird and the only son of our chieftain. We can nae loose him when Lyam is tae old to produce another heir. This shedding of blood in oath given before the Mistress of Ravens is an unholy thing," he continued, the apprehension of it showing in his wide eyes. "Although I hae never seen a man slain by the Morrigan for breaking the oath made before her, I still hae heard of the curse finding the oath breaker. It is a horrible thing, and I for one wi' nae be responsible for our laird's death."

"Aye," added another retainer. "I hae heard the same things."

Shaking his grizzled head, Conner muttered, "I ken that it is a horrible thing. That is what makes it worth doing. If the lad is speaking the truth he has nothing at all to worry about. Is nae that right, Dunmoore?"

"He is correct, and my word is my bond," James agreed tightly. "However, ken this Conner MacNee: when my sworn word is proven to be without guile, ye wi' be from henceforth, discharged from the service of House MacNeish. Faithlessness wi' nae be tolerated from one who has vainly accused me as a liar and a coward. Yer property which was given for loyalty to my father wi' be bought back from ye at a fair price, Conner, but ye must leave our lands and seek another master," the laird declared, his mild tone not detracting from his judgment. "I would hae greatly appreciated a continued loyalty to me as ye gave my father. I may nae be the man Lyam is, but I am his loving son and heir to our kindred," he added with a sad sigh.

The older man's face had taken on the shade of ashes as James spoke, but pride would not allow him to relent from the harsh words he had already spoken against the old chieftain's son. Bowing stiffly, Conner acknowledged his master's right to discharge him from service and the protection of the Laird of Dunmoore.

"I ask that ye assist me one last time as a MacNeish retainer, Conner," requested James, crossing over the few steps to the small camp fire, the bared blade of the dirk in his hand catching the orange light of the flames. "Ye ken how to prepare me."

Nodding briskly, the old retainer joined the young laird. "Sit there, Master," he said, indicating a bare spot just beside the fire.

Ashes from the fire were scooped out with the old man's calloused fingers before he turned again to face his captain. "Now, lad, ye must take one of yer own blades, that bonny dirk wi' work just fine, and draw yer own blood with it. The blood is what serves to seal the oath," Conner instructed him bluntly. "As yer blood drips into the flames ye must call out to the Morrigan and offer it to her."

James nodded curtly. "What then?"

The older man swallowed audibly. "Th-then, as yer blood continues to drip, ye must let it mingle with the ashes in my hands. Until ye do sae it is nae tae late to change yer mind," he volunteered, appearing as he spoke to age before the laird's eyes. "Once ye hae done sae it is tae late to turn aside. Ye must use the paste of ashes and blood to hae a figure of a raven drawn upon yer forehead and yer bared chest. Once I hae finished doing sae ye must relate again to us the complete tale about what compelled ye to lead us away from the field of battle. Do ye understand?"

Silently nodding his understanding, James slowly raised the sharp dirk in his hand from his side and allowed the firelight to glint across the blade. Lifting his eyes to those of the man crouched before him, the young laird and captain brought the keen blade to his left hand and rested the edge on the palm of his right. Drawing forth a deep breath of the clean night air into his lungs to calm himself, James clinched his jaw and with a jerk he slashed the steel deep into the flesh of his hand!

He's a tough lad, thought Conner, from where he crouched before the laird. *I was sure he would cry out or even change his mind. Ye old coot, why did ye hae to believe the worst about the lad? He's spitting image of his Da and he has the same spirit as well. It's tae late to go back now, but I've wronged him and that's for sure*, the old retainer finally admitted grudgingly to himself.

His lips curled back from his teeth in a wordless snarl of pain, James growled more like a wounded animal than a man. And in a rough voice with his head thrown back, he howled at the starless sky.

"Morrigan! Morrigan! Hear me and smell the blood I offer ye from my own veins and shed by my hand," he chanted over and over again. "This is my blood I present to ye; it is hot and pure and true. Accept my oath of blood, Battle Mistress!"

Even though he was well acquainted with the traditional dark ritual, Conner's own blood ran cold in his veins as he listened to the words of the young laird, who knelt bleeding before him, as he cupped his leathery hands to catch James' blood. Suddenly Conner's head snapped upward as his ears caught the screaming cries of ravens. *There must be scores of them*, thought Conner with a shudder. Aloud, he declared, "The Lady Morrigan has heard yer cries, lad, and *she* is here. *She* is here!"

Hearing the tremor of awe in the old retainer's tone roused James from within his pain induced trance, and he riveted his eyes to Conner's wondering face. The captain's fierce grin nearly unnerved the other watching soldiers, but Conner disregarded it as he dabbed the bloody ashes to the young laird's forehead. Carefully he traced the rune of a raven in flight with a sure finger onto him. When he had completed his task there he moved to James' bared chest and fastidiously repeated the same rune, before sprinkling the remaining paste of blood and ashes into the fire.

"Ye are ready, Captain."

Regaining his feet, Conner backed away from his young master and moved to join his fellow soldiers, who were now standing and glancing about them in wide-eyed fear. They could all hear the loud rustling of wings beating the air and the stark, raucous cries of teeming numbers of the large birds coming from every direction, but each was unable to spot even a single raven in the darkness.

The ravens had gathered by the scores, if their cries were any indication, as James raised his voice and once again recounted his tale of what transpired earlier near the base of the hilltop trail, and which had caused him to flee from the field of battle. His seeming abandonment of General MacSean was related once again, in a voice raw with emotion as he shouted into the night. He told of Duncan's orders to seek escape and the dire mission that he was charged with to locate Devlin if he could, but to find the king's army in hopes of routing reinforcements to the survivors of the northern army before the Duke of Argyll and his allied forces could destroy it altogether.

An eerie silence reigned over the temporary camp once James had finished his story. So immediate had all sound and traces of the multitude of ravens vanished that the company had stared in shock into the night with wide frightened eyes. All sensible men feared the might of the Morrigan, and those men were very sensible indeed.

James quietly stood up and regarded the fearful soldiers for a long moment. "If its nae to much trouble, how about someone find something to bind my hand, wi' ye?" he asked, glancing down at his bloody palm. His eyes abruptly widened in shock and James gasped, "I do nae believe it! Conner, look ye here!"

As James held out his bloodied hand for inspection, the grizzled retainer blinked uncertainly at the laird, and ran a leathery finger before his eyes in a sign to ward off evil before he hurried back to his side. "It wi' be alright, laddie, the cut was nae sae deep as all that. Seeing ones own blood always comes as a shock; we'll hae it bandaged up for ye just fine," he promised, arriving to look over his master's wounded hand.

"Look at it, Conner!" he demanded.

Old Conner's eyebrows seemed to raise clear to his hairline as he smeared the dark blood around with a finger. He raised astonished eyes to stare at his captain. "By Lugh's long arm! James, yer hand is healed!"

"Aye, but how?"

The man shrugged his shoulders uncertainly, but his eyes betrayed what he knew to be true. "Perhaps The Morrigan did sae to prove yer honesty. Who can say for sure? The ways of the ancient Sidhe are strange, but they hae always possessed amongst them a clear code of honour which they always lived by. Honour in battle was The Morrigan's most rigid law, and ye hae proved yerself to *her.*

"I am sorry for my doubt and for believing the worst of ye, James. I accept that ye hae rightful cast me from yer service, but could ye find yer way to forgiving an old goat of a retainer his skepticism, who should hae thought with his heart instead of his head?" he asked, ducking his head before the young master.

Not one to hold a grudge, James allowed a small smile onto his face. "Aye, that I can do, Conner. And, if ye would continue serving me as ye hae my father, take my hand in friendship." Holding out his blood encrusted hand, he smiled openly as the older man took it firmly and pulled him into a rough embrace.

Afterward, James accepted the hand of friendship from the others of his company and slaps on the back as all the recent wounds to the spirit were healed.

Once the excitement of the evening was over and everyone had resumed their places around the fire and each reclined on his saddle, except those who were on sentry duty, a friendly banter began which had been lacking before. The dry rations still lacked for any taste, but that did not seem to matter like it had. Redwood had pulled his saddle over to one side of his captain, and Conner had situated himself on the other side.

"I can nae say with any confidence what has befallen the general, but we must accept the possibility that he was slain in battle. Considering the enmity that Colquhoun bears against Duncan and his brother, I doubt he could hae escaped; and surrender was never an option," James murmured, not willing to accept that possibility in his heart of hearts. Realizing that he must not allow his own fears for the general's well-being to keep him from accomplishing his mission, the captain tried his best to put all such hopeless thoughts from his mind. He knew there was nothing that could be done for Duncan, at least not immediately, except to carry out that commander's final orders to the best of his ability. And that was exactly what he planned to do.

"If the general is nae dead," James continued steadily, "he is almost certainly held prisoner by the Archbishop of Saint Andrew's. To my own mind, if Duncan *is* held in the clutches of Colquhoun, that is very likely worse than being dead. I hae heard of how the bishop is quite fond of torturing confessions from people who hae crossed him. It does nae matter whether they are innocent or guilty, every man has within him a breaking point and wi' say anything just to make the pain stop."

The MacNeish laird shuddered inside as he thought about what Colquhoun would do to the general, and made himself put the grim thought aside. He did not want his dreams plagued by images of what Colquhoun might do to someone he considered to be a sorcerer, and forcibly changed his line of thought.

"Anyway, it is my mission, and yers, to reach the king and warn him about the dire straights of his northern army. Finding Devlin is a plus, but I believe the most critical that is to report to the king," he said gravely. "That is what General MacSean wished and we must nae fail him. If he is still alive as a prisoner of the bishop, then only King Gregor and the main army wi' hae a chance of securing his rescue in time. I hae taken the blood oath and ye ken I speak true," he reminded them. "Can I count on ye to follow me, or must I continue on alone from here?"

The entire company, though not sitting beside the captain as did his lieutenant and old Conner, had heard every word he had spoken to the two men. Looking on, they raptly waited for what those men's response would be. All of them respected Redwood and his opinions, but they also looked on the old sergeant as a father figure and tended to follow his lead, especially when uncertain in their own minds.

Conner noted their undisguised interest and he grunted an apology to his master, chagrin plain on his bluff face, before speaking so all could hear his words. "I believe that Lord Duncan did indeed order the captain here to leave the battle and seek out the king to beg for reinforcements," he stated in his rough voice. "I go with James."

"As do I," pledged Redwood.

Many of the soldiers appeared relieved to hear those men affirm their support to the laird, and one by one the MacNeish men stepped forward to confirm their pledge of loyalty to the chieftain's son. James, for his part, was gracious in accepting those oaths as he knew that one day he would be their chieftain and head of the MacNeish sept. He also knew that no Scot was ever really ruled, but allowed themselves to be led from time to time by those they trusted and respected.

"Well then, now that those matters hae been attended to, we had better get some sleep. The night is nae getting any younger and neither am I," growled Conner, slapping James on the shoulder good-naturedly as he passed on his way to gather up his bedroll. "Lugh kens that we wi' need to be fresh tomorrow and the days following, if we are to find the king's army quick enough to make any difference."

Ye are right about that, Conner, the weary laird agreed. Returning to his saddle he arranged a blanket under him and laid down. Unbuckling his plaid, James shook the folds out and arranged the wool to wrap around himself. He closed his eyes, and before other men's snoring could disturb him, he was sound asleep.

Having taken advantage of his nephew's offer to preside over the evening staff meeting away from their tent, Gregor had retired early. Stripped of his armor, he had even been afforded the luxury of a bath; a wide wooden barrel carried along in the baggage was filled by several buckets of heated water carried by his page and a few others. Clean and feeling refreshed for the first time in days, the king stretched out on his cot for some well deserved sleep. It took barely a moment before his baritone snoring could be heard by the amused guards posted outside the entrance of the royal pavilion.

Gregor had already been enjoying a deep and dreamless slumber for a couple of hours before the Warlord had finished his nightly rounds and finally laid down on his own cot for some much needed rest as well. Sleep, however, did not come so easily for Sean as it had for the king as his restless mind refused to allow it. It was sometime near the midnight hour as he still remained awake, that a ruckus broke the stillness of the night and seemed to be coming from the northeastern perimeter of the large camp. Sleep being denied him anyway, the Warlord threw off his coverings and rose from his cot to go and investigate what was happening. Fumbling in the dark for a cloak and his sword, Sean bumped into the camp table situated between his and his uncle's cot and rattled the cups sitting on it, and quietly cursed the noise.

In an instant, Gregor was wide awake and blinking his eyes furiously to get them to focus in the dark, while he fumbled beside his cot to draw his sword. Rolling off the back side of his camp bed the king succeeded in drawing his sword while pulling a dirk from beneath his pillow. Even through the fog of the sudden awakening, which was fading rapidly from his head, Gregor was reminded of prior kings who had had their reign cut short by the blade of an assassin in the night.

"Hold Gregor! It is only I, Sean," whispered the embarrassed nephew of the king as he backed safely away to the other side of the tent. "I'm sorry to hae wakened ye, I was seeking a cloak when I rattled the desk between us. I wi' be back shortly, Sire. Something has alarmed the sentries and I'm going to take a look. Please, go back to sleep if ye can, and I wi' take care of everything."

Confident now that it had only been Sean, the wary king rose from his defensive crouch and released his grip on his sword while tucking the dirk back into its place under the pillow.

"Bloody hell, Sean!" he exclaimed, releasing a pent up breath he had not realized he had been holding. "When ye startled me awake just now I thought assassins had gotten into the tent and come to-"

Before Gregor could finish what he was saying, a sudden rustling outside the tent entrance interrupted him. A sentry ducked his head inside the dark tent and held up a shaded lantern and exclaimed, "Sire! My lord, please excuse this intrusion, but a large party has arrived just now from Lord Duncan's army. A Captain MacNeish leads them, and Sir Devlin, the general's son, is with him. They wait outside having demanded to be brought to ye immediately. It must be urgent, Sire; their mounts are in sorry shape."

Gregor and Sean exchanged a surprised glance. "Send Devlin in, Sergeant, along with Captain MacNeish," the king ordered briskly.

"Aye, Sire."

Brushing past the opened tent flap, Devlin strode inside and knelt before Gregor. "Sire, I hae come on the command of my Da, to beg Yer Majesty's urgent assistance. We were led into a trap by Duke Domeric and his ally, the Archbishop Colquhoun," he said in a rush, "and I fear my Da and his cavalry may all be slain or captured by now."

Speaking for the first time, James took up the tale where Devlin had left off and related to the king and his marishal the circumstances of the well laid ambush and the battle of the defile. While he gave his report, Gregor could picture in his keen mind the images of what had happened. Fighting to hold the bottleneck of the gorge leading to the hilltop: battling and nearly defeating Lord Stevenson's clan warriors supported by heavily armed warrior-monks, and then finding Colquhoun personally entering the fight and cutting off their brave attempt to break through and rejoin main body of their forces led by Lord Kirkland. Colquhoun had ridden under his clerical banner, gloating over how he had outwitted his Sidhe adversary, and sealing the trap with several hundred of his heavy cavalry and horse archers. He saw in his mind's eye as Duncan issued curt orders to Captain MacNeish to take his company of Border Dragons and escape however he could to come and alert him of the location of the Campbell main army, to secure the person of Duncan's son if he could, and report of the extreme peril to the northern army if it were not reinforced as soon as possible.

Gregor shuddered at the stark pictures James' report had allowed him to paint so vividly within his mind.

"Ye hae done well to find us as quickly as ye hae," commended the grave Warlord as he shot a glance at Gregor. "Three days. This army is a hardy lot, but they could never march that swiftly. However, with Captain MacNeish and his lads to direct us there, our cavalry could make the trip in roughly the same amount of time, Sire" he added for the king's benefit. "Shall I alert the commanders?"

King Gregor nodded thoughtfully after a moment. "Aye, do sae immediately. We can leave Lord Donald in command of the infantry to follow in our wake with as much speed as he can muster from them."

I only pray we can arrive in time to reinforce an army still fighting, and nae to just bury fallen kinsmen and comrades, he grimly added to himself.

*   *   *

"After all that you hae put this wretch through, do ye still actually believe he kens the whereabouts of The MacGregor?" Domeric asked with incredulity, his tone cold, as he regarded the prisoner strapped to a long table within the archbishop's tent.

"Of course he does," snapped Colquhoun. "This misbegotten creature is one of Gregor's closest advisors and a nephew to boot, is he nae?"

Feigning continued unconsciousness, Duncan listened to the quarreling exchange between his enemies standing a mere few feet away from where he lay. He was fairly certain that the hulk of a torturer, Toby, had finally broken the remaining joints of his toes and wondered what would be done to him next. *My fingers probably,* he suspected grimly and cringed at the morbid thought. *Well, maybe it wi' take my mind from the blinding agony of my poor mangled toes.*

Why, for the love of God, does Colquhoun keep putting off having me executed? I'm sure he would find great satisfaction in watching me die, he thought with certainty. *He must realize I do nae ken where Gregor and my brother are, despite what he says to Argyll. Maybe he just has nae thought of something sufficiently degrading to inflict on me yet. The bastard wi' probably hae me flayed. Aye, that's probably what he'll hae done to me next,* Duncan concluded remotely, through his pain induced delirium, right before he gratefully passed out once again.

Some unknown period of time passed before something very cold and wet struck Duncan's face and chest, rousing him with a gasp from his fevered sleep, like a slap and brought the misery of his existence crashing back to him. The pain in his feet was unlike anything he had ever experienced and he cried out in anguish.

"Ah, that's better. It's sae good to hae ye back with us again, MacSean," the bishop's oily voice purred. "Ye hae been very uncooperative sae far. Toby, here, has been quite anxious for ye to talk, as hae I. If ye deem to continue refusing to make use of the tongue our dear Lord hae blessed ye with, well, I fear that just perhaps I must hae to order Toby to remove it. Is that what ye wish, MacSean?" asked Colquhoun gently, a falsely benign smile curving his thin lips as he gazed down at his captive.

Duncan slowly rolled his head from side to side. "Nay, Bishop, I do nae wish it," he whispered through parched lips, turning his fever glazed eyes toward his tormenter. "Whether it be my wish or nae, ye wi' still do as ye like with me, Colquhoun. I already hae much to give to the credit of yer tender mercies, O most foul bishop of Satan! Threats of further abuse wi' nae loosen my tongue to betray the king."

Henry nodded with mock sadness and reached out to smooth his prisoner's hair almost tenderly before grabbing a handful of it, wrenching Duncan's head up from the table to glare balefully at him from just inches away. "Ye are a dead man, MacSean, only ye do nae ken it yet!" he spat vengefully, a sudden sadistic smile touching his cruel mouth as a glint of madness grew in his ice blue eyes.

A bleak croak of laughter issued from Duncan's throat. "Ye are wrong there, Colquhoun; I knew I was dead as soon as I fell into yer loathsome grasp."

Opening his hand suddenly, the bishop released his captive's head to let it bounce painfully against the heavy oak table with a crack. Moaning pitifully, Duncan screwed his eyes closed while waves of nausea rolled over him, only opening them when the dark tide subsided to a tolerable level. "Ye bastard-"

Colquhoun was already speaking again before Duncan could finish what he was going to say. "-hae ye flayed one strip of flesh at a time, and then before ye are allowed to die, I'll hae ye hoisted onto a cross and tied there like a common thief," said the bishop, cackling with glee. "The crows wi' nae even wait for ye to be dead before they begin to dine on the choicer morsels of yer body. Of course, they wi' pluck out yer eyes first since that is their favorite tidbit, but I'm sure ye already knew that," the rebel bishop continued happily. "I hae heard that they also hae an obscene appetite for dining on a man's balls. Did ye ken that? Nay? Ah, well, I would nae worry about it tae much, since ye wi' hae the opportunity to quite soon to discover the truth of it for yerself, MacSean! Oh, aye, ye wi' indeed!" The man's wild laughter hooted with lack of restraint and the captive general screwed his eyes shut with sudden despair.

"Ye are mad, Colquhoun," Duncan moaned. "Completely mad."

"Silence, sorcerer, or I wi' hae yer foul tongue removed!" raved the Archbishop of Saint Andrew's, his laughter abruptly cutting off. Turning to glare at the patiently waiting torturer, he sneered, "I was given to believe ye were a master of yer craft, Toby. Ye must be loosing yer touch; ye hae nae even broken this pathetic sorcerer's spirit yet! I give ye just one last chance at him; if he has nae loosened his tongue by morning, ye wi' find out first hand the wrath I hold for those who fail me. I *must* ken the bloody MacGregor's whereabouts sae I may inform the Lord Domeric. Am I clear?"

The mute torturer nodded quickly to the irate bishop and hastily bowed. When he straightened, Toby held up one hand with gap-toothed grin. Clasped in that hand was a scalpel-like knife that glimmered sharply in the meager light. Moving the blade slightly from side to side he grinned wider as the glow from a brazier caught the instrument's keen edge and reflected its amber light.

A wicked grin stretched across Henry Colquhoun's narrow face as he dipped his head with appreciation toward the hulking torturer. "Ah, perhaps ye do possess the master's touch after all, but we shall see. If that does nae loosen MacSean's tongue for us, I think maybe nothing wi'," he said approvingly. "See that ye use it with care, Toby. I would be sorely disappointed should my prize die prematurely."

Toby bowed again, his tongue less mouth kept shut, and when he looked up again the bishop was already gone, leaving him alone with his plaything.

Being nothing, if not diligent about his task, the immense pain-giver set himself to his work bearing the razor-sharp blade. Moments later, Duncan had feinted once again as a thin portion of skin had been expertly stripped away from one foot. The last thing he saw before yielding to fevered oblivion was Toby's grotesque face leering excitedly down at him as he screamed in untold suffering.

The torturous sessions seemed to be endless, and Duncan swiftly lost count of how many times he was reawakened for the misery to be continued. Some time later, as consciousness fully returned to the miserable general, it was to a voice he recognized as belonging to Domeric Campbell, the falsely crowned pretender king.

"For the love of God, Colquhoun, look at the wretch! If he knew anything of value to us, he would hae begged for us to hae it by now. More torture gains us nothing at this point," he declared with disgust. "Just let the bastard die."

"What's wrong with ye, Yer Highness, are ye getting soft? Ye do nae feel sorry for this vile creature, do ye?" Colquhoun chided sarcastically. "I was given to understand that *ye* employed the services of a torturer in yer citadel. My sources could be wrong, I suppose, especially since ye do nae seem to possess the stomach to even witness what a true master of his craft can accomplish with the proper motivation."

"Aye, it's true that I employ a torturer when the need arises," grunted Domeric, casting a slow glance across Duncan's ravaged body, his expression betraying his horror at what had been done. "But *never* would I allow or condone such grisly business to be done in my dungeon. Nay, nae even to my worst enemy would I do such as this. If God wishes this sort of ghastly behavior from us, perhaps it would be best if I find some other to worship and offer my prayers to."

"Blasphemy! How dare ye blaspheme sae in my presence?" howled Henry in a strangled voice, a wild look of madness again growing in his eyes. "God should strike ye down for such an affront, Campbell!"

Snorting with contempt, Domeric fingered the hilt of his sword and thought how good it would feel to drive its blade into the loathsome cleric's guts. Meeting the bishop's glare with one of his own, he snapped, "Shut yer flapping lips, Colquhoun! I'm nae sae sure of who ye worship anymore, but my God does nae desire such foulness as this." He indicated with one hand the whimpering captor strapped to the table, and winced as he again looked on Duncan's wretched condition. "I remind ye that ye follow *my* banner and ye wi' obey ye commands, or ye may leave the field," he said flatly. "I wi' condone nay forth torture of this man, sae either be done with the poor wretch now, this moment, or I wi' hae my own headsman do it for ye! Are my orders clear enough for ye, Henry? Ye are done here, and I wi' wait idle nay longer!"

Colquhoun's eyes fairly bulged from his head in outrage as he struggled to curd another withering retort from escaping his lips. "As ye wish, *Yer Majesty,*" acquiesced the furious bishop, his words dripping scorn like acid. "Wi' *His Majesty* permit this humble priest the task of having this prisoner flogged before he is crucified?"

The Duke of Argyll, and self-styled King of Scotland rolled his eyes with a sigh of exasperation before nodding curtly. "Very well, if that's what it takes to be done with this sordid business. Do what ye must," he agreed reluctantly, pointedly ignoring his ally's sarcastic tone, "but be quick about it. I hae an entire army, camped around this tent of yer's, sitting idly by and getting more restless every hour because of this one prisoner. If we tarry here much longer, we need nae worry any longer about discovering the location of The MacGregor's army because Gregor wi' hae found us!"

Henry gave a derisive laugh. "I doubt that."

"Oh, ye doubt it, do ye?" Domeric mocked with undisguised disdain. "Perhaps ye hae forgotten about MacSean's second in command, that Lord Kirkland of MacPherson fellow? Aye, his troops may hae been scattered and chased from the battlefield after the fall of their general, but what do ye suppose they hae been doing these few days while we just sit here on our collective arse? The first thing any semi-intelligent officer would hae done would be to dispatch couriers to speed word of their defeat to Gregor with an appeal for aid and reinforcement," he explained slowly, speaking as if to a dimwitted child.

"Well-"

"Of course he would; would ye nae do the same in his position?" The Campbell answered his own question over the top of the man's reply, the whole while glowering darkly from under lowered eyebrows. "By now, Gregor wi' ken where we are encamped, possibly hae an idea about our defenses, and ken about how many troops I hae and what types of troops they are.

"Then, of course, we hae Duncan here," he went on harshly. "He is Gregor's own nephew *and* Warlord MacSean's dear brother. Give those cunning minds enough time, which we may hae already given, and it's a safe wager to bet that they wi' attempt some sort of rescue with a plausible degree of success.

"Duncan, here, is nay poor tactician but is as a child to the art of war compared to his brother, Sean, The MacGregor's warlord. That was how I was able to snare him in our trap," admitted the Campbell lord. "Sean, on the other hand, wi' nae be sae tricked or out maneuvered; I ken this from personal experience as he has already defeated my clan in a number of past border raids, and once in a pitched battle. He knows what he is doing and it would be foolish to underestimate him."

"Ye fear him!" Henry accused.

"Nay, but I do hae a healthy respect for his abilities as a general and a cunning opponent. Ye are the one that should fear him, especially when he discovers what ye hae done to his brother," he advised, casting a significant glance over at where the bishop's tortured captive lay bound and moaning in pain.

Henry gulped. "What wi' ye do then?"

Domeric shrugged his broad shoulders. "Hope that our lads are better than his and pray for the best," he replied with a sigh. "The lads hae found a new confidence in us and in themselves after the victory we achieved over Duncan's army. That wi' count in our favor with morale sae high; though it dwindles the longer we sit inactive."

"And me?"

"Ye must continue to lead yer clansmen and those warrior-monks ye hae brought with ye, Bishop. Other than that, in the meantime, ye should pray. Pray, Colquhoun, for God's will to be with us throughout the rest of this bloody war or both our heads wi' be on the chopping block," replied the duke, slapping his palm against the trusty basket hilt of the sword hanging t his side. "Aye. Pray hard, Colquhoun."

"Bring the vile wretch," Colquhoun commanded some time later, once he had summoned two of his dutiful warrior-monks to the pavilion, that most everyone else but Toby, carefully avoided and gave a wide berth.

Without removing the heavy iron chains shackled to his wrists and ankles as they lifted him from the blood stained, oak table, Duncan was roughly dragged from the large tent between the brawny soldiers. Outside, the condemned general was hauled past the gloating bishop and a sneering Lord Stevenson as he was conducted to the place of his execution. Domeric Campbell was there as well, but would not or could not force himself to meet the ill-used prisoner's flat and emotionless stare. *Domeric, apparently, can nae look upon the handiwork of his henchmen,* Duncan thought with a little surprise. *Maybe the old duke has a conscience after all, though nae enough of one to put a stop to this foul business of Colquhoun.*

As his guards led him on, Duncan caught sight of the waiting cross which had been erected for his honour, but had little time to think about it as the gravely silent men warding him halted before two more of their waiting brethren. Those two warrior-monks were impressively large and burly men mounted on powerful destriers, and each took hold of a chain bound to his wrists. Being held thus, Duncan waited stoically for the pain of the whip to add its torment to his already ravaged flesh.

Ach, I doubt this can be any worse than when that hulking brute, Toby, broke my bloody toes, Duncan thought resignedly, bracing himself against the strike of the lash that he knew would soon be coming. He was wrong.

Striding eagerly forward, to a point two paces and directly behind the secured prisoner, Tearlach Stevenson uncoiled the cat-of-nine-tails he brought with him. He had had it specially made just for such an occasion as this. On the end of each tail was knotted a small but jagged sliver of steel, designed to pierce flesh and then rip it away on the back stroke. *What flesh he has left when I'm done with him wi' be ribbons,* Stevenson reckoned as he allowed himself a satisfied smile. *I'm going to enjoy this.*

Duncan's agonized scream echoed throughout the entire encampment as the nine wickedly designed tails slapped into his body to tear at the flesh. Each successive time the lash struck, Stevenson laughed with glee and goaded the helpless man shrieking before him. "How does my sweet cat's caress feel, MacSean? How many more of its strokes do ye think it wi' take before it has flayed every morsel of flesh from yer body?" he gloated. "Ha! Ye whimper more like a bairn than a man. Scream for me, MacSean! Scream!"

Dear God, help me, Duncan's thought cried as he grounded his teeth to smother another scream. *I do nae ken which is worse: the brutal touch of that cursed lash tearing apart my flesh or that hellspawn's mad giggling and rantings!*

New flashes of white-hot pain racked through his body at each strike and the cold sweat streaming from his pores dripped into the bloody gouges torn into his back, sides, and front of his torso where the tails wrapped around and sliced into him. Sagging more and more heavily against the chains holding him up, Duncan wondered if that was how he was going to die, instead of the promised and dreaded cross.

"Curse it all, Colquhoun, call off yer dog! Is this nae enough to satisfy even yer lust for the poor man's blood?" Duncan vaguely heard, as the Campbell lord growled at the smirking bishop, the words barely registering through the red screen of agony raging in his mind. "He can nae take much more from that madman lashing him as if one of the devil's demons possess him! Or is it yer wish now that MacSean perish under the lash rather than on yonder cross?"

The smirk died on Colquhoun's narrow face as he regarded his ally with a look of disdain. "I begin to think this sorcerer has taken ye under his spell. This is the third time ye hae pleaded leniency on his behalf, my dear duke. Hae ye been bewitched, Domeric?" asked Henry, one eyebrow cocked elegantly in feigned curiosity. "Or is it that ye just do nae hae the heart for doing the Lord's work?"

Domeric snorted. "*This* is the good Lord's work? Perhaps, God in His wisdom, may demand a man's life to be forfeit for wicked deeds or the use of sorcery, but torture such as this? I think nae. Such unrelenting torment as this is nae the way of a forgiving god," he replied coolly. "Hae ye even asked the wretch for a confession of his sins? Of course nae. Bishop, I tell ye true on my word of honour, I would nae do thus to any man nae even to my worst enemy!"

Colquhoun's lip curled with undisguised contempt before turning away from the duke to watch as Duncan cringed under the painful stroke of his friend's whip yet again. "Lord Stevenson! Thank ye, but that should suffice," the bishop called out, regret plain in his tone. "We would nae wish to deprive the cross, which yer men labored to erect, of its intended victim, would we?"

Stevenson glanced back and lowered the whip, disappointment written across his cruelly handsome face. "Nay, Yer Grace."

"Hae ye the sign I asked for?"

"Aye, Yer Grace. My captain has it ready," Stevenson acknowledged, motioning for his officer to bring him the mentioned sign.

"Good man," Henry said with a smile. "Please hang it about the prisoner's neck sae all may read of his crimes as they witness his just punishment.

Stevenson returned the smile. "Of course, Yer Grace."

Sidling arrogantly up to the nearly unconscious prisoner, the bishop's erstwhile friend slipped the engraved wooden sign around Duncan's neck. "Yer time on this Earth is about at an end. This placard bears a proclamation of yer guilt, MacSean," he goaded softly. "All who read it wi' ken of yer evil deeds performed in the service of yer lord Satan, and how the kirk deals with yer brand of wickedness! Soon ye wi' be joining yer foul master of darkness in the fiery pits of hell for all eternity. I trust yer journey to meet him wi' be a slow and excruciating one."

"If ye seek someone that serves Lucifer look nae to me, but instead cast yer glance in a looking glass. He is yer true master, nae mine," croaked Duncan, the broken words coming through bleeding lips as he raised defiant eyes to meet his tormenter. "Lucifer awaits ye, Stevenson, and I pray my brother sends ye to meet him!"

Emitting a wild cry of rage, Stevenson smashed the captive general across the face with the handle of his whip. Hate radiated from the bishop's henchman as he cocked his hand back to deliver another blow.

"Enough!" cried Henry, afraid of losing his prize too soon to his ally's fit of rage. "Tearlach, give over, the cross awaits him, and I hae faith it wi' yet humble this sorcerous dog adequately, but he must live long enough to hang from it. Can ye nae see that he is trying to goad ye into slaying tae soon, and depriving us the satisfaction of watching him suffer a lingering death for his sins?" he inquired coolly.

Reluctantly, and visibly fighting for self-control, Stevenson turned his back on the bishop's prisoner and curtly nodded. "Aye, Yer Grace; his spell would hae worked tae, if ye had nae recalled me to my senses in time."

"Guards, secure the condemned creature to the cross," Henry ordered, his tone far more cool than his inner thoughts were. Eyeing Duncan triumphantly, the rebel bishop went on, directing his next words to him. "Yer fate is upon ye, Duncan MacSean. Oh, but I realize ye can nae read the sign hanging across yer chest, can ye? I wi' read it for ye," purred Colquhoun. "It says,'

Here dieth a most foul sorcerer. *Behold the fate of all who worship Satan!* What do ye think that, wretch?"

Duncan wheezed in what the surprised Archbishop of Saint Andrew's interpreted as a laugh. "Ach, but ye are pathetic, vile priest! I hae never worshipped Lucifer, but I would be happy to summon him here to collect yer black soul if I knew how," the general groaned, bending nearly doubled over as a dry racking cough nearly gagged him. "Aye, but at least I hae the consolation of knowing the devil wi' hae it some day sooner or later, ye dark hearted servant of-!"

The force of Colquhoun's sudden back-handed blow wrenched the weakened general's head violently around. The savage blow silenced whatever else he would have said as he groaned miserably before recovering dazedly. The cuffing dealt him failed to add very much to the pain that Duncan had already experienced since his capture, and another dry and wheezing chuckle escaped his bleeding lips.

"Crucify him!" Henry shrieked madly, spittle flying from his mouth.

The burly monks unshackled the chains from about the prisoner's wrist and ankles without a word before seizing him the arms and dragging him to the cross which had been assembled for his execution. It was, Duncan faintly realized, a Saint Andrew cross that he was laid down upon to be secure to. Too soon, the condemned general found himself tied fast to the cross by strong, dampened, rawhide straps; his arms and legs spread apart in the semblance of an X. Moments later, Duncan felt himself raised into the air as soldiers hoisted the saltire cross up and slipped the main beams into the holes, especially prepared to hold it erect, with a sudden jolt that nearly pulled his arms from the sockets.

Duncan gasped wretchedly as sinews popped and his whole body jerked against the bindings, only an abiding pride keeping him from screaming while new pain rushed through his nerves. He had lost weight since his capture, though it had only been a few days, from the total lack of food and water and from the all too constant torture that he had been subjected to from his enemies. Despite that, gravity still dragged his body down against the leather straps binding him and caused the tight, dampened straps to cut cruel grooves deep into his bleeding flesh.

Sae, it appears that perhaps I wi' die this way after all, he admitted to himself with a hint of despair, directing his pain sharpened gaze down at his enemies. Defiantly, he forced a rictus-like grin onto his bloody face. *This is certainly nae the heroic death I had envisioned for myself, but at least I go to meet my Maker knowing I hae lived a good clean life and hae nae shamed nor dishonoured myself before God or The Morrigan.*

Staring up at his victim with a self-satisfaction tempered with an equal amount of frustration, Henry Colquhoun forced onto his narrow face a smile of malicious delight for the benefit of his defeated quarry. Deliberately turning his head away to regard his loyal henchman, the bishop nodded curtly to Stevenson, who stood scowling up at MacSean, waiting nearby at his right hand like a well trained dog.

"Inform me immediately when he begins to swoon, my friend," Henry ordered quietly. "I wi' nae allow him to die as the blessed Saint Andrew did. Instead, I would hae MacSean cut down and splayed between four strong horses, sae that his body may be quartered while there is still breath in him."

"With pleasure, Yer Grace."

As he hanged limply from the saltire cross, Duncan understood how it was that a cross truly killed its victim. *I'm going to suffocate. I can barely draw breath into my lungs, stretched as I am*, he realized dejectedly, even as he dug his heels into the rough wooden beams to raise himself to gulp sweet air into his burning lungs. Sagging down once again, the king's younger nephew hung lethargically from his bonds as he felt a wave of despair flare anew within him. An unreasonable fear tightened his scrotum as he awaited for the cold hand of the angel of death to descent upon him and pull his immortal soul from the dead husk of his corporeal flesh.

Rallying himself by sheer force of will, Duncan again pushed himself up to gulp another lungful of air. *Ach*, he chided himself silently, *at least I can show this lot how to die well. Aye, I wi' prove to Colquhoun and his lackeys that a MacGregor clansman faces the hand of death with dignity and show them nay fear! I hae had a good life, albeit one tae short. I hae many friends from among my clan and from other clans as well. They wi' avenge me*, the dying general knew in his heart, *my dear brother and Gregor wi' see to that beyond a doubt. I would nae want to be Henry Colquhoun when they discover what he has done to me, and finally catch up to him! Sean wi' surely hae him flayed alive, an inch at a time. A very slow death that, and excruciatingly painful as well, as I hae found to a small degree, but exactly what that foul bishop sae richly deserves!*

Duncan allowed a mocking grin to curve his lips. *Aye, and then auld Colquhoun can go to meet his true master in hell, for he is certainly nay servant of God. Nay true priest would hae done, let alone condoned, even a portion of the hellish atrocities that bloody Henry has reveled in.*

The general struggled for another breath and when he sagged back down against his tightening restraints he tried to swallow to ease his parched throat but could not. As his vision began to tunnel, Duncan closed his eyes and to try and take his mind off his own torment, pictured in his mind's eye how his most dire of enemies would die. With vindictive approval he watched as Colquhoun was staked to the ground and slowly, methodically had his skin peeled from his body in a long and bloody sheet, to reveal the corrupted muscles and sinew lying beneath . . .

"The evil wretch is smiling!" exclaimed Henry, gaping in disbelief as he returned to his cohort's side and looked up at Duncan. Low murmurs of consternation began to ripple through the ranks of warrior-monks assembled to bear witness to the first execution of a man condemned as a sorcerer, as well as the first crucifixion decreed since the time of The Recovery.

"Yer Grace! Look ye there, toward the hills," gasped Stevenson, pointing with one hand to the southwest. "That must be why the bastard is smiling; he sees the approach of friends and thinks The MacGregor can rescue him from his fate!"

Domeric, likewise, had noticed the glittering of polished steel and the dust kicked up from the royal army's advance as well. Cursing the bishop's foolishness he summoned his mount, and he and his senior officers were already bellowing orders to assemble all of the cavalry troops and infantrymen into formation.

Horns blew the alarm and all through the camp frantic soldiers armed themselves, while their officers tried to organize the mob of surprised highland and lowland men alike into an orderly fighting force

Red-faced with fury, Domeric raged at the lack of discipline and wondered what had become of the outriders who were charged with warning him of any approaching body of men. *Bloody hell, if we can nae meet them beyond the confines of our tents they wi' trap us within our own camp!* Bagpipes began blowing the scurling notes of advance as the first battalions were at last formed up. They marched out to meet the approaching enemy to buy time for the rest of the surprised army to organize. *I pray they can hold long enough to prevent a total slaughter,* Domeric thought grimly.

Caught up in his daydream of retribution as he was against Colquhoun and his chief henchmen, Duncan failed to take notice of the royal army's appearance from the hills. Nor was he even aware of when the two opposing forces, urged on by the strident call of the great highland bagpipes, began their struggle.

CHAPTER ELEVEN

"*The MacGregor!* King Gregor MacGregor of Scotland! For the king!" went the mighty shout, leaping from many throats advancing from the hills and plains to the south and west of the frenzied army camp of the Duke of Argyll.

The fiercely burning sun cast its dazzling rays to gleam brightly from polished armor and brandished weapons as the Royal Army of Scotland, led by her king, streamed down onto the flatlands of Achriabhach that lay south of might Ben Nevis to force the unprepared Campbell host to battle. Immediately the balmy air was filled with the sound of ferocious clan warcries: *Gregalach* and *Ard Choille* being among the most prominent among them, as proud banner bearers trotted forward carrying high their clan standards. Foremost of these standards was the proudly borne red lion of Scotland and the white cross on blue of Saint Andrew.

In his weakened state, Duncan slipped in and out of consciousness, stirring only when his lungs protested insistently for more much needed oxygen. He was barely aware enough to understand that something was happening to cause a stir among his enemies. In fact, the ill-used general did not realize that the king had come at last, too preoccupied with gaining his next breath to think about anything else.

The warrior-monks that had earlier gathered around the cross to bear witness of his execution were gone now, arming themselves for the coming battle. Their commander remained, however, alternating between screaming and shaking his fists at the coming army of King Gregor, and dragging bundles of wood to pile around the cross that bore his prisoner. Meanwhile, Lord Stevenson, forced to leave the side of his ally, was hurrying to rally his clansmen and the mercenaries he commanded to reinforce the duke's forces as best as his squire rushed to buckle on his armor and sword.

Domeric's Campbell levies and those clans whose chief had given loyalty to him were becoming more organized thanks to the more able officers and their solid cadre of veteran non-commissioned officers. In their hasty defense, the first battalions which had gone forth at the onset took heavy losses but averted disaster by somehow repulsing the first initial charge of the royal army's heavy cavalry. Although he had been surprised by the appearance of the king's army, Domeric was an able and canny opponent and put the brief respite to good effect. Mounted on his favorite chestnut gelding, the duke assumed personal command for the time being, and ordered them back in an orderly withdrawal to more defensible ground before Gregor's commanders could reform their cavalry for a second massed charged on his position.

While all this was happening, Colquhoun at last succumbed to the good sense of his lieutenants and reluctantly agreed to follow The Campbell's wise example to likewise withdraw his forces to a better fighting position and leave behind his prisoner. But before doing so he found a lantern filled with oil and smashed it among the bundles of wood he had quickly stacked around the cross. His last act before accepting the reins of his horse was to take a flaming brand and toss it upon the shattered lantern. As flames raced across the dry wood, Colquhoun shook his mace up at the nearly lifeless general.

"Duncan MacSean!" he bellowed to be heard above the cacophony of battle. "May God damn yer soul to hell for the wicked sorcerer ye are! I pray that ye writhe within the flames I send for ye before ye feel the unrelenting hellfire ye go to meet, but if ye should survive this day ken that this is nae finished! This wi' never be finished until I see with my own eyes yer charred remains," Colquhoun raved madly, lost in an impotent rage of frustration. "I wi' search ye out to the ends of the world and hae yer unholy guts roasted on a brazier, even if I hae to do it by myself! I wi' harry ye for the remainder of my days if I must, until I hae ye in chains again and can finally send yer black soul screaming to meet the eternal flames of hell!"

For Duncan everything appeared dimly and doubled as his vision began to fail from a lack of breath drawn into his heaving lungs. To his horror, there appeared to be two Henry Colquhouns screaming curses at him with wild gesticulations and two large maces being waved at him. The last thing General MacSean saw before passing out from suffocation was the hateful bishop astride his mount and riding away, with many a backward glance, at the head of a column of warrior-monks and his clansmen.

"My Lord!" shouted Captain MacNeish, pitching his voice to cut through the din of battle, as he angled his horse toward the king's marishal. "The cross! Do ye see it, near the center of the camp? They hae yer brother hanging from it; and I see flames beginning to grow higher around it even now!"

Jerking his head around to follow James' pointing finger, Sean quickly located the object and nodded brusquely. "Aye, I see it. Are ye sure it's Duncan? 'Tis tae far for me to make out who it could be."

"I hae the eyes of an eagle," he stated with no sign of boasting in his matter of fact tone. "It is General MacSean, I'm sure of it. He is nae moving even though the fire grows and nears his legs. He'll burn if we do nae get to him soon!"

Utilizing a talent that was like second nature to him after so long, the Marishal compartmentalized his mind to deal with multiple problems at the same time. *This is more an overgrown skirmish rather than a true battle*, Sean considered. *Already they are retreating to more favorable ground as our cavalry regroups. We wi' be forced to piddle around with their rearguard before engaging them again. If Henry has left behind my brother, it likely as nae means Duncan is dead already, but why set fire to the cross if he is dead? Bloody Colquhoun actually had the gall to crucify him. Crucified my brother! By Lugh, if Duncan is dead, I wi' personally see that Colquhoun* . . . Sean shook his head vigorously to break that line of thought, and glanced at the captain.

"Pray that Duncan is still alive, Captain," he told James quietly, before turning away to peer through the dust and heat haze at the cross once again. "We wi' ken for sure soon enough; once we hae broken through the Duke of Argyll's rearguard we wi' ken if we hae prayed hard enough for God to listen." The MacGregor Warlord hardened himself and isolated his emotions to a closed put of his mind as he formulated the best and most swift way to eliminate those standing between him and his brother.

Sooner than the Warlord had expected, given the situation, the elements of the Campbell rearguard abandoned their weak position and retreated with alacrity to rejoin the rest of their organizing army. Sean immediately signaled a general advance and horns sounded throughout the army; the army marched forward to the skirl of bagpipes and the heavy cavalry moved forward at a trot, remaining in formation to screen them should the enemy have some surprise in store.

"I wi' ride with yer company, Captain MacNeish. Let's go save Duncan from the flames, whether or nae he is still alive," Lord Sean ordered. Together they galloped into the abandoned camp, earnestly making their way toward where Duncan hanged limply from the roughly hewn cross located at the very center. In just a few moments they pulled their mounts to a halt within yards of the burning cross of Saint Andrew.

My God, he's already dead, Sean groaned silently in anguish, vaulting from the saddle to join the sobbing Captain of the Border Dragons. "Ye others, scatter the burning wood surrounding the cross! Come, Captain. Help me get my brother down from there; he may yet be alive," he ordered, rushing to the cross and continuing to plead to God that his beloved brother yet lived.

In short order, the wood had been scattered and the flames put out, and a moment later the cross had been lifted from its postholes and laid gently flat on the ground. Lord Sean knelt beside his stricken brother as James hurriedly hacked away the leather bonds tying the general to the stout timbers. Tears streaked Sean's cheeks like rivulets through the powdery dust coating them, turning it to mud as he suddenly caught his breath in a relieved gasp. Looking up at the grieving James, he laughed for joy, "He's alive! By the grace of my dear God Almighty, our prayers reached the ears of Heaven!" exclaimed the hard-bitten warlord, weeping joyful tears. "Duncan is alive!"

"By God, he looks like death warmed over," growled Gregor, shaking his head with equal parts anger and relief. "That bastard Colquhoun has surely outdone himself this time; when I get my hands on him, he wi' pay for this I swear it! What could hae possessed him to do such a thing?"

Sean spat on the dirt floor of the surgeon's tent. "He's my brother and that's all the reason he would need; Colquhoun considers both of us to be sorcerers because of the abilities granted by our Sidhe blood, nae to mention the ancient sciences we both hae studied and learned to use. Anything he can nae understand he condemns. Besides all that, I believe the bishop is mad, plain and simple, Uncle," stated Sean, his eyes bleak.

"Poor Duncan," he said sighing, before glancing up at Sean. "I can see that he was tortured, but what all was done to him?"

Sean shook his head helplessly and nodded for Father Lyle, an experienced battle surgeon, to give answer to the king.

"Well, Sire, he was really worked over for some time and, aye, he was tortured," the priest muttered, his worry evident. "I would wager, if I were the betting type, that a trained torturer was employed. See his hands and toes? Each nail has been extracted with the precision of a surgeon," he explained professionally, pointing out the raw pink flesh with an edge to his voice. "Next, each and every joint of the toes of both his feet hae been broken and left dislocated. The general wi' probably never walk right again, if at all. It seems that some sort of foul drug was also administered as a means to force him to impart information they wished to extract, but I ken nae what it might hae been. The rest," the priest sighed sadly, "ye can plainly see for yerself. His feet were partially flayed, and of course he was lashed mercilessly with some cruel instrument. The beatings he received were numerous, but luckily, Lord Duncan has nay internal injuries that I hae been able to detect; still, he wi' be a long time in recovering. As to his mental state, well, only time wi' tell whether his mind was able to withstand use abuse."

Duncan suddenly stirred weakly, moaning in obvious pain from where he lay on the cot, startling everyone present. "Devlin? Is Devlin here?"

"Summon Lord Devlin immediately!" Gregor sharply commanded an orderly, as Sean moved swiftly to his brother's side and knelt, clasping Duncan's hand carefully but as if he would never let it go. He forced himself to meet his brother's unfocused gaze and smile as if everything was right in the world.

"Duncan, how is it with ye?" he asked softly.

Duncan tried to smile but his battered face was too swollen to allow more than a parody of one. "Ach, I wi' be fine, just as long as ye do nae break my hand. My friends among the other camp hae done enough of that already," he whispered hoarsely and tried to laugh, but a hacking cough quickly ended his weak attempt at humor. "It is good to see ye, but I hae been ill used, brother. It appears that ye hae somehow cheated that mad bastard of a bishop, Colquhoun, of my early demise after all. My thanks for that; I owe ye one, Sean," said Duncan, opening his eyes once again to regard his worried brother, once the coughing had stopped. "Ye hae to get that madman before he does this to anyone else, I beg of ye; a demon has him, I think, and possesses his mind," the stricken man added with haunted eyes. "Colquhoun claims he serves God, but the God of our fathers never asked for or desired such service as Henry offers up. In his madness or possession, whatever it may be, he serves nae the Heavenly Father, but some evil power like Cromm Cruac or perhaps even Satan himself. I ken nae what for sure, except that it is wicked and corruption incarnate."

"I wi' avenge ye, Duncan, and put a stop to Colquhoun. Nay unholy power wi' keep me from it," promised Sean.

"Father!" cried Devlin, rushing into the tent to the injured man's side, kneeling next to his uncle. "I did as I swore to do! But, oh, Da! What hae they done to ye?"

"I ken ye did, laddie, or I would be dead right now," Duncan replied, grimacing as he other hand was grasp with enthusiam.

"By God, I thought I would nae live to lay eyes on ye again, Devlin. Ye are unhurt?"

"Aye, I'm well with nary a scratch," the young man assured. "Ye hae nothing to worry about, Da, except resting and healing."

"Aye! That goes for me as well, General MacSean," Sean suddenly broke in, a broad smile spreading across his face. "Ye are ordered to sit out the rest of this little war of ours, and concern yerself with nothing but getting well. Yer wife would never forgive me if I let anything come between ye and going home to be nursed by her. Ye ken how the Livingstons can be when they're riled!"

Duncan's good humor was short lived as he recalled Father Lyle's earlier words concerning his recovery, and a dark cloud covered his bruised features. "What if Father Lyle is right and I am nay longer able to walk?" he demanded. "What good am I to ye or anyone else as an invalid?"

Sean kept all expression from showing as he regarded his younger brother. "Ach, ye wi' be nay invalid, and besides, ye do nae need to walk, Duncan. Ye are a cavalryman, remember? Why walk to battle when ye can ride?" replied Sean, an impish grin hiding his true feelings, as he wondered what the future held in store for Duncan as well.

Blue eyes twinkled as Duncan tried to smile. "Such compassion!" he remarked, chuckling in his familiar good natured way. "Perhaps ye are right, except that I would hae to live in the saddle until someone helped me off. But what if I fell off?"

"I could hae ye strapped on?" suggested a smirking Sean.

"Wi' ye two continue bantering on all evening or could yer king, perhaps, get in a word or two?" inquired Gregor, smiling to himself as he moved to stand at the foot of Duncan's cot. "I must say that even though ye look like hell, Duncan, but it does nae seem to hae affected yer tongue any! I trust ye gave as good as ye got."

The ill used general looked up at his uncle with chagrin and wagged his head. "As to that, Sire, it was a bonny fight right to the very end for me. I managed to crack more than a few of their skulls before I went down," Duncan replied, his eyes unfocusing as he thought back to the frantic battle that had surrounded him. Only a few days had passed, but to him it seemed as if it had been weeks. "It became apparent to me as sae many of their men went down to my sword that they had been given orders to take me alive, nay matter the cost. "As it was, I had nay such compunction as far as that lot was concerned. Things turned rather badly after I was unhorsed, but still I fought on and took several more with me before matters turned even uglier and I was borne under by a press of bodies. Once I was subdued, Colquhoun was in none tae charitable a mood during my visit with him, I must admit. He seemed to be a bit out of sorts about the toll my lads and I took of his clansmen and his precious warrior-monks."

Gregor snorted. "Ye hae a talent for understatement."

Duncan shrugged uncomfortably. "Aye, maybe sae, but it does help to rehash it, Uncle. If only it were possible, I would be more than happy to completely strike those particular memories from my mind; then perhaps all the bloody nightmares would stop plaguing my sleep," he replied quietly.

"Pardon my thoughtlessness," Gregor apologized. "Ye are right, Duncan; I'm sure it does nae help ye to continue speaking to us of it."

"Sae, wi' ye wait until tomorrow to renew the attack against the duke's army or wi' ye press the advantage ye hae already gained today?" inquired Duncan, adroitly changing the subject, and glancing for at the king and then his brother, unsure who would be making that decision.

"We fight tomorrow," Gregor said simply.

"Aye. Tomorrow is soon enough," agreed the Warlord with a nod. "The lads hae marched far in the last couple of days and are weary from the swift pace that was set to them. Besides, Domeric has surrendered the field to us already, along with his camp and nearly all his stores. We eat well tonight, and after short rations for weeks it wi' be nice to hae a full belly before going to battle. Plus," Sean went on with a smirk, "it wi' be dark soon and I want to see Colquhoun's spitefully snarling face when I remove the head from his shoulders. I wi' be sure to bring ye his head in a basket as a trophy, if ye wish it," his brother offered, only partly joking.

"Bring it to me on a pike," growled Duncan.

"I could hae it pickled for ye," Sean suggested.

Duncan shook his head. "Nay; on a pike wi' be just fine. I hae nay wish to keep it, but just as proof for my eyes that he is truly dead. Afterward, ye can do with it what ye wi'; it might make an excellent ball for hurly."

"Gentlemen, I am sorry to intrude," apologized Father Lyle, interrupting them as he stepped back inside the convalescent tent. "General MacSean needs his rest, despite however much the patient might protest. Rest wi' help in aiding the healing process, and he has much to heal thanks to a certain bishop of his acquaintance."

Gregor nodded his understanding. "Of course, Father, ye would ken what's best. Take good care of him; I'll need him back in the saddle as soon as ye can manage it. As it is, his leadership wi' be sorely tomorrow when the battle begins anew."

"Aye, Yer Majesty," Lyle acknowledged, bowing as the king departed.

A few moments later everyone had departed the surgeon's tent; the last to leave had been the patient's son, who stooped to place a kiss on his father's sweaty forehead and give him a gentle hug before leaving and promising to return as soon as Father Lyle gave him permission to do so. Alone with his thoughts, Duncan was able to relax and close his eyes, but sleep came slowly. When he did finally drift off to sleep it was not a sound restful slumber, but filled with more nightmares and terror of his time spent in the enemy camp-of Toby and Colquhoun and Stevenson leering at him as he felt the cruel assortment of tortures all over again.

In spite of the sleeping draught Father Lyle had given him, Duncan woke from the dreadful dreams more than once throughout the night in a cold sweat, embarrassed to find the sheets beneath him soaked with perspiration. As morning approached, the general realized that only one thing could bring an end to his night terrors. He prayed that Sean would take his vengeance on Henry quickly and deliver the man's head as promised. Only then was he sure of again enjoying peaceful sleep.

CHAPTER TWELVE

"Here they come, just as ye said they would," King Gregor murmured, not taking his stormy eyes from the battlefield laying before him, and missing the brusque nod from his marishal who silently watched events unfold.

Morning had dawned with a welcome coolness that had been missing for several weeks and the morning mists had invigorated the waking highlanders. Although it was still not quite noon, the air was retaining a little of the earlier crispness and many hoped that the unusual heat wave had finally snapped.

In what seemed to be an ocean of shining steel-tipped lances, with their various colored pennons fluttering in the morning breeze, began to move forward borne by strong warhorses. First at a walk and then smoothly transitioning to a trot, the enemy cavalry advanced as the royal kinsmen looked on with interest. The forest of lances swept down smartly to point ruthlessly forward to The MacGregor's allied forces as if performing a precision drill. Soon The Campbell's packed squadrons of heavy cavalry was breaking forward like a frothing tidal wave of charging horses and riders toward the waiting center ranks of the Scottish king's royal host.

The confident rebel heavy cavalry swept forward, charging in a double wave of racing horseflesh and glittering steel; riding stirrup to stirrup in a flexing but solid line, they came with the sound of thundering hooves in a formation more than two hundred yards across. From his position among the ranks of his waiting company, Captain James MacNeish watched intently as the enemy neared and lowered their lances; seeing his cue, James raised his sword on high and waited patiently until that steel tide surged within range of his lethal longbowmen. Flashing a savage grin of satisfaction he swept down the shining blade of his father, and as he did so nearly a thousand catgut bowstrings snapped forward in their distinctive twang to deliver their deadly cargo.

Arching high into the air flew the first long distance volley of clothyard arrows, these tipped with lighter but with razor sharp tips. They sailed nearly three hundred yards before beginning their descent to fall like deadly rain among the enthusiastically charging cavalrymen. Even before the first volley struck home, a second was already launched and on its way. A third volley soon followed and was in flight as the first began finding their targets and visibly staggering the once orderly ranks. The hail of arrows continued to empty saddles and soon the first wave of knights appeared as hardly more than a rabble with gaping holes in their lines. Wounded and dying horses and riders fell screaming beneath the flashing hooves of those coming behind in the sudden chaos, and often this caused those following too close behind to stumble and collapse in bone crushing heaps, becoming easy targets for the well trained archers.

The rebel squadrons of charging knights and warrior-monks were coming too fast to stall out altogether by then, particularly the second wave which fared somewhat better than the first. Captain MacNeish understanding this, signaled to his archers and they deftly slipped back behind the line of sunken pickets they had purposely shielded until that moment. Loosing one more hasty volley into the nearing enemy ranks at point blank range, the highland archers withdrew with alacrity to safety behind the dense mass of infantry led by Lord Donald.

The devastated initial tide of heavy cavalry was utterly shattered as they plunged into the cleverly revealed wooden pickets before they could reach the waiting units of bristling pikemen arrayed before the deep ranks of regular infantry. The second wave of charging knights, who had fared better than their comrades, hammered through the line of pickets but lost much of their momentum as they were forced to swerve around fallen horses and what remained of the sharpened stakes.

Waiting for them were several ranks of stalwart pikemen ready to receive their charge. The front two ranks knelt, and in well-drilled unity, grounded the butts of their chosen weapon firmly into the ground and angled the long poles outward, aiming those fifteen feet of hardwood tipped with another foot and a half of sharpened steel. Behind their fellows, the other packed ranks of pikemen stood ready and braced themselves for the collision with weapons aimed over the heads of the front ranks to stab at the coming cavalrymen, and to absorb and reinforce against the shock of the assault.

The shock they expected never came. The battle trained mounts had never been conditioned to hurl themselves against such a wall of bristling weapons. As they neared those waiting schiltrons the warhorses shied from the obvious danger and tried to swerve aside to avoid the obstacle or simply slid to an abrupt halt sending their rider tumbling head over heels. Rearing fearfully as other thundered into them from behind, more riders were unseated mere feet from the gleeful faces of their enemy.

No more than a dozen lances struck home among the braced pikemen, and those knights were quickly and methodically dispatched, spitted on thrusting pikes. Hundreds of the heavily armored cavalrymen had been annihilated and the survivors dumbstruck by the carnage inflicted by the lowly highlanders.

Mounted astride his muscular Clydesdale, Lord Donald watched and laughed as the enemy quickly fell to his troops. He waited as the remaining force of knights began to dismount, their charge stalled, and started to form a wedge to attack on foot with drawn broadswords. Before the bewildered knights could organize, Donald waved his sword in a flourish over his head and bellowed, "Charge!"

Several of the dismounted knights succeeded in forming a hasty wedge and trotted forward to engage the pikemen. Using their shields they were able to deflect the clumsy, oversized spears and close with the front rank, hacking vengefully at those men with an intensity borne from desperation. Occupied as they were with those initial troops, they stood no chance as the soldiers beyond used their reach advantage and the confusion to thrust their glinting steel at them with deadly intent. Hundreds more knights died, skewed on the ends of the long spears, cut off as they were from friendly forces.

Emerging from the dust kicked up by the now destroyed charging knights, a fresh threat presented itself as they cantered nearer. Nearly five hundred lightly armored, horse archers appeared and loosed their shafts on the move, firing into the unarmored pikemen to great effect. Wheeling adroitly they raced across the flat ground parallel to the force they attacked, launching arrows as they went.

Donald, Lord of the Isles, kneed his great mount in agitation as the horse archers continued their scathing attack and slew more of his men. He swore angrily with language colorful enough to have pinked the ears of any priest that might have heard it.

"Lord Fraser!" he bellowed, his voice a bull roar. "Lead out yer infantry; I'll stand for nay more of this shite! Captain MacNeish and his archers wi' fall in with yer lads, and under the cover of yer shields, wi' take out those bloody, buggering mounted archers or send them running before they chew up my pikes any more than they already hae!"

"Aye, Donald!" replied Mhoram Fraser with an acknowledging shout. Turning, he bellowed orders of his own to those eager officers of the blood hungry infantry under his command, and to the waiting commander of the Border Dragons. Urging his war mount forward, the Earl of Inverness brandished his sword and led them at a trot.

The scathing rain of arrows halted briefly as the horse archers reached the western end of the royal battle lines and reformed to sweep across the field a second time. As the heavy royal infantry advanced the rebel horsemen were obliged to engage them as their avenue across the front of the tightly packed pikemen was impeded. Altering their course the horse archers cantered across the exposed formation of infantry and loosed a strafing barrage as they came, fearless as they engaged their earthbound adversaries.

The troops following Lord Mhoram were no easy pickings however, as they raised their large rectangular shields and intercepted the incoming missiles. Having waiting for such an opening, Captain MacNeish and his Highland hunters stepped out from behind their guardians and loosed deadly shafts of their own at the swift light cavalry as those men sought to bring another arrow to string. Although the rebel horsemen posed a moving target, they were nevertheless at point blank range for the MacNeish men and an easy target for hunters of their skill. The affect was withering and instantaneous as riders and mounts fell like wheat under a giant scythe. Scores of horses with empty saddles ran away toward the enemy lines, eyes rolling in fear as they went. Many more bore wounded riders and followed in the wake of their stable mates to escape the sudden carnage.

The remaining mounted archers who barely numbered two hundred now, and not possessing the heart or pride as the heavily armored knights had, turned tail and fled as swiftly as their mounts could carry them. In doing so they abandoned the survivors of the two waves of heavy knights that still desperately fought on. Those proud few numbered less than two score now, and fought on knowing there would be no rescue and expected no quarter from the enemy surrounding them. They did not watch as the horse archers ran away from the fight like whipped dogs: whining in fear with their tail between their legs.

The rebel knights shouted derision at their ally's retreat and battled stubbornly on, but they went suddenly silent as they saw their doom approach in the shape of Lord Donald's pikemen. That lord led a flanking movement of fresh troops to bear down on their rear and caught the beleaguered knights in a complete envelopment. Many fought to the very end, but some in tiny pockets of two or three knelt and lowered their weapons in hopes of being spared for ransom. In token of surrender those few knights extended their swords reversed, offering the hilt to officers of the victorious pikemen.

From his viewpoint atop his mount and at the crest of a knoll behind the royal army, King Gregor, along with Marishal MacSean, observed the opening foray of the battle unfolding before him with approval. *God grant that the day ends as well as it has started. I would hae an end to this conflict, once and for all.*

"Well, that's bloodied their nose," commented Lord Sean, chuckling with dark humor as he watched the beaten rebel horse archers reached their lines several hundred yards away. "Domeric wi' be having a fit about now!"

Gregor nodded in agreement. "Aye. But what wi' happen next, Sean? Surely old Domeric wi' ken better than to try Donald's pikes again with cavalry," wondered the king out loud, unconsciously stroking his peppered beard in thought.

"What cavalry? Most of what he has remaining are Colquhoun's warrior-monks, and he wi' nae be sae eager to offer them up to slaughter.

"He wi' send in his own archers," replied MacSean, pausing a beat at his uncle's skeptical look. "Nay, nae those mounted puppies; they hae nae the heart or stomach for a stand up fight, nor is that what they are trained to do. Nay, the duke wi' send in his real archers to gall our lads, protecting them as ye saw Lord Mhoram screen ours," explained the Warlord. "Hae faith in Lord Donald, I hae already given him his orders for when The Campbell comes at us again, Sire. He wi' be ready when the time comes, and sae wi' our heavy cavalry." His confident air, as much as his words soothed the king as they waited for events to unfold before them.

Gregor resumed stroking his graying ginger whiskers. "Lord Kirkland and old Alister MacAlpine lead our heavy cavalry today. A pity Duncan was nae able to assume command," he remarked, glancing over at his nephew.

"Aye," Sean agreed, his eyes tightening, "but they ken what they are about."

"I suppose they do make a bonny combination. Kirkland is rash and spoiling to avenge Duncan," Gregor said, smiling slightly, "and Alister is smart, with experience enough to keep our young MacPherson chief in line should he start to allow his lust for revenge to make him tae reckless."

"Aye, that's just the way I saw it tae, Sire," replied MacSean, directing a look of approval and a grin at his king. "Perhaps, by the end of all this, I wi' transform ye into a true warrior-king after all, Uncle."

Gregor laughed suddenly and slapped the blonde warrior's armored shoulder with paternal affection. "Perseverance is the heart of being a Highlander, true son of my dear brother. Perhaps ye wi' succeed before I die of old age!"

"Form phalanx!" commanded the burly Lord Donald of the Isles, jumping down from his huge horse with a crash of heavy armor. "Mhoram, The Campbell is sending his archers, just as the Marishal claimed he would, with the heavy infantry to ward them. Remember to leave the rear and centers of yer turtles open for our own archers. I wi' maintain position here and wait for the command to sally forth," he informed his ally. Grinning, he added, "Good hunting, and save some for me!"

The Chief of Clan Fraser chuckled and threw up a salute to his friend. "Aye, and to ye as well. May Lady Morrigan smile upon us both!"

Across the battlefield, companies of rebel archers marched in step within their position mingled with two advancing regiments of heavy infantry. Twelve company sized formations completed the core of the enemy offensive, while on their right a squadron of light cavalry warded their flank and on the left rode forth an equal number of the heavy cavalry composed mostly of Colquhoun's warrior-monks.

Held in reserve was the balance of the Duke of Argyll's army, composed mostly of clan troops and lighter armed Highlanders. Those men formed the bulk of his army, but watched and waited for the order to charge into battle.

The infantry were commanded by Fergis, Duke of Hamilton, and marched steadily across the dusty pasture land in a massed formation until they reached the halfway point between the opposing forces. By design, the units of foot began to dissect into their twelve parts and as they did so each shifted to the same turtle-backed formation as the royal infantry. Showing a precision earned through drill, the turtles separated and spaced themselves out diagonally from one another, allowing each to support the other's flank and be supported in kind. Arranged thus, they denied the foe a chance of a rout; a single unit might be defeated and chased from the fight, but the others, being independent would remain to continue battling.

Marching under the weight of their massive door sized shields, the phalanxes started forward at a measured pace to match that of the rebels. Maintaining a position within the centermost turtle, Lord Mhoram Fraser personally commanded his regiments in the king's name. As his infantry neared the enemy position a shower of arrows hummed through the air and clattered harmlessly off the heavy shields locked atop their heads and fell to the ground. Mhoram laughed as more volleys of incoming arrows struck innocuously against the armored hide of his phalanx and littered the field. "If they keep that up, they're apt to waste all their precious arrows with nothing to show for it! Their officers most hae little sense and nay experience."

"My lord, we are in position," reported the phalanx captain.

"Good enough!" he replied with anticipation, turning to where the commander of his archers waited patiently near at hand. "Captain MacNeish, are yer lads ready to teach those rebel bastards a lesson for me?" inquired Mhoram, a ferocious grin splitting his bluff features as he regarded the young officer.

"Aye, my Lord."

"Hae at them then, laddie. It's time to roll the dice!" declared the exuberant earl, laughing with relish as he slapped Captain MacNeish on the shoulder.

Grinding to a brief halt, the royal phalanxes smartly drew themselves up and stood defiantly, less than twenty yards directly before the approaching rebels. Enemy arrows continued to fly, whizzing overhead to strike among the advance lines of Lord Donald's pikemen as the rebels belatedly realized their attack had no affect on the nearer armored formations and switched targets.

Spilling unseen from the open rear of each royal phalanx, skilled hunters and the yeomen of the king's archers quickly formed into shallow ranks behind their armored allies with swift and practiced meticulousness. Redwood and Lieutenant Gaston looked to their captain in anticipation for the signal to shoot.

There were two hundred men in all bearing longbows, and each one a member of Captain James MacNeish's personal company of *Border Dragons*. All those present had volunteered to follow James into the hazardous duty of marching onto the field to strike a blow against the rebel army. Now they were poised between the two massed armies and prepared to sell their lives, if need be, to inflict a telling and significant blow on those that dared to bear arms against their lawful king. Now was the moment of truth, and James prayed that Marishal MacSean's gambit paid off. Saluting his lieutenants with a fist to his chest, James drew his sword.

Laird MacNeish swept his sword down in a flash of steel and instantly the strings of two hundred longbows snapped forward and a concentrated volley of clothyard arrows arched out over the protecting shield wall of the Campbell phalanxes. The barbed arrows tore into the ranks of the light infantry beyond with devastating effect. As if struck mute by magic, Campbell clansmen and their allies watched in open-mouthed bewilderment as comrades before and beside them tumbled to the ground clutching futilely at arrow shafts that suddenly bloomed from their bodies. A second and third volley was loosed by the time the first reached its destination. The arrow shots were from long range, but massed as they were, the rebel levees had nowhere to go but forward.

A lusty cheer rose from the MacGregor ranks as they saw their enemies begin to fall as the hail of arrows rained down upon them.

Loosing three more volleys in rapid succession, James signaled his company to fall back and scatter within the approaching ranks of pikemen as the royal phalanxes started forward again to the screamed orders of their officers. The armored squares pivoted and charged, wedge first at the opposing formations, colliding with them in a crash of shields and bristling swords. Men on both sides screamed and died in the sudden heat of melee, battling mightily shoulder to shoulder with their fellows.

Angered rebel bowmen viciously fired on the charging pikemen in response to the royal archers, dropping men as their enemies rushed forward. Scores of pikemen fell, along with several of the royal archers who flooded their ranks, but on they came while Captain MacNeish reorganized his company.

Forming ranks, the Border Dragons faced their opponents and returned fire, their target being the rebel archers this time. And as the archers skirmished between each other, the Royal Army began its slow advance until the balance of its archer corps to reach just within the extreme range of their longbows.

Duke Domeric saw the ploy and the danger it posed, but was not able to counter it as his enraged clan levees howled with blood lust and charged on their own. Streaming across the battlefield the Highlanders ignored their own archers and embattled phalanxes and continued to charge deep into the Warlord's trap.

Disengaging from the ferocious hand to hand combat with the opposing heavy infantry, Lord Mhoram signaled a fighting withdrawal of his regiments. Following his prior orders, the Earl of Inverness retreated to merge with the advancing main army as the Warlord's plan had called for, should the enemy swallow the bait.

The heavy infantry and advancing pikemen intersected one another and as Lord Donald rode up on his massive horse he accepted Lord Mhoram's salute with a grin. "Well met, my friend. The trick worked very well, I'd say. Reform yer lads into a bonny shield wall and my pikes wi' form behind them."

Lord Donald turned as Captain MacNeish approached with a bow in one hand and saluted with the other. "It is time, Captain," he rumbled. "Pass the word to yer lieutenants and to the other archer commanders to begin concentrating an arrow barrage on that lot of idiot rebels racing this way. Let's see how they enjoy the full taste of a thousand missiles falling on their heads at one time!" he added viciously.

The wildly charging irregular infantry never knew what hit them as soon a deadly hail of clothyard arrows tipped with wickedly barbed heads showered down among them. Wearing no armor to protect themselves the screaming rebels fell in heaps under the onslaught as the air was suddenly filled with hissing arrows. Their bravery did then no good as hundreds of rebel clansmen fell under each withering volley. Unexpectedly and for no apparent reason to those hapless warriors, the lethal rain of arrows halted, but then, like a continuous peel of thunder, steel-shod hooves rumbled closer and the very ground beneath their feet trembled as hundreds of the royal heavy cavalry charged them from the left. The rebel's highland charge faltered then in the face of this new threat, as the deadly arrows had not been able to do, despite the terrible losses they had inflicted. Like death incarnate, the armored knights spurred their heavy destriers down upon the remnants of Duke Domeric's rebel clansmen and spitted many on the end of their long lances, while others were simply ridden down and trampled under the flashing hooves.

Pausing only long enough to dress their ranks, Marishal MacSean's proud knights continued on across the field to engage the terror stricken rebel archers. Those who tried to hide themselves among the heavily armored infantry, as they retreated toward their previous position across the battlefield from the royal army, avoided deadly fate. Those that sought to run away were quickly rode down and butchered by knights that fought with the all too fresh memory of what had been done to the courageous and well loved Duncan MacSean.

From his vantage point upon a slight knoll that swelled behind The Campbell's Alliance Army, Duke Domeric Campbell cried out in horror as he saw all too well what was happening to his army. Already it was too late to do anything but watch helplessly as his army's archer corps was slaughtered all but wholesale by the unchecked charge of the royal heavy cavalry. Adding insult to injury, Domeric knew without seeing the fluttering banner of crimson on deep green that Lord Sean MacSean was personally leading the king's heavy horse and for the moment commanded the field.

Nearly speechless with anger, Domeric glanced around for an aide-de-camp and finding one gestured for the man to attend to him. "What fool was in command there?" he pointed at the devastated remnants of his archers and the fleeing units of mostly intact heavy infantry. "Who was the blithering idiot that commanded those regiments tasked with protecting my bloody archers and failed sae completely?" demanded the duke, his voice a rasping whisper of pent up rage.

The aide swallowed. "His Grace, the Duke of Hamilton."

Domeric's expression grew even more bleak and he howled a wordless curse. "If Hamilton somehow survived that debacle I want the fool brought immediately to me in chains! Is that quite clear, Captain?"

The duke's military aide swallowed again and nervously looked down and made a thorough study of his dusty boots. "As ye wish, Yer Grace," he replied slowly, wishing it was anyone but him that had to speak his next words, "but are ye certain that's the most wise course? Meaning nay disrespect, Sire, but the Duke of Hamilton's clansmen might take exception to it and they anchor our right flank," he said finally, finding enough of his courage to look his leader in the eye.

The furious duke stared balefully at his aide for a moment. "Aye, perhaps ye are right," Domeric at last admitted darkly, glowering from behind bushy gray eyebrows as he paused to reconsider his last order. "Ach, very well. Do nae arrest him, Captain, but ye wi' escort Hamilton to me at once, if that is he still breathes this Scottish air. Aye, if he yet lives I wi' deal with him then."

The aide nodded with relief. "Aye, Yer Grace. At once."

The next few hours, following the opening gambits and early clash of battle, dragged on slowly as the opposing armies sparred with one another with the intent of feeling out each other for weaknesses. As the afternoon wore on the generals of both sides would not quite commit themselves and their troops to a strategy that would fully engage the posturing enemy.

The Royal Army of Scotland appeared to hold an advantage with their heavily armored knights, whose squadron was fully intact; and, though they had been bloodied to a certain extent, their archer corps remained in good spirits and outnumbered their humiliated counterparts by at least three to one. The rebel Alliance, however, retained a considerable force of stolid, dependable heavy infantry and despite their earlier losses they still held a numerical advantage. The rebel knights had suffered a considerable blow early on, but yet the two thousand-mostly warrior-monks commanded by Archbishop Colquhoun-posed a serious threat to any all out attack.

Lord Sean MacSean, the king's stalwart Warlord and Marishal, stood beside his liege and coolly contemplated the Duke of

Argyll's forces waiting across the battlefield with a spyglass pressed to one eye.

The Marishal pulled the glass from his eye and snapped it shut against his thigh with an audible click. "If Domeric wishes to bring the fight to us again this day he wi' hae to do it soon. There are perhaps two hours of daylight remaining to him, but nay more," surmised MacSean, thoughtfully rubbing thumbs into his throbbing temples in a futile effort to banish the ache growing in his head. "If nae, he may hae some ploy in mind that he wishes to save until after darkfall. If that is the case, we must be vigilant and prepared for whatever may come. Domeric may be detestable, but he is a cunning fox."

"Ye were correct in yer first theory, Sean. Look," Gregor ordered, pointing out with one hand the movement among the duke's rebel army.

Sure enough, as both royal leaders looked on, blocks of rebel infantry began to rattle swords and spears against shields and targes, shaking large Lochaber battleaxes at those standing arrayed against them. Officers on horseback rode among them and shouted orders as they shifted into new positions. The drone of bagpipes sounded before their wild scurling began and signal horns blew as the army prepared to renew the battle.

In answer to their enemy's posturing, the Royal Army immediately went on alert with the clarion call of their own horns. Not willing to be outdone, pipers of the clans in support of King Gregor brandished their own weapons and began playing a crisp melody. Lifting up their voices, the royalist troops sang the words to the old Gaelic tune. Although the voices might have been rough and somewhat out of tune they were enthusiastic, and succeeded in drowning out the opposing army's sword rattling and fierce warcries.

Seeking to counter the lively response to their challenge, the rebels lifted up their own voices to the call of another martial bagpipe tune. Afternoon faded and turned to evening as the two rival army's coarse voices clashed as resoundingly as if they wielded arms against the other, both seeking to out do their enemy.

A great cheer suddenly rose between songs from the royalist side as King Gregor, astride his handsome warhorse, trotted out to take his position at the army's center along with his royal bodyguard surrounding him. The king raised a gauntleted fist into the air in salute and ordered his personal banner unrolled beside that of the cross of Saint Andrew and the rampant red lion on gold. As those banners were unfurled the cheers turned into a roar as the soldiers acclaimed their chosen and decreed leader.

Standing tall in his stirrups the king gestured for silence as he regarded his army of brave soldiers with a broad affectionate grin. "I must say," he began, pitching his voice so all could plainly hear him, "if all battles were won by the army with the most lusty and loud troops, ye, my loyal countrymen, could never suffer defeat! I am most proud to hae such fierce and faithful friends to fight with against my foes."

A wordless shout of approval pealed throughout the ranks and across the trampled battlefield as the royal troops brandished their weapons until the king again waved for quiet before he could speak again.

"Waiting out there before us is our enemy," shouted Gregor, pointing an accusing finger at the drawn up ranks of the Campbell Alliance Army. "Who they are and what they stand for makes them our enemies much more than any foreign invader. They hae raped and pillaged, even among their own clans folk! They hae murdered innocent women sworn in service to God! What crime could be worse than doing such to yer own people and making war against one's own brothers? Are we nae, one and all Scotsmen?" demanded the king, a tremor of emotion entering his voice that made his righteous anger all the more terrible to behold. "Aye! Of course we are, and I see before me a whole army of my countrymen willing to make a stand and put a stop to their villainy. By Lugh, Duke Domeric Campbell and his henchmen lead an army bearing arms against the right and legal King of Scotland. They divide our land in a dreadful civil war that could leave us all at the mercy of our neighbors to the south! Divided, as The Campbell makes us, we are weak; the English can nae help but ken this and look eagerly to our borders for land they hae always coveted. Is this nae the most terrible sort of treason?"

"Aye!" shouted the king's soldiers.

"Should we nae make our nation whole again and destroy the rebellious Duke of Argyll, and put an end to this bloody clans conflict?"

"Aye!"

"What should be the fate of Domeric Campbell and the rest of those lords who hae falsely risen against their rightful king?" he demanded.

"Take their heads! Take their heads!" cried the booming voice of the royal army, rising to a fevered pitch.

Sitting his mount beside the king, Marishal MacSean nodded with approval at the way his uncle rallied the troops, admiring the force of his charisma. Standing erectly in his stirrups, so that he could be seen and heard, Lord Sean shouted in his loudest parade ground voice, "Who is our beloved king?"

"Gregor MacGregor!"

"Long live the king!" cried Lord Sean.

"Long live the king! Long live King Gregor!" erupted the enthusiastic throng, passionately repeating the mantra over and over again.

Brandishing his sword overhead, so that it flashed in the crimson rays of the late day sun, Gregor yelled exuberantly, "Brave Highlanders! Stalwart Lowlanders! Valiant men of the Isles! Wi' ye fight with me for love of Scotland and the victory over those enemies that stand arrayed against us?"

"Aye! For Scotland and King Gregor!" roared the army. The volume of the cheer and acclaim rose higher and louder with each shout until it reached a crescendo so great that the sound of it literally caused the king's ears to ring. His face flushed with a ruddy glow, Gregor turned and beamed a determined smile over at his devoted nephew who wore a smile of his own. "I'd say the lads are ready," he mouthed.

Nodding agreement, Warlord MacSean turned his attention to a waiting officer and signaled the horns and bagpipes to sound the *To Arms*. Moments later he took his place at the head of the king's royal cavaliers, whom he would personally lead in battle.

Soon, the battle for sovereignty of Scotland was joined in earnest.

CHAPTER THIRTEEN

The clamor of the two opposing armies rose in such a clash that the force of it seemed to shake the heavens. As Scot battled Scot, and Highlander raged against fellow Highlander, the much anticipated confrontation began late that afternoon. It seemed as if the elements themselves were at battle in the red-hewed sky as thunder pealed and lightning flashed, while a chilling rain started to pour down in a relentless driving shower upon the men below striving to kill one another. It was not long before the trampled field of battle was transformed into a churning quagmire of mud, and strewn with the hacked and crumpled bodies of dead and dying warriors.

Afternoon ended and shadows lengthened as evening progressed under a hostile sky, and the massed armies continued to strive one against the other to a bitter standstill, neither gaining nor giving up any significant ground or advantage. To the good fortune of Duke Domeric's forces, the downpour of rain which had turned the ground to mud, had all but negated any numerical advantage that the royal army could have capitalized on to batter his rebel infantry. Deepening mud served to bog down any cavalry charge aimed at the rebel flanks, so much so that each royalist attempt at such an attack was repulsed. Although not easily done, defending infantry fought off each attack at much less cost to themselves than what normally would have been incurred. Those small successes were minor victories that were hard won and served to buoy the rebel morale.

Darkness began to encroach of the evening hours wore on and still the bloodied ranks of infantry fought valiantly on, neither side gaining any clear advantage. At last, the signal horns sounded their clarion call of withdrawal and soon a parley was agreed on, in which both sides arranged to stand down until dawn. When the two armies disengaged and retreated to opposing ends of the churned battlefield, neither side could claim victory, despite many acts of personal heroics performed by soldiers of both sides and the typical brand of resolute bravery Highlanders were known for. Any sort of decisive triumph for either army had been dashed early on: for the rebel forces this was attributed to the major losses they sustained to their heavy cavalry in an ill-conceived charge that was met by an infantry force prepared with concealed pikes; in the case of the royalist forces, they lost what benefit they had gained by the effects of the change in weather which rendered their cavalry's shock value mostly ineffectual. On those rare occasions during the day when either side had achieved some amount of success and briefly gained the upper hand, neither army had been able to make appropriate use of heavy cavalry to follow up on their infantry's success. Neither side proved able to capitalize on their hard won advantage nor prevent those commanding the other side from rallying their troops to avert a rout and avoid being chased from the field in defeat.

Despite all the differences the two armies and their leaders had in regard to beliefs and politics, the Scottish rivals were evenly matched in both talent and numbers. As the tallies were taken, once the temporary truce had been agreed to and unarmed soldiers had gone back to retrieve their dead, it turned out that from the evening battle that both sides had lost men in equal numbers. Roughly a thousand rebels had perished, and a like sum had fallen from among the royalists. Nearly every one of those troops, rebel and royalist, had been among the infantry struggling amid the rain and mud.

Sometime during the night, lost amid the cries of the wounded, the thunder and lightning had subsided, and the rains had passed off to the east. Dawn seemed to arrive more soon than it should have for the weary soldiers of both armies, but by the time the sun had peeked over the, not far distant mountains, battle lines had been drawn once again in preparation of resuming the undecided battle. In contrast to the previous day, the sun shone molten at its rebirth and burned away the morning mists soon after it appeared. Fluffy white clouds rode high in the azure sky, having chased away the earlier black ones that had swirled so tempestuously with violence the evening before. The ground was still damp from the heavy rains, but the dry soil had hungrily absorbed much of the needed moisture and already showed signs of firming up.

Even as the sun was in the process of burning away the last vestiges of clinging fog, skirling cries of bagpipes sounding their fervent martial music beckoned the armies of opposing Scotsmen to march with strident cadence into the fray. Pockets of mist still swirled across the battleground as orderly squares of infantry and hedgehog-like blocks of pikemen marched resolutely forward, as if they were wraiths, sometimes visible to their enemy and sometimes not. None uttered a sound except for the tangle of armor until the foe appeared before them in like fashion no more than a hundred yards distant. As if they had received some cue, the fierce Highlanders' vociferous voices suddenly overpowered even the shrill music of the war pipes, as they screamed their ferocious battlecries over and over again until they met with a mighty clash of arms.

The collision of men and weapons was staggering as the two sides converged in the center of the trampled field. A multitude of warcries resumed after the initial impact and could be heard even over the din of combat, with nothing able to silence them except the death of an army.

In an early gambit to test the strength of the royal army's left flank, which was warded by a squadron of heavy cavalry and another of light horsemen, the Duke of Argyll send Lord Stevenson, commanding the remaining half-strength force of his mounted archers, to assail that position for any weakness. Assailing the royal cavalry also meant assaulting a battalion of troops expertly armed with longbows that were interspaced at regular intervals among the horsemen. The rebel aim was to strike at those archers and any other soft targets they encountered, while posing a moving target in return, and should the maneuver prove too costly, sweep away as swiftly as they had come and return to their former position to await further orders.

Stevenson skillfully led forth his horse archers and conducted a series of swirling assaults to try and soften the royalist flank for the infantry while attempting to curl around it engage the rear, but to no good effect. He was matched and surpassed in skill by the experienced leadership of Marishal MacSean, who expertly countered every such effort. Not yet realizing that all his actions would continue to be balked on that front, no matter what ploy he chose to employ, Lord Stevenson regrouped his fleet horse archers and set out for another strafing attack. Finally, after a number of game attempts to outmaneuver the wily marishal, the chief of Clan Stevenson at last broke off his unsuccessful raid and retreated in good order back to the Campbell's allied lines to report what he had learned to Duke Domeric. Although disappointed, Stevenson was not surprised that his attack had been so easily rebuffed by his determined adversary.

Hours passed since Stevenson's first aborted attack upon the royalist left flank, and the noon hour approached with the bright sun nearly directly over head. Weary troops were regularly rotated to the rear to rest as fresh soldiers came forward to relieve them and the fighting continued with little abatement as the day wore on.

Sallying forth from his leftmost flanker position with several hundred knights, Marishal MacSean personally commanded a number of successful lancer charges against the rigid phalanxes of rebel infantry. Inflicting considerable damage to those troops, he still failed to accomplish any significant impairment to the enemy formations.

From his position, once again warding the king's left flank, the Warlord of Clan Gregor waited and watched with intense concentration as he witnessed several battalions of reserves, formerly held back by Duke Domeric, thrown into battle near the center to bolster their front battle lines. Seeing this sudden commitment, Lord Sean reached for his helmet and spurred to the head of his waiting knights. *The time to act is upon us*, thought the Warlord, loosening his sword in its scabbard.

The royal marishal knew the time to act had come because he well understood the martial part of the mind of Domeric Campbell, who commanded the rebel army. Through a lifetime of experience he realized the duke would not commit such a large portion of his reserves unless the situation was critical or he had decided the time was ripe to seize the initiative in hopes of turning the tide of battle in his favor. *Aye, he sees something and is readying to act. A breach of our center could be disastrous and possibly even win the day and the battle for him, and perhaps the war, should he begin a rout. Now,* considered Sean, *if I play it right, we may be able to resolve the outcome of this battle in the king's favor while Domeric is preoccupied with his own plans.*

Both arms of cavalry, Lord Sean's most effective offensive weapon available, stood poised and ready for his command. Astride his mount and ready to lead the heavy cavalry under the Warlord's overall command was Alister, Earl of Atholl; nearby as well was Lord Kirkland MacPherson who would lead forth the light cavalry.

"Gentlemen, it is time we acted to make an end of this battle and assure Gregor is the victor," declared the Warlord. A moment later both cavalry commanders had been given their orders, and each returned to their respect command to await the signal. In the meantime, Lord Sean summoned one of his swiftest scouts to serve as courier to relay a message to the king informing him of what he intended.

Marishal MacSean raised the silver chased horn to his lips and blew. The clarion note seemed to hang in the air for an eternity before fading away at last, but time seemed to slow as thousands of horses were spurred forward. The rumble of their advance grew louder as they sped from trot and then to a canter, and finally a ground devouring gallop toward the rebel army which stood at arms against them.

The ground began to tremble under their feet and then the rebel infantry heard the frightening noise of thundering steel shod hooves bearing down on them. Those rebel troops along the Duke of Argyll's right flank faltered as they realized that they were the target, with none but the battered warrior-monk cavalry under Bishop Colquhoun to come to their aid, and quailed in fright.

The Highlanders, under the king's banner, fighting there noted what was taking place and took heart with spirited cries of encouragement to their allies, redoubling their own brave efforts against the enemy before them. Soon, those rebels who had up until that moment had been pushing back their opponents, found themselves forced to return the ground briefly gained. Their lines began showing signs of buckling as the heartened and revitalized royal Highland troops surged forward with fresh vigor.

The battle raging hotly at the center of the lines and toward the royalist right flank however, was not going in the king's favor as fresh rebel troops rushed into the fray. Taking the brunt of Duke Domeric's reinforced assault from the insertion of his fresh reserves pouring into the fight, the royal army was taking a battering and was pushed stubbornly backward while King Gregor desperately ordered forward his own reserves to try and stem the dangerous enemy surge. Already his lines were bowing in the center and appeared near the point of breaking. Realizing that his reserves might not be enough to rally his flagging forces, which were showed growing signs of buckling under the ferocious onslaught, Gregor rode personally into battle. Leading his enthusiastic company of royal bodyguards forward, the king came to his men's aid.

The response was immediate and beneficial.

"The King! The King is come to fight with us!" called voices from among the troops of the royal army until it became like a mantra. Cries of *Gregalach* carried above the fray from the throats of his clansmen until the chant was taken up by all those that strived for his cause. The royal troops' fervor carried over to their fighting as well, as they stubbornly refused to surrender another step before the rebel aggression. Stemming the tide, the royal battle lines began to firm, stiffened by the influx of reserves and the added physical and moral support of the king and his hard fighting bodyguards.

In moments the rebel assault began to falter and then crumble in the face of the king's timely intervention. Soon it was the rebels forced to give ground or break instead of the royalist troops, and it was Duke Domeric who found himself obligated to enter the fighting, along with those of his household guard, to halt the ebbing tide of his attack.

Gregor, blast him, may nae be the general that MacSean is, but he is a mite more capable than I gave him credit for. Ach, the maneuver should hae worked, but at least I was able to stop his counterattack. Tae bad I could nae hae salvaged some of the gains we fought sae hard for, thought Domeric, as he began to consider a new stratagem in his plan of attack. *Perhaps a decoy around the loch would give him pause. Aye, perhaps. That might make Gregor pull back those reserves of his.*

As the lines stabilized, Duke Domeric withdrew from the fighting, and flagging a courier to his side he began issuing instructions to be relayed to one of his generals, Lord Alfred Cameron, commanding his right flank. While he was busy doing so, another scout-one converted to courier duty-rode his lathered mount pell-mell in the duke's direction and pulled up, agitation showing clearly on his young face. The stark fear in his wide eyes told the duke something was terribly wrong even before the wide eyed lad could deliver his message. Once Domeric heard the scout's report, he refused to believe it without seeing for himself. If true, it was a genuine calamity in the making.

Lord Alfred, although not a man Domeric Campbell would have ever called his friend, was the duke's most trusted and loyal ally, and now he was dead. The right flank Cameron had commanded had been mauled by the surprise all-out assault conducted by the royal cavalry led by Gregor's warlord. That this had happened while The Campbell was in the thick of the fighting at the center of the field was of little consolation as the duke witnessed the ruin of two full battalions of his infantry. To make matters worse, most of the army's remaining heavy cavalry under the command of Bishop Colquhoun had been routed. As he watched with growing anger, Duke Domeric saw the kirk knights flee the field before the pursuit of a large force of light lancers.

The remaining royal cavalry were already in the process of spearheading a fresh infantry surge to exploit the broken flank while junior officers of the rebel cause sought to rally their troops. It was too little and too late. By now the undefended flank was being curled under the weight of staggering cavalry charges led by the Warlord as he made short work of the demoralized and frightened rebel Highlanders that remained standing before the might of his lances and swords.

Archbishop Henry Colquhoun's once clean white surcoat was now muddy and stained with blood and drying gore. His once fine and shining, purple plumed helmet was dented with its proud plume sheared off by a lance that had come very close to shearing off his entire head. The nasal piece, crafted to protect his face, was bent off to one side and now served to obscure his vision.

The Archbishop of Saint Andrews was not a happy man.

Of his once formidable body of warrior-monks, Colquhoun retained at his beck the services of barely two dozen knights and twice that many men-at-arms. Not that a single monk had deserted their bishop; their loyalty was proven by the bodies of so many of their fellows strewn upon the battlefield. Marishal MacSean's concerted attack had been the final blow that broke their stiff and unyielding back; even then they would not have fled if their leader had not given the command to do so.

Gradually the more fleet light cavalrymen closed the distance between themselves and the fleeing bishop's ragged and bloodied force. The exultant pursuers began to shout challenges, after the beaten monks and their leader, along with humiliating insults. In tribute to their professionalism, the warrior-monks were able to ignore the taunts for a while, but finally it became too much for even them to bear.

"Yer Grace!" shouted the kirk knight's only remaining officer, nudging his mount alongside that of the bishop as they continued to flee. "We can nae hope to escape! Their horses are more fresh than ours are and less encumbered. Please, let us turn aside from this shameful flight and fight them. We are knights in the service of God; let us prove the valor of our militant order upon the bodies of these rascals that presume to ridicule us and cast vile insults upon our honour!" he pleaded furiously.

Colquhoun cast a wary glance over his shoulder at the relentless royalist pursuit, gauging them less than an arrow shot behind the rearmost of his men and grimaced before returning his attention to the agitated officer riding at his side. "Ye ken that none wi' be spared if any of us should be taken alive, do ye nae, Lieutenant? They are out for blood, particularly after what I had to do with their precious Duncan MacSean; withstanding the fact that he is a sorcerous devil in human guise, they love him still. Are ye prepared to die this day? Surrender is nae an option; that would tantamount to suicide. Do ye understand, Lieutenant?" demanded the bishop.

"Aye. Nevertheless, I would willingly perish as a knight should, selling my live dearly at the point of a sword," replied the fiery officer with resolute assurance. "It would be much better to do that than continue running away from the fight our enemies offer, like some whipped dog from its chastising master!"

The bishop's eyes narrowed as he regarded the man's admonishment. "Very well, Lieutenant," he allowed after a moment. "Pass the order round that we wi' rally upon yonder hillock, the one bearing a lone pine standing at its top. We wi' make a last stand there," Colquhoun clarified, checking the lay of the ground about it with a critical eye. "If needs be, the grade wi' aid in a single charge in whatever direction we choose."

The officer nodded, favoring his superior with a tight lipped smile. "Of course, it wi' be as ye say, Yer Grace."

A few moments later the small force remaining to Henry Colquhoun had gained the designated hillock and hastily deployed into a tight circle to face outward against the fast approaching pursuers. So arranged the kirk troops awaited their enemies, ready to defend the little hill and prepared to fight in whichever way the attack might come.

Forming a noose around the shallow hill the royal cavalry deployed without delay to surround the drawn up rebels to prevent their escape. Once they had moved into a ring about their quarry, the horsemen held position easy bow range and awaited further orders from General MacEwan. Meanwhile, he conferred with Lord Devlin, who was present out of courtesy to General Duncan MacSean, and his other officers as they discussed the best plan of action for dealing with the band of rebels.

"Nay, sair. I do nae think ye should do it," balked one grizzled officer, shaking his head at Devlin. Duncan's son had just spoken his wish to offer single combat to whatever champion the rebels might choose. Aiming a pointed look at the general, hoping for a word of support from his commander, the outspoken officer paused before adding, "Sair, we clearly hae the upper hand; there is nae need for ye to risk yerself in such a way. If a challenge must be offered I wi' do it instead. Yer father would be sorely displeased with us if any wayward thing should happen to ye."

General MacEwan removed his helmet to run fingers through his thick mop of gray hair. "Dgunal is correct to suggest caution, but the decision lies with ye, Devlin. One thing there is that I must say, and it is this: the challenge must be issued directly to Bishop Colquhoun, as it is he to whom honour must be satisfied in the name of yer father. It wi' be up to Colquhoun whether he decides to accept the challenge or designates another to fight in his place."

"I understand," said Devlin, offering a nod of thanks to the general. Turning, he addressed himself to the older officer, "Thank ye for yer kind offer, Dgunal, but I must nae send another to stand for my father's honour; that is my duty. Should I fall, tell my Da that I did my best to avenge him. However, should I triumph, then it wi' be in the minds of every man among these proud kirk knights that we are the equal of any of them, and the pride of their knightliness wi' be lowered by my deed."

Riding forward with the older general's blessing, his favorite Lochaber axe in his hand, Devlin guided his mount several horse lengths beyond his allies. Halting then the young lord raised the crescent blade and saluted the enemy band as he stood erect in his stirrups. "Hail the enemy! I am Devlin MacSean, son of Duncan MacSean," he stated, boldly raising his clear tenor voice to address them. "I hae come to offer challenge to one that has dealt most foully with my noble father. Henry Colquhoun! Stand forth and fight one who calls yer honour into doubt, if that is, ye hae enough honour remaining in ye to accept such a challenge in good faith!"

A low murmur passed among the rebel kirk troops as they heard Lord Devlin's challenge and waited for their leader's response. In the meantime, Devlin watched Colquhoun's reaction and smiled to himself as an officer, denoted by the ornaments on his armor, whispered fiercely with his commander. Shortly following the heated exchange between the two, the red faced officer trotted his mount ahead until he sat alone before the circle of his comrades-in-arms and planted his lance in the ground.

Presently, the knightly officer raised a hand to his visor in salute. "I am Alexander MacClintock, kinsman to the good bishop, Henry Colquhoun," he introduced himself curtly. "Despite the fact that ye are nae of acknowledged knightly rank, I judge that ye hae the courage and determination to become one someday, should ye live to achieve it. I wi' nae insult ye by naming ye a sorcerer, but as yer father has been judged by His Grace to be one, I must beseech ye to nae use such power against me if such magic should be in yer grasp," shouted MacClintock, a thick mustache of ginger whiskers hanging down to cover his upper lip. "If ye wi' give me yer most solemn word of honour to abstain from any skills beyond yer martial prowess with steel and a strong arm I am willing to accept yer challenge most gladly.

Devlin nodded, though inwardly he seethed at the accusation of his father, or he, being a dabbler in the black arts. "I am nay sorcerer, I assure ye Sir Knight. However, to ease yer mind and that of Bishop Colquhoun, I wi' pledge ye my word," replied Devlin, a note of irony coming into his voice. "I swear to ye before God and these witnesses, on my honour and the honour of my clan, that this wi' be a fair contest of single combat. Force of arms alone wi' determine as to whom wi' be the victor and nay use of any supposed eldritch power wi' be employed, sae help me God."

"Well and nobly said, sair; I accept yer word as bond enough," answered the rebel champion, nodding his head in approval. Retrieving his lance by pulling the long broad head from the turf beside him, the knight went on, "Furthermore, I accept yer challenge on behalf of myself and Archbishop Colquhoun. Prepare yerself to receive my charge," he warned in a commanding tone. Reaching up he slammed shut his visor with a clank and shouldered his heavy lance, ready to commence the combat.

The combatants trotted their mounts away to a neutral area a small distance from the others so no one else could impede their contest. An expanse of about a hundred yards lay between the opponents as they wheeled about to face one another with a brief salute. Spurring their mounts to a ground devouring gallop the two champions hurtled forward without hesitation. The armored riders thunderously charged straight at one another and as their paths intersected Devlin caused his mount to swerve slightly at the last instant. Whirling his great, long-handled axe above his head, he delivered a heavy downward chop that sliced cleanly through his foe's lance just beyond the sharp steel point. Without breaking stride the war trained mounts thundered on, momentum carrying the riders past the other before Devlin could bring his axe around to strike his disarmed adversary.

As the combatants reached a goodly distance from the other they wheeled about their snorting horses and prepared for another charge. Urging his mount back into action, Devlin spurred toward his opponent, whom had taken the opportunity to discard his lance and draw a shining broadsword from his hip into a gauntleted hand. They hurtled toward each other and for a second time Devlin swerved as they converged, but this time to the opposite side as Sir Alexander anticipated the same maneuver and guarded against it with his sword. Unlike most men, Devlin was a left-handed fighter, and though he had been taught to fight with the right hand, 'as was proper', he had insisted on equal training with his dominant left hand and could fight equally well with both. His ambidexterity served him well now. As he stretched forward and high in the stirrups, the general's son brought down his whirling Lochaber axe with such force that he surprised even himself. The keen crescent blade swept down with a whistle of steel that swept aside the knight's attempted parry and struck the man's armored head such a powerful blow that it sheered clean through Sir Alexander's helmet, his skull, and deep into the stricken knight's brain. With a sharp crack on the mighty impact, Devlin's arm went suddenly numb and the axe's stout oak handle splintered down its length, nearly shivering to apart under his fingers.

The sword fell from Sir Alexander's loosened grip and tumbled to the ground beside his horse a second before the knight pitched sideways and hit the ground from a resounding crash. Blood stained the man's face as his unseeing eyes seemed to gaze up at the victorious Highlander who stared dumbfounded down at the slain knight.

For a long moment stunned silence reigned among all those that had watched with avid interest the single combat. The hush was so total that Devlin was sure that every man there could hear the wild hammering of his heart as he looked up, forcing his eyes away from those of the dead rebel knight. Then, all of a sudden, a wild shriek of fierce voices took up the MacGregor's ancient Gaelic battlecry, in honour of his victory, until it echoed triumphantly in the ears of the bewildered rebels. "Ard Choille! Ard Choille!" *The Woody Heights! The Woody Heights!*

While their stirring cries of *Ard Choille* were yet filling the air, General MacEwan led his lightly mounted Highlanders in a bold charge up the occupied hillock toward an enemy that milled about in consternation. The royal soldiers were halfway up the incline before the rebels at last shook off their shock. Already to was too late to mount a charge down the hill, and with that advantage lost they braced themselves for the coming attack as the screaming Highlanders rapidly closed on their position.

Armed with long handled battleaxes or basket-hilted claymore and spike fronted targes, the light cavalrymen who wore only light weight armor neared the top of the shallow hill. Before reaching their enemies each Highlander slipped nimbly to the ground, and using their mount as a shield, they advanced again with menace showing in their eyes to meet the rebels before them.

Colquhoun and his warrior-monks belatedly realized their mistake as MacEwan and his men swarmed in and around the heavily armored and ponderous knights, quickly overwhelming them with two and three attacking each of them. It was a ferocious fight as the warrior-monks were skilled and hardy veterans of war and their mounts were well trained for battle and lashed out at the attackers with deadly steel shod hooves. As man and beast worked together as a fighting unit, the kirk soldiers proved a formidable foe, and each fought with courage and pride as they rallied to protect their leader. Ultimately, the number of foes assaulting them proved too much as prized horses were hamstrung beneath them by one enemy, and others pulled them from the saddle to be dispatched with no regard to any chivalrous code.

"Colquhoun! Colquhoun, I'm coming for ye!" cried Devlin, pulling free his sword from the armpit of the knight he had just run through. Laying about him with the fallen Sir Alexander's broadsword he fought furiously to battle passed the bishop's bodyguard. Hacking viciously into the exposed neck of another knight's horse, Devlin forced the big warrior-monk on the defensive as he fought to control his floundering mount, and waited for the opening he knew must present itself. What happened next surpassed anything the vengeance-seeking young lord could have hoped for. With a dying groan the knight's handsome steed shuddered in agony and stumbled back on buckling legs into the bishop's own horse. Everything seemed to slow in Devlin's mind as the surprised Colquhoun was suddenly thrown to the ground as his mount screamed and reared in fright. The rebel bishop landed hard on his back with a crash of plate armor and lay stunned, the breath knocked from his lungs, as he tried to lever himself from the trampled earth.

Seeing the Archbishop of Saint Andrews go down the remaining warrior-monks gave a great cry of lamentation, and the fight quickly went out of them, believing their leader to be dead. Soon, those kirk knights that had continued to fight were throwing down their swords as they asked for quarter, surrendering themselves to the fierce and bloodied Highlanders howling with triumph.

Having regained his breath, the shaken bishop lurched to his feet and stumbled away from his pursuer, somehow maintaining a grip on his flanged mace. Desperate to flee the disastrous fight, Colquhoun sought for a horse, any horse, which could bare him away from certain death. Noticing one several yards away he limped as fast as he could in that direction, all thoughts of injured dignity cast aside in his haste.

"It's over, Colquhoun, surrender yerself!" growled a blood spattered Devlin, while he dismounted to follow after the hated bishop. "Yer precious monks saw ye go down and they now hae the good sense to surrender themselves. Look about ye, if ye do nae believe me," he shouted with annoyance. "Stop, blast ye!"

Intent on escape, Colquhoun refused to so much as glance about him or back at the furious lord, his mind focused solely on the waiting horse. *I can nae allow myself to fall into the hands of sorcerers or sorcerer lovers!* he told himself over and over while he shambled ahead on his injured ankle, gasping in pain. Something suddenly caught at his long purple cape, and as he paused to frantically rip it free Henry glimpsed the young MacSean behind him hanging on to the end of it. He screamed with fright, and with a surge of strength borne of fear, ripped the cape from his shoulders and staggered away while wildly waving his mace. *His father's torture has surely driven the son mad! If he gets a hold of me, I ken he wi' certainly kill me; I'm sure of it!* whimpered the terrified bishop within his depraved mind.

The trampled ground suddenly seemed to leap up at Henry as he felt a heavy blow strike him in the back. Colquhoun struggled to get his feet under him and somehow rolled free for an instant, but again Devlin tackled him back to the turf. An almost inhuman shriek of rage issued from the bishop's mouth as his bid for escape was thwarted. A growing terror of capture and being held captive by the son of his dreaded enemy, a man he truly did believe to be a sorcerer, lent him a strength he normally did not have. Henry pulled free his arm and sought to plunge the dirk he still held into the young warrior's throat, but found himself fighting for possession of his weapon as the blade wavered mere inches from the man's bulging artery.

"Oh, dear God, nay!" Henry cried frantically. Try as he might, he could not get the blade to budge, though his muscles quivered with the effort. "Let go of me, ye spawn of a sorcerer! I wi' nae suffer a witch to live, as God gives me strength!" he screeched through bloody lips, his face drawn in a rictus of hate.

"Ye had better drop the bloody dirk right now Colquhoun or I swear I wi' break yer filthy wrist, ye bastard!" Devlin growled viciously, the words coming from between tightly clinched teeth. "Let go of it *now!*"

That was when Henry could hear and straight away began to feel the grinding and snapping of bones, followed immediately by blinding pain that flashed from his crushed wrist up to his elbow and then directly to his brain. He screamed in agony then as his vision began to narrow, and the world spun crazily beneath him.

"Ahhh! My arm, ye hae broken my arm," Henry whimpered, even as he felt the dirk wrenched from his useless fingers. "Ye filthy get of a black-hearted devil, how dare ye treat a servant of God in such a manner when ye ken He can strike ye dead for it? I can nae believe even ye, foul spawn of Satan, would goad God sae!"

Devlin snorted humorlessly. "Did I nae give ye fair warning to release yer hold on the dirk, ye foolish bastard?" demanded the furious Highland lord. Hissing his next words in the wailing bishop's ear so only he could hear them, Devlin added, "Tempt me any further with more of that shite coming from yer lips and I should be most happy to break the other one for ye tae, ye miserable worm!"

The defeated bishop's eyes went wide in panic and seemed to bulge as he shook his head violently side to side. "Nay! Nay, please-please do nae hurt me anymore!" Henry pleaded, nursing his crushed wrist protectively to his chest.

MacEwan hurried over to where Devlin crouched over the bishop, along with two of his men, and helped the young lord to his feet while his retainers took charge of the prize prisoner. "Well done, Devlin! Yer father would hae been proud of the way ye hae conducted yerself this day," congratulated the general, smiling broadly. "Duncan wi' indeed be pleased when he finds out that this evil man wi' be tried and, without a doubt, be executed for the torture and vile crimes perpetuated against him.

"When there is time, I would be honoured to place the spurs of knighthood upon yer feet when the king dubs ye," MacEwan added, returning Devlin's sword to him and they watched the bishop bound to the back of a horse for transport.

"Thank ye, general, ye honour me," Devlin replied with a weary smile. "For now, however, we should finish getting the prisoners rounded up to head back to our lines; the king may still hae need of us with bringing this battle to an end."

"Indeed," agreed the old veteran.

*   *   *

The rout of the Duke of Argyll's entire right wing was complete as all those who remained alive and able-bodied had fled the field of battle however they could. The clans loyal to Domeric Campbell banded together as best they could under their respective clan banner and scattered in every direction like leaves before the wind. In a matter of only minutes, the solitary cohesive force remaining to the beaten Campbell duke was his own faithful clansmen and the core of stubborn Hamilton men. Those Lowlander warriors had found it necessary to turn to Duke Domeric for leadership when their own duke had fallen under the onslaught of Marishal MacSean's devastating cavalry attack. Only a shadow of Argyll's formerly impressive army survived, it being reduced to little more than a thousand troops in fighting shape, while several hundred more bore wounds of one type or another. These men Campbell led from the field in a general retreat in the hopes of reaching a place of sanctuary to lick their wounds and regroup.

It was King Gregor, in no mood to allow his adversary to slip away and return at some other time to plague him in the future, which personally led a large well-armed band of royal troops after the fleeing remnant of the Duke of Argyll's army. While those under Campbell's direct command fled in good order toward Inveraray, the other rebel clans took flight in what ever route their own leader chose. It was a race the Campbells and their allies were destined to lose. As for Domeric Campbell, the powerful lord over the vast expanse of Argyll lands and master of its capital's most impressive castle of Inveraray, he would never again lay eyes on his ancient and opulent home, except through the staring, unseeing gaze of a corpse.

Due to Domeric's head start, brought about by Gregor's careful marshaling of his victorious army, the king's pursuing force was not able to hunt down and close with the main rebel army before nightfall. Wary of any surprise attack that might materialize out of the darkness, Gregor halted his pursuit just after dusk and set half of his soldiers on a rotating two hour watch throughout the night.

No attack came that night or the following night, and by dawn of the second day as the royal forces again resumed their hunt, with refreshed and fed men and horses, they hoped to track down the fleeing rebels. It was drawing nye unto noon before they again caught sight of their quarry near the lochside village of Annat and effectively pinned Domeric's forces against Loch Awe, where the duke waited in hopes of ferrying across the deep waters and making good his escape.

King Gregor was swift to deploy his forces of heavily armed knights and the lighter horsemen armed with their deadly bows to hem in the rebellious duke before he could have a chance of escaping. The king could see that Domeric would either be forced to make one last desperate stand or accept the king's terms of surrender as the ferry boats came from the distant quay across the calm waters.

The rebel leader was blessed with a final vestige of good fortune in his time of need while fleeing the trailing king. Early on the same day as the pursuers caught sight of his ragged army, Domeric had been joined by a tardy warband of MacGinnes clansmen pledged to support him in the fight against his enemies. They had been expected a week earlier, but had been unexpectedly detained due to a heated running skirmish with a marauding band of Gordons, led by their fiery young laird.

"Sae, ye hae come at last, uh Alec? Ye come tae late for the battle; one more day and ye would hae missed the war," declared Domeric, his lightly spoken words dripping with cool sarcasm and disappointment toward the tardy MacGinnes chief. Around the two noblemen, the duke's officers moved with alacrity to redeploy the relatively fresh clansmen among their own exhausted troops. The newcomers swelled their thinned ranks to nearly fifteen hundred men able to fight. "Ach, forgive my hasty words, Alec; none of us could hae expected our faithless Gordon allies to turn on their friends. But ye are here now, and glad I am that ye hae come because my need is great.

Perhaps yer arrival wi' tip the balance here, and ought to give our *king* Gregor something to think about; he wi' nae expect my army to be sae reinforced while on the run. Mayhap, he wi' nae hae brought forces sufficient to contend with the additional Highlanders ye hae brought me!" he exclaimed, savoring his good fortune.

Across the rippling fields of barley, Gregor brought his divided forces to a halt and ordered his officers to form their troops into position. Riding at the king's right hand was Lord Donald and they quietly discussed what tactics to use during the impending battle, Gregor offering his old friend some observations that his nephew had shared with him from previous engagements with Domeric.

"Auld Domeric wi' seek to out fox us if given the opportunity, sae we must be wary of being lured into some trap he might hae in mind," Gregor cautioned, frowning as he looked over his enemy's forces. "The fox seems to hae more lads with him than when he fled the field a couple of days ago, would ye nae agree, Donald?"

Donald nodded slowly as he considered the deploying rebels. "Aye, ye are right. Campbell must hae met up with some allies arriving late to join the battle," replied the burly island lord. "It looks to me like he has somewhere between twelve hundred and fifteen hundred lads with him now; he did nae hae that many men before, even counting the walking wounded. His newcomers wi' be more fresh than those he had already tae; more fresh than our own, most likely."

"Can we take him with the forces we currently hae, do ye think?"

"Ach, aye!" snorted MacDonald. "We hae nearly two thousand of our best lads, including those bonny, mounted archers commanded by that young MacNeish fellow. We're in fine shape to finish Campbell off, one and for all. Trust me."

In an uncharacteristic show of humor, Gregor slapped his friend on the shoulder and broke into a wolfish grin. "By Lugh, thanks for reminding me! I had nearly forgotten about that promising lad; I had it mind to promote him for his excellent service."

Twisting about in the saddle the king caught the eye of an orderly and shouted, "Find me Captain MacNeish and bring him to me at once!"

Moments later a worried looking James MacNeish, along with his huge red haired lieutenant cantered up to the king's position. Drawing rein, both officers pulled up and sketched respectful salutes. "Sair! Captain MacNeish reporting as ye ordered," the young Highlander said, removing his helmet and holding it in the crook of his arm.

"Good day to ye, Captain," greeted Gregor, a smile still lingering on his lips. "I hae heard reports of yer valor and fine leadership from men that I trust beyond doubt, and I intend to reward such bonny service. Skilled officers are a valuable commodity to me and to Scotland, especially during these trying times. What would ye hae as a reward for the excellent and faithful service to yer king?" he asked.

James was nonplussed by the question and it showed on his youthful face. "Sair, ye are my kinsman and chief, therefore it is my honour to render such service. What duty I perform in yer name is only right and just for our clan and kingdom, for I love both," he replied slowly but with feeling. "I do nae seek nor require any reward for any service I hae rendered ye, but I thank ye for yer confidence and yer generous offer."

"Children of the Mist wi' long endure while men of yer distinction continue to wear our proud tartan, laddie," commended Gregor, while Lord Donald looked on with a smile of approval at the young MacNeish. Drawing off a gauntlet, the king extended his hand and added, "Wi' ye accept my hand in friendship, First Captain?"

"Aye, sair; it is my honour to do sae," James replied at once with a delighted grin, reaching out to clasp the king's hand. It was only then that he realized King Gregor had addressed him by a new title. "Thank ye, sair!" he exclaimed.

The MacDonald smothered a chuckle that tried to rumble up from his throat. "The day is wasting away while we tarry here. Ye had best see to yer men, First Captain," he recommended, showing the officer a toothy grin. "We still hae some bloody rebels to send on their way to the halls of Hell."

Accepting the order with a respectful salute, James and his burly lieutenant put spurs to mount and thundered off to rejoin their men. As the two leaders watched them ride away they laughed as Redwood reached over slapped his friend a congratulatory slap on the back and howled a warcry, his bright red hair streaming behind him.

Time halts for no man, and it was well nye unto dusk before the battle lines on each side had been drawn as both leaders did what they could to outwit the other, using bold stratagems as well as more subtle maneuvers. Charges between cavalry had been exchanged, though they had been more an act of feeling out the enemy than anything else. Companies of infantry had also clashed briefly, but that fighting had been nothing more than minor skirmishes. The MacNeish Border Dragons had inflicted a share of casualties on the rebels with their superb archery even as the daylight began to fail, and shadows grew long until the darkness began to grow across the still waters of Loch Awe.

Neither side had gained an advantage from the minor engagements that had been conducted, but Gregor enjoyed playing the cat to The Campbell's mouse. As it was, the duke's reinforced army, already with inferior numbers, was slowly dwindling and hoped for a reprieve as the sun was sinking behind beneath the horizon.

Even while the last rays of the glowing sun peaked over the distant mountain tops to the west, the Border Dragons let loose a volley of clothyard arrows at their enemies which was followed by three more withering barrages loosed over the heads of Lord Donald's infantry. Fully committed, the Lord of the Isles charged forward with his men in a wild rush, barely retaining any kind of true formation, drilled discipline all but forgotten in their bid to put an end to their struggle with the renegade Scotsmen.

The skirling wail of great Highland bagpipes urged the Highlanders on into fierce battle and bloody hand to hand combat. Wild and ferocious warcries were screamed from raw throats as each clansman threw himself with abandon at his equally unrestrained foes. Swords rang on swords and against armor and shield; bloodied blades and axes thudded mercilessly into flesh; bones were smashed, and all the while brave and courageous men from both sides were dismembered and worse as others were slain by the score. As men fell, never to rise again, their fellows fought on. In the dark of twilight more lives were taken and lost as the field of barley grain was crushed under foot and hoof, until the whole field was stained crimson and fouled by the reek of loosened bowels.

Slowly but surely the grim contest began to swing in favor of the royalists, as their superior numbers and better supplied men began to overwhelm the faltering rebels. Not willing to concede, The Campbell stubbornly refused to heed any advice that involved surrendering, and urged his soldiers on with an ardent determination.

Laird Alec, Chief of clan MacGinnes, wrung his hands in concern as he watched his clansmen take the brunt of the royal assault. "Yer Grace, please, we must parley with Gregor for an honourable surrender, or at the least attempt to flee from this place! I hae found some few boats that can ferry us across the loch. A rear guard could buy many the time needed to escape across the waters and to safety," suggested MacGinnes. "Our lads, my lads, are being slaughtered for nay good reason! The day is lost, but if we flee now we can live to fight another day!"

Domeric stared angrily at his ally. "Nay, the fight is nae yet decided! By God, ye hae become as spineless as any Lowlander, MacGinnes!" he growled with contempt. "I wi' nae run one step further, nor wi' I *ever* surrender and bow the knee to grovel before any thrice damned MacGregor!"

The MacGinnes chief stiffened as though he had been slapped. "Very well, if that is yer final word, Yer Grace. Ye force me to act in a manner that I would rather nae; I am sorry, but since ye wi' nae take sound council against the folly of continuing this-this slaughter, I must withdraw my clansmen from this hopeless endeavor," he replied with regret, stoically enduring Domeric's terrible anger as the duke cursed him roundly until his face was flushed crimson. "I *am* sorry, Domeric, but I wi' nae stand by and hae my clansmen sacrificed for yer stubbornness, nor watch them be butchered before my eyes for some impossible dream that is fated to fail."

Taking his leave of the incensed duke, Alec MacGinnes rode away to rally his clansmen and ordered his clan's pipers to play their call of retreat. While the men of that clan sought to disengage from the battle, and then swiftly retired from the field, seeking the boats awaiting them, Domeric Campbell wept bitter tears and cursed with impotent rage as he watched long awaited dreams of dominance shattered before his eyes.

By way of the withdrawal of the Clan MacGinnes fighting men, the end was all but inevitable as the rebel army lost hope and began to disintegrate in the face of their unrelenting foe. Left with barely two hundred troops of his formerly imposing army, the obstinate Duke of Argyll still refused to back down. Although he sought to rally his men by joining the fight with his bodyguards, Domeric's clansmen gave ground and fell with heavy losses as they were all but slaughtered around their chief. None ran away, refusing to yield as long as their chief yet fought, but they pleaded with hopeless eyes as more fell every passing moment. Domeric knew in his heart then that all was lost.

"My duke!" cried out one of Argyll's remaining senior officers. "The king's men are seeking to redeploy and use their numbers to surround us!"

"I'm nae blind, Captain; I can see that very well for myself!" Campbell snapped impatiently, himself laying about with his blood stained sword in the heat of the fighting with his surviving bodyguards, and weary beyond measure from the long day and evening of the ongoing battle. Overriding the orders of his own officers, Domeric bellowed to be heard over the deafening crash of melee, "Left and right flanks shift and backstep! Center on me and form circle! Form circle!"

It took only moments before the royalist forces had formed into a wide crescent and had the beleaguered Campbells completely pinned against the shore of the wide loch, where they began to tighten their envelopment. Soon the rebels found their feet being lapped by Loch Awe's cold waters, and they cried with despair at their plight.

Viewing the position in which the rebels had been maneuvered in to, King Gregor relayed the command through his officers to temporarily cease fighting and to pull back several yards as he rode forward. Remaining well within his own orderly ranks the king reined to a halt and lifted his voice to hail his adversary.

"Domeric Campbell, I call upon ye to surrender yer force! Ye must ken that ye are beaten, and hae nay hope of escape. Continuing to fight is foolish and does nothing but invite the annihilation of these brave clansmen," shouted Gregor, indicating the weary men crowded about the shore, while the rebel duke wheeled his tired warhorse in a tight circle searching with growing despair for a way out.

There was no weak point to be found through the royalist lines and no where in which to try and punch a way through. It was now much too late to hope to reach any remaining boats to attempt to cross the loch. *I should hae listened to Alec when I had the chance,* Domeric suddenly berated himself as he cast a forlorn glance over the remnants of his army and saw how few still remained.

What had once been a grand army now amounted to little more than an oversized warband and Domeric knew in his heart that to remain at arms against such a formidable force, that so vastly outnumbered him, was nothing short of suicide. Peering about him, the duke recognized some of the survivors as close kin who looked to him not only as a lord, but also as a member of their extended family.

The rebels were a desperate group of hardy clansmen and all the more dangerous for their hopeless position with their backs against the dark waters of Loch Awe. They stared suspiciously out at the king's soldiers as those men moved slowly back to make a neutral space between the combatants. Taking the opportunity to catch a breather the rebels milled about mostly in place, packed into a half circle centered on their mounted leader. Most eyes remained riveted on the silent foe as they waited for a renewed assault; bristling with an assortment of bloodied weapons, they stood firm and still proudly defiant, as only a Highland man could, and prepared to fight to the death for their chief if he asked them to do so.

Separated from the rebels by no more than several yards, Gregor sat his mount and impatiently awaited The Campbell's response. He hoped for a clean end to hostilities, sickened by the forced killing of his own countrymen, but determined that the rebellion would be stamped out one way or another.

"Surrender now, Campbell, and hae yer men throw down their weapons!" Gregor repeated angrily. "Dreams of yer wearing the Crown of Scotland are over. There is nay avenue for ye to escape from justice, Domeric. None! Put aside yer pride and consider the welfare of yer brave and loyal clansmen; I assure ye that they wi' be dealt with fairly," the king urged, hoping this new appeal would get through to the man.

"What argument ye hae is with me, Domeric. Yer animosity is personal, just as it has ever been, sae why continue to involve others in our dispute? My claim to the throne is by right of closest kin and blood," he stated flatly. "I was proclaimed king in Edinburgh shortly following the tragic deaths of King William and Prince David, an act that was conducted nearly a fortnight before I received news of those fateful events. I did nae seek out the crown, nor had ever hoped for it, but the duty has fallen to me to bear," Gregor informed the rebel duke. "I do nae expect ye to believe my words, but they are true, and I willingly stake my honour and my life on them.

"Let us, just ye and I, settle this dispute between us over crossed weapons. If ye fall by my hand let it be known that yer cause is finished," Gregor proposed. "But should I be slain by yer hand, then I swear that ye wi' be given leave to go safely from this place to continue to plot against my son for the Throne of Scotland. What do ye say, Domeric? Are those terms acceptable to ye?" asked The MacGregor with a grim smile. "Yer force is beaten and weak against the might of my lads standing before ye. Wi' ye accept my invitation of single combat, Yer Grace?"

Domeric stared in stony silence at his old nemesis for a long moment before he deigned to respond. "Just why exactly should I do as ye suggest, MacGregor? What act of treachery is it that ye plan?"

"Treachery?" Gregor barked a forced laugh. "Look about ye! I hae nay need for treachery and ye ken it, Domeric! And as for why ye should face me-why nae? Ye hae nothing to lose, but much to possibly gain should ye lay me low."

The Duke of Argyll's once fine armor was dented and battered as he flexed his arms, and he bled freely from several painful, but clearly not mortal wounds he had sustained during the fighting. His face was pale with fatigue and expression bleak as he wearily lifted off his helmet and hung it from his saddle. When he raised his bloodshot eyes to meet Gregor's, they were sharp with defiance and old hate. Long had the ancient clans of Campbell and MacGregor feuded and fought throughout the centuries, but never had either of those proud clans been beaten into submission. *Histories wi' nae write that I am the first to capitulate to a bloody MacGregor! I may hae been beaten, but I refuse to be broken!* Domeric resolutely vowed in his heart.

"I can nae, and I wi' nae surrender to bow the knee to ye Gregor or to any other MacGregor," he declared, anger clipping his words and causing his mount to snort and prance uneasily. "Where would be the honour of leaving my lady wife, my kinsmen, and my clanfolk undefended and at yer mercy while I merely stood aside? My obligation is clear: I must fight to defend all, even if it is necessary that I should give my life fulfilling my sacred duty!" Domeric snapped harshly.

"A duty is sacred when it is done selflessly to protect those in one's charge," the king replied mildly. "Live or die in single combat facing me and ye hae satisfied every obligation to kith and kin that could ever be demanded. Refusing to do sae and continuing in this folly is merely suicide, which puts yer soul at risk. What say ye, Domeric? Wi' ye nae accept my challenge as honour demands?"

"Sae be it," blurted the rebel duke. Grabbing his dented helmet, Domeric pulled it on and raised the heavy visor. "I accept yer challenge and wi' face ye in single combat, to the death, MacGregor. I shall ask for nay quarter and nay quarter shall be given! There is, however, one boon that I am loath to request as I, unfortunately, hae nay more lances in which to use. Might ye hae one I could borrow?"

"Sire, I hae one the duke may use," Lord MacDonald offered.

Gregor nodded. "The Lord of the Isles has a spare lance. Is that acceptable to ye, Yer Grace?" asked the king, lifting his helmet to place it on his head.

"Aye, and with my thanks, Lord Donald," agreed Domeric.

The combatants approached a lane of open ground separated from the two armies by about one hundred yards. Lord Donald continued to the far end of the makeshift lists along with his friend and king. He chuckled grimly as he rode at the silent Gregor's side and murmured, "Ye do realize how foolhardy this is, do ye nae, Gregor? Why risk yerself in a needless gesture? It's nae that I hae any doubt about yer ability to take him, ye ken, but what if the old fox gets lucky?"

"He wi' nae."

"If ye say sae," Donald muttered under his breath.

"Do nae worry," remarked Gregor as they reached their position, "leave that sort of thing for my wife; it does nae suit ye."

The big man snorted but said nothing.

Across the way, The Campbell sat mounted beside his second and waited at his end of the improvised list and hefted his borrowed lance into position under his arm. After the king had turned his eager mount he reached down to accept the lance Donald handed up to him. Once the opponents were set and ready they dipped their lances in salute, and then without delay they were spurring toward each other with leveled lances glinting softly in the moon's silvery light.

The two heavily armored men thundered across the level ground as they urged mounts to speed. Gregor's lance head scored a glancing blow to the rebel duke's shield and skittered off with little affect, while successfully dodging away from the blow leveled at his own. Then they were passed one another and continued on to the opposite end of the tilting ground to turn for another run.

As the knights galloped at each other a second time, from out of the darkness a single arrow streaked in from Gregor's right as the adversaries neared, and struck the king's lance near to where he gripped the shaft. Startled by the unexpected impact, Gregor's hold on the lance faltered and he dropped his weapon just as Domeric's swept in to strike squarely on his shield. The force of lance's blow jarred him from his seat and caused the king to fall heavily to the trampled ground with a resounding clash of armor.

A glint of moonlight reflected from a steel helmet and betrayed the lone Campbell archer drawing back to release another arrow as he stood concealed within a cluster of aspen trees growing near the bank of the loch. The archer was well hidden in the shadows but the reflection was enough for Lord Donald to pick out the assassin.

"'Ware Gregor! An assassin hides near the shore!

"Treachery! Treachery!" cried Donald, outrage lending strength to his voice. "The Campbell dogs dishonour the truce and attack the king! Kill them, kill them all and allow none to escape our vengeance!"

Leaping onto his charger, Donald jammed spurs into the flank of the horse and rushed toward where his friend had fallen in hurried desperation. He sobbed in impotent rage as he saw that he was already too late and watched as the rebel leader had already wheeled about his snorting mount and leveled his lance at Gregor, whom had rolled under the belly of his horse to dodge away from another arrow and sought to lever himself back to his feet. Coming up, Gregor pulled an axe from the frog hanging at his waist.

The sharp lance dipped with deadly intent aimed at the now standing Gregor's chest, but as if time had slowed for an instant, the island lord watched helplessly, still too far away to do anything. Quick as the angry strike of an adder, the king bellowed wordlessly and swept up his favorite single-handed battleaxe and struck a mighty blow just beyond the lance's steel head. The well-honed axe chopped clean through the thick wooden shaft an instant before it would have impaled him.

Mouthing a venomous curse, Domeric threw the ruined lance down at his enemy in frustration and urged his mount past the unhorsed man. Wheeling his horse around in a tight, half circle the rebel duke drew his sword and prepared to renew the attack on his sworn enemy with ruthless determination.

"What treachery is this, Campbell?" Gregor accused furiously, dropping into a wary fighting stance. "Ye spoke sae much about honour before, worrying that I might hae some deception in mind, but I say it is ye that has nay honour! A common brigand has more honour than ye and I am ashamed to admit ye bear Highland blood!"

The Campbell lord's only response to the accusation was to kick spurs viciously into his mount's flanks and charge directly at the king. Issuing a hoarse warcry, Domeric closed with his foe wielding his well-used broadsword with the deadly intention of lopping off the head of his accuser. Before the duke could complete his attack, he found that he suddenly had no target in which to strike down as Gregor abruptly dropped to the ground with an astounding show of agility and leveled a stroke of his battleaxe into the charging horse's vulnerable belly. Driving the keen, crescent blade deep into its guts he disemboweled the unfortunate animal. The mortally wounded beast ran on for another pace or two, due to its momentum, before collapsing with a wrenching scream.

Swearing, the chief of Clan Campbell kicked free of his stirrups and was thrown clear of the floundering animal, but was nevertheless winded by the not inconsiderable fall and only groggily gained his feet by leaning heavily on his sword. Shaking his head to remove the cobwebs, Domeric glimpsed the approach of his sworn enemy carrying his bloodied axe at the ready, slanted diagonally across his chest. Mouthing another curse the duke raised his sword before him to defend against the coming attack.

"Yer mother should hae taught ye to nae use such offensive language," Gregor commented dryly. His approach was slow as he took the measure of his opponent, and noted the duke's wobbly stance. "Did ye like my little trick, Domeric? I hae been saving it for a special occasion," he stated amicably, halting a few paces away.

Domeric grunted. "Ach, aye, ye dirty bastard. I had nae seen it done before," he growled with grudging appreciation. "Where did ye learn it from? The bloody Irish, nay doubt. They never had any regard for a fine horse."

"As a matter of fact I did. How astute of ye to guess," replied Gregor, coming forward again as the two warriors began to warily circle one another. "I was sincerely hoping it was a maneuver ye had nae seen before."

"Fortune smiled upon ye."

"Aye, and she still is!" cried Gregor, darting toward the man to deliver a swift chopping swing of his battleaxe at the duke's head. Instinct alone allowed Domeric to duck behind his raised shield in time to deflect the powerful blow. Nothing, however, could stop the vicious backswing of the weapon as it split the man's shield nearly in two and drove him backwards and momentarily off balance. Perceiving that his foe would be moving in to finish him off, Domeric threw the ruined shield at the king's face and took a hasty step away to place himself beyond the range of the descending axe. The move gave him a brief reprieve but the king would not surrender the initiative.

Knocking the wrecked shield aside with a sweep of his own, King Gregor paused temporarily to jerk off his helmet and cast it to the ground at his side. Rounding on his old enemy the king barked with tightly controlled wrath, "It is time to hae an end to this once and for all, Campbell. Prepare to meet yer Maker!"

Driving forward, Gregor lunged at the rebel leader and swept his battleaxe in a whistling arc that abruptly halted short of its intended target as Domeric raised his sword just in time to strike Gregor's opposite shoulder with enough force to shear through the chain hanging below the plate warding it. As it was, the Campbell chief did not have the stamina remaining in his weary arm to follow through on his advantage.

Stumbling back with a groan of anguish, Gregor dropped to one knee. Allowing the axe to dangle from its chain about his wrist he brought that hand up to cup over the wound which came away slick with blood. "Bloody hell," he muttered to himself, "I'm getting tae old for this foolishness!" Reaching his hand down to his kilt the king wiped the bloody free from his hand and took a fresh grip on his axe.

Although he was more exhausted than he would have cared to admit, Domeric nevertheless saw his chance to finish off his old enemy, and uttering a wild incoherent warcry, ran at the kneeling king. Holding his sword at high guard he closed to deliver the killing stroke on his wounded opponent. A light of triumph gleaming in his eyes the duke cried out, "Aye! Ye should kneel before me, before I end yer ill and miserable life! Kneel before the better man, MacGregor!"

Gregor hurriedly climbed to his feet but had no opportunity to get a proper grip on the axe hanging from his wrist. In desperation he began swinging his wrist in tight circles carefully outstretched to avoid harming himself, in that way he caused the weapon to whip around before him in a figure eight. It was more of a defensive move than anything else, but he had no time to think of something better.

As Domeric charged in at his wounded enemy all thoughts of defense were overshadowed by an irresistible urge to plant his sword in The MacGregor's chest. As it was he left himself no time to guard against the flailing axe, having already committed to his attack. The deadly arc of the axe whipped up between the duke's body and the reach of his descending sword, and struck powerfully into his unprotected armpit. With a meaty thud the crescent blade chopped like a hammer into Domeric's yielding flesh and cleaved his arm almost completely from his body so that it hanged by a narrow strip of flesh and tendons. Blood pumped bright and red from the raw stump as the Campbell lord shrieked in agony and stumbled to his knees at the feet of the king.

Lord Donald's sudden arrival did not even register in Gregor's mind as he stood enthralled and at the same time revolted at the carnage he had just inflicted. He had never seen so much blood spurt from a man before and watched in stunned shock as tendons ripped apart, his enemy's arm tearing from his body to fall to the trampled earth.

"Finish it, Gregor, I beg ye!" cried the mortally wounded Domeric, blood and tears running down the cheeks of his ashen face. "Hae mercy and finish what ye hae done, MacGregor! Kill me please, I beg of ye. Please-"

Coming out of his shocked daze, Gregor slowly moved a step closer to his old foe to pull off the duke's helmet and grabbed the man by a handful of hair to draw his face up just inches from his own. "I should let ye suffer, ye treacherous fool," he growled in a voice thick with contempt. "Yer bloody assassin very nearly completed his foul mission for ye, Campbell, but his aim was just slightly off the mark. However, despite such an act of deceit, here I stand and the right has triumphed after all!"

Domeric shook his head emphatically from side to side. "Nay. Nay, I did nae give any order to dishonour the single combat. Hate ye I certainly do, but I would nae stoop to such a thing. I swear it," cried the dying man, groaning as the world began to spin and a tunnel of darkness started closing in around him. "I wanted nothing more than to hae yer bloody dripping from my sword, nae some assassin's arrow."

"His words certainly seem to hae the ring of truth in them," Donald interjected, coming to stand at the side of his friend.

"-the man must hae seen an opportunity to do me a final service and took it upon himself to take advantage of the situation and feather ye," Domeric indicated weakly. "I admit that I shamefully took full advantage of the opening he gave me, when ye were unhorsed, but that is all."

"Perhaps I am a rebel in yer eyes," admitted the weakening duke as hot blood continued to pump from his shoulder, "and I may hae committed treason in persisting with our long feud into this godforsaken war, but I am nae a dishonourable knight! Please hae mercy, Gregor; end my suffering and allow me to die now before my clansmen, with my honour intact."

The frowning king swore one of his favorite oaths under his breath. He did not owe this Campbell anything, God knew that, but he felt inclined to demonstrate at least that small mercy towards the man. Domeric Campbell had been his lifelong enemy and chief rival, but also had been a worthy adversary and fellow knight. He weighed the cost of mercy and found it to be negligible compared to the benefit of goodwill it might buy with Clan Campbell, as well as the burden lifted from his conscience.

"God help me, Domeric, but I believe ye," Gregor admitted grudgingly. "Sae be it. Domeric, Duke of Argyll, I send ye to yer death with the knowledge that nay reprisals wi' be visited upon yer wife kin. Nor shall yer clanfolk feel my wrath as long as they stand down and nay longer bear arms against me as their rightful king.

"Now prepare yerself, Lord Domeric," warned Gregor. "Hold steady and I wi' make yer end as quick and clean as possible."

"Thank ye, MacGregor."

King Gregor of Scotland gripped his well used axe and raised it over the duke's extended neck, and whispered, "May God hae mercy on yer soul and permit ye to rest more easily in the next life than in this one." Aiming a mighty blow at the duke's neck, the sharp crescent-bladed axe hurtled down and with a muffled wet *thunk* cleaved the proud head from its body on the first stroke. Slowly the corpse toppled sideways to the ground, while the duke's severed head dangled by the hair from Gregor's hand.

The ever loyal following of Gregor's Highlanders, whom had followed the chief of Clan Gregor from the beginning, gave a great cry as their triumphant king raised aloft his trophy and presented it to them. Although he should have rejoiced in his victory the king felt only a deep sadness as he thought of so many of his countrymen that now lay dead as the expensive cost of that triumph.

Laughing good-naturedly amid the raucous cries of acclaim for his old friend and new king, Donald clapped Gregor on the back in congratulations. "Smile for the sake of yer men, Gregor. This bloody war is all but over now, thanks to ye," proclaimed the burly Lord of the Isles, beaming at the somber king. "Come on, Yer Royal Majesty; let us go find something to eat. I'm sae hungry I could eat a calf by myself!"

*   *   *

Elsewhere, headed toward the west of Scotland to skirt around the north shores of Loch Feochan and riding in the direction of Kilbride, Marishal MacSean was leading a force in pursuit of the rebel chief of Clan Stevenson and his fleeing clansmen. At his side rode Lord Kirkland, who came along in hopes of further avenging the tortured Duncan by tracking down Colquhoun's chief henchman. Although Tearlach Stevenson might not have tortured the general personally, Kirkland knew that the man, Toby, had been in his paid employment and therefore proved his willing involvement.

Kirkland glanced over at Lord Sean, his friend's older brother, and shuddered to think what the man would do to avenge

Duncan once Stevenson had been caught. *It wi' nae be a pretty sight, that's for sure. Sean is a decent fellow, for all his ominous dealings about the Sidhe, but I doubt he has any thoughts towards mercy right now.*

Along with the two noblemen came an all mounted force of about three hundred men, all eager to find Stevenson and his clansmen, and make them pay for the ill treatment Duncan had undergone at the hands of the rebels. The royal force had been on their trail for nearly a day before a MacPherson scout returned with poorly suppressed excitement. Guiding his mount to Kirkland's side, the scout whispered a hasty report to his chief and the MacGregor Warlord.

Sean's bleak smile did not touch his eyes and nearly froze the blood running in his companion's veins with its cold and deliberate maliciousness. "Stevenson; such a fool to think he would escape sae easily. The villain wi' be ours soon," he said, allowing himself a ruthless chuckle. "It surprises me that he has survived sae long when he is foolish enough to halt and pitch camp when he should ken we would nae just let him run away. He apparently does nae even realize we are behind him!"

"How many men does he hae?" Kirkland asked his clansman.

"Less than half of our number," replied the scout.

The Warlord nearly purred. "Good."

Concealing a shiver at Sean's tone, Kirkland dismissed his man and trotted off to pass the news to his and the marishal's warband. Alone briefly with his thoughts, Kirkland considered the Warlord. *I'm glad that we are allies in this war, because I would sure hate to hae him as an enemy. Sean is fair and evenhanded as a lord and leader, both honest and gracious to his friends, but with his enemies he is like a hungry wolf and totally without mercy! He's ruthless when his mind is set upon victory or vengeance. Thank God,* MacPherson thought, crossing himself self-consciously, *that I hae never done anything to cause his ire to be directed at me!*

Barely more than an hour later, while Kirkland rode among those clansmen he had brought with him, a scout dispatched from the Warlord reined in beside the lord to match his mount's gait. "Lord Kirkland, Marishal MacSean sends his regards and wishes that ye join him as soon as is convenient. He said to let ye ken that we wi' soon be within sight of the rebel Stevenson's camp," he reported.

"Thank ye. I wi' join the marishal directly."

When the two leaders had spoken earlier it had been agreed that instead of merely coming upon the Stevenson warband unawares, the sole piper accompanying the royalist war party would play a challenge to alert the enemy of their approach. Kirkland had not liked the idea of relinquishing the surprise so cavalierly, but MacSean had reminded him of the knightly code. They already outnumbered the rebels two to one, and to seek further advantage was less than honourable.

Now as Lord Sean and The MacPherson led their troops forward into the secluded vale, Stevenson's clansmen were drawn hastily into formation to meet them. Their lines were somewhat ragged but they appeared determined to stand and fight.

Lord Tearlach Stevenson calmly sat his mount at the head of his clansmen and watched silently as his adversaries drew within hailing distance. As they neared he stood erect in the stirrups and made a brave show of drawing his sword. "I suppose I should nae be surprised that ye came along with Duncan's sorcerous brother, Lord Kirkland. Hae ye come to help the mighty Warlord exact vengeance upon me?" goaded the rebel chief. "Sae, would ye like to ken what I hae to say to that? I say, come and try to take it if ye think ye are man enough!" he added with a sneer.

Mere seconds passed after Stevenson had delivered his taunting message before the two sides were charging at one another with wildly screamed warcries. With a resounding clash, made all the more loud for taking place in the short twilight before full darkness, the opposing clansmen met in joined melee. It was not pretty nor epic in scope; there were no special tactics or tricks employed and there was no place to hide. What the fight was was bloody and vicious melee with no quarter asked and none given. It was made all the more terrible for the animosity borne by the royalist forces and the utter desperation grown in the heart of the rebels.

Battling his way through a stout wall of Stevenson warriors, Kirkland found that he was being swept away from his household guards. The writhing tide of bodies pulled him inexorably toward where the Stevenson chief's position as he continued to hack and chop down the stubborn enemy. "Stevenson! Ye are mine, ye black-hearted wretch! Oh, get of a mangy dog, my sword cries out for yer blood!" bellowed Kirkland, spitting insult after insult at the man as he drew nearer to his quarry, hoping to goad the enemy chief into personally crossing swords with him.

At last Kirkland forced his way within striking range of his hated foe. "I hae come for ye, now defend yerself dog!" he shouted hoarsely. Spurring his snorting destrier at Stevenson he swung his basket-hilted claymore in a mighty blow at the rebel's head, but the lowland chief managed to interpose his blade in time to parry the killing strike the his sword's cross hilt with a grimace.

"Well met, MacPherson!" gasped Stevenson, giving ground to buy a little time, his wrist momentarily numbed by the shock of his opponent's initial blow. Guiding his mount with only his knees he took his sword into a two-handed grip just in time to meet the young MacPherson chief's ferocious all out attack.

Giving voice to a blood-curdling warcry, Kirkland launched himself at his foe only instead of targeting the man he aimed his blow at lightly barded head of the man's horse. Surprised by the tactic, Stevenson failed to ward the blow and it connected with a meaty thud, easily piercing the leather barding and cleaving nearly halfway through the beast's neck. Both horse and rider went down, the animal screaming and thrashing about in agony, while Stevenson was fortunate enough to kick free from the stirrups and jump away from the flailing hooves. Although he landed heavily and had to regain his bearings after the sudden fall, the Lowlander took advantage of the few seconds he was granted as Kirkland dismounted and humanely put down the wounded horse with a slice of his dirk across its throat. By the time the Highland chief turned back to seek him out, Stevenson had mostly recovered and was levering himself to his feet.

"Stand up, Stevenson, I do nae hae all night!" growled Kirkland, stepping away from the dead horse. "By Morrigan's black wings,

I want the pleasure of cutting ye down fairly! Come, Toad! Coward! Do nae tell me ye are afraid to face someone capable of defending himself? Perhaps I am tae much for ye to handle?" he goaded mercilessly, a fire gleaming in his smoldering eyes.

Lord Tearlach's face flushed red with rage at the well aimed insults. "Ye barking whelp, I wi' show ye to nae insult yer betters! Ye had better hope ye hae the teeth, little puppy, to back up yer yapping," he shot back angrily. "Come on then, puppy. If it's a lesson ye seek, I wi' give ye one ye'll never forget!" Beckoning to Kirkland with the blade of his sword, Stevenson sneered a smile full of disdain as he finished standing and crouched into a practiced defensive posture.

Shrieking a throat wrenching warcry, Kirkland raised his sword and rushed across the intervening ground separating them in a frenzied attack on the villain he had sworn vengeance upon. The contest of swords was joined in earnest as their blades met with a clash, steel screeching in a discordant melody as the combatants danced in stately grace exchanging thrust, parry, and repose with deadly skill. The sound of their fighting grew loud in the night as the other fighting slowly waned. All around the battling chiefs, the melee ground to a halt as they waited to see whom would emerge the victor. Kirkland attacked his foe like an avenging angel while Stevenson traded him stroke for stroke, drawing energy from his growing desperation, frightened that his younger opponent was the more skilled swordsman.

Anger at the fear he felt quickly replaced Stevenson's anxiety, and galvanized by this new emotion he took the initiative and went on the offensive. Raining a barrage of strengthened blows on his antagonist the rebel chief began to beat down Kirkland's guard and little by little forced him to retreat before his brutal onslaught. Becoming more bold as his confidence returned the rebel leader became less cautious in warding himself as he reveled in the delightful thought of striking down the young upstart.

Realizing the change in his opponent, Kirkland decided to take a gamble while he still had the stamina to do so. Following another stunning barrage of steel that the rebel chief rained down upon him, MacPherson fainted slightly away from the other warrior and purposely lowered the point of his sword. Spying the apparent opening in his foe's defenses, Stevenson rushed in with an overhand blow meant to chop a diagonal slice through the base of the other man's neck, his blade cleaving on through the sternum and into the chest and the beating heart beneath.

Ha! He's taken the bait! exalted Kirkland, throwing up an armor-plated arm to intercept the descending blade. *Now to put an end to this.* Even as he registered that thought, white hot pain coursed from his arm to his brain as the sword penetrated through the armor and laid open a deep, ugly gash the length of his forearm. Without conscience thought, but rather a warrior's instinctive reaction, MacPherson thrust out his sword in a straight armed jab. The still keen point of the blade darted forward with all the strength he could muster toward the overextended rebel chief. Stevenson saw the blade coming but could do nothing to prevent it. Unable to check himself in time, he felt the cold steel of the claymore pierce through the finely wrought hauberk he wore, as his momentum carried him forward following his own sword. He grunted as the length of razor-sharp steel smoothly slid deep into his guts and completely impaled him as the bloodied point punched an exit from his back.

Mortally wounded, Lord Tearlach Stevenson's dark eyes widened in surprise and dawning horror, both of those emotions coming in equal measure. *Oh, gods, the pain!* he cried out in his mind, though amazingly not his mouth. *Sae cold and yet sae hot at the same time. I've long wondered what dying must feel like. It's nae sae bad as I imagined it to be-I wonder if Henry is already waiting for me?*

Kirkland stood grasping his sword buried in his enemy's body and watched the man dying by his hand without expression. The rebel chief sagged against his foe and his hand suddenly twitched with a muscle spasm from holding the heavy sword. Losing their strength his fingers released the hilt and the broadsword tumbled to the ground at their feet. Not quite conceding to the inevitable, Stevenson rallied what reserves of strength he still possessed and forced his cold limbs to answer his mind's commands; grasping hold of the sword buried in his stomach with both hands and smiling at the man who had just slain him he began pulling the crimson stained blade from his guts.

"Ye fight well, MacPherson, and better than I had expected. I salute ye," he said, forcing the words from his lips. Coughing weakly, he slipped slowly to his knees and dragged Kirkland down with him. "This is really nae such a bad way to die," he added softly, blood beginning to bubble from his mouth. Looking away from his killer and to the blade still remaining in his guts, Stevenson put all his concentration toward his shaky hands in a supreme effort of will. A little smile came to his lips as he grasp the sword by its hilt and gave it a quick twist, turning the blade inside him and ripping wide open the terrible wound he had taken just a moment earlier. Uttering a soft cry the clan chief sighed his last and toppled to the ground, eyes rolled back into his head.

The chief of Clan MacPherson remained standing where he was and just looked down at his dead enemy and fallen rival chief. "Aye, Stevenson. And ye die well," he whispered so softly that no one else could hear. Then stooping, Kirkland reached down to pry the dead fingers from the hilt of his sword and pulled his dependable blade free of the dead carcass who had once been his hated adversary. Quietly he knelt and carefully wiped the length of bloody steel clean on the Stevenson tartan.

Kirkland heard the soft fall of footsteps approaching him and turned to discover it was the king's marishal. "Stevenson is dead, and Duncan is avenged," he volunteered, though there was no need to state the obvious. "He fought well; I even thought he might beat me for a moment there, but God and the Morrigan brought me through."

"Aye; I saw yer duel," replied MacSean. "I made sure that ye were nae interrupted by keeping the peace about the two of ye as the death dance was waged. Morrigan, I dare say, was pleased by it and the outcome," he added reassuringly. "Are ye alright, lad? It appeared like the swine delivered a nasty parting blow to yer arm."

"Ach, it's nothing some stitches can nae take care of. How fared we in the battle? I lost sight of it in my desire to hunt down my enemy," he admitted, somewhat sheepish as he glanced about him for his horse.

The Warlord bared his teeth in a grin that resembled a wolf's feral snarl. "The men of Clan Stevenson were all bark and little bite; they fought out of duty to their chief, but had nay real stomach left for it after being chased from the battle. As it was they were like sheep, for the most part, coming to the slaughter. The lads are finishing off the last pockets of resistance right now," he replied with satisfaction. "Some few managed to flee into the forested hills just to the northwest. We lost a dozen of our lads and another two wi' probably nae see dawn, but it went as well as could be expected."

Less than an hour later, once the last of their men had given up their pursuit of the fleeing enemy and returned to the vale, Marishal MacSean and Lord Kirkland formed up their force and moved toward the southern end of the valley to set up camp for the night. When dawn came the triumphant warband of Highland troops headed out, their dead tied across the saddles of their horses, and began retracing the route they had taken over the last couple of days. Having little need to be wary with the enemy subdued they made good time and found themselves back at the site of the main battle in just over a day. The warband was greeted with cheers at their return but the field was an unwelcome place as piles of allied dead burned in huge funeral pyres.

Far across the trampled field, prisoners of the rebel army labored to stack their fallen comrades, much like cordwood, so they also could be burned, though without so much ceremony as those pyres of the royal host's honoured dead. The stench of burning corpses was terrible and men were quick to dampen rags with anything from vinegar to water for tying around the nose and mouth.

The forlorn cries of wounded and dying soldiers still wailed throughout the nights sounding like nothing other than the chilling howl of banshees. As he made his way toward the recently erected medical tents near the edge of camp, King Gregor grimaced at the oppressive stench of blood and gore that permeated the cool air and again wished he were back within his own tent. The incense burning from the brazier was a luxury he was happy to have as it kept the stink at bay. He was not sure which was worse, the burning smell of smoldering flesh or the more fresh corruption coming from the surgeon area.

Other tents had also been erected for the housing of prisoners, but many had been set up for the wounded of his own men and it was to one of these that he braved the foul odors to visit. Before the tent he approached a pair of alert MacPherson clansmen stood sentry with bared steel and smartly saluted at the king's advance. One held open a flap for him. As he ducked to enter the second guard volunteered, "Sire, Lord Kirkland and yer Warlord are waiting inside for ye, and they hae a bonny gift for ye to see."

Leading Gregor inside, the older, higher ranking guard stood aside and announced the king, before quietly returning outside to his post with a proud smile. His kinsman returned his smile. They were trusted with guarding the king!

Once he had been announced, King Gregor was greeted warmly by Lord Sean, his nephew and marishal. "Uncle! I'm relieved to see ye returned safe and triumphant from yer excursion against old Domeric. Are ye well?"

Gregor nodded. "I'm quite well, and I'm glad to see ye are the same. And was yer mission a success as well? The sergeant outside spoke of a bonny gift, but I see nay bottle of old scotch anywhere," he commented, smiling at his nephew.

"Alas, we hae nay scotch to share, and mores the pity," Sean replied, "both of us could use some of that as well. However, our friend, Lord Kirkland has claimed a trophy for ye and for Duncan. It rests on that cot over there," he informed the king, indicating a blanket covered portable cot sitting in the corner.

Gregor nodded and promptly marched over to where it sat. Pulling back the thick blanket draped over the form of a man. Revealed was a knightly warrior in a bloodstained purple surcoat so dark that it appeared almost black; a plaid was brooched across his chest and over one shoulder, also stained with blood. The plaid matched the pattern on the man's kilt, but the tartan was not immediately recognizable to the king. *He does look familiar, but I can nae place his face,* he thought with a frown.

"Do ye recognize him, Sire?" asked Kirkland.

"One of Colquhoun's senior officers?"

"In a manner of speaking, but more aptly his chief minion. That is Lord Tearlach Stevenson, chief of his rebel clan, and the villain that provided the foul bishop with his pet torturer," grated Sean, utterly failing to conceal his disgust as he surprised the king by reaching out and striking the corpse's jaw a sharp blow. "Uncle, this jackal is the same man that gave Colquhoun the means to torment my brother!" he exclaimed. "May his black soul roast in hell and maggots chew the marrow from his bones! I only wish that Duncan could hae been able to strike down the vermin himself."

Taken aback, the king frowned anew. "Sae, this is Stevenson. His death was well earned from all I hae heard about him; Scotland is well rid of his like," he commented, flipping the blanket back over the dead man's face. "Well done, Kirkland. I would hae ye do me another service for Duncan's sake."

"Aye, anything, Sire."

"I want ye to hack off the criminal's head and hae it pickled. Ye may keep it until ye deem fit to present it to Duncan," stated a dour faced Gregor. "As for the body-hae it burned with the rest of the rebels; this *lord* has nay right to a pyre of his own."

Outside, the entire camp suddenly seemed to erupt as many voices began to shout and cheer. The mounted force gone in pursuit of Bishop Colquhoun and led by Devlin MacSean and General MacEwan had last returned. With them came one of the greatest prizes of the war bound to the saddle of his horse.

CHAPTER FOURTEEN

"Sae, Devlin," Gregor began, regarding his great-nephew with an intent gaze. "Ye hae done a great service for yer father and myself in capturing such a vile enemy this day. Such gallant service deserves to be well rewarded. Kneel before yer king, young Devlin MacSean," he commanded with a barely concealed grin, drawing the sword girded at his side. "For yer acts of courage and bravery, as well as for faithful service rendered to the Crown, I, Gregor I of Scotland, dub thee Knight-Lieutenant of the most Royal Order of Scotland!" the king pronounced proudly. "Arise, Sir Devlin!"

Once Devlin had accepted the king's hand to pull him to his feet he fought off the urge to nurse his shoulders where Gregor had smacked him with the flat of his sword. In place of doing so the new knight beamed with pride, first at his Uncle Sean and then back at his great-uncle, the king of Scotland.

"Thank ye, Sire. I am honoured beyond words."

"Nae sae, Sir Devlin, the honour is mine to confer upon ye yer due as justified by yer gallant actions," replied Gregor, gently correcting his nephew with a fond smile. "Ye were a knight in yer heart before I ever made ye one in name. Scotland wi' always hae need of knights such as ye, Sir Devlin.

"Sae, tell me, what of Colquhoun?"

"Sire, the prisoner is secure and under heavy guard. However," replied Devlin, "I must warn ye that the man is raving mad and seems as if taken by some vile spirit. It may be best if ye were to wait for morning before interrogating him."

The king's green eyes suddenly grew cold and hard as agates and it took every bit of Devlin's willpower not to shrink before that icy stare. "Sire, please forgive me if I seem impertinent, but Henry Colquhoun is wicked enough on any normal day to tempt even a saint to violence. This day is worse; he acts like one possessed by the spirit of one of the damned," the young elaborated. "If I had nae been restrained, I might hae slain him during the return. Knowing what he had done to my father, I was tempted sore, and I was the one who accepted his surrender. He purposely goaded me, with his ill speech, in what could hae been nothing more than malice to cause me to slay him."

Gregor barked a laugh, though it was a harsh sound. "I hae dealt with his kind before; never fear, I wi' nae slay him out of hand. I wi' watch him die once a proper tribunal has decreed it sae. Justice wi' be served even to one such as he, though I admit it would be a pleasure to straggle the life from him myself," growled the king, unable to conceal the hate he held for the rebel bishop.

"I share those feelings, Sire."

"I think Devlin has the right of it, Uncle," spoke up Sean, standing close to the king's right hand. "Why nae let it wait until morning? Let Colquhoun squirm for a while as our captive; if he truly believes we are all a coven of sorcerers he'll sweat the night away with nary a wink of sleep. The longer we allow him to worry over his fate at our hands the more pliable he's likely to be."

Considering the cool logic of the Marishal's words, Gregor closed his eyes briefly before finally nodding acquiescence. "Very well. Yer arguments hae merit, though I chafe at the delay. Let us all be off to our cots and then tomorrow we shall confront Colquhoun and interrogate the villain at our leisure."

"Aye, Sire. Come the morrow it shall be as ye say and in the blessed light of day we wi' delve what information we may extract from that bishop's corrupt mind," agreed Sean, casting the king and his nephew a wry grin. "In truth, listening to Henry's wagging tongue is nae something that I look forward to."

"Nor I," admitted Gregor.

"Most likely, we wi' all hae nightmares for weeks once we ken what lurks within that warped mind of his," Sean added, his grin having vanished. "It would nae surprise me much to discover that he is possessed of some dark spirit, as twisted as his mind seems to be-I mean, dear God in heaven, he is supposed to be a priest! Surely, he could nae hae been this way when he took his vows."

"Perhaps Henry has fallen under the influence of a demon," Gregor allowed, shrugging his broad shoulders, "but that is nay excuse for all he has done and allowed to be done. Come; let's find our beds and whatever sleep we may find. Mornings light wi' be here sooner than we would like, and having to deal with the likes of auld Henry Colquhoun wi' tax us enough as it is."

Emerging from the confining tent where the rebel Bishop Henry Colquhoun was held under close guard, both king and marishal breathed deeply of the fresh morning air as if to cleanse themselves of some rotten thing that had soiled them by its uncleanness but their necessary exposure to it. Feeling sickened they were grim faced and more than a little shaken at the prisoner's dementia as they silently regarded each other.

The interrogation of the mad prisoner had lasted mere minutes, but being in his presence had seemed to stretch into an eternity. There was no further doubt that the rebel bishop had indeed become possessed by a demon. Neither the king, nor his nephew, could determine when Colquhoun had been stricken, but under the influence of hypnosis, Henry had spoken without regret of his dabbling with black magic and of his summoning of a spirit that he had been too unskilled to keep under his control. That same spirit had swiftly acted to overpower the foolish man and take over his mind until nothing good and righteous remained. In that instant, the man that had been Bishop Henry Colquhoun ceased to exist. Driven insane by the evil consciousness that controlled him, Henry or what had previously been Henry, had retreated into a tiny corner of his mind which remained sealed away from the evil presence. There the man lived in unending terror and cowered, paralyzed in a faded existence to witness all that happened around him.

Once they had retreated to within the confines of the royal pavilion and their privacy was ensured, Gregor allowed himself a groan of dismay and flopped down atop his cot. For his part, Sean muttered darkly to himself and eased down onto his own, reaching for a bottle of aged Scotch resting on a small wooden foldable table near his cot. Uncorking the bottle he drank deeply of the amber spirits and let the fiery liquid course down his throat. "Care for a drink to cleanse yer insides?"

Gregor shook his head in refusal. "Nay, thank ye, an entire bottle would nae be enough after what we hae just been witness to."

"Aye," growled Sean in agreement. "Although I must admit that was perhaps the most loathsome duty I hae ever been forced to carry out, we were able to ascertain some understanding of what led to his downfall. Do ye realize that there is a part of Henry that is still hidden from the evil possessing him?"

"Aye."

"Do ye still plan to hae the bastard executed, Uncle?"

Gregor's head came up sharply at the inquiry. "Ach, of course I do! What else is there that I could possibly do with him?" he demanded, an uncompromising tone in his voice. "Every man, lass, and bairn all over Scotland has nay doubt heard by now what Colquhoun has done and ordered done. Do ye actually believe any one of them would understand a decision to allow the madman to live? I sincerely doubt it, thank ye very much! I would lose their trust straightaway, and understandably sae.

"Furthermore, sae what if Colquhoun was possessed and forced to do all those despicable deeds, especially concerning Duncan? He was the fool mad enough to dabble in the black arts *and* sufficiently wicked to summon forth a demon!" Gregor ruthlessly pointed out. "That man called an evil into the world, as if there is nae plenty enough evil here already, sae to my mind he deserves whatever fate is dealt him and I wi' offer him nay pity whatsoever! If that means that Henry Colquhoun is condemned to perish along with that fell demon in his mind, then I say, sae be it!"

Weathering the heated passion of his uncle's tirade, Sean sat silently by until the man who was king had finished before clearing his throat to speak. "I did nae mean to imply that the bishop should nae be executed, Uncle; I hae my own special interest in that, ye might remember" he stated patiently. "I merely wished to ken if ye remained determined to slay him. Technically, he is still a prince of the kirk, even though we ken he does nae deserve such grace. I for one wi' be most pleased to watch as Henry breathes his last, but his fellow bishops may nae."

Gregor smiled thinly at the mild rebuke, but before he could respond one tent flap was raised suddenly and the older sentry on duty poked his head inside. "Pardon the intrusion, Sire," he stated respectfully, blinking in the lantern light. "If it pleases ye, Lord MacDonald desires to speak with ye."

"Let him in," said Gregor with a nod.

Immediately, the sizable frame of Lord Donald ducked through the entry flap and ambled into the confines of the royal tent, accepting the seat that Sean offered beside him on the cot. "Bonny morning to ye both," he greeted cheerfully. Stretching his long legs out before him and causing the cot to groan under the strain, he chuckled. "My lads tell me that ye two hae already been to visit our captive bishop this fine and glorious day. Sae, what did the crusty auld coot hae to say for himself, besides his usual ranting, that is?" he asked, his manner, as usual was blunt and straight to the point.

Gregor grunted at his old friend's cheerful mood. "Ach, rant was what he most certainly did, although between the two of us we were able to extract a bit of information that we had nae known beforehand. It was nae a pleasant experience," he replied with distaste. "We now ken for a fact that Catherine, the Campbell's duchess, is holed up in Inveraray Castle with what is left of the Campbell Household Guard and some of the other rebel forces. Yer thoughts on that matter are confirmed, Donald," the king added with a wry grin. "She wi' ken his husband is fallen."

"When do we start for Inveraray?" inquired Donald.

"Dawn tomorrow," stated Gregor. "We wi' bring the prisoners on the march with us, and root out whatever resistance Catherine may offer. Once we hae taken Catherine, by force if needs be, a tribunal wi' be held to pass judgment on the leaders we hold from this treasonous rebellion. Sentences wi' be carried out on the spot," he added sternly, "and, there wi' be nay appeals permitted. None."

"When we start out tomorrow, Colquhoun should be kept strictly separate from all the other prisoners," recommended the MacGregor Warlord. "He was one of the main rebel ringleaders, and he would happily seek to enflame the others to revolt. I ken nae what influence he may still hae over them, but it's best nae to leave anything to chance where he is concerned. Nothing would beyond him, especially at this point, and he wi' seek some way of escaping his fate."

"Wise idea," commented a grinning Donald. "Make the bastard sweat all alone with his villainous thoughts."

Gregor nodded in thoughtful agreement. "Aye, see to it, Sean. My friend," he went on turning his attention back to MacDonald, "Sean and I were going to see Duncan before seeking out our breakfast. Would ye care to join us? I think he would enjoy seeing a face that was nae ours for a change and maybe yer cheerful attitude would do the lad some good. God only knows the two of us are anything but chipper right now."

"Sure, why nae? I doubt I wi' starve over a brief visit."

Chuckling, the three of Scotland's mightiest nobles exited the royal pavilion and made their way in the direction of the infirmary area. Conversation among them immediately halted as each man covered his face with a vinegar soaked rag to block the worst of the stench as they walked side by side.

Lying on a cot and covered with blankets, his head propped up with extra pillows, Duncan impatiently allowed his son to feed him a tin cup full of savory soup along with a biscuit of journeyman's bread. The hard biscuit he had Devlin soak in the broth to soften it before trying to chew it, but he still chafed at being nursed like an invalid. Although the general remained thin and shockingly pale, the clearness of his eyes showed that his fever was at last gone. He felt better, though still somewhat weak, and thought he would soon be his regular self again before long.

Both men glanced up at once as the king, along with Sean and Donald following immediately behind, and Duncan smiled greeting at his visitors around a mouthful of the softened bread. Three answering grins greeted his own before Gregor remarked, "I see that yer infamous appetite hae returned. Ye must be feeling better."

"Ye seem to hae something growing on yer face, General, who is that a side affect of yer confinement?" asked Sean, he chided with false severity. "Perhaps ye should hae yer nurse shave the scraggly thing off before anyone else sees ye."

Duncan snorted at the friendly teasing. "Come to harass the bed ridden, I see. And a bonny morning to the lot of ye as well," he rejoined with mild sarcasm. "Ye gentlemen wi' excuse me if I do nae stand to receive yer pleasant greetings more respectfully, I trust. The healers tending me promised to do me more harm than Colquhoun and Stevenson's pet if I should be foolish enough to violate their orders."

"My father thinks that just because he is still able to breath and eat, he should rush back to his normal duties as if nothing has happened," volunteered Devlin. "Sire, perhaps if ye or Uncle Sean would be good enough to tell him how truly close he came to dying, he would believe it for true. Da has made quite a poor patient thus far."

"He had better believe it," stated the king, glowering down at the recovering man with a critical eye. Snagging a stool and scooting it close to the foot of the general's cot, Gregor sat down as he continued to regard his stricken nephew. "Ye had *better* believe it, Duncan, every word of it is nothing but the truth. Ye are lucky or perhaps blessed to be alive after what those bloody bastards did to ye."

Duncan sighed resignedly. "Alright, I believe it. I *do* remember what was done to me; it's a wee bit difficult to forget. But ye had better nae leave me behind," he warned, directing a dark scowl at each of the men gathered about his cot. "I deserve to be there to witness the end of this mess and to see Colquhoun hanged and quartered for his crimes! I would nae be robbed of that right."

"Do nae worry about that, brother. I promise that ye wi' nae miss anything, after all, ye are a key witness in the charges laid against him," Sean reassured him quietly. "Ach, as to missing out, Uncle, hae ye dispatched a courier off with news to Glenorchy about our victory? If nae, I wi' see to it if ye wish."

"Nay, I hae nae," he replied, shaking his head, "though I should hae thought to do sae. Elizabeth and Grigor need to be notified that this war is very nearly resolved. Once we hae compelled Catherine to surrender her castle the victory wi' be complete at last." Gregor smiled at the satisfying thought.

"I wi' hae a letter drawn up to be signed and sealed straightaway."

"Aye, Sean, ye do that," the king confirmed. "Alright then, let's prepare for our little march to Inveraray and a date with its unwilling hostess Catherine Campbell. We would nae want to keep the grand lady waiting, would we?"

"Nay, we could nae hae that."

Soon the medical orderly returned with orders from Father Lyle to look in on the patient and urged that the gentlemen allow Duncan to rest. The general rolled his eyes, but everyone could see that despite what he would have them believe the visit had tired him and it would not take long for sleep to claim him.

Following the foiled plot at Glenorchy to assassinate Prince Grigor, the royal heir, he and his mother along with Alastair Fletcher, Archbishop of Edinburgh had each taken turns at interrogating the captured assassins involved in the plot. It had not taken long to discover a pattern from the garnered answers, despite the fact that none of those men had been entrusted with the full details of the murderous scheme. What they had uncovered was a conspiracy devised to put Prince Grigor as well as the new queen, along with as many of the royal household as was possible, to the sword. This vengeful plot, carried out by Campbell clansmen, appeared to have been instigated by Bishop Colquhoun without the knowledge or consent of the Campbell chief, Duke Domeric.

As Bishop Fletcher strode into the private chapel within Castle Glenorchy, he noticed at once the kneeling form of Elizabeth offering prayers at the foremost rail and glided up quietly beside her. Without a word, Alastair knelt alongside the queen, bowed his head and crossed himself piously and waited for the woman to notice him while he offered up a brief prayer of his own.

"Good evening, Yer Grace," she whispered after a moment.

"And a pleasant eventide to ye as well, daughter," he replied mildly, offering a smile at the queen. "I had presumed that all had gone off to their beds by this late hour. I hope that I am nae disturbing yer prayers?"

She returned his friendly smile in kind. "Nae at all, Yer Grace. Yer presence is never a disturbance," she answered softly. "I came here to add one last prayer for my dear husband before seeking out my bed. I fear for him and miss him greatly. I would nae ken what to do if something were to take my Gregor away from me," Elizabeth confined in a whisper, a single tear sliding down one fair cheek. "Forgive me, Father. I-I should nae be sae lacking in faith, but I can nae help myself."

The bishop nodded sympathetically. "Ye are stronger than ye ken, daughter, as is Gregor. Coming here and offering fervent prayers for a loved one is proof that ye do nae lack in faith. We must all trust in God to protect the right, and ken that He does sae. Today was proof of that as He stood by us all in preventing the fell plot aimed at slaying both ye and yer son," he said, in kindly reminder. "Trust in the Lord with all yer heart and with all yer mind and He wi' see Gregor through this trial put before him and keep him safe for both ye and for Scotland."

After giving the bishop a reassured nod, Elizabeth returned to her prayers and before long crossed herself piously as she raised her head. Bidding the considerate bishop a whispered good night the queen rose from her knees and quietly departed the chapel to leave Fletcher alone with his devotions. While the kind-hearted priest went before God his thoughts and prayers were offered up for the sake of the inexperienced king and queen of the ancient kingdom of Scotland, a land once known to her first inhabitants as Alba.

The following day found the arrival of Marishal MacSean's courier bearing the letter signed and sealed by the king, just as Bishop Fletcher's own message would have reached the royal army encampment. In the cleric's letter was a brief outline that spoke of the foiled assassination plot instigated by the dark-souled Bishop of Saint Andrews. It was well that Fletcher was not present to hear the language used by the king and his two nephews when those men read the missive.

As frightening as an assassination plot could be, especially aimed at one's family, the attempt had failed and so had the rebellion after so many long months. The end was near and soon Gregor's triumph, which was another victory for Scotland, would at last be complete. Once again, that ancient and proud land and people would be whole and undivided, united under a strong and wise king.

The Royal Army of Scotland had been on the march since dawn, headed for the final showdown at Inveraray in the heart of the Campbell territory of Argyll. By Highland standards the massed army moved slowly, its pace measured by the speed of their supply wagons. It would be three days before King Gregor and his army neared their destination. In the meantime, couriers bearing messages relayed welcome news that nothing had changed in Glenorchy since the original correspondence sent by Bishop Fletcher that had spoken of the failed plot to kill the king's family.

Duncan continued to recuperate from his ordeal and grew steadily strong with every passing day, although he complained continuously about being carried by wagon like an invalid. On the third day of the march from the flatlands of Achriabhach the army had crossed Loch Awe by ferry. Only a day or two from Inveraray, Father Lyle relented at last and permitted his grumpy patient to mount his horse and ride a portion of the day before returning to the wagon for rest. Although the general still appeared pale and haggard following his unassisted rides, the change of traveling mode seemed to return to Duncan a portion of his proud bearing. He continued to tire quickly, but Duncan knew that the sight of him riding following such a tribulation as was inflicted on him must have been a bitter brew for Colquhoun to swallow.

Taking grim satisfaction from riding where the rebel bishop could not help but see him, Duncan laughed each time

Colquhoun glanced his way with a scowl and began to mutter to himself in frustration. A petty revenge perhaps, but it still was sweet and well worth the effort it took to sit erect and pretend his injuries were of no consequence.

Meanwhile, King Gregor deployed the Royal Army into position to lay siege to the sprawling town surrounding Inveraray Castle, his forces further strengthened by the late addition of formerly rebellious clans. Following the rout of the Campbell Alliance Army, several clans yielded to the king and swore him their allegiance. Most prominent among the former rebels to join Gregor were: Clan Cameron, Hamilton, and MacGinnes, in exchange for the king's word that no reprisals would be made against the folk of their kindred. The captured Colquhoun clansmen and the troops of Henry's Episcopal guard, including his warrior-monks had been disarmed and rode under the watchful eyes of the alert company of archers commanded by First Captain James MacNeish. Those soldiers following the captured bishop had yet to swear allegiance to Gregor as king and therefore had wisely not been given the king's parole.

Once word of the outcome at the Battle of Achriabhach spread of Gregor's victory and the civil war was all but decided, a dispatch was delivered from Montrose, stating that James Graham, Duke of Montrose and chief of Clan Graham, pledged his tardy fealty to the new king along with the swords of all those men bound to him.

The ripening bodies of Domeric Campbell and Richard, his executed nephew, had been coated in salt and wrapped in linen before being sealed within pine boxes for the journey. None of those things did much to alleviate the stink emanating from those dead bodies, especially that of the rough coffin holding the remains of Richard Campbell. Such a nauseating smell rose from the wagon containing the coffins that the soldiers forced to march near it began to complain and horses shied away from it; before long everyone gave the wagon and its poor driver a wide berth.

The sun rose the following morning hidden behind a sky full of dark clouds that promised a soggy day. The king's army had arrived the previous evening, but already the townsfolk of

Inveraray were in a state of near panic as they kept a wary eye on the many campfires spread in a great circle around the low town wall. A flag of parley flew from a pike, raised by order of the king, for those within the castle to clearly see. Gregor hoped that Lady Catherine would be reasonable enough to surrender without causing the need for further bloodshed, but held out no hopes of such.

Riding forward with Sir Devlin at his side, that man bearing a smaller white banner, Gregor made his way slowly to the extreme range of arrow fire from the fortified town wall. Among the king's party were his martial nephews, as well as his old friend Lord Donald of the Isles. These leaders were escorted by a token force of a dozen of Lord Kirkland's finest light cavalrymen bearing slender lances with brightly colored pennons which fluttered in the freshening breeze that continued to grow in intensity. Coming behind the other riders rode a bound Henry Colquhoun under the watchful glare of Lord Donald, who kept that man's reins tied to the cantle of his saddle to prevent the rebel from trying to escape. Considering the bright glimmer in his eyes, MacDonald appeared eager for his prisoner to attempt just such a foolish deed.

Following an irritatingly long wait a heavy, iron bound sally port located beside the barred main gate swung open long enough to permit a single rider to exit before it was pulled shut with a solid bang. The man was armored and fluttering above him, tied to the tip of his lance, was a white flag as the knight cantered toward where his counterparts waited with growing annoyance.

The knight slowed as he approached and pulled up a couple of horse lengths from where the king sat his mount; lifting the fancy black plumed helmet from his head he addressed himself to the distinguished MacGregor. "Greetings, my lord, to ye and to yer companions. I beg yer pardon for the wait, but we were nae prepared for visitors. My Lady, the Duchess of Argyll, bade that I come forth to inquire as to what yer intentions are in Inveraray, Gregor, Laird of Glenorchy," the knight stated courteously, his bow only a shallow one, but properly respectful for the rank of laird.

"*Our* intentions?" wondered Gregor, forcing a laugh, as he used the royal plurality with such ease that the knightly herald's eyebrows twitched. "*We* would believe that *our* intentions were rather obvious under the circumstances regarding the upheaval currently plaguing this land. Would ye nae agree, Sean?"

"Certainly, Sire," he concurred with a nod.

At the strategic naming of the infamous Warlord, the herald visibly paled and his mount pranced sideways at its master's sudden apprehension. The knight calmed his horse with practiced ease and met Sean's clearly amused gaze suspiciously for a moment, as if he expected to be stricken with a bewitchment or something worse. As he sought to regain his poise the knight quickly looked away from that steady blue gaze with relief, thankful that he must only speak with The MacGregor and await his response.

"Her Grace must ken what Our intentions hae to be, after all, it was that lady's own husband that took the field to oppose Us in rebellion and disregard for Our legal rights as Master of Scotland," stated Gregor, his patience wearing thin. "And this rebel," he paused to indicate Henry with an air of disgust, "who is bound and stripped of all his priestly insignia, is none other than Henry Colquhoun; formerly the Archbishop of Saint Andrews and a general under the command of Duke Domeric, yer lady's husband; he now languishes as my prisoner. Our army has taken many captives, and others formerly sworn to fight under the duke's banner hae abandoned his cause to ride under the royal standard. It seems that most hae lost heart and do nae wish to stand in further rebellion against a resolute King of Scotland who is sae rich in friends.

"Ye ken what Our intentions are, but what are yer lady's wishes?" demanded the scowling Gregor. "Wi' Lady Catherine open these gates in welcome and submit to her king, begging forgiveness? Or wi' she hae to be forced into submission by the might of a powerful army and crushed along with all who stand with her?"

The herald quailed before the ruthlessness of Gregor's demands. "I-I hae nae the authority to speak such on behalf of my mistress, but if ye would send an emissary with yer terms, I wi' personally assure him safe passage and see that Her Grace wi' receive him straightaway," he offered, seeking to placate the king. He held up one hand before adding hastily, "My Lady wi' hae one stipulation. She fears the presence of those whom she considers wielders of witchcraft and sorcery, my lord King, and wi' nae allow any such person to come within her halls."

The king growled under his breath as he glanced sidelong at his nephews, even though he had been expecting such nonsense to crop up again. Turning in the saddle with a creak of leather, Gregor motioned for Lord Kirkland to join him before the herald. The choice had been made beforehand, when it was brought to light that Catherine was a distant cousin of the MacPherson chief. Kirkland had reluctantly agreed, but adamantly swore that he had no familial love for the arrogant lady.

"This is Lord Kirkland MacPherson, chief of his noble clan and a beloved friend," Gregor introduced, indicating the stalwart general. "He wi' go with ye as my ambassador to speak with yer duchess, Sir Knight. I accept yer offer and place him under yer care and protection until he is safely returned to my side."

"Ach, lord King," stammered the herald. "Ye may nae ken, but My Lady and her kin of noble Clan MacPherson are somewhat estranged-"

Gregor impatiently waved the knight to silence. "Lord Kirkland is my choice to go before the duchess nevertheless. Nay Sidhe blood runs within his veins, and is therefore a suitable emissary. Estranged or nae, there is news of a personal nature to pass on that is best shared by a kinsman," the king maintained, his voice firm. "With that in mind, wi' yer lady guarantee my Lord Kirkland safe conduct or shall I be forced to withdrawal to my army and prepare to raze Inveraray to the ground?"

The herald drew himself up stiffly in indignation. "Lord King, I assure ye that Lady Catherine is an honourable woman! Yer threats are nae necessary!"

"I'm sure that she is, but I must insist."

The knight gazed at Kirkland narrowly and nodded. "On behalf of Her Grace, I promise that safe conduct wi' be rendered to her kinsman. In token of this pledge, I offer myself as hostage until Lord Kirkland's safe return."

Gregor smiled thinly. "That wi' nae be necessary, Sir Knight. As long as my lord has been returned to me here in one hour, yer town and its citizens wi' remain at peace. Their welfare rests in yer lady's hands; nay treachery wi' be tolerated."

"I shall inform Her Grace of yer warning, lord King," the knight muttered.

"Ye do that. We wi' be waiting."

The short ride through the fortified gate and into the town beyond toward the elegant and ancient castle was a silent one as the affronted herald pointedly ignored the MacPherson chief riding at his side. In truth, there was little to be said, but the tacit discourtesy still grated on Kirkland's nerves. A war had been waged, against rebels who had taken up arms in opposition to their rightful king, and won, but the outcome was not a pleasant one to the vanquished. The Campbells had always been a proud clan and would continue to harbor animosity towards their ancient enemies; nothing that he might say at this point would change that. Any enemy emissary who bore news of his opponent's defeat and came to offer terms for accepting their surrender could hardly expect to be a welcome guest, not that Kirkland would have expected a warm greeting regardless. He was certain the audience with his kinswoman would not be a pleasant affair in the best of times, though he had no particular reason to fear for his safety.

Deferring to his temporary selfless position as a royal emissary, rather than as a lord and Highland clan chief, Kirkland had donned a clean kilt with his spare riding boots and bore only a dirk at his side, rather than his customary armor. As a sign in honour of keeping to the dictates of a truce he bore none of his usual arsenal of offensive weapons. A four cornered plaid lay brooched at his throat and the MacPherson tartan swept over one broad shoulder. On his head sat a Tam O' Shanter bearing the badge of his clan along with the traditional three eagle feathers that denoted his rank as chief of that respected clan. Kirkland smirked at the spring in his step, at the lack of heavy armor he had become so accustomed to wearing nearing every waking hour.

Self-conscious of his uncertain welcome among so many scowling faces, yet still confident about his mission, Kirkland rode along at the Campbell knight's side as they made their way through the prosperous town's streets. Soon he found himself entering the castle courtyard, the cobblestones clicking solidly beneath the steel hooves of his horse.

The prominent main entrance to the castle keep lay up a set of broad steps that Kirkland remembered from a previous visit. Once they had dismounted, the Chief of Clan MacPherson handed off his reins to a stableman and followed his silent guide within the walls of the impressive castle. As the brooding herald led him down a long corridor and then up a flight of stairs, Kirkland glanced around at the many fine wall hangings and other displays of wealth. A second flight of carpeted stairs ended in another corridor, this one wide and bearing colorful banners with weapons and armor lining the white-washed walls which continued on to a pair of carved wooden double doors situated at the end of the hall; as the hall reached those prominent doors it split off to the left and right, leading to different sections of the massive keep. Beyond those stylishly carved oak doors, he recalled, lay the keep's imposing main hall where important visitors and guests were usually met by the residing duke and duchess.

The herald, curtly bidding his charge to wait, left the clan chief before the doors and entered through a smaller door off to the side in order to inform his mistress of the arrival of the king's envoy. A few minutes passed before the closed mouthed herald came back out and signaled for the waiting Kirkland to follow him through a different door that lay down the right corridor which offered a smaller, more private chamber.

The Duchess Catherine was already seated and waiting for him within an intimate sitting room, the richly carpeted chamber lit by standing candelabras and a cozy fire within a small bronze plated hearth. Ribbons of muted sunlight cast their feeble rays through high-set windows that were tall and slender, and appeared to have been widened versions of former arrow slits before the castle had been renovated. The lady had taken up a seat in an armed and deeply cushioned chair, as if the flames could insulate her against the cool greetings that Gregor had sent with his agent. Standing opposite the hearth from the lady were clustered those bishops and priests which had thrown their support behind both, the Campbell bid for the throne, as well as the captured Henry Colquhoun. The duchess' face was as Kirkland remembered it, both handsome and stately at the same time, but more drawn and pale that he had ever seen it. When she turned his way, as the herald led him into the chamber, and recognized her cousin as King Gregor's envoy, her cheeks flushed with anger and her lips pursed whitely as she glared at him.

When Lady Catherine finally spoke, she succeeded in curbing her ire, and in a cool, measured voice said, "Sae, my dear Kirkland, I should hae known that the upstart would send ye to speak for him. Ye look well, considering ye are the little added salt he rubs in the wound of an all but vanquished foe. Being Gregor's lap dog seems to agree with ye," she stated acidly, a dry, brittle forcing its way from her taunt lips. "Does it please ye much, young MacPherson, that yer elevated cousin is now sae brought low from the lofty perch she sought to enjoy?"

Sketching a careful salute before the bitter woman, Kirkland continued into the chamber and halted a couple paces from before her seated form. The clergymen furiously whispered amongst themselves as he declined to acknowledge their presence and leveled a frank gaze at his estranged kinswoman.

"Ye could nae be more wrong, Cousin," he began calmly with a sad shake of his head. "It does *nae* please me whatsoever to see one of clan brought low, but what is sae much worse than that is to see she whom achieved such a lofty and respected position just stand by and allow her husband to throw it all away! Yer bairns are dead, Catherine, and wasted on some futile and treasonous dream of rule; greed and ambition are what killed them, along with a hate that could nae hae been yers! Why would ye quietly go along with arrogant husband of yers and nae be content with what ye already had?" he demanded, speaking candidly as one cousin to another, rather than envoy to foe. "Did ye nae ken that the Royal Council in Edinburgh had already proclaimed Gregor king according to the Law of Scotland? Of course ye did, ye had to hae known and why they did sae; Gregor, after all, is wed to our deceased king's eldest daughter, Elizabeth.

"What was Domeric's claim to the throne?" demanded Kirkland, before going on to answer his own question. "Was it nae some bastard son of the late king that would never be permitted to ascend to the throne? That only that, but a bastard that the king had never even admitted to parenting, let alone to putting forward as a prince of the realm? And on top of all that," he continued, like a horse with the bit between its teeth, and rolling his eyes heavenward with unconcealed contempt, "yer Domeric even claimed that the bastard's mum was in fact the duke's very own daughter! I hae seen sweet little Helen and I can tell ye that I hae never met a more innocent maiden, and that's for sure! Bearing that in mind, I find it quite difficult to believe that sweet Helen could hae been sneaking about behind the queen's back and bedding our late king," he stated derisively, snorting a cold laugh. "It is even more unbelievable that she could hae possibly carried a child of her own when she yerself is nae but a young blossom and barely come of age."

From where she sat, Catherine stared at her younger kinsman wordlessly with a face that had swiftly lost all color, leaving her as pale as the simple linen dress that she wore. Seeing the lady seen to shrink within herself, Kirkland curbed his unplanned tirade with a sigh, fearing that she might faint if he continued.

"Forgive me, Cousin-I regret that I make a poor envoy as my tongue leads before my thoughts," he murmured in apology. Reverting back to his proper roll, Kirkland stood more erect and forced his visage to one of an expressionless mask. "Yer Grace, it was never believed that ye would receive any envoy from yer sworn adversary with joy, but His Majesty thought that perhaps ye would prefer to hear the news I bring, if nae the king's terms, from a kinsman. As The MacPherson, I am still yer kin, albeit one to whom ye are estranged. The folk of clan Campbell are nae yer kin," he reminded gently, "but the MacPherson are yer family and wi' nae turn ye away; even though ye may hae forgotten the old ties of blood these last years, yer family has nae."

Composing her features carefully in an effort to conceal from Kirkland her shock, Lady Catherine clamped her hands down on the hard wooden arms of her high backed chair until her knuckles turned white. What her cousin claimed was unbelievable and at the same time appalling. Simply implausible, though his words carried the ring of truth. She had always adjudged herself to be a wise assessor of honesty, but uncertainty chilled her as she regarded the man standing before her. *Domeric said nothing to me about any of this,* Catherine thought, a small knot of dread taking form in her breast. *Surely this was nae the claim my husband had pursued in the name of ambition? Nay, it can nae be sae; nae only must it be untrue, but it would also be insane or at the least diabolical that Domeric should hate Gregor sae much! My Domeric would nae hatch such a plot to try and steal the throne without the rightful claim I believed him to hae, would he?* Tears unbidden welled up in her big brown eyes. *Did Domeric rebel to usurp the throne?* The duchess shook her graying head and regarded Kirkland with a fresh outlook.

"I was never privy to what claim Domeric had pressed for gaining the throne; I simply believed it was an honourable one when he said his justification was clear. That was all I needed to ken," she stated quietly. "Ye are *quite* certain that what ye hae told me is accurate, and that it is nae *ye* whom hae been misled, Kirkland? Domeric may nae be perfect but he is my husband and I love him. I would be shamed to allow idle rumor or outright falsehood to turn me from him in the least, especially now when he has need of my love and support the most. However, if he has behaved devilishly in the pursuit of a false dream and injured my Helen's reputation, then I curse him for a fool."

"As much as I regret being the bearer of such tidings, Yer Grace, I assure ye that everything I hae spoken to ye is true and proven beyond any doubt," he attested, laying a hand over his heart. "Ye hae my solemn Word on it."

"I see," she whispered in a forlorn sigh. "He has been a good and affectionate husband for many years, but now I see that I wi' hae to be divorced from him. I can nay longer trust him after this breech of faith," admitted Catherine, her voice shaky as she wrung her hands feebly in her lap.

Kirkland murmured, "That wi' nae be necessary."

"What do ye mean?" Catherine demanded, looking up at him sharply.

"The news I bear may be best given in private, my Lady."

She glanced at the anxious clerics and shook her head. "What is this news? Ye may speak of it before these men; they are bound by oaths of discretion," she whispered gravely. "Kinsman, has Domeric fallen?"

Kirkland nodded slightly. "Aye. I am sorry to bring ye such news, but the duke is dead. He was slain some days ago by Gregor in single combat," he imparted carefully. "He died bravely, and in the end seemed to be at peace."

Tears trailed down her cheeks as she screwed shut her eyes. "I feared as much when Gregor's army appeared and nay word had come from him this past fortnight. What word hae ye of my nephew?" she asked softly.

"Richard also is dead, my Lady."

Catherine nodded in sad acceptance but frowned slightly at the strange tone she noted in his voice. "Ye report his death, but ye fail to tell me the manner of his death," the duchess noted. "Tell me, that I may properly grieve."

Kirkland grimaced in discomfort under her stead gaze. "Richard was taken, along with those remaining among his warband, at Lochay. He was trialed and convicted of his crimes against the Crown," MacPherson reported, while adding, "as well as other felonies perpetrated against the populace. The king initially gave the order for him to be executed by hanging, but mercifully relented, and allowed him a swift death by headsman. Both bodies hae been borne here for a proper burial."

A keening wail escaped the duchess' lips before she was able to stifle her sudden feelings of loss, and the anguish that went with them. Unabashed tears leaked from her eyes and down pale drawn cheeks as silent sobs wracked her body. The ill news seemed to age Catherine right before her kinsman's very eyes. Instinctively, a number of the rebel prelates moved toward the stricken duchess and tried to offer words of comfort. Only one elderly man, clearly a bishop by his dress, turned to Kirkland with a question in his troubled blue eyes before quietly asking, "Lord MacPherson? Might ye hae any news concerning Bishop Colquhoun? Do ye ken if Henry yet lives, or is he fallen as well?"

Kirkland leveled a frosty glare at the man. "Ach, aye; he yet lives, at least for the time being. He was taken following the rout of the Duke of Argyll's army," he replied coldly, his loathing for the evil bishop far from diminished. "He rides a prisoner of the king and is in our tender care I assure ye, Bishop Sutherland. Of course, he lives at the king's sufferance, and I doubt he wi' remain in that care much longer."

"How sae? Wi' Gregor release him into the custody of the Church to be judged by a panel of his peers?" the elderly bishop wondered aloud.

The MacPherson chief shook his copper-haired head emphatically with an air of grim satisfaction. "Nay, nae hardly. His crimes are against the state and the citizens of Scotland as much as church law. There are several charges leveled against him that he must answer to," he said, a feral grin darkening his face. "Colquhoun wi' stand trial before the king for his war crimes and other felonies, and then I am sure that creature wi' be executed as he sae richly deserves. King Gregor has but to decide the method in which he shall be dispatched to hell! Some of his worst crimes were committed against the person of Lord Duncan MacSean, the king's own nephew. I'm sure that the sentence wi' be appropriate, as the king is nae in a lenient frame of mind just now. Perhaps hanging and quartering," he suggested, shrugging his shoulders carelessly. "That would be my recommendation. Whatever it may be, it is well deserved for what he's done!"

The bishops eyes widened in shock. "But that can nae be! His Majesty can nae summarily judge such a priest of his rank!" exclaimed Sutherland, shaking his gray head emphatically. "Henry is God's servant to judge!"

"Gregor MacGregor is God's appointed sovereign of this land, and as such is sae granted authority of high and low justice over all his subjects," Kirkland asserted boldly. "Twice over is Gregor king and lord of Scotland. The Royal Council has proclaimed him by formal writ as our lawful king throughout these lands and in the capital of Edinburgh as well. Furthermore, Gregor has vanquished all opposition that has been arrayed against him in the field of battle. Gregor is king by rule of law and by the right of conquest!" he stated in such a succinct manner that the shaken bishop stared at him wordlessly. "He may do what he wishes and when he wishes; who dares gainsay him?"

No one within the hushed chamber dared to answer his challenge. Catherine sat with bowed head silently sobbing, while the clergymen exchanged worry glances at one another, none willing to meet the fierce MacPherson glare.

"King Gregor indicated one hour to deliver news to ye regarding yer husband the duke, and the royal terms of yer formal surrender; that time grows short," spoke Kirkland, abruptly breaking the stunned silence within the chamber. "His Majesty, Gregor I, sends me with the terms he is willing to offer the Duchess Catherine of Argyll in exchange for her immediate surrender. I hae been instructed to read ye those terms, Yer Grace. Are ye now willing to hear them?"

"Aye," Catherine sighed tiredly, as if she had no more willpower to offer further resistance. "Let us hear what mercies Gregor has to offer."

Reaching down to the top of one riding boot, Kirkland pulled forth an oiled leather tube and shook out a rolled up scroll of parchment. Using his thumbnail he broke the wax seal and carefully unrolled the document; MacPherson cleared his throat and began to read the text word for word.

"From the high and mighty Lord Gregor Iain Malcolm MacGregor, by the Grace of God, King of Scotland, Prince of the Isle of Man and Duke of Edinburgh, unto Lady Catherine Campbell, Duchess of Argyll," he stated, beginning with the preamble, his voice clear and steady for all to hear.

"Greetings: First of all, ye should be aware that any further resistance on the part of ye, yer clansmen, and all henchmen in yer service in now futile. Continued defiance will be dealt with severely and shall be considered as an act of deliberate treason against yer lawful king. I have nay desire whatsoever for the spilling of more Scottish blood, but any persistence in this rebellion shall force Us to command the immediate proscription of the name and clan of Campbell. The possible extermination of the former shall follow when a writ of fire and sword is signed and sealed by Our hand, much as one ancient Duke of Argyll caused to befall the Clan of Gregor to be proscribed and hunted down like dogs, in times long before the Recovery.

"Our terms are quite simple," Kirkland continued with the document. "If your ladyship will effect an immediate and unconditional surrender, and willingly renounce all claims for herself and future generations, including of all of Domeric Campbell's line, to the proud Duchy of Argyll, We are prepared to offer the following concessions. First: nay reprisals, now or in the future due to this rebellious war, shall be inflicted upon the Clan Campbell, however, at an as of yet uncertain date hereafter, the nobility and all military officers of that clan shall be required to swear oaths of allegiance to Us as their rightful sovereign and liege lord over the Kingdom of Scotland. Any failure to comply will be punished by imprisonment; breaking of such oath or foreswearing of it shall meet with a sentence of immediate summary execution. Furthermore, should those persons or Clan Campbell openly defy the laws of Scotland, in so much as harm is caused to others, the law breaker shall be dealt with on an individual basis before a royal court.

"Second." Pausing briefly to take a deep breath before continuing, Kirkland drew himself up and readied to deliver the following concession.

"Respectfully granted to Lady Catherine is permission to collect the bodies of the slain Domeric Campbell and that of her nephew, Richard Campbell for their honourable funeral rites and interment here at Inveraray. Leave is given to attend such sad and solemn ceremonies for the deceased, and a short period of time up to one week is granted in which the bereaved may mourn the passing of their loved ones."

The lady crossed herself piously. "Gregor is merciful to allow for such. Ye may tell him that such a courtesy is cherished and shall nae be forgotten," stated Catherine, her voice breaking with curbed emotion as she regarded her cousin. "The king has my sincere thanks on behalf of myself and Clan Campbell."

"His Majesty sought to be sae," replied Kirkland. "And I shall convey yer words of thanks when I leave this place."

Catherine nodded thoughtfully. "Cousin, ye hae nae yet deemed to tell me fully as to why my nephew was executed in such an informal manner. Is there some reason ye hae failed to do sae?" she speculated, revealing her innermost thoughts. "For what reason did Gregor's mercy nae include Richard?"

Kirkland glanced away from her frank gaze and studied the tiles of the floor, taking a long moment to compose a response before again meeting the duchess' intent stare. "Yer Grace, please, the knowledge of such wi' nae reassure ye and I seek only to spare ye a grief that ye would hae nay desire to bear. The grief ye bear already is more than enough for one day, and I would nae cause ye more distress," he said, pleading with his tone. "It is better to nae ken of it, Catherine."

"Even sae."

He sighed in grudging acquiescence. "As ye wish."

Allowing the parchment to roll up on itself for the time being, Kirkland used the few seconds to ponder how best to tell his cousin what she demanded to hear without breaking her heart. It was not possible he realized with dread. Even as he sympathized with Catherine, he would not and could not bring himself to feel remorse for the young Campbell lord, knowing what the loathsome lordling had done to deserve his fate. Still, the foul crimes committed by her nephew, Kirkland knew, would cut her deeply.

"Nae much more than a fortnight ago, at the Argyll town of Lochay, Lord Richard was captured and taken prisoner along with the remnants of his command," he began slowly, reiterating what he had already reported. "Reginald MacNab, chief of his clan of renegades, led a fruitless assault on the king's forces but failed to escape. As was his right as a clan chief and laird, MacNab challenged the king's chosen champion to a contest to the death. He fought well that afternoon, but met his fate at the mighty hands of Lord Donald of the Isles. Richard, for his part, surrendered and was taken along with his men. The following day once he had been trialed and convicted he was confessed and soon afterward executed. Among the crimes he was found guilty of committing was treason against the Crown, and—and of the heinous felony of rapine upon the noble personage of the Duchess Lauralee of Ulster," Kirkland allowed the words to hang briefly in the hushed chamber before continuing. "The rape was witnessed, and when confronted with that fact, Richard confessed to the crime."

Catherine's already pale visage branched further as the grim tidings struck home with the force of a blow and she swayed in her seat. "Dear God in heaven!" she gasped disconsolately, her knuckles white where she gripped to arms of her chair. "And ye say that Gregor allowed him to be shriven?"

"Aye. Gregor permitted it," affirmed Kirkland, "as Lord Richard had convinced him of a genuine regret for his actions."

Composing herself as best she could, Catherine bade her cousin to continue with the list of terms and murmured, "Ye were correct, of course, it would hae been better had I nae known more of Richard's disturbing crimes. I was amiss to question Gregor's mercy and I wi' nae press ye for any further particulars, thank ye."

"Very well," replied the royal herald, carefully unrolling the parchment in his hand to resume reading. "Third. In addition to the forfeiture of Argyll, the titles and lands pertaining to the Marches of Lorne are stripped from ye and revert to the keeping of the Crown. Furthermore, the honour of bearing of the Great Seal of Scotland, which Lord Domeric had the privilege of holding is withdrawn.

"We would not have the prosperous Clan Campbell impoverished, but return to the good graces of Scotland by way of guarding a portion of her borders from invasion," he continued to read. "Therefore it is Our will that the title and corresponding lands of the Earldom of Arran remain in keeping to your clan, to be bestowed upon the new chief of Clan Campbell once he has presented himself to Us and swore proper fealty."

Catherine snorted suddenly. "The Earldom of Arran. "Does Gregor actually seek to purchase the good will of he, whom shall be chosen from among his kin, to be chief of Campbells?" Catherine inquired snidely.

"Nay, Lady," denied Kirkland. "Rather, His Majesty seeks to demonstrate fair and wise leadership toward the future of a noble clan.

"Four," continued without pause. "Should the Lady Catherine swear a binding oath before God that she will never in future allow arms to be raised against the rightful King of Scotland, namely Gregor I and his heirs, the former shall be permitted to retire to a convent of her choosing for the remainder of her life or until such time as the king shall allow her to return to her honourable kin of Clan MacPherson."

"It is very generous, Yer Grace," murmured Bishop Randolph Campbell, standing close by his aunt's side. Steeling himself, he raised his troubled eyes toward Kirkland. "What of myself and the other clergy whom supported Duke Domeric?"

By way of answer, the king's herald glanced at Randolph and the other priests gathered around the former duchess and read on. "Five. Upon determination of their degrees of civil culpability, the bishops and priests involved with the rebellion led by the Duke of Argyll and Archbishop Colquhoun shall answer before a tribunal of the Church of Scotland. That body shall be convened by Alastair Fletcher, the esteemed Archbishop of Edinburgh, at his earliest convenience. We shall abide by the ultimate ruling of that ecclesiastical tribunal," he finished a last, allowing the document to roll back into his hand. Looking up, Kirkland added, with a measured look at the gathered clergy and his cousin, "Further terms and concessions are nae open for debate."

For a long moment the chamber was deathly quiet as all within waited for what decision Catherine would resolve to make. "Ye may tell Gregor that, though his terms are harsh, they are still within reason," muttered Catherine, an old spark of her spirit still gleaming in her cold eyes. "Due to the gravity of the situation, I require a short time to make my decision. He shall hae my answer before two hours hae passed."

"I wi' deliver yer message, Yer Grace," promised Kirkland, passing the rolled document to her extended hand and bowing politely.

"Go then, I must confer with my advisors as to whether there wi' be peace or if this war shall continue unabated," commented the haughty duchess, giving Kirkland leave to depart. As the king's emissary bowed again and turned to withdrawal, Catherine threw up a hand to bid him halt. "Wait! Kirkland," she exclaimed suddenly, "as my kinsman I must ask me one question. As ye ken the sort of man Gregor is, do ye believe that he wi' keep to his word and abide by the terms and conditions he has offered?"

"Aye," he said, nodding fervently. "That I do. Gregor is an honour man and does nae give his word lightly."

The lady let her breath out in a long resigned sigh, as if suddenly weary beyond all endurance, and nodded curtly. "Very well. Thank ye kinsman; the sworn word of The MacPherson is assurance enough. Tell yer master to expect my answer in two hours—and Kirkland, it has done my heart well to ye safe and well."

He spared his cousin a small smile. "Thank ye, Cousin. The blood never forgets, and my enemies are wise nae to try and touch this cat without a glove for fear of drawing back a bloody stump!" He alluded to the ancient clan motto.

Catherine chuckled dryly and nodded her understanding.

Once the king's envoy had departed, Catherine rose wearily from her seat and made her way to one of the tall slender windows overlooking the primary town of the Duchy of Argyll. Gazing out with a forlorn sigh she shook her head in regret.

"Randolph," she called to her priestly nephew, reluctant to take her damp eyes from the familiar sight arranged below in neat orderly streets, "gather what advisors I hae remaining and bring them to me in the great hall. There is an important decision laid out before me that must be made, and it should nae be mine to make alone."

Catherine dabbed the tears from her sad eyes with the corner of an embroidered handkerchief, and only turned when she heard the door close behind her nephew, slowly stepping away from the window. "Well, my loyal friends, shall we adjourn to the great hall for this portentous discussion?"

CHAPTER FIFTEEN

It was nearing the noon hour when the tall, sturdy gates of the town of Inveraray opened to permit a solitary rider, bearing a rippling parley flag flying from an ash staff, to ride through and trot toward the king's party midway between the town and the impatient royal army. Behind the approaching rider, the town's gates remained open in mute answer to the duchess' decision in token of her submission to the king.

The rider who reined his mount to a halt before the waiting Gregor proved to be the same Campbell knight that had met the king earlier. He bowed stiffly in a reluctant but solemn obeisance, a further acknowledgment of Catherine's acceptance of Gregor's sovereignty, before beginning to speak.

"Yer Royal Majesty," the herald stated respectfully. "My mistress, the Duchess Catherine of Argyll, has bid me convey to thee compliments and to acknowledge in yer royal presence that she accepts yer terms of surrender. My Lady invites ye to join her in the great hall this evening where she wi' attend ye, if it pleases Yer Majesty to do sae. I am given to understand that Lady Catherine desires to ask of boon of thee."

"A boon? She would hae a boon of me?" exclaimed an incredulous Gregor, his surprise clear in his voice. "Lady Catherine would hae the gall to presume such a thing in the face of all that has transpired between her house and mine? What exactly is this *boon* she would hae of me? Surely nae leniency?"

"Nay, I do nae believe that is her ladyship's intent, Yer Majesty," replied the herald with a shake of his head. "My Lady did nae confide her request to me, but it may be that she desires to ken the fate of Lord Oliver and his family. We hae had little news from Arran, but what has come was that the island was taken. Nay word has arrived as to what fate has befallen the duke's brother and his household. My Lady has fretted long over what may hae become of Lord Oliver's wife and children."

Gregor's sudden anger died stillborn. "I see. If such is yer mistress' boon, then it wi' most assuredly be granted, Sir Knight."

"She sounds sae contrite, now that we hae her back pinned to the proverbial wall," quietly muttered the king's marishal, waiting at his master's right hand.

The Campbell knight bristled with outrage. "I hae nae come to listen to my Lady be sae spoken of! Once only wi' I overlook yer discourtesy for the sake of this parley," he cried, staring daggers at MacSean. "If ye should sae speak of the duchess again I wi' be forced to answer the insults of yer foul tongue with steel, that ye never again abrade her sae! Of that, MacSean, ye hae my solemn word of honour!" His words, although ones of warning, came out as a personal challenge.

King Gregor glanced aside at his nephew and saw the Campbell herald's death written there in those cold blue eyes. "Sir Knight," the king hastily intervened, hoping to avoid further bloodshed. "I hae nay desire for another death on this of all days; we meet to lay this war to rest. Think of that if ye value yer own life sae little, as Lord Sean has nay qualms about using yer body to scabbard his sword," admonished Gregor. "Withdraw yer challenge before yer lady is required to send forth another envoy to replace ye, and to carry away yer bloodied corpse."

"I ken all tae well who the notorious Lord Sean is, and even sae, I wi' nae back away in cowardice," the resolute knight replied, his voice shaking with emotion. "I am Sir Dominic, Lady Catherine's sworn knight, and I refuse to allow snide and discourteous words be spoken of her. It does nae matter from whom they may be uttered. My life is my Lady's, and her honour is my honour!"

For a moment Sean's face remained a stony mask, but then to the surprise of his uncle, the Warlord suddenly grinned. No less taken aback was the knight whom had laid down the challenge, prepared as he was to lay down his life for his mistress' honour. His eyebrows raised in disbelief, the knight held the man's gaze, but wondered at the deadly lord's sudden humor.

"Ye hae bollocks of pure brass, Sir Dominic," admitted MacSean, nodding with approval. "Perhaps I was remiss in speaking of yer lady as I did. That being the case, ye hae my humble apology. Mayhap, once this solemn affair has been completed, ye would honour me with a friendly duel?"

The brash knight stared a moment at MacSean in astonishment. "Ye want to-that is, aye. I would be honoured to do sae, my lord."

Shortly, Lady Catherine's herald had saluted the king a final time and departed, returning to within the confines of the walled town to deliver word of the conquering king's acceptance. He was still shocked to be alive, having been certain that he had met his death a few moments before.

Once he was gone, Gregor turned to his marishal, cocking an eyebrow. "What prompted ye to back down and allow the lad to live, Sean? I ken very well that he would hae been easy meat for ye, sae tell me," he insisted curiously.

MacSean snorted. "The lad was just a misguided youth trying to up to a knightly ideal in defending another's honour. Despite a palpable fear that I could almost smell-whatever tales Colquhoun and his ilk must hae spread about me had to be incredibly dreadful-young sir Dominic won a valiant fight over his terror in standing up to me, and I respect that," replied the Warlord, shrugging his shoulders. "Anyone that can master his fear can accomplish anything. Aye, I could hae slain the lad out of hand due to a fault in my judgment, but that would hae been wrong and a waste of a promising and brave man to do sae," he admitted with more than a little chagrin.

"Ye never cease to amaze me," remarked Gregor. "I was quite certain that ye were about to cut the lad down without sae much as a blink of yer eye and leave his carcass to feed the birds. Catherine would nae hae been happy."

"I'm nae that ruthless!" cried the taken aback Sean.

"Ach, ye usually are," Gregor corrected.

"Uncle, ye injury me to the quick!"

Gregor was still chuckling at the wounded expression on his nephew's face when Lord Donald approached in the company of the stern-faced Niall Abernethy, Bishop of Aberdeen, both appeared curious as to the king's humor.

"Ah, Donald," greeted the widely smiling king. "We hae been invited to enter the Campbell bastion this evening to accept their surrender. Ye wi' assume command of the army in my absence," he informed his burly friend. "If anything untoward should happen while I am within the lion's den, I expect ye to take Inveraray by storm using whatever force is necessary. Ye are to show nay mercy for any treachery."

"Yer Grace," said Gregor, turning his attention to the waiting bishop, "I would ask that ye accompany my party, and act as escort for the bodies of Duke Domeric and his nephew Richard. I expect Lady Catherine wi' wish to hae them taken directly to their family's private chapel; once there, ye may leave them in the care of the lady's chaplain."

"Of course, Sire," agreed the bishop.

"Good," pronounced Gregor, glancing around him to see Lord Kirkland and his recovering nephew join the small knot of noblemen. "For now, we wait, but when we enter I would hae ye, Duncan, and ye, Kirkland, among our group. Sean, until we reach the castle, I would hae ye ride at my back to ward me from any treachery that our Campbell hosts might attempt.

Sean nodded acquiescence. "As ye wish, Sire. And by the Sidhe blood that flows in my veins," swore the Warlord, his tone solemn and bleak, "I swear that none shall gain past me to draw a single drop of yer blood. Any who dares to deal treacherously with ye wi' pay for his crime on the length of my blade."

It was still just the outset of evening when King Gregor and his retinue entered the town of Inveraray. Thunder had begun to boom off in the distance and black clouds were moving in from the west threatening a stormy night. Paying no heed to the weather, the Scottish king rode down the main avenue in the manner of some ancient conqueror fresh from a triumphant campaign. Preceded by two columns of heavy cavalry, with a company of royal archers marching between them, and two hundred pike bearing infantrymen, the king's party made their way toward the impressive Campbell stronghold as if on parade. A plain circlet of hammered gold shone where it rode on Gregor's helmet, and in the crook of his arm he bore the antique sword that had been handed down from his father and his father before him, in the place of a scepter.

No resistance greeted the royal party as they rode through the eerily hushed town and the king's martial show was met with silence and the bitter countenances of the wary populace even as Gregor's knights drew up before the grand stone castle. The knights swiftly redeployed to form a protective cordon that extended to take in the whole of the courtyard adjoining the keep, the royal cavalry posted themselves as best they could in a fashion designed to thwart any attack on the king.

Gregor sat his horse and motioned for a groom to come forward, handing the young man his reins. He glanced around as he pulled off his red stained, leather gauntlets and nodded slightly as Sean moved to wait a pace behind him, a hand resting on the worn hilt of his sword. Seeing that a squad of archers and a company of infantrymen had gone within to secure the castle and its great hall the king waited. Not as patient as its master, Gregor's impressive white charger snorted at the groom and stamped steel shod hooves on the cobblestone yard until an officer reported that it was safe for the king to enter.

In honour of the occasion, Gregor had donned a tabard bearing the royal crest with Scotland's rampant lion on one side and regal unicorn on the other. A long sweeping cape of rich purple hanged from his broad shoulders, which fluttered in the freshening breeze. Every inch the royal master, The MacGregor at last dismounted and proceeded to climb the weather worn, broad steps leading into the proud castle. The tall iron-bound double doors were opened wide for him and flanked by two sturdy MacDonald clansmen who nodded respectfully to the king as he strode purposely inside.

A modest group of nobles and ranking Campbell retainers and family were lined about each side of the massive hall by the time Gregor reached that place, most appearing anxious when they spied their triumphant enemy. On the far end of the vaulted hall sat Lady Catherine, Duchess of Argyll, perched on a handsomely carved, tall-backed throne, who was completely clad in deepest black as a sign of mourning. Nestled upon her gray, coiffured head was the elegant ducal coronet of Argyll.

Casting his sharp gaze to the left and the right as he marched down the center of the hall's black and white mosaic, stone floor, Gregor made note of his troops lining the perimeter of the massive chamber while his archers commanded the upper galleries, with clear fields of fire, should it be required. The quiet competence of those soldiers was a profound reassurance to the king as he continued toward the far end of the hall.

The hall was a grand place and regal in its collection of battle standards which ranged from recent times to the ancient. Numerous captured banners hanging from the walls and rafters high overhead spoke of the power and might of Clan Campbell through the centuries. An enormous collection of various weapons adorned the walls as well, which had been added to for close to a millennia.

Abruptly, complete silence fell as the ducal chamberlain rapped his tall staff of office sharply against the polished marble floor before barking in a strident voice, "Her Grace, Catherine, Duchess of Argyll, doth welcome into her demesne a most esteemed visitor: His Royal Majesty, the High and Mighty Lord Gregor Iain Malcolm MacGregor, by the Grace of God, King of Scotland, Prince of the Isle of Man, Duke of Edinburgh, and Defender of the Faith!"

Gregor suppressed a sigh of relief as he heard the royal titles announced as they should be, but allowed himself a satisfied expression as he strode purposely down the center of the hall and approached the waiting Catherine. The gold of Gregor's informal circlet glimmered red in the light of the numerous oil lamps illuminating the hall and the occasional flash of lightning that flared from the many tall, narrow windows which ringed the hall with their elaborate panes of stained glass.

At last nearing the ducal throne set upon its raised dais, Gregor, with a show of solemn dignity, passed his sword to Duncan who kept a pace behind and to the right. He removed his crowned helmet and handed it off to Lord Kirkland, marching at his other flank, before halting at the edge of the raised platform. Both of those gentlemen stepped back a couple of paces while Marishal MacSean moved to stand behind the king's right shoulder, being his proper station as King's Champion.

An arrogant mask of composure etched Catherine's face as she rose stiffly to her feet. Staring coldly down at the man she still considered an upstart and interloper, and then casting her gaze out with stubborn pride at her nobles and ranking clansmen, she at last deferred to the king with a terse, albeit respectful curtsey. In response, those nobles of Clan Campbell bowed as well, but they went ignored as Gregor ascended the shallow steps to stand directly before the duchess. The king's back was ramrod straight as he halted a pace away from the regal lady and matched her stare for stare. A hint of a faint sigh, loud enough that only Gregor could hear, escaped the woman's pursed lips as she sank on shaky knees before him. Carefully, Catherine reached up and pulled the ducal coronet from its place on her gray haired head. She clutched it to her breast, bowing to stare at it regretfully, hands shaking ever`so slightly. A moment passed, and then with a tear rolling down`one drawn cheek, Catherine lifted the beautiful coronet up in extended hands toward the waiting king that he might accept it.

Although he had not intended to, Gregor glanced down again at the submissive lady and met her tearful gaze. Unexpected compassion filled his heart at he looked upon a woman that had lost virtually everything she held dear. Her husband, son, nephew, and many other close kin were dead in the Campbell bid to usurp the throne.

Accepting the coronet, Gregor absently passed it into the keeping of his Warlord, and extended his hand to assist Catherine to her feet. *I do pity her for all she has lost; I can nae imagine how I would cope with the loss of Elizabeth or Grigor.*

"It was conferred to me by yer knight, Lady, that ye wished to ken of the fate of Lord Oliver and his family," Gregor stated gently, once she had gained her feet and before she was ushered to one side by a waiting Kirkland.

She nodded. "Aye, Sire. God grant that his bairns and wife still live."

"Be assured then, my lady, that they do indeed yet live," promised the king, a smile coming to his lips at her sigh of relief. "Lord Oliver and his family are alive and well, confined in their former residence on the Isle of Arran.

"I must say, yer niece, Heather, is quite a lovely lass," he said, glancing sidelong at Duncan with a slight grin. "She is a fiery one to say the least, and I'm afraid that she may nae immediately be happy with the fate that I hae decided for her future."

Catherine frowned and whispered suspiciously, "What fate?"

Gregor chuckled to himself, eliciting an answering glare. *Is this the type of poor reputation I hae earned for myself by harboring supposed sorcerers?* he wondered; then replying aloud said, "As matters stand, I had it mind to hae the bonny lass wed to my nephew. Are ye acquainted with General Duncan MacSean?"

"Nay," she croaked with dismay.

"I can see that ye misjudge my nephew by a false reputation put upon him by the one time bishop, Henry Colquhoun," Gregor stated coldly. "I can assure ye that Duncan is nay sorcerer, nae more than is his brother, Sean; although Colquhoun has done all that he could to persuade everyone to the contrary."

"And I should accept yer word over his?"

Gregor snorted. "My honour has been my life from before I was dubbed a knight by our late King William. And it is nae my word or honour that hae ever been in dispute, Lady," he retorted, adding in a cool tone, "and aside from the matter of my word, what reason could I hae to lie to an old, helpless woman?"

Lady Catherine bristled at the callous manner in which he spoke to her, but wisely heeded the warning in the king's tone and curbed her caustic retort. "It is my belief that dear Heather is tae young for marriage, but if ye are determined to force such a match on the girl, I only hope that Lord Duncan wi' be an easy master to one of her tender years. She has a fiery temper, as ye hae said, but she is barely a woman and still sae innocent that her family has permitted nae suitors to court her," the duchess confided.

"Duncan is a patient man, and he has already borne witness to Lady Heather's temper tantrums. I believe she wi' warm to him, given time and the general kindness he is known for," replied Gregor, smirking as he recalled the tale of one of her tantrums.

Impatient to bring an end to the assumption of power, Gregor signaled Kirkland to escort the former duchess aside. Reclaiming his ancient sword from Duncan the king stepped up to the ducal throne and lowered himself down unto the thick velvet cushion, laying the naked blade across his knees. He directed a slight nod to Sean, whom taking the cue, motioned for the nobles of Argyll and the royal guardsmen to usher the most notable prisoners of war to advance from the far end of the hall toward the dais. When the escorted prisoners neared the platform tragedy reared its ugly head.

His wiry frame exhibiting surprising strength, lent no doubt to his extreme hatred, Colquhoun broke away from his armed escorts. Drawing a slender-bladed stiletto that lay well hidden within a cunningly concealed sheath inside his riding leathers that had been covered by his clerical surcoat, he charged up the dais.

Caught up in the belief that the defrocked bishop sought to attack the king, the soldiers moved to defend Gregor, but instead the snarling prisoner rushed at Duncan who was facing his uncle and unaware of the drama transpiring behind him. Before anyone could move to intervene, or the archers stationed above could draw a bead on the agile madman, Colquhoun swiftly closed on the hapless nephew of the king with a murderous gleam shining in his eyes as he raised the sharp dagger.

Gregor, staring with wide-eyed horror, and Duncan's brother only had time to scream a desperate cry of warning to their kinsman. Both shouts came too late.

Even as the startled Duncan began to turn, the madman reached him wearing a feral grin. One wiry arm wrapped around the general's neck as Colquhoun slammed the long blade into the small of his back, the slender point easily sliding through the mail links of Duncan's armor until only the quillons and hilt remained visible. His sudden gasp of agony was overwhelmed by the shriek of exaltation that issued from Henry as the madman pulled out the blood dripping blade to plunge it again and again into Duncan's back. Both men fell to the floor in a heap as the general slumped and pulled his nemesis along with him, Henry still clinging tenaciously to the dripping, blood slickened hilt.

"Nay!" Sean cried despondently, watching as his brother slumped to the floor in a pool of his own bright blood. Whipping out his sword with a snarl the elder MacSean jumped from the dais and hastened to where the two men lay tangled on the reddened marble tiles, Colquhoun seeking to extricate himself from his victim.

As he glanced up at the cry, Colquhoun saw his stricken prey's brother closing on him and laughed, brandishing his blood-slickened blade at him once he regained his feet. "Stay back, MacSean! God has given one sorcerer into my hands already, but it would be my pleasure to slay a second one!" he crowed.

A cry, that sounded more beast-like in its fury than martial, burst forth from the throat of the enraged Warlord as he pounced in on his prey. His heavy claymore swept through the air in a gleaming arc as Sean pressed in, slicing a hissing diagonal path at his hated foe. A blow intended to cleave through the whole of Henry's arm came a fraction of a second too late as the mad bishop jerked back his arm in more alarm than skill. Instead, the broad blade struck the much smaller weapon and shattered the quillons with a sharp chiming ring and a tiny shower of blue sparks as it sheared through the man's fingers. Without pause the claymore drove through bone and muscle until Colquhoun's hand rose, severed from the arm, into the air to land several paces away, at the feet of one ashen faced noblewoman who straightaway fainted at the grisly sight.

Nearly mad with rage and grief, Sean drew back his blade for another cut, this one intended to remove the wicked man's head. At the last moment, somehow the snarling Warlord checked his attack and instead of the death blow, punched the howling man in the face with the sword's brass basket-hilt. Colquhoun screamed in anguish as blood, amid a shower of shattered teeth, flew from his ruined mouth. The Warlord's face was a stony mask as he wiped his sword free of blood on the fallen bishop's surcoat and slid the blade away in its scabbard. Cold blue eyes regarded Colquhoun as he drew back a mailed fist and punched the man in the face, then a second time, and a third time, until the evil priest's features were so mangled that they were barely recognizable.

Grabbing the former bishop in both hands by the surcoat, Sean lifted his mewling victim high into the air and suddenly screamed an incoherent cry of fury-filled sorrow as he shook Colquhoun like a rag doll, with a might charged by pure adrenaline. In a final cry of desolation he flung the moaning man away from him toward the dais, where Henry landed in a bloody heap against the platform's broad steps.

"The sword is far tae easy a death for the likes of ye, Colquhoun!" howled Lord Sean, before falling to his knees at the side of his unmoving brother. "My brother did nothing to ye to deserve this! Duncan was innocent of any crime, of any guilt, but still in yer madness and pride ye were determined to slay him nonetheless," accused the Warlord, casting a scowl over his shoulder at the groaning man. His bright eyes found Gregor's, tears streaming unabashed down his bearded face, and demanded, "Sire, I beg to invoke the ancient laws of blood vengeance, which allow the kin of a murdered relative the right to name what the penalty shall be for the killer!"

The stern face of the king was still pale from the sudden fiendish murder of Duncan and he immediately nodded his assent. "Sae be it! Nay trial is necessary in this circumstance, as the accused is already condemned by his foul actions before the eyes of every one within this hall. Does anyone here dispute my decision?" Gregor demanded, daring anyone to speak as his eyes swept to Lady Catherine and over each of her retainers.

"Very good! Henry Colquhoun," he stated, glancing contemptuously at the man who moaned feebly below him, "ye are duly judged and found guilty of murder. Such sentence as Lord Sean deems fit shall be carried out at once!

"Kinsman," he inquired, turning his gaze upon Sean, "what sentence do ye name that should be applied to the convicted?"

"Death by slow torture."

Gregor swallowed but nodded assent. "Very well. What manner of torture do ye demand?" asked the king, noticing several nobles, including Catherine, flinch as if they had been struck when they heard the exchange.

"The nails of his hands and feet shall be drawn, as was done to Duncan," began Sean, his tone hard with suppressed rage. "Emasculation after that, followed by his being paraded through the streets for all to ken of his shame, until he is brought back to the town square and posted to a cross with a sign listing his crimes.

"While he yet hangeth from that cross, I would hae a burning brazier brought sae that his intestines, once they are drawn from his belly, may be roasted before the wretch's eyes. Only then would I consent to allow his death," he stated coldly.

"Nay!" cried Catherine, distress tingeing her shaky voice, as she jumped to her feet. "Ye can nae permit such barbarity, Yer Majesty! What Henry Colquhoun has done is unforgivable, but he is a priest and a prince of the church-!"

"A prince of Satan more like!" MacSean interjected hotly.

"Enough!" shouted Gregor, rising to his feet and glowering down at the Lady Catherine and the entire assembly. By the time his vengeful nephew had finished with pronouncing the sentence, even he had been shaken by the depth of Sean's wrath but knew it was within his rights according to ancient law.

"It is yer right to demand these punishments, Kinsman, but are sure that this is what ye truly want?" asked Gregor. "I fear for the weight ye shall hae to bear on yer conscience once all is done. Surely, ye would nae hae me thought a tyrant?"

The Warlord returned Gregor's look steadily and shook his head. "Laws of blood debt are a part of Scotland's ancient code, and as such, ye are responsible only for seeing to their enforcement. The king must uphold the law nae dictate it," Sean replied evenly. "Yer people wi' nae believe ye a tyrant, but merely ken that yer Marishal is ruthless and nae a forgiving man toward murderous criminals."

The king held his nephew's gaze a moment longer before at last nodding. "Sae be it. Sentence has been named and shall be carried out according to Scottish Law," he said in acquiescence. "Lord Sean, ye must ken, in accordance with the code that ye must be in attendance for the administering of these punishments.

As the kin who has invoked the ancient law, it is sae required of ye."

"I would nae miss any of it, Sire," declared MacSean, the savage coldness in his eyes belaying the stoniness of his features. "Henry Colquhoun is an evil man and that evil deserves a much more dire fate than I could ever call down upon him. The sooner he goes to meet his infernal master in hell the better for us all."

"If any deserves such a fate, it is he," agreed Gregor, before turning to address the stunned people within the hall. "After punishment has been concluded, the body of the convicted shall be burned and the ashes scattered that none may make use of his corpse for any foul ends. May God grant Henry Colquhoun rest if it be His will do sae, but for what he has done I agree wi' Lord Sean-it seems to my mind that God shall cast that man's dark soul into the abyss, where Lucifer shall provide him with everlasting torture!"

From where he lay at the base of the platform, Colquhoun began to recover his senses somewhat from his pummeling and sat up groggily. "MacGregor. O wicked king, as there is nay justice or mercy to be had in yer court, I must demand appeal to the church for those things! I hae served the church for all my life; allow me the right of being judged by my peers, I beg of thee."

"Bishop Abernethy," the king beckoned, "as the ranking prelate, I bid ye come forward, as yer presence is *begged* for by the condemned. Perhaps," Gregor continued, "ye should make use of this opportunity to shrive the prisoner and administer last rites, that his soul may be given a measure of peace before sentence is carried out."

"Sire-!" cried Sean, outrage plain on his face.

"Nay, Nephew," stated Gregor, forestalling him with a raised hand. "Ye hae been granted the right of naming punishment, and they are sufficient for his offenses. What follows is out of my hands and up to the wisdom and authority of the archbishop."

Returning his attention to the assembly, King Gregor searched among those whom were gathered about the former duchess for another he must judge. His gaze fell upon Bishop Randolph Campbell. "Bishop Campbell, come forward and kneel before Us that ye may hear Our judgment of ye."

Reluctantly, but lacking surprise, the named individual moved solemnly forward. Fear was written in stark measure across his youthful countenance as he fell to his knees before the king. He looked fearfully up at Gregor and cried, "Hae mercy, O King! It is true that I stood behind my kinsman's claim and his banner, but I hae never loved Henry Colquhoun. We would hae been better nae to hae had his support," he admitted shakily. "Had I known of that man's crimes, I swear before God, that I would hae renounced him as a fallen priest. Please believe me, Sire."

"As a matter of fact, I do believe ye, Yer Grace," replied Gregor, as he intently regarded the kneeling man, "however, the measure of yer treason must be determined and answered for. Bishop Abernethy wi' head a board of clerical inquiry to establish yer level of guilt and culpability in the rebel schemes."

"Yer Majesty, please," cried Catherine, suddenly rushing to Randolph's side and falling to her knees. "Randolph but followed the call of his blood! I swear there is nay evil intent in his heart, and I beg mercy for him!"

Gregor sighed heavily in resignation, somewhat embarrassed by her outburst. "My Lady, please! Do be silent a moment and ye wi' find that I am disposed to be merciful in this case. I deem it likely yer kinsman was hoodwinked every bit as much as many others were by the machinations of Henry Colquhoun," he admitted gently. "We thank ye, Lady, for speaking to the character of this man. Now, if I may continue . . .

" . . . hear Our judgment, Randolph, Bishop of Lochay," the king went on. "It is Our wish that ye be confined within the monastery located near the east coast, at Saint Andrews, in Fife, and under the care of Bishop Abernethy. That bishop wi' administer that archdiocese until a suitable replacement is elected by the church. Ye are to remain there until such time as His Grace and I are equally convinced of the part ye played in the rebellion and are confident of yer repentance toward yer crimes. Only then shall it be determined if ye should resume the duties of a bishop to the Scottish people."

The kneeling bishop stared in wide eyed wonder at the king, unable to believe the remarkable leniency of the royal judgment. "Yer Majesty, I promise to show ye that yer mercy is nae ill-placed. However, Sire, if I may hae yer permission, I would speak of something while I am yet before ye."

Gregor nodded. "Ye may speak yer piece."

"Thank ye, Sire," Randolph said, ducking his head respectfully. "Of all things, I would first beg for yer forgiveness, Lord King. I can see plainly now how I hae wronged ye, and it shames me. Truly, I did nae ken much about Yer Majesty, as a priest I hae little regard towards politics and clan relations, except that ye, as a MacGregor and chief of that clan, hae long been at feud with the clan of my birth," admitted the young bishop, picking his words with care. "It was wrong of me to name ye enemy merely because of the name ye bear. With that said, on behalf of Clan Campbell and the See of Lochay, I would humbly ask ye to nae make the same mistake I am guilty of. Aye, my clan stood in rebellion against ye, but the common folk are innocent people who hae followed the commands of their chief. They do nae deserve to live in fear, quailing in their homes, as they wait for fire and sword to fall upon them."

Gregor considered his words. "Honour is never served by shedding the blood of innocents. If I were still just the chief of a clan the Campbells would hae something to fear from MacGregors as we raided yer cattle and sheep," he admitted, finding himself warming to the man before him. "However, I am more than I once was. I am king to all the people of Scotland, and nay honest person has need to fear me. There shall be nay reprisals nor retribution brought upon yer clan or any other which submit to my authority. The king's justice shall be fair and for all Scots, in equal measure."

"My thanks, Yer—" began Randolph, only to be cut short by a sudden outburst of raving by an incensed Colquhoun.

"Guards! Gag this lunatic!" barked Abernethy. The normally reserved bishop shook with righteous anger, showing more emotion than Gregor had ever seen the man demonstrate in his presence.

The captive former archbishop was roughly hauled from his feet and a rag stuffed forcibly into his mouth as Abernethy stalked forward and bowed curtly. "Sire, I declare this man," he indicated Colquhoun with a stabbing finger, "excommunicated. Nae just for his crimes of treason and murder, but for foul blasphemy he spouts! His rights of benefit of clergy are permanently revoked immediately!" Abernethy pronounced coldly, giving the king no opportunity to say a word. "There shall be nay attempt permitted from any quarter to allow this filth to regain those sacred rites. MacSean was wise in the choosing of that vile man's punishment, and I am ashamed to acknowledge that Colquhoun was once a priest, much less a prince of the church!" spat the irate bishop.

It was clear to Gregor that whatever the former bishop had said to the typically quiet and reticent Abernethy the words had struck a raw nerve. As he glanced toward Catherine and her shaken entourage the king could see that whatever the captive's ranting had been about had left the entire group ashen and wide eyed in shock.

Returning his royal attention back to those ranged before him, Gregor watched as one guard, without waiting to be ordered to do so, cuffed the recalcitrant prisoner once again into a temporary state of submission. The other guard seized the opportunity to stuff the gag more securely in place between the man's teeth even as dismayed murmurs began to break out throughout the crowded hall.

As quickly as the murmuring began they subsided into silence as King Gregor stood up from the ducal throne and walked across the platform and down the steps to come face to face with the convicted man. Locking gazes with the ex-bishop the king's fierce green eyes glittered like polished agates within his rugged face. Paling in the face of his grim enemy, Colquhoun cowered suddenly and would have turned and fled if he had not been forcibly restrained by the guards pinning his arms to his sides.

"Ye stand convicted of treason and murder; for the foul slaughter of prisoners in yer charge and the torture of others are ye condemned. Furthermore, ye stand accused, by the good Bishop Abernethy, of blasphemy before all these witnesses," Gregor stated coldly, emphasizing his statement by yanking Colquhoun's head back with a handful of the man's greasy gray hair. "Ye are guilty of rebelling against yer rightful king and for the dreaded crime of breaking faith with God and His Holy Kirk."

Unable to speak with the wadded gag shoved into his mouth, Colquhoun did the one thing he could manage. Twisting his right hand, the one-time archbishop wagged his fingers to gesture obscenely at his antagonist.

Eyes widening in a swift anger that flushed his face crimson, Gregor instantly retaliated with blunt force. Roaring an oath the outraged king swung a white-knuckled fist at the offender, the powerful blow striking flush on the man's chin and snapping back his head with a crunching of bone. Drooping in the grasp of his guards, Henry moaned as blood flowed from his mouth where he had bitten off the tip of his tongue. The jaw hung at a painful angle, dislocated, and his chin shattered from the assault.

Nodding with grim satisfaction, Bishop Abernethy curbed the bleak smile that sought to reach his lips and covered it with a respectful bow to the king. "This creature had that coming and more, Sire. I was much tempted to do that myself, but I'm glad ye beat me to it," he murmured softly. A harsh chuckle burst from Gregor lips, and he clapped the bishop on the shoulder without comment.

Pointedly ignoring the dumbfounded stares aimed his way by the murmuring crowd, King Gregor strode purposely back to the ducal throne and lowered himself back onto its cushioned seat. "Take the prisoner away," he commanded, "and confine him in the dungeon below to await his sentence. The rats abiding down there should prove fine company for the likes of Colquhoun. Do ye nae think sae, Yer Grace?"

Trying unsuccessfully to suppress a grin, Abernethy nodded. "Such grand accommodations should suit him perfectly, Sire."

Dragged kicking and squirming from the hall, in a futile effort to escape his guards, Colquhoun found himself being hauled between two of the king's brawniest men. Once out of the grand hall they took their charge down several flights of ancient stairs, worn smooth with age, and deep into the bowels of the old castle. The short procession halted briefly at an iron door as the former bishop's guards spoke through the bars of the portal to the jailor on duty. Once the door was opened they resumed their way into the dimly lighted dungeon, the stale air thick with dampness and the foul stench of human excrement. The tread of their boots on stone in that dark and forlorn place the only sounds aside from the scurrying of mice and rats.

Leading the little group through a second heavy gate of blackened iron the lone jailor held aloft a torch and beckoned them to follow him down a side corridor the reeked of decaying excrement. Ambling past a row of cells the dungeon guard rattled his keys across the bars of each to further torment those held within and cackled merrily as he led them on. At last, he stopped before the final cell on the left hand side and pushed open the door which screeched noisily on its hinges. He stepped aside, humming to himself, as he allowed the prisoner's escorts to inspect the cramped cell.

"This be it, laddies," he commented needlessly and cackled again before adding, "our finest guest suite. Is this nae a fine place to store away yer wretch?"

One soldier snorted humorlessly.

"A filthy, stinking pit of doom is what this place is. I would rather be dead than cast away and forgotten in this foul place," muttered the other guard. Together they dragged the feebly struggling prisoner into the cell and cast him onto the floor amid a stinking heap of moldering straw and rat droppings.

"Tae good a place for this maggot, if ye ask me," grunted the first guard, kicking Colquhoun as he tried to crawl back out. "Come on, Jocko, lets get away from this nasty hole. As it is, we probably already carry this stench on us like we hae been on sodding latrine duty for a solid bloody month."

The two prisoner escorts backed out of the reeking cell and into the corridor, and the jailor slammed shut the iron door on his newest guest. Leaping at the door with a howl, Henry pressed his face against the bars and screamed obscenities, ranting anew in his demented state. The retreating backs of his guards did not pause nor give indication that they heard him as they continued on, speaking quietly amongst themselves.

"It's a good thing yer Mary is nae here to catch a whiff ye about now, Murdoch, she'd probably up and divorce ye on the spot," jested Jocko.

The man snorted. "And what if yer sweet little Dierdre were to get a good nose full of ye with shite on yer boots, Jocko, my lad? Why, she would wrinkle up her pretty nose and nae let ye near her or yer house until ye had washed out in the cold with a bar of lye soap *and* had burned those boots. That's what *I* think!" claimed Murdoch, laughing good-naturedly at the chagrin on his friend's face and slapping the younger man on the shoulder. Both men chuckled as they exited the dungeons; Colquhoun was already cast to the back their minds as they plodded back up into the castle proper.

"Gentlemen and ladies of Clan Campbell and those of ye that in the past months hae chosen to join the leaders of that clan in their rebellion at arms against Us, take heed to Our judgment," King Gregor declared. "The time has come for Us to speak of what wi' be the fate of yer lands and titles and various estates. In times past, many hundreds of years ago, the lands of Argyll were only in part a possession of Clan Campbell; many parcels and glens of these fine rolling lands-moors as well-were lived on, farmed, and used for grazing by families of MacGregors. Over time, due to wheedling and trickery, by political double-dealing and treachery, those lands were seized; the name of MacGregor outlawed, and their honour besmirched, all for the ambitions of a power-hungry earl that wished to become a duke. Only now, after sae very long, is it finally possible to right that wrong and see that justice is done for their ancestors."

Murmurs of apprehension and dissent to grow steadily as the king spoke until he at last paused to allow his words to sink in. After a brief moment, Gregor signaled for the Argyll chamberlain to command the hall to silence. The boom of that officer's staff striking the marble tiles cut through the babble of voices to restore order until all those present quieted and returned their attention to the king.

"Lords and Ladies, by the authority of the Crown of Scotland, We, Gregor I, hae accepted the Duchy of Argyll and all subsidiary lands and titles from the keeping of Lady Catherine Campbell, save for the Earldom of Arran" he stated, inclining his head toward the former duchess. "In sae doing, We lay legal claim to all these lands and all estates thereupon. All lands and titles subordinate to Argyll are released from their former ties and are returned to ownership and custody of Clan Gregor.

"It is Our further wish that this Duchy of Argyll, including Castle Inveraray, be placed into the care of Our loyal and noble friend, Lord Donald of the Isles," he said, a smile coming to his lips as he glanced at that stunned man. "It is known to Us that Clan Donald has also been dealt with by blood and treachery at the hands of Clan Campbell, particularly in a place called Glencoe, and should nae be forgotten.

"All transfer of titles shall be formally completed once We hae reached Edinburgh and installed ceremoniously upon the Throne of Scone."

King Gregor paused briefly to swallow down emotion that threatened to enter his voice before continuing. "The Royal Army of Scotland, formerly called 'the Army of the North', which was led by Our nephew, Lord Duncan MacSean, shall be placed under the able command of General Lord Kirkland MacPherson. His force shall remain to enforce a peaceful transfer of ownership of all affected lands and estates.

"In regards to those which wi' swear allegiance to Us in good faith and cooperate with Our appointed officers with honour, ye hae our royal word that ye wi' be dealt with in all honour. Pardon shall be granted for previous offences and a general amnesty given to all members of yer immediate household, save those members who may hae violated laws of war and chivalry in their own right. For the better part of ye, We are sure that this wi' allow ye a fresh start under Our rulership. Ken this, however," he went on sternly, "it would be better for a man or woman to *nae* come forward at all, should they seek to swear falsely. Be assured that We and Our Marishal wi' ken who deceitfully gives their oath. All who swear shall do sae on their knees, yer hands between Ours, and ye wi' place a solemn kiss upon the Holy Bible held by Bishop Abernethy; furthermore, ye shall place a kiss of peace upon the blade of Our ancient sword when it is offered to ye by Lord Sean, Our strong right hand," he added, squashing the smirk tugging at his mouth, as those assembled reacted with consternation.

His address complete, King Gregor nodded to the chamberlain, and that officer again rapped his tall, bronze capped staff on the tile at his feet, before barking, "My Lords and Ladies! Attend our lord King!"

Hesitantly at first and then with more alacrity, a single line formed before the dais as previously rebellious nobles came forward to swear allegiance to the king. Several of the gentry and ranking Campbell clansmen cast fearful glances up at the infamous Sidhe warlord standing near the king's right hand while they waited their turn. Notwithstanding those misgivings, the oath taking went smoothly and without incident, just as Gregor had expected considering his nephew standing by with bearing his naked sword. As each came forward on their turn and placed their hands between the king's own, Lord Sean was able to ascertain to each person's honesty by reading of facial expression and body language, although those kneeling believed a more arcane method was being used to read their truthfulness. In the end each had given an honest enough account of themselves to satisfy the MacGregor Warlord of their intent to hold to the homage pledged in his presence to the king.

Once those formalities were completed, King Gregor reclaimed his sword from MacSean and held it casually in the crook of his arm, in place of what would soon be a scepter, and stood. "Lady Catherine, may I escort ye from this hall to yer chambers? We shall nae rush ye in packing nor in bidding goodbye to yer family." He stepped away from the throne and down to where the lady stood beside Bishop Sutherland.

Catherine shook her head, though she accepted his arm with a restrained bow and accompanied him from the great hall. "Thank ye for the kind offer, Sire, but nay, I hae other matters to attend to first."

"Aye, of course," Gregor replied quietly as they reached the wide hallway outside. "Perhaps ye would hae me accompany ye to the chapel? The coffins of yer husband and nephew hae been laid there. Bishop Abernethy has offered to perform a service over the deceased, unless ye would prefer another to do sae."

The former duchess nodded stiffly seeking again to quell her emotions. "That is most considerate of ye, Sire. Please convey to His Grace my appreciation and acceptance of his thoughtful offer."

A moment later they reached the secluded chapel which deeper within the keep. As one of the royal guardsmen opened the doors to admit them, Catherine gasped with a hand coming to cover her mouth as she saw for the first time the pair of pine coffins laid out side by side before the private chapel's altar.

The stricken lady pulled her hand suddenly away from her escort's arm and rushed ahead, all thought of dignity forgotten as she hiked up her skirts and ran to the sealed coffins and fell to her knees before them with a pitiable sob. Her entire frame shook from weeping that escaped her lips, and Catherine tenderly touched each wooden box as if to comfort those dead whom laid within them.

Gregor held back a distance out of respect for her grief; after a moment the lady turned to glance back at him and asked in a whisper that he could barely hear to come forward. "Sire, in which does my Domeric lay? He was my husband since I was little more than girl, and is whom my heart grieves for most of all. Do ye ken?"

Gregor could only shake his head, but as he did so, Abernethy stepped within the chapel and strode to the widow's side to lay a consoling hand on her shoulder. "Daughter, I ken that this a difficult time for ye, especially now," he said softly, compassion earnest in his voice. "Under yer left hand lieth yer departed husband. Perhaps if ye would deem to pray with me for a time, even for the soul of Lord Domeric, it would grant ye a measure of peace as well as that of yer husband. Nae withstanding his crimes, ye should nae forget a prayer for Richard; that young man's soul must needs require all sacred helps it may in finding a measure of peace."

"Thank ye, Yer Grace, ye are quite correct," said Catherine, sniffing as she wiped tears from her cheeks and looking up at the gentle priest as fresh tears gleamed in her eyes. "I would very much appreciate yer prayers along with mine. It seems prayers and God are all I hae left."

"They are all anyone needs," he assured her.

"I see nay reason why we must remain much longer in this misbegotten place, Sean," intimated Gregor, walking through the courtyard with his nephew. "I would hae yer brother taken home where he may be put to rest. An eye must be kept on Devlin, lest he do something rash in his grief; wi' ye see to it?"

Sean nodded gravely. "Of course, Sire."

"Before we leave Inveraray I need time alone with my thoughts and perhaps to pray for wisdom," murmured the king. "If ye could hae a private chamber cleared while we await the appointed time for Colquhoun's execution, I would appreciate it."

"I wi' see to it, Sire," promised a subdued Sean.

"Thank ye. And, Sean? Hae word passed about to our officers, including the new officers sworn to me from Clan Campbell, that I wi' hae a briefing with them at dusk once our last piece of unpleasantness has been taken care of," ordered Gregor, absently rubbing at his forehead where the coronet sitting there was already giving him a raging headache. "We still hae some final points to go over before we take our leave of this place and depart tomorrow for Edinburgh. I must be certain that I do nae leave behind me any misunderstandings to plague us all later; I hae nay wish to be called back to this place if it can be avoided," he added grimly.

A short while later, while the king wandered through the ducal palace, Marishal MacSean found him sitting in one of the castle's gardens alone, but under the watchful gaze of two well-armed soldiers. Together they strode back within the keep and Sean led his weary uncle to the chambers he had arranged for him. The hallways were empty accept for royal troops tasked with patrolling them lest some rogue rebels rise up and seek to do harm to the king or his appointed officers.

Once Sean had gone the king removed his armor and weapons, laying them on a chair near at hand, and eased himself onto an identical chair with its thick cushions. Only then did Gregor allow his eyes to close, willing himself to relax for the first time in days, stretching his long legs out before him and crossing them at the ankle. Try as he might, even behind closed eyelids, the king's mind could not slow down and intruding thoughts of the immediate future and the impending execution came unbidden to him.

Soon, once all of our honoured dead are buried, including my poor and foully used Duncan, Gregor grieved privately, *I must begin to establish my rule and put this kingdom to rights. The citizens of Edinburgh wi' expect a triumphal entry into the city with my victorious army at my back and I must act the part, though my heart bears little but grief for what we hae all lost these past months.*

The official coronation must be performed before the existing Royal Council; the Throne of Scone must be brought to the capital before that may be done, of course. Only then wi' I truly be able to perhaps find the time to relax a little. Then I can set aside the mantle of commanding armies and become a proper king.

Meanwhile, as the king sat alone with his thoughts of the future, MacSean was about his uncle's business. He preferred to remain active and not allow his own thoughts linger on his slain brother, lest he give in to the sorrow he had tucked away deep within. Hailing several of his commanders and fellow noblemen, Sean informed them of the king's orders. On he went immediately after, seeking out any matter to attend to in the service of the king, finding some comfort in the knowledge that he served a noble master, a master that would soon be formally honoured as King of Scotland.

The final matter in which Sean dedicated himself to was insuring the prisoner held for the brutal murder of his brother was secure in his cell. Once he had looked in on the former bishop, MacSean posted two of his best men to remain with the jailor to see that Colquhoun would be delivered promptly on time for his execution. The Marishal knew that only when his brother's murderer was at last dispatched would he gain any measure of peace and closure in his heart.

The war between the Scots was over, but one final enemy was yet to die.

A little more than an hour before dusk, Sean watched with burning eyes as Henry Colquhoun gasped his last rattling breath and joined his infernal master in hell.

CHAPTER SIXTEEN

The journey to the ancient Scottish capital of Edinburgh for the royal army was an eager one tempered with sadness. An army marches only as swift as its slowest elements, and the victorious Highlanders were a weary lot following a long season of warfare. The better part of a fortnight passed from the time King Gregor led his army from Inveraray until they at last reached the sprawling streets of the city's Old Town. Looming above those busy streets sat proud Edinburgh Castle keeping solemn watch over its people from high above on its majestic and volcanic Castle Rock.

The king's spirits rose suddenly as his army reached the Royal Mile and began its presession through the heart of the capital. Mounted on a fine white charger, Gregor led his proud army up the avenue toward the castle and his waiting queen.

Citizens of the great city gathered in clamoring throngs along the wide avenue to cheer their new king and his triumphant army. Meanwhile, many others peered from windows and doorways, waving and shouting throughout the procession route as they waited to see the impressive martial force, and in hopes of catching a glimpse of King Gregor and his knightly lords and officers. And as the king led his army further into the Old Town, the gathered folk spied Gregor at the forefront of the proud column and took note of his regal bearing, nodding to themselves with approval.

Slowly at first but with growing momentum, a chant began to whisper through the crowds that swiftly spread until it rang above the loud clattering of the many steel-shod hooves striking the cobblestones of the mounted cavalry. Louder still the chant grew as a multitude of voices in resounding concert cheerfully cried out, *'Long live the King! Long live King Gregor! Long live King Gregor!'*

The first afternoon following Gregor's jubilantly cheered arrival into Edinburgh, he and his noble allies-notably those various clan chiefs and titled noblemen which had backed his fight for the throne-met in a council of state. Joining those men were a number of lowland lords whom belatedly had come to throw their support and endorsement behind The MacGregor. Between them, they had successfully established a new twelve member Royal Council, but although this process went smoothly enough on the surface, Gregor had been quick to discover that he still had a disquieting number of enemies among the gentry. Perhaps the most prominent among them was Francis, the succeeding Duke of Hamilton, brother of the slain Fergis, and his wife Marlena.

Immediately preparations began for the coronation of the new king. Although a royal coronation was nothing more than a formality to Gregor, he realized the people of Scotland needed that formality as a reassurance that peace was truly at hand. He desired to have the ceremony completed as soon as possible so that he and rest of Duncan's family could lay their loved one to his eternal rest. The crypt was already prepared; now the family just required the opportunity to say their last goodbye and time to mourn a beloved and fallen kinsman.

The honours of Scotland were polished and cleaned; those involved in the ceremony rehearsed their rolls in the event; and preparations were made for the day long trip to Scone Abbey with the Stone of Destiny and the royal entourage. Much of the planning had already been done before the king's arrival in Edinburgh and Gregor was pleased continue on to the ancient site so soon, knowing he would be reunited with his wife at Scone.

The morning dawned fair and bright on the appointed day of his coronation and Gregor sought to put aside all thoughts of contrary nobles as servants robed him for the ceremony to come. In the end the impatient king was properly dressed in all the regalia of his exalted office and already complaining about the bulk and heat of it all. Yet tetchy about the heavy and constrictive garb, Gregor was ushered to his appointed position inside the intimate abbey on Moot Hill.

Glancing aside at the sound of approaching footsteps, Gregor found his nephew coming to join him with an encouraging smile lighting upon his lips. In the crook of the Marishal's arm lay cradled the ceremonial sword of state, jewel encrusted hilt winking with enough precious stones that it could have purchased another kingdom.

Following his uncle's gaze, Sean grimaced. "It's a pretty enough sword to look upon, but utterly useless as a weapon."

Gregor chuckled. "Aye. Of course, I'm nae dressed for combat, as ye can see."

Behind the king's marishal followed the notable bishops: Abernethy and Fletcher, both men responsible for conducting the upcoming ceremony, the latter having just arrived the previous evening from Glenorchy along with Elizabeth to be on hand for the coronation. Both princes of the church nodded with polite respect and murmured their own encouragements to Gregor before continuing on their way to the front of the abbey and the dais erected there. Each of them paused to genuflect before the cross arranged behind the ancient Throne of Scone before moving to their positions for the ceremony. Although each of those church leaders were bedecked in attire as richly adorned as the king, they seemed much more at ease in the finery than did the monarch.

The time to begin the ritual came at last and the cue was given for the procession to start forward as a sweet-voiced choir of young boys and girls began singing from on high, along the balconies set along either side of the church nave. Moving at a slow, stately pace the entourage went forward, a deacon coming behind with a golden censer swaying back and forth, spreading its sweet odor of incense into the air as he followed up the central aisle toward the bishops atop the royal dais.

Then it was Gregor's turn to march down the aisle toward the waiting bishops; trailing immediately behind him and charged with carrying the hem of the white mink robe of state was the king's great-nephew, Barak. Two paces behind the royal page followed Marishal MacSean and the youthful looking Lord Kirkland, striding shoulder to shoulder. The former bore the gem-encrusted sword of state and the latter carried on his palms a gold velvet cushion which cradled the royal signet.

Ahead stood Bishop Abernethy, his face composed and serene, appearing as regal as Gregor himself while wearing the clerical finery of holy office. In robes of deep purple, a gem encrusted crosier cradled in the crook of his right arm, and a tall white miter trimmed with gold sat atop his erect head. To one side of his fellow bishop and slightly behind stood Bishop Fletcher as he held the formal Crown of Scotland in all its glittering magnifecence upon a polished golden charger. As Gregor drew near, Fletcher cast an encouraging little smile at the nervous man.

Piously crossing himself before the altar erected upon the dais, Gregor knelt and bowed his head while uttering a brief prayer, while the reminder of the royal entourage moved into their positions. At last the king opened his eyes and looked up to find the impressively vested bishops waiting patiently; ready to proceed, Gregor gave them a brief nod to indicate that he was prepared to continue.

Abernethy came forward and with a reassuring smile offered Gregor his hand to help him to his feet. Once the king was standing, the bishop turned him to face the mass of people packed within the abbey's nave to witness the coronation, and as he did so, he raised Gregor's right hand above his head.

"My lords and ladies, I present before ye the rightful King of Scotland," the bishop announced in a solemn and carrying declaration. "Do all that hae come here offer loyal service and homage to God's chosen sovereign of this kingdom?"

"God bless King Gregor!" cried their acknowledgement.

Gracing the enthusiastic spectators a solemn nod of his head in acceptance of their reply, Abernethy turned to Gregor and urged him to mount the steps up to the altar. From his place behind the altar the bishop, with identical gravity presented forth a large volume of the Holy Bible to Gregor; piously he bade the king lay his hand upon the sacred book before continuing on to quote the oath of coronation. As the bishop did so he spoke looud and firmly so all in attendence could hear.

"Lord Gregor Iain Malcolm MacGregor, are ye willing, before God and all these witnesses, to accept the binding oath of coronation?"

"Aye; I am sae willing," agreed Gregor.

"Sae mote it be," intoned the presiding bishop.

"Lord Gregor, ye cometh here before Almighty God and all these witnesses as the designated heir, and are therefore sae confirmed as the rightful and legal heir of our late, beloved King William and his only son, the late Crown Prince David, of the House of Stewart. In accordance with the temporal authority given the sovereign of the Kingdom of Scotland, do ye solemnly swear to keep the peace between the citizens of Scotland; to govern yer people according to our ancient laws and customs; and to remain, in all yer dealings, a true and honest servant who is faithful to God?"

"I do solemnly swear all these things," he replied.

Abernethy nodded gravely in approval. "Furthermore, wi' ye to the utmost of yer ability and power cause our laws and justice, both high and low, to be kept faithfully while tempered with mercy in all of yer judgments, my Lord?"

"I pledge to do sae."

"And wi' ye also pledge before God and these witnesses gathered here that all forms of evil which may arise, including the wickedness in all forms of the worship of Satan and his demons, shall be subdued and condemned according to the laws of God, while supporting and asserting the Almighty's commandments?" Abernethy demanded, fierce-eyed and with a voice filled with ecclesiastical authority.

"I solemnly pledge to do sae according to the wisdom in which God has blessed me with," declared Gregor with total honesty.

A tiny frown creased the bishop's brow and then with a flourish he presented a scroll. Unrolling the parchment he laid it on the altar before the kneeling Gregor and offered the man a quill pen and opened bottle of ink. As the uncrowned king accepted the pen with a grateful nod, Gregor carefully scrawled his new signature with a shaking hand, *Gregorus Rex*; and then lifting the sheet up for all to witness he replaced his hand upon the Holy Bible offered by the officiating bishop.

"All things to which I hae sworn wi' I perform and uphold all the remaining days of my life, sae help me God!" Gregor firmly declared.

Abernethy allowed a small smile to grace his lips and while the witnessed looked on he took up a vial of consecrated oil and annointed Gregor's proud head. When the ritual was completed the youth choir in the galleries broke forth in joyous song.

Finally allowed to regain his feet, Gregor controlled his impatience as best he could and allowed deacons to come forward and fasten the scarlet and gold robe of state above the snow white one he already wore about his shoulders, and to buckle about his waist the ceremonial sword belt of scarlet-dyed leather. Following those things, a triple stranded torque of gold, silver, and bronze was settled around his neck as a token of his roll as overlord of all the clans of Scotland.

A muted clash of what sounded to Gregor like steel ringing on steel could be heard outside and somewhere beyond the closed wooden doors of Scone Abbey. Casting a questioning glance at Bishop Abernethy the king felt a queasyness grip his vitals, but the bishop merely raised his eyebrows in confusion and bade Kirkland forward with the royal signet. Taking the ring in his hand, Abernethy uttered a brief prayer over the large ring before holding it up to slip upon Gregor's right hand.

The royal signet on the king's finger, Abernethy motioned for MacSean to bring forward the ornate sword of state and waited patiently while the MacGregor Warlord stepped to his side with a concerned frown lowering his eyebrows. The warrior carefully placed the ornamental sword across the serene bishop's outstretched hands. Another short prayer was spoken over the sword and then Abernethy laid the additional token of office across Gregor's raised palms with a formal bow.

The sword in hand, Gregor responded with a slight nod of thanks before raising the blade to his lips and kissing the shining steel. As he slid the long blade into the tooled scabbard hanging at his side the sounds of disruption could be heard more clearly now. The king shot his nephew a worried glance as he gripped the hilt of the jeweled sword and mentally prepared himself for what might come.

It was clear that fighting was taking place outside the entrance to the abbey as the martial noises continued to increase in intensity and grow more pronounced. MacSean no longer pretended to hide the scowl from his face as he loosened his ever-present sword within its scabbard and stod poised to defend his king.

In a display of remarkable determination, Bishop Abernethy continued with the ceremony and bestowed on Gregor the golden, jewel-adorned scepter of Scotland, when suddenly the doors at the entrance to the abbey burst open sharply. Cries of consternation broke from among the congregation as armed men charged into the church yelling in exaltation with waving swords and axes.

As MacSean turned to face the sounds of chaos coming from the entrance at the rear of the abbey and his fingers tightened on the hilt of his sword as he saw the armed men and who led them intrude onto holy ground. Astounded surprise widened his cold blue eyes and he cursed softly to himself. *This can nae be; I watched him die!*

Gregor could hear the heavy tread of booted footsteps coming down the aisle-way, but forced himself to not turn and look, though he was fully aware that some determined adversary approached and had come with enough men at his command to defeat the company of royal guardsmen ordered to ward the abbey. The bishop standing before him had paled and seemed on the verge of being sick and his hands shook with fear.

Uncertainty gripped at the king's vitals and he cast another glance over at Sean and noticed not fear but hate burning in his eyes; the Marishal's hand was instinctively gripping the familiar hilt of his favorite sword, but his knuckles had turned white with tension as the tendons stood out on his hand. Sean gave no notice of the king's attention as his eyes remained riveted to the interloper and clenched his jaws with such ferocity that the muscles in his cheeks twitched.

Returning his attention to the distressed bishop presiding before him, Gregor caught his eye and nodded for him to continue with the ceremony.

With eyes wide with alarm, Abernethy turned to lift the formal crown from the cushion silently offered by his fellow bishop. As he again faced the king who knelt before him he held the crown at his breast and bowed his head to gather his thoughts and utter a silent and fervent prayer over it.

"Halt!" bellowed a deep, gravelly voice with a note of command.

Abernethy jerked his head up suddenly as if he had been slapped and glared out at the intruder. "Who *dares* break into this house of God with weapons of war to intrude on such a solemn ceremony?"

His building fury, mingled with more than a fair measure of wonder, caused Sean to miss the bishop's outraged demand and any reply that might have been given. All was made silent by his own anger consumed thoughts as he continued to glare at the face of the all too familiar intruder. *By the Morrigan! I saw this vile wretch die! How can he be here to plague us yet when, with my own eyes, I watched as he was castrated and hung from a cross? I saw his belly slashed open and his guts drawn; I smelled the stench of his of his innards roasted over a brazier as he shrieked in agony!* thought Sean, trying to reassure himself with the memories still fresh in his mind. *I did nae look away as that filth of a man died on a cross and had his body quartered and burned to ashes. His skinny bald head I posted on a pike with my own hands! Is Satan sae taken with the vile creature that he would return his shade to haunt us all like some foul ghoul to strut even into such a holy place and try to prevent Gregor's coronation?*

Interrupting Sean's bewildered thoughts and startling Gregor as well, causing the king to flinch despite himself, a ringing clash of steel striking stone rang throughout the hushed abbey. The king forced composure onto his features before he rose and turned to face the brazen challenger. Stony dignity covered the anxiety he felt like a mask, covering all the emotions awash within him, as Gregor glanced down to see a mail gauntlet laying near the base of the steps leading to the altar. It was, of course, the formal token of an offered challenge; curiosity suddenly brimmed within him as he raised questing eyes to meet those of his unexpected antagonist.

What he saw was the face of a man he had never expected to see again. That hawkish face, thin to the point of gauntness, with its large slender beak of a nose ranging below frigid blue eyes, and all topped by an untidy mop of iron gray hair. Situated on the man's face was the same familiar and hateful smile; a smile it was that did not reach those eyes, but full of unmitigated contempt and malice. Shocked beyond words, Gregor allowed his gaze to travel past the man to take in the two score highland warriors clad in their clan's tartan and armored in mail with bared weapons in hand. His mind raced as he tried to compose himself, *How is this possible?*

The man chuckled dryly, though there was no hint of humor in the sound. "I see that my appearance has taken ye by surprise, MacGregor. How could I possibly be here after ye murdered me—that must be the question ye are asking yerself; aye?"

He drew the sword from its scabbard as the king descended from the platform and bent down to pick up the thrown gauntlet. "I assure ye that I am nae a ghost; Henry and I were born twins, of course. It's strange, but I swear that I could feel the moment of my brother's death," he stated amiably.

"Ye must ken the reason for my uninvited presence," he said with a sneer of hate. When he continued, Colquhoun raised his voice so that it carried easily throughout the entire abbey so all there could hear. "I am Lord Robert Colquhoun and I hae come at this time, in this place, to avenge my dear brother whom ye had executed. Furthermore, on behalf of Clan Campbell, I call ye out Gregor MacGregor and challenge yer right to the kingship of Scotland; I find ye entirely unworthy to be our king!"

"As I must assume ye consider yerself a man of honour but somehow ignorant of church law, Lord Robert, I find myself compelled to inform ye that the church frowns most severely upon armed parties of warriors barging into the house of God," responded Gregor through clenched teeth.

Colquhoun snorted. "Be that as it may, MacGregor, I wi' nae leave this place until my challenge has been accepted. Ye hae taken up my gauntlet now give me satisfaction," the man growled deep in his throat. "It is yer death that I hae come for. Nothing less than my sword in yer guts is acceptable!"

"Very well. I had hoped for the bloodshed to be at an end, but I see that more must be shed," agreed Gregor, making up his mind. "As the anointed King of Scotland, We accept yer challenge. Under the ancient laws of personal challenge Our champion wi' do battle with yers at whatever time and place that is acceptable to ye while the choice of weapons is mine. Do ye honour these terms?" he asked, knowing he would not and that Sean would be his own choice of champion, and furthermore that his nephew could easily dispatch any opponent in a fair fight and most others in an unfair contest.

The vengeful Colquhoun's avian-like visage twisted into a scowl of rage but then smoothed as he reluctantly nodded. "Very well, MacGregor; squirm if ye must, but ye merely delay our own combat for a time. I wi' continue to call ye out for single combat until ye agree to meet me yerself, *Yer Majesty*," he hissed sarcastically.

"That shall nae happen as long as Our champion stands!" countered Gregor.

"Hae it yer way, MacGregor, but ye just put off the inevitable. *My* champion wi' meet yers here and now," he said contemptuously. He gestured toward his left at a mighty and thickly muscled warrior to step forward. A sinister smile played about the warrior's fleshy lips, his hand hovering near the hilt of his long sword as he glided with surprising grace up to his master's side.

Steel rasped slickly from the well-oiled scabbard hanging at the warrior's side as he drew the heavy blade; still smiling he sketched a disdainful bow to the king. "So, now," he spoke for the first time, his voice thick with an accent Gregor did not recognize, as he gestured menacingly with his sword, "will your champion come forth to do battle? Or must I be denied the satisfaction of honor by coming upon a coward and slaying him where he cowers?" he inquired with an air of cool arrogance.

MacSean quietly descended from his position upon the dais steps with a calm grace, the measured gait of some great hunting cat, drawing his sword as he came. "Perhaps ye should save yer arrogance until ye hae proved yerself against my Scottish steel, foreigner. Nay man, much less some dirty Spaniard, has yet defeated me in combat, duel or otherwise," growled the Sidhe lord. Upon reaching the base of the dais steps he accepted the gauntlet from Gregor on the tip of his blade and flipped it carelessly back at Colquhoun. In a loud clash of its steel links the armored glove fell before the offending lord and skidded to a halt at his feet.

"In the name of Lord Gregor MacGregor, King of Scotland, I gladly accept yer challenge of single combat!" stated MacSean as he stepped forward.

"You are overconfident, Sir Knight," the mercenary countered coolly, gliding toward his opponent and smoothly moving into a fighting stance with the casual grace of an experienced fighter. "I can change that."

Anticipating the coming combat, the retainers of Lord Colquhoun edged back into a loose circle to give the men room to maneuver while the two combatants closed. They circled one another, studying and probing for weaknesses, as the distance closed between them. Meanwhile, Gregor retreated from his position and moved off to one side as the chosen champions squared off.

"My name is Pablo Garza de la Manuel," the Spaniard volunteered, carefully sizing up MacSean, the tip of his blade moving in lazy figure eights before him. "I would not want ye to die by my hand not knowing the name of your killer."

Sean subdued a smirk and politely bowed his head at the warrior before him. "That is most gracious of ye, O Mercenary. I am Sean MacSean, Warlord of Clan Gregor and Marishal of Scotland."

Sean continued to keenly study his adversary, watching every little movement of the Spaniard's sword and noted with professional appreciation the man's stance and economical use of footwork. The foreigner moved with a smooth and effortless gait, as if stepping to some music-less, precise dance. Instantly Sean was on his guard as he realized the brawny warrior squaring off before him was no typical sell sword.

The Scottish Marishal had no more reservations about this combat than he had had about any of a hundred prior contests he had fought in his career; he was a seasoned veteran of many battles, a swordmaster, and more skilled than any man he had crossed swords with and he knew it. In all honesty, he had never lost a duel since his early training as a squire and he had no intention of allowing that streak to be broken, especially when his uncle depended on him. However, he recognized a gifted opponent and was justifiably wary and on his guard against this mercenary's unknown skill with a blade, despite the quiet confidence he felt of another triumph.

Those in attendance within the abbey watched in rapt silence as the two warriors circled each other with wary caution, probing steel flicking out to be countered by the opposing weapon. In an explosive burst of motion, Pablo attacked with a vicious lunge as he sought to surprise his adversary by striking swiftly to pierce MacSean's defenses, but the wily Warlord was not fooled by so common a tactic. He nimbly parried aside the darting blade and struck back with a ferocious riposte that forced the bigger warrior to retreat a few steps. Instead of forcing the attack, MacSean smoothly withdrew as well, as he realized this victory would be no easy feat. The Spaniard gave MacSean a slight nod before springing forward, his blade moving like an extension of his arm as he pressed a withering assault on his opponent.

Biding his time, MacSean continued to study the brawny warrior, shifting with deadly elegance into a defensive style of fencing that allowed him to conserve his energy as the attacker spent his on seeking to penetrate a singing steel barrier the Marishal wove about himself. He gave ground before the bigger man a step at a time, but easily deflected each of Pablo's new and more elaborate attacks with the shining net of steel he spun in the air before him. The Marishal restrained himself from going on the offense, content to watch and learn the mercenary's fighting style and habits.

Sean did not know how long the contest had been going on, but at last he saw the opening he had been waiting for and in a flash changed his stance to catch the opposing warrior momentarily off-balance. Darting in on the Spaniard with deceptive speed he attacked and deftly brought to bear a unique technique which he had been saving for just such an occasion. His keen blade slashed through the mercenary's oil darkened jerkin and skittered across the mail shirt lying beneath until the sharpened tip found flesh, digging a shallow furrow across one vulnerable shoulder. Uttering a surprised grunt, the wounded warrior stumbled back in more shock than pain, clasping a hand briefly to his bleeding shoulder before raising the blood covered fingers up to glare at.

The mercenary's swarthy face flushed furiously at the sight of his own blood, despite the slightness of the shallow wound, instantly loosing the calm coolness which had marked his earlier demeanor. Pablo was proud to the point of arrogance about his skill with a blade and was well aware that he was an excellent swordsman. He had never dreamed he might meet his match, let alone bargained for taking any sort of wound; it was something that had *never* happened before. He did not like it one little bit!

Pablo fixed his dark eyes, filled with a new-born hatred, at the Highlander and charged back into the melee with a vengeance, flinging himself headlong at his foe. No longer did he fight with cool detachment, but instead attacking with more raw emotion than good sense. It was just what MacSean had been hoping for.

Soon a growing frustration began to take hold over the Spaniard with his cunning opponent's maddening ability to withstand every attack he threw at him. Pablo began to take more risks in order to catch the Highlander off-guard, while at the same time opening himself up for counterattacks. The latest such risky assault, MacSean ducked under a heavy back-handed riposte, and the Spaniard knew immediately that he had left himself out of position to properly defend his flank from attack.

Noting that the mercenary was over-extended, MacSean struck without hesitation in a blinding flash of steel. And although Pablo desperately parried the Marishal's initial blow, the viper swift riposte that followed penetrated his defense on the left and Sean's razor-sharp blade sank deeply into his upper flank. The claymore pierced through both protective armor and yielding flesh beneath like warm butter.

The heavy broadsword sagged in Pablo's suddenly nerveless fingers and the blood drained from his bewildered face. Silently, MacSean withdrew his dripping blade and stepped back a pace watching as blood streamed from the mortal wound he had inflicted. The Spaniard staggered drunkenly on his feet for a few seconds and fear at last took the place of bewilderment in his dark and already glazing eyes. A moment later he groaned wordlessly and collapsed bonelessly to the tile floor, his forgotten sword clattering to the floor with him. Bright blood bubbled like scarlet foam from his mouth and red droplets flecked his lips as he coughed weakly. A heartbeat later the dark brown eyes of the fallen warrior glazed over completely in a dead man's blind stare.

No emotion showed in MacSean's calm face, and although he felt no regret for killing the sword-for-hire, he did respect his foe's skill with a sword. Nonchalantly he bent over the dead warrior and wiped his blade free of blood on the man's tunic before straightening again to turn and fix Colquhoun with a cold stare. He stalked calmly across the floor heading toward his and the king's new-found, but familiar enemy, contempt flashing in his cold blue eyes. Still clutching his trusty claymore in one fist, MacSean advanced on the suddenly wary Colquhoun, prepared to make a bloody end of that man's bid to derail Gregor's coronation once and for all.

Lord Robert, the twin brother of the defrocked and executed Henry Colquhoun, retreated behind his retainers and ground his teeth in agitation at MacSean's approach. He had hired the big Spaniard at a heavy price from the King of Spain, and now Robert had been forced to watch in humiliation as his vaunted champion was laid low before his eyes. It had been a short albeit intense fight, but to Colquhoun's eyes his champion was defeated with what seemed relative ease by a man his brother had hated passionately.

"Do ye now yield, Colquhoun, to the king's champion?" MacSean demanded, leveling the tip of his sword toward the interloper.

Pointedly forcing himself to ignore the waiting Marishal, Robert slowly turned his head away to fix a glare at the king. "MacGregor, yer pup has bested my champion but my challenge yet stands. I call on ye to accept that challenge and face me personally in single combat," he called out in a grating tone. "I swear by all that is holy that I wi' send one man after another to face off against yer champion until ye do agree to meet me and put yerself to the hazard, instead of hiding behind the mighty sword of this creature. Come and prove yer own honour if ye would be king. Come and let us finish this now," he added, a note of hope in his words.

Gregor glared back at his antagonist and then nodded his head. "Hae it yer way, Robert. A second Colquhoun lord dead begins to appeal to me. Very well, I wi' fight ye just to be rid of yer wagging tongue," growled the king with impatience. "Yer hateful countenance is one I had trusted never to behold again and I would rid myself and my family of it forevermore."

A look of concern was betrayed in MacSean's eyes as he glanced away from the treasonous lord and looked askance at his uncle. "Sire, please, ye do nae hae to do this. Let me fight him," he advised, jabbing the point of his sword toward Robert. "Ye should nae risk yerself now that the throne is finally yers. I wi' gratefully fight as yer champion against any who might stand against ye. I assure ye that I wi' make short work of this foul troublemaker and any ruffian he may send."

Gregor shook his head and offered his stalwart nephew a grim smile as he strode forward to confront his adversary. "Nae this time, Sean; the pleasure shall be all mine, although I would request the use of yer sword." He halted his advance several paces from Colquhoun and slowly looked the man up and down, as if he were a man inspecting the condition of an animal before deciding to purchase it. Gregor did, however, stop short of seeking to physically check the lord's teeth. At last, with a nod for his clan's warlord to back away, Gregor accepted the proffered sword. The weapon in hand he grinned at the superb balance, and then bowed slightly over it at his foe.

"Here I am, sir, just as ye desired," rasped Gregor. "On guard!"

"Well met, MacGregor," remarked Robert, a smile coming to his face as the long blade of his sword hissed free of its scabbard.

Cautiously they began circling each other, evaluating the skill and swiftness of their opponent. Neither was a young man, both middle aged, but like the quick strike of an adder the two warriors leaped simultaneously into action. The shrill ring of their blades rang and echoed in the hushed abbey while the onlookers held their collective breath and wondered what the outcome would be.

Lord Robert appeared an exact duplicate of his dead twin brother, but he fought with a skill no priest could hope to match as he battled furiously to breach the formidable defense the king wove about himself. To Gregor, the likeness was uncanny and he found it difficult to believe he fought anyone other than Henry Colquhoun. The face of the Colquhoun chief was flushed bright red with the veins standing out tautly in his forehead as he assaulted the king's shield of weaving steel. With a stubbornness born of hate he charged headlong on the attack, intent on wearing down Gregor's stout defense to quickly cut down his foe before his own stamina began to wane.

Round and round the two battled, trading blows that were parried with grunts of effort as they sought the blood of the other. The king and his challenger appeared to all present as so equally matched that neither man could gain an advantage and for long moments they fought to a standstill. Becoming weary from the prolonged duel, Gregor's guard drooped slightly and Colquhoun was swift to strike a blow that the king was just barely able to knock aside. The challenger followed up on his sudden advantage to rain a series of ringing blows against the king's guard but failed to score a hit. Growling with the strain of his assault he charged in with a heavy-handed swing intended to remove the king's head in one vicious chop.

From where he tensely watched the fight, MacSean blanched as he took note of his uncle's sagging defense, unaware that the move was a daring stratagem by the king to entice the sort of attack which his foe had unleashed. He involuntarily gasped as he saw Colquhoun dart forward with a bestial snarl to close in for the kill.

The blow leveled at the king was a powerful one; tendons stood out on the ropey arms of Colquhoun as his lips drew back from his teeth in a rictus of effort as he swung a killing strike down at Gregor's neck. An instant before the cleaving stroke could land the king pivoted to the side and deflected the blade away. Sensing his foe off-balance Gregor answered with a swift riposte before the man could recover. The point of his sword darted toward his challenger's chest, yet somehow Colquhoun avoided the impaling lunge by desperately twisting his body away. The sharp point of the claymore missed its intended target and only succeeded in slicing through his doublet sleeve and piercing the mail shirt lying beneath. The deep gash, although not a critical wound, pumped forth bright blood that rapidly stained Colquhoun's sleeve clear to the wrist as he cried out in pain.

Backing quickly away, Robert clutched at the wounded limb protectively with his opposite hand and glared balefully at the king while vigorously cursing the man and his lineage in general as he did so.

As he cautiously remained on his guard, Gregor lowered the bloody point of his blade slightly and demanded, "Yield to me Robert Colquhoun-"

The king was unable to finish his demand before the enraged lord suddenly lunged at him with a vicious snarl—a move calculated to catch him by surprise. "Never!" he screamed. "I wi' never surrender to ye; now die ye upstart bastard!"

Desperately, Gregor parried aside the lethal strike and the heavy two-handed blows that followed after it which rained down upon him like hammer strikes on an anvil by his infuriated enemy. His sudden desperation lent the king an untapped reserve of energy to meet the foe head on and adroitly confounded the frenzied assault.

Following another wild flurry of powerful sword strikes, their blades ringing with the sharp impacts, Colquhoun began to visibly tire from his exertions as well as from the loss of blood continuing to stream from his arm. He leveled another vicious slash that whistled through the air as the king ducked under it, but he proved too slow in recovering and Gregor, seeing an opening at last, pounced. Darting inside the lord's guard, with a move seemingly too nimble for a man of his age, the king extended his blade and lunged with all his might! In less than the space of a heartbeat the broad bladed claymore pierced smoothly through the breast of Colquhoun's doublet and on through the mail armor to sink deeply into the left side of his chest. The cold steel cleaved Lord Robert's heart in twain and the bloody point exited his back by several inches, tenting out the mail from the rear of his body. Gregor growled suddenly and using both hands savagely twisted the blade in his stricken challenger's breast.

Amazement bloomed clearly on Colquhoun's hawkish face as he stared at the sword buried deep through his body. Weakly he clutched at the hilt and pushed himself off Gregor's blood slickened blade inch by painful inch as his blood flowed from the mortal wound. Free of the killing yard of steel his heart's blood pumped scarlet in great spurts that stained the king's finery. The dying man gaped in horror as he helplessly watched his life's blood pump out of his chest in time with his weakening heartbeat and quickly grow into a red pool at his feet. Opening his mouth in a silent cry, Lord Robert tottered on powerless legs and slowly slumped to his knees. He stared up at his killer and tried to speak, but then his eyes rolled up into his head and he pitched face forward into the pool of his own cooling blood. He was dead before he ever hit the floor.

The sound of Colquhoun's lifeless body smacking into the unyielding and wet tile was enough to cause many present to cringe, and more than one lady to faint. The holy ground of the ancient abbey, moments before so pristine and unspoiled, had in moments been sullied and turned into a killing ground.

King Gregor stood looking down with distaste at the dead man laying at his feet, feeling somewhat dazed from his hard won victory. A long moment passed before he recognized the shouts ringing through the confines of the old abbey. The cries he heard were those of acclaim, which arose from the numerous lords and ladies gathered within and had been forced to stand aside to watch and hope for their anointed king.

Moving wordlessly to his uncle's side, Sean nodded respectfully and accepted the bloodied sword the king passed to him, and stooped to carefully wipe the blade clean on Colquhoun's rent doublet. As he did so he kept a gimlet-eyed stare fixed on the dead lord's henchmen lest they do something foolish.

As he followed the direction of MacSean's gaze, Gregor seemed to suddenly shake himself from the haze of battle, and shouted, "Guards! Attend yer king! I want this dirty Colquhoun carcass immediately removed from this kirk. And see that the head is added to that of its twin, on a spike, above the gates of Edinburgh," he commanded. He fixed a hard glare at the milling mass of Colquhoun retainers and stabbed an accusing finger at them. "These armed intruders hae burst into this holy place with their laird intent on spilling the blood of their rightful king. Disarm them and take the lot of them away to a suitable dungeon until they may be tried for their treason."

Later in the afternoon, there remained no trace of Robert Colquhoun's corpse, nor any of the blood he had so copiously bled all over the abbey floor. The retainers that had appeared with that fallen chief had been rounded up and were on their way to Edinburgh, where they were to be given accommodations deep within the bowels of that mighty fortress. A little more than two hours had passed since the interruption of the coronation ceremony and now the court officials were prepared to resume the ritual. The floors had been laboriously scrubbed clean of blood and gore; incense wafted throughout the abbey, chasing away the stink of death; and those in attendance were once again seated along the hard wooden pews, eager to see their king properly installed on the Throne of Scone. All there prayed that this time no untimely incident would take place to cause any further disruption to the occasion.

A light tap on the shoulder brought Gregor out of his tense reverie and he glanced over that shoulder to see Sean calmly awaiting him.

"Uncle, I believe ye hae a coronation to complete," he remarked lightly, an easy smile softening his stern features. "The bishops and the court await yer convenience; let's just hope nay more of bloody Henry's relatives make an appearance, uh?"

Gregor grunted in agreement. He turned stiffly and marched with a resolute air back to his appointed place upon the dais.

Before the altar he crossed himself and nodded to the bishops that he was ready to continue. Those gathered in the congregation cheered as the king knelt and MacSean moved behind him to drape the royal mantle over his broad shoulders. For the sake of the ceremony, Gregor once again sank to his knees down on the steps before the altar and humbled himself in pious submission before God.

Before the kneeling king, Bishop Abernethy took his place at the altar and gave Gregor his personal blessing, resting a hand upon the royal head. That done, he motioned forward his fellow bishop bearing the jeweled crown of state. Solemnly, Bishop Fletcher came forth and lifted the heavy crown from its bed of velvet, chanting along with his church brother the ancient formula of king making.

"O Thou most mighty King of Kings and Highest of Lords, we humbly beseech Ye to grant Your holy blessing upon this earthly crown," the bishops cried as Fletcher lifted and held the splendid crown aloft above his head. "O Holy Lord of Heaven, may Ye consecrate Your servant, Gregor, upon whose head this crown may rest. Strengthen him, guide him with Your perfect wisdom, and grant him, by Your infinite Grace, every holy and proper virtue sae that he may be an example to all his people. In the name of the Holy Trinity, whom reigns forever and ever as our Almighty King, Amen."

With slow dignity Bishop Fletcher lowered the blessed crown down onto Gregor's head, and smiling added one further blessing, "Long life and prosperity to thee and thy entire house, King Gregor of Scotland!"

The heavy state crown at last resting on his brow, King Gregor was helped to his feet and then formally vested with the remaining articles of regal insignia to his new office. Once the investiture was complete the proud king did not even try to hide his sudden smile as a sea of expectant faces regarded him as he turned to look out upon them. At long last the throne was his and the Scottish people *his* people.

During the last of Gregor's investiture the rough hollow wooden chair, holding the ancient Stone of Destiny within for its seat, was carried forward and placed near the edge of the shallow dais leading up to the altar. As the congregation's acclaim for their king quieted, Abernethy offered Gregor his hand and slowly escorted him to stand before the greatest of all Scottish treasures.

Reverently, the king reached out a hand and brushed his fingers across the solid surface of the oblong block of red sandstone, the hairs rising on his arms. He looked out at the expectant faces watching and proclaimed, "It is nae lightly that I would sit upon the *Lia Fail*. This unassuming stone *is* Scotland, and he shall sit upon it has the grave duty of protecting and preserving this land above any other obligation." That being said, Gregor slowly lowered himself upon the stone. All the attendance jumped up and cried out in a loud unified voice which rang joyously throughout the abbey.

The jeweled sword of state resting across his knees, Gregor sat stiffly erect on the rustic throne before the eyes of scores of Scotland's lords and ladies, however his own emerald gaze was fixed adoringly upon one particular lady who approached. She walked down the center aisle toward the dais in stately fashion, the glistening in her eyes making the crystalline azure of their hue sparkle brightly. She wore a richly brocaded gown of palest blue and her long thick mane of chestnut tresses was braided and looped on either side of her erect head. Bound about the lady's elegantly coiffured hair, in the place of a tiara, was a simple band of woven heather and other Highland wildflowers. She was the most beautiful woman Gregor had ever laid eyes on, and Gregor smiled warmly as she drew near, his eyes full of the love he held for her.

The lady reached the base of the shallow dais and gracefully knelt with both knees resting on the scarlet runner before the throne. She lifted up her radiant face to smile at Gregor, and said, "Yer Majesty, as is my right, I come before all others to offer my pledge of loyalty and homage to my king."

Rising smoothly from his regal seat, King Gregor descended the three shallow steps to stand before the kneeling lady, motioning at the same time for Bishop Fletcher to attend him as formerly arranged.

His attention returning to the lady bowed before him, Gregor thought, *It has been tae long since I hae gazed into her beautiful face.* He smiled affectionately at Elizabeth as he gently took her hands between his own and accepted her heartfelt oath of fealty. His adoring eyes did not stray from his wife's as he took from Fletcher's hands a smaller and more delicate jeweled crown. Gregor lifted exquisite crown up above the lady's head for the entire congregation to clearly view.

"This is the crown which We would place upon the most faithful head of Our Lady Wife, that she might be queen to stand at Our side," he stated resolutely to all the nobility filling the abbey. Gregor returned his gaze to his lady's comely face, Elizabeth's shining azure eyes so like a cloudless sky were wide and full of her love as she smiled up at him, and he forced himself not to wink at her. "Elizabeth Maeve Stewart MacGregor," said the king, slowly lowering the crown toward her fair brow, "with this blessed crown, We, Gregor I of Scotland, do signify and confirm ye as Our Queen of Scotland, that ye may rule at Our side as long as We may live."

The graceful crown touched the lady's head and Fletcher moved quickly to help affix it securely in place. Satisfied with it at last, the bishop smiled at the king and his queen before gliding smoothly back to his original position.

Taking Elizabeth's hands in his own, Gregor carefully helped his wife to stand and, although not according to protocol, impulsively hugged her to him in a rare show of public affection. Motioning that a seat should be brought forward and placed beside the Throne of Scone, the king for it to be in place before he escorted his queen forward and helped to her sit. Only then did Gregor resume his own seat and signal to the royal chamberlain that a line should be formed of those who would next offer their pledge to him according to their rank and title.

The next to come forward offering the solemn pledge of homage was Grigor, the king's only son and heir apparent.

Immediately following the prince were the gathered ranking clergy, bishops and archbishops, considered as princes of the church.

Once the bishops of the realm had offered their fealty to the king and queen, the gathered peers of Scotland came forward one at a time in their turn. As close kin, Sean MacSean stepped before the enthroned king and sank to his knees with cat-like grace as his uncle regarded him with a frank gaze. Placing his calloused hands between those of the king, Sean lifted up his voice so that it rang out strong and sure throughout the hushed abbey, where most nobles remained unsure and anxious about the Marishal's official position and status within the new order.

"Yer Royal Majesty, I, Sean MacSean, do willingly offer solemn pledge to ever be yer loyal servant as long as I may live with both limb and heart. It is with all good faith and truth that I humbly wi' serve ye in honour, to live or die against all manner of persons which may defy yer rule. This I swear, sae help me God!"

The king nodded in acknowledgement, retaining his nephew's hands between his own. Clearing his throat, Gregor spoke, "Lord Sean, We accept yer pledge and wi' hold ye to it by means of further obligation. We are pleased at this time to bestow upon yer head further responsibilities, should ye be willing. Is it yer wish to accept from Our hand those duties We would place upon ye?"

"It would be my honour to do sae, Yer Majesty."

The king allowed a small grin to touch his lips that only Sean could see. "Sean MacSean, in token of the regard I place on yer long and unswervingly loyal service and for the renowned prowess of yer exploits at arms, We proudly name ye Our champion! Furthermore, We also would be pleased to hae under yer firm leadership the Duchy of Strathclyde, while continuing to be Marishal-General of the armies of Scotland," Gregor declared, scarcely able to conceal a wider smile as he noted Sean's astounded expression. "In token of yer acceptance of these charges, place yer kiss of peace upon the blade of Our sword, my lord duke," commanded Gregor as he went on, extending the sword of state under its shining blade rested on his nephew's shoulder.

Once the king's newly appointed marishal had formally pressed his lips to the blade as directed, Gregor nodded with satisfaction. "Arise, Sean, and ken that We are well-pleased with ye, my valiant champion and Duke of Strathclyde!"

As he rose to his feet, MacSean smiled hesitantly as he opened his arms to receive the royal embrace from his uncle, the king. And then his turn before Gregor was finished; gracefully, the once Warlord of Clan Gregor, stepped aside to take his place a pace to the right and slightly to the rear of the man he was sworn to protect. Already the recently crowned monarch was motioning for his chamberlain to send forward the next nobleman to come before him and swear homage.

He who followed immediately after the King's Marishal was Donald MacDonald, lifelong friend and ally of Gregor. The burly warrior marched proudly to the edge of the dais and knelt with a wide smile splitting his grizzly bearded face. He reached out and placed his broad hands between those of the king and promptly gave his oath.

"I, Donald MacDonald, Chief of Clan Donald and Lord of the Isles, do solemnly pledge to be yer liegeman. I offer to Yer Majesty both life and limb and heart in loyal service; in good faith and truth, I furthermore swear to follow and keep yer rule of law throughout all lands under my stewardship and uphold the king's justice against all yer enemies, both foreign and domestic. All this I swear, sae help me God!"

Unable to resist smiling at his enthusiastic friend, Gregor chuckled softly and gave a nod of acceptance. "We acknowledge yer pledge, Lord Donald. Long hae ye been Our most staunch friend and supporter, and that shall never be forgotten. In regards to that, We are moved to honour such loyalty with new responsibilities at this time. My lord, are ye willing to serve yer king and Scotland in a broader role?"

"Of course, Yer Majesty."

This particular promotion pleased the king most of all. Not only had the massive warrior battled long against the large Campbell clan's incessant aggression against her neighbors on his own and alongside Gregor and his clan. It was well known at this time that the late Domeric Campbell had by no means limited his vengeful plots and general ill will to just the MacGregors. The hate he bore had extended toward the MacDonalds as well, a people he had also long hated and despised for reasons known only to himself. And although he reserved his hate for those two clans, Domeric had ever been more than willing to use whatever means necessary against his neighboring clans to sate his thirst for power and an overwhelming ambition to expand his territories.

"Very well. Lord Donald, it is Our pleasure to bestow upon ye a Crown property recently returned to Our safe keeping. It has need of a just and lord and We can think of nay one more qualified than ye. Therefore," Gregor went on, extending his sword to touch upon the warrior's head, "We confer upon ye the title of Duke of Argyll and all the lands and duties pertaining thereto." The king allowed himself another smile as shock shone in his friend's wide eyed stare.

"We remember, all tae well, yer unswerving friendship, especially when it was depended on most in these most recent trying times of the clans conflict," stated Gregor. "We believe ye hae justly earned this lofty title formerly held by the late and rebellious Domeric Campbell. Aye, and also, Our steadfast Lord of the Isles, We furthermore do bestow unto thee the rank of Sealord. This is a new creation which shall from henceforth be granted to Scotland's highest ranking admiral; equal in rank to Marishal, ye shall sail and command the surrounding seas against all Our enemies from wherever port they may seek to assail Our beloved Scotland.

"In token of yer acceptance to serve in all these charges, place yer kiss of peace upon this blade blessed of God," Gregor commanded quietly, moving the sword from the man's head to one mighty shoulder.

As the gleaming blade touched the huge warrior's shoulder, Donald raised his bearish head to regard the king with a look of brotherly love. One glistening tear rolled silently down his cheek to disappear into the thick growth of whiskers that was his bristly red beard, and pride shone in his bluff face at the honour his friend had conferred upon him. With no hesitation at all the big island lord pressed his lips firmly to the waiting blade, as was the ancient custom, and thereby sealed his oath.

The regal sword carefully withdrawn and handed off to his champion, Gregor offered his hand to personally help his large friend to stand. "Arise, my lord," he commanded, "as Our Duke of Argyll. And let it be known by all gathered in this holy place that We hae always been well-pleased with ye, and proudly name thee publicly as Our friend." Once Gregor had finished that last proclamation he stepped forward and impulsively embraced his huge friend with a chuckle and slapped the warrior's back heartily with brotherly affection.

Afterward, the remaining nobles of the island realm came forward in a steady stream to bow and offer the king their oaths of fealty in turn. While at King Gregor's side the King's Champion took up the sword of state and held it blade pointing toward the heavens to ward his charge, but to also have it at the ready for the sealing of oaths as the lords, ladies, and great peers of the realm came to swear their allegiance. It was not until several hours later that Gregor and the rest of the royal procession at last took their leave of the ancient abbey at Scone to depart for Edinburgh.

Great was the expectation outside the abbey as the substantial crowd filled the small courtyard and lined the rustic avenue leading from the abbey to the well kept King's Highway. And as King Gregor emerged at the head of the royal procession, the fair queen on his arm, the gathered spectators erupted into joyful cheers. A wide smile stretched across the king's handsome face that he could not have contained even had he tried. His people were all cheering for him, their newly crowned king.

Jubilantly the throng cheered with heartfelt cries that carried across the land. *God save the king! God save the queen! Long live King Gregor!*

And all throughout that war torn kingdom the people breathed a collective sigh of relief at the crowning of their new king. Their hopes and prayers of peace and prosperity rode upon the broad shoulders of Gregor MacGregor and the stability only a strong leader could provide in the days to come. As a whole the folk of Scotland were contented that at long last the civil war was indeed finally over.

EPILOGUE

In just scant months following the ascension of Gregor I to the throne of Scotland the ancient Scottish kingdom was awhirl with sweeping changes that would affect every citizen of that land. The king had set for himself and his government a rigorous schedule to put forward the political changes he demanded, and had accomplished much during his short time as sovereign-something not easily done in light of so many older noblemen who were set in ways and stubbornly set against any change. To be sure, what Gregor had achieved, with the help of his allies, in the beginning months of his reign was remarkable and well worth speaking more about.

The very first act which King Gregor sealed into law was the establishment of his Royal Council and the strictures set to govern this austere body. The Royal Council would consist of a body of twelve of Scotland's most able and ranking noblemen, or noblewomen, should her rank be appropriate. Since the time of Gregor I creating this body, the Council has served as a governmental cabinet whose authority was in large part subject only to the authority and approval of the king. Below is a record of the original members of the King's Royal Council:

King Gregor—Overlord

1. Donald MacDonald: Duke of Argyll, Lord of the Isles, and Sealord.

2. Mhoram Fraser: Duke of Inverness and Lord General in the Royal Army.
3. Sean MacSean: Duke of Strathclyde, King's Champion, and Marishal-General of the Armies of Scotland.
4. Grigor MacGregor: Prince of the Isle of Man and heir apparent.
5. Marlena Hamilton: Duchess of Hamilton
6. Kirkland MacPherson: Marquess of Northumbria and Lord General in the Royal Army.
7. Robert Graham: Earl of Montrose and General in the Royal Army.
8. Alister MacAlpine: Earl of Cluny and General in the Royal Army.
9. Byron Sinclair: Earl of Sutherland and General in the Royal Army.
10. Angus Douglas: Earl of Moray and General in the Royal Army.
11. Niall Abernethy: Primate of Scotland and Archbishop of Saint Andrews.
12. Richard Fletcher: Archbishop of Edinburgh.

One of King Gregor's priorities of his fledgling reign was to formally have his son, Prince Grigor, recognized as his heir and Crown Prince and to have the young man added as a full member of the Royal Council. The first step in seeing these things achieved was to have the prince dubbed as knight. This was perhaps the most simple of all accomplishments, as the prince had already been in training for the knighthood since he had been just a lad in Glenorchy.

The requirement for any man to hold the title of knight and enjoy the privileges of that station are two fold and important, in that a man must be a knight if he would be granted a place of authority or hold high military command. Firstly: without combat and martial training and experience the gentry in general (and for good reason) would not recognize a man's authority-even though he might be a prince-to command in the heat of battle until he had attained knighthood by stringent training and trial in arms. Secondly: although this might seem the same thing, it differs in degree toward command and high authority. No man may be put forward to be king in Scotland or carry out princely powers unless he first is a member of the knighthood. Normally a young man is permitted to seek the trials of knighthood on his seventeenth birthing day, however the young man's lord may seek an exemption should circumstances warrant.

It was for those reasons in which Gregor as chief of his clan had seen to the rigid training of his son. In true MacGregor fashion, Grigor had excelled in his training and sought the respect of his instructors as he desired to follow in his father's footsteps. As a knight the prince could be trained in the art of martial leadership and expect the respect of the gentry and army commanders.

It was only a few months shy of his seventeenth birthing day that Prince Grigor was dubbed a knight by his proud father, while on the same day being confirmed as the royal heir. So confirmed, Grigor became Prince of the Isle of Man with his own estates and an honourary rank of general. The rank would remain honourary until such time as his Lord Sean and Lord Donald deemed him fit and able to lead in his own right; only then would the rank become his in fact.

The final but most difficult part of King Gregor's agenda was the installation of his son within the Royal Council. Some dispute was raised about Grigor's tender age and his lack of experience in any sort of governing capacity by those whom saw themselves as more capable in such a prestigious position. The king's sole argument was obvious and quickly overcame what grumbling there had been. *What better way for the young prince and heir to learn and lead than to gain that experience from the wise councilors already sitting upon the Royal Council?*

During those early months of King Gregor's reign there were few changes which took place that the common folk of Scotland could readily see, but those changes would be sweeping and portentous while pleasing those folk greatly. For instance, the system of taxation was moderated, in that it was balanced much more evenly and according to each individual's means and by the amount and quality of landed property owned.

Further changes which were included in the new king's program were the complete abolishment of any type of enslaved labor, indenture, and keeping of serfs. Open kitchens along with the establishment of lodgings in exchange for labor were initiated as a means of assisting the needy and homeless, especially within and near many of the larger cities, like Edinburgh and Glasgow. Another program began was a system of revitalization and the enlargement of the Royal Navy, which had sadly been allowed to deteriorate over the last several years. In this regard, the Crown authorized the hiring of many skilled jobs and even more posts for regular labor to any that were able-bodied and in need of income and willing to work for it.

Of all the changes which King Gregor wrought, the most startling and recognized was his achievement in bringing about self-imposed political reform. At this time there are still numerous difficulties to be worked out, as many ranking members of the nobility stand against such changes. However, the final result will likely be as the king foresaw from the beginning, which is a triple-tiered governmental structure. In this structure the common citizen, if a land owner, will possess the right to vote on certain issues and elect representatives to speak for them in the new government.

It is for all of these reasons that King Gregor has quickly become a well-loved ruler to his people and the respected overlord to much of the gentry, though this respect is grudgingly given by some. Furthermore, throughout every part of Scotland and even into England, Ireland and Wales, the man whom had at one time not so long ago been known as The MacGregor, was by now commonly called: Gregor the Just.

This is the end of Chronicles of the New Earth: The Clans Conflict. The saga will continue in Chronicles of the New Earth: The War for Northumbria.

Lightning Source UK Ltd.
Milton Keynes UK
UKOW02n0225030215

245554UK00002B/32/P